WEAVING

MAN

BY

TOVE FOSS FORD

INSPIRED BY AN IDEA FROM BRIAN D. FORD

FIRST BOOK OF THE PROPHECY SERIES

This book is a work of fiction. Names, characters, businesses, places, events and incidents are either the products of the author's imagination or used in a fictitious manner. Any resemblance to actual persons, living or dead, or actual events is purely coincidental.

Cover Art by Tove Foss Ford
http://www.eirdon.com
ISBN: 978-0-9981549-1-6

DEDICATION

To all whose "eyes see forward", past and present.

TABLE OF CONTENTS

WEAVING MAN

PROLOGUE

The wind lifted whispering voices from the Sea of Grass, the great plain that stretched across the hillocks and shallow valleys of northern Mordania.

Tharan-Tul, Great Shaman of the nomadic Thrun, crouched with his back to a roaring fire, watching the night sky revolve above Eirdon. His gnarled, large knuckled hand gripped his wooden staff. The wind tugged at his long hair and the folds of his heavy, embroidered robe. The fire flared behind him.

He had watched many nights now. As Shaman, he read the sigils and interpreted the circles that were woven through all life on Eirdon.

Toward the east, two stars rose and began to climb. Then, finally, a third star equally as bright as the pair crested the horizon and began to ascend the great dome of the sky into the gathering of stars called The Weaver, glowing with diamond brilliance against the deep velvet night.

It was the conjunction of three planets, as Tharan-Tul had expected.

He smiled knowingly, and nodded to himself.

"So," he said to the soft voices whispering from the grass. "So... it has begun... again."

CHAPTER I
BANISHED

He had many names.

Aylam Josirus, Lord Stettan, The Surelian Solution, who used his dead mother's tribal name - Menders - as his sole identity, stood alone outside the door of the royal birthing chamber in the Great Palace of Mordania. With the exception of two guards blending into the shadows cast by flickering gaslights, the only other person in the corridor was a sharp-faced young woman. She was visibly sulking.

Menders ignored her. He had no interest in anyone else's despair.

Menders had been commanded to Court that morning when an official summons arrived for him at the home of Commandant Komroff, headmaster of the Mordanian Military Academy. He'd returned to the capital city, Erdahn, the previous night from an in-depth and extremely dangerous covert mission in Surelia.

This mission had taken him two years to complete and had resulted in the elimination of a threat to Mordania that had become known as "The Surelian Problem". Menders' success had required the sacrifice of the last years of his teens and a romance that would have ripened to marriage. He had arrived at Court expecting to be rewarded with the position of Court Assassin. At the age of twenty, he was considered the greatest assassin who ever lived.

Instead, he had been made guardian of the Queen's second child, which she was laboring to bring forth at that moment. Not even the Heiress, but "the spare", whose impending birth had never been announced.

Worse still, Menders was to go with the newborn child and the rest of her household to a remote royal estate in Old

Mordania, more than two days' train travel from Erdhan.

The posting was for the first sixteen years of the child's life. By the end of that time Menders would be far too old to be an assassin, the necessary bodily flexibility and lightning reflexes diminished by advancing years. His career was over. There would only be years buried away in the country as the official guardian of a little girl.

He was angry, confused, run through by the spear of betrayal. He should have been celebrated as a hero. Instead he was being sent into exile.

Menders was of an unprecedented age for anyone to be appointed Head of Household for a royal child. Such positions went to retiring military commanders or Courtiers who had become obsolete, often men with families of their own. They would hire nurses, governesses and tutors to raise the child, taking little interest in the proceedings. Menders had yet to acquire wife or family, and considering the remote location he was being sent to, his chances of doing so would be nil.

He had been handed professional and social death.

Perhaps the child wouldn't survive the birth, or would be a boy, who would be snuffed out before he drew breath. Only Queens ruled in Mordania.

There was a sudden bustle behind the doors of the birthing chamber, followed by the thin wail of a tiny baby. Menders closed his eyes and then swallowed. The child hadn't died and it would never have been allowed to cry if it had been a boy. It was a girl and his fate was sealed.

The door of the chamber opened and a woman beckoned to the sharp-faced girl. She scurried inside.

Moments later the Queen herself walked out, followed by the usual crowd of sycophants who fawned on and scraped to her day and night. She was tousled and reeking from her confinement, her red hair soaked with sweat. Although she had delivered a child only minutes before, she was heading back to the

Great Hall, where she and her entourage would doubtless drink into the night. No bed rest for her. Mordanian Queens were bred to be tough.

Menders performed the formal obeisance of the Mordanian Court, slowly lowering himself to one knee, his head inclined against the other, his arms outstretched at shoulder level. According to Court protocol, this position was sustained until the royal personage acknowledged the one who performed it. Menders managed a covert glance toward the Queen in time to see her shoot a scathing glance at him from beautiful aquamarine eyes. Her lip curled in distaste and she walked on without acknowledging him or releasing him from his humble and uncomfortable posture.

Menders' comprehension of his miserable situation became perfectly clear.

Should Morghenna VIII take a dislike to anyone at Court for any reason, that person disappeared. It was obvious from the way the drunken bitch looked at him that she disliked him - for reasons unknown.

Menders rose slowly as the Queen and her followers moved away down the hallway. He was sickened by the odor of unwashed bodies. He'd heard the Queen was prone to fits of melancholy and did not bathe regularly or groom herself. Menders' nose wrinkled in nauseated disgust. It wasn't only the sweat of labor — this was the reek of days, even weeks without washing.

The Queen's Chamberlain burst from the birthing chamber, holding a bundled blanket. He rushed over to Menders and shoved it into his arms.

"Lord Stettan, I present you with your ward, Princess Katrin Morghenna of Mordania," he said briskly, looking in the direction of the Queen and her party, obviously desperate to follow them. "You are to leave immediately. The Royal Train is waiting for you at the station. Further instructions will be forwarded to you. You are supplied with a wet nurse, cook, guard and physician. All the documentation you require will be provided before your departure."

With that, the man scurried in the wake of the Queen and her Court, leaving Menders standing there holding a newborn baby.

He'd had no experience with infants. Children were part of the scenery, little things that clung to the hands of women or who dashed about and got underfoot in the street. He held the infant at half arms' length from his body, stiff and uncomfortable, as if holding it close might break it.

I could kill it, he thought. Babies die all the time for not much reason. They die in their cribs, in their sleep. A pillow would do the trick, or a bit of poisoned water in its food. Then he would be free of his sentence as this lump of flesh's guardian for a decade and a half. He'd killed so many and this was hardly a person yet.

He looked down at the bundle, and saw that they hadn't even bothered to dress the child, that it was still slightly wet and naked except for the folds of blanket. It seemed to be asleep, and he was surprised, after hearing that newborns were red and crumple-faced, to see that it was a delicate pink, with a damp fuzz of downy golden hair on its head.

Just then the baby wriggled. Menders instinctively drew it closer to his body, cradling it in his arms. It made a tiny mewing noise, and opened its eyes.

They were a startling electric blue. They looked up into his as if this minutes-old child saw him, knew him and accepted him entirely, for exactly what he was.

Menders shifted her into the crook of his left arm and extended his right forefinger in her direction, touching the back of her tiny hand.

She grasped the tip of his finger with strength he would have never expected from such a miniscule piece of humanity.

Her fingers were delicate and perfect, tiny dimples showed where each finger met her hand. There were pearly fingernails, so minute that they were funny and touching at the same time.

Menders felt a torrent of warmth in his chest. A sudden lump rose in his throat while tears stung his eyes. He smiled, then kissed the tiny hand as if acknowledging the most elegant lady at Court.

If this child is to be given to me, then she is my child, he thought.

In all his years of service, Menders had never failed a mission. At that moment he swore an oath to himself that he would never fail this Princess of Mordania.

"You are my little one," he whispered to her, feeling drawn into the depths of those blue eyes, stricken with love he had never felt before. He would be with her forever, so long as his heart beat, this tiny, precious, pink and golden girl who had been given to him with no more thought than if she had been an outworn shoe or greatcoat. If her mother had no love for her, he had love to give that would more than make up for it. He would protect her and care for her all of his days.

He became aware of commotion all around and looked up to see that the luggage of Katrin's household was being dragged out the door and loaded onto sledges. His own case and trunk, which he had been ordered to bring to the Palace, were being loaded with everything else.

The sharp-faced girl caught his eye. She tried to take the baby but he shook his head and cuddled Katrin close to his heart. He wrapped her securely against the cold and followed the luggage out into the long midwinter twilight.

CHAPTER 2
BAND OF OUTCASTS

Menders snapped awake, suffering the unnerving confusion of one who regains consciousness after a short sleep to find he is nowhere he recognizes.

It came back. He was on the Royal Train. He looked down at the child in his arms, and knew it had not been a dream. The infant Princess really had been given to him to protect and care for.

He looked through the carriage window at the winter sky, his attention drawn by the brilliant new star that had been reported in all the newssheets. His reflection in the carriage window caught his eye.

He could be considered attractive, with an aquiline nose and long, flowing dark hair. His chin tended a bit toward weakness, but it was well camouflaged with a jawline beard and elegant moustache. He wore dark corrective spectacles in all but the dimmest light because a familial trait had saddled him with an eye condition that rendered the irises of his eyes such a pale grey that at any distance his eyes appeared to be completely white. His vision was corrected to some degree by the spectacles – without them, he was, essentially, blind.

Weak eyes, painfully sensitive to light, should have been a disadvantage. Menders had made them into an asset. His night vision was like a langhur's. Anyone who was unprepared for his white eyes was unnerved by them. He had formed a habit of looking over his glasses at those he wished to unsettle. What was the need for dark corrective spectacles compared to that?

Menders' body had been honed to the hardness and flexibility of steel, despite his being weak by nature, with an inherent shortness of breath. He had attained physical strength and power through years of self-discipline and training; he had forced his reluctant lungs into efficiency. His razor sharp mind was equally well-schooled. All for a career that was no more...

The bundle in his arms shifted and he looked down to see that Katrin's eyes were open. She was watching him. He smiled, the rising bitterness in his soul receding.

"There is a new star in the sky," he whispered to her, smiling as she gazed up at him raptly. "Only just risen in conjunction with Calthor and Aphrus. It has the scientific men in a frenzy to name it and explain it, but most people are saying it's a sign of great things. Of course they don't know I just saved their nation, do they? Most people don't even know men like me exist."

Katrin gave a funny little sigh, as if she commiserated with him. Menders pulled the curtain across the window to block the cold seeping in.

"We're going to a strange and distant place, my Little Princess," he said. "I know a story I can tell you." He adjusted his position, putting his feet up on the seat opposite, reclining comfortably with his wonderful baby resting on his breast.

"Once upon a time, there was a tiny princess, only just born. It was the wish of the Queen that the princess be taken to a magical land to be raised in safety so she would be the most accomplished and wise woman in the world. The Queen ordered her bravest and purest Dark Knight to accompany the little princess far away to the top of the world, where the forests are deep and the mountains are always covered with snow.

"The Dark Knight, upon being given the little princess, felt a sudden warmth in his breast, and saw a magical cord grow from his heart, just as one grew from the tiny heart of the princess. The cords twined together in a knot that could never be untied or broken, and the Dark Knight at that moment swore an oath on his life.

The Dark Knight said, 'You will not be raised as I was. I won't let anyone do the things to you that were done to me. You will be cherished and loved and I swear that you will never come to harm so long as I am alive, my Little Princess, no matter what I have to do to keep you safe."

Menders let his voice die away as Katrin's eyelids drooped and closed, and he bent so that he could kiss her hair. Then he leaned his head against the back of his seat, the baby held safely against his heart.

"I protect the future of Mordania," he murmured.

The train thundered on into the night.

***

Later, with the baby asleep in the crook of his left arm, Menders drew a slender, leather-bound volume from his pocket, opening it to a clean page. The Royal Carriage was beautifully equipped, down to being furnished like an elegant drawing room. From the writing desk that was conveniently provided, he located a pen and ink and began to write.

I find myself in a strange circumstance, with a child in my care. Though this is not the fate I had expected, an assassin must play the hand dealt him. As the Thrun say, "turn as the circles do."

I have yet to formulate an opinion of the people who have been thrown in with me on this mission.

Menders dipped the pen again, and paused to think about the six people who had been pressed into service as the Princess' household. He had met them only briefly at the station, and they were presently all in the carriage ahead, avoiding him. Menders had the Royal Carriage to himself. It was little used, now that the Queen had taken up a life of drunken docility. She had not left the Palace in years.

The doctor seems the most capable. He's a large and hearty fellow.

He delivered the Princess and pronounces her in fine health. He is the least afraid of me. He and the cook are Old Mordanian, like myself.

The cook is a robust woman of early middle age. As to whether she can cook remains to be seen. Lucen Greinholz, the guard, is recently detached from the Royal Regiment. He is of pensionable age but seems a forthright and loyal sort. He alone has family to bring with him, a plain but seemingly pleasant wife and a very spoiled boy of three. They're Southern Mordanians.

The last of the four is the wet nurse, another Southerner. She seems distant and indifferent, and has yet to strike me as maternal. With no child of her own with her I can but assume she has lost one recently. This may prove to be a problem.

Katrin stirred and began to cry.

"I suspect you may be hungry," Menders said to the child. "And at this stage, that is not something I am equipped to handle myself." He settled her in the bassinet that had been provided, then opened the carriage door and walked onto the platform.

He gasped, realizing that they must be well into what was known as Old Mordania, the rugged eastern lobe of the nation. How hideous the cold could be out here, far from the tempering effects of the ocean! Pulling his jacket close, he stepped across the gap and hauled on the door handle of the next carriage, revealing the guard's startled face.

"Can you send the nurse in, please?"

The big man nodded, the door closed and Menders moved hastily back to the warmth of the Royal Carriage. Presently, the sharp-faced young woman came in, bringing a swirl of snow with her.

Menders took her cloak.

"I'm called Menders. I think she's hungry." Menders lifted the baby from the bassinet. The young woman nodded and took the child, then sat on a straight backed chair beside the bassinet with Katrin nestled in her arms.

"I'll have to feed her," she said unenthusiastically. "I'm Ermina Trottenheim."

Menders nodded, standing with his legs braced slightly apart against the motion of the train, his arms folded across his chest.

"I would prefer some privacy." Mistress Trottenheim scowled.

"Yes, I understand," Menders replied. "You may proceed." He rotated on the spot and stood with his back to her. There was a mirror above the sideboard across the carriage that afforded him a view of her. At this stage, with an untried group of people whose motivations and loyalties were not yet certain, he would take no chances.

She undid her dress quickly and put the baby to her breast.

"I find your lack of trust offensive," she said peevishly.

"Do you?" Menders replied. "You wouldn't if you bothered to think about it. I have no information about you. The Princess' safety comes first and foremost with me. Think on this... given your close proximity, how quickly do you think you could break that little one's neck?"

"I would never do such a thing," she snapped indignantly.

"Good. I'm glad to hear it," Menders responded. The child fed in silence for a while before he spoke again.

"You have lost a child of your own recently."

Her eyes flashed up, surprised. She had not spoken of it and he had made a statement rather than posing a question, so no doubt she wondered how he knew. Assessing situations quickly was one of an assassin's many skills.

"Born dead five days ago. Who told you?"

"No one. A simple deduction on my part. If you had a newborn, you would have brought it with you. Since you haven't, yet are able to be a wet nurse, you must have lost a child. Also, you seemed ill at ease which led me to believe you hadn't nursed before."

She looked past his shoulder to the mirror on the wall and

gasped.

"You said you wouldn't look!"

"I said no such thing. I merely turned my back to ease your discomfort. But at this stage I am not about to take my eyes off the Princess for a minute."

Mistress Trottenheim fastened her dress quickly and put Katrin down in her bassinet. Menders sat in the chair before the writing desk.

"Tell me about yourself." It was not a request and Ermina Trottenheim knew it.

"My husband died in battle three months back," she said waspishly. "I've been a nurserymaid for Princess Aidelia for four years and was given this position because my baby… died and I had milk. I'm in the Royal Family, distantly related." She looked at him haughtily.

"I'm Royal Family too," Menders countered. "Very closely related. Second cousin to the Queen."

"I've never been to Old Mordania," she said after a tense silence. Her tone made it obvious that she considered being sent to Old Mordania the worst fate imaginable.

"I was born there," Menders responded, looking at the dark window. He could see her reflected in the glass. She was watching him closely.

"I have clothes for the Princess, Mister Menders," she finally offered, obviously wanting a change of subject. "She'll need a diaper now that she's eaten and she'll probably sleep for a while, so she'll be fine in the bassinet."

"Dress her by all means but I'll hold her when you're done," Menders directed decisively. The young woman dressed Katrin and wrapped her in a fresh blanket, then handed her to Menders with open annoyance. He ignored her expression. He was not about to confide his feelings for the child.

"I had best get back to the others," Mistress Trottenheim said. "There'll be supper on soon. Shall I send some in?"

"No," Menders replied, deciding he had better not keep too far removed from the rest of the party. The gods only knew what stories would begin to circulate about him, and he was going to need these people in the weeks and months ahead. "I'll come forward for it. The Princess will also need attending to at odd hours. It would be best if you and she were in the same carriage. "

"Surely you don't mean to have the child fed on demand? She should be on a schedule." She was looking at him as if he'd gone mad.

"Deprive a hungry baby of food? Surely you cannot be serious." His tone hardened. Having been deprived as a child himself it was a bitter notion to him, despite the fashion of 'toughening' children practiced in the Royal Family and high society.

"Scheduled feeding is how a child should be raised," she retorted, assuming an air of authority. "It is what the Queen would wish."

"The Queen is not here. I am," Menders replied. "I have full authority over the Princess."

"And you're an expert on child rearing, are you?" Mistress Trottenheim sniped.

"Since you have no notion of my knowledge and capabilities, I think it would be unwise on your part to make any assumptions at this point." Menders answered, his tone frigid. "We do things one way. My way. Do you understand?" He removed his dark glasses and stared at her.

She opened her mouth to reply but one look at Menders' eyes closed it again.

He was sure he had not heard the last of the matter. She was not the type to leave things alone. He replaced his glasses on his nose and began to open the carriage door, then paused with his hand on the big brass handle.

He looked intently at Ermina Trottenheim. She stiffened slightly in response.

"You've been nursemaid these last four years to the Heiress, Princess Aidelia?" he asked.

"I said I was."

"What's your personal opinion of her?"

"Aidelia? I... well, she's..."

"This is not a test of your loyalty," Menders added, sensing her apprehension. "It's not to see what you might say or not say, with the idea that I would report it to the Queen. This is strictly between you and me."

After a pause, she lowered her voice and answered," Well, she's... strange."

"How so?"

"She's... I don't know how else to say it. Strange. Fits of temper, biting, violent outbursts, hates being touched, goes wild if anyone tries to bathe her. She's been like that since birth."

"Does she seem to be ill?"

"Oh no, not at all. She's fit as a bull, strong for her age and size. Look." She rolled up her sleeve and there, just below the elbow, was a bite mark. It was yellow, purple and black. "When I was ordered to brush her hair."

"A child did that?"

Nodding, she rolled her sleeve down.

"I see." Menders nodded and gently bit his lower lip. "Thank you Mistress Trottenheim. I'll be along shortly." He pulled the door back, and the wet nurse made good her escape.

After closing the door, Menders saw Katrin was slumbering peacefully and sat at the writing desk, picking up the pen again.

The wet nurse is a problem. No question. Snide, bitter, contemptuous – just the sort of person to cause trouble. I will have to consider other options as soon as possible. If she is this difficult with someone she hardly knows, what will she be like upon further acquaintance? Is her behavior the reason why she has been sent away from the Court? Surely other wet nurses could have been sent. Adding a difficult and unmaternal nurse to

***

Menders studied his reflection in the sideboard mirror. He looked sinister and displeased. No wonder the others were staying in the parlor carriage.

He looked down at his black suit and then at his black greatcoat thrown across a seat nearby. He must have presented a very intimidating figure to them back at the Palace. Of course he had, he'd deliberately cultivated just such an image for years. He had no change of clothing available in the carriage, so he would have to appear in his assassin's garb, but he would also appear holding a baby, not a weapon. Hopefully that would help break the ice a bit.

Menders rose, pulled on his overcoat and then lifted Katrin from her bassinet. She stirred and mewed in protest.

"All right, all right. Now, it's under my coat you have to go, because we're going into the next carriage, and it will be cold on the way." With that he tucked her against his side, snugging the blanket around her, buttoned his greatcoat and opened the door.

He crossed the platforms rapidly and opened the door of the parlor carriage, bursting inside with a gasp. He shucked off the coat, taking Katrin from its depths and cradling her in his arms.

Menders looked up to see six people staring at him.

"He's only a lad!" the cook burst out. It was the first time some of them had seen Menders up close. "What madness is it to send a boy out here with a tiny baby girl?" She rose and beckoned to Menders. "Come here, Mister Menders, have some supper. Let me take the little mite so you can eat. A boy your age probably eats seven times a day if I'm not mistaken."

"I don't know if she'll cry, she does anytime I put her

down," Menders said as he walked over to the group, then transferred Katrin to the woman's arms.

"Spoiling her already?" She smiled at him and he knew that she wasn't in the least intimidated by black clothing or black looks. "I know a trick or two with babies, so you have a break from being papa and have some of my stew." She eased back the blanket that covered Katrin's face and began to coo.

"Isn't she the loveliest baby," she warbled as Mistress Trottenheim silently served a plate and set it on a small table at the end of the carriage, nodding to Menders. "Here now, she looks as if she's already a week old and only born yesterday. Hemmett, see the pretty baby?"

The little boy, who Menders had guessed might be three years old, craned up to see Katrin.

"Gimme the puppydog!" he demanded, holding out his arms.

"She's not a puppydog!" the cook laughed. "She's a little girl and your Princess."

"Gimme the puppydog!"

"A man of single mind, our Hemmett," said the doctor as he pulled out a chair and sat, setting his own plate in front of him. "Glad you joined us. I'm Rainer Franz, Court Physician – or was." He was a hearty, blond man, tall, in his thirties.

"She's a little baby, and you can't touch her just yet," the cook was saying to the implacable Hemmett. "When you're allowed to you must always use gentle hands."

"Gimme the puppydog!"

"Oh dear. Hemmett, show the baby your toy horse," said the woman Menders assumed was Hemmett's mother, though she appeared to be in her mid-forties. She rose to distract the little boy from his determined course to take Katrin in his arms and play with her like a 'puppydog'.

"Mister Menders," Doctor Franz said, as Menders ate voraciously, "do you have any idea of the condition of the house we're going to?"

Menders' fork stopped halfway to his mouth and he stared at the doctor, looking over his glasses. The doctor blinked but then covered up very professionally, as if he was confronted with people who had white eyes every day.

"I thought one of you would," Menders said, realizing that he looked like an idiot. "The only thing told me is that the house is called The Shadows and that when the train stops, we'll be there."

Lucen Greinholz, the guard, hauled up another chair. He was nearly seven feet tall and appeared to be in his early fifties. Hemmett ran over to him and began to clamber onto his lap. At first, Menders thought the man too old to be Hemmett's father, but the little boy kept demanding his attention by calling out 'Papa!' loudly and poking at him.

Lucen placed a wax-sealed, leather billfold on the table. "We were told to give you this, sir."

Really, Menders thought. Obviously, no one was in a hurry to bring it to me, we've been traveling for hours. The gods only know what they thought might be in this… their writs of execution, perhaps. He was glad the men were coming forward, but the women, he noticed, were still keeping a wary distance.

Menders took the billfold, broke the seals and withdrew a single sheet of paper. He scanned it quickly.

"It's the charter giving me guardianship of the Princess," he said, feeling at a complete loss. There was no other information; if money was to be provided, how much and when, where they were going, if the house was habitable, if there was a town nearby – nothing.

Menders looked up at Lucen Greinholz, who shrugged.

"We'll manage, we don't have much other choice," the big man said placidly, as Hemmett thumped his chest repeatedly with a toy horse. "Here now, son, leave off," he continued with amusement. Hemmett paid no heed, misbehaving with such confidence that Menders knew it was a longstanding pattern.

A look at Doctor Franz was more satisfying, because he was obviously feeling the same frustration Menders did.

"What concerns me is the fact that we have a newborn infant here and might be going to a place where there is no fuel or food," Menders said.

He put his fork down and looked around the group before speaking.

"Some of you are Northerners but does anyone know the area we're going to? I was born in Old Mordania, but in the far eastern part. I haven't been in Old Mordania since I was eleven."

"I'm from Old Mordanian stock, but born in Erdahn," Doctor Franz said apologetically. "I've never been out here."

"I was born near here, in Erdstrom," the cook volunteered. Menders looked over his glasses at her and sighed as he saw her start. She fell silent.

"Would you be so kind as to dim the gaslights?" he said. Doctor Franz reached up and turned down the gas.

Menders swiveled his chair around so that he faced all of them.

"Now," he said, removing his glasses, "These are my eyes. I know that they can bother people but since we're all thrown in together I can't have everyone jumping every time they happen to see them. I don't see well without my glasses, which have to be dark because I can't bear a lot of light. I wear them almost all the time. My eyes have always been like this, it's a quirk in my family." Menders had become accustomed to the questions people asked about his unusual visual organs and had developed this speech to save time.

He looked from one person to the next, holding each gaze until the initial flinching was over and they'd had time to get used to his peculiarity. There was a general murmuring of interest and the cook said, "I think they're quite attractive once you get used to them." Menders couldn't help smiling at her. He replaced his glasses and the lamps were turned up again.

"Now then," Menders said to the cook, "What should I call you?"

"Cook is good enough. My name is Valdema Fersten and I was born in Erdstrom some fifty miles from The Shadows. It's called that because it's in the shadow of The Giants."

"Giants?" Doctor Franz asked. Menders said nothing, concentrating on his plate, nodding his thanks when Mistress Trottenheim placed more food on it for him. He knew what The Giants were. They occurred in several places in Old Mordania.

"They're great stone pieces of bodies, hands, noses and suchlike, poking up out of the ground," Cook answered. "Like parts of statues, but huge. You can see them from the train line and if the snow's not too deep we'll have a look at them today. They're found in this part of Mordania, more of them the further north and east you go. No-one knows who made them."

"What about the house?" Doctor Franz asked.

"I've never seen it," she replied. "It's the only royal house in this part of the country and the furthest one north, they say. There are other great estates around and there is a small village within five miles - or was before I left the area."

"How long ago was that?" Menders asked.

"Some ten years. I wish I could tell you more," she sighed.

"Does anyone know if word was sent that we're coming?" Menders asked, starting to feel a bit of panic.

No-one spoke.

"Gods," he muttered. For all they knew, they were about to arrive at a frozen waste, with no shelter, no notion of where the house was, nothing. And with tiny Katrin as vulnerable as a human being could be.

He let his mind start churning, sorting through the information he had, precious little that it was. After a moment, he had a plan.

"When we arrive, I will make them hold the train. That way no matter what, there will be shelter for us. Cook, how much food is left?"

"Plenty, enough for two or three days. I planned for a possible delay. The trains often get stopped or slowed during the winter," she replied. "And if need be, the train could go on to Erdstrom where there would be an inn and food to be had, if the tracks are clear. Some winters they're completely blocked for months but this winter hasn't been hard from the looks of things."

"I might need someone to help me convince the driver that we're going to hold the train," Menders said to Lucen Greinholz.

"Oh, I don't know... you look like you could be very convincing to me," Lucen grinned. "But whatever help you want, then I'm your man." He slid Hemmett off his lap, having apparently grown tired of being pounded with a toy horse. The pounding had gone on throughout the entire conversation without Lucen making a move to put a stop to it.

"Good. Doctor, I'll need you to help me find if there are any resources there at all or anyone who can tell us where we're going, if there's transport available, that sort of thing."

Doctor Franz nodded and Menders realized that everyone looked relieved.

"There now, I told you that he'd have something figured out, they don't take dolts to be assassins," Cook said to the group at large. Menders managed to bite back a laugh, then sat back and looked around at the little group.

"I don't know what you might think of me," Menders began, then paused. That wasn't quite true – he did know what they thought of him. People always thought assassins were murderers, cold blooded killers, madmen. They didn't know or understand that an assassin was not just a contract killer or thug. An assassin was as highly trained as any specialist in any technical field, and was skilled at espionage, intelligence gathering, subterfuge and sabotage. Assassins killed without compassion, it was true, but also without any other sort of emotional involvement. Menders had always considered himself a sort of surgeon, quickly and carefully removing cancers and infections that threatened the healthy body of Mordania.

"But the charter I have been given is quite clear," he continued. "I have full legal authority over the Princess and I am to see to her needs, comfort and security. In those respects I am the final authority." He cast a sharp glance at Ermina Trottenheim, who looked away. "However, I don't want you to think that I have that same authority over you. I am not the lord and master and you are not my servants. Instead, I see us all as having been thrown in together. We'll have to help each other."

He watched their faces closely and saw his words had lessened some of their apprehension.

"But you are still... in charge of things, right?" Lucen asked with concern.

"In some respects, yes. I am to be responsible for the estate of the Princess, assuming there actually is an estate there to be responsible for."

"Good!" Lucen beamed with a relieved grin. "I'll follow any sort of order you care to give but I'm not keen on giving them myself."

"That should work out then," Menders said. He turned back to the table.

"How did you come to be sent out here, Mister Menders?" Cook asked.

"Just Menders, please," he told her. "I seem to have drawn the dislike of the Queen. I saw a look she gave me as she passed me yesterday."

The group looked around at one another, and Cook nodded sagely.

"Another one then. Me, I got into a fight with that idiot

they call a cook at the Palace. Filthy bitch, never scrubs out the pots properly, leaves food out all over the place. The kitchens there are a disgrace. I finally got into a slapping match with the vile woman and that was the end of me, off to the end of the world I go."

"I caught a bullet right below the knee two months ago when two fools decided to duel in the Palace courtyard," Lucen Greinholz added. "I'm just as hardy, but I can't stand at attention for hours any longer. I'm glad to be away from The Palace. We're looking forward to a new place."

"I had the temerity to suggest that Princess Aidelia carving designs into her arms and legs with a knife isn't the activity of a normal child." Doctor Franz contributed bitterly. "Since the Queen ascended the Throne a couple of months back, she's been getting rid of royal staff left and right, putting her own flunkies in. So here I am."

There was a ripple of discomfort as the Doctor mentioned the behavior of the Heiress and a sudden silence, unbroken even by Hemmett's continual jabbering, settled over the carriage.

"Mister Menders knows how I'm here," Mistress Trottenheim said after a moment. She got up at a glance from Cook and took Katrin. "She's hungry and I have my orders." She gave Menders a look and went to the end of the carriage, where she was shielded from view by the seats.

"What do we have with us in the way of supplies, Doctor Franz?" Menders asked.

"Please, call me Franz," the doctor said. "No point in formality. I have medical supplies, plenty of them. I had warning a day ahead of time that I would be sent out with the baby, and I depleted the Palace stocks considerably. Medicines, bandages, sutures, instruments – we have enough to see us through anything but a plague."

"What about clothing for the baby?"

"Mistress Trottenheim has that. It's sufficient for a while, and baby clothes can be made up of anything, old clothing, sheets. There are plenty of blankets."

"I have some old baby things of Hemmett's that she can have," chimed in Greinholz's wife. "I'm Zelia. I like to sew, so I can run up anything the little Princess needs. We also brought most of our household goods. There would be enough sheets and blankets for everyone to start with, if there's nothing ready at the house."

Menders gave her a nod of thanks and she smiled shyly.

"Lemme see your spooky face!" The demand came from around Menders' knee. He looked down to see Hemmett staring up at him, trying to see behind his glasses.

"I can't take my glasses off with the lights turned up. It would hurt my eyes," he answered. Hemmett decided to remove that obstacle by attempting to climb on the seats to reach the gas lamps, but his mother took him down and bore him away to the end of the car where she started chatting with Mistress Trottenheim. Cook rose from her seat and came to the table.

"I was told that there are dishes and pots and pans at the house," she said. "If any of you gentlemen is a dab hand with a gun or crossbow, there should be plenty of game in the district. I can cook anything so long as I have means of heat and some knives to cut it up. So we shan't starve."

"I could say I'm a dab hand with a gun or crossbow," Menders said. "I'm more experienced with shooting men, but I imagine I could probably hit a deer with a bit of luck."

"Best you do then, because I won't be happy about you bringing me a man to cook," Cook said, and burst out laughing.

CHAPTER 3
THE SHADOWS

The train finally stopped in the bright light of late morning, at a desolate wooden platform blessed with one small, forlorn building. An old sign, faded almost to illegibility, proclaimed 'THE SHADOWS HALT. NO SCHEDULED SERVICE. SIGNAL WITH FLAG OR LANTERN TO STOP TRAINS'.

It wasn't a very encouraging sign.

Doctor Franz went to see if there was anyone inside the building and found it locked. He rubbed at a grimy window pane with his sleeve, then peered inside.

"Hasn't been used in years by the look of it," he called.

Menders immediately walked forward to the engine, hastening against the biting cold. He climbed up to the footplate, figuring that the driver wouldn't move the train with one of the passengers hanging from the engine window. Lucen had disembarked on the other side and made his own way forward to the engine.

"Where are we?" Menders demanded as Lucen Greinholz climbed up and grinned at the driver through the other side of the cab. His grin was very imposing.

"Shadows Halt, sir," the driver said. "Here, what's all this about?"

"We've been sent out with no idea if anyone is going to know we're coming, and we have no idea where we're supposed to go," Menders replied.

"Let us out of here, and we'll get back in the carriage and have a talk," the driver said, looking from Menders to Lucen with some amusement. "Don't worry, lad, I'm not going anywhere. Our orders were that you disembark here, we go on to Erdstrom to turn the engine and head back light. But I'm not about to abandon you, if it seems you've been left in a hard spot. There's no regular service here, you know. We don't stop, most times. People just leave us parcels and such to pick up and we set out what's theirs. Papers and mail, and the like. If there's no-one turning up soon, we'll carry you up to Erdstrom, there's plenty of lodging there."

Menders drew a private breath of relief that the driver wasn't some timeserver determined to keep to a schedule and stepped down to the platform. The driver and fireman climbed down behind him, and then scrambled up into the warmth of the parlor carriage.

"I've driven this run for years, when the track is open," the engine driver explained between gulps of scalding coffee. "The Shadows is about two miles from here. It hasn't been used by the Royal Family since I started some eight years back. There are tenant farmers on the estate. Sometimes they come to the halt to catch a train. So why are you people here?"

"We have the Princess with us. The Shadows is to be her home," Menders said, taking the baby from Mistress Trottenheim and holding her where the driver and fireman could see.

They rose and bowed.

"We weren't told. Just said to run a special express up to Shadows Halt," the driver explained. "Had no idea you didn't know what was happening – but that's the way it is in Mordania these days, isn't it? Likely someone nearby has seen the smoke from the engine, we'll hear soon enough."

Indeed, it was only a few moments before someone hallooed outside.

Menders swung down into the bright daylight to see two sledges pulled up at the halt and two men heading his way.

"You're the people from Erdahn?" one of them called. He looked relieved when Menders nodded. "We only got the letter about you coming with the child two days back," he puffed, sliding on some packed ice and jumping off onto snow where he could get better footing. "No idea when, because at the point the letter was written the child wasn't even born yet, there was no way to know. So we've been watching for a train. Sorry not to meet you, but it takes some time to hitch the horses."

"There are eight people altogether," Menders told him. "Two small children, a three year old boy and the Princess, born yesterday. The children can't stand the cold for long."

"Neither can I, let's get in the carriage," the man said, blue eyes twinkling intelligently between his heavy fur hat and well-wrapped scarf. "I'm Spaltz, one of the tenant farmers on The Shadows." He hauled himself up into the carriage. Mister Spaltz was a great heavy boned man, broad more than tall, with huge large-knuckled hands, a genial face and hair the color of burnished copper.

"So... you would be?" Mister Spaltz said, casting a quizzical glance at Menders.

"Menders. Guardian of Princess Katrin, second rightful Heiress to the Throne of Mordania." Menders indicated Katrin.

"Ah, I see." Mister Spaltz bowed respectfully to the Princess before looking at Menders again. Menders could not help thinking that the farmer had been expecting a more senior man. "So, I guess it's you who'll be in charge then, sir?"

"So it seems."

"Right. My eldest girl and two of the other farmer's wives have been trying to make some headway with the house, and they've got enough cleaned for you not to be drowned in dust or et up by spiders," he said. "We shouldn't tarry too long, it's bad for the horses to stand in this cold. So we'll save the introductions for later. Best to get these children to better shelter."

Mistress Trottenheim gave Katrin to Menders. He felt entirely extraneous as the women flurried around, gathering belongings and chattering about being glad that someone had opened the house and begun cleaning it. They seemed cheerier now that they knew there were actually people around The

Shadows.

"Lemme see your spooky face." A tug on his trousers let Menders know that Hemmett was at his side. Another tug threatened to half-undress him and because Hemmett's mother was busily stowing things in a hamper, Menders crouched to the child's level and obliged him by looking at him over his glasses. Hemmett giggled, not the least unnerved by Menders' eyes.

"Spooky face! Gimme puppydog!"

"This isn't a puppydog," Menders said firmly, moving Katrin's blanket aside so Hemmett could see her. "This is the Princess. No more asking about a puppydog."

He had observed enough of Hemmett's behavior to know that he must make it very clear to the little boy just what would be permitted and what wouldn't. Menders had spent the second night of traveling in the carriage with the others and had watched as Hemmett refused to lie down to sleep, rifled people's belongings and sat up playing while everyone but Menders was dozing. He was a child who had obviously never been disciplined. If Menders was going to live in the same house with this youthful wild man, the line had to be drawn, the sooner the better.

Hemmett goggled at Katrin. "Pretty baby," he cooed. "Who her papa?"

"I don't know, Hemmett," Menders answered.

"You're her Papa." Hemmett leaned against Menders' knee and gazed at Katrin. He reached out carefully and patted her blanket.

"We have to take good care of her, because she's very small," Menders said firmly. The little boy nodded. Menders rose from his crouch just as Mister Spaltz, returned with an armful of furs.

"My wife sent this down so you could wrap the baby in it," he explained. "Those blankets aren't going to be enough for this weather, she'd freeze in a minute. Put the fur to the inside, right by the child, then wrap around until they're all snug, then put the blankets around that. He helped Menders swaddle Katrin with a level of expertise that let Menders know he was no stranger to children. Then he grinned down at Hemmett.

"Want to ride alongside of me and help me drive the horses, young man?" he asked.

In Spaltz's sledge Menders cuddled Katrin close while Hemmett sat beside him, flapping the ends of the reins that Spaltz held further up with heavily gloved hands. It was far too cold for much conversation and

halfway through the ride, Hemmett turned and burrowed under Menders' arm, hiding his face from the chill. Then Spaltz gestured and Menders saw they were approaching a house.

It was massive, four stories high, turreted and decorated in Old Mordanian style with intricate carving and fretwork. What windows Menders could see were intact. Smoke rose from several chimneys, a comforting sight. The entire building was laden with snow. Thank the gods it looked secure and warm – although he didn't like the roof. It was forested with chimney pots, elegantly domed spires and steeply gabled windows. Far too easy for someone to hide up there.

Mister Spaltz drew up to the massive stone steps of The Shadows and Menders hurried inside with the baby, Hemmett clinging to his trouser leg.

Two women and a girl were bustling about. They stopped suddenly and bobbed awkwardly to Menders. The girl, seeing that the women were mute with shyness, spoke.

"I'm Eiren Spaltz. Please, bring the baby right into the kitchen, it's the warmest room now." She beckoned. The kitchen was more than warm, as three enormous iron ranges were all glowing hot, pots and kettles simmering away.

"Shall I take the baby for you, sir?" Eiren Spaltz asked. Menders shook his head and placed Katrin on the table, unwrapping the tight bundle of blankets and furs until she was free.

"What a lovely girl!" Eiren said in surprise. "When was she born?"

"Only yesterday," Menders responded, watching as she adjusted Katrin's little dress and felt her hands to see if they were warm. The girl was thin and wiry, with red hair in two long braids and a mouthful of teeth too large for her face. She might have been thirteen, but though she was still quite a child, she had an air of experience with Katrin – and Menders didn't like the idea of Ermina Trottenheim as nursemaid for the Princess.

"Only one day old and she's so pretty. Usually new babies are red and squashed," Eiren said, smiling up at him. "My baby brother was born two weeks since and he's still like a red monkey."

Menders removed his overcoat and hat. "Do you have much experience with babies, Miss Spaltz?" he asked.

"That she does!" said one of the farmer's wives, who had come in to look at the baby. "Got five little brothers and sisters and her the eldest. She brought her own baby brother into the world just two week ago and saved her poor mother what was bleeding half to death. Eiren's a good hand with children, my Lord."

Menders saw Eiren go pale. The youngster stopped smiling and bent over Katrin, tickling her belly lightly. There was a question to be answered there.

The front door banged open and the rest of Katrin's household blew in with various exclamations, moans and curses about the cold. Eiren and the other women hurried to help with coats, bundles and bags.

"Grahl's teeth!" Doctor Franz gasped, his breath still steaming as he blustered in the door. "That's wicked cold out there, Menders!"

"Oh, but you should have been here for winter proper!" Eiren laughed, taking the doctor's coat. "We're past the worst clasp of it now!"

"What a cheery thought," Franz said as he warmed his hands over one of the stoves. Eiren took his coat and gloves. Franz gave her a grin and a quick tug on one of her braids.

Cook busied herself inspecting the contents of the pantry and the scullery full of pots.

"This'll do. We can be going on for a while here," she said cheerfully but with great authority, gratified that she had discovered a deer hanging in the larder, plus as a sizeable portion of a pig. "Now, Menders, I observed that you like to eat – what sort of food do you like?" she asked, happily inspecting canisters.

"Everything," Menders said with conviction. Cook laughed.

"Well then, you like to eat, I like to cook, we'll get on famously," she declared. "I knew you had the appetite of a younger boy, you don't even look like you're finished with your growing yet. However, while the others are looking around, I do want to ask you something. Why would a very pleasant and decent young man like yourself become an assassin?"

"What makes you think I'm pleasant and decent?" Menders asked, perching on the edge of the table and lifting Katrin to rest against his shoulder.

"All I have to see, young man, is how you love that baby there, to say nothing of being concerned for the welfare of all of us and very kindly tolerating Hemmett's nonsense, which can be trying to say the least."

"Yes, well … unlike many other boys sent into Special Services work, who are chosen and told that they will undertake the training, I volunteered to become an assassin."

She shook her head in bewilderment.

"I can't say I see it, but I suspect you had your reasons. I certainly won't hold your being an assassin against you, and after all, you won't be assassinating anyone now."

Menders couldn't help laughing. Who knows, he thought to himself. I will do whatever it takes to keep this little child safe.

But for Cook's sake, he made light of it.

"No, I'm sure I won't be. Cook, do you think that deer and pig are from these farmers' winter provisions?"

"Very likely. They've been hanging a while, you can't just shoot a deer and carve off a chop right away, meat has to age," she replied.

"We can't simply take it and leave them with nothing," he said.

"I'm sure they've kept something back, and you'd insult them by refusing their gifts," Cook cautioned him. "Take your weapons out tomorrow and assassinate a couple of deer with them, take them by these farmer's houses in exchange. That's the way people do things out here."

Only some do, he thought, remembering how his father, on a country estate similar to this one, treated his tenant farmers with callous indifference.

"It's a good custom when living in the big house to be of service to the people who live on the estate. It's best to have something ready on the stove all the time, so that not only can young assassins have something to eat whenever their stomach starts growling, but so can anyone from the estate who needs a meal." Cook was chattering away, oblivious to Menders' thoughtful silence.

"Would you see to that?" Menders asked. At that very moment, his stomach began to rumble.

"There's soup there done enough to eat," Cook responded gleefully, much amused by the sound.

"I shall endure for a while and take a look around the place," Menders replied with as much dignity as he could muster, while his stomach added an obligato of growls. He started for the door with Katrin, snatching a slice of bread from a cut loaf lying on a bench. Cook saw him and he could hear her laughing after him.

The entryway was cobwebbed and dusty. A great clock

stood in solitary splendor opposite the huge, double front door. Its wooden casing was burled heartwood, darkened with age, the large brass pendulums and balance weights hanging unmoving behind the grimy glass door, like ancient lost treasures seen through a murky sea. The vast face was faded; the ornate hands of aged and darkened bronze stood motionless at three minutes past two. Cut outs in the clock face showed much of the inner workings, but it was obvious the brass and bronze gears and cogwheels had not turned in many years.

Menders opened the clock's glass door. Inside was a key, thick with dust. He set the balance weights and by stretching up, could just reach the hands to set the correct time. He slid the key into its slot and began to wind.

To his surprise, the winding gear moved with relative ease. The spring tightened, Menders gently set the pendulum in motion.

The old clock began thrumming out a slow and steady thump, like a giant mechanical heart.

Time began to move in the dark old house. Katrin cooed. Menders smiled at her and with the clock pulsing away, he began inspecting their home.

Cobwebs hung in the corners like lace curtains, dust was thick on the floor and windows were grimy. Menders looked into several rooms. There was a considerable library, though the smell of musty books was so overpowering that he did not linger. There was a room furnished as an office that he particularly liked, where the Head of Household would see to the running of the estate.

And he was the Head of Household, and what he knew of running estates was… nothing.

Katrin whimpered and he was suddenly very sure that she needed a clean diaper.

"All right then, Little Princess, we'll find your charming wet nurse and the diapers, shall we?" he asked, looking at the dust on the floor, seeing the multiple footprints that had gone up the massive wooden stairs. He followed them upwards, hearing voices as he came to the first floor.

This was apparently where the bedrooms were located. There was much movement, laughter and gossip as the women chatted while flinging open cases. Lucen pried open crates and boxes and Franz sorted through piles of medical supplies while Hemmett went gamboling about and got in everyone's way.

"There you are," Zelia Greinholz said cheerfully as Menders stepped into the midst of them.

"We're looking for diapers," he answered.

Mistress Trottenheim came and took Katrin from him. The baby's whimpers rose to yowls of protest.

"You're spoiling her terribly," she said with venom. "I'll see to her." She walked away into an adjoining room. Menders followed her silently.

Mistress Trottenheim started when she found him behind her in her bedroom.

"I'll be here until we can get the nursery sorted out. It's on the next floor up, and it's a wreck. I'll see to her, thank you."

"I'll see where you have the diapers and other things and I will see how you change her diapers, thank you," Menders responded.

"Mister Menders, it isn't necessary for you to carry her about and do these things. I'm her nurse," she sniffed.

"Do you want to be her nurse?"

Caught by surprise, she immediately answered, "No." Then she flushed red and glared at him. "Do you want to be her guardian?" she snapped waspishly.

"Yes. I want to be her guardian. What concerns me is that you don't really want to be her nurse. I can certainly understand why and I'm not naïve enough to believe that someone else's baby can replace yours, but I want this child to have all the love it is possible for her to have."

She turned away and busied herself by changing Katrin.

Though she was not ungentle, she handled the baby briskly. Katrin began to wail. The nurse fastened the diaper and then tried to hand the baby back to him.

"She's hungry," he said, as Katrin sucked her lips in between shrieks.

"It isn't time for her to eat yet," Mistress Trottenheim declared.

Menders stared at her. "If she's hungry now, feed her now."

To his annoyance, she opened her mouth to retort. He whipped off his glasses and glared at her without blinking until her gaze dropped and she flushed red.

She angrily put Katrin to her breast. Menders was gratified to see her surprise when the ravenous baby latched on vigorously.

"The other people here will consider you quite highly placed, and I will not have you being blatantly rude and disrespectful to me," Menders said as the baby suckled and Mistress Trottenheim looked thunderous. "If you truly don't want to be here, and don't want to be her wet nurse, I won't insist that you stay longer than it takes me to find a replacement. Until then you will have to be civil to me and I will do the same for you."

"I didn't say I wanted to leave," she retorted.

"No, you didn't, but I won't have her nursed by someone who resents her," Menders answered. "You are free to return to Erdahn. You're the only one of us who is able to do so, because you were assigned to be her wet nurse and nothing more. Claim to have lost your milk and your responsibility is over. I can't shed my responsibility. The Doctor and Greinholz can't either, neither can Cook. But you're free to go."

She did not reply. When Katrin finished, she handed her back to Menders, buttoning up quickly.

He positioned Katrin more comfortably in his arms and began to leave the room.

"Mister Menders, you don't have to take her with you everywhere," Mistress Trottenheim said behind him. "She can go in her bassinet for now, until the nursery is cleaned. Or I can take her."

He turned, and gave her a very small, very cold smile.

"I have asked everyone to call me Menders. You are the only person here who refuses to do that. After seeing how you handled her while you changed her diaper, I am in no hurry to leave her in your care."

He was glad to see her look away in confusion.

***

An inspection of the first floor found that he had been left the largest bedroom. Menders took a jaunt around it with Katrin held against his shoulder while he rubbed her back. He'd seen the nurse do it before and had also noticed that she'd neglected to do so after the baby's recent feeding. Within a few seconds, Katrin released a gusty belch and he laughed softly.

"So she thought she'd hand me a baby with a bellyache and then triumph over me when I didn't know what to do, eh Little Princess?" he said, snuggling her into the crook of his arm again. "She doesn't know old Menders, does she? Probably thinks because I'm a man I can't possibly pick up a trick or two through observation – or that I'll overlook her deliberately placing you in the position of being uncomfortable and ill."

The bed hadn't been made up yet and was covered with heavy canvas as protection from dust. Menders made the mistake of touching the heavy bed curtains just as Eiren, passing in the hallway, saw him and said frantically, "Don't touch the curtains, sir!"

A shower of dust made him sneeze violently and then Katrin sneezed too. He fled sheepishly into the hall, while Eiren took Katrin and rocked her until he stopped bending and sneezing like some sort of bizarre clockwork.

"I think the first thing we'll do is get the bed curtains outside and beaten," he gasped, wiping at his streaming eyes. "That is, if it gets warm enough."

"Oh yes! It should warm up nicely in the middle of the day," Eiren giggled, much amused by his performance. "We'll get a ladder in and haul them all out. There just wasn't time after we swept all the spiders from the kitchen." Spontaneously she cuddled the baby close and kissed the top of her head. Menders watched as he wiped his eyes and nose with his handkerchief, his mind working.

***

From Menders' Journal:

The rest of the household have retired, and I will not be far behind them. It has been an exhausting but productive day making the bedrooms habitable, so that we could fall into clean beds from exhaustion.

Doctor Franz declared war on cobwebs and was a comical figure, flailing about with a broom, swathed in a huge apron he found somewhere, his head wrapped in a cloth. Much giggling from the ladies. By the end of the day he'd rousted most of the cobwebs in the living quarters and was very proud of himself.

Lucen Greinholz is worth his weight in gold when it comes to miserable, dirty tasks, particularly in removing nests of mice from drawers, which caused much consternation when discovered, to say nothing of shrieking, again from the ladies.

I have spent the day on top of ladders, scaling woodwork and crawling across beams to unhook and re-hook hangings, drapes and curtains, being the smallest of the men, and the most agile, thanks to my training. I have only been so dirty once before in my life, in that hiding in a ditch incident I don't care to remember.

I find the members of the Princess' household to be cheerful and ready to make the best of our situation, with the exception of Ermina Trottenheim, who continues contemptuous and moody. I can excuse some of her behavior because of her situation, but I foresee nothing but trouble coming from her. The other women, including the wives of the estate farmers who helped out today were shunned by her, or ordered about peremptorily until I put a stop to it. She is going to be a problem, and the sooner I make her disposable, the better.

With that end in mind, I have engaged Marjana Spaltz, the wife of Mister Spaltz, estate farmer, in the post of wet nurse for the Princess. She has a surfeit of milk, and would be pleased to help out. I have also hired her daughter, Eiren, as the first of the Princess' nursemaids, and have been told that there are several other likely girls on the estate who would be glad for a similar position. Eiren is exceptionally bright and naturally fond of children, though I was told in confidence by one of the farmers' wives that she was badly frightened by her mother's recent delivery. She is tender and loving with Katrin and I believe will be an excellent nursemaid for her.

Menders rubbed his eyes and put down his pen. Enough journal for one day. He rose and made a trip down the hall to look in on Katrin, who was tucked into her traveling basket in Mistress Trottenheim's room.

He found the wet nurse getting into bed.

"Am I to have no privacy?" she snapped.

"I was just looking in on the Princess."

"She's asleep, which I soon hope to be."

Menders walked into the room, picked up the basket and a handful of diapers, and walked out. He wasn't leaving his baby there.

"What will you do when she starts screaming for the breast at three in the morning?" Mistress Trottenheim shot after him.

"I'll bring her here," Menders answered back over his shoulder. "So I wouldn't sleep too soundly, if I were you."

He closed and bolted the door of his room, setting the basket on the desk. Katrin was awake now and gazing up at him.

He lifted her out and got into the bed holding her.

"Why don't you just sleep here with me tonight, until we get your nursery sorted out," he said conversationally. "I think you'll find it much more comfortable than in that basket on the desk." He made a little nest for her on the empty half of the bed, where he could reach her easily, and blew out the lantern on the nightstand. His body slowly relaxed and he sighed, reaching out to touch Katrin's head.

He leaned over and kissed her tiny, velvety cheek.

"Everything is all right – sleep well, Little Princess," he whispered.

CHAPTER 4
STRANGE AND VIOLENT WATERS

I have declared a rest day after two solid weeks of cleaning and refurbishing the portions of the house that we will be using. Much of the house has been sealed off, access doors locked and spiked shut, chimney flues closed and latched. It would be nearly impossible to access The Shadows in any clandestine way.

Everyone went back to bed after breakfast, except for Cook, who is happily thumping away in the kitchen, kneading bread. Mister Spaltz stopped by and took Hemmett back to his farm with him, giving us all a much welcome break.

The nursery is now clean and habitable and as Eiren Spaltz and Kata Brogen are able to begin work, Katrin will be sleeping there. She has been in my room, and I must admit that I will miss her, though having a full night's sleep will be welcome. At the moment she is snugged up here in the bed beside me, asleep after some play where I dangle my watch for her to look at. She can't quite follow it with her eyes, but she can focus on it. Franz tells me that this is advanced behavior for her age.

Mistress Ermina Trottenheim will now be extraneous and it is my intention to have her leave for Erdahn at the earliest opportunity. She has not attempted to fit in or endear herself to anyone, and her attitude toward me is cool and contemptuous. She shows no interest in the baby and nurses her begrudgingly. Katrin is uncomfortable with her as a nurse. So Mistress Trottenheim will have her walking papers once the new routine is settled.

After setting his journal aside, Menders stopped off at the kitchen and then went toward his office with a handful of cookies and Katrin in her basket.

He was distracted by noises from Doctor Franz's office and detoured. The doctor was there, rattling around with some bottles.

"Can't sleep in the daytime either?" Franz asked with a

grin.

"Never really could." Menders set Katrin's basket securely in one of Franz's armchairs. He described the plan for Mistress Trottenheim to be sent back to Erdahn and Franz nodded in agreement.

"Franz, do you know why they sent Katrin here?" Menders asked. He had formulated his own theories but now wanted some input from others.

Franz sighed and sat down, gesturing for Menders to do the same. Menders set his handful of cookies between them and Franz pounced hungrily.

"I have a pretty good idea," the doctor replied. "I've deduced much of it, but can't prove it. Katrin's father wasn't in the usual run of Prince Consorts. They're generally chosen for or by the Queen for the sole purpose of conceiving a child – and they tend to vanish conveniently afterward, so they don't get ambitious and try to seize power. He wasn't a Prince Consort at all, frankly, but someone who was at Court for years. The Queen knew him from the time they were youngsters and I believe she was in love with him. This was quite an irregular situation. My suspicion is that Katrin's been sent here to be forgotten."

"I have begun to think that Katrin is here so that she is protected from her sister," Menders replied.

"It's possible," Franz conceded. "Who can say, really, what moves through the mind of the Queen? She drifts from crystalline lucidity to drunken dullness at a whim."

"Being banished up here may be to our benefit," Menders replied.

"How so?"

"I don't want Katrin involved in the Court in any way," Menders explained. "Not after what you and Trottenheim have told me about Princess Aidelia." He quieted, remembering the gruesome stories.

Aidelia hated being cuddled or held. She fought anyone

who picked her up. Worse still, she reveled in cruelty, torturing animals, pinching and gouging her nurses. She would claim that no-one could make her cry and then would rake her arm with her fingernails until blood flowed, laughing the entire time. Her most recent hobby had been getting hold of any sort of blade and using it to cut designs in her arms and legs. She sickened any reasonable person who saw her, because of her continually roving eyes with the white showing all round and because of her filthiness, as she fought viciously against being bathed or groomed. All this in a child not much past her fifth birthday – a child who was the Heiress to the Throne of Mordania.

"Tell me," Menders said carefully. "Is there a chance that Katrin will be like Aidelia?' Inside he was screaming in agony at the thought.

"Different fathers," Franz answered immediately. "Aidelia's father was completely demented, mad as a spoon. Did that eye-rolling Aidelia does. His favorite hobby was killing puppies, loved watching torture, once got out of his carriage and bludgeoned a man to death with a walking stick for no reason anyone could find. He ended up deciding to fly off the Palace roof one night when he'd been drinking more than usual."

"Oh yes?" Menders murmured. He knew how to help people to 'fly'. Two people took an arm and a leg apiece, then one... two... three... Very likely Aidelia's father had been assisted in his flight.

"Who is Katrin's father, please?" Menders said in the bland, calm way that often tricked people into speaking before they thought.

"That tone is a doctor's trick too, Menders," Franz responded, just as blandly. "However, I will tell you. Bernhard, Lord Markha."

Menders blinked in surprise.

"I know Lord Markha," he said without thinking. "He was one of my tutors at the Military Academy and at Special

Services training."

"I wondered if you might have known him. He was teaching at the Academy during the time you would have been there."

"*Was* teaching there," Menders repeated softly.

"Yes, he's dead," Franz answered "Shortly before Katrin's birth. It's presumed the Queen had it arranged."

Menders was silent. Bernhard Markha had been an intelligent, blond man from an Old Mordanian family. In every way Markha was the foil to Menders; tall, fair, far more outgoing. He was friendly, compassionate and had been protective of the younger cadets. He'd been assigned as Menders' tutor when it was found that Menders' education prior to entering the Academy had been lacking. Later, Markha had been one of Menders' circle of friends.

"For someone like him… with the Queen. How could he?" Menders said with distaste.

"The Queen has her better moments," Franz answered gently. "And she isn't mad. She's a drunkard, yes, and of late she's a slattern and has gotten worse with time. She had times of being most attractive before her latest pregnancy. She and Markha had a long association. His father was attached to the Court and Markha was around it from the time he was a boy. They were of an age, he and the Queen. Also – you're very young, Menders."

"I'm not an innocent, nor am I without experience," Menders retorted with a bit of heat.

"My apologies. Some men are attracted by dissipation in women. It draws out their protective nature. Markha was one of them. He had great feeling for others and a great desire to help her, and for a time it seemed that his attentions would change the Queen – she was still the Princess then. She improved greatly, had a sense of purpose. Then the old Queen, "Morghenna the Terrible" finally died - and he was no more."

Menders sat silently for a while, looking at Katrin asleep

in her basket, her fist curled under her chin. His relief that she didn't have the same father as Aidelia was palpable. Then he felt a sudden and startling surge of regret for Markha, the caring and decent man he'd known, who'd decided to swim in strange and violent waters.

"The Court eats people," Franz sighed, leaning back in his chair and putting his feet on his desk.

"So it seems. More reason to keep Katrin away from it."

"Menders, if the Queen summons her there, you'll have no choice," Franz replied.

Menders looked at him over his glasses, and Franz turned away.

"We'll see. I'm very resourceful," Menders told him.

"No doubt, we will. You're an amazing young man."

"You talk like you're an old grandfather," Menders answered.

"I'm hard on thirty. I was married. I'm widowed and have no desire to remarry. I've been a Court Physician and let me tell you, that jades a man rapidly. So forgive me if I sound like a sage," Franz sighed. He sought out a cigar and offered the box to Menders, who declined.

"You seem to adapt quickly," Franz continued, lighting the cigar and puffing, opening the window behind him to let out the smoke, while Menders draped a light blanket over Katrin's bassinet to protect her.

"It's considered an essential trait for an assassin," Menders answered.

"Yes, but for an assassin to become a country squire and foster father?" Franz grinned.

Menders shrugged. "Yes. It's a matter of mental discipline. At this time, I'm the father of a baby girl and managing her estate. So I rise to the challenge."

Franz shook his head.

"There are men who spend a lifetime learning to adapt

that way," he said.

"I've had practice."

After a few moments of companionable silence, Franz sighed.

"What are we going to do about women way the hells out here?" he said, cocking an eyebrow at Menders.

"In all honesty, after the last two weeks, that is absolutely the last thing on my mind."

"Springtime will change that," Franz teased.

Menders grinned. "Springtime will make me even busier, I'm afraid. I'll have to conserve energy. If you're feeling amorous, go romance Cook."

"I might not survive the experience, she's far too energetic for me," Franz laughed. Cook was a force of nature, up before any of them every morning, devoting her entire day to the endless preparation of meals, preserving and butchering between times. She was badgering Menders to dig a kitchen garden as well. Menders pointed out that it would have to wait until the ground wasn't frozen hard as stone. She was a good natured woman, widowed because of a war as so many were, with a nearly grown son in Erdahn who was a journeyman tailor.

"It could be a wonderful match," Menders jibed.

"You romance her," Franz snorted.

"Me? She treats me like I'm her son. The other day she rapped
my knuckles with a wooden spoon."

"Brave lady, thrashing the sinister assassin," Franz laughed. "I'm sure Cook will find her own man given some time and it won't be you or me. Of course, there's Mistress Ermina Trottenheim, but that's more misery than I'm willing to take on. So hire some buxom housemaids, one for you, one for me."

Menders felt his face go still and hard.

"I'm joking," the doctor protested. Menders worked to gain control of rising temper.

"Your father was a right bastard, wasn't he?" Franz asked very quickly, catching Menders off guard. "First rights, and all that nonsense?" Franz hammered on.

"Worse. People were objects to him," Menders said coldly. "Particularly girls."

"I apologize, Menders," Franz replied. "I had an idea, but I wasn't sure. I have no intention of cutting a swath through the farmer's daughters, don't fear. I don't treat people as objects. I joke a lot. It eases things a great deal when one is a doctor and dealing with life and death all the time. I still miss my wife and she's been gone for four years. Any romancing I do will be discreet, as well as lasting, never fear."

"Thank the Gods I'm too tired to consider it," Menders grumbled, rattled that this man had gotten so much information out of him.

"Understandable," Franz grinned. "Your attention is engaged at present by putting this disused place together and loving and caring for that magnificent little baby. Enjoy your new fatherhood, Menders, and don't worry about the salacious natterings of an old fart like me."

"Speaking of the baby." Menders excused himself, rising and lifting Katrin's bassinet, wanting to take her to his room to settle her in her crib.

"Yes, the day marches on," Franz answered. "I'm going out on calls."

Just as Menders was about to go through the door, Franz spoke again.

"You can look at me with your white eyes if you like, but I can't help wondering – doesn't an assassin treat people like objects too?"

Menders turned toward him but spared him the eyes.

"Some do. I didn't. I saw them as people the world would be better off without. People who should be removed, as you would remove a splinter before it goes septic."

Franz raised his eyebrows.

"I think I'm glad that you're a country squire now," he said. "I wouldn't want to find you creeping up on me in the dark."

"If I were going to kill you, you would never know I was there. One moment you would be alive, the next moment you would be dead. I would hand your death to you as quietly and intimately as if I had slipped a note into your pocket."

"That's a form of mercy, I suppose," the doctor remarked.

"Very much so. An assassin is a trained professional, as skilled as any craftsman or artisan. We are not sadists who enjoy and relish killing. Any who develop such tendencies are shunned, driven from our ranks and - eliminated."

Nightmare images flashed across Menders' inner eye, the story of the great assassin Ranfeld, who had gone mad and begun to kill savagely and indiscriminately. The tales had been whispered in the dormitory of the Military Academy and later in the private rooms of the Special Services department – and Morshall Komroff, Commandant of the Academy, made it a point to tell the grim story to every young assassin.

No-one had been able to stop or eliminate Ranfeld, whose talents as an assassin made him slipperier than ice. Eventually he had been hunted down like an animal by his fellow assassins. Mounted on armored horses, armed with rifles, pikes and lances, they cut him down on a misty plain south of Erdahn. Even so, Ranfeld had managed to kill two of them before they finished him.

Menders would never forget the Commandant's eyes as he told the story. He had been in the group that had gone after Ranfeld, having been an assassin himself at the time. Because they were shunned by other people, assassins tended to consider one another brothers. It had been a
terrible burden for those men to kill one of their own. The

Commandant had been more than a brother to Ranfeld – he had been the man's bonded lover. His eyes were wells of grief when he told the story, again and again, so that young men being sent on their first mission would take heed and remember...

"I have removed many enemies of the state, both within and without Mordania's borders, and I have helped keep a tenuous peace between Mordania and its neighbors so that others might live," Menders continued, giving no outward sign of the inward workings of his mind.

"I... hadn't thought of it like that," Franz said, somewhat shamefacedly. "You're a hero. You should have been given a medal."

"Assassins are never openly commended or acknowledged. We work in the shadows of history. Heroes are loud men who charge the enemy waving a sword. That's what the public expects and wants. In fact, should I have been killed or captured on a mission in another country, Mordania would disavow any knowledge of me. I would have been erased from all official records, and would never have existed."

"Hardly seems worth it," Franz said. "All that risk with no reward?"

"We serve. We do not seek reward," Menders responded, rising. He went to his room with Katrin. She woke after her short nap and he lifted her out of the bassinet.

He held her, looking into her eyes.

"I think I'm going to have to be all things to you, my little one," he whispered. "Do you mind? You see, I can be anything. It's something I learned a long time ago."

He could swear she smiled. He rocked her gently.

"A man just told me that I love you," he said, patting her back while her eyes closed. "He's right, you know."

CHAPTER 5
HEAD OF HOUSEHOLD

From Menders' Journal:

Finally received money from The Palace for Katrin's and the household's support. Will repay Franz and myself what we've forwarded from our own incomes, as there will now be regular payments from the Crown. It seems they haven't entirely forgotten about us these past months, although I am unsure how I feel about that. Perhaps it would be best if they did.

Purchased a farlin for myself, a primitive horse-type creature, though their resemblance to the common horse is limited to the fact that they have four legs and a long neck. They are used by the Thrun herdsman on the Sea of Grass. He's largely unbroken and wild, but intelligent and a likely mount, very fast and with a fiery temper. His name, Demon, suits him.

With the roads passable after the thaw, I have made contact with the estate farmers so I can learn how to run this place. They're the ones who know. I'm sure they expected me to be an arrogant little shit, but I am hoping they will be accommodating when they find I'm ready to learn from them and not tell them what to do. Several have already made use of Franz's services and Cook's endlessly simmering pot of stew. They seem wary of all of us, of me in particular. This is to be expected. The Gods only know what stories have circulated about me already. It seems a farmer will ride all the way across a snowy cold landscape to the big house on some pretense or another, just to get a look at an assassin.

Have to cut a lot of wood. Woodlot horribly neglected, much dead wood and many overgrown trees. Thank the gods Lucen knows how to manage a woodlot. He's good with an axe and I'm skilled with anything with an edge on it. Wood is used for all heating and cooking, even in summer, as it's always cold enough at night to warrant lighting the fires. We cut wood for hours every day and the stoves and fireplaces eat it in no time. Will see about bringing in some loads of coal or chabron before next winter. Lignus is preferable but expensive; also the Artreyans don't want to sell much to

Mordania. Must look into more efficient heating.

I'm in a quandary regarding running the household. What I know of housekeeping is minimal and I simply do not have the time to devote to such concerns. This spring I must become a farmer, an estate manager, continue being a father for Katrin as well as coping with all problems that arise. I asked Zelia to try the job but from the look of panic in her eyes she is no more anxious to have a position of authority than Lucen is. Cook is working flat out now and keeps the kitchen running admirably, feeding seven people regularly with more from the estate when there is illness or injury on one of the farms. So I am making sad cobbling of the household management and accounts. Where to find a housekeeper out here?

Katrin is growing fast, thriving with Marjana Spaltz as wet nurse and nursemaids giving her bottles at night. So it is high time to tell Mistress Trottenheim to move on. I hope she will be as relieved as I. She has no purpose here and continues to be sulky and disrespectful to all, myself in particular.

Voices filtering through the window from outside distracted Menders from his journal. His well-trained ears discerned a group of the estate farmers, stopping by the kitchen at lunchtime, discussing him.

"Have to say he's a good one. Shook his hand the other day – like iron. Stronger than mine. He's no stranger to hard work, even if he is gentry."

"Seen the little bastard with that axe? It goes around so fast you don't even see it, then splits flying everywhere. Swings it from the ground he does."

"He uses a good old-style saddle on that farlin of his too, not a great cushiony Artreyan saddle. Can ride astride and sidewise too. Saw him jump down and back up yesterday without the farlin stopping. He's a horseman, I'll give him that."

"Watched him walk across the ridgepole of the house the other day to see to those broken roof tiles. Like he was walking across the ground. Never even held his arms out to balance."

"My girl's one of the nurserymaids there now and she says he's a perfect gentleman. Not like some great people can be when there's a young girl in service at a house. And he loves the little Princess. Always takes her with him. She's the light of his life. He's cut out to be a family man."

"Sound like you're fixing to get him saddled with your Kata."

"Be a step up for her, if I could."

"And you too, no doubt. You old fox."

The men laughed and walked away.

Menders had to hide a smile. Intrigue was everywhere, even at The Shadows. Kata Brogen was a pleasant young girl and a devoted nurserymaid for Katrin, but lacking in curiosity or native wit – and a mere child as well, of absolutely no interest to him. He had no intention of finding a lady for The Shadows, but if he did, she certainly couldn't be farther from little Kata.

***

"Where would I go?" Mistress Trottenheim cried, her face crumpled in dismay.

"Back to Erdahn I would imagine," Menders replied, staying across the room from her. He had not expected her to respond to being relieved of her duties as she had. "Surely you have family, or your late husband's family…"

She shook her head. "My parents are dead. My husband was older and had no family. I have nowhere to go – and the Queen ordered that I was to come here!" Her voice had risen to a shout.

"Mind your tone," he said, not wanting everyone else in the house to hear their exchange. "The Queen ordered you here as a wet nurse. You didn't wish to hold that position. You've made it very obvious that you do not like being here, that you have no feelings for the baby, that you are contemptuous of me. You haven't tried to get along with anyone."

"They haven't tried to get along with me!" she retorted.

"That is patently absurd. You have – sit down." She had burst into tears and was pacing back and forth. She flung herself down on a chair, her eyes streaming. Menders turned away and looked out the window of his office. As he expected, once he was not watching her,
Mistress Trottenheim quieted.

"Now," he said, keeping his eyes turned to the window, "There is no reason for you to be here. Why not return to Erdahn? I can give you a recommendation. Surely having been nurserymaid for Princess Aidelia, you can get a recommendation from someone at Court as well. You might even be able to find employment with the Court again."

"I would not want to be nurserymaid to that child again," Mistress Trottenheim said, her voice grating with tension.

"That's understandable, but surely there are other children in need of care."

"You need a housekeeper."

Menders blinked. She'd shifted direction so quickly that he had no reply.

"You need a housekeeper," she repeated. "You haven't the slightest idea how to run this house and you're going to be busy with running the land. The place needs laundresses and cleaners and someone who can organize things. The Princess is growing out of her clothing. I can run the house."

Menders turned and looked at her. There was an avid light in her eyes that he distrusted.

"What experience do you have?" he asked.

"Before I married, I helped my mother run our household," she replied eagerly. "It was a very large house with servants, a cook and gardeners. I did the household accounts and directed the servants."

"There are no servants here and Cook needs no direction," Menders said in a calm tone he knew would irritate her. "What is needed is organization of duties. No-one is to be ordered around."

"Of course not," she replied quickly. Too quickly.

Menders turned away and looked out the window again, letting his mind tick over.

Of all the people in the household, he knew her least. He'd avoided her because he sensed she had a histrionic nature. He suspected a desire for power was behind her offer – but he had few options and was running short of time and energy for all that needed to be done. It could take months to find someone trustworthy and suitable for the task. Menders didn't have months. The spring and summer in Old Mordania were short and would be filled with managing the estate, so that sufficient food was put by for next winter. Still, the idea of giving this woman a position of such importance was daunting.

He shrugged slightly. A sickening pain shot from his overworked right shoulder joint all the way down into his hand, reminding him of the endless labor he performed, except for a few hours of sleep a night. It made the decision. He was not a housekeeper and for now one had presented herself. It would buy him time to locate a better person for the job if Mistress Trottenheim proved unsuitable.

"I'll try you at it," he said, turning back to her. "Take warning. If you should begin to throw your weight around or treat anyone with less than complete respect, I'll see you on the next train to Erdahn and inform the Queen, my cousin, of the reasons behind my actions."

He saw anger kindle deep in her eyes, but she held herself in check.

"It would also be best," he went on, "if we agree to keep a mutual distance. Your behavior so far has done little to win my friendship, Mistress Trottenheim."

***

Hemmett crept quietly along the hallway behind the kitchen, where the door to the backstairs was.

He knew Menders was there. Menders' face had been tired and grey and when it was like that, he always went to the backstairs.

The backstairs were forbidden. Hemmett wasn't supposed to go near them because Papa said they weren't safe. Maybe Menders didn't know they weren't safe, because he would go and sit on them. He did it almost every day after he'd chopped wood for a long time.

Hemmett listened hard. He could hear Menders there, sitting on the third step as he always did. His breathing was rough, as if he had run hard, but Hemmett knew he hadn't. He'd just walked in from the woodlot.

Hemmett peeked around the doorway and saw Menders there in the dark, sitting with his head down on his knees, rubbing slowly and steadily at his right arm. It must be hurting. Menders groaned softly and rubbed his arm harder.

Hemmett followed Menders a lot. Menders was fair and he let Hemmett know what he could and couldn't do. He never changed his mind for no reason. He made up good games and gave Hemmett things to do that made him feel important. Mama and Papa were good but they never stayed the same. One day they would tell Hemmett not to do something, but if he did it the next day they would just pretend they didn't see. He didn't know where he was with them. He always knew where he was with Menders.

"There's a little mouse in this stairway," Menders said quietly, not moving his head from his knees. Hemmett shrank back around the doorway and didn't even breathe. He didn't want

Menders to know he was near the forbidden stairs.

"You aren't supposed to be around these stairs, Hemmett," Menders went on. "You could get hurt here. I don't want you here again. You don't need to worry about me. I'm just resting for a few minutes. There isn't anything wrong."

Hemmett didn't say anything, just stood against the wall, waiting. After a while, he heard Menders stand and walk slowly up the stairs. Hemmett began to follow, but then ran around to the front stairs, which were all right for him to climb, and went up to the nursery that way. He knew that was where Menders was going.

Hemmett watched from the stairs as Menders went into the nursery and picked up Katrin, who started her funny laughing as soon as Menders went in the room. Then he sat down slowly and stiffly in the big chair, holding her.

"Hello, Little Princess," Menders said softly. Katrin crowed and snuggled against Menders. "I've cut at least a cord of wood today. Not really, but my arm feels like it. Sometimes I wonder if you can die from cutting wood."

Hemmett crept across the nursery floor toward the chair. Menders sounded so sad. Hemmett wanted to help.

He saw Menders sniff slightly and then smile as Hemmett reached his side. Hemmett plucked at Menders' sleeve.

"Hemmett too?" he asked. "Hemmett too?"

"There's always room for you too, manling," Menders smiled, reaching down to help Hemmett climb on his lap. Hemmett snuggled down once he was there while Katrin cooed and reached out to him. Hemmett touched her hand gently, remembering how Menders always told him they had to take great care of her because she was so small, to always be careful.

Hemmett settled back against Menders and slid his thumb into his mouth. Menders' arm around him was warm and strong. Hemmett closed his eyes. He felt safe here.

CHAPTER 6
MADAME HOLZ

When Katrin was six months old and just starting to crawl, with the short northern summer in full bloom, Lucen Greinholz returned from Shadows Halt where he met the weekly train to collect mail and parcels. He came into Menders' office with a royal decree in his hand.

Menders opened it and perused the contents. Then he flung it viciously on his desk. He rose and stormed down the hall to Franz's office.

"It seems we're about to acquire a head nurse," he said when the other man looked up in surprise.

"Grundar shit! Why?" Franz exclaimed.

"It seems someone has remembered we are here and has decided to send along a Madame Holz to see to the Princess' upbringing," Menders snapped in reply.

"Oh no."

"Why, 'Oh no'? You know this Holz woman?"

"Let's go for a ride," Franz said, rising from his chair. They'd formed a policy of talking about certain topics away from the house. Some issues concerning the Princess were best kept between Franz and himself.

The summer landscape was radiant, glowing green and gold but Menders was blind to it.

Franz came straight to the point.

"Madame Holz, my dear Menders, is Princess Aidelia's head nurse and she was the Queen's nurse as well. She reigns supreme in the nursery at the Palace. She's a drunkard and a great proponent of toughening children."

Menders did not respond.

"I'm talking about toughening, the very old style discipline," Franz continued. Menders remained silent until Franz burst out, "Well? Don't just sit there looking at me like a drowned fish. I'm talking about routine beatings and near starvation, Menders! Princess Aidelia is barking mad because her father was, but this woman's treatment of her certainly hasn't helped the situation! It's what led to the Queen being a weak creature who runs to the bottle every time she's challenged or uncertain!"

"I'm well aware of the kind of discipline you're talking about!" Menders shouted, startling Demon. The farlin bolted and Menders had a struggle to quiet him. After a moment Franz caught up to them.

"I know what you're talking about," Menders said again. "All too well."

"Close to the bone, eh?" Franz looked at him intently.

Menders nodded.

They rode on in silence for a few minutes.

"And fish don't drown. You can't drown something that breathes water," Menders said quietly, embarrassed by his outburst.

"You know everything," Franz joked, and smiled. Menders didn't respond.

"I saw on your official orders that your title is Lord Stettan," Franz continued after a moment.

"Yes." Menders spoke reluctantly.

"I know a little of your late father, but was he..."

"A believer in toughening? Yes," Menders replied bitterly. "From birth. The harsh tutors, before them, nurses who hit me if I cried. No blankets in winter or fire to keep the nursery warm, food when they decided I would eat, and precious little of it. Having to memorize endless sagas and recite them, being beaten if I forgot so much as a word. I loved being sent away to the Military Academy. It was a much easier life."

"Grahl's teeth, Menders, I'm sorry. But that's what's in store for the Princess if this woman comes here and is her nurse," Franz said worriedly.

"My childhood is a done thing, but hers shall be nothing like mine, not while I can draw breath," Menders muttered.

"When is this woman arriving? Perhaps we can do something to keep her from leaving Erdahn at all."

"She's already on her way," Menders answered.

Franz swore. "I don't suppose we could blow up the tracks?"

Menders burst out laughing

"Don't tempt me," he replied, relieved to have an ally.

"What puzzles me is why she's being sent," Franz mused. "Normally, the royal head nurse is in control until the Heiress is ten years old, when a governess and tutors take over. I wonder if she's in disgrace? Princess Aidelia is only five."

"Considering The Shadows seems to be their idea of a dumping ground, I wouldn't be surprised," Menders sighed. "But she's the last thing we need here."

"I'll help you get rid of her – whatever needs to be done," Franz said, his voice shaking a bit.

"Perhaps Madame will be amenable to an agreement." Menders replied. He looked around, seeing the beautiful afternoon for the first time now that his mind was clear and formulating plans.

"Race you back," he said suddenly, slackening Demon's reins. The farlin took the bit between his teeth and raced away before Franz could turn his big gelding. Menders laughed a little as he heard the doctor yelling after him, calling him all sorts of names.

***

From Menders' Journal:

Now midsummer, the days are long, only two hours of full darkness at night. Madame Holz arrives by special train this evening.

Mistress Trottenheim says Madame Holz is worse than Franz believed. She practices "blanket training" of babies. Child is placed on a blanket, is struck whenever it crawls off of i, until it stays there out of fear. This restricts its movement and frees the nurse for other tasks.

It is hoped by one and all that Madame will find the Shadows not to her liking, and can be persuaded to leave. Should that not be possible, then something else will have to be done. As has often been the case in many final solutions... I will provide that something else.

***

Madame Holz was heavyset, disheveled, ugly as a mangy hog and furious.

"What is the meaning of keeping me waiting, sir!" she demanded. Her voice had the annoying full richness of someone accustomed to being obeyed.

"Sit down," Menders said without preamble or greeting. "You must have documentation with you. Let me see it." He sat behind his desk, hands folded together with fingers laced. He had deliberately let the woman wait and she was at just the fever pitch of rage he'd hoped to reduce her to.

She produced an envelope and flung it at him. He perused the documents with excruciating slowness. He willed something to be out of order so that he could send her away. He could find nothing.

"There is nothing as to why you've been sent here when Princess Aidelia is still so young. Has the Royal Family acquired another head nurse?" he asked coolly.

"I have been sent here because of my vast experience in raising children of the Royal Family," Madame Holz blustered angrily. "I have not only been head nurse to Princess Aidelia, but to the Queen herself."

"And who is Princess Aidelia's head nurse now?" Menders asked.

"Princess Aidelia is a very advanced child because of the thorough training she received from me. She now has a governess. "

Menders knew she was lying.

"I do not feel, as the head of Princess Katrin's household, that we have need of your services," he said. "You may stay here as our guest until the weekly train departs in six days. It is unfortunate the communication regarding your arrival only arrived two days ago or we would have sent word before you left."

"Who do you think you are?" she thundered. Spittle flew from her mouth, sprinkling his face and the papers before him on the desk. Menders hated people who did that.

"I know who I am. Lord Stettan, cousin of Her Majesty, head of Princess Katrin Morghenna's household." Menders removed his glasses and fixed her with his ghost-like eyes.

"Well, Lord Stettan," she snapped, "that documentation is a Royal Command, and you know it. You aren't fooling me. And don't think I'm afraid of your eyes either, I've seen freaks like you before. Her Majesty wants me here to raise the Princess properly and that is what I intend to do."

"I would suggest, Madame, that you decide on a place for retirement and I will provide you with the funds to go there and settle comfortably," Menders countered. "Perhaps Surelia? I own a luxurious villa there which could be deeded to you – as my gift."

She hesitated just long enough to let him know the idea tempted her.

"Don't be absurd! I was sent here by Her Majesty," she spat in response. "It is my duty to obey her command. Her Majesty would be very interested in the offer you've just made me, sir."

"Why? Does my cousin wish to retire to Surelia too?" Menders asked, allowing himself a superior smirk.

Madame Holz bristled at his levity.

"Princess Katrin is being raised in a manner that I approve," Menders went on. "She has a wet nurse and two nurserymaids. She is growing well, is healthy and happy."

"Happiness is not my concern, sir. Royal children must be toughened, so they can endure the rigors of ruling. This has been done since the time of Morghenna the Wise. It is the express wish of the Queen. She would be indignant to find that my services were refused."

She gave him a triumphant glare. Stalemate, he thought. I have nothing left to play right now.

"In that case, I will show you to the nursery, but there are some conditions under which you will begin your duties," he said. "In the first case, there will be no physical punishment of the Princess. She is six months old. That is far too young for a child to be corporally punished. Secondly, there are two nurserymaids employed here who see to her needs. They will continue the nursery routine that the Princess is accustomed to. Lastly, the wet nurse, Mistress Spaltz, is to have access to the Princess at all times, to feed her on demand."

"On demand, sir! Absurd! Since when is a royal child fed on demand! She should have been put on a schedule from birth!" Madame Holz drew herself up in towering indignation.

"The Princess shall not be physically punished or starved," Menders said deliberately, staring up into her eyes. She quailed and went silent.

"I will show you to the nursery," he continued, rising. "Breakfast is at eight. If you prefer something sooner, I can arrange it, though the kitchen is closed for the night."

"Perhaps a glass of wine?" she asked.

"While on duty, Nurse?" he responded with disdain. "That would be entirely inappropriate. Follow me please."

He went upstairs briskly. She was heaving by the time they reached the third floor nursery. Eiren looked up at Menders in dread as Madame Holz flubbered in.

"Madame, this is Eiren Spaltz, one of Princess Katrin's nurserymaids," he said evenly.

Madame Holz didn't acknowledge the girl. She clumped over to the crib and glared down at Katrin.

"This child is disgustingly fat," she announced. "I shall inform the Queen of her condition. It will take much work to correct the damage that has been done here. Royal children are not fed until they're the size of suckling pigs!"

"May I suggest that Madame has had a long day and should retire," Menders replied. "If you wish to discuss Princess Katrin's upbringing further, you may see me tomorrow."

He left her standing there and beckoned to Eiren. He walked her away from the nursery.

"If she does anything at all to the Princess, I want you to scream loud and long," Menders confided in a low tone. "Fight her if you have to. I'll be right outside the door. Don't hesitate, do you hear me?"

Eiren was trembling, but nodded.

"Good girl." Menders walked her back to the nursery, then watched from the darkened hallway until he saw she was in her place beside Katrin's crib. Madame Holz, it seemed, had dragged her bags into the nurse's room.

He went to tell Franz what had transpired.

"Sounds charming," Franz said flippantly but Menders could see he was deeply troubled.

"Hopefully she'll just go to sleep tonight," Menders said. "I'll be standing guard but I don't want her to know I'm there. Eiren is watching, and she'll fight tooth and nail for Katrin,"

"Do you want me to watch with you?" Franz offered.

Menders shook his head.

"I'll probably need you tomorrow, so get some rest," he answered. "Let's just get through the night."

Menders went to his room to change into black shirt and trousers, then situated himself outside the nursery, melting into the shadows. Eiren saw him but gave no indication that she knew he was there. After a short while, he heard resounding snores from the nurse's room, and breathed a sigh of relief. At least Madame Holz wasn't going to try toughening Katrin this night.

***

"The Great Sow wants breakfast taken up," Eiren announced, coming into the dining room, Katrin on her hip. She looked harried, her long red braids frowsy; she hadn't taken time to dress her hair.

"Tell her we don't... no, you sit down, have breakfast," Menders said, rising and helping her put Katrin in her high chair. "I'll deal with Madame."

Up the stairs again to the nursery. Old times, he thought, considering he'd just spent the night on the floor outside the nursery door. He walked in and was treated to the sight of Madame Holz standing there, arms crossed, steaming with fury like a red-velvet-clad railway locomotive.

"We live simply here," he said bluntly. "No-one has breakfast taken to them unless they are ill. If you wish to eat, you will come down to the dining room. It will give you a chance to meet the rest of the household."

"Where is the Princess?" she demanded.

"In the dining room with the rest of us, as usual," Menders answered.

"That is absurd! She should not leave the nursery!"

"Breakfast is on the table," Menders responded, turning on his heel, walking out of the nursery and back down the stairs. After a moment, he heard her following him.

Madame Holz's introduction to the rest of the household was not the social success of the year. Within three minutes of her appearance in the dining room, she had mortally insulted Mistress Trottenheim and Franz. Hemmett took one look at her, realized she was the living embodiment of every horror his young mind could conceive and screamed uncontrollably until he had to be removed by his mother.

Madame ordered Cook to fetch her tea instead of coffee. From his vantage point Menders saw Cook spit into the cup in the kitchen. Lucen Greinholz took it upon himself to grin madly at Madame, which she found extremely unnerving.

Menders' job today was to rasp at Madame Holz's nerves until she was at the screaming point. He was rather looking forward to it.

Halfway through the meal, Madame demanded wine.

"At breakfast, Madame?" Menders asked in a very pleasant and social tone of voice. "That is far too sophisticated for us in the country. Has it become the custom at Court?" He saw Franz cover a smirk with his napkin.

"I feel a chill," she responded curtly.

"I'll build a fire in the nursery for you," Menders answered.

"There should be no fire in the nursery, it's not good for the baby," she retorted.

"Well then, you'll just have to endure the chill. I would suggest woolen underwear, it can be quite cool here at any time of the year," Menders responded calmly, finishing his coffee. Missing your wine are you, he thought, noticing that her hands were trembling. Good thing I've locked up all the bottles. You'll feel demons dancing under your skin before long, if I'm not mistaken.

After breakfast he took Katrin and went with her to his office. On cue, Madame erupted through the door.

"What is the meaning of bringing the child in here?" she trumpeted.

"I keep her with me a good part of the day. I am her guardian after all," Menders responded.

"She must be returned to the nursery!"

"No."

Madame came up short, blinking as if slapped. It seemed that no one had ever tried a simple but effective 'no' on her before. It was as final as the cast iron bumper stops at the end of a railway line and had about the same effect.

"I... I shall write to the Queen immediately," Madame Holz bellowed. Katrin winced and began to cry.

"I find that you are not attending to your duties," Menders said. "Might I suggest you return to the nursery?"

"There is no point to me being in the nursery without the child! The child goes with me. I am her nurse!"

"Katrin stays with me. To the nursery with you, Madame."

"I am writing to the Queen," she said again.

"When you're done, bring the letter to me so I can send it for you," he answered. "All correspondence in or out goes through me - a precaution for the Princess' safety." She glared and stormed out, banging the door shut.

"Come with me, little one," he said to Katrin. "We'll go see what Lucen is doing. I'll let you wear yourself out for a while and then we'll get some sleep before I fall down."

He tucked her up in one arm, walking outside and around to the back of the house where Lucen was tending the kitchen garden, much hindered by Hemmett, who was thriftily collecting worms into a pile as they were exposed by Lucen's hoe. The young worm rancher was greatly dismayed as his captured quarry continually escaped by burrowing back into the ground. He was approaching the yelling point of frustration when he looked up and saw Menders and Katrin approaching. He ran to them.

"Lemme see Katrin!" he bellowed.

"When we get over to your father," Menders replied, extending a finger for Hemmett to hold. Hemmett latched on and tried to pull Menders along faster. Lucen looked over and stood up straight, leaning on his hoe.

True to his word, once he reached Lucen, Menders crouched and let Hemmett stare at Katrin. She reached out toward him. Very carefully he extended a finger, just as Menders had to him, and grinned when she grabbed it.

"My baby!" he announced. Then inspiration struck him. He went to retrieve a worm, with intentions of presenting it to Katrin. Menders, knowing Katrin's proclivity for putting things in her mouth, stood up while the worm wrangler's back was turned and grinned at Lucen, who grinned back.

"How does the gardening go today?" Menders asked.

"At a snail's pace because of my helper here. Hiding from that harpy?"

"Just being lord of the manor," Menders answered, handing Katrin to Lucen, who began to swing and toss her, which she loved. Menders took the opportunity to rub his eyes, which felt as if they'd been sandpapered.

"So what are you going to do about her?" Lucen asked after making a circuit of the garden holding Katrin at arms' length, as if she was flying.

"At the moment, ignore her, because as soon as I take the edge off this one's energy, I'm going to go to sleep," Menders answered as Lucen handed Katrin back over. He bent and set her on the ground, holding onto her hands as she pushed with her legs.

"Want me to watch tonight?" Lucen asked.

"No, I'll do it."

"Can't watch every night forever, Menders," Lucen observed.

"I know that."

"Why don't you let Zelia take the baby for a while? You get some sleep," Lucen said after a moment. "Madame won't have any idea where to find her."

"It's better if I know exactly where Katrin is right now," Menders said, lifting the baby and holding her high while she kicked with glee and giggled.

Lucen stepped very close and spoke very softly.

"You let me know if you need me to do something," he muttered.

"Thank you," Menders nodded. "I think Madame will probably leave on her own very soon."

"However she leaves, it won't be soon enough," Lucen answered. He picked up his hoe, looked around to be sure Hemmett wasn't about to stick a hand under it, and attacked the row of beans again.

Menders walked around the house, letting Katrin look at the flowers that were blooming. The midsummer air crackled with insect buzzing and birdsong. He glanced up when he was beneath the nursery to see Madame Holz glaring out at him. He waved up at her pleasantly.

Franz's office was his next stop. The doctor was reclining in his chair, turned toward the window, a heavy book open on a small table before him. He was switching his attention from the book to a row of bottles, then back to the book. Menders walked forward silently and looked over his shoulder.

Poisons seemed to be the reading matter for the morning. Menders suspected the book text coincided with the contents of the bottles. Another one, Menders thought. Katrin, you never need to doubt Lucen and Franz's love for you, that's certain, and I will never doubt their loyalty.

Katrin reached toward Franz and crowed. He nearly fell out of the chair, closed the book with an almighty bang and wrenched around, staring at Menders.

"You white eyed little bastard!" he gasped. "You don't walk, you float around!"

"I could take that very badly if I chose," Menders replied, setting Katrin on the desk so the doctor could take her. Franz, badly rattled but covering well, tickled the baby and then blew loudly on her stomach, releasing a cascade of giggles.

"I'll be sleeping for a while," Menders said quietly. "I'll keep her with me. If you would watch for Madame for me?"

"Consider it done," Franz answered.

Menders' last stop was the kitchen, where Cook was fuming and viciously sharpening her longest knife. Menders restrained himself from laughing. Another amateur contemplating murder.

"I need to rest, Cook," he said, making sure she knew he was there first. He didn't want her wheeling around waving that knife.

"Do you want to leave the little love with me?" she offered. He shook his head.

"You're my last line of defense. Make sure Madame doesn't get to my room, would you?"

"She won't get past me," Cook replied belligerently.

"Also, would you do something for me? Take several bottles of wine out of the cellar and put them out on the sideboard."

She nodded silently. He finally made his way to his room, bolting the door behind him.

"At last," he sighed to Katrin, depositing her in the middle of the bed, putting up pillows as barriers lest she roll off. Katrin immediately wiggled in his direction, smiling at him.

"Now, I'm hoping you'll go to sleep," he whispered, rubbing her back and letting her snuggle close. Thank the gods her eyelids were drooping...

He slept for a couple of hours, because the patterns of sunlight and shadow were entirely shifted when he woke to Franz shouting his name. Katrin lifted her head and began to whimper anxiously. He scooped her up and went toward the noise.

Madame Holz was blocked in the hallway by three people determined to keep her from getting to Menders. Franz continued to shout. Cook was giving Madame Holz the dressing down of a lifetime, while Lucen barred the way to Menders' room, looking completely immovable. Menders watched as Ermina Trottenheim emerged from her own room. She made no move to join the other members of the household in their campaign.

"You will not take that baby and hurt her and treat her badly!" Cook thundered.

"I have orders from the Queen herself!" Madame roared back. "All of you are going to be very sorry indeed for the way you've allowed things to slide here!"

"Madame! What is the meaning of this disturbance?" Menders said, his calm voice scything through all the ranting.

"Sir, I have come to take that child back to the nursery where she belongs!" Madame Holz was glaring and he could see that her hands were shaking. So you're beginning to feel the lack of wine very badly, he thought with satisfaction.

"She does not spend the day in the nursery," Menders countered.

"That is absolutely irregular and absurd!" the woman shouted. "A child's place *is* the nursery. Children *must* know their place!"

"You do not decide how things are done in this house, Madame," Menders replied dryly, easing Cook in the direction of the kitchen. He caught Franz's eye. The doctor moved forward rapidly, taking Katrin. Madame moved as if to intercept him as he walked back toward his office, but Menders stepped forward and held Madame's gaze.

"Do not touch that child," he said, cracking his voice like a whip.

"Who do you think you are?" the woman bellowed. "I am the Royal Head Nurse!"

"You know who I am, Madame, as I have explained before. My patience is wearing thin," Menders answered. He stepped closer. He could smell the rage on her, to say nothing of her wild desire for something to drink. Her very eyeballs were vibrating.

"I will offer one more time while Sergeant Greinholz is here to witness it. Choose a place of retirement and I will give you a generous sum of money to go there and settle."

"How dare you! I have orders, sir, and I will do whatever I must to follow them!"

No hesitation this time. She'd considered his suggestion and was not going to play. She had no moves left – but Menders did.

"Well then, what are we going to do?" he said conversationally. "I won't let you have the care of the Princess if you're going to subject her to the toughening you do so well. That is the beginning and end of it."

He rambled toward the sideboard, feeling her eyes on him. He could hear her swallow as he walked by the bottles of wine Cook had put out.

"You will lose your head as soon as I send word back to the Queen."

"And how do you intend to do that?" he asked. "Any letter will have to go through me or one of my agents."

"I will leave and go to the nearest town where I may send a letter."

"There isn't a train for five days. However will you last without wine for so long?" Menders said caressingly. His fingers ran the length of the neck of a bottle of Rembenheitz, a particularly fine deep red, almost twelve years old.

"I serve the Queen," Madame Holz blustered, her voice trembling. Menders picked up one bottle, and then another, perusing their labels. It was all very fine stuff indeed – Cook had chosen well. He removed the cork from one bottle before reaching for a wineglass. He poured the glass full and sipped.

He thought Madame's eyes were going to fall out of her head. Lucen stood as if transfixed, watching the woman drooling.

"Thirsty?" Menders asked pleasantly, taking another sip.

"Perhaps… perhaps we can come to some meeting of the

minds," she quavered.

"Perhaps. But I will not listen to you so long as you think you can force your will on me. Perhaps if you show that you are willing to compromise, I will be able to work with you. I am a reasonable man... when others are reasonable."

She looked ready to faint. Menders deliberately placed another wineglass and filled it. Her eyes were riveted on the red liquid.

"I too am not unreasonable," she said, taking an involuntary step forward.

"Do you think you could care for the Princess overnight, according to my standards?" he asked. "Her nursemaid was up all of last night and could use the rest. The Princess usually sleeps very well. It's very easy, really. I'm sure a woman with your experience can manage it."

"Yes, of course, yes, I can do that, very easily," she said eagerly, watching as he took another sip of wine.

"Then you will take night duty in the nursery tonight," Menders said, favoring her with a slight smile. "If you manage that without feeling that you must toughen the Princess with mistreatment, we will see what else can be done." He picked up the other wineglass and held it out to her. "Care for a glass of wine?"

He thought she was going to knock him over. He hid his distaste as she guzzled the contents of the glass, wine running down her chin. Lucen grimaced and left the room. Menders set his own glass down, nodded to Madame Holz and walked noisily away, making sure his footsteps were audible to her.

Then he walked back silently and watched as she swilled down the contents of her own glass a second time, then drained the one he'd left behind. She looked around furtively and grabbed two bottles of wine, uncorking them before rushing away to the stairs, climbing toward the nursery.

"She'll be falling down drunk by tonight," Franz said a

few minutes later, leaning in the doorway of Menders' office, Katrin on his hip.

"I'm aware of that," Menders answered. "I need a reason to send her back, and she's going to supply me with one."

"Using Katrin as bait?" Franz said, raising his eyebrows.

"I won't be far," Menders replied.

CHAPTER 7
AN AWKWARD SEA BIRD

Katrin was wailing in the nursery.

It was very late, well after midnight, and the house was asleep – except for Menders, who was sitting silently in the hallway just outside the nursery.

The wailing went on. Menders waited.

He tried to force himself to block out the escalating howls. Sooner or later Madame Holz would have to do something about whatever it was that was making the baby cry. He was sure, despite the fact that she'd been drinking heavily all afternoon and evening, that she was still awake.

Katrin's wails switched to gasping sobs. The sobs went on and on, punctuated by despairing howls that twisted in his heart. He had never heard Katrin cry like that, not from the moment she had been born.

Menders rose to his feet.

Katrin was hungry, sick or in pain, and Madame Holz was doing nothing about it.

The nursery night lamp was burning low, but there was no sign of Madame Holz. The fire was dead, something that was never permitted to happen. Nights were cold at The Shadows, even at the height of summer. Menders moved across the room swiftly and looked down at Katrin.

Tears, a red crumpled face, sobs. No blanket in the crib at all, the fire gone out, the room cold, and the reek of a very foul diaper, something that had never been permitted. Katrin was always kept clean and fresh smelling. Forgive me, little one, for letting this happen to you but it's the only way I can keep you safe, he thought as he picked her up.

"So, Lord Stettan, what are you doing here?" Madame Holz had come out of her room, at last.

"Why is this baby in this condition?" he asked, keeping his voice cool.

"It teaches her, sir, to endure discomfort." She was swaying drunkenly. A miasma of soured wine surrounded her.

He took Katrin to the changing table.

"Oh, you're going to rescue her yourself, young man?" Madame Holz said, drunken jollity deepening her voice. "This should be amusing." She lurched closer.

Menders ignored her, and bent over Katrin.

"All right, Little Princess, I'm here," he murmured and was gratified when she turned her head toward his voice, though she wasn't ready to stop wailing. At least she knows someone is going to help her, he thought, pushing up her little nightgown and opening her filthy, saturated diaper, closing his mind off to the stench. He peeled the vile garment from her and flung it into the bucket nearby.

He clenched his teeth when he saw her reddened and chapped skin. Forcing himself to remain calm, he concentrated on removing the filth from Katrin, drying and powdering her before wrapping her in a clean diaper and fastening it.

"What a clever young man," Madame Holz said sarcastically. "Perhaps you'd be better suited to a position as under-nurserymaid instead of a trumped up little freak who thinks he's a gentleman."

Menders lifted Katrin and held her against him, pressing his lips to her downy little head for a moment. She'd stopped wailing. Her crying was that of a tired baby who was ready to sleep.

"You have not abided by the agreement we made this afternoon and you have neglected your charge. You're also intoxicated while on duty. You're dismissed," he said to Madame Holz, keeping his voice down so that Katrin didn't startle. "You are to leave tomorrow."

"Very well, sir," she smiled. "I will be glad to let Her

Majesty know just why I have returned to Court. I'm sure that you will also be leaving here very soon after that."

She went back to the nurse's room, and a moment later he heard the clink of a bottle against the rim of a glass. Can't leave it alone, he thought with satisfaction.

Katrin was dozing off. He put her back in her crib, found her blanket and covered her. There was no further sign of Madame Holz. After lighting the fire, Menders hurried to his office, stripped off his coat and collar and unbuttoned the top buttons of his shirt before rolling up his sleeves to show his forearms. He untied his hair and raked a comb through it until it was loose and flowing over his shoulders. Then he rapidly traversed the hallway to the kitchen. He uncorked a bottle of wine and rinsed his mouth with it, spitting it into the kitchen basin. Taking two wineglasses, he started upstairs toward the nursery.

The light was burning in Madame Holz's room. Menders replaced his dark spectacles with clear ones and arranged his features into an expression of anxiety and mildly drunken petulance, positioning himself in her doorway.

Madame Holz was very intent on her drinking, and didn't notice him until he carefully clinked one of the glasses against the wine bottle.

"Ah, you're back, young man," she said, looking up at him with a drunkenly sly expression. Her eyes slid to the bottle greedily.

"I thought we might have a talk," Menders said, pitching his voice low, so that the seductive husk in his lower register was very apparent.

"Do sit down, little night owl," the woman said expansively, waving her hand vaguely toward the chair opposite hers. "Been having a few drinks yourself? Thinking about what will become of you when I tell the Queen about how you dismissed me against her orders?"

Menders pretended to be embarrassed by her sagacity and

sat, setting out the glasses and pouring them full of wine. She glommed onto hers ravenously, draining half of it in a gulp. He poured it full again and gave her a smile.

"Well now, you're a pretty young man when you're loosened up and have those blasted black spectacles off," she said. "The eyes take some getting used to, but they're exotic. You're Old Mordanian, I see."

"Indeed," Menders answered, pretending to sip his wine. She was far ahead of him in drunkenness, and he wanted to keep it that way.

"I can tell by the slanted eyes," she informed him. "Same as with the baby in there. You mustn't think that I'm a cruel woman. The toughening regimen has come down through the Royal Family and the finest Old Mordanian nobility from the days of Morghenna the Wise, after weakness led to the execution of Queen Clearheart and the occupation of Mordania by the Surelians." She sounded like she was reciting something that had been pounded into her brain by rote. "I have my orders. By the time I'm done, this one will be toughened to the point where she can endure anything."

"It seems a hard thing to leave a tiny baby in a foul diaper while she screams," Menders said, setting his tone to sound as if he wasn't exactly sure of such a surety.

"I'm sure it does to a sensitive young man like you," she replied, leaning forward, blatantly letting her dressing gown gape open. "It's obvious that you're fond of the child. But learning that she has to tolerate discomfort is an important part of her training. It's groundwork for what she has ahead of her."

Menders nodded as though she was giving him pearls of wisdom while his mind played briefly over the sorts of things this woman would consider tormenting a baby groundwork for – beatings, hunger, inadequate bedding in a cold nursery during the winter, no time to play, endless memorization and recitation, repression of natural talent, harsh discipline, vicious criticism, lack of love.

"Now that I understand why you raise the royal children in the way you do, I'm confused as to just why the Queen has sent you away from Princess Aidelia," he said earnestly.

"She is… angry with me. I had some wine and fell asleep. Anyone might have done it. The Princess got out of the nursery, was playing on the stairs. She fell and broke her arm. Just a childhood accident, I tried to tell Her Majesty, but she sent me up here. Took me away from the Heiress and sent me to the end of the world. It isn't as if the Queen isn't fond of wine herself."

She pouted and tried to refill her glass. Menders took the bottle away before she poured it all over the table, filling the glass himself. She drained it instantly.

"That's the sort of thing that could happen to anyone," he said soothingly. "I hear Princess Aidelia is a handful."

"Oh, she's a wretched, wretched child. But she'll be a strong Queen. It's taken harsh discipline to break her, but I know my job. You think all this pampering and loving is good for the little Princess, but it isn't. Mordania needs strong Queens and I know how to make them. Toughening is the only way."

Menders suppressed nausea as he saw that the thought of inflicting cruelty on children was arousing the wretched woman. She was beginning to pant and had a lustful light in her eyes.

"Perhaps I was hasty in telling you that you're dismissed," Menders murmured, letting his voice resonate sensuously, pouring more wine into her glass. "I have to admire a woman who, for the sake of Mordania, will deny the natural impulse to care for a baby in distress. I misunderstood your motives."

"Oh, entirely. I can be very tender, under the right circumstances." She flicked her tongue out and licked the rim of her wineglass, looking into his eyes. "With the right person," she added.

Menders took a sip of wine, swallowed, and leaned his chin on his hand as he replaced his wineglass on the table, the image of a young man who was definitely feeling what he was drinking and starting to respond to the advances of a woman.

"What sort of person would that be?" he asked, slowing his words just enough to create the illusion that the wine was affecting his head.

"Oh… young. Like you. How old are you, little night owl?"

"Twenty." He picked up the wineglass again but didn't drink, holding it at a level to draw her gaze to his eyes.

"Twenty. So young," she mused, gazing into his eyes just as he'd intended. "You must be very lonely here. So far away from everything, without a wife, without company."

"The Shadows *is* very isolated," he said, leaning forward slightly, as if mesmerized by her bloodshot orbs.

"I'm sure it is. You must feel deprived without the love of a woman," she whispered, fingering her flabby cleavage.

"I have been very lonely," Menders ventured, dropping his eyes long enough to seem uncertain. Then he looked up at her, making sure that he looked like a sad little puppy desperate for love.

"Poor little Head of Household," she slurred, quaffing more wine. Then she leaned across the table, knocking the bottle over. She kissed him, thrusting her tongue into his mouth.

He forced himself to kiss back as if he was completely enamored, ignoring the sour taste of her lips and tongue, closing his nose to the reek of her unwashed armpits. The wine oozed across the table and began to drip on the floor.

Madame Holz sat back and stared at the spilled liquid.

"Oh no," she mourned, looking at him coyly. "I've spilled your lovely bottle of wine. I am a bad girl."

"I know where to get more," he grinned, as if he was as drunk as she. He made a point of gulping down the contents of his wineglass. He could afford to at this point, and it would wash the nauseating taste of her out of his mouth.

"Where?" she asked eagerly, as if they were conspirators.

Menders leaned back in his chair and ran a hand through his hair, fixing his gaze on her eyes while his other hand slipped his own wineglass into his pocket.

"In my room."

"Why what a bold suggestion," she smirked, scrambling up from her chair.

"My room is also much warmer and I have a much larger bed," he tempted, taking her hand and drawing her to him. She began slobbering toward his mouth. He kissed her, several times. Then he glanced toward Katrin's crib, visible in the nursery by the light of the dwindling fire. There was no time to build it up again, just now.

"Don't bother about her, she'll sleep for hours," Madame Holz panted, trying to climb his leg, suddenly inflamed with desire. "Let's do it here."

"Oh no, I want more to drink," Menders pretended to laugh "Don't you want more wine, my dear? And perhaps I have a few tricks hidden away that might amuse you... but they're in my room."

She grunted and nearly smothered him with a repulsively slimy kiss, then pulled him eagerly toward the nursery door.

The cold of the hallway damped her ardor a bit and he squired her across the floorboards of the landing, smiling and holding her close as they descended the stairs to the first floor. The stairwell was flooded with the full moonlight of Ito, the smaller of Eirdon's two moons.

Menders paused at the top of the stairs. He kissed Madame Holz several times and ran his hands up and down her doughy body before drawing her attention to the view of the moon through the stairwell window.

"Look how beautiful," he murmured, standing behind her with his arms around her waist. He nuzzled her thick, sweaty neck.

"Oh, isn't it," she responded, looking, drunkenly swaying on her feet. "It's so beautiful."

"Not as beautiful as you are," he whispered in her ear, following his words with an exhaled breath. She leaned her head back and closed her eyes.

He released her and stepped back.

He lashed out with a powerful kick, balancing himself to deliver maximum force to the small of her back.

The impact snapped her spine, launching her into the stairwell like an awkward sea bird. She arced through the moonlight with a faint fluttering of cloth that sounded like stunted wings trying to fly, too drunk to struggle, too surprised to cry out.

She hit the stairs where he'd calculated, about halfway down, tumbling with a sickening looseness to the bottom, making little noise on the thick wooden risers. She finally came to rest on the landing with a nearly inaudible thud.

Menders ran soundlessly down to her, pressing his fingers against her throat, feeling for a pulse. Not dead. He waited a moment, needing her blood to keep moving so that she would have bruises in case the Queen wanted the body returned.

He did not laugh or gloat over his triumph. Grimly silent, he took Madame Holz's head in his hands. With a rapid motion, he twisted it round as if he was trying to screw it off. There were multiple snapping sounds, like a handful of dry twigs breaking. He felt for the pulse again.

Dead.

Bright eyes gleamed at Menders from a dark recess, then silently withdrew into shadow. He did not see.

Menders dashed for his office, closed the door, rebuttoned his shirt, refitted his collar, pulled on his coat, tied back his hair. He rinsed his mouth and face until he was sure that there was no trace of wine on his breath and that her slobber was off his moustache and beard. He removed the wineglass from his pocket and pushed it behind some books on a shelf, making a mental note to return it to the kitchen tomorrow. Then he walked back to Madame Holz's body with a lantern.

Excellent. The bruises were already in evidence. For the sake of the others in the household, he would play the scene out to the end.

The Princess' nurse, having drunk far too much despite being on duty in the nursery, had overturned her purloined bottle of wine. Further complicating her misdoings by neglecting her charge (as she had previously neglected Princess Aidelia), she lost her footing while going after yet another bottle, tumbling to her death down the stairs in the dark. The fall neatly broke her back and neck. Menders, awake later than the rest of the house as was his habit, had heard the noise of the fall, but it was too late to render any aid to the stricken woman. How unfortunate.

He shouted the house up. Everyone came running, pulling dressing gowns on over their nightclothes. Soon, a candlelit circle of people were staring down at the rapidly cooling body of Madame Holz. Doctor Franz attended her and pronounced her dead. He pointed out the bruises to the assembled group as evidence of her fall.

No-one was particularly heartbroken over the demise of Madame Holz. She had stepped on more than one set of toes. Menders saw Zelia and Cook exchanging relieved glances. He caught Mistress Trottenheim giving him a measured gaze that turned fearful when he met her eyes. She retreated to her room without a word. Franz promised to write the necessary letter and death certificate, and he and Lucen helped Menders carry the body down into the cellar, where it would lie until morning.

When the household had settled down, Menders climbed the stairs to the nursery. Eiren was there, building up the fire.

"It had almost gone out. This place was like an icehouse with that poor baby covered with only one blanket," she said in a sharp whisper. "I've put some more covers on the little lamb.

That woman left a shitty diaper sitting beside the crib in the bucket, the reek was sickening!"

"That's all over now," Menders said, bending over the crib and putting a hand under the blankets, rubbing Katrin's little back as she slept. He felt her tiny feet. She was warm. She would be fine until the nursery heated up again.

Only a fool would think this episode would be the only threat to darken Katrin's life. Living in Mordania, where plots and political intrigues swirled like windblown leaves, meant threats would always have to be faced.

When the inevitable dangers arose, Menders would be waiting.

"There's wine spilled all over the room in there," Eiren whispered in disgust. "She upended more than half a bottle. There are two other empty bottles as well."

"I'll write a letter tomorrow that will keep us from having any more head nurses sent out," Menders replied, turning toward her. "I found out that she let Princess Aidelia fall down a flight of stairs, which broke her arm."

"Funny that she managed to fall down the stairs and kill herself," Eiren answered. "But good riddance."

Menders bent over Katrin's crib and saw that she was sleeping soundly.

"Everything is all right," he whispered to her. "Sleep well, Little Princess."

He knew sleep would elude him for the rest of the night. It would take some time for him to estimate all the Queen's potential reactions to Madame Holz's demise.

He would calculate a response to every possible repercussion. That alone would keep his mind active until sunrise.

CHAPTER 8
TIGHTENING THE WEB

Nothing happened.

Of all possible official responses to Madame Holz's death, the one Menders hadn't anticipated was silence. Routine correspondence between The Palace and The Shadows came and went, but nothing was said about the late head nurse or about providing a replacement.

It was as if Madame had disappeared like a puff of smoke one night. No-one missed her. No-one mourned her passing.

When it became apparent that there would be no inquest, Menders, Lucen and Doctor Franz took the body from the cellar coolroom late one night, dug a grave in a corner of the estate cemetery, and interred Madame Holz.

***

Two weeks later, Menders sat at his desk, penning a letter to a woman who had once been his lover and was now his friend.

The Madame Holz incident had made one thing clear – not only was Menders isolated here at The Shadows, he was also blind and deaf to events at Court. It was time to begin cultivating contacts in Erdahn. He needed a network of eyes and ears.

Cahrin Velten and Menders had been very close in their late teens and he had hoped for marriage as time went on. Cahrin had the special temperament needed to be an assassin's wife, having been an assassin's daughter. She was well acquainted with the tensions and stresses that were part of life for those assassins held dear. Menders' two year assignment in Surelia had put more than physical distance between them. Now, despite some regret, Menders felt it was for the best that they had parted, as he had been sent to The Shadows within two days of his return from

Surelia.

Cahrin's husband, Olner, had survived his time on overseas missions and was now involved in surveillance and intelligence work in Erdahn, working with Thoren Bartan, the Court Assassin. He was a perfect candidate for Menders' network of contacts.

Menders' letter told of his orders and predicament in masked terms that would be easily decipherable to a fellow assassin. He made clear his desire for news – all kinds of news – from Erdahn. He knew Olner would understand what he meant. That done, he sealed the letter, added it to a pile of similar missives and sat back.

This was only the beginning of his plan to extend an intelligence network beyond The Shadows while increasing the security within the estate. Menders knew that no plan was infallible, that by the very nature of her lineage Katrin would always be at risk. He had to minimize that risk in any way he could.

He had begun to tutor the men of the estate in advanced and improvised fighting styles. This was well received and taken on as a sort of sport, even by Doctor Franz, who took a fancy to knife fighting mostly because he thought it made him look dashing. It didn't but Menders hadn't the heart to tell him so.

It didn't end there. The women needed to be able to defend themselves and the Princess.

"Imagine that somehow, someone has gotten past all the men and other people on the estate. Suddenly, he's in here, with you and the Princess," Menders said to Cook. As if on cue, Katrin gooed from her high chair. "What would you do?"

Without hesitation, Cook looked around and picked up a long bladed carving knife from the massive cutting block that sat in the middle of the kitchen.

"I've got this knife," Cook said. She waved it menacingly.

"No!" Menders reprimanded her. "Don't show it to me.

Never show an enemy your potential. By the time you do that, he's already figured out three different ways to disarm you. No assassin is going to be scared off by a knife. Drop the knife down by your side, beside and slightly behind your leg. Good. You can bring that knife up fast and surprise your adversary."

Cook did. The knife was a flashing arc of silver.

"Good! Keep it closer in to your body. Never get a weapon too far out, it can be taken away from you. With it close in you can lunge and drive with your whole weight. Aim for under the ribs, the gut, try to bring the blade up with a thrusting motion." He stepped back and took an aggressive posture.

"Now... I'm an assassin and I've come for the Princess. I'm not afraid of you. Without a weapon visible, I don't even see you as a threat. What are you going to do?"

Cook dropped her arm and hid the knife out of sight behind the folds of her skirt. As Menders stepped forward, Cook flashed the knife up, lunging at him.

He caught her wrist as the point of the blade stopped perilously close to his midriff. For a pudgy, docile looking woman, Cook could react with startling speed.

"Yes... very good."

Just then, Doctor Franz wandered into the kitchen. He looked at Menders and Cook in their combative embrace and paled.

"Oh dear. Not arguing over dinner are we? I can come back later."

"No argument, Doctor," Menders replied, placing the long bladed knife carefully on the cutting bench. "Just showing Cook how to carve fillet of man."

Katrin's nurserymaids received special training as well. Menders opted to start the young girls with something they might have at hand in the nursery – fire pokers.

Of the two, red-headed Eiren had the most potential, being bright, very much a chip off her father. Kata tended to look forlorn, keeping her eyes on the floor and holding the poker as if it was a live snake, but Eiren was all business, intent with purpose. Though always polite, she was never subservient in her attitude when addressing him. She always looked him in the eye.

"Now, every measure is taken to ensure your safety here at the Shadows, as well as the safety of the Princess. But suppose someone got in and was coming at you? What would you do?" Menders waited as they looked uncomfortable.

"I... I could hit them... with this poker?" Kata ventured.

"Yes, you could try. Eiren, what about you?"

"It would depend," Eiren said.

"How so?"

"On how afraid of you I was."

Good answer, Menders thought. "All right, suppose you are afraid but you still have to do something. I'm coming to hurt you, perhaps kill you. What then?"

"But... I'm not afraid of you, Mister Menders," Eiren replied.

"All right then," Menders said. "If it's not me you're frightened of, then imagine I have come for the Princess. I'm going to kill her, not you, and there's just you and me and that poker."

Eiren straightened, resolution in her eyes. Gods help the man who tries to lay hands on this one, Menders thought. Eiren gripped the poker like a short thrusting spear and held it at waist level, while Kata looked on wide eyed.

"That's good. Now, come at me... come on Redhead, do your worst!"

Reacting to his use of a nickname she hated, Eiren took a quick step forward and thrust at him. He deflected the poker with the palm of his hand.

"Good! Put more weight behind it. And that was an obvious move, you need to strike unexpectedly, not signal your mo – gods!"

Eiren had brought the poker up fast as he was talking, He just managed to step aside enough to avoid being emasculated. The poker struck him a stinging blow on the inner thigh. Eiren gasped and dropped it with a clatter.

"Oh, I'm so sorry!" she blurted. "Did I hurt you?"

"It's all right," Menders gasped, trying to keep his voice from coming out thin and strained, like that of a constipated flea. He cleared his throat. "Very good. Clever move."

Eiren stood there, her hands open before her, unsure of what she should do. Menders leaned against the changing table and rubbed his thigh. Of all the scrapes he'd been in over the years, to have a mere girl damn near break his leg with a poker!

"I think, you're getting the idea," he finally managed. "Let's continue tomorrow, shall we?"

Once outside the nursery, Menders allowed himself the luxury of a muffled curse. Behind him, he heard Kata's shocked voice:

"Eiren! You nearly knocked his nuts off and then he'd be no use to any woman!"

Laughing under his breath, Menders made his painful way to Doctor Franz's office.

***

Menders knocked the knife from Ermina Trottenheim's hand. It skittered across the floor, coming to rest against the far wall of the Great Hall.

"Well done," he said quietly.

"I said I knew how to defend myself with a knife," she replied petulantly.

"You do indeed." Menders went to the knife and picked it up. "But would you defend the Princess, if need be?"

"Whatever else you might think, I am not a monster," she snapped. "Of course I would. I didn't want to be a milch cow for the child, but I certainly would defend her if necessary."

"Very well." Menders sheathed the knife. "I would like to know where you acquired your expertise."

"My husband taught me, if that's any of your business," she responded.

"Oh, but it is my business," Menders replied softly. "You just used a technique familiar to assassins. You told me your husband was a soldier and I am not aware of a Trottenheim being a member of Special Services. So I would like to know who taught you that trick with the knife."

Mistress Trottenheim glared at him. "I've told you – my husband. I don't know where he learned it. I imagine it's possible an assassin showed it to him!"

"Unlikely." Menders simply watched her. She remained indignant long enough to let him know she was telling the truth.

"All right then," he capitulated. "Let's just hope your loyalty never has to be tested. I'll be watching."

He left her sizzling with fury, went to his office and began a series of letters enquiring into the identity of Ermina Trottenheim and her husband.

CHAPTER 9
WINTER

Menders always felt the moment when seasons changed. Autumn would flirt with the end of summer for weeks, chilly nights making a few leaves brighten. Then a crisp day coupled with a cold wind and the tang of smoke from a wood fire would announce that autumn was here, all flaming colors and achingly blue skies.

For weeks, random snowflakes would drift down on grey autumn days and frost rime would harden on the ground – but it was the smell of snow on the air and a leaden sky showing a sudden molten streak of sunset as the wind rolled over from autumnal crispness to the bite of true winter cold that let him know winter had arrived.

He was in the woodlot one late autumn afternoon with Lucen when their second winter at The Shadows arrived. They had paused in their work to drink from a jug of scalding coffee. A sudden gust of wind carried the smell of fresh ice and snow before it, and a scatter of snowflakes pattered against the trunks of the trees.

"Here he is," Lucen said in his deep voice. He bowed formally. "Welcome, Winter. An old friend, with a new white coat."

Menders leaned on his axe handle, amused by Lucen's lyrical performance. The Shadows was prepared for the season and he was looking forward to the challenge of their first full winter in the far north.

"Did you know the Thrun call winter The White Beast?" he asked.

"Appropriate."

"At least we're ready for it," Menders answered. "Not like last year where we ended up here like fish out of water."

"You managed all right. Got us through it," Lucen grunted, preparing to swing his axe again.

"I like to think it was a co-operative effort," Menders said.

Co-operative efforts were typical of the denizens of The Shadows. When they learned of Menders' letter writing campaign to his associates, they began writing to friends and relatives in Erdahn or other cities to get news, information and a notion of the mood of people across the country.

Mordania's current war with Artreya over disputed colonial territories was not progressing well. Of immediate concern to Menders was the danger of Mordanian army deserters, who were fleeing their units to avoid deployment abroad. Disgruntled, desperate for food, desirous of drink, it was common for them to raid homes, particularly large ones. Menders and Lucen were painfully aware of the amorality of disaffected military men. They ordered a large supply of ammunition and procured several new guns. Menders had his assassin's weapons, but Franz and Lucen had arrived at The Shadows unarmed. Menders insisted on procuring lightweight weapons and drilling the women in their use. Ermina Trottenheim and Eiren proved to be the best shots, though he wouldn't like Cook having a go at him either.

Another danger to be considered was wolves. The Northern or Old Mordanian wolf was nothing like the common lowland wolf, which was a variety of big shaggy dog. The Northern wolf was best described as a short-tailed, long-legged Surytamian crocodile with ears and a brain. Fierce and wickedly intelligent, they hunted in packs, with coordinated movements. They stood chest high to a tall man.

During warm weather when game was plentiful, Old Mordanian wolves shunned humans, but as winter drew on and the animals struggled to find food, they gravitated toward settlements, preying on livestock. They had been known to kill people who were alone, particularly after dark. Legends about packs chasing sledges and breaking into snowbound railway carriages abounded. In some particularly hard winters it was said that they had broken into buildings to attack people. More reason to have ammunition and firearms at hand.

When the first heavy snowstorm came, Menders launched The Shadows on its winter season. Winter madness was not unheard of in this part of Old Mordania, particularly when people were thrown together for long periods of time due to snowbound conditions. Menders had made exhaustive lists in his notebooks, planning many activities that would keep the denizens of the estate happy and healthy through the cold months.

The estate farm families were enthusiastic over his suggestion of regular dances. Traditionally they held such events themselves, usually in an empty hay barn which was cold and inhospitable. They were delighted with the size and comfort of the Great Hall and Menders was thrilled that they could provide a rough but enthusiastic band. Menders had thought he might have to use The Shadows' ancient spinet to provide music for dancing. He played very well, but his idea of a good time was not thumping away at a jingly and fragile spinet while other people danced.

The farmers looked on dancing as an enjoyable wintertime activity, good for keeping the blood moving. The wilder the music, the better they liked it. Occasionally the ragtag band would attempt a javot or valtz with varying results, usually humorous, but the farmers really felt their mettle when they roared into the holta. This was an Old Mordanian country dance requiring great energy and a prodigious memory, as the figures were complex and varied. The physical effort expended during the holta was staggering.

The first time Menders got pulled into the holta, he was nearly knocked off his feet as Marjana Spaltz grabbed his hands for the first turn and swung him around like a sack of grain. He saw quickly that this was nothing like the tame ballroom holtas he'd experienced when in military school, and laughed aloud as he leaned back against the swing of the next turn. He was then passed along to the next woman in line, who happened to be Ermina Trottenheim.

Having been at Court, she was a skilled dancer. She could make any man look to his steps, though she was so small that she was often swung off her feet during the holta by some of the more hardy country boys, and was tossed into the air by the same during the lift. Now she latched onto Menders' hands and leaned back as he swung them around in the full circle required by the turn and launched into the tricky sidesteps that moved the entire line of dancers around in the complex curving undulations of the dance.

"Why sir, I had no idea assassins could dance," she laughed breathlessly.

"We dance very well, we're required to learn," he answered her.

"Why is that?"

"Assassins are tutored in dance to blend in at various occasions, to say nothing of cultivating balance. Espionage isn't entirely creeping around in the dark wearing black, Mistress Trottenheim. Get ready for the lift." He grasped her waist and lifted her clear of the ground as he handed her to the next man in line.

His next partner was little Eiren. Menders intended to temper his style to her size and tender years until she, having been born to this country dance, nearly yanked his arms out of their sockets. She shrieked with delight when he tossed her high into the air on the lift. She left him laughing.

The eccentric band attempted a valtz next and Menders found Mistress Trottenheim before him, curtsying. He bowed politely and took her onto the floor.

He realized they were making a sensation, because they were the only couple who knew how to reverse step. When valtzing, the farmers and their wives circled relentlessly in one direction until watching them made people dizzy. Menders' and Mistress Trottenheim's graceful switches of direction were drawing more than a few eyes. Unfortunately, some of the dancing couples decided to try it without knowing exactly how and there were immediate collisions and upsets. The valtz disintegrated as the musicians began to guffaw and eventually the only way to restore order was for Menders and his partner to give an impromptu reversing lesson.

As real cold set in, Menders cleared the soft snow from part of the frozen lake, and during the sunniest hours of the short days, skaters appeared on the ice. Lucen would hold Hemmett in his arms and skate along while the little boy hooted and howled, delighted by the echo of his voice in the winter stillness. Children from the tenant farms skated on carved wooden blades. Franz constructed a tiny box sled for Katrin and took her, bundled up until she looked like a little bear cub, down to the lake for outings, pulling her behind him. Cook was fond of taking a turn on the ice and loved to grab Menders' hands if he happened to be there, turning them in dizzy circles until they both sat down with their heads spinning.

Near sunset on his twenty-first birthday, the shortest day of the year, Menders was shoveling more snow off the ice, enlarging the skating area so that the children could race.

Feet crunched on snow behind him and he looked around to see Ermina Trottenheim in grey furs, just sitting down to put on her skates.

"It's getting cold," he remarked, standing upright and leaning on his shovel.

"I like this time of day. I like the cold green color in the sky after the sun sets," she said, rising and skating away from him. He watched as she turned gracefully and skimmed over the ice, her skates leaving thin white lines behind her.

No-one he'd ever known had mentioned that green tint in

the winter sunset sky. It was rare, something he watched for. It was icy and clear and it touched his heart in a way he couldn't explain.

Mistress Trottenheim skated back to him.

"Are you just going to hold up that shovel all day, or are you going to be a gentleman and skate with me?" she asked, smiling up at him. He looked at her dubiously – she had never really smiled at him in the time he had known her. It changed the aspect of her features from shrewish to bewitching. He didn't trust this sudden change in attitude toward him, though she had been friendlier since the first dance of the season a few weeks ago.

Menders shrugged, dug his shovel into a snow bank and offered her his arm. She took it.

After almost a year at The Shadows, Menders and Ermina Trottenheim had reached an unspoken arrangement. They no longer clashed, as she kept to her duties as housekeeper and didn't interfere with his management of the estate or the Princess. He dealt with her mainly by avoiding her.

"Why don't you be polite and ask me how I am?" she asked, a little kittenishly.

"All right then, how are you?" Menders felt uncomfortable.

"Fine. I wanted to thank you for how hard you've been working to keep us all happy this winter. You don't think anyone realizes what you've done, but we do. It could have been horrible. You've made it very special."

"There's plenty of winter to come yet," Menders replied.

"Yes, and I'm sure you'll think up something like a hopfootle tournament or a pillow fight," she teased.

He smiled then, she laughed and they skated on in silence.

"I didn't have a childhood," he said suddenly, surprising himself. "I think I'm having it now, this winter."

"You're nothing like a child. Let's spin," Ermina

Trottenheim answered, swinging around in front of him and grabbing his hands. "But not until we fall, nothing is harder to fall on than ice."

He caught her hands and leaned back, starting them spinning. Slower than when Cook whirled him around, slow enough to be able to see her laughing. He couldn't help smiling.

They spun to a stop and stood there dizzily. Then she shivered and Menders realized that the sun had dropped completely.

"Go inside, it's getting very cold," he suggested, helping her over to the bank. "I have to finish this and put the shovel away."

"Getting rid of me?"

"No, looking out for your welfare. And I thought you didn't particularly like me, Mistress Trottenheim."

"You're not so bad," she said with another smile. "I expect I've gotten used to you. You'd think after all this time you might call me Ermina. After all, I don't call you Mister Menders anymore."

She removed her skates and walked away toward the house without a backward glance.

Menders retrieved the shovel and continued with the expansion of the skating area, not going in until Cook bellowed out the door that he would go without his birthday dinner if he didn't get in to the table right now.

***

Dear Menders,

We were delighted to hear from you! Olner learned through Thoren Bartan that you had been sent away with the baby Princess. Before he told us, we feared you had been hurt or killed and removed from the official records.

Olner says you are wise to be concerned about plots. Of course, there is always something brewing isn't there, dear friend? I am enclosing a list of details. After all, this is Mordania. No wonder our Queens are so hard. None have been deposed from the Throne since Clearheart, but it hasn't been for want of trying.

Our present monarch is in her cups much of the time now, very ineffectual, and people are frightened by the stories that go around about Princess Aidelia. Olner fears an overthrow may be in the offing. As far as we know, little is known about the existence of Princess Katrin.

Regarding your enquiry about your housekeeper, it sounds as if you've been saddled with Ermina Trottenheim. She's a shrew, manipulative and self-serving as well. I shall intrude enough to warn you not to get involved with her. She has had some tragedy in her life, but even before then she was not a pleasant person. She caused a great deal of trouble at Court by spreading rumors and setting people up against one another. Of the people you were sent out with, she is the one most likely to cause you trouble. Olner has made enquiries about her husband. He had nothing to do with Special Services, but was good with a knife, so it's likely Mistress Trottenheim did indeed learn that knife trick from him.

I have given your address to your particular friends Haakel and Bertel. Menck and Commandant Komroff told Olner that they had heard from you and will be writing soon. Ifor Trantz has suffered an injury and his partner, Falk, was killed in the same incident – which you probably know, as you were in Surelia at the same time. We have lost track of where Ifor is. Rumor has it that he is in dire financial straits since being demobilized from Special Services with no pension.

We are well. We miss you at our socials and dinners. Do write soon again, we will be very glad to keep you informed.

Affectionately,

Cahrin

Menders finished the letter, put it down and sighed a little. He missed his friends and the social life he'd had in Erdahn. He had no close family alive, only first cousins he'd never met. His friendships had filled a gap in his life.

The news of Ifor Trantz having disappeared was particularly disturbing. Trantz had been one of his tutors at the Military Academy and Menders had worked with him in Surelia as well. To know that Ifor was struggling now was exasperating, considering the man's excellent record and years of self-sacrifice and service to Mordania.

He looked ruefully at Cahrin's warning about Ermina. Cahrin's letter had been delayed by bad weather which had set in on his birthday, the evening he and Ermina had skated together. Trains had not gotten through for almost two months. Menders, contrary to his usual caution, had gotten very drunk at the birthday party put on for him by the household.

He had ended up in bed with Ermina – and he was well aware that it wasn't a love affair. It satisfied a need, but he feared it had opened a door to unwanted complication in his life. He also knew that he had been manipulated in that direction by Ermina and had taken the bait like an absolute fool.

***

Franz paused in Menders' office doorway.

"Want me to tell you something you don't want to hear?" he asked.

"No," Menders answered. He was preoccupied with simultaneously writing an order for kitchen staples and holding Katrin, who was bouncing on his lap and trying to take things off his desk.

"My young friend, I'm going to say it anyway, just so I clear my conscience," Franz persisted, stepping into the office and closing the door behind him.

"Why can't I just order three hundred pounds of flour all at once and be done with it for a year?" Menders asked.

"Because if you do it gets full of weevils before you get to use it up," Franz answered, perching on the edge of the desk and making faces to make Katrin laugh. "Everyone knows that."

"Right." Menders took a pencil out of Katrin's mouth and returned to his order, refusing to look up at Franz. He knew what the doctor was going to say and he didn't want to hear it. Katrin retaliated by slapping the desk with her open hands and singing wordlessly.

"You and she are not compatible," Franz said quietly.

Menders looked up at him without a word.

Franz rose and walked across the room.

"I was afraid of this," he sighed. "You're stuck out here together, you're of an age, she's a pretty thing and it's obvious she's decided to set her cap for you. I know it's pointless for me to say this, but it would be best if you stopped before things went any further."

Menders still didn't respond. He put his pen down and lifted Katrin over his head. She was now a year old, robust and bright. She knew that she was distracting him and wanted him to stop writing and play with her instead.

"Menders, there is no way that you are going to be able to give Ermina what she wants. I don't think any man could do it, because no matter how much you gave, it would never be enough." Franz turned away from the window and put his hands in his pockets. "She has a difficult disposition and it hasn't improved. I thought at first it was because of the deaths of her husband and child, but I'm starting to believe it's inherent. Some women are that way."

"Age speaking to youth?" Menders said sarcastically.

Franz sighed. "Past unhappy experience. Wasting my time?"

"No," Menders replied, settling his baby on his lap again. "I appreciate your honesty, and your friendship."

"She'll want you to marry her. Maybe not now, but in

time."

"I will never marry," Menders said, looking up at him.

"That's a bold statement," Franz said, "although I had assumed as much."

"I'll tell her that before things go any further. I've intended to," Menders went on.

"She won't believe you. She'll think she can change you. She'll try to be first with you and she'll be jealous of Katrin."

"Katrin will always be first," Menders said quietly, looking at the child. She repeated her name and patted his face.

"Are you in love with Ermina?" Franz asked quickly.

Menders turned away and said nothing. He wasn't, and that truth made him feel that he was using her. He was also painfully aware that she was using him.

Franz waited for a few moments, and then left without a word.

CHAPTER 10
CUT DOWN

Ermina raised herself on one elbow and leaned over Menders in a cascade of dark hair before kissing his mouth. He looped an arm around her smooth back and held her close.

He had some gratification from the physical side of their relationship. She wasn't bad in bed, though he was aware that a great deal of her performance was purely theatrical and not genuine. He needed the physical release. He was young and virile and, in some ways, needed to remind himself of the fact. His responsibilities and heavy workload often made him forget that he was only twenty-one.

Emotionally, he was left cold and feeling less than chivalrous, boxed in by the situation. He was making the best of it, hoping that Ermina would be satisfied with what he could give and that she wouldn't begin demanding what he could not offer her. So far she had been quite sweet and openly adoring – but he felt that a lot was lurking under the pretty surface of the situation.

The affair had put distance between Menders and the rest of the household, as it could hardly be kept secret when everyone lived in such close proximity. The others disapproved. Ermina had never done anything to win friends among the residents of The Shadows. It hadn't occurred to Menders at the time, but elevating Ermina from wet nurse to housekeeper last year had been perceived as favoritism by everyone.

"She had better not come down here to my kitchen and start trying to lord it over me," Cook rumpussed at the time. "I'll give her a crack across the noggin with my spoon!" Cook had a favorite wooden spoon, nearly the size of a small boat paddle, which she wielded as her rod of authority in the kitchen. It had rapidly become known as 'Cook's particular spoon' and was given a wide berth by anyone seeking to sample the cooking.

The room was growing brighter as the sun rose and he nudged Ermina gently.

"I need my glasses," he said as she sat up, looking at him inquiringly.

"Poor eyes," she smiled, moving so he could reach over to the nightstand for his spectacles. He perched them on his nose.

"The well-dressed gentleman this year will sport dark glasses and his birthday suit," she said.

"I should walk out like this and look in on Cook."

"She'd whack you with her particular spoon." Ermina settled back on her pillows and stretched.

Petite, bird-boned, delicate. He would never have guessed that she'd borne a child only a year ago. She'd been tightly corseted since childhood and he found her bizarrely small waist off-putting. Sadly, she was not even the physical type he was attracted to; he preferred hearty and healthy women with natural curvaceous figures, though he certainly would never intimate that to Ermina. She could no more help her tiny frame than he could his white eyes. She tried to be pleasant and intimate and he could certainly do the same, if only out of a sort of sympathy for her.

"What does the lord of the manor intend to do with the day?" she asked.

"Oh, I shall call in my mistresses and have my way with them for several hours, followed by an orgy with my Surelian slaves," Menders answered, giving her a squeeze. She was in a nice mood this morning.

"You'll be a very busy boy," she said. "I'll be looking out the linens today while you're wallowing in lust."

"In reality, I have to sort through the woodpile a bit, see about that broken window in the nursery, make some progress on the accounts I've been neglecting when I'm dallying with you in the afternoons, see Franz about this blasted eye again, ride out to Spaltz's to see how Eiren's getting along after being sick, and see the blacksmith about straightening the nursery fire poker, which has been severely bent. That should take me up to lunchtime."

She laughed merrily and then stopped when she saw his surprise.

"You're actually serious? All this before lunch?"

"It's a normal day. After lunch, time with Katrin of course, order seeds and supplies for the kitchen garden, and rope off the skating area. The ice is too thin for it to be safe anymore."

Ermina sat up and shook her head. "Give me the accounts. They're ordered like the household ones, aren't they? I'll do them, you're doing enough. You never stop moving, Menders."

"I'm afraid it's the way I'm put together," he sighed, rising and stretching mightily.

"Very nicely indeed is the way you're put together," she flirted as he pulled on his trousers and shirt and let himself out into the hallway.

He made his way to the kitchen and depleted Cook's supply of hot water. After a bath in his room, he shaded the window and studied his left eye in the mirror.

A splinter had flown up under the bottom of his glasses while he was splitting a log a week ago. It lodged in the corner of his left eye. In a reflex action he'd rubbed it. Franz had extracted the splinter and the damaged eye was responding to treatment, but slight infection of the injury was causing an irritating sensation of itching and burning.

His eye was filmed with tears, even with the low light and it looked redder than it had been. Menders decided to see Franz as soon as he was in his office rather than fooling around with woodpiles and windows. Perhaps a change of medications was needed. He felt unusually tired and his thoughts were moving very slowly this morning.

While waiting for the good doctor, Menders went up to see Katrin.

The nursery was still quiet, with no indication that either

Kata or Katrin were awake. Menders opened the door a crack and peeped in. As usual on fine mornings, it was a bright and cheery place, flooded with sunlight.

Katrin opened her eyes and rose in her crib, grinning and shaking the crib bars resoundingly.

"Menders, Menders!" she shouted, bouncing on her toes.

A groan came from the nurse's room where Kata was still trying to sleep. Menders hushed Katrin as he lifted her out of the crib.

"Noisy Little Princess," he smiled as she put her arms around his neck and snuggled against him. He took her to the nurse's chair. She stood on his lap and grinned into his face delightedly, ready to start the day, overjoyed that he was with her.

"Do you know that it's going to turn green outside soon, Snowflower?" he told her. "There are snowflowers coming up through the snow. Just like your nickname. I'll take you out later so you can see them. They're white and gold, just like you are. We'll get your sled out and you can have a ride around the garden." He went on with similar chatter while Katrin alternated between listening intently, as if she understood every word, and crowing happily.

Suddenly she reached out and pulled his dark glasses off.

Pain flared from his damaged eye to his brain. The brilliant sunlight flooding his retinas felt as if someone had thrust the stem of a broken wineglass into his eye.

Menders cried out, squeezing his eyes shut as they streamed with tears. He groped for his glasses.

"Here, Mister Menders," Kata said. She put the glasses into his hand. He could hear Katrin beginning to cry fearfully.

He shoved the glasses on his nose but still couldn't open his eyes. The pain was too great. Katrin was crying abjectly and he gathered her close.

"No, don't cry, it's all right. Shh. You couldn't know what taking those off my nose would do. Don't cry." With similar soft words, he comforted her as he worked his eyes open. He could see her blearily, reaching out with her little hands to pat his face.

"Menders," she said mournfully, her forehead wrinkled with worry.

"See there, now I have my eyes open," he told her. The pain was incredible and tears were running down the inside of his nose. "Everything is fine." He held her close and kissed her several times.

"Kata, could you take her? I have to see Doctor Franz. Don't scold her. Try to comfort her, it isn't her fault."

He stumbled from the nursery, then groped for the stairs. He could just manage to keep his right eye open, but the left was pure agony if light struck it.

He managed to get to the first floor and heard Ermina gasp as she came out of her room.

"What happened? Menders, darling, what happened?" she said shrilly.

"Nothing serious. Katrin pulled my glasses off and that damned eye is so sensitive. Can you help me get to Franz's room?"

"That wicked girl! Poor love, here."

"She's not wicked! Don't be absurd," Menders snapped, as Ermina put an arm around his waist and led him down the hallway to Franz's office. "It was an accident, she didn't mean it. Don't you go chastising her."

"All right, all right... just let's get you to the doctor first."

In moments he felt Franz's hands on his face, gently drawing off his glasses and carefully opening his left eye. Even the shaded light was excruciating.

"I'm sorry to have to do this Menders, I can't see a thing without more light," Franz said, regret in his voice. "Ermina, could you run down to Cook and ask her to fill some clean towels with ice? Bring them back here."

Menders could hear her pattering away down the hall.

"Let me look. Brace yourself." Franz's voice was very serious. "I'm going to have to shine a light into your eye."

Menders gritted his teeth, gripped the edge of the table Franz had perched him on and nodded. Even so, he cried out at the pain and fought to get away from Franz's hand on his head.

"Damn!" Franz swore as he looked at the eye. After several agonizing moments while tears flowed down Menders' face, he mercifully removed the light just as Ermina opened the door.

"Here's the ice – Grahl's teeth!" Ermina gasped.

"It's worse than it looks," Franz said quickly. "It isn't uncommon. He needs something for pain. Could you run back to Cook and ask her for the ramplane syrup?"

"You aren't dosing me with ramplane, you idiot, it'll knock me cold!!" Menders blustered angrily. Then he heard Franz bolting the door.

"Now you listen to me," the doctor replied heatedly. "You have a serious hemorrhage in that eye, caused by infection and the sudden contraction of the eye muscles when the light hit it. Your entire eyeball is flooded with blood. It's bright red and swelling. Combined with the infection from your injury this is a very serious situation."

"How the hells could that happen? I've borne light like that before," Menders growled.

"Not when you've had an infection. Your eyes are not normal."

"Tell me something I don't know!"

"Listen to me, you stubborn bastard, do you want to go blind?"

Menders felt an icy claw of fear sink into his heart. Blind! No, impossible... how could he care for Katrin if he were blind?"

"Now, before Ermina comes back you have to hear this. I've made a mistake by not doing this before with that eye infected, but it seemed to be healing. Now I have no choice. You have got to get in bed and stay there until this eye is completely normal again."

"*What?* For how damned long?"

"A minimum of two weeks."

"I can't stay in bed for two weeks!"

"Menders, stop roaring and trying to scare me and listen," Franz said in a very low voice. "Your eyes are very delicate at the best of times. The injury you had was infected, but was responding to treatment. Now your eye is extremely compromised. What happens to one eye can happen to the other. Infections can spread. You have no choice. You must allow your body to heal or you could lose your sight."

Menders said nothing.

"Now, I won't bandage your eyes if you're able to lie quiet…"

"You will *not* bandage my eyes!" Menders was astonished to hear himself shouting. What the hells was wrong with him, carrying on like a lunatic? He had dealt with pain and serious injury before. He'd risked his life more than once and knew how to control fear, but something about facing a possible dark and uncertain future shattered his composure.

"All right, I'm not going to try to explain any more, I'm just going to tell you one thing. Do you think that the Queen will keep you as Katrin's guardian if you go blind? What do you think will happen to Katrin if you're replaced?" Franz's voice was cool and controlled.

"That's exactly what I was thinking." Menders began to breathe deeply, clenched his fists and then released them.

"At least we're of the same mind now," Franz said. "Ermina's at the door. Shall I let her in?"

Menders nodded. The door was unbolted.

"Here's the ramplane," she said shakily. Menders could feel her touching his hand. "Doctor, his hands are ice cold!"

"Yes, he's frightened," Franz said calmly. "Hand me that

spoon, would you dear? And leave us alone."

When she had gone, Menders heard Franz say, "I don't want to have to resort to holding your nose and incurring incredible injury from you. I think today you would do better with a dose or two of this, not only for the pain but so you can rest. I don't know why you're so terrified, but you are. Perhaps you don't know why you're terrified either. It doesn't matter. This will help you through some of the time."

"Through all things, I have always been able to rely on my own resources," Menders replied, forcing the words through chattering teeth. "But not if I can't see. The idea terrifies me."

"Then do as I say and we'll see about saving your sight." Franz tipped the syrup down Menders' throat. "Now it's bedtime," he continued.

"I can manage to put myself to bed, thank you," Menders snapped as Franz took his arm when he slid unsteadily to the floor and tried to walk to the office door.

"You could if you could see." Franz walked him toward his bedroom.

Menders could feel the ramplane taking effect. His fear was being replaced by a feeling of simply not giving a damn. Before he knew it, Franz was divesting him of his clothes, festooning him in a nightshirt and pushing him toward the bed.

"Go ahead," the doctor said with amusement. "I promise not to tuck you in."

"You gave me enough to knock me out, you bastard," Menders slurred, feeling the ramplane hit him like a hammer.

"Serves you right for getting belligerent with me. Now, I'm putting an ice pack on your left eye. Leave it there. Lie still or I'll just shoot you like an old horse."

The ice pack was a blessed relief. So was the ramplane. The savage pain was vanishing, replaced by dull throbbing.

He woke hours later to heat and agony. He raised his hand to his eye and found a horrible swollen lump. Someone pushed his hand away.

"You mustn't touch it," Franz said.

"Here, darling, here's some water," Ermina said on the other side of him.

He drank gratefully. His mouth was foul and dry. He could feel a crust on his face beneath the injured eye.

"I'm going to clean your eye and get some medicine into it," Franz explained. "It isn't going to be fun, but you have enough ramplane in you to blunt the worst of it."

The cleaning was agonizing, though Franz was very gentle. Menders could barely work his uninjured right eye open. When he did, his vision was completely blurred.

"Both your eyes are infected," the doctor said quietly. "It's very bad. Be still now, I have to put the drops in."

The drops stung terribly and after a moment Menders could feel them trickling into his nose. Franz gave him a handkerchief and told him to blow gently, that he must not sneeze if he could help it.

Ermina wiped his face with a wet cloth. Desperate to escape the fever and pain, he swallowed another dose of ramplane and slipped back into sleep.

This time he dreamed and the dreams were terrible. He could hear Katrin screaming and saw a dark shadow coming close to her while she held out her arms to him and cried. As he reached to lift her away from the darkness, a cane descended on his hand viciously, shattering his bones. Katrin's screaming grew louder and more frightened and then he jerked awake and realized the screams were his own. Sweat was pouring off him and someone was pinning him to the bed while Franz held his head, calling to him and telling him that he was dreaming.

He slid back into the darkness to find one of his tutors waiting for him, the one who'd seemed kind at first and who had turned out to be the worst of all. Menders came screaming out of sleep again, fighting against the hands that held him motionless and turned his face into the pillow so he couldn't breathe and couldn't fight as the tutor played his painful, sickening games.

"Menders! You must lie still!" a distant voice that seemed part of the dream said.

"The ramplane's got him off his head, I've seen it go through soldiers like that." The deep voice vibrated in Menders' ear and he realized that Lucen was holding him securely. He stopped fighting. The two men turned him over. He tried to help, but was as weak as a reed. The sheets and his nightshirt were drenched.

"Menders, are you with us?" Franz asked.

"Yes. Sorry," he whispered.

"Don't be. I had no idea you'd have that reaction to the ramplane. Have you ever taken it before?"

"Small doses, only for pain, not to sleep."

"Well, you can't tolerate it. The fever is making you delirious. It's broken for now, so you'll have some time to be lucid. I'll get some clean sheets and we'll get that sweat off you."

Menders couldn't see a thing and felt a jab of fear. His hand went to his eyes. They were bandaged.

"Franz didn't have a choice, you kept clawing at them," Lucen said. Menders nodded very slightly. Both eyes and the space between them were enormously hot, heavy and throbbing.

"Don't move your head," Lucen continued gently, his big hand touching Menders' forehead. "If you need anything, just tell me and I'll get it for you."

"Water," Menders whispered. After Lucen held the flask for him he asked, "What time is it?"

"Five in the afternoon. Same day you fell ill."

"Katrin?"

"She's well, playing with Hemmett up in the nursery. Don't worry about her, Kata's with them."

The door opened and closed and Menders could smell Franz – a wafting scent of tobacco and medicine.

"Now, let's get you civilized again," he said. With a minimum of fuss Franz and Lucen changed the sheets. Menders' sodden nightshirt was removed and replaced. Lucen began sponging the sweat from his face.

"You're proficient," Menders breathed.

"I was assigned to a soldier's hospital at one time," Lucen answered. "If you want a bed bath, I'm your man."

Menders couldn't help smiling. "I'll bear it in mind."

"Fair warning," Franz said. "You'll have these fevers for a while and a bed bath will be very welcome with enough sweat on you. How's the pain?"

Menders was about to minimize it, then simply said, "Awful."

"I don't want to give you more ramplane," Franz said.

"I'd rather have the pain," Menders answered.

"I'll do what I can for it. Do you want to see Ermina? Better do it now, because your fever is going to rise again."

After Ermina came in, Menders regretted agreeing to see her. She was beside herself with concern. It was more emotional drama than real worry and he ended up having to comfort her when he really only wanted to take whatever Franz could give him and try to escape through sleep. She kept touching him unexpectedly and fussing with his bedclothes, chattering away about nothing after she got over her crying fit. He tried to smile and be cheerful but she made him so nervous that he wanted to scream.

He wanted to see Katrin, very much. His eye was oozing under the bandage, and he felt as if a wire was being drawn tight around his head. The heat in his face let him know that the fever was rising.

"Bring Katrin," he whispered abruptly, cutting Ermina off in mid-sentence.

"Oh darling, she's fine, she's just had dinner and Kata is getting her ready for bed," Ermina said, adjusting his blanket for the fifth time and unexpectedly touching his forehead, which startled him so that he blinked, sending shooting jabs of pain into his brain.

"I didn't ask how she was, I asked to see her," he said, keeping his voice even. He heard Franz's footsteps approaching the door, and knew that his voice had carried. His ears were starting to ring and he felt very sick.

"But love, it's getting late, and you'll be able to have her visit tomorrow. Let this be our time…" Ermina began.

"I want to see Katrin!" Sweat was breaking out on his forehead and he began to tremble.

"You're far too ill!" Ermina said bossily.

"Gods damn it! Don't tell me what I can't do! I want my baby!" he shouted.

"Go get her, Ermina!" Franz said sharply. "Have you no better sense than to argue with someone who is this ill?"

She began arguing with Franz. Menders felt something snap in his mind.

"Let me up! I'll go to her myself, don't tell me I can't see her, I want her here! I want my baby!" he roared, fighting against Franz, amazed when he made no headway. He had no strength. He heard Ermina running away.

"No, no, don't thrash around!" Franz commanded. "You must lie still! Lucen's gone for the baby, he'll have her here in a minute. Here!" He leaned Menders over the side of the bed just before he vomited. "It's all right, there's a basin there, let it out."

"What will happen to her if I die?" Menders gasped when Franz eased him upright again. "You have to take her if I die. Please don't let them have her."

"Shh. We're going to do everything we can to keep you from dying but you have to help us. Lie still and try to rest."

Menders reached out, viper fast, and seized Franz's shirt front. "I cannot lose my sight! I *cannot!*"

"Like anyone else, you can and you will if you don't stop

fighting me!" Franz yelled.

Menders let go. "Promise me. Promise that you'll take her. Take her out of Mordania, say she's your daughter. Don't let them have her."

"Yes, of course. Calm down. Lucen's coming with her now."

"If anything happens …."

"Yes, I'll take her. You know I'd defend her with my life. Now here she is. Don't frighten her."

Suddenly Katrin was placed in his arms and he felt her patting his face. He held her to him and let himself relax. His head had to be on fire, it burned so.

"I'm going to give you something for the fever now, it's going up fast," Franz said from across the room. "No, you can keep holding her. Just keep holding her. That's right. No-one is going to take her away. Now, open your mouth for me. It isn't ramplane. It tastes horrible. I have some water here just as soon as you swallow it."

An intensely bitter trickle down his throat and then the blessing of water to wash the taste away. Katrin nestled against him and didn't try to get him to play. She kept patting him and babbling in a soft little croon.

"My Little Princess, little Snowflower," he whispered. The medicine was making him drowsy, but he held her close.

He woke with a jerk, drenched with sweat. Katrin was gone. With his eyes bandaged he couldn't tell what time it was. He lay still and listened.

Someone was in the room. His nose told him it was Lucen, wearing the old jacket he gardened in. Menders could smell soil and mulch. From the sound of his breathing, Lucen was asleep. The house was quiet, no noises from the kitchen, no voices. Menders sniffed. The fires smelled banked. It was late then, possibly past midnight. In the entryway the ticking of the giant old clock was a familiar heartbeat.

He always checked on Katrin at night. He had every night since she was born. It assured him that she was safe, wanted for nothing, that the nursery was secure and the fire was keeping it warm.

He sat up, his head throbbing and slid over the side of the bed to the floor. His nightshirt clung to him, drenched with sweat. He was weak and shaky. He'd been fine this morning, had been ready to go and throw logs around. Now he was staggering, as if a wet nightshirt was too heavy for him!

Lucen didn't stir as Menders made his way into the hallway. He could find his way around the house at night, even if there was no light at all. A trained assassin could walk a tightrope blindfolded. He would just go up and check on Katrin, then slip back into bed and no-one would be the wiser.

Halfway down the hallway he collided with a hallstand. It fell with a clang and he tumbled over as well, landing hard.

"Grundar shit!" he hissed, trying to untangle himself and the clammy nightshirt from what seemed to be several fire irons and umbrellas.

"What the hells? What are you doing?" Franz was suddenly there, big hands gently lifting him. "You're supposed to stay in bed, you blasted idiot, not go crashing around the house like a clumsy ghost!"

"I need to check on Katrin," Menders said, feeling with his feet for the scattered contents of the stand before stepping around them and continuing toward the stairs.

"You mad little bastard, she's fine, safe in the nursery."

"No. I always check on her, always before I go to bed. I can't not check on her." Menders heard his voice rising.

"You are far too ill to go up there," Franz cried in exasperation.

"I'm going. I always check on her."

"Menders, please listen – look out!"

Menders' foot had caught something scattered by his

collision with the stand. He fell again, more heavily than the first time. All his feline assassin's grace and agility seemed to have deserted him. Franz swore and was at his side.

"You're going back to bed if I have to pick you up and carry you there," he said angrily.

Menders wrenched away and heaved himself up, only to step on the hem of the nightshirt and fall again. Completely shaken and disoriented, he groped around him before reaching up to pull the bandage away from his eyes.

All was dark. He began to crawl. He couldn't fall again if he stayed down.

"Gods, you stubborn…" Franz was behind him again. "Here, I'll help you. Lucen, we're taking him up to the nursery, there's no point in fighting with him. We'll chair lift him."

"I can walk!" Menders hissed in a defiant whisper, although his crashing around had probably awakened half the house.

"I've never struck an unarmed and sightless patient before," Franz snarled, "but by the gods, Menders, you're tempting me!"

With their hands under his arms, they supported him up the stairs to the nursery. It was warm - the fire doing its job. It was also quiet. They guided him to Katrin's crib. He ran his hands over the bars and then down and across her mattress until he felt her, warm, snuggled under her blankets in her little nightgown with the soft lace ruffle at the neck. He straightened the blanket and stroked her hair, then turned to the fire. He sniffed and then held a hand out. It was burning well.

"It's fine, built up for the night," Lucen whispered.

Menders turned toward the windows and felt the latches. Secure. Then he went toward the changing table, felt over the piles of diapers, the bottles of oil and powder. All in place. Nearby were extra blankets, cups, shawls, all the accoutrements a baby needed.

He turned back to the crib, helped by Lucen and Franz, and kissed Katrin's forehead.

"Everything is all right – sleep well, Little Princess," he whispered.

By now he was very sick and dizzy. They got him down into his bedroom.

"Hold him up while I get these sheets changed," Franz said to Lucen. Menders swayed in Lucen's strong grasp, shivering violently.

"How can you see to do that in the dark?" he asked blearily.

"It isn't dark, there's a lantern. You can't see because your eyes are gummed shut," Franz said briskly. "There, a decent bed again. Now, we divest you of your nightshirt and put another one on and back we go for another round."

Menders was incredibly grateful for the bed. Funny, he often climbed all three flights of stairs twenty times a day or more, but now going up one flight had completely exhausted him. He only wanted to lie still.

Franz leaned over him.

"I am not going to fight you about going up there every night, but you must let us help you. And if you don't lie still and do whatever you can to recover, we won't take you up there. Do not ever pull the bandage off again. I'm going to clean your eyes now. A wet cloth will be touching your face."

Menders lay still, shivering with fatigue, until the painful process of cleaning and drops was over. He was relieved to see a blurry, dim glow from the lantern when his right eye was clean. He wasn't blind – yet.

"Now please, let us get a few hours' rest. If you decide to go out and chop down trees or walk on the roof tonight, I swear to you that I will kill you." Franz said fliply.

Sleep came swiftly, like a great onrushing wave.

CHAPTER II
CAROUSEL OF NIGHTMARES

Menders lost the distinction between dream and reality. Dreadful images loomed; old memories, new terrors, suffocating black wells of fear, fits of screaming. Scenes swept by like blurry, half-remembered images from a faded watercolor book.

Lucen's strong hands holding him down when he came tearing out of a nightmare, screaming and fighting. Franz's endless ministrations. Constant bed and nightshirt changes, burning drops in his eyes, medicines tipped down his throat. Then more sleep, more nightmares, more terror.

Sometimes he couldn't hear Franz and Lucen speaking at all. Other times their words were clear as a bell on a winter night.

"What in the name of all the gods happened to him?" he heard Lucen say at one point when he'd come howling out of yet another dream of tutors, fighting with all his strength.

"Enough to send most people mad," Franz responded. "It's that iron will of his that kept him from going completely off his head, but now that he isn't in control of himself it's all coming back to haunt him, poor little bastard. Gods, he can fight!"

"He's like soldiers who've gone battle mad. What about his eyes?" Lucen asked.

"Right now I'm just trying to keep him alive and keep Ermina away from him. The last thing I need now is dealing with the histrionics of a self-centered bitch."

He wanted to let them know that he heard them, that he appreciated what they were doing, but couldn't speak. Then his head grew hot again and the dreams, colored red and black, returned.

Running in terror through the rooms of the house where he had been born, desperate for help. Running to his father as a last resort, knowing that his tutor, the one who had seemed kind at first, was behind him. Finally bursting into his father's study, dashing across the pool of light cast by the lamp, hiding behind the chair where his father sat glaring at him. Words of apology from the tutor in the doorway – and then his father's hand closing on his wrist, dragging him from his hiding place, handing him over to the tutor. His father closing the door, leaving him to his fate.

He sat up, screaming, fighting, was calmed and restrained, slept again, dreamed again, screamed, wept and fought. The procession of days was lost to a grinding carousel of nightmares.

Every night he fought his way to consciousness and checked on Katrin. Often he could barely walk. Lucen and Franz bore more of his weight than he did, but he saw to it that she was safe and warm in her crib, whispered to her that everything was all right, to sleep well.

Then his moments of clarity grew scarce and the fever raged without breaking. The dreams ceased and he lay in a listless torpor, hardly able to swallow the medicines. If he took more than a couple of spoonfuls of water or broth at a time, he would vomit. He was aware that he was never left alone and sensed Franz with him almost all the time, as well as Lucen, though sometimes he could hear Cook or Zelia talking to him. Cook brought Katrin in to him often. He lived for the time she was there, when he could hold her. He didn't hear Ermina and didn't want her there because she worried him so.

He became used to being hot, constantly hot, burning up. There was always a foul taste in his mouth that water couldn't wash away. Often he couldn't move, couldn't speak. The pain in his eyes and head raged on, but it didn't matter. Nothing mattered.

Then a sudden sense of peace came upon him, and he felt himself drifting.

"Gods! Franz! Franz!" Lucen's voice came to him dimly. The blankets ripped back.

"He's burning up, water!" Franz's voice was frantic. "Get the shirt off him, I'll get ice."

Menders felt Lucen turning him on his belly, using his big hands to rip the nightshirt down the back. Franz's footsteps in the hallway, then in the room. A splash.

They sponged him, but he didn't even feel the cold water. He heard Ermina calling out in the hall.

"Shut the door, bolt it. She's the last thing we need," Franz snapped. "Menders! Can you hear me? Pack ice into a towel, wet it and hold it on his head."

He could hear them working over him but drifted higher, no longer feeling the pain in his eyes or the icy water they were splashing over his body.

"I can't tell if he's breathing," Lucen said frantically.

They turned him onto his back with a thump and Franz bent over him.

"Barely. Gods, if the infection has gone to his brain - Menders, you won't thank me if I save you to be an idiot. Get hot water, we'll put his feet into it, we've got to draw this heat down out of his head."

Lucen going out the door and speaking abruptly when Ermina started shouting at him in the hallway. Franz speaking in his ear.

"Menders, you're dying. Come on, damn you! Breathe!"

It didn't matter. Nothing mattered.

Dimly, he heard Lucen coming back, felt hot towels slapped over his feet. It was wasted effort. It didn't matter.

Franz slapped his face, hard. He didn't feel it.

"We've lost him," Lucen said, standing upright.

"Keep that hot water on his feet! I don't give up that easily." Franz dumped ice water directly on Menders' head, then suddenly flung the contents of the basin over his body, drenching the bed.

It didn't matter.

Franz spoke low in his ear.

"I guess you won't be seeing that Katrin is safe tonight," he said, his tone fierce. "You're going to die and leave her alone in the world."

The physical pain returned, stabbing Menders' eyes like twin daggers. He began shivering from the fever and the ice water that was pooled all around him in the bed. He tried to sit up.

"That brought you back," Franz said, attempting to sound sarcastic, but failing. He supported Menders, feeling his head.

"The fever's broken. Lucen, put him in my bed for a while, until we can get this mess sorted out."

Lucen lifted Menders as easily as he would a child, taking him into Franz's room. Suddenly, Ermina was there, clawing at Menders' hand.

"You look so terrible!" she gasped. "They haven't let me near you in all this time!"

"Please don't talk so fast, it makes my head hurt," Menders breathed.

"Tell them to let me be with you!" she demanded, talking even faster. "I've been so afraid! What would happen to me if you died?"

"Ermina, leave him alone," Franz's voice came from the doorway. "This is the last thing he needs right now."

"Why won't you let me help?" she protested.

"Because you aren't a help! Lucen, see her out." Franz waited as Lucen removed the protesting and then wailing Ermina. The doctor sat on the side of the bed.

"How are you feeling?"

"Terrible... but alive," Menders croaked. He felt his breath hitching in his chest and was humiliated to realize that he was crying. The tears were searing.

"Thank you for everything," Menders gasped, trying to bite back the sobs.

"I'm a doctor. I take care of sick people," Franz

answered. "You've been through hells and you aren't finished. You're going to be in bed for a long while yet. The fevers aren't over either but I'm hoping that this one might have burned out the worst of the infection."

"What about my eyes?"

Franz sighed. "Not good. Very swollen, very infected. I'll do everything I can."

Menders sighed in despair and tried to lie back, but Franz held onto him.

"Listen to me," Franz said. "Two years ago, if anyone had told me that I would ever admire a twenty year old boy who hadn't even finished growing, I would have laughed out loud. Then I witnessed you being handed that baby and I saw you rise to the challenge of loving her, though it was obvious that becoming her guardian was the last thing you expected. I watched you come out here and rise to the challenge of running this estate. I watched you finding a way to get us all through the winter. You haven't been afraid to take on every challenge that has come your way, Menders. Now, what you have to do is look at this illness as another challenge. That will give you a fighting chance."

Menders nodded. He was too weak to do any more.

CHAPTER 12
WAITING TIME

Fevers came and went in the next few days but Menders found a sort of peace and managed to reflect on his situation with clarity.

"Do you know what the worst of this sickness was?" he asked Franz one day.

"The fever, I expect."

"No. The fear."

"That's understandable."

"Not for me. I'm an assassin. We are trained to deal with fear, to master it. During every mission there is a possibility that you may be killed. Accepting this brings rationality of thought and clarity of purpose. But this was something else. This was a fear that... wasn't anything I was expecting."

He felt Franz sit on the edge of the bed. Menders was lying on his back, hands folded across his chest, his eyes still bandaged.

"You've had to experience what the world is like for us mere mortals then," Franz joked. "You nearly died, so fear is understandable, as I said."

"No... you still don't understand. It wasn't fear of death. It was fear of becoming something useless."

"Blind."

"Yes. Unable to fulfill my obligation and commitment to Katrin."

"I watched you climb those stairs every night, even though we had to carry you more often than not. I was impressed, although in a lesser man I would have been concerned that it had become a mania."

"An assassin must have purpose. We need something to believe in. Otherwise, we are nothing more than killers for hire, no better than any nighthawk street thug."

"I hadn't thought of it quite like that," Franz said after a pause.

Smiling, Menders answered, "Most people don't. Did I ever tell you what I did on my last mission?"

"No," Franz replied. Something in his tone made Menders think Franz might not want to know. "You said once it was somewhere abroad."

"Surelia. I was there two years."

"Two years?" Franz marveled.

"Yes, deep infiltration. I speak the language like a native. Not only that, but I adopted the mannerisms and habits of a Surelian. In short, I became one. As you know, there had been a fragile peace between our two nations for some years, until recently."

"Yes, ever since we gave them a right old shellacking at the Battle of Tastian Island," Franz said proudly. "That put them in their place."

"That defeat stuck in the minds of some more militant members of the Surelian Royal Family and the Military Council. Some of them were bitter about losing control of Mordania after deposing Queen Clearheart, because of the uprising that returned Morghenna the Wise to the Throne. Do you know much about Clearheart?"

"The general story," Franz admitted.

"She was a great Queen. When the Surelians invaded Erdahn, she sacrificed herself for her country. She gave her newborn daughter to a trusted courtier. He fled with the child and Clearheart allowed the Surelians to capture her, to give him time to get away. They tortured her to death in full view of the people – and raised a sentiment in the population that eventually led to the uprising that put her daughter, Morghenna the Wise on the Throne. I read up on her back in Erdhan, because it was my ancestor, the first Lord Stettan, who took the child and raised her in seclusion. Someday I hope to write a biography…"

Menders' voice had grown soft and dreamy. Doctor Franz could tell that his mind was distracted by the tragic story of Mordania's most famous Queen. Even now, more than two hundred years later, the battle cry "Clearheart" was commonly used by Mordanian soldiers.

"I die with a clear heart, for I protect the future of Mordania," Franz quoted, echoing the doomed Queen's final words.

Menders started a bit and smiled sheepishly over his lapse.

"Anyway," he went on, "it came to our attention that a small but powerful group was plotting to infiltrate the Mordanian military, overthrow the Queen to destabilize the country, then invade and settle what they call "The Mordanian Question" in Surelia's favor once and for all. They were very secretive. It took quite some time to winkle them out."

"Two years time?" Franz asked.

"About that."

"Then what happened?"

Menders smiled. "Oh, one night, there was a party with nearly two hundred people invited… then came shootings, stabbings, and an explosion that leveled most of the place."

Franz gasped. "By the Gods, you don't so things by halves!"

"No point. If you want to destroy a nest of snakes you must do it while they're all in one spot, before they slither off in a thousand different directions."

Menders could hear Franz scratching at his moustache. "Didn't the old King of Surelia die suddenly at about that time?"

"Yes… wasting sickness. Very tragic."

"You again?"

"Not directly, no. That was the work of a brilliant Mordanian assassin named Falk and his partner, Ifor Trantz. The new King was a surprising choice, with a benevolent viewpoint toward Mordania."

"He seems a decent sort of chap," Franz noted. "The new Queen seems nice too."

"Yes. She likes horses, he likes guns and hunting. Their outdoor pursuits make them well suited. She has Fambrian heritage too, which helps break 'The Old Family's' stranglehold on the Crown."

Franz had heard rumors of the network that had footholds in the Royal House of Surelia, influencing it to their own ends. They were secretive and shadowy people, always simply referred to as 'The Old Family'.

"We have finally settled the 'Surelian Problem' and gotten them on side with us," Menders continued. "So that leaves the Artreyans as Mordania's main threat… those popinjays."

Franz laughed at the idea of comparing the people of the new and powerful nation of Artreya to the raucous, colorful birds that infested hedgerows in the summertime and caused no end of mischief and damage.

"So you helped save Mordania from an invasion and removed a serious long term threat at the same time. I was right before, you're a hero!" Admiration rang in the doctor's voice.

"No, sir," Menders replied. "I am a servant of my country. The assassin named Falk, who eliminated the old King of Surelia – he made the ultimate sacrifice, shot to death while on that mission. His partner, Trantz, was permanently and severely injured, unable to serve any longer. He was released from service with no pension and has been struggling to survive ever since. There are no accolades for those of us who work in the shadows, Doctor."

Franz had no reply.

***

Doctor Franz nursed a contemplative pipe in the sanctity

of his office, musing over his conversation with Menders. Then he opened his medical record book.

Patient file, Menders

Patient continues to improve in general health, though much debilitated. Eyes still seriously infected and swollen, but the amount of involvement seems to be decreasing. At this point, it is impossible to assess what, if any, vision he will have at the outcome of his illness.

Franz sat back, put his pipe on the desk and sighed. He sat still for some minutes before writing again.

Menders poses many questions for me, both as his doctor and as his friend, for I believe that I have become his friend by this time. In our conversation today he confided his sense of service to Mordania to me, and though admirable, it is also a matter for concern. Menders is a young man who needs a strong vocation, and his extreme devotion to Katrin and The Shadows (and all the people who dwell there) gives him the sense of dedication that he requires. How he will cope if he loses his sight and is unable to be of service to the Princess and Mordania is questionable.

I know more about Menders now, as a great deal of his childhood has been revealed to me during his fits of delirium. I knew a great deal about his father, who was an infamous reprobate who had been banned from Court by Morghenna the Terrible prior to Menders' birth. It is not difficult to see that Menders' extreme upright morality is in direct reaction to his father's lack of the same. However, I fear that he is setting too high a bar for himself, requiring a standard of behavior that will be impossible for him to sustain. As it is, his unfortunate association with Ermina has strained his emotional health, as it goes entirely against the grain of his morality – and I would venture to say that the concomitant stress has, very possibly, weakened his resistance to the infection. It is certainly not an affair that will sustain or help him in any way.

To make matters worse, Mistress Ermina is throwing her weight around in her role of housekeeper now that Menders is not able to keep an eye on her, and is creating household dramas on an ongoing basis. I have told the others to keep this from Menders, as he is far too weak to contend with the situation now. Time enough when we have some idea if he will regain his vision and health.

What sort of country trains children to be killers? Knowing that Menders was put into training as an assassin at the age of eleven and sent out to kill when he was fifteen has made me understand a great deal about him. In any other occupation, he would have been considered a youth – but as an assassin, he had to become a man long before he was physically or emotionally ready to be one. The damage this has done to his mind is considerable. I fear that his life will never be free of the impact of those years where he killed so many.

The doctor sat back and considered the conundrum of boys being sent into the dark to kill in the name of a Queen who probably didn't know of their existence.

***

Once Menders was no longer critically ill, Franz permitted visits by the household. Cook would sit by the bed, chatting away as she peeled a basket of potatoes or kneaded bread in a bowl. Lucen brought every news sheet in and faithfully read every word aloud, slowly and laboriously. Zelia dropped by for brief visits with Hemmett, which were lively and often hilarious.

Ermina came to Menders' room as well, but he couldn't be glad about it. She fussed and fidgeted, moved suddenly, chattered constantly and was always bossy. Being completely blind with his eyes still covered, it drove Menders near madness. He felt exhausted after she'd been with him. Sometimes when he heard her coming he would pretend to be asleep, just so he didn't have to listen to her or refrain from lashing out and swatting her hands as they fluttered around him constantly, like giant moths.

Franz helped pass the time. Katrin was a healthy child and though Franz ran a practice from his office, seeing to the medical needs of the tenant farmers and other people in the locality, he had plenty of spare hours. He would read to Menders or talk, and Menders had persuaded him to play DeGratz, having Franz call his moves out loud and telling Franz where to move his own pieces. Menders had won two out of three games that way. Franz scolded him fiercely and had refused to play since.

As spring progressed, the work of the estate was in full swing. Menders spent much time alone, unable to see. It became tedious very quickly without his notebook, sketchbook or anything else to occupy himself with.

Eiren was a saving grace. She was a bright child who loved to read. She often asked for books from the estate library, usually requesting one 'with adventures in it'. When Menders could have visitors she'd talked to her father, who came to see Menders.

"I know that you've always made a point of never being alone with the young girls and as a father I appreciate that. But I know you would never do anything improper, Mister Menders. Our Eiren has told me that she would like to read to you, if you had a mind for her to do that. I wanted to let you know that I have no objections to her sitting by you and reading or talking while you're in your sickbed."

Mister Spaltz was a forthright man and Menders made an exception to his rule of never being alone with one of the nurserymaids, though he insisted that the door be kept open during Eiren's visits.

Now she was at his doorway.

"Well, hello Eiren," Menders said pleasantly. He smiled at the sound of her indrawn breath.

"How did you know it was me?"

"By your walk. You have new boots and one of them squeaks. The right one, I believe." Menders was guessing which boot it was, purely for effect, figuring he could only be fifty percent wrong. He imagined her staring down at her feet.

"I thought you might be asleep," she said.

"No, just taking a walk around the estate with my ears."

Eiren muffled a giggle. "With your ears?"

"Yes that's right. Sit down, close your eyes and listen very carefully." He heard her settle on the bedside chair. "Now, tell me what you hear."

"I... I don't hear anything," she said shyly.

"Nonsense! There is always something to listen to. Now, imagine you walked downstairs from this room and out into the yard. See in your mind's eye what you would pass, then listen for those things."

"I hear... my breathing. And yours."

"Filter those out and listen further afield."

"I hear... oh! Katrin and Kata, playing in the nursery."

"Yes. They're playing with blocks, you can hear them click together."

"Oh! So you can!"

"What else?"

"Um... the big clock in the entryway! It's almost like a heartbeat. Funny, I've never noticed how it sounds before. And then... Cook, in the kitchen, moving things, talking to someone... no, arguing with someone... has to be Ermina."

Menders smiled at the way Eiren mouthed the name Ermina, as if she were spitting out bitter berries.

"Listen further away, outside and across the estate," he prompted.

"Wind in the trees, yes... and birds! Popinjays, forest strutters, a red warbler, I think."

"Do you hear someone working in the woodlot?"

"Oh that's much too far – no, wait! Yes, yes I can!" Eiren's voice had become breathless with excitement. "Big heavy strokes! Has to be Lucen, nobody can swing an axe like he does.

And then, just past that, the bells on Kleint's cows."

Menders strained his ears and then finally located the sound. Gods, even he hadn't heard that at first! She really can do it, he thought to himself. What a rare little bird!

"Very good." He smiled.

Eiren inhaled sharply. He imagined she had opened her eyes and was looking at him. "That was amazing! I almost saw myself there."

"It's a trick assassins use to focus and concentrate. It passes the time. I have a lot of empty hours, I'm afraid."

"Would you like me to read to you? I looked in the library and found a new book with pirates in it. And I brought you some flowers. I'll put them in the glass. They're jewelflowers and hide-tights."

"Pirates sound just right," Menders said, turning on his side and getting comfortable, at least for a while. Who would ever think that lying in bed day after day would actually start to hurt?

Eiren clinked around on his nightstand for a moment, poured water and then took his hand, touching it to individual blossoms as she told him which was which.

"I can smell them and if they're as pretty as they smell, they must be the best jewelflowers and hide-tights in the entire garden," he complimented her.

"They don't have much smell at all," Eiren protested.

"They do if you can't see. I can smell all sorts of things now. If you can't use your eyes, you'd be surprised by how you begin to notice things like that."

"How do they smell?" she asked.

"Thin and green. Like springtime."

"You can't smell those things!" She was laughing, which made him smile. "You can't smell shapes, and colors."

"They smell thin and green nonetheless. And I can smell that you stopped off in the kitchen and ate two of Cook's best ginger biscuits."

"How can you tell I had two?" she asked.

"Ah, that is a mystery for only me to know," he teased. She always took two of things, because she was too hungry to stop at just one and three would be greedy. This applied to slices of bread, cookies, sweets and helpings at meals. Of course, she had no notion that he'd observed this, just as he observed everything about everyone. At least, he used to, he reminded himself.

"I would have brought you some, but Cook says you still can't eat them."

"No, but I'm glad you thought of me." He could hear her pulling the chair closer and settling herself again. His diet was very restricted, as his stomach was somehow involved with the infection and he vomited frequently.

"How's Katrin?" he asked, before Eiren could get launched on the pirates.

"She's had a good morning and ate a big lunch. She didn't want to settle for a nap, so Kata's playing with her, like we heard. Shall I read now?"

"Of course, let's hear about the pirates." He tucked a hand under his cheek and listened while she launched into the book, which was intended for a child her age. She read easily, having been taught by her father, who was the most literate of the estate farmers. When Eiren lost herself in the story, she became very expressive and would vary the voices of the characters. Sometimes her performance was unintentionally funny, and twice he had to hide the fact that he was smiling at a passage that was supposed to be particularly dramatic. Finally he slipped and grinned just as she was giving a grand impersonation of a particularly wicked pirate, with heartfelt growls and an attempt at a Surytamian accent.

"Mister Menders! This is supposed to be thrilling and you're laughing!" she protested.

"I'm sorry, Eiren, it is thrilling. It just reminded me of something funny that happened when I was little," he said quickly. "Tell me, what would you like to do when you're older?"

He heard her close the book. "I like it here at The Shadows," she said slowly. Eiren had a fear of being discourteous.

"Yes, but I know you don't want to be a nurserymaid the rest of your life, or a farm girl either. Katrin won't need nurserymaids forever. It's just for now, while she's little."

"Well... no. Not that I don't love Katrin. I do, very much. She's such a funny, sweet baby. But I would like to teach. I can read and I can do figures well. I think that if I read enough books, I could have a little school in that old unused building on my father's farm. I would teach the children from the other farms, so that they would know how to read. Someday I want to know all the things you know, Mister Menders."

"Oh, I know a great many things," Menders said, thinking that some of them weren't suitable for little girls to know.

Being a nurserymaid was sufficient for now. It gave her experience and a salary, and it also relieved her family of having to keep her. They had eight children to provide for, with only Eiren old enough to work. But as he'd come to know her, he'd begun to realize that Eiren was not content with her lot, and he'd pondered on what this girl, isolated in a remote place, might want to do with her life.

"That's quite an ambition," he prompted, "To be a teacher."

"I think it would be a great thing," she said quietly. "You're right. I don't want to live on a farm forever. It's a hard life for a woman."

He was about to laugh and say that she wasn't a woman, but then remembered that most girls on the estate were married and expecting their first child at sixteen. Eiren was fourteen. She was being realistic.

"My mother... Mister Menders, she's had eight children

and she's lost at least one tooth for each one of us. She's only thirty-one. She works all day and the work is never done. I work here, but there's Kata to do some of it and when the day is over, it's over, unless Katrin needs a diaper in the night. But Mama is up before anybody else, she goes to bed after everybody else and her hands are never still. And when she had my brother, right before you came to The Shadows – Mister Menders, it was terrible. I was the only one there to help her and the baby came wrong and there was so much blood..." Her voice trailed away, quivering.

He knew about that birth, where Marjana Spaltz had nearly died while Eiren struggled frantically to save both her mother and her youngest brother. It was said that the girl hadn't spoken for a week after the birth, only coming out of her shell when he had walked into The Shadows with Katrin in his arms on their arrival from Erdahn. The damage done to her young mind was obvious. Her mother's predicament had obviously made her think seriously about her choices in life – or lack thereof.

He heard Eiren shift in the chair, as if she had forced herself upright from a slumping position.

"It may be wrong and ungrateful, but I don't want to be like that. I love my mother and our farm has given me everything I have, but I don't want to be like that," she continued fiercely. There was sudden determination and a touch of desperation in her voice.

"That's understandable, Eiren," he replied. "I think your idea of a school on the estate is an excellent one. Having more people who can read would be an improvement."

Indeed it would. Most of the farmers couldn't so much as read the almanac or manuals for farm equipment. It was seldom that Menders rode anywhere on the estate without someone running to their gate and asking if he would read something for them. He'd had the heartbreaking experience of being handed an official letter, which had been kept unopened for two months because the farmer and his wife couldn't read, to find that it was informing them of their only son being killed in Mordania's latest military action. The poor couple had been completely unknowing, and were devastated because the letter had been lying on the table for so long while they had believed their son to be alive.

"Do you know that there are schools for teachers, where you can go not only to study different subjects but also to learn the best methods of teaching?" Menders asked.

"There are? But that would cost a great deal of money," Eiren replied. Her voice trembled a bit with excitement.

It would be something to ponder, during all the hours he had to lie here doing nothing. He had money of his own from his personal estate, wisely invested and with no-one to spend it on since Katrin had a royal income. Perhaps he could sponsor Eiren to attend teacher's college someday.

"Eiren! What are you doing here? Shouldn't you be in the nursery?" Ermina's peevish voice cut into his thoughts. He'd been so absorbed that he had failed to hear her approach.

"I asked her to read to me for a while, Ermina," Menders said.

"I didn't hear any reading," she sniffed. "Kata could use some help with the nursery laundry."

"This is Eiren's free afternoon, Kata's on duty now," Menders said, snapping his voice. It got her attention.

"Well, she needn't stay here. I'll read whatever you want," she responded, sounding as if he was two years old. Her tone made Menders bristle.

"Since I have the afternoon free, I'll walk over to my parents' house and see if Mama needs any help," Eiren said quietly. "I'll leave the book." With that she was gone; Menders could hear her footsteps retreating down the hall.

There was a rustling of pages and then Ermina let out a snide little laugh.

"Pirates?" she said sarcastically. "Very deep reading. I'm

sure you were fascinated, considering your usual reading matter is incomprehensible to mere mortals."

"Yes and that child would have loved to spend her free time today reading just that book. Now she's going to walk two miles to work hard for the rest of the afternoon," Menders said angrily.

"Oh darling, don't be upset, it isn't good for you. Why don't you lie back and I'll read whatever you want."

"No."

"Don't be grouchy. Is your head hurting?"

"It always hurts! My eyes are still the size of fists and running rivers of pus," he answered viciously.

"I'll bathe them for you."

"No."

"You *are* being difficult." Smugly, as if she was speaking to a fractious child she knew would have to do her will sooner or later.

"Do you know, Ermina, that Eiren would like to be a teacher? That she's afraid of ending up like her mother, worked half to death and an old woman at the age of thirty? That's what we were talking about when you decided to come in here and interrupt." He pulled away from her hands, which were patting and tugging and adjusting the bedclothes, his hair, the bandage around his head, his nightshirt.

"Well you shouldn't encourage such unrealistic nonsense, it's simply not possible for a farm girl to be a teacher," she nattered. "No wonder she's half in a dream all of the time. I've been thinking about letting her go."

Menders sat upright and turned his head in her direction.

"You have nothing to say about who is employed here," he said coldly.

"I'm the housekeeper!"

"You have nothing to say about who is employed here," he repeated, gritting his teeth.

"Well! You must be running a fever, if you want to play with the little girls and get angry if I wish to dismiss a lazy servant!"

Menders knew this could go on for hours. He'd been round it before. Ermina liked arguing, if you could call it that. Baiting and contradicting was more like it.

"Leave me alone," he sighed. "I'm tired. I want to sleep a while."

"Here, I'll help you settle down …"

"For the Gods' sake, Ermina, I can manage to go to sleep by myself!" he shouted.

"What a pisspot!" He could hear her flouncing out.

He dropped back against the pillow, feeling ill. He'd been better today but now his head was spinning. He'd worked himself up into a fever. Wonderful. Nothing like a few hours of bad dreams and a foul tasting mouth. Thank you, Ermina.

He heard someone at the door and fired a pillow in that direction.

"Hey, be careful there, Head of Household," Franz said, his tone telling Menders that he was grinning. "Good thing you didn't fling that at the fair Ermina, they'd be hearing her yowling down at Spaltz's." He came toward the bed, thumped the pillow down on Menders' lap and then sat against the bedpost. Menders could hear the rattling of a DeGratz set.

"So you heard," Menders sighed, repositioning the pillow.

"Couldn't help it. Want a suggestion? Dismiss the housekeeper, not the nurserymaid."

Menders grunted. He didn't want to discuss it.

"Here, let's have a look at your eyes." Franz got up and unwrapped the bandage.

Menders worked his eyes open. He could now see light and blurry shapes, but not much more because of the swelling in his eyes.

"I won't use the lantern, I'll just put the drops in and

change the bandage," Franz said.

The fresh bandage did feel better, as did the clean and temporarily cool pads over his eyes. He didn't ask Franz what his eyes looked like. His prognosis was still uncertain. No point in talking about it or wondering if he would ever have more vision than he had now.

"I'll let you torment me through a game of DeGratz now that I've seen the last sticky baby for the day," Franz announced jovially, clicking the DeGratz pieces into place on the board.

"I was talking to Eiren," Menders said, surprising the doctor. He usually pounced on the opportunity of a game of DeGratz like a starved weasel. "She wants to set up a school in that vacant building on her father's farm."

"Indeed? Interesting, very interesting." Franz's voice was thoughtful.

"She could set up an informal school now, but when I told her that there are places where she could learn to be a teacher, she brightened up - until she thought of the cost."

"Now I'm intrigued. It wouldn't be a bad thing to have a school on the estate. Some of the ignorance I deal with... well, I won't dwell on it," Franz sighed.

Menders nodded. He saw it all the time on the estate farms. Both human and animal suffering were made worse by ignorance. It wasn't that the farmers were heartless. They simply didn't know that there were better ways of doing things.

"What say that when little Eiren is about to be unneeded in the nursery, we have a talk with the Spaltzes and send our protégée to learn to be a teacher," Franz said outright. "Between the two of us we can afford it. I'd hate to see that little girl married by the time she's sixteen and starting a string of babies. I doubt you'd have any resistance from Spaltz, other than that he'll insist on doing some kind of work to offset the cost of school and board for her."

Menders smiled and leaned back against the pillows. He

would have ruminated over the entire affair for days and even weeks, while Franz was inclined to act outright.

"Now then, let's get on with this game, and mind you don't cheat," Franz cautioned. They began the game, calling out their moves to each other. After a short struggle, Menders won and smugly said "DeGratz!"

"Oh grundar shit!" Franz groaned. "Talk about a mind like a steel trap!"

Menders grinned.

CHAPTER 13
CLEARING VISION

"What do you see?" Franz asked as Menders set his glasses in place on his nose.

Menders looked around.

"Everything – but I'm going to need a new correction, it's blurred," he answered, smiling with relief.

"Good. That's the best we could hope for, considering the swelling and the length of time your eyes were infected. I'll make enquiries as to whether there's a proper optometrist in Erdstrom - otherwise you'll have to go to Erdahn."

Menders smiled and lay back, looking at the beautiful blurred world through his glasses. "Put up the shades," he ordered.

"Yes sir," Franz answered, and did so.

Menders blinked.

The world was green. Of course he had known that spring had come during the tedious weeks in bed, but it was still a shock, for his last view of the world had been a study in white and grey.

"Winter has marched on," Menders said quietly.

"Just be glad you're marching with it, Head of Household and not ploughed under the sod," Franz replied. "What is it, Eiren?"

Menders looked around. Eiren was standing in the doorway, fuming.

"Mister Menders, I know it's not for me to criticize and Doctor said we weren't supposed to bother you with what she does, but you should know. Ermina won't let me give Katrin anything to eat and she's hungry."

Menders listened carefully. Katrin was crying upstairs.

"Ermina says Katrin has to start having meals on a schedule," Eiren continued belligerently.

"Thank you," Menders replied, climbing out of bed. He started for the door but couldn't face the idea of confronting Ermina wearing only a nightshirt. "I'll be there as soon as I'm dressed."

He went to the closet, grabbing a pair of trousers and a shirt. He could hear Katrin's crying escalating.

"I can go up there and bring her down," Franz offered.

"No, I have to do this," Menders responded, pulling the nightshirt off over his head. He drew on his trousers and began to button the waist.

His hands slowed. He'd been swallowed up in voluminous nightshirts for many weeks.

"Gods," he whispered. He'd always been lean but if he didn't hold the trousers up with his hands, they would be down around his ankles.

"Well, at the Military Academy they always said I was like a greyhound, all prick and ribs, but nothing like this," he muttered to Franz, wrapping the loose waistband a quarter again around his waist. "I need one of Katrin's diaper pins."

"You'll fill out quickly the way you eat. For now, use this." Franz dropped just such a pin into Menders' hand from the collection of odd items that infested his pockets. Menders pinned his trousers, pulled on the shirt, which draped on him like a deflated balloon, found his shoes and headed for the stairs with Franz at his heels.

He was winded by the time he reached the top. He leaned against the wall, catching his breath while Katrin's wailing turned into despairing sobs. He gritted his teeth, clenched and unclenched his fists, then walked into the nursery.

Katrin held out her arms to him, crying his name. He went and gathered her up, glaring at Ermina. At that moment, Katrin's belly rumbled and she whimpered.

"Why are you letting her cry?" he asked, his tone cold and low.

For once Ermina was dumbstruck. Obviously she had not expected him to be up and about. When she'd seen him only this morning he'd still been bedridden, with his eyes swathed in bandages.

"And since when does anyone in this house not eat when they are hungry?" he continued, walking toward her. Katrin snuggled against him, rubbing her teary face on his shirt.

"It's high time she was given some sort of schedule and discipline," Ermina said, having found her tongue. "She's been very difficult during the time you've been in bed."

"Where I should be right now," Menders said. "Katrin has a schedule, and always has. She gets up in the morning, goes to bed at night, has meals with the rest of us and additional food when she's hungry. That is how it will remain. Franz, would you take Katrin down to Cook for something to eat, please?"

He glared at Ermina until Franz took Katrin away. Then he grabbed her by the shoulders.

"What are you doing in this nursery?" he growled, giving her a shake. "Who the hells do you think you are?"

"Menders, it's only a half hour until time for her to eat! She needs to learn that she can't have everything she wants the moment she wants it," Ermina began in the shrewish tone that infuriated him.

"A half hour! That's an eternity to a child Katrin's age! What possible purpose could it serve to make her stay hungry for half an hour?" He felt himself building up to a rage and released her. If he didn't, he might just shake her to death.

"She's terribly spoiled! The nurserymaids give in to every whim she has! You're just as bad!"

"You are not in charge of Katrin, the nurserymaids are. You are not a nurse, you are a housekeeper. Katrin is my charge, not yours. Get out of this nursery, and stay out. You have nothing to say about how Katrin is raised."

"It's always Katrin with you, isn't it? Why are you even

out of bed?" she snapped.

"Because I heard my baby crying while you just stood by and did nothing," he answered. He waited until she slammed out of the room, then leaned against Katrin's crib wearily. Even though he'd been in bed for weeks and had been desperate to be free of the confinement, he wanted to be nowhere else now.

"Come on," Franz said in the doorway, "Back to bed. Baby is happily eating a slice of bread and butter, Ermina has flounced off to her room and you're about to fall down."

After a slow trek down the stairs, Menders got into bed gratefully. A few minutes later, Eiren brought Katrin in to him.

"Menders!" she cried, smiling and putting her arms out to him.

"I can see you now, Little Princess," he said, taking her and holding her close. "When I have new glasses, I'll be just like I used to be." He held her on his lap while she patted his face and then gently put her hands to his glasses, but left them in place.

"No, no," she murmured. He smiled.

"That's right, leave them where they belong," he said. She was sleepy after her crying fit and the food she'd had, so he settled her onto the pillows and eased down beside her.

"No one will ever starve you, my Snowflower," he said, stroking the golden hair that was beginning to grow long. "Not even for half an hour. Why don't you stay here with me for a little while?"

Franz had pulled the shades down so Menders removed his glasses. Soon he would have a new pair made, so he could see properly. He would be able to start eating normally again. Before long, he would begin building his body back to the strength it had before he fell ill.

Katrin turned over and smiled at him before she closed her eyes.

CHAPTER 14
"HOW MANY BOYS HAVE YOU BEEN EXPECTING TO STEP OUT OF THE DARK?"

It was early summer before Menders finally let himself into the dim, aromatic stable. Two heads appeared over stall doors and in one stall noisy kicking began.

"Hello there, fat boy," he murmured to Franz's big grey gelding, rubbing the horse's neck and feeding it a couple of sugar lumps. The greedy animal lipped at his hand long after the sugar was gone. "You eat too many of these, you soft Artreyan lapdog," Menders laughed.

The kicking further down the stable increased and Menders left the affectionate horse, walking down between the slanting shafts of early morning sunlight that fell through the high windows.

His farlin, Demon, snapped at him in greeting.

"I see you didn't miss me," Menders smiled, paying no attention to the farlin's dramatics. "No sugar for you if you don't love me anymore."

With a bit of eye rolling, Demon leaned his head against Menders' shoulder.

"Ah, that's better. You're very sweet, so you can have your sugar – but if you nip my hand, I'll give you a clout around the head you won't forget," he said, offering the sugar. Demon took it and crunched happily.

"I'm not supposed to ride out on you yet," Menders said, patting the sinuous, striped neck as Demon nosed his pockets, hoping for more treats. "I've been sick, so I'm going out on your pudgy friend over there."

When he walked away Demon went back to kicking his stall door. Menders turned back to him, laughing.

"So you did miss me," he said, rubbing Demon's

forehead. He could see the farlin was restive. He'd been cooped up for weeks. Franz wasn't about to ride him, being far too large for Menders' Mordanian saddle and it was the same story with Lucen. Franz's Artreyan saddle would swim on Demon's lean body. One of the younger tenant farmers had taken Demon out for some exercise and had returned looking, as Cook said, like he'd been dragged through a hedge backwards. The farmer had refused to try riding Demon again. Eventually even Lucen wouldn't lead Demon anywhere because he kicked and bit out of frustration. The farlin had spent the last two weeks stabled.

"I'll put you in the pasture," Menders said, reaching for the lead. He hesitated.

He truly didn't care for riding Franz's gelding. The gelding was a good horse, but riding him was as easy as sitting in a chair. Demon, on the other hand, was prone to bolt and buck, shied at everything and had a particular trick of whipping his head around in a snakelike motion to nip his rider on the foot. He adored Menders and obeyed him out of love, but he was still a handful, with a wild strain in his bloodline that was downright lunatic.

"What say we go against doctor's orders and have a ride?" he asked the farlin, who knew the word 'ride' and went back to kicking his stall door resoundingly. "Stop that. Wait for me."

In a moment Menders was back with his saddle and bridle. He saddled Demon quickly while avoiding the animal's playful but painful pointed teeth. He mounted with one leg wrapped around the high pommel of the saddle, the traditional sidesaddle riding posture of Thrun herdsmen. That way when Demon bolted, which he was sure to do, he wouldn't run out from under Menders – that is, unless the saddle girth broke.

The moment Menders rode out of the stable, Demon tore down the road toward Spaltz's farm as fast as he could go. Menders bent low over the animal's neck, feeling the wind rush at his face and stream his long hair behind him. Eventually the farlin quieted and was content to walk along when Menders reined him in.

It was well worth going against doctor's orders. The wild ride had cleared Menders' head and he could think clearly and sharply again. He'd been plagued with a tendency toward drowsiness and lack of energy – now he knew why. He'd needed exercise, not more rest.

Menders began thinking about the dreams that accompanied his weeks of high fever. He'd come to terms with many of the terrifying memories they'd contained. For the first time in his life he no longer consciously blocked his memories of childhood and now had little to fear, even from his worst recollections.

During the two years Menders had spent in Surelia, several stressful incidents had brought his traumatic memories floating to the surface. For the first time since becoming an assassin, he'd been unable to find any sort of mental peace. No matter how he tried to clear his mind, his brutal childhood continually confronted him, particularly the memories of the tutor who had used him sexually.

Upon his return to Erdahn, it was easy to find Hartsen Trentov. Menders gained entry to the man's house the night of his return, determined to kill his former tutor. He'd moved through the darkened rooms silently, finding his quarry sitting alone before the fire.

The stench told him the story before the man even knew he was there. Menders didn't need to kill him. Trentov's own body, stricken with one of the slow growing rots that consumed people painfully from the inside, was already dying.

Menders stepped out of the shadows right beside Trentov, who looked up slowly, his face pallid and full of dread.

"Tell me, how many boys have you been expecting to step out of the dark?" Menders asked. "More than a few, I expect."

"Aylam?" Trentov quavered, shielding his eyes from the firelight. In response, Menders removed his dark glasses. When the tutor saw the white eyes that identified his ex-pupil, he shuddered.

"How did you get in here?" he whispered.

"How many boys have you been expecting to step out of the dark?" Menders repeated.

"Gods, if you're here to kill me, just do it. You'd be doing me a favor," Trentov groaned.

"There are some things I want to know first," Menders said. "Did you know you were hurting me?"

The man looked away.

"So you did. You knew you were hurting me."

"You fought. If boys don't fight, it doesn't have to hurt. Some like it." Desperation rang in Trentov's voice. "Your little cousin, Kaymar, I taught him after leaving your home – he loved it. He loved me. There were no complaints from him until I left for another posting…"

Menders blanched. He had never met his cousin, Kaymar, who was six years his junior. He would have been just out of the nursery at that time. This man was babbling about meddling with a little boy, even younger than Menders had been when Hartzen Trentov first raped him.

"You sicken me," he snarled. "The idea that monsters like you walk the world sickens me."

Trentov sat, wringing his claw-like yellow hands in the firelight. There was silence. Menders turned away, ready to leave.

"Aylam, please."

Menders turned back. Trentov was staring at him from hollow eye sockets, his face lined with pain.

"Aylam, kill me. I know you intended it when you came here. Do what you came to do."

"No. You'll die sooner or later. Until then, when the pain is tearing away at you – remember your student, Aylam." He leaned closer, his pale eyes hard as alabaster. "When you're feeling your guts sizzling and want the pain to stop, and you know someone could have made it stop and didn't, then… remember me."

He faded back into shadow and had almost reached his point of entry when he turned and made his way back to the firelit room. He was not surprised to see Trentov in tears.

"I would have been merciful enough to kill you if you'd done one thing," he said, making the man jump violently in his chair.

"What?" he gasped.

"If you'd apologized." Menders greatly enjoyed the stricken look on Trentov's face. "If you'd only apologized."

With that, he left the house and had determinedly put everything that the tutor had ever done to him out of his mind until it emerged during his fever and delirium. It seemed that some things, even when dealt with, are never really over.

Now, on a clear summer morning under a sky of blazing azure lightly sketched with thin brushstrokes of cloud, he could confront all his memories and know that they were of the past and could never hurt him again. If nothing else, being sick had freed him from the exhausting effort of consciously keeping the nightmare recollections at bay.

Menders reined Demon around toward The Shadows.

"We've got to head back now," he said. "The sun's getting high and I'm starving. I'm sure you could use something after that run."

In answer, Demon tried to bite his foot.

"Little bastard," Menders said affectionately, swinging his leg around and settling himself astride. One advantage of an Old Mordanian saddle was the ability to sit either way, which prevented fatigue. His muscles were soft from lack of use and he was starting to feel the ride.

"We'll have to do some work on you, until you're safe enough for Katrin to ride with me," he told the farlin, who swiveled his ears back and forth, listening. "Otherwise I'll have to go and get a big chubby Artreyan nag like Fatboy back there at home."

Thinking of Franz's horse brought thoughts of Franz himself to mind.

When Menders first recovered his vision, he'd been shocked to see that Franz's face was full of old contusions, including what must have been a horrendous black eye. He'd asked the doctor if he'd fallen and got a typically sarcastic but affectionate reply.

"No, Head of Household, I ran into a threshing machine named Menders."

It was then that Menders understood just what Franz had done for him. Coping with an ex-assassin with muscles like steel who was lashing out in delirium had been a dangerous and damaging ordeal. He'd tried to apologize, but Franz brushed it off. Later, Menders saw similar marks on Lucen's face. Lucen was embarrassed and wouldn't talk about it, so Menders queried Cook as she sat by his bed, punching away at dough in her bread bowl.

"When you were at your worst they both looked like they'd been thrashed by a prizefighter," she said frankly. "You were that far off your head. They wouldn't let me, nor Ermina, nor Zelia near you for fear you'd hit one of us and kill us outright. Because you were delirious nothing held you back and you swung and kicked as if you were fighting off a wild animal."

Both men had nursed him devotedly and they had literally saved his life. They'd also managed to do something for him that he'd never thought would happen. They'd helped him to overcome the intense reserve he'd felt around other men since he was a child, something that had come courtesy of Hartzen Trentov and other cruel tutors, to say nothing of his father.

He'd been friendly enough with other boys at school, but always at a remove. He'd always gone into a cold sweat when one of the ones who was attracted to other males would make advances toward him, though he never thrashed them as some of the other boys were wont to do. But after the weeks Franz and Lucen had to do everything for him, dressing, undressing, bathing, bed changes, he'd lost the compulsion to pull away from them. They were his friends and they were helping him – and that was all.

It made a free and easy relationship between Menders and Franz possible. Their friendship had always been warm, but at times Menders had found himself wondering if Franz's closeness had an ulterior motive. Franz was a physical man. At first Menders had been wary, and it had shown. Franz had never let that sway him in the least. He was simply one of those big, bluff men who thought nothing of throwing his arm around another man's shoulders, mock wrestling with him or calling him by ridiculous and affectionately abusive nicknames. Now Menders could reciprocate without feeling compromised in any way. He was glad of it.

He was also grateful for another thing that showed Franz's mettle. While delirious, Menders had begged Franz to take Katrin out of Mordania if he died and he'd thought Franz had agreed simply to humor a sick man off his head. But later Franz had come to him and reminded him of the promise. Menders' illness had brought Katrin's vulnerability home to both of them.

Together they had come up with a plan. Should Menders die or be incapacitated, Franz would take Katrin to Erdstrom and sail for Surelia. If the weather was unfavorable, for Erdstrom was sometimes ice-locked in winter, they could wait in a safe house that Menders had acquired there and sail by the first available boat. Menders owned untraceable property in Surelia, a legacy of his final mission as an assassin. There, Franz would raise Katrin as his daughter. She would effectively disappear from the face of Eirdon.

"The painful thing will be that you couldn't have contact with anyone at The Shadows or in Erdahn, not even to let them know that you and Katrin are alive," Menders warned. "Letters could be intercepted and traced."

"I'm aware of that," Franz replied. "It would be a complete break, as effective as if she and I had both suddenly died." They both went silent.

"If you were incapacitated, but alive, I would take you too," Franz finally said. "That has to be part of the agreement."

"What, if I went blind or the like? Tie yourself down with that? No. Absolutely no." Menders clenched his teeth.

"Shut up and don't be so noble all the time, it's a damn bore. If you're living, you'll go with Katrin and me if I have to drag you strapped to a pallet. You can be the blind uncle or half-mad cousin. If you were living, you couldn't be separated from her and I would refuse to go without you. It would be a cruelty to deprive Katrin of you. So we'd best settle it now. If alive, you will go with us. Take it or leave it, Menders."

Unwilling to show the surge of emotion that went through him, Menders stared at Franz through his darkened glasses.

"And don't try glaring at me through those goggles, because it doesn't work," Franz added fiercely. "Save us a lot of time and just nod."

After a moment, Menders nodded.

"Good. Now, enough of a grim subject. See to it that you don't end up incapacitated or dead, because I forbid you to ever get sick again. Damned if I'll put up with you beating my brains out another time."

Demon caught sight of The Shadows and decided he was going to gallop home. Menders was glad to let him go, releasing his memories of Franz and their conversation. His stomach was clamoring for food. The faster they got home, the better.

Of course they were caught red-handed by Franz, who was standing by the stable, looking thunderous.

"You damned idiot!" he raged as Menders and Demon

slid to a stop in the yard and Menders dismounted. "I told you to ride my horse, not that circus animal! Are you trying to get yourself killed?"

"Franz, I think I should ask you to marry me. You nag less than Ermina," Menders said, grinning at the big man. Demon took a nip at Franz and got a whack for it from Menders.

"Gods, I give up. I spend weeks putting you back together and the first thing you do is go out on that demented animal!"

"Yes Mama," Menders purred. Franz stormed off into the house while Menders unsaddled Demon and turned him out to pasture. The little farlin, far from being weary from their long ride, bucked, whirled and tore away across the grass as if his feet were on fire.

CHAPTER 15
DECEPTION

One look around the breakfast table let Menders know that the Shadows residents were not happy. Eiren was red-eyed and had obviously been crying. Cook was tight lipped and silent. Lucen and Zelia were intent on their plates and Hemmett, for once, was cowed by the atmosphere. Menders said nothing, sat down and kissed a delighted Katrin, who was in her high chair at his side.

Once Menders was no longer bedridden, Ermina had ceased to treat him like a child, but now there was a struggle for power between the two of them that wasn't pretty. It caused a disruption of household harmony. Menders was unwilling to sacrifice the peace and unity he'd worked so hard to create.

Menders found Cook to be in a perpetual bad mood when he was released from bed rest. Through careful questioning he'd found that Ermina had been meddling by trying to alter the way Cook organized meals.

Cook had always served a sit-down breakfast and dinner, with the midday meal self-served from the kitchen sideboard. There was always a pot of soup or stew simmering on the back of one of the ranges, so that food was immediately available at any time for members of the household, estate farmers who were doing work on or around The Shadows or families in need. A plentiful supply of bread, cake, cookies, cheese, sweets and cold meat was always at hand. Cook worked incessantly from before sunup until dinner was done. The pick-up lunch was a good system, because at midday people could be anywhere. Trying to have a sit-down meal with everyone together would have been a logistical nightmare.

During Menders' illness, Ermina had decided to order a sit-down meal in the middle of the day. Cook resisted successfully but apparently there had been quite an altercation. It was still on Cook's mind when Menders was released from bed rest, because Ermina kept nagging at her about it. Ermina could worry an issue like a dog worried an old bone.

"The middle of the day has to be free because that's when I do the baking," Cook told him when he'd gone to see why she was banging pots around. "It's no easy feat feeding eight people, to say nothing of the estate folk in need."

"I'm well aware it isn't, Cook," he'd agreed. "I'll deal with Ermina. You know exactly what you're doing and don't need to be ordered around by anyone."

She'd given him a huge slice of nut cake to take back to his office, as well as a big smile and a kiss on the cheek.

The argument with Ermina over that issue had raged for an hour and gotten him nowhere. She was convinced that her official position as housekeeper gave her the right to order the rest of them around. She'd gotten a taste of power while he was ill and nothing was going to shift her now.

He'd come to realize that Ermina was limited in her mindset, had little empathy for people and was very conventional in her views. To Ermina, servants could be commanded by anyone who was their social superior, children stayed in nurseries and had schedules and men who slept with women proposed marriage and made babies.

Things were progressing just as Franz had predicted. Ermina was pressing Menders to marry her. In a moment where he was feeling extremely dejected, fearful that he'd always be an invalid and that he would never regain enough vision to function, Ermina had climbed into bed with him. He'd been glad of the contact and distraction at the time but since then she'd begun to insist that he go to the altar with her.

No matter what he said, she argued with him. Arguing with Ermina was like punching a sponge. No matter how hard you hit, it made no impression.

Menders had known as soon as he'd begun to love the baby given to him that he could never marry, because he could never put anyone before Katrin. It would be cruel to enter into marriage with a woman and then continually expect her to put another woman's child before herself or her own children. Katrin would always be first in his heart, as long as he lived. He'd tried to explain this to Ermina, with no success.

"That's nonsense! She's someone else's baby. You couldn't possibly put her before a wife." Ermina scowled at him.

"I could and I would. She's my baby."

"She is not! She's the Queen's baby. I think you've lost your mind!"

"I felt the same way before I was sick. I told you the same thing then and you had no difficulty accepting it."

"I've changed my mind," she said smugly.

"Well I haven't."

"Menders, if you would just marry me, we could have children of our own, and then you would be able to put Katrin in her place. She's someone else's child and one day she'll either grow up or be summoned to Court and then where will you be?"

"With her. I'll serve her and protect her, always. I'm sorry, but that is the way things are. You can sit there and think up arguments all day. I will not change, ever!" He'd made the mistake of letting his voice rise in irritation. She jumped all over that weakness, knowing she was wearing him down.

"That's ridiculous and you know it. You don't have to stay with her. All you have to do is make sure that her upbringing is being carried out properly. You could live somewhere else. You could have your own house on the estate, a wife, children that are yours, not someone else's! You don't have to be a nursemaid to her!"

"I've made my choice and it isn't going to change," he said, gritting his teeth.

"What would you do if Katrin and I were both

drowning?" she shrieked. "Which one would you save?"

"You would drown!" he shouted back. Ermina slammed out of the room dramatically.

Now Menders waited until his plate was filled, because he was ready to chew through the tabletop. He ate half his breakfast and then looked up.

"I'd like to talk to all of you about something," he said. "Since I fell ill there seems to be some confusion regarding who gives orders in the household and who is in charge. I thought we had an understanding about how things work, but that seems no longer to be the case.

"I want all of you to know that I am the head of this household. This is set out in the charter given to me by Her Majesty, the Queen. If anyone is going to give orders, it will be me. I have never given orders to any of you and don't intend to begin, because we live here as a family, not as servants and master. Should I be away or should something happen to me, Franz is the person to go to with questions. Ermina, you are to stop ordering people around. That is my order."

He didn't watch as she jumped up and fled from the room.

"You've got balls," Lucen muttered.

"You'll certainly hear about it," Franz added.

"That isn't anything for anyone else to worry about. Kata, Eiren, you continue with the regular nursery routine, just as you always have. Cook, the same for the kitchen. Lucen, I don't have to tell you what to do. As far as I'm concerned, none of you are servants. You're my family. Now, if you would be so kind as to fill my plate again, Cook, I would be most grateful."

"I'd say things are back to normal, with you eating enough for three," Cook grinned, filling his plate generously and passing it back down. Menders tucked in, gratified. He'd have another scene with Ermina, that was to be sure, but the rest of his people were happy again.

One thing was now resolute and clear in his mind. Ermina would have to go.

***

"I'm going to have a baby"

Ermina stood before Menders in his office, smiling broadly in the wake of her announcement. She tried to snake her arms around his neck, but gasped in dismay as he pushed away and sat down behind his desk.

Menders had called her into his office tell her he was going to seek another position for her. Well, she seemed to have upset that idea. He had to admit, grudgingly, that her timing was brilliant.

"What's the matter, lover?" she wailed in dismay.

"You even have to ask?" Menders snorted in disgust. "I've been very careful and used preventives any time we've been together. You agreed to do the same. I've told you why I cannot and do not want to have children and you agreed to those conditions."

"I changed my mind," she interrupted.

"I see. You didn't inform me, of course," Menders replied coldly.

"You'll be happy about it, you'll see," she cooed, going all fluttery. "You like children, darling! Once you have a child of your own, you won't have to dote on Katrin so. All that is just love wasted, because she can't ever be your child."

"Get out of my office. I don't want to talk to you right now or listen to your nonsense."

Ermina waxed furious.

"Turning me out won't change the fact that I'm carrying your child!" she sniped.

"Whether you are or not will remain to be seen," Menders said quietly. "But I'll tell you this – I absolutely will not sleep with you again. It was a mistake to go back to it when I was sick. Believe me, once I learn a lesson, I learn it for good."

"Well, you learned this one too late," she railed. "You have to do the right thing by me now!"

"And that is?" Menders asked, deliberately crossing his legs, looking up at her over his glasses.

"You have to marry me unless you want your child to be a bastard," she hissed.

"Even if you are pregnant, which I sincerely doubt, I will not marry you," Menders replied, his voice like ice.

"You'd have to!" She stood there glaring at him, sharp faced and scowling.

"Do not begin, for even one moment, to think you will ever be in a position to tell me what I have to do! You would have to prove that the child was mine and even then I would only be obligated to support it, not to marry you."

"Are you saying that I'm unfaithful?" Ermina shouted in righteous indignation.

"I think you would do anything to get what you want," Menders replied. "You haven't proven to me that you're pregnant and I wouldn't put lying about it past you. Now, get out of here."

"I am pregnant! I'm two months along!" Ermina shrilled.

"You're fabricating this entire thing," Menders responded calmly. "You underestimate me."

Ermina gasped and glared and then dashed to the door.

"We'll just wait then! Likely it'll have freak's eyes like you and then you won't be able to deny it!"

She believed that making remarks about his eyes hurt him and almost never failed to do it during their increasingly frequent and violent arguments. Ermina had no qualms about people hearing them quarreling. She had the ability to drive Menders to the roaring point as well as a talent for identifying his vulnerabilities and hammering at them until he was ready to kill her. Nonetheless, twitting him about his eyes did not work. After twenty-one years he was immune to anything anyone could say about them. In truth, he was proud of them.

Menders had spent the first eleven years of his life on the Sea Of Grass, the enormous plain in far eastern Mordania. The area, including the vast property of his father's estate, Stettan, was inhabited by bands of Thrun, the nomadic tribesmen of the far north and east. Menders frequently fled Stettan for days at a time to escape abuse and "toughening". He had been accepted and embraced by the local Thrun clans, The Menders and The Tailors. His own mother, who died at his birth, had been half Thrun and of the Menders clan.

When Menders was only five years old, a chance meeting with a young Thrun boy, Tharak Karak, had brought him into the Thrun world. Young Aylam Josirus had been weeping in the shadow of an enormous stone hand, one of The Giants rising from the grassy plain, when Tharak happened upon him.

Tharak immediately appointed himself young Aylam's protector. He took Aylam home to his parents, who made him welcome. They tended the welts left on his back by a brutal beating. They were intrigued and enchanted by his unusual eyes and presented him to the shaman of their clan, Tharan-Tul, who took one look at Menders and named him Thartan a'a' Tharak, Magic In The Eyes. Being given a Thrun name made Menders part of the Thrun. Those remarkable people considered his white eyes an asset, one greatly to be desired.

So Mistress Ermina Trottenheim would make no headway in deriding his eyes to him, just as she would make no headway with her claims of pregnancy. If she really was carrying his child, he would cope with it by taking it from her and sending her away with a pension, as would be a father's right. He would never let anyone as spiteful and unstable as Ermina raise a baby. He was thankful that he'd removed her from direct involvement in Katrin's life as early as he had.

He got up, disgusted with himself at having continued the

affair with her during his illness. It was a weakness that a woman like Ermina lived to exploit. He'd been foolish – very.

Leaving his office, he came face to face with Franz, who was waiting for him in the corridor.

"Troubles, my fine young friend?" Franz asked bluntly.

"Ermina just informed me that she's pregnant," Menders answered, just as bluntly.

"The hells she is," Franz snorted.

"Let's take this to your office," Menders replied. They went there and settled into chairs.

"Now, why do you say 'the hells she is'?" Menders asked, looking closely at his friend.

"My boy, I specialized in women's care. That's why I delivered Katrin. Ermina is not pregnant. She's due to start a monthly any day. After observing her for eighteen months, I've noticed a pattern. She starts acting like a lunatic for a week before her monthly, followed by being down in the mouth when it starts."

Menders' eyebrows went up. He'd noticed the same behavior since he'd started sleeping with Ermina. He'd dreaded the week when her shrewish nature was intensified a thousandfold, combining with her natural belligerence to make her truly detestable. She would be cruel and scathing to everyone, particularly the two children. Hemmett openly despised and feared her, and Katrin avoided her whenever possible.

"She has no power in the household now that you've laid out matters for everyone, so she thinks that she'll get it by becoming Mistress Menders," Franz continued. "She had a taste for power playing when she was at The Palace, but it's gotten worse now that she's here and thinks she has a chance to get in the driver's seat. Don't panic and do something foolish."

Menders snorted with laughter. He did not panic. He'd already managed to do something foolish, however, by getting involved and staying involved with Ermina.

"Have no fear," he said sardonically. "Even if she is pregnant and it is my child, I would not marry her. I'd take the child and then be rid of Ermina by one means or another."

Franz studied him silently for several moments.

"I believe you would," he finally said.

"Oh, I'd try to pay her off to go to Surelia or such," Menders said. "I'm not one to kill off a lover for convenience's sake. However, after speaking to you I'm confident that I will soon have a very good excuse to put her on a train and never see her again."

"It will be a relief to one and all," Franz said bluntly. "Bad enough to be isolated out here without the endless quarreling going on."

"That's at an end, I assure you," Menders replied. There had been several vociferous arguments between Ermina and himself that had resounded through the house. The last one had frightened Katrin so badly that she wailed and cried for half an hour. No-one was going to reduce Menders' little girl to such a state.

"Remind me not to cross you," Franz said quietly.

"You may cross me at any time. I consider that constructive criticism. It's being used, deceived and treated as if I'm an idiot that gets my back up," Menders answered.

***

A week later, Menders used a lockpick to get into Ermina's room. The glum behavior Franz predicted had begun and Menders was ready for the entire sorry business to come to a head and be over with.

He didn't have to rummage much. Within seconds he had found a pair of bloodstained bloomers wrapped around two bloody cloths. He looked under the bed to find more cloths soaking in a pot there. He bundled the soiled items under his arm and descended to the ground floor, making his way to Ermina's office where he unfurled the entire damp mess on her desk.

"Explain," he snapped, his voice like the edge of a knife.

Panic flared in her eyes. It was swiftly replaced by rage.

"How dare you go in my room without my leave!" she shrieked.

"Explain this right now," Menders said, keeping his voice low.

"I… it started only this morning, I must have miscarried," she said faintly, realizing that her rage wasn't going to make him back down.

"Absurd. If you were miscarrying, you'd have screamed the house down," Menders countered.

"They aren't mine," she said desperately. Menders almost gaped at the bizarre, bold faced lie.

"Get packed," he ordered. "There's a train through today, thankfully. I won't endure your presence in this house any longer. If you aren't ready to be at the halt by noon, I will take you there without your belongings, because you are getting on that train. If you make a scene, if you start howling or screaming, or doing anything that will upset this household, I will cut your throat and have an end to this charade once and for all."

She opened her mouth, but then closed it and glared at him.

"I'll tell the Queen about how you killed Madame Holz," she hissed.

"I didn't kill that fool of a woman, she fell down the stairs," Menders said calmly, watching her reaction. If she really knew, she'd hold fast. He was sure she was bluffing.

She was. Her gaze fell and she started to snivel.

"Crying won't help either," Menders said. "You've overstayed your welcome here."

"Don't you love me?" she asked, looking up with eyes brimming.

"Oh for the gods' sakes, I never said I did. Just as you don't love me. You have two hours to get ready to leave. If I were you, I'd do it with some dignity."

"Where will I go?" Ermina stared at him. He realized that the stupid woman had never even considered the notion that he might actually evict her.

"Go away from here. That's all that matters to me," Menders answered brusquely. "A word to the wise, which means it's wasted on you – if you want to catch and hold a man, deriding, ridiculing and deceiving him isn't the answer. I'll be ready at half-past eleven to take you to the halt. I'll give you your wages when you get on the train."

"What about a recommendation?" Ermina snapped.

"Do you think I would recommend someone like you to any unsuspecting employer?" Menders asked. "Deceitful, dishonest, hateful to children?"

"Without a recommendation I won't be able to get work!" Ermina cried.

"My name means enough to me that I would never put it on a bogus recommendation," Menders said evenly. "Should you write one for yourself in my name, you will be very, very sorry. And I will know about it." He turned and walked toward the door.

"I'll tell the Queen that you aren't raising Katrin properly," she snarled.

She found his hand gripping the front of her dress and a knife pressed against the skin of her throat. His spectacles were off, his white eyes inches from hers. She didn't recall actually seeing him move. One moment he was at the door, the next he was holding her fast.

Ermina's mouth opened and closed repeatedly, like a fish gulping air, but for once no sound came out.

"If I kill you right now, no-one will know or care," he whispered. "I'll just bury you out in the woodlot and say you went off on the train. Do you want that?"

Ermina gaped at him.

"I said, do you want that?" Menders whispered.

She shook her head.

"If you trouble my cousin the Queen, I will find you," he continued. "I was a famous assassin and I always found the people I needed to find. You've run out of options. One more word other than 'yes' from you and I will make my life a lot easier and yours a lot shorter."

He released her and she scurried from the room. He was alone, holding his knife and looking at the bloodied pile of cloth on her desk. He bundled it up, carried it into the kitchen and thrust it into the fire in the iron range, opening draft and damper completely so that it would burn fast.

He turned away to find Eiren standing in the doorway, a wide grin on her face. He smiled in response.

"Life is about to be much more peaceful," he said.

"She's really packing, Mister Menders," Eiren responded.

"Good. How's Katrin?"

"Tried twice this morning to slide down the stairs on her bottom so she could visit you," Eiren smiled.

"Intrepid little princess," Menders smiled back. "Keep her up there for the rest of the morning, would you? I don't want her to be upset if Ermina decides to make a scene. I'll take Katrin out this afternoon, once I've seen Ermina off."

Ermina was silent and sullen in her room at the appointed time, her trunk and case packed. Menders hefted the trunk, indicated wordlessly for her to take the case and motioned her ahead of him into the hallway. At the front steps, he heaved the luggage into the phaeton and then handed Ermina up.

"You don't need to wait with me," she said abruptly when they reached the halt and Menders hoisted the signal so the train would stop.

"I'm taking no chances of you managing to miss the train

and spending one more minute at The Shadows," he replied just as abruptly. "You'd wander into the woods and then claim that you had lost your memory or been chased by bandits. You're getting on that train and you're never coming back here. As far as you're concerned, you've never seen the place. You will not speak to anyone of who lives here or what goes on here. Do you understand?"

Ermina looked ready to argue for a moment, but then nodded and sat on the bench provided for waiting travelers.

When the train pulled up, Menders loaded her luggage. He handed her the purse containing her wages when she was on the platform of the carriage.

"Remember, you've never seen this place," he said quietly.

Ermina curled her lip.

"Freak," she spat.

Menders started to laugh. Vicious and cruel to the end – and she wondered why he didn't want her with him.

Ermina started and then scowled, stumbling into the carriage as the train pulled away.

Menders waited until the train went out of sight, to be sure she didn't get off it somehow. He took what felt like the first deep breath he'd drawn in weeks. It was a beautiful early autumn day.

CHAPTER 16
KATRIN IS NOT SAFE

Dear Cahrin and Olner,

I take time from counting out loud to write to you.

Yes, that is a strange opening but I have been counting everything these days, as Katrin is at that age where she is learning numbers. I count stair risers, cobblestones, cookies and stars in the sky. Fence railings, flowers, pebbles. It interests and delights her, so I don't mind.

One of our nurserymaids has left The Shadows to marry and after the drama with Mistress Trottenheim, I am not anxious to hire in any servants. The other nurserymaid, Eiren, is working toward going to teacher's college, though she still cares for Katrin. At this point, I have been the housekeeper for some time. It makes life very busy and is often burdensome but I prefer the extra work to the risk of bringing another problem into this house.

Manners have become an issue here, of late. Since we all work like peasants to keep the place running, we have become very casual at table and eat like peasants as well. This has rubbed off on the two children.

The other day, Katrin climbed out of her high chair and walked along the top of the table to the breadboard, retrieved a slice and returned, carefully avoiding stepping in any dishes. Hilarity ensued but I have begun to watch my own etiquette and notice that everyone else is doing the same, with the exception of Hemmett.

That young man, when asked by me to pass the bread last night, hurled a slice onto my plate with killing accuracy, causing a great spray of gravy. Katrin dressed him down, calling him "bad pig boy". Hemmett was cowed and has eaten "like a sissy" ever since. Katrin regally approves of this, giving him kindly nods throughout each meal, which he watches for assiduously while I try not to laugh out loud.

Continuing in this lighthearted vein, our dear Cook has tried to set me up with an attractive young widow from the district. You will doubtless be disappointed that I have declined, though the young lady is very attractive, doe-eyed and dark with two charming little children — but I think I have managed to convince Cook that I really am not in a position to marry. It would be vastly unfair to marry and have a wife and children come second to Katrin. I'm in no hurry to have another liaison.

I have to close now, as I need to have a talk with Doctor Franz. My best to both of you, and to the small ones. Write soon.

In friendship,

Menders

Franz was leaning back in his chair, a thick book in his hands. Intent on his reading, he was oblivious to Menders' approach, and nearly went over backwards when Menders spoke.

"Damn! I'm going to put metal soles on your shoes so I can hear you walking!" he swore, uprighting himself. "Why don't you sing loudly or something when you're creeping around so you don't startle people?"

Menders ignored his scolding, and took the chair opposite.

"I've received some information," Menders said. "There is a serious threat to the Queen from a faction formed around one of the royal cousins. "

Franz looked at him closely. "And this means?"

"It could mean nothing. The Queen and Council have excellent intelligence gathering resources. It's very likely they know all about it and have had Bartan take steps. If the Queen was overthrown, a new ruling Queen could want Katrin eliminated. At this time, Katrin's entire protection consists of me, you, Lucen and Eiren. We won't have Eiren for much longer."

Franz raised his eyebrows.

"There's always the plan to leave for Surelia," he responded. "We could do that if there was danger."

"Yes, I know. I would take that route if I knew about the danger and couldn't find a way to avert it. What concerns me is the danger I don't know about. If someone wanted to remove the present royal line they wouldn't announce it and blow a fanfare. They'd come suddenly, without warning."

"How likely would that be?" Franz asked with concern.

"Franz, there is always a danger I don't know about, be it an armed squad of fifty men sent to kill us all, an assassin in the night or a mad wolf in the forest. I have to assume that danger exists at all times or I'm going to end up failing Katrin. I have an idea, but I need your support before I can begin to act on it."

"Tell me what you're planning," Franz said after a moment.

"What I intend to do is gather a group of men who will function as a special Guard for Katrin – an unofficial one."

"It's illegal to raise a militia in Mordania," Franz groaned. "If word got back to the Queen, we'd all be dead and Katrin would end up with some guardian who wouldn't give a damn about her, or worse, back at the Palace at the mercy of those lunatics."

Menders nodded. "Yes, I know that," he said quietly.

"Who would make up this unofficial Guard?" Franz asked, a frantic edge to his voice.

"I've written to Olner Velten about contacting one-time Special Services officers," Menders answered.

"Special Services?" Franz interrupted him. "What the hells is Special Services?"

Menders sighed.

"I'm Special Services," he said levelly and deliberately. "It's the branch of the military that deals in covert actions. Spies and assassins. Men I consider my brothers and trust with my life."

Franz shook his head. "Special Services or not, Menders, you're looking to lose your head. Surely you've considered how this might look at Court? You, secreted away in the country with an Heiress to the Throne under your control, raising a small private army to protect her... it would look like you're planning a coup!"

"I'm not going to march around in a parade announcing what I'm doing," Menders replied. "The Queen and her Council will not know. I need men who would be loyal to Katrin no matter what happens to the Queen. Men who've been drummed out of Special Services are excellent choices because they have no love for the Queen, yet have intense loyalty to Mordania. Many of them are financially desperate, like my friend Ifor Trantz."

Franz nodded reluctantly.

"The right men would feel loyalty to Katrin and be disillusioned enough with the Queen that they would fight a force sent at her command," Menders continued very softly. "Having been removed from service, they would no longer be under oath to the Crown."

Franz clutched his head, thumping it down on his desk.

"Gods, Menders, you're beyond having your head taken off, you're marinating for the roasting spit, do you know that?"

"Franz," Menders said, in a low and terrible voice that made the stricken doctor look up in surprise. Menders rose, removed his glasses despite the daylight, and leaned across the desk, nose to nose with his friend. "I live to protect and care for Katrin. I will do anything. I will kill anyone. I will stop at nothing to protect her, not if I have to cut the throat of our drunkard Queen in front of her entire Court of toadies. Nothing will prevent me from doing what I've sworn to do."

Franz closed his eyes for a moment and then shook his head.

"All right. Put your goggles back on and sit down."

Menders did so.

"You're really afraid of this faction, the ones plotting against the Queen?" the rattled doctor said after a while.

"To a degree," Menders replied. "But it's also certain

there will be other plots in the future. If I recruit a Guard they could keep Katrin in sight and serve as lookouts while going about their other tasks. I desperately need help with all the physical work to be done around here and if any threats arose, we would be ready."

Franz said nothing.

"The worst time to decide to do something is when it's already too late," Menders continued quietly.

Franz was silent for a few more minutes, staring at the top of the desk. Then he drew a long breath.

"I know you killed Madame Holz," he said softly.

"I was quite sure you did," Menders responded. "It was the only solution. I offered her several ways out. You know that."

Rainer Franz erupted, springing to his feet. His chair crashed to the floor.

"Damn it!" he cried. "Here you are, ten years younger than I am, looking like a slightly sinister schoolboy who would think that saying 'grundar shit' is the last word in being naughty. I think that I know you. I see you being kind and decent. You work yourself to exhaustion for us. You're up before all of us, you go to bed after all of us, you're up in the night checking doors and windows and making sure the fires don't go out. You love that little girl as purely and tenderly as I've ever seen a father love. Then you sit there and tell me that you're a cold blooded killer as calmly as you would tell me that it's starting to rain and you talk treason as if you're discussing a dinner menu! What the hells kind of man are you?"

"I'm every man," Menders replied, rising to his feet and sauntering across the office. "Every man has the same capabilities but most won't admit it to themselves. Inside every man is a loving father, or a cold blooded killer – or a slavering animal. What makes the difference between the loving father and the cold blooded killer is a matter of choice. Most men choose not to be a killer. In my case, I accept all these aspects of myself and make use them as is necessary."

Franz stared at him.

"Haven't you ever killed a patient when they were dying horribly?" Menders asked in a very gentle voice. "When it would be a mercy to release them from pain that has become constant agony? Did you ever let a baby deformed beyond all hope die at birth rather than slap it into life?"

His voice was just seductive enough that Franz, taken off guard, nodded.

"Then aren't you a cold blooded killer, my friend?" Menders almost whispered, keeping his tone low, the pitch that he knew could evoke a confidential response in both women and men – the sound that made people let down their guard and say what they would normally keep to themselves.

"It comes to most doctors. It's merciful," Franz replied, staring at Menders.

"Yes, taking a life that way can be merciful. Where is the difference between that and taking a life to protect a life?"

"Menders, I'm not saying I regret what happened to Madame Holz. Any woman who was literally aroused when contemplating tormenting a six month old baby is best removed from the face of Eirdon. I don't look down on you and I don't consider you despicable, but gods, you sometimes befuddle and terrify me!"

Menders sat back, breaking the intense contact he'd formed with Franz. The doctor didn't know it, but the last several minutes had been a test - the ultimate test of Franz's loyalty. He'd passed, handsomely.

"For that, I'm sorry," he said in a more normal tone. He could see Franz blinking, probably wondering just what had happened between them. "It's a very difficult thing for most people to accept. I am not a working assassin now. I even wish that mad bitch Holz had just taken my offer of a nice villa in Surelia."

"How many kills do you have?"

"You don't want to know," Menders replied quietly. "Please don't ask me that again. I'm not ashamed of it, I'm not proud of it. It is just something I did. I will kill if I have to. I'll decide not to kill if I can."

Suddenly Franz extended his hand across the desk. After a moment, Menders reached out and gripped it.

"All right, you mad little bastard, I'm with you. We'll get an illegal Guard for our Princess – and when they put you on the roasting spit, I'll be right beside you. At least we'll be able to talk to each other as we slowly sizzle."

"I'll bring the onions."

***

Morschall Komroff, Commandant
Mordanian Military Academy
Erdahn, Mordania

Dear "Father" Sir,

I am hoping that this finds you well and the Academy ticking along nicely. Things move along well enough here – it is still a great deal of work for me, as I have been continuing with the housekeeping organization as well as the estate management, but it's a price to pay for peace that is well worth it.

Sir, I am in the process of recruiting a private Guard for the Princess. I could use your advice and assistance in contacting those men who have left Special Services for one reason or another. I am aware that Harcort Menck and Ifor Trantz are both demobilized and in desperate straits, having been given no pensions. Can you let me know who else might be interested in living here at The Shadows? They would need to be willing to take on some physical work as well as helping me with the network I am building and creating a security protocol for the Princess.

As you know, I am venturing into perilous waters, but it is necessary. There have been several plots to date and Bartan has managed to eliminate a couple of assassins before they started on their journeys to The Shadows. I fear that if I hesitate longer I will have made a very dangerous error.

If you have Ifor's address, I would be glad to write to him directly. Also, any addresses of any of the other "boys" who are no longer in service, or who wish to leave it soon would be enormously appreciated.

With all love and respect,

"Son" Menders

CHAPTER 17
PLANS MOVE FORWARD

Menders was pacing the length of the Great Hall, hands on his slender hips, eyes on the floor, his usual attitude for serious thought. Katrin, approaching four years of age, played nearby with several sheets of paper and a soft pencil he had provided.

He looked toward Katrin to be sure that mischief wasn't in the offing. She was lying on her stomach, knees bent, feet in the air, singing to herself as she drew assiduously on the paper. She would be occupied for several more turns of the Hall.

A decision must be made as to who would be the "mind" of his developing network of informants. He was considering two longtime friends, both brilliant with codes, espionage and organization.

Through his growing network of contacts, Menders received reports about the status of a number of governments, the personal lives of the Queen and Princess Aidelia and the doings of various factions which revolved around royal cousins who were in the Throne line.

In return he supplied information on the social atmosphere and mood in his particular part of Old Mordania, which he derived from another network - the extended families and friendship circles of the tenant farmers and landowners in his area.

It was like weaving a web. You started small, close to the center, then slowly expanded into a wider circle. What he needed was the spider that kept the web stable and growing.

The two men he was considering, Ifor Trantz and Harcort Menck, were intelligent and inventive. Each could be ruthless when necessary.

Ifor had been his history and languages tutor at the Military Academy. Five years Menders' senior, Ifor's mind was a beacon, brilliant when it came to codes and strategy. He'd had an estimable career in espionage as the partner of the equally brilliant assassin, Falk. Both were part of Menders' mission in Surelia where an ambush took Falk's life and left Ifor with a bullet lodged dangerously close to his spine. It gave him episodes of agonizing pain where he could barely care for himself.

Now Ifor, dismissed from Special Services because of his disability, was struggling somewhere, fallen out of sight of his friends, family and colleagues. He'd lost one job after another as his physical condition made it impossible for him to carry out work duties. While Menders was in Surelia, he had paid Ifor for breaking coded messages. Commandant Komroff had sent him a monthly allowance until Ifor vanished, leaving no forwarding address, unable to bear taking charity even from the man he, like Menders, called "Father".

Harcort Menck had also been a spy and was another of Menders' tutors from the Academy. His specialty had been mathematics and logic. His mind was the most well-ordered Menders had ever encountered. His memory for people, details, places and events was prodigious. During his career he had been most gregarious and knew more people than Menders could name. He would be invaluable in expanding Menders' network of contacts.

Menck had also been injured in the line of duty, falling down the façade of a four story building during a mission. The accident had left him with a badly damaged spine and two shattered legs. Though he had healed well initially, he was becoming progressively paralyzed. Like Ifor, he had no pension forthcoming. Currently he was living with family members who were resentful of his presence and increasing debility.

It wasn't a situation where Menders could write a letter and ask these men if they were interested in a position that would result in them being tortured to death if it was ever discovered that they held it. In other circumstances, he would have gone to talk to them directly, but recently he'd found he could walk up behind Franz, Lucen and Eiren without them taking notice. He must stay with Katrin at The Shadows at all times.

So the decision must be made as to which man to approach with his very unconventional offer – then he must sort out just how to make contact – particularly difficult in the case of Ifor, as no-one knew his whereabouts.

Suddenly he heard soft, rapid footsteps and Katrin was beside him, hands on her hips, walking along with him. She watched him carefully and then mimicked his stance and gait.

He looked down at her.

"Well, Snowflower, what are you doing?"

"Walking like you. What are you doing?"

"I'm thinking."

"Walking."

"Thinking while I walk."

She nodded, wrinkled her brow in "thought" and continued to pace alongside him. She seemed very happy with this new activity so he continued his perambulations.

Normally he would trust a message to the mails, as he did his letters to Cahrin and Olner, but regarding this matter - no. He also couldn't spare anyone from The Shadows to deliver his proposal to the man he chose.

Menders turned and Katrin turned with him. Her motion was so funny that he couldn't help smiling. He bent, lifting her quickly and tossing her up in the air, which she loved. She shrieked and laughed and then threw her arms around his neck when he caught her and pulled her close.

"I've had enough of walking and thinking because I'm getting nowhere with it," he said to her as she settled on his hip. He extracted two sweets from his waistcoat pocket and held them up for her to see.

"Now what colors are these?" he asked.

"Red. Green." Katrin pointed to the correct colors.

"And which one would you like the best?" Menders smiled, amused by the avidity in her eyes. She had a terrific sweet tooth. "The red one tastes like springberries, and the green is like winterleaf."

Katrin grabbed both sweets and crowed, "Both!"

Menders laughed – then grew silent. Both. He'd ask both men. If they both accepted, one could function as the coordinator for Menders' network, while the other would be the senior officer of what would be Katrin's new Guard. A simple solution for a problem of his own making!

Menders tossed the little girl again and then caught her up under one arm like a hopfootle ball, running the length of the Great Hall with her while she squealed and laughed and clapped her hands.

"You're such a smart girl, perhaps I can send you with messages to Mister Menck and to Commandant Komroff for Mister Trantz," he said at the end of their romp, settling her on his hip again.

"I'll do it," she responded helpfully.

"It's a little far for you to go right now," Menders smiled, walking from the Great Hall with her. "When you're as old as Eiren is you might go that far. She's going where Mister Menck and the Commandant live when she leaves for school in a few months."

He slowed, his mind whirling.

Eiren – to school.

He could trust Eiren to carry out the task. She was bright and devoted to Katrin and himself. He would keep the messages very innocent in appearance, so that no danger would come to her.

"An hour of walking and I was getting nowhere and then a few moments of conversation with you and I've waxed brilliant, my Little Princess," he grinned at Katrin. "Shall we go have a talk with Eiren about being my messenger girl?"

***

Eiren looked positively wretched for a girl setting out to fulfill a dream. She'd been crying, and that made her look very red – red hair, flushed red face, red eyes. Worse still, the dress provided by her parents as a going away present was red.

"I wanted to thank you again, Mister Menders," she quavered. "For the opportunity and all. You and the doctor."

"If you're going to thank me, thank me by doing well," Menders smiled. "And try not to look too heartbroken about going."

"I'm not! I'm heartbroken about leaving." Tears welled up in her eyes again. She had never been away from her family for so much as a day before.

"I know it, child, I'm not scolding you," Menders said gently. "It's hard for you, but if you look on this as something exciting and interesting, you'll be surprised how fast you stop being homesick."

"Did you go away from home to school, Mister Menders?" she asked, rubbing at her eyes with the back of her hand.

Keeping his tone light, he answered, "I did, and when I was much younger than you. I was only eleven. It was a bit frightening at first, but before long it was very comfortable." And a hells of a sight better than home, he added in the sanctuary of his mind.

"Eleven! That's very young. Our Ertoldt is only eleven and I can't imagine him going far away to school!"

"It was young, but it was the custom in my family. And it worked out well, as you see." He posed a little and she actually giggled.

Eiren was traveling with family friends who were moving Erdahn. She'd qualified to take a two year teacher's course and had been given passes for a couple of classes already due to the high quality of her admission exam.

At sixteen she was still very much a child, with few signs

of maturation yet. Teeth still too big for her face, hair in long red braids, but she had a keen and active mind. She would do well.

Menders had nearly offered to pay for her to travel home for Harvest Day and Winterfest but diplomacy made him refrain. Mister Spaltz had been grateful to accept her tuition being paid but Menders knew that the farmer would feel compromised if more was offered. This meant that Eiren would be in Erdahn without returning to The Shadows for the two years of her course, as her parents would never be able to afford the fare and would never consent to her traveling alone.

"Now, can you try not to break down in front of the Princess?" Menders asked, trying to sound a little more formal. "She's very upset as it is."

Eiren nodded and then lunged forward abruptly and awkwardly, hugging him around the waist.

"Thank you! I know this was your idea and you made it happen," she whispered.

Startled, Menders patted her back and then eased her away. He tugged one of her braids.

"Make me proud," he said gently. "And write to all of us. Now, wipe your eyes and we'll go see Katrin."

Katrin had been given the room next to his in the long hallway on the first floor because he didn't want her in the nursery by herself. She'd begun to have nightmares of a creature she called 'the blue frogmouth', an apparition which made her seek the safety of Menders' bed. The idea of her waking alone in the nursery, far away from the other bedrooms, was far too painful.

Katrin looked up as Eiren appeared in the doorway of her room. She had been crying.

"I have to go now," Eiren said, managing to sound cheerful. "Won't you come and say good-bye?"

Katrin jumped off the bed and ran to her. Eiren picked her up. Katrin threw her arms around Eiren's neck and held on like a limpet.

"I'll write you a letter just as soon as I get there and tell you all about the train ride," Eiren said to her. "I'll write all the time so it'll seem like you're there with me. Then when you grow up and go to Erdahn, it won't seem like a strange place to you."

"I wish you would stay here," Katrin whispered.

"I'll be back before you know it and you'll be such a big girl then, almost five years old! Riding a pony and able to read big books, I'm sure. Now, I have to go or I'll miss the train."

Menders felt his heart ache as tears flowed from Katrin's eyes. She released Eiren, gave her a kiss and allowed herself to be put down, dragging her sleeve across her face.

"Goodbye, little darling," Eiren whispered. She turned away, her eyes closed, then forced them open and said, "Goodbye, Mister Menders."

"Goodbye, Eiren."

Eiren nodded solemnly. She left the room without another word.

He stayed with Katrin, who cried as she heard Eiren go down the stairs. He sat on her bed and held her while she sobbed.

He didn't say any of the things people say to crying children. There was more than enough time for distraction when she'd calmed down a bit. For now she needed the security of someone who loved her holding her.

It worked. Once she'd had her cry, she sat up on his lap.

"When I'm a big girl will I go away to school?" she asked fearfully.

"I think you'll have school here with me," he answered. She smiled.

"Good. I don't want to go away from you on the train," she replied, snuggling against him.

"Well then, you won't."

Lucen appeared at the doorway.

"Would someone here like to ride her new pony?" he

asked, winking at Menders to let him know that Eiren and company had departed and were out of sight. Menders had been determined to avoid a farewell scene at the halt. Eiren's entire family of ten was going to be there, as well as people bidding farewell to those she was traveling with. It would have been overwhelming for Katrin, far too sad and upsetting.

"I would!" Katrin cried. The pony, Snowflake, was a new addition and she didn't know how to ride yet. Lucen's infinite patience meant that he would hold her on the pony's back for as long as she wanted.

"Come along then," Lucen said, scooping her up. "Let's go see if that boy of mine is around and you can have a ride together."

Menders went to his office. He meant to put away the pile of books Eiren had used and picked up several volumes to return them to the bookshelves. He lost heart, put them back on the desk and then sat down, turning his chair to look out the window.

He hadn't realized until this week, while Eiren was busy preparing for her journey, just how much of his time had been occupied with planning her lessons and explaining the material to her. Franz wasn't much of a teacher. He could select study material, but was worthless when it came to instruction so most of it had fallen to Menders since Eiren had started prepping for her entrance examination.

They'd been at The Shadows for almost three years now and for the first time Menders was feeling restive. He'd been no further away than a day trip to Erdstrom to be measured for new glasses after his illness. It was coming into autumn, the time when work slowed. For the first time since arriving at The Shadows Menders was not looking forward to the approach of winter.

He'd steadfastly refused to become involved with any woman on the estate since sending Ermina away and wasn't interested in anyone in the neighboring village or on the nearby estates either. All available women were looking for one thing, a husband, and that he couldn't be.

Of course, Katrin was his delight and the light of his life. Teaching and spending time with her took up much of his time. Hemmett needed help with his schooling as well and that was a challenge, because he simply didn't learn when taught in the traditional way. Franz was there for conversation and games of DeGratz. There was always much physical work to be done, to say nothing of the estate business and the housekeeper's job.

I should not be bored, Menders thought. I have a great deal to do, and I have to continue seeing to Katrin's safety and staying informed about what is happening at Court. There are all those farming methods I was going to read about this winter. We'll be having the dances as usual, and plenty of other things that will need to be arranged. I should not be bored!

He couldn't quite admit it to himself that he wasn't bored at all. He was lonely.

***

Hemmett watched as Katrin ran across the garden. He was her guard now. Menders had said so. He had to be very sure that she didn't go too far or get hurt, but he had to be kind and careful too because she was smaller than he was. With Eiren gone now, there was one less person to take care of her.

"Come on, Bumpy!" Katrin called, dropping to her knees under a willow tree. The leaves were starting to fall and she loved to play with them.

When Eiren was still at The Shadows, she braided Katrin's hair like her own, but Hemmett liked it better the way Menders or Cook did it, with it held back off her forehead with a band or ribbon bow and falling loose down her back. It reached her waist and was the prettiest color, like the hair of the princesses in Hemmett's storybooks. He couldn't read yet but he looked at the pictures and made up his own stories about them.

He liked to think that one of the handsome princes in the pictures was how he would look when he grew up. Right now his hair was shingled short after he'd gotten glue in it and he thought his head was shaped like a potato. He'd have to improve a lot before he looked like the prince in the picture.

He knelt beside Katrin in the fallen leaves.

"This is money," she announced, holding out handfuls of golden leaves for him to take. Yesterday the leaves had been magic dust. She had crumpled them until they were very fine. "We're pirates, finding a treasure!"

Hemmett laughed and helped her heap up piles of leaves, being a very good pirate with lots of growling and evil laughing and saying "faw!" It was his favorite word. He made it up himself because Menders had stopped him from swearing.

The wind came along and lifted the golden willow switches, sending more leaves spiraling down around them. Hemmett looked up into the whirling gold, then at Katrin's hair, which was tossing in the breeze as well.

"You're like the willow tree, with all gold hanging down," he said, touching her hair in wonder. It was so pretty, shining like the sun, while his own hair was brown as dirt. Katrin looked down at her hair and then up at the willow branches. She looked and looked, smiling as the leaves fell down.

"I'm going to have a special name for you, just like you do for me," Hemmett announced suddenly. Katrin had called him Bumpy since she was a little baby and just starting to talk. Nobody knew why. "I'm going to call you Willow."

She looked at him and smiled. Hemmett felt perfectly happy.

***

Dear Mister Menders,

I wanted to let you know right away that I arrived safely in Erdahn and am settling in. I'm not ashamed to say that I was really surprised at how many people there are here. I'm sure I'll get used to it soon, but right now it takes my breath away when I see all the people in the street. All the different colors of clothing and hair are dazzling.

I have started classes. I like school a great deal and I don't find it hard, not nearly as hard as some of the things you had me learning! I have been very interested to find out that K is very far beyond children her age in the things that she can do. I am the only person in my class with experience actually taking care of a little child, which I find funny. Most of the students are from well-to-do families where I swear they have never had to do a lick of work! I tell them about life on the farm and looking after a little girl and they are amazed. Don't worry, I don't tell anyone who K really is.

I hope everyone there is well, especially you and K. I was sorry that you were having problems with your digestion when I left and asked my sister if she knew of anything that might help you. She was very pleased about being asked for advice. My elder sister says a good egg should ease nervous tummies. You might try it, she's very informed about these things.

I will write soon again. Right now I have to study history. The stories of Morghenna the Wise's war against the Surelian overlords fairly got my blood moving, especially since I remember you told me your ancestor was her Royal Advisor and military commander during the war! I miss you all very much.

Affectionately,

Eiren

Menders' eyebrows went up when he read the part about his digestive problems. What could she be on about? The remark was deliberate and not some odd oversight. As for "nervous tummies", that was very unlike Eiren. She wasn't one for baby talk or cute words. On top of that, there was no sister of hers living in Erdahn…

Suddenly he looked at that peculiar sentence alone and

laughed aloud. She had gotten his messages to Harcort Menck and Commandant Komroff. Reading only the first letters of the words, they spelled 'message sent'.

"Smart girl," he said, admiring the way she'd woven it into her narrative. She would do beautifully at teachers' college. He had already coached her in subjects at a difficulty level far beyond anything she would encounter there.

Now to wait for a reply from Menck. So far no-one had been able to trace Ifor Trantz, who seemed to have disappeared into the southeastern part of Mordania.

Menders sighed and put the letter down on his desk before looking out the window at the leaves glistening from a recent rain shower.

He'd go for a ride. It would ease his feelings of restlessness. First, he would need to be sure Katrin was happily occupied.

He heard her laughing in the kitchen and poked his head in. Cook had her festooned in a large apron and they were busily compounding something in a bowl.

"Now, stir it around. Don't slop it up the sides, keep it in the bottom, like a big girl does," Cook was saying.

"If you ladies are going to be occupied for a while, I'll go for a ride," he said, smiling as they both looked up. It was a tie as to who was covered in the most flour.

"Oh, I want to ride too!" Katrin cried.

"I need to take Demon out, Little Princess, he's been in his stall for two days. Let me work the kinks out of him and when I come back, I'll take you out to ride Snowflake," he offered.

"By then we'll be done," Cook told her. "Don't want to leave your good dough to waste, Katrin."

Katrin nodded happily, belaboring the contents of the bowl with the spoon again. "We're making animal cookies," she announced.

"I look forward to them," he replied, stepping over to her

for a floury kiss and then making good his escape.

Demon was restive. He snapped and kicked and generally showed his displeasure at the world until Menders jumped into the saddle and wrapped his leg around the pommel. Demon ran as if the road was on fire, tearing along far beyond the Spaltz farm before Menders could get control of him again.

"You're as grouchy as I am these days," Menders said as the farlin swung his head around, snapping at Menders' foot. "I'll let you run some more soon, just cool down now." They jogged on for a while but Demon was still jittery.

Menders let him canter while he went through a series of stunts; jumping to the ground while Demon was moving, then bounding back into the saddle, picking up objects on the ground from the farlin's back. Eventually he felt confident enough to vault over Demon's back from one side to another, boosting himself with the saddle while the farlin was in a full gallop.

Such displays of horsemanship were a Thrun sport, popular for carnivals and festivals. Menders had learned the tricks in his boyhood during the times he had run away from home and stayed with the Thrun. Those days in their camps were his most treasured memories. What would his life have been like if he's accepted the Thrun's offer to go and live among them on the plains of the cold far north? It certainly wouldn't resemble his present situation, that was certain.

The exercise finally knocked the edge off of Demon's foul mood. Menders felt, if not happier, at least pleasantly weary.

As he reined Demon down to a walk, he saw that Franz was watching them from a distance, seated on his gelding. He must have been out in the area making calls – he had an extensive patient load now. Menders urged Demon over to him.

Demon approached the gelding cautiously. He had terrorized the gentle horse for months until the day the gelding had enough and swung around, taking an enormous mouthful of Demon's neck and shaking his head wildly while biting as hard as he could. They weren't good friends but had formed a sort of truce. They could tolerate each other's company.

"You're deliberately trying to kill yourself," Franz said calmly.

"I've done those stunts since I was a boy," Menders replied.

"Grundar shit."

"No, we had Thrun herdsmen on the estate where I was born. I learned from them. Where are you heading home from?"

"Frohmoff's. His wife is still very ill from the birth," Franz replied, reining the gelding in beside Menders as they started back to The Shadows.

"I'll take some food over tomorrow then. They'll need it," Menders said.

"Yes, they will. She's not going to live," Franz sighed.

"Grahl's teeth," Menders hissed. There was a terrible ongoing cycle in Old Mordania of women suffering complications in childbirth and dying, while girls married young and started babies immediately. Many of the farmers in the area had been through multiple wives. The hard work on the farms and the endless childbearing wore women down and often killed them.

"I'll see what else they'll need then. There are eight children?" Menders asked.

"Nine with the baby and Frohmoff without a notion of how to cook."

"We can get them over the worst of it without difficulty," Menders said after a moment. When the farmers were widowed they tended to remarry quickly. It wasn't that they didn't mourn their wives, but here was an urgent need for someone to tend motherless children and do the woman's work on the farm. Mordania's constant warfare eroded the supply of marriageable young men, so there was a plentiful supply of unmarried young women for widowed farmers to choose from.

"A couple of the children are pretty threadbare as well,"

Franz added.

Menders took out his notebook and pencil, wrapping Demon's reins around his wrist while he wrote. There was now a stock of castoff clothing at The Shadows, gathered from the farms and other holdings, which was then distributed to anyone in need. He would also arrange for some of the farmer's wives help the Frohmoff family for a while.

"That's the brightest I've seen you in some time," Franz observed. "You're down at the mouth this autumn."

Menders shook his head. He didn't want to start a string of confidences. What good would it do?

"Why don't you come with me next time I go to see Kara?" Franz suggested. Kara, Lady Keel, was the very attractive widow who owned one of the two estates adjoining The Shadows. Franz had been keeping company with her for some time. "You might meet someone you could spend some time with."

"No."

"You would feel better."

"For a while. And then I would feel much worse. If that sort of thing would work, I'd have done it by now," Menders replied, swinging his leg over Demon's head to sit astride, replacing his notebook in his pocket.

"Experience taught you that?"

Menders nodded. "My time in Surelia taught me that. I want more. I like the physical part but then I want to talk about history, or go to dinner and stop by an art gallery. Or play the spinet while she sings. I want it all. If I can't have it all, I'd rather have nothing."

Franz groaned. It wasn't in jest.

"Living way out here that's not too likely a possibility, with restaurants and art galleries thin on the ground. You may have to settle for what you can get."

"No."

"You're a romantic and there is no cure for that," Franz sighed. "My young friend, you will have a difficult life if you can't compromise. What you want is married life with someone like yourself, but you refuse to marry."

"I can't compromise. Not on this. Not on much of anything, unfortunately. It's always been all or nothing at all. I can't be happy with half measures."

Franz opened his mouth to reply, obviously ready to remind him of his affair with Ermina, but stopped himself.

CHAPTER 18
THE WHITE BEAST

Menders looked up toward the halt as he heard train brakes squealing, accompanied by a shrill whistle. It was the weekly scheduled service coming through, probably one of the last regular trains before winter really closed in and the tracks became impassable a good part of the time. There would be mail on the train. A few moments later, Lucen drove by from the stables, on his way to the halt.

Menders went back to shoveling snow into a mound that would eventually be a snow castle for Katrin and Hemmett. It got it off the steps and this year both children were big enough to play outside in the cold for long enough to enjoy it. Katrin was happily picking up bits of snow, making miniature snowballs and throwing them toward Hemmett, who usually caught them and tossed them back very gently.

"Will we finish the castle today?" Katrin asked, looking over at him.

Menders, sweating inside his heavy clothing, smiled at her use of the word 'we'.

"No, it will take a while," Menders told her. "Winter is very long, so it will be something to do."

She nodded and returned to her snowball making.

Menders leaned on the shovel handle, watching the road for Lucen. Katrin scooped up a handful of loose snow and flung it at him. He laughed and reciprocated. Within seconds, a lot of snow was flying as Hemmett joined in, though Menders kept him from getting hold of the shovel with which he would have gained instant weapons superiority and also would have probably managed to hit someone in the face.

During a brief lull, as his combatants went into a war council about possible strategies to overthrow him, Menders looked up toward the road to see if Lucen was coming back.

He was, at a desperate pace. He bypassed the drive entirely, hell bent for the stable, shouting something inaudible.

A sudden howling wind hit Menders and nearly knocked him down. It swirled the snow up from the ground in a thick white curtain.

The White Beast had turned on them with sudden, savage fury. A northern Mordanian blizzard was something few people outside of the area had experienced. Those caught out in one rarely lived to tell tales.

Menders grabbed Katrin's hand and Hemmett's jacket, struggling up the steps to where Franz had the door open. Menders started back down to locate and help Lucen. Within seconds Lucen came running into view, waving a fistful of mail and laughing a bit at his predicament.

"Just beat it home," he panted in the entryway where he and Menders shed their snowy outer garments. "Engine driver told me that he's been trying to outrun this storm all day long. He hopes to make Erdstrom ahead of it. It's a monster. From the halt I could see that the sky was completely black to the west."

Another massive gust hit the house, rattling the windows violently. Katrin and Hemmett were at the first landing window, laughing and pointing at the swirling snow and blackened sky. Menders climbed the stairs to them and picked Katrin up.

"Neither one of you is to go outside for any reason," he told them seriously. "In a storm like this you could be lost very quickly. Do you understand?"

Katrin nodded. "Yes," Hemmett answered solemnly.

"Now, we'll be indoors for a while," Menders went on. "What would you children like to do?"

"Read my book," Katrin said proudly. Menders smiled. Katrin was indeed able to read. She had learned by listening and looking at the text when he read to her and was now engaged in reading a small children's book. It was slow going at times, as there were many unfamiliar words, but she loved it and read every day.

"Faw! Not for me, sitting around reading a book!" Hemmett announced, springing onto his father's back from the landing. "Giddap, horse!" he shouted and Lucen obligingly trotted away with him. It was a typical Hemmett reaction. He was having a hard time learning his letters and was intimidated by Katrin's prowess. Menders had exhausted several ways to teach the boy the alphabet but for some reason he could not connect the written letters with their names.

Menders and Katrin repaired to the armchair in his office and he handed her the book. She had not been content with a primer comprised of repeated words and phrases and wanted to read a more advanced story. She was doing well enough with it that he doubted any harm was done by not subjecting her to the tedium of "See the dog. See the dog run. Run, run, run."

As Katrin started on the adventures of a particular green bird, Menders thought about the weather that had just surprised them.

Their previous winters at The Shadows had been long but mild, what the local people called "Open Winter" - snowfalls were fairly predictable and of short duration with fair weather in between. This made travel by sledge possible for visiting and social events.

"Closed Winter" was a situation dreaded by the locals. Those seasons were typified by relentless snowfalls and blizzards that sometimes lasted for days, with such massive accumulations of snow and ice that even movement between farms on the estate was nearly impossible. There were fearsome stories of men who had been lost and frozen to death within a few feet of their own front doors or of entire families who had gone winter mad after being cooped up together for months with resulting murder and suicide. Such "Closed Winters" were presaged by sudden violent blizzards, like the one howling outside - the White Beast of Thrun legend.

"Menders?" Katrin piped forlornly. He realized that she hadn't been reading aloud for several minutes, while he'd sat there ruminating.

"What, Snowflower?" he asked.

"This one." She pointed to the word 'flew' and he pronounced it for her, showing her the sound for each letter. She nodded, finished the sentence and then closed the book.

"Menders, why are you sad?" she asked, craning around to look at him. He turned her so she was more comfortable.

"I'm not really sad. I'm concerned about this big storm."

"The house is very strong. It's been here a long time, you said," Katrin assured him.

"It is indeed," Menders smiled. "What concerns me is getting around, to the stable, or the henhouse. We'll have to work out a way so that nobody gets lost in a blizzard like this."

"If you got lost, what would happen?" she asked, her blue eyes riveted on his.

Menders didn't hesitate. Both children lived in a place that could be fatally harsh and they needed to know the truth.

"If you got lost in a storm like that one, you would probably die of the cold," Menders said. "In such a storm it's impossible to see and the wind comes from all directions, so it's easy to lose your way. This is why I told you and Hemmett that you must not go outside until I give you leave. That won't be until this storm is over."

"We'd better tell everyone else," Katrin said with some urgency. "What if someone decides to go out and ends up dead?"

"I think all the grownups know not to go out but you could go and remind everyone," he told her, setting her on the floor. "And then you and Hemmett could go around and make sure all the windows are shut tight." That would be some harmless occupation that would make the little ones feel as if they were doing something important.

"Faw! That'll be fun!" she cried, running away into Franz's office to lecture him about the dangers of going outside, which the well-padded doctor, very fond of his creature comforts, was not about to contemplate. Franz rose to the occasion and listened to the various dire consequences that could come from going outside, adding phrases like 'human icicle' to Katrin's vocabulary. Finished with Franz, Menders heard her running down the hall to Cook to begin her warning speech again.

***

Menders woke to find he had pulled his covers up over his head. His room was frigid.

Something moved against the small of his back. He smiled and looked under the covers.

"I think someone must have given me a dog in the night," he teased, looking down at Katrin nestled in the warm recesses of the covers, her eyes sleepy. She made little barking noises and giggled.

"Stay there, sweetheart, it's like ice out here," he told her, reaching for his dressing gown, glad for the heavy felted nightshirts that were vital to comfort in this part of Mordania. "Let me build the fire up."

With a quick raking of embers, a few hearty blasts with the bellows and several small seasoned logs, the fire burst back into life. Menders shivered, his breath visible on the air. He went to the window and looked out.

The snow was up to the bottom of his window – and his room was on the second floor. Twelve feet of snow.

"Grahl's Teeth!" Menders gasped. The air was thick with huge, solid clumps of snow falling from an iron grey sky.

"What's wrong?" Katrin asked from the bed. She jumped down from her perch, squealing as her feet touched the cold floor.

Menders picked her up, carrying her to the window. She was gratifyingly astonished at the snow covering the entire ground floor. Menders deposited her back in his bed and drew the covers up over her.

"You stay there now until the room warms and I'll get the fire going in your room so you can dress," he told her. Excited by the unusual situation, she grinned and snuggled down in the blankets.

Menders went to her room and got the fire roaring. As he braved the icy hallway again he saw Lucen coming toward him, breathing steam like a fairy-tale dragon.

"Nice morning!" Lucen grinned. "I'll get the ranges stoked in the kitchen while you see to the Princess. Cook's coughing like a sick seal and Zelia's trying to convince her to stay in bed."

"I'll come with you, Katrin's all snugged up in my room," Menders answered. "Better see if we can get outside at all."

"Doubt it. We'll have to get out the first floor windows and shovel away from the doors."

"Will the doors hold up to the weight of snow?" Menders asked.

"They'd stand a battering ram, those doors. And the storm shutters were all closed on the downstairs windows, so those are safe too."

"It'll be a thankless task, trying to clear the doors," Menders warned him. "It's still coming down and the sky toward the west is black. Lots more where this came from."

Between them they had the kitchen ranges blazing in minutes. All the ground floor windows were thickly coated with a layer of ice on the inside. Those in the kitchen began to drip as they thawed.

With the exception of the small store of wood kept inside to be convenient to the fireplaces and ranges, the rest of the fuel was outside, under tons of snow. More wood was going to be necessary, and soon. A worrying situation, with someone in the house already ill.

Menders went upstairs to Cook's room. Franz was already there, seeing to her.

She looked bad but was sitting up, preparatory to getting out of bed. Then she coughed – not a deep cough, but a rough one.

"No young lady, do not get out of that bed," Menders said heartily, going to the fire and putting two more small logs on, depositing the rest of the wood in the hod and picking up the poker.

"There, you see?" Franz admonished Cook. "That's exactly what I've been telling her, Menders."

"Listen to the doctor. You have to get over this quickly because we're going to be snowed in for a while."

"You poor men, having to get through that snow to the woodpiles," she rasped. Getting to the woodpiles wasn't such a problem, it was digging down to them that was going to be tricky, but Menders didn't worry her with those details.

"Don't bother about that." He sat on the edge of her bed and then tucked his feet up, glad to get them off the chilly floor. It was cutting through the bottoms of his slippers. "Now, tell me what you had planned for the day and we'll see to it."

"There's porridge on the back of the range, as always, one pot of stew and one of soup," Cook croaked, reaching for her glass of water on the bedside table. Franz handed it to her along with a small paper cone filled with white powder. "There's a roast of venison ready to go into the oven about mid-afternoon. Zelia knows how I do it. We've bread for a couple of days, plenty of baked things around. I always have food ahead, just in case."

"You do indeed. A woman after my own heart," Menders grinned.

"After your bottomless pit of a stomach, you mean," Franz added.

"Marry me and cook for me the rest of my days," Menders teased, ignoring the doctor's jibe.

"Anyone who had to cook for you would be dead of overwork in a week," she teased back. "Anyway, I'm about to marry Mister Ordstrom."

Menders laughed and then looked at her.

"Really?" he asked. He exchanged a surprised glance with Franz. They knew the retired farmer, who now lived in one of the crofter's cottages. He was one of Cook's best customers but there'd been no sign of romance.

"Yes indeed. You've been moping so much lately that you haven't noticed, but I am. I won him over with my hot venison pies."

Menders leaned over to kiss her in congratulation but she held him back. "Not only should you not be kissing engaged women in their beds but you don't want to catch this cough and carry it to Katrin," she said quickly.

"As always, you make good sense," Menders told her, checking to be sure the fire was burning well. "Anything else?"

"If Zelia would make up a bit of honey and lemon I wouldn't complain," Cook said. "Now off you go to start coping with the situation, my boy."

He gave her a pained expression that only made her laugh.

"Oh, you live for it, lad," she said. "A catastrophe like this snow is a tonic for you. Get yourself out of here!"

Outside Cook's room, Menders and Franz paused as a blast of wind actually shook the house, rattling the upstairs windows viciously. It came in wild gusts, battering the building. Moaning, mournful notes, like those of a deeply resonant organ, rose from the open chimneys, as though the old house protested the wind's treatment. The Shadows was a massive construction of heavy wooden timbers and beams, some thicker than a man's waist, set into a deep stone foundation. The men exchanged worried glances as they felt the mammoth building shudder.

"We're going to be all right, aren't we?" Franz asked quietly.

"Yes," Menders said firmly. "One way or another, I'll see to it and get us through." Franz smiled with relief.

After breakfast, Menders, Franz and Lucen spent the day clearing access to the woodpiles. They worked until it was too dark to see. By then all three men were at the point of collapse but Menders was able to relax, knowing they now had sufficient wood in the house. Even if the well in the cellar ran dry, there was more than enough snow for water. And more snow kept falling. Now Menders realized why the centre roof beam of the house rivaled a bridge beam in size. The snow on the roof was six feet thick in places and the great ridgepole creaked under the weight.

He began to go out before dinner to re-shovel the hard-won ramps under lamplight but ended up standing exhaustedly in the doorway, unable to force himself out into the cold one more time.

"Leave it," Franz said abruptly behind him, reaching around him to close the door. "It will be there tomorrow. We'll shovel out again if need be. I'm in agony, so you're probably not much better."

Menders didn't argue.

***

It snowed.

It snowed for days and then it snowed some more. When it wasn't snowing, it was threatening to snow. The wind never stopped, great hammering blows rattling the house, shaking the storm shutters in their mountings. The incessant moaning from the chimneys raised hackles and quickened tempers.

Sometimes the wind scoured away some of the accumulated snow. When this happened, it was possible to go outside for short distances. Menders would go to the stable, to check on the stablemaster and the animals. Demon was not happy. Every time Menders thought he could trust the snow to hold off for a few hours, he would tear up and down on the maddened little farlin, raising a shimmering rooster tail of dusted snow from the hard frozen road.

"That isn't an animal, it's a leather bag full of piss and fire," the stablemaster said one day after Menders had run Demon around for two hours and was still kicked and bitten when he tried to put him in his stall.

"He isn't particularly happy," Menders groaned, rubbing his shin.

"No, doesn't care for this snow at all," the stablemaster agreed. "Myself, I'm more than glad to rest and read. It's definitely a Closed Winter."

It was indeed. The snowstorms blew up in minutes. The furthest Menders went was to Spaltz's farm to get news of the other families on the estate. He was nearly lost trying to get back home. Snow started flying thick and heavy, the wind swirled in circles and tore at him and he couldn't see a thing. He finally gave Demon his head, praying the little farlin would find his own way home.

The made it to the stable half frozen. Menders still had to reach the house, setting out with a rope tied to the stable door so he could find his way back if necessary. He struggled along, berating himself for not having laid a chain line out to the stable as he had to the woodpiles.

With the temperature dropping rapidly and the wind cutting through his greatcoat as if it was a silk shirt, Menders slipped and fell on the icy path. The rope ran out before he reached his goal, and he was terrified to find he couldn't even see the house, though he must be very close. Just as he was sure he was lost, and was going to return to the stable, he bumbled into the house's west wall. He groped his way to the door. As he tried to turn the handle, the door opened. He fell forward into the blessed warmth.

Someone pulled the frozen coat off him. Franz raked his hair back from his eyes and helped him retrieve his glasses, which he'd tucked into his shirt pocket for safekeeping. Menders' hands were numbed to the point where he could not grasp anything.

He could see that Lucen was holding Katrin, who was sobbing. Lucen made her turn around.

"Look who's here," he said gently. "See? He's all right, he was just a little late."

Menders held his arms out and took her. He could feel someone pushing him into a chair and unlacing his shoes.

"Feet are all right," Franz said quietly, shaking his head. "Still warm. You're lucky."

"Lucen, would you take a rifle outside and fire it into the air, please?" Menders said. "The stablemaster is waiting to hear it. Don't stir a step away from the door. It's impossible out there."

"Here now, Snowflower," he smiled at Katrin as Franz chafed his feet into a semblance of warmth. "I got back all right, no need to keep on crying."

"I thought you were gone forever," she sobbed. "I thought you would be frozen under the snow like an icicle and you'd break apart if we hit you with a hammer!"

He couldn't help laughing at the image and Franz did as well, making Katrin look up and forget about her misery. Outside Lucen fired the rifle. A moment later, a distant shot was heard.

"Now then," Franz said heartily, lifting Katrin onto her feet, "everyone is safe and it's time for us to have some dinner. Why don't you put the cutlery on the table? Hemmett, would you help her please?" He set Katrin on the floor, wiped her face with a clean handkerchief and then sent her on her way to the kitchen.

Once she was out of earshot, he spoke softly to Menders.

"Feel up to coming back to my office? It's warm."

Menders rose with his help and hobbled down the

hallway. Every joint ached.

"Shirt off," Franz ordered briskly when the office door was closed.

"What are you on about?" Menders asked.

"I'm checking your heart and lungs. Take a look in the mirror and you'll see why," Franz said, rummaging in his bag.

Menders was shocked when he saw himself. He was ashen, his lips blue and purple, his eyes red-rimmed.

"Grahl's teeth," he muttered. Franz gave his chest a good sounding.

"It all still works, but take it easy for a day or so. Those weak lungs of yours are rattling a bit and you've had a shock," Franz said as Menders put his shirt on again.

"I didn't realize you knew about my lungs," Menders said quietly.

"I can hear them, you fool," Franz snapped, tapping the framed medical diploma hanging on the wall. "I do know the symptoms. You're wise not to smoke. Give you much trouble, do they?"

"Not since I went to military school and got in good condition," Menders answered. "They only make themselves known with a lot of exertion."

"Well, you need to rest until I give you leave to return to normal activity."

"Believe me, I don't feel inclined to do anything else," Menders answered. "I feel worse than I did after the day we dug through twenty feet of snow."

As he rose, he saw that there were three lanterns on the doctor's office windowsill.

"Trying to burn the place down?" Menders jibed, pointing to them.

"You didn't notice? They're in every window of the house. We lit every lamp, candle and lantern we could find and put them in the front windows so you could see your way home… what? Sit down!"

Menders felt Franz pushing his head down to his knees and went limp, feeling his heart pounding with fear while his head spun. It took several minutes for him to be able to sit up and speak.

"I never saw them," he whispered. "I was right next to the house before I saw it, and I couldn't see any light at all. Right by the front windows – and I never saw any light. The snow was that thick and blowing that hard."

Franz squeezed his shoulder, hard. "You're a lucky man," was all he said.

The White Beast was a merciless foe.

CHAPTER 19
THRUN

Katrin and Hemmett were in the process of defending their snow castle from vicious brigands. Hemmett was in command.

"Fire on these men coming on the left!" he roared. Katrin rushed to one side and scooped up snow, making snowballs as fast as she could. She flung them out the window.

"We've repelled them!" he hollered, climbing down from his perch on the icy wall of the structure. "Hoorah!"

Katrin cheered too, panting for breath. It had been a terrible battle and she was worn out. It had been much easier to scoop up the snow when they still had the chamberpots they'd taken from the bedrooms, but Zelia had come out and depleted their war machinery while delivering a severe scolding. Katrin wondered why. The chamberpots were clean and no-one really used them because everyone used the privies.

"Next time I'm the King, Bumpy," Katrin panted.

"You can't be the King, you're a girl," His Majesty reasoned.

"Then I'll be the Captain. You just stand up there and tell me what to do and I do all the fighting and get all hot."

"I'm sorry, Willow," Hemmett said regretfully, pulling off her wool cap and smoothing her hair, which was straggling into her face after the rigors of battle. "Too bad we don't have our scoopers any more."

"I'm tired of playing war anyway."

"Let's ride on the sled then."

"No, I'm hot and we have to climb up." Katrin looked around. The yard had been white for so long now that she'd almost forgotten what it looked like when it was green. A huge frozen drift ran down from the roof of the house on one side, and they used it for sledding. It seemed funny, but there was so much packed snow on the ground that they were walking up higher than the tops of the shrubs and hedges.

It had finally stopped snowing all the time and now it was very cold. Every day the sky was blue and it seemed to be higher than it was in the summer. The sun seemed smaller and far away, like a lantern light in the distance.

Katrin took her cap back from Hemmett and tugged it on.

"Well I want to sled," Hemmett said.

"I don't."

"I do! I'm older! I was alive before you were born!"

"So go and sled by yourself," Katrin announced. "I fought all those bad men, I'm too tired to go climbing up there!"

Hemmett grabbed the rope of their sled and went stomping up the slope of the drift. As he turned around at the top, he stopped and shaded his eyes with his hand.

"There's someone on the road," he said.

"Is it Mister Spaltz?" Tiredness forgotten, Katrin toiled upward to stand by him.

It certainly wasn't Mister Spaltz.

It was a great many people – and animals like nothing Katrin and Hemmett had ever seen. There were farlins, like Demon, but the other animals looked like giant mountains of hair. They were dark, lumbering shapes against the snow with their breath steaming like train engines. They hauled tall brightly colored carts piled high with rolls of cloth and other bundles. The sound of heavy bells could be heard across the snow.

"Let's go see!" Hemmett yelled. Forgetting all admonitions about approaching strangers, both children jumped on the sled and flew down the slope, then ran toward the road.

An enormous sound made them stop in their tracks. It was louder than the biggest thunderclap. It vibrated and echoed across the yard and forest and Katrin could hear icicles crashing off the house and trees. Then there was another sound, low and drawn out, almost so low you couldn't hear it. It made the snow under their feet shake. Hemmett covered his ears but Katrin was fascinated.

They saw that the travelers were turning and coming up the entrance road to the house. They were playing strange music, with bells ringing, drums pounding, more of the low droning sound and smaller crashing sounds like the first enormous sound.

She could see the people now. They were big! Bigger even than Lucen. They wore brightly colored clothing covered with embroidery and flashing metal buttons, lots of jewelry and huge hats ringed with fur. Their boots were huge too, with turned up toes, fur tops and more embroidery. They walked in time to the wild music with a measured, swaggering stride.

Katrin and Hemmett stared, mesmerized. The procession drew nearer and they saw one man who was even bigger than the other big people.

He wore a long gown of many colors, covered with embroidery and flashing spangles. His belt buckle was the size of a dinner plate, all loops of metal that twisted around and under themselves. Strands of bells and many knives hung from the belt. His boots flashed with silver. He had a beard, moustache and long dark hair like Menders but his hair hung all the way to his ankles. His eyes were very dark and turned upwards. Instead of being round, they were shaped like almonds — and they were looking directly at Katrin.

He smiled, a big smile full of large white teeth.

"I am Tharak Karak a'a' Thrun, Highest Chieftain of the Thrun," he said.

Katrin curtseyed as Menders had taught her to do.

"I am Princess Katrin Morghenna of Mordania," she answered, smiling up at him.

Tharak Karak bowed. Then he reached out and took off her cap — and smiled when he saw her hair.

He picked Katrin up and tossed her high, like Menders

used to do before she grew too big, then held her high above his head for the people behind him to see. She could hear Hemmett yelling for Tharak Karak to put her down but the big man paid no mind. He called out something loudly in words she didn't understand and then looked up at her.

"Light Of The Winter Sun," he grinned, holding her high over his head, while the crowd chorused a mighty cheer.

***

Menders and Lucen were in the middle of turning a mattress at Zelia's direction when the sound of an enormous gong shook the windows. It was followed by the shattering crash of scores of icicles falling from the roof eaves. Then came the long low drone of the garzan, the deep-toned, hand-beaten bronze horns Menders remembered from his boyhood.

"It's the Thrun!" he said.

"Katrin is running over to them!" Lucen cried from the window.

"They won't hurt her."

Menders dashed to the front door, throwing it open to see a huge Thrun man holding Katrin up over his head. The crowd of Thrun roared its approval.

"I don't believe it!" Menders gasped. "Not only are they Thrun but I know this chieftain!"

Franz appeared behind them, breathless and holding a large rifle in his hands.

"Who in the gods' names are they? Some kind of savages? Are we being attacked?" Franz asked excitedly.

"It's all right, they're friendly," Menders replied, trying not to laugh at the good doctor's alarm and awkwardly handled weapon.

"Menders says he knows them," Lucen added.

"Knows them!" Franz blustered. "Knows them my arse! I

mean... just look at them, they didn't pop by on the bloody train from Erdhan! And they've got Katrin!"

"It's all right," Menders said firmly. "Franz, please put that damned rifle away before you kill someone and we'll go meet them." He grabbed his greatcoat from the hall rack and led the procession out the door.

The large Thrun holding Katrin bellowed in Thrun and the crowd roared again. Then he turned toward the house, saw Menders approaching and roared "Magic In The Eyes!" in Mordanian.

Hemmett came running toward Menders.

"He's got Katrin!" the little boy yelled anxiously. "I tried to protect her but there are too many of them!"

"It's all right," Menders assured him, taking his hand. "Come on, you'll see. He's an old friend."

Menders and Hemmett reached the Thrun, who were smiling up at Katrin and applauding, cooing, waving. Lucen and Franz came along at a cautious distance. Katrin looked a bit startled, but not frightened. She was certainly secure, being held aloft by the huge hands of the Chieftain.

The enormous man lowered Katrin to the ground. Menders walked across the last few feet of snow between them, looked up and tipped his glasses slightly so the Chieftain could see his eyes clearly.

"Tharak Karak, my brother," he said in wonder.

They gripped forearms and then Menders was smothered in a strong embrace.

"These are prophesied times," Tharak said softly, releasing him. He looked down at Hemmett, who was standing back shyly, clinging to the skirt of Menders' coat. Tharak crouched down and held out a hand to the boy.

"And you, my small man, you too have a Thrun name," he said gently in Mordanian. Hemmett, curious, took Tharak's hand and was pulled over to stand before the giant Thrun. "Your

Princess is Light Of The Winter Sun because her hair is golden and because one day she will light the way in a dark time. Menders is Magic In The Eyes because of his white eyes and the way he can see inside people's souls and watches for danger. You are Light Brighter Than The Sun for something you will do when you are grown."

"Will I be brave?" Hemmett asked in wonder.

"Bravest of them all. Your name will shine like a beacon."

"Faw!"

"Let's not go filling the boy's head with stories, shall we?" Menders said in a tone of quiet reproach.

Tharak reached out and ruffled Hemmett's curls, the elation of the moments before giving way to quiet solemnity.

"There are those things that will be. The circles are cast, and will roll forward. This you know, my friend." Tharak replied.

"Yes, well... for now that's just between us."

The Thrun chieftain nodded.

"Why are you here?" Hemmett asked. The Thrun were unloading carts, unpacking bundles and generally acting as if they owned the place. Strange, loping creatures the size of a medium dog, with rough orange brown fur, pointed ears and mad yellow eyes wove through the commotion. They didn't seem to belong to anyone in particular but moved around with casual indifference, doing whatever they pleased. It was said that you never actually owned a Thrun thryge – they just tolerated your presence and accepted your servitude.

"We have come to have a carnival!" Tharak announced to the children, smiling and standing upright again. "We have farlin races and games of chance! We eat a lot, tell many stories, trade all sorts of things. Our home is where our tent poles stand, so we will show you true hospitality! We will celebrate Light Of The Winter Sun and the future that shall come to pass."

He lifted Katrin to ride on his shoulder, clapped Menders affectionately on the back and set out toward the house.

Hours later, the Thrun had set up their tents in the open areas around The Shadows. The Chieftain's men were in the process of trampling down a circular racecourse with their farlins. Intrigued, Franz walked along with Menders, watching the entire process.

"How do you know this king of theirs?" he asked, watching as Tharak Karak strode along, Katrin perched on his shoulder, a Thrun-made fur hat on her head in place of the red woolen cap Tharak had removed. "Some fellow leads half the Thrun nation in here like he's got deeds on the place and you just happen to know him?"

"We both grew up in the same place. We were very close friends when we were boys. I haven't seen him since I was eleven and went to the Academy..."

A little Thrun girl ran up to them. She grinned at Menders and held up her arms.

"Hugs, Uncle!" she demanded in heavily accented Mordanian. "Thahlia my mother!"

Franz stood thunderstruck as Menders laughed and complied with the request, lifting the child into his arms.

"So your father let you in on the secret, little Thira?" Menders asked, before lapsing into Thrun, speaking with the child for several minutes before putting her down again. "I'll be over soon to see your mama," he continued. The little girl nodded, gave Franz a shy smile and ran off.

Franz stared at Menders.

"Uncle? Do tell," he said sarcastically.

Menders gave him an amused glance.

"You know the sort of man my father was. He had many bastard children, and that little girl's mother, Thahlia, is my half-sister" Menders replied. "My father never supported her or any of the others but the Thrun always treated me as their own. Thalia is Tharak's first wife. They have three boys and little Thira, who is the youngest. I haven't seen Tharak and Thahlia since I was eleven and I've never seen the children, but I've stayed in touch by letter. These people are my family, Franz."

"So he knew you were here? Or was this coincidence?" Franz asked.

Menders shrugged and shook his head.

"I haven't been in touch with him since we came here or while I was in Surelia, because that was a secret mission. For the last few years Tharak's people have been isolated on their island because the ice bridge didn't form in the warmer winters we've been having. But Tharak wouldn't do anything by coincidence. From what he's said, they've heard about Katrin."

Franz looked sharply at him. "How? And heard what about Katrin? To most people she's Mordania's best kept secret. How can a bunch of Thrun isolated on an island know about her!"

Menders stopped playing with a farlin colt that was making advances toward him.

"There's a Thrun prophecy that a child with golden hair born into the Royal House of Mordania will change the course of history and bring about an era of peace. They call this prophesied child Light Of The Winter Sun. I heard him call her that as he held her up for the rest of them to see." Menders looked out across the snow as he spoke almost reluctantly.

"Dear Gods!" Franz said. "That's quite a task for her."

Menders said nothing, looking grim.

"Come on, Menders, don't tell me you actually give credence to prophecies and such nonsense!" Franz scoffed.

"Of course not." Menders turned and looked at him. "I've heard all sorts of Thrun stories, over the years. They have a legend and a prophecy about everything. Katrin will live her life according to her choices as much as possible, so long as I live." He sighed. "But I must admit that there have been moments where I've remembered those old sagas about Light Of The Winter Sun."

"Well this Tharak is very taken with her," Franz said, obviously wanting to leave mysticism and prophecies behind. Then he looked around at Menders so sharply that the bones in his neck crackled.

"Wait a minute! He did know you were here," Franz said. "He shouted something up to the house after he picked Katrin up. Something about eyes. You were hardly out of the house and he hasn't seen you since you were eleven."

"Don't be absurd, he couldn't have known I was here," Menders replied.

"Frog bollocks!" Franz said. "He hasn't seen you in more than ten years! You must have changed somewhat in that time, yet I'm supposed to believe he picked you out at a hundred yards distance on a bright day with terrible snow glare? He knew all bloody right!"

Menders shook his head and walked on. Franz, realizing that he would get no further short of starting an all out argument, changed the subject, and followed in his wake.

"So what are these carnivals like?" he asked. "They've brought enough provender to outlast a siege."

"This is as nothing," Menders answered. "When I was a boy they still had the Great Confluences. Thrun clans came from all over Eastern Mordania, including the specialist clans that mine and work metal. The Great Confluence went on for weeks as they traded with each other, made marriage agreements, socialized."

"I didn't know Thrun mined," Franz said. "I thought they were all herders and such."

"The specialist clans are scattered now since the incursion of Southern Mordanians into the old Thrun lands. The Thrun mine where ore is near the surface, like an open pit or along river banks. They won't work in caves or down in shaft mines."

"Why not?"

Menders put his hands in his greatcoat pockets, and thought about it. "I'm not sure. There is an ancient Thrun belief that they must always be out under the sky, where it can see them."

"Eh? Where the sky can see them?"

"That's what they say," Menders said with a shrug. "You see, Doctor, the Thrun are a very conceptual people. They believe in a series of interconnected concepts which are linked together to bring order to all things."

"Like their prophecy about Katrin?"

"Something like that," Menders replied coolly, not wanting to be drawn back into that discussion. "They call themselves the first people of Eirdon, or the 'one people'. All other people are called 'downworlders', as if the world was dome and the Thrun lived at the top."

"What a damned queer notion," Franz said with surprise.

"The Thrun legends say that a god… well, not even really a god, but a power that is called Thrun, brought forth the first people from the heavens. They fell to Eirdon in a falling star. The first people were also called Thrun and they were let to live and prosper on the lands that were, in turn, also called – "

"Let me guess," Franz put in. "Thrun?"

"Yes, that's right."

"That's a lot of uses for one word."

"Yes, it is," Menders laughed. "You see, Thrun is more than just a word. It's a concept. You have to have a flexible mindset to keep up with it. It requires a sort of mental gymnastics to think as they do, at least for Mordanians, although Old Mordanian families are closely related to the Thrun."

"My family is Old Mordanian," Franz said proudly.

"Well there you are!" Menders grinned. "Perhaps it's time for you to reclaim your Thrun heritage." He could tell that Franz was quite taken with the idea. No doubt within a few hours, he would be wearing big boots, an oversized embroidered coat, a fur hat and a belt with an enormous buckle.

"You'll have plenty of time to get acquainted with them.

We can expect several days of farlin races, horsemanship contests, saga telling, wrestling matches, dancing, drinking and trading. They have furs, carpets and rugs, jewelry, farlins, weapons, saddles, all kinds of things they'll trade for money or goods. If you're sharp, they'll trade you one of their wives."

Franz laughed out loud.

"How many wives do they have?" he asked.

"Most men take three, if they can support them. The Chieftain can have seven, though Tharak mentioned to me that he only has six at the moment."

"Only six," Franz said, sounding awed.

"It isn't nearly as salacious and tempting as you think," Menders grinned. "The Thrun have more girls than boys for some reason, so there are always more women than there are men to support them. It's also a way to keep from wearing wives out with childbearing. Once a woman has had the children she's willing to bear, she encourages the husband to take another wife. The women help each other with their work and childrearing. And no, despite that lustful gleam in your eye, they do not sleep with the man at the same time. Each marriage is separate and private."

"So much for running away with them," Franz sighed. "Since Katrin is well cared for at the moment, show me around. I want to see these trade goods. I need a new hat."

Menders guided him on a tour of scores of bundles of trade goods. Franz was agog at the piles of furs, gems, jewelry, weapons and more and had to be restrained from trading away everything in his pockets.

"We'll wait until they're ready – and don't trade with them without me, or you'll get skinned!" Menders laughed, dragging Franz away from the piles. "Anyway, we need to contribute to the feasting, so come and help me drag out some meat to give them to roast."

"How much debauchery can we expect?" Franz asked.

"Considerable. They make a drink called Kirz out of the milk their borags give – those animals there." Menders indicated the huge shaggy beasts that drew the carts. They looked like huge hairy oxen with long, flexible tails and enormous curling horns. "It's deadly. Fermented, frozen and only the alcoholic part kept. Guaranteed to knock you cold."

"Interesting," Franz said, then caught Menders' look and added, "I'm interested in its medicinal properties, you understand."

"If being unconscious has medicinal benefits, then kirz is your drink. You've been warned. If you wake up with your head on fire and your eyeballs feeling like they're going to explode, without your pocket watch or your wallet, wearing one of those hats and with a Thrun wife, don't blame me."

Menders started through the crowd of Thrun to fetch some meat from the larder to add to the festivities. Franz trailed away toward the nearest Thrun arranging his display of trade goods.

Cook was carving up an enormous joint of pork in the kitchen and looked up at Menders with a happy grin.

"I haven't seen a Thrun carnival since I was a girl," she said. "I know what they'll be wanting, pork and venison, and we've plenty of both. I've put on all the big pots full of potatoes to boil and good thing, because some of them were almost not fit to eat. We'll put them out in a big tub of butter once they're done."

Menders began checking the stores of salt. The Thrun loved salt and used it as a unit of trade. He pulled out several bags of salt and added bags of flour, another prized item. "They'll have dried fish, Cook. Can you use some?"

"That would make a wonderful change, yes, please do get some," she said, flinging another slab of meat onto the pile she'd already cut.

Menders took the bags of salt and flour to Tharak Karak. The High Chieftain was walking around magisterially, Katrin on his shoulder, overseeing all unpacking and tent raising. From time to time he handed something up to her and Menders could see that she was already laden with gifts, including a beautiful set of child-size white furs, strands of gems and pieces of jewelry.

Tharak was pleased with Menders' gifts and handed Katrin over while he distributed them among his wives. Franz had been drawn into trading for furs with a man who wanted his pocketknife. Menders and Katrin hurried over to watch the show.

"Take no less than five for that knife and don't back down," Menders warned Franz, settling Katrin on his hip. "Want to go and look around some more?" he asked her. She nodded, putting one of her strings of gems around his neck.

"Tharak said I'm going to be prophecy. What does that mean, Menders?" she asked.

Menders shot a scathing look at the tall Thrun's back. "It means a big man can't keep his mouth shut." Katrin looked startled. "Sorry, little one," he amended, damping his temper. "It just means he thinks you will grow up to be someone he already knows all about."

Katrin considered this for some time, her brow furrowed. "I don't see how."

To distract her from the topic, Menders carried her around the encampment, explaining various things, showing her the piles of trade goods and trading a small amount of salt for a blue dress covered with gold embroidery.

Everywhere he went with her, Thrun deferred to them and then followed behind. He could hear them repeating the Thrun words for Light Of The Winter Sun as they passed.

"They'll have great fires tonight and tell stories," Menders told Katrin.

"Can I stay up and see?" she asked eagerly.

"Oh, I think so."

She wiggled with excitement.

**

Katrin felt as if her feet hadn't touched the ground in two days. Everywhere she went, she was carried on the shoulder of Tharak Karak or on Menders' hip.

Official bedtime was abandoned. So were regular meals. There was always food cooking in the Thrun camp. Huge joints of meat turned over big fires, pots of stew simmered, strips of meat were thrown on a sizzling hot metal plate. The moment Katrin came near anyone cooking, they ran out with something for her to eat. The smell of freshly cooked, heavily spiced meat was wonderful.

Katrin had a special seat for the farlin races and screamed with delight when Menders and Demon won most of them. She was surprised when she saw him let Tharak Karak win the last race, pulling Demon down from a full gallop with obvious effort while the Thrun chieftain thundered past.

"Why did you let him win?" she cried as he came to get her after the prizes had been given out.

"I let him win because he's the Thrun chieftain and my friend," Menders said, lifting her high and then giving her a hug. "It's being polite."

"Everybody could see what you did. It didn't fool anybody."

"Of course not. They know that I let him win. It's a point of honor and respect. At your age the idea may seem a bit complicated, little one."

It didn't make sense to her. But she liked Tharak Karak. If it made him happy to win when he really didn't win, that was fine.

All the farmers came to the carnival too and traded axes and cloth for the Thrun's furs, jewelry and knives. She was glad. It seemed like forever since she had seen some of the other estate families, because of the snow. The men drank a lot of the Thrun's special drink and got very silly.

The nights were the best of all. The Thrun built huge fires, played music and danced. They told stories. When they did,

Menders would sit with Katrin on his lap and explain the stories to her, because she couldn't understand the Thrun language yet.

The stories were wonderful, about old times and heroes and gods that blazed across the sky on a ribbon of fire, then came down to where men lived. Some of the stories were about three children and the Weaving Man. Menders didn't say much during those stories and when she asked him he said he didn't know all the Thrun words. That was silly, because he spoke Thrun as well as Tharak Karak did.

The storytelling and music went long into the night, and she would fall asleep, only to wake up in her bed the next morning. She would get up, run to Menders' room and wake him by tugging on his toes. Then they would race to see who could get dressed first before they went back outside to see the Thrun.

She didn't ever want the Thrun to leave.

***

Menders sat in Tharak Karak's personal tent with Katrin asleep on his lap. It was the fourth night of the Thrun's stay. The day of contests was over, and Menders was considerably enriched after winning all races but one, several of the horsemanship competitions and one knife throwing contest. He had furs enough to last him and Katrin for years and she had a stock of jewelry that any woman would envy. He'd traded for and won enough rings to have one for every finger, twice over. He had several wickedly sharp knives with elaborately carved bone handles, just because he wanted some new toys, and he'd traded cleverly for a little farlin with a red Mordanian saddle for Katrin, to say nothing of several highly decorated saddles for Demon.

Tharak Karak swallowed a long draught from an ornately decorated silver goblet and passed it to Menders. It contained a watered down version of kirz

"So, Aylam, you never came back to your lands," Tharak

smiled. "Your tenants are good. They care for the land well."

Menders nodded. Several of the Thrun had told him this. He drank and passed the goblet back.

"We have not had time to speak together before now. How is it that you are the father of the Princess?"

"I'm not truly her father."

"In the important way, you are her father," Tharak refuted him. "To father a child – it can take seconds. To be a father to a child takes a lifetime. You are her father and a good one. How did it come to be?"

Menders told him about his assignment as Katrin's guardian. Tharak nodded.

"So instead of bringing death, as you once did, you nurture life. For you the circle has turned, and will again. Now tell me – is she in danger?"

"Why do you ask?"

"I see it in your eyes."

Menders sighed, and reached for the goblet, which Tharak handed over. He drank and then settled down to speak, shifting Katrin slightly so she rested more comfortably against his shoulder.

"There is always danger. My greatest fear is that her mother will recall us to Court. That means I would no longer have control over Katrin's life and her safety. The way the Queen wants her to be raised is a terrible one."

"Do you think I have forgotten the way you were treated when we were boys?" Tharak asked quietly, his eyes turned toward the fire, where they gleamed in the amber light. Most Thrun had dark eyes, though blue eyes were not unknown. Tharak's were almost black. It gave the chieftain an enigmatic facial expression. Unable to read the elegant brown faces and impassive eyes of the Thrun, Mordanians found them mysterious and difficult to understand. Unfortunately for the Thrun, what Mordanians didn't understand, they considered untrustworthy at best, a threat to be eliminated at worst.

"I'm deliberately disobeying the express orders of the Queen," Menders said, not answering Tharak's rhetorical question. "What's more, there have been several attempts on the Queen's life since Katrin was born. There are factions seeking to have the Queen removed so her daughter, Princess Aidelia, can ascend the Throne. Aidelia is mad."

"Yes, we have heard stories," Tharak said, smiling as Katrin stirred a little and then settled more snugly against Menders' chest. "To us she is Tareg Tal'ula."

"The mind of broken shards," Menders translated out loud. "An appropriate name for Aidelia."

"We fear reprisals against us were she to become Queen."

"Should that happen, they would also come after this child," Menders said softly, snuggling Katrin close.

"If that danger arises, come to us," Tharak said immediately. "Live with us. We will honor her as a chieftain and she will never be in danger. Every Thrun would die to protect her."

Menders pondered the offer. Several plans that could be put into effect should there ever be immediate danger to Katrin's life were already in place, but Tharak's suggestion was welcome. If he took Katrin to live with the Thrun, one hundred thousand Thrun warriors would ride out against anyone who sought to harm her.

"I thank you, my friend and brother," he said quietly.

"You, likewise, are my friend and my brother. You always have a home with us." Tharak took back the goblet, drank and sighed. "Tomorrow must be our last day here," he continued. "We have much trading to do in other parts before going back over the ice."

Menders nodded, feeling regret. It had been a wonderful interlude and seeing his first friend again had been comforting after the lonely and frustrating months just past.

"So tomorrow night will be our best one," Tharak went on. "Do you remember the Chieftains' Dance we learned as boys?"

"You're talking to me," Menders grinned. "Of course I remember."

"Then we will dance it together tomorrow night, the Highest Chieftain of the Thrun and the Head of Household of Light Of The Winter Sun. To say... not to say goodbye. To say 'until the circle turns again'."

Menders nodded. It was an elegant tradition.

"Speaking of goodbyes, or at least goodnights, I need to get this little one off to bed," he said, readying to lift Katrin.

"She is asleep already," Tharak said swiftly. "Stay here in my tent tonight, Aylam. We'll talk longer and the child is safe and comfortable."

Menders agreed. The household would already be asleep, save for Franz who was probably carousing somewhere, being more fond of kirz than he should be. Menders snuggled Katrin into the furs next to one of Tharak's seven children, and settled down to drink and talk the rest of night away.

***

Katrin woke to a gentle push on her shoulder and was surprised to see Thira grinning down at her.

Menders was sound asleep beside her, his cheek pillowed on his hand. Across the tent, Tharak Karak was snoring resoundingly and there were other children and some of the wives there as well. They must have stayed so late that she fell asleep and Menders decided to camp here. She'd slept in a Thrun tent! Wait until she told Bumpy!

Thira beckoned and they slipped out of the tent together. A Thrun woman was cooking nearby. She gave them bowls of savory stew and stroked Katrin's golden hair wonderingly, as if there was magic there that could be felt to the touch.

After they'd eaten, Thira ran to her farlin and jumped up. Katrin couldn't do that, but climbed on a rock while Thira kept the farlin still so she could slide onto its back. Katrin held on tight to Thira's waist as they jogged through the camp.

It was nice the way all the Thrun liked to see her and came out to wave or bow. They always had time for children, not like at The Shadows where people were often too busy and told her to go and play and let them get on with things. Except for Menders. He never sent her away and if he was busy, he let her be busy with him.

She heard Hemmett calling and looked around to see him riding up on his pony, Smoke.

"There you are!" he said, reining Smoke in. "I couldn't find you nor Menders in the house."

"We stayed in Tharak Karak's tent last night," Katrin said proudly.

"Faw! You didn't!"

"I did!" Katrin retorted.

"Faw!" Hemmett repeated vehemently.

Thira decided there was too much talk for her liking and chirruped to her farlin, which set out at a run. Hemmett whooped and came riding after them. They made a wild circuit of the camp before they heard Menders whistling for their attention. He was in front of Tharak Karak's tent, watching them.

When Thira rode over, Menders plucked Katrin from the farlin's back and settled her in her usual place on his hip.

"So you've been up to mischief this morning, getting up at first light and riding around bareback," he smiled. "This is the last day the Thrun will be here, so we need to make the best of it."

"Oh no!" Katrin said.

"They have to move on. They have a lot more trading to do before they go back home," Menders explained. "We'll hope they can come back next year. Since you'll be their guest of honor this evening at the celebrations, I think a bath and your new dress might be in order. So we need to get back to the house."

When night fell the Thrun's fires were built up, including an enormous triangular tower made of logs. The music began and there was dancing. The women made pretty circles as they danced to slow music that sounded like smoke looked. Then the men leapt into the circle and the music turned into fire. They grabbed the women's hands and spun them around and then the men and women separated into two lines, moving far apart and then back together to spin again.

Tharan-Tul told a story and Menders whispered the Mordanian words to Katrin. It was about how the world was made by the god called Thrun. The Thrun were the first people, so they were named after the god. They lived in a magic place at the top of the world where the fishing and hunting were good, where there were precious metals and gems and where a magical light always shone in the sky. The world became warmer and the children of the Thrun moved through it, living in many lands. There were other men who were not Thrun, who made war against them. Soon the world was full of war.

The stories were exciting, scary and terrible, all at the same time. Katrin decided that war was not good. The idea of war left her feeling cold, as if dark circles had been drawn inside her.

The Thrun were told by their god that a child with golden hair would be born who would be called Light Of The Winter Sun. The child would change the way of war to the way of peace and bring a new day to the world.

"That's what they call me!" Katrin said as Tharan-Tul stopped speaking.

"That's right," Menders said, putting a hand on her hair. "Tharan-Tul wants you to go to him."

"You come with me," she urged, tugging Menders' hand. She was a little afraid of Tharan-Tul, though he was very gentle when he spoke to her. He looked fierce, with bright blue eyes shining sharply in a haggard and weatherbeaten face. He had a very twisted leg that made him limp.

"No. This is something you have to do alone," Menders smiled. "It's all right, Snowflower. Go ahead."

Katrin walked to the place where Tharak Karak sat on his jeweled chair with Tharan-Tul beside him. There was a small table in front of Tharan-Tul with a big leather bag on it.

When she reached them, she curtseyed in the formal Mordanian style and heard the Thrun draw in their breath with appreciation.

"It is time for me to give you a very special present," Tharak Karak said to her. He wore clothing that looked as if it was made of gold. The firelight made all the gems on it sparkle. "You may look at all the things that are in this bag, but you may only take one for your own. It is up to you to choose the one that is best."

Tharan-Tul opened the bag and slowly took out one sparkling strand of gems after another. He held each strand up to glitter in the firelight and then placed them one beside the other on the little table. When he was finished, he looked at her.

"Choose well, little one," he said in his rasping voice.

Katrin clasped her hands behind her back, as she had seen Menders do, and looked at the glittering strands.

One was red and glowed like coals. She liked it very much but she wanted to look at all of them first. A blue one caught the light. It matched her eyes. There was a heavy chain of gold that looked like a snake and another chain of silver strands that twisted around and under themselves. One was yellow as sunshine and another was orange and blazed underneath with green. One strand was plain grey, the color of an old fire in the hearth on a winter's morning and yet another was as green as the leaves in summer.

The only sound was the crackling of the fire.

Katrin looked along the row of strands again, one at a time. She picked up the red strand and held it at eye level, then put it down, then began lifting the other strands. The colors of the stones were fascinating. Red! Blue! Green! The metal chains were rich and heavy.

She was about to choose the red gems when she noticed the grey strand again, the plain one, the one nobody would really want, the only one she hadn't picked up. She turned her head slightly, still looking at it.

Deep golden light jumped in the misty grey depths of the stones. She moved her head another way and blue flashed where the golden light had been, with green at the edges. It was like sunlight shining through grey clouds full of snow. It was like the light of the winter sun.

She picked up the grey strand.

"This one," she said clearly, looking up at Tharan-Tul. A soft gasp went through the crowd.

"You have chosen the right one, Light Of The Winter Sun," he said quietly.

Tharak Karak, his face split into a huge grin, stood and swept her up high over his head, turning her to the crowd.

"Light Of The Winter Sun!" he roared in his own language. The Thrun roared back.

When he'd hugged her and put her down she ran to Menders, to show him the magical fire in the dull grey stones.

Did you see? I chose the ones that aren't pretty until you really look at them! Was that good?"

"Yes, that was very good," Menders hugged her close but he did not smile.

Katrin was showing Hemmett the lights flashing in the stones when the music began again, a low steady drumbeat like the beating of a heart. Thump-pa, thump-pa, thump-pa! Katrin looked up and saw that Menders and Tharak Karak were alone in the dancing area, at separate corners of the wooden floor.

"What are they doing?" she asked Hemmett in a whisper. He shrugged, staring.

Tharak and Menders moved slowly toward each other in a pattern, taking turns at altering the dance steps, then mimicking each other. They stamped their feet and turned toward and then away from each other. Tharak Karak's huge boots with the turned up toes made thumps on the floor when he stamped; Menders' slender black shoes – that Doctor Franz called Surelian road slappers – made sharp raps when he stamped. The drum beat faster and they moved close to each other.

Suddenly they drew out long, wicked looking knives. Katrin squeaked in dismay as the firelight glinted on the blades.

Both men lunged and the knives clashed with a terrible noise. Then they were apart again, circling, stamping, moving the knives with sinuous grace, weaving golden traceries of reflected light in the smoky air. Just as soon as Katrin could see a pattern, it changed, while the drum beat ever faster. The mock fight continued, becoming more heated and frightening. She held tight to Hemmett's hand, afraid that Menders would be cut by Tharak Karak's whirling blade.

Then the men threw the knives so that they stuck, quivering, in the floor. They clasped hands, laced their arms together and pulled close to one another, so close there was no space between them. They turned in a circle with their arms intertwined so tightly that if one of them made a false move, both would fall.

They danced around and over the two knives at their feet, never looking down but never touching them. The drums pounded so fast that the separate beats blended together into solid sound. Then, as the two men drew so close that their bodies seemed to be one, the drums fell silent – a silence louder than the drumbeats.

Menders and Tharak Karak held the position for a moment, then embraced while the watching Thrun stamped and whistled through their teeth. Menders bowed to Tharak and then to the applauding audience before coming back to Katrin and Hemmett.

"What was that? What was it about?" Katrin asked.

"It's the Chieftain's Dance. It's a story about how two rival Chieftains gave up fighting and became friends," Menders told her.

Thira ran over to Katrin and tugged at her hand, beckoning. "May I go play?" Katrin asked.

"Run on, Little Princess, but when I tell you it's time to go, it's time to go, understood?" She put the strand of grey gems in his hand and ran away with Thira.

***

Menders woke, groaning. He'd had far too much kirz the night before, not only in the Thrun encampment, but also afterward as the household sat around and had drinks before bedtime. It was the famous Chieftain's Reserve, potently pure. Now he had to get up and get outside so he could farewell Tharak and the Thrun.

Kirz should have a label that read WARNING: MAY CAUSE REGRET.

He rolled over leadenly and sat up, holding his throbbing head for a moment. He somehow got into his shirt and was pulling on his trousers when his senses were assailed by a strident honking in the dining room. Holding his ears, because if he didn't his head would split in half, he advanced on the noise.

Franz was sitting upright at the table, where Cook lay unconscious with an empty glass clutched to her bosom, apparently having crawled up there to stretch out after enough celebration. Franz, wearing a pointed Thrun hat, was tooting a Thrun horn in Cook's insensible ear.

"Gods man, stop it," Menders groaned, confiscating the

horn.

"I'm playing music for her," Franz said, his eyes rolling. He wasn't hung over – yet. He was still very drunk. He managed to focus on Menders.

"Go to my office. In the locked top right drawer of my desk you'll find a pistol. The key is on top of the doorjamb. Get the pistol and keep it with you all day," Menders said.

"What in the gods' names for?" Franz slurred.

"Because when you finally come down off the bender you're on, you'll wish for a quick and merciful death."

"Oh ha ha, most robust and jolly," Franz retorted. "So tell me, little fellow – just who is Weaving Man?"

"Been talking to our Thrun guests, have we?" Menders replied dryly, slumping into a seat at the table. He stared dully at Cook. She began to snore.

"Weaving Man is someone in a legend and nothing more," he finally said.

"Ha, you little liar. Ought to nick the end of your tongue with my scalpel for that one. They say you're the Weaving Man. That you hold the threads – 'cept you only have two yet and there should be three. Haven't found the third, they say."

"The Thrun say a lot of things. That doesn't automatically make them true."

Franz tried to reach for the remains of his kirz, but Menders beat him to it. "Gimme drink, you little white eyed bastard," Franz grinned.

"You've had enough. Sleepytime." Menders reached over and pressed gently on a pressure point at the side of Franz's neck. The doctor collapsed forward into slumber on the table, his hat still rakishly askew on his head.

The next to be attended to was Cook, to get that glass out of her hands before she dropped it and surrounded herself with broken glass. She clung to it and stopped snoring long enough to mutter soft expletives but he finally worked it free and returned it to the kitchen.

He looked in on Katrin, who was sound asleep, then made himself walk down the hallway to see if Zelia and Lucen were still alive. Groaning could be heard. He opened their door in time to see Hemmett holding up a small gong, for which he'd traded a cherished toy. He was preparing to hit it with a wooden mallet.

"Don't do that, there's far too much pain in the world already," Menders ordered, snatching the mallet away. Lucen was dead to the world while Zelia moaned and turned away from the light coming through the window.

"I'm hungry!" Hemmett protested. At the notion of food Menders' stomach nearly turned over.

"Bread and butter in the kitchen to hold you, then run down to the Thrun. Someone will give you breakfast," he directed, getting hold of the gong. "No, I'm keeping the gong. No, you can't have it right now. You can't ring it in the house, that's a firm rule. Go on now."

Hemmett ran off and Menders went to his own room and hid the gong away. No-one in the house was going to be able to endure it being struck for at least two days, given they all had hangovers the size of borags.

After washing and a clean set of clothes made Menders feel human once more, he looked in on Katrin again.

She smiled and sat up, fresh as a flower.

"You're the happiest person here," he smiled back, sitting beside her.

"I'm sorry the Thrun are leaving," she said. "I'll miss Thira." She peered at him. "Are you all right?"

"I drank too much kirz. That isn't a good thing, but I'll be fine soon."

"I'm hungry."

"I'm not. Unless you want soup for breakfast, I suggest we go down and get breakfast for you at the camp and then say goodbye. They're packing up now and need to be on their way."

The cold air did Menders good. When a Thrun woman supplied Katrin with a bowl of stew, he felt able to accept one himself. He'd yet to have the hangover that his appetite couldn't overcome. Menders' stomach had been likened to a steam locomotive during his schooldays. It demanded a lot of fuel and was very difficult to derail.

Tharak, looking worse for wear, was supervising the packing process, and stopped by for a bowl of stew himself.

"I've seen you look better," Menders teased him.

"Ah, a good walk and I'll be fine, eh Light Of The Winter Sun? Will you miss us?" Tharak smiled.

"Yes, I will," Katrin said between bites. "Will you come again next winter?"

"So long as the ice bridge forms across the sea, we will come to see you," Tharak promised. "If it is a warm, soft winter we can't come, but so long as the winter is hard and real, we will be here."

"You could get boats, you know," Menders teased.

"The Thrun are not a sailing people, as well *you* know," Tharak replied with a grin. He lifted Katrin onto his knee and gave her a hug.

"Keep well, little one," he smiled. "Go and say goodbye to Thira."

Katrin scampered away and Tharak turned back to Menders.

"Well, my friend, the first prophecy has come to pass," he began.

Menders held up a hand to stop him.

"I don't care to know," he said quietly. "I don't want to expect extraordinary things of Katrin because of a legend."

"You know the prophecies, Aylam. You've heard Tharan-Tul chant them many times," Tharak responded.

"I've forgotten," Menders answered sharply, with finality.

"Katrin and Hemmett deserve to grow up free of believing that the courses of their lives are predetermined. It's going to be hard enough for Katrin because her life is so limited by her rank."

"All right, Weaving Man," Tharak said, sighing dramatically.

"Don't call me that! I'm Thartan a'a' Tharak, Magic In The Eyes," Menders responded, anger sharpening his tone.

"You are both, the first person ever to bear two Thrun names," Tharak answered calmly. "There will be only one other whose Thrun name will change from one to another – if the prophecies come to pass this time." He rose and stretched, then shook Menders' hand before enveloping him in a firm embrace.

"Take care of your children, Magic In The Eyes," he said, stepping back.

"Hemmett isn't mine," Menders protested.

"Sired by you, no. Yours all the same. Sometimes children find their parents," Tharak replied. He turned and strode away, circling the wagons and borags, bellowing out directions and orders, very much the High Chieftain.

With amazing swiftness, the Thrun formed their procession with Tharak at the head.

The enormous gong was struck, shattering the calm. Menders was ready with his hands over his ears. Distant screams of hungover agony could be heard from the house.

The garzan sounded. Tharak stepped out across the snow and to the sound of drums and bells, the Thrun began to leave. Soon they were away up the drive, then down the road, then finally gone, leaving only the lone figure of Tharak silhouetted against the snow.

He extended both arms at shoulder level, hands toward the sky, then brought them together over his head to form a circle, fingertips touching.

Menders repeated the gesture. Tharak turned and was soon lost in the bright glare of sun on snow. An eerie stillness settled over The Shadows.

"What did that mean?" Katrin asked Menders.

"It means 'until the circle turns again'," Menders answered softly. "It's how the Thrun say goodbye."

CHAPTER 20
FATHER AND DAUGHTER,
MOTHER AND SON

Katrin leaned close to the mirror, looking at her eyes. Eyes were suddenly of great concern to her.

Hers were blue, very blue, but that wasn't what she was looking at. It was the shape that interested her. It was puzzling, the way her eyes were shaped. They were something like the eyes of the Thrun – not so slanted, but the same shape.

She went to look at Doctor's eyes.

"Hello there, little one," he smiled. "Got something for me to take care of? Boils to lance, sore throats, broken dignities?"

She laughed, peering at his eyes.

"Ah, a staredown."

"No, I'm just looking at your eyes." They were soft blue, not sharp blue like hers were and they were shaped like hers. She thanked him and ran down the hall to the kitchen to look at Cook's eyes.

"And what are you looking at?" Cook laughed.

"Your eyes. They're like mine."

"Silly girl, my eyes are brown, yours are blue," Cook said.

"Not the color but the shape."

"Yes, they're eye shaped. Here, have a cookie."

Katrin took two and ran to Hemmett's room.

"No girls!" he said as she looked in. He was building something. It looked like a kite.

"I have a cookie for you. I want to look at your eyes."

He made a horrible face, pulling down his eyelids and turning up his nose so she could see the inside.

"When you do that you look like a boar," she said, holding the cookie out. He stopped pushing his face around and took it while she got a good look at his eyes. They weren't shaped like hers.

"No girls!" he said again, turning his back on her.

"Old toad! Boys are toads!" she responded, closing his door hard.

Katrin skipped out into the hallway again, stopping at the big mirror to study her eyes some more. If she pulled down on the sides of her nose a little, they looked even more like the Thrun's eyes. She didn't understand it, but she knew who would.

Katrin poked her head around the door of Menders' office. He was bent over something he was writing and didn't look up while he spoke in a funny voice.

"My wonderful magical powers tell me that a little girl is looking at me." Katrin giggled and went over to him.

"How did you know it was me?"

"Short light footsteps, a distinct smell of lemon soap and Cook's spice cookies," he said, looking up and grinning at her.

"What are you doing?"

"Writing in my notebook about things I'm going to change here."

"Like what?"

"A bathroom with a huge tub and a boiler to have water hot all the time. No more heating bathwater on the stove. Things like that."

Katrin was trying to look around his dark tinted glasses.

"What do you want, Little Princess?" he asked.

"Can I pull down the shades? I want to look at your eyes."

"Give me two more seconds to finish this and then you may," he said. She liked that. He didn't always ask why she wanted to do things. When she finished writing she pulled the shades down, making the room dark enough for him to take off his glasses.

"Here, sit up close," he said, setting her on his lap. She looked at his eyes.

Most people didn't like them but she did. They were silvery white. Nobody but Menders had eyes like that.

"What do you see?" he asked.

"They're like mine. The same shape. More the same shape. They aren't like Lucen's or Hemmett's but they're like Cook's and Doctor's – but more. And they're like the Thrun's eyes, but not so much."

He smiled at her attempt at quantification.

"Should I explain it to you?"

She nodded.

"Hemmett, Lucen and Zelia are Southern Mordanians. You, I, Doctor and Cook are Old Mordanians. We're related to the Thrun. That's why we have eyes shaped similarly to theirs, like an almond. Southern Mordanians have rounder eyes."

"Really? We're Thrun?"

"We're definitely Thrun. But from a long way back."

"But the Thrun's eyes are brown or black. And your eyes look more like the Thrun's eyes than mine. The shape, not the color."

"That's because my grandfather was Thrun. Your Thrun ancestors are farther back. And remember Tharan-Tul? His eyes are blue. It happens sometimes among the Thrun."

"Why are your eyes white? Or almost white, they're not really white."

"That's something that runs in my family. Some of us don't have the color in our eyes that most people have," he explained.

"Do you mind?"

He shrugged. "If you've never known anything different you don't miss what you don't have. Now, if you'll put the shades back up, I'll show you something."

When she climbed back up on his lap, he had a map on the desk.

"This is a map of the world we live on," he said. "Do you

remember the name?"

"Eirdon."

"That's right. This is as if you took the planet's skin off, and flattened it out, like peeling an orange."

"Mordania," she said, pointing to the word.

"Yes — this is like a picture of the world from up in the sky, as if you were a bird flying over it. The blue is water, all the oceans. The colored parts are land. This is Mordania, and this," he explained, taking a pencil and making a cross on the map, "is where we live at The Shadows."

"Then what's all the rest of this?" she asked in astonishment, looking at all the colored parts of the map.

"The rest of the world. We live in only a part of it."

"It's a big part."

"Indeed it is," Menders smiled. Mordania was the one of the largest free standing land masses.

"These are other countries. And this island," Menders said, pointing to a white shape near the top of the map, "is where most of the Thrun live."

"It isn't very far," Katrin said, looking at the paper, walking her fingers across to the Thrun island.

Menders laughed a little.

"It doesn't look like it, but it's very far. More than five hundred miles."

Katrin wrinkled her forehead. She couldn't even think of five hundred miles.

"Long ago," Menders continued, "the Thrun traveled from this island over the ice bridge into Mordania, where many Thrun still live. This part of Mordania we live in is called Old Mordania, because it's the first part of Mordania that people lived in. Down here is the part called Southern Mordania. The people who live there look different from people who come from Old Mordania, because Old Mordanians look more like the Thrun, who are their ancestors."

Katrin nodded.

"The Queens of Mordania are descended – are part of the same family that the Thrun are part of," Menders went on. "They have always been tall women with red hair. Once, long ago, there was a woman chieftain of the Thrun and her daughter was the first Queen of Mordania."

"I don't have red hair," Katrin said. She knew what red hair looked like. Eiren had red hair.

"No, you have golden hair because your father had golden hair, like I have eyes like the Thrun because my grandmother was Thrun," Menders answered. Katrin looked at the map again.

"Where was I born?"

"In Erdahn, here." Menders pointed to another place on the map. "Then you were given to me and I brought you on the train from there, all the way around this water, to The Shadows."

"Is it a long way?"

"Very. It took two nights and a day and the train never stopped. It couldn't go fast because of the snow."

"Where is my mother?"

"She lives here in Erdahn, at the Palace, because she's the Queen," Menders answered. Katrin knew that, but she didn't realize how far away it was. It was as far away as the Thrun's island.

"Why doesn't she come to see me?"

Menders sighed a little. "Queens of Mordania don't see their children much."

"I think that's bad," Katrin said.

"I don't think much of the custom either," Menders smiled. "But we have a nice family. I'm your second cousin, so I'm part of your family and then everyone here has become a family as well."

"What's a cousin?" Katrin looked at him in surprise. She hadn't known this.

"We have the same ancestor, the same great-grandmother.

We're relatives called cousins."

"Do I have other cousins?" Katrin asked excitedly. Menders laughed.

"You do indeed, quite a few of them. Maybe when you're older you'll meet some of them," he replied. "For now you'll have to make do with a cousin who gets to be your father."

She put her arms around his neck and hugged hard. Let her mother just stay where she was. She had Menders and everyone else and they loved her even if her mother didn't. Although she couldn't understand why her mother didn't.

"Tell me about these other places," she said, looking back at the map. She liked all the different colors.

"This is Surelia. It's warm there and they make wine. You're learning their language. This part here is Samorsa, where the food is hot and spicy, and this part here, that's Fambre, famous for its linen and music."

Katrin frowned. It was all one big lump, right in the centre of the map but different parts had different names, unlike Mordania.

"But… isn't that all just one?" she asked.

"Try telling them that, Snowflower," Menders laughed. Samorsa and Surelia had been arguing over their border by force of arms for decades.

"This is Artreya, which is a very large country far across the sea. It reaches all the way from the top of the planet to the bottom. It's where boorish upstarts come from." Menders picked up a round, carved marble paperweight and traced his finger from the top to the bottom of it.

"It stretches from pole to pole, like this. The people there look different from Mordanians. They usually have dark hair and eyes that are round like Southern Mordanian eyes."

Katrin looked at the map.

"It's so big," she sighed. "I can't keep all of it in my head."

"Well no, not all at once," Menders laughed. "We'll look at it many more times but now I think a good way to learn about how maps work is to make our own map of The Shadows. Maybe Hemmett would like to watch while we start it."

Katrin shook her head.

"He won't let me play with him. He keeps saying 'no girls!' So I called him an old toad," she explained.

Menders laughed. "Boys are known to do this and they can be old toads at times," he said. "We'll start on our own then and let him join in later." He put the map to one side and pulled over a big sheet of paper, the kind he used for drawing, uncorked an ink bottle and picked up his fine point pen, the one Katrin wasn't allowed to draw with.

"Now, the top of the map is north, so we'll draw the north wind blowing from there, so you remember it," he said, quickly making a drawing of a cloud with big eyes and fat cheeks blowing snowflakes out of its mouth. Katrin laughed.

"This is east, where the sun rises, so here's the sun waking up." Menders drew a bed with a sun peeking out over the covers. "In the west is where the sun sets, so here he is, ready for bed." Another sun in a nightshirt with sleepy eyes. "The south is where the south wind blows warm, so here she is." This time, a lady cloud with big curls, blowing flowers out of her mouth.

"Here's The Shadows," Menders went on, his pen flying, drawing a picture of the house – then a moment later, a little girl who looked like Katrin standing in front of it. She clapped and watched excitedly while Menders drew the drive and then the road, and then drew himself holding her hand when she asked him to.

"Now, Snowflower, if that is where the house, drive and road are, where would the stables go?" he asked.

Suddenly she understood perfectly, and pointed.

"Smart girl! That's exactly right, by the bend of the road where the drive meets it. So here's the stable – and here's

Snowflake." Suddenly there was a drawing of the stable with her white pony standing by it.

"Put Demon in," she smiled. He did, making Demon look skinnier than he was and with a wicked face.

They went on, with Menders drawing in the road that led to Spaltz's farm and then a drawing of the farmhouse and the Spaltz family standing outside, from the old granny down to the littlest Spaltz. Toward the south he drew The Giants, the huge stone hands and noses that poked up out of the earth. Katrin could just remember Menders walking over to them with her one day when she was really little. He'd drawn a picture of her sitting in the palm of one of the hands. It was in a frame on his desk.

"We'll do more tomorrow and soon you'll have a map of the entire estate," Menders said. "It sounds like it's getting to be dinnertime, so you need to run and do your chores." He kissed her and set her on the floor. She was about to run out of the room but then she turned around and looked right at him.

"You say you get to be my father," she said. "Do I have a father?"

"Yes, little one but he died before you were born," Menders answered gently, stroking her hair.

"I think that's sad," Katrin said, feeling her eyes prickle. "I didn't get to know him. Maybe he would have come to see me."

"Yes, it is sad, but I knew him. He was my tutor when I was in military school and we were good friends, Bernhard and I. You look very much like him."

"Was he a good man?" Katrin asked. "Would he have loved me?"

"Yes, Little Princess, he was good and he would have loved you," Menders smiled.

"Not as much as you do," Katrin said, suddenly feeling very certain.

Menders looked like he was going to say something very

serious for a moment, but then he just smiled.

"You might be right there," he said. "I love you very much indeed. But Bernhard would have as well, if he'd had a chance to know you. Now, time for you to get to work or we won't have any dinner tonight with no forks out to eat it with."

Katrin laughed, bent over and kissed his hand where it rested on the arm of his chair, then ran off to the kitchen.

***

Borsen could hear the heavy raindrops drumming on his mother's cloak. She held it over his head like a roof, so he would stay dry. He was a little boy, very small for his age. He stood beside her on the seat of the bench they'd picked out, his face pressed close to the pictures carved into the shimmery, white stone base of the big statue that blocked some of the rain. Borsen had weak eyes and he could see things well only if they were very close.

"She was a great Queen, The Great Glorantha," his Mama said softly, her words rocking along from tone to tone in a soothing singsong, the inflection characteristic of the Thrun language. "The Surelian invaders killed her husband and children and burned her village, as they had killed many other Mordanians and Thrun. Glorantha rode out against the conquerors, a woman all alone. It inspired the people of Mordania and they rallied behind her in a great army. They drove the wicked Surelians out of Mordania and then joined in a great, strong tribe, all together."

Borsen ran his thin little hand across the wet, slippery stone, over the carved figure of the great Queen in her chariot. Pale sunlight slanted through the clouds for a moment and lit the stone. It sparkled inside, glinting under the smooth white surface. Borsen traced a fine dark green line that ran across the carvings.

"Mama, what is this stone?" he asked softly.

"I don't know, my Little Man," she smiled. "It is not

familiar to me. The Thrun do not use this stone. It is the old bones of the world. Pretty, isn't it?"

Borsen nodded, unable to take his eyes off the tiny lights glinting inside the stone. He watched until the sun went behind the clouds again. Then he looked up at Mama, who was smiling down at him.

"Where I grew up, on the Sea of Grass where you were born, my Little Man, there were great stone statues different from this," she said. "They are parts of people, great hands or feet, thrusting up from the ground. They are called The Giants. When you were very small, I took you to see them, before we moved from there."

"Who made them?" Borsen asked, moving closer to her so he could see her face clearly.

"Nobody knows. The Thrun believe they are the life of Eirdon. Old bones, coming out of the ground. There is a poem about them. It goes like this:

> *There are Giants in the ground,*
> *There are Giants in the sky.*
> *When clouds are thick and rolling,*
> *You see them striding by.*
> *When the snow drifts deeply,*
> *There are giants far below.*
> *Sleeping in the places,*
> *Where all men's bones shall go."*

"Where are The Giants now?" Borsen asked, looking around, squinting into the rain.

"They are everywhere. They are what make everything live," Mama smiled. "You can't see them but they are there. They come from The Light At The Top Of The World, where everything on Eirdon came from and where everything goes when it dies."

Borsen turned back to the carved pictures, bringing his

eyes close to them, running his fingers over the wheels of the Queen's chariot. Was she one of The Giants, he wondered. He leaned against Mama and rested his hand against the cool, wet, glistening stone.

"Here, get away from there! Bloody City Thrun! Get off, you trash!" A man's voice boomed from nowhere, making them both start.

Mama cried out softly and bent over her shin. Borsen nearly fell and clung to her as she rubbed the place where the man had kicked her.

"Please, sir…" she gasped, speaking awkwardly in Mordanian.

"Move along or you'll get worse!"

"Come, Little Man," Mama whispered, gathering Borsen to her and rising with him. He wrapped his legs around her waist and held on tight, turning his face from the man who was driving them away. It was better not to look at them, although all he could see was a human-shaped blur. It was better to walk away.

Mama limped into an alleyway. Borsen could tell that the leg that the man had kicked pained her badly. They had to stay near the statue because they were waiting there for Borsen's father, who was looking for places he could steal from. Borsen tried not to cry.

"Do not let that trouble you," Mama said gently, cuddling him close. "He is just an unkind man, not worthy of notice. You are more than he will ever be, my Little Man. Always remember, you do not have to follow the way of those who do wrong, like your father, like that man. Always follow The Way Of Light, the way of the Thrun."

The rain began to drum down harder and Mama drew her cloak up over her head and Borsen's, making a warm, snug cave for them both.

"Always remember that you are Thrun, my son," she whispered. "Remember you are from the first people of Eirdon."

CHAPTER 21
MENDERS' MEN

"Wondered where she'd got to," Menders said as he came level with the door of the room that now belonged to Ifor Trantz. He could see that Katrin was sound asleep beside the big man — she must have made a late night visit to The Shadows' newest inhabitant.

"She was very concerned about you earlier," Menders continued, settling in the bedside chair. "Gets on pins and needles if anyone is ailing in the house."

Ifor was indeed ailing. The haggard man who had been helped off the train earlier that day bore little resemblance to the reticent but brilliant tutor Menders had known. Body-bound with agonizing pain, Ifor could barely walk with Menders and Lucen supporting him. Franz had wrapped him in a brace to support his back.

Only then had Ifor managed a shy smile, because Katrin ran forward with her hand out, offering to help him.

Katrin was four years old —Ifor Trantz was a huge, bearlike man. He was not as tall as Lucen but he was probably as heavy when in good health. Menders had immediately taken in the way his clothing hung on him.

Ifor had been living in abject poverty for five years while trying desperately to remain employed. His injured back led to his dismissal from one job after another, as he could not maintain any posture for long. Several months ago, Ifor had re-injured his back when he slipped while walking along the shore of the Southern Ocean and fell into a tidal pool. He had remained half submerged all night in late winter weather, rescued by passersby just as the tide that would have filled the pool, drowning him, was coming in.

Months of complete invalidism as a result of his accident

meant Ifor had been facing the choice of living with his sister's family or traveling to Erdahn where Commandant Komroff had offered him a

home. These options were nothing Ifor wanted.

Ifor was of a proud people, the legendary Southern Mordanian fisherman of the far southwest coast. Fiercely independent, huge statured and strong, they fished the Southern Ocean with nets thrown from shallow skiffs. Their trade was difficult and dangerous but they were tough, hardy people who took care of their own. Ifor's father had been killed at sea in a sudden storm. Determined that her son would not follow in his father's footsteps, Ifor's mother had sent him to school. It was there that the young boy's brilliance was discovered and Ifor was given an entrée to the Mordanian Military Academy and then to Special Services training.

He was an unlikely spy. Ifor's bearlike, outsized build and awkward unattractiveness seemed designed to make him stand out in any crowd. His face was heavy and slablike, giving him a superficial appearance of stupidity. Perpetually untidy, coarse black hair and a habit of avoiding eye contact with others completed the picture of an extremely socially withdrawn, retiring man who seldom spoke and withdrew from most human interaction.

But if Ifor was given a role, he was transformed. During his years at the Academy and then as an assassin, Menders had watched Ifor become diplomats, artists, street musicians, beggars, military officers, butchers – all undercover roles that allowed him to infiltrate situations to gather information or commit sabotage. Menders remembered him posing as a swashbuckling sailor just in port, flirting openly with men and women, rollicking along in a crowd that had been swept into his wake by his jokes, snatches of song and open pockets. All the while, Ifor had been dropping explosive charges that would be detonated later when a certain Surelian dignitary arrived at the same port on his yacht, very much simplifying the Surelian Problem.

At the Academy, Ifor had been a gentle and patient tutor for cadets who were behind in schoolwork. A plague of ill-educated tutors had worked their way into the network of noble and wealthy families
in Mordania. They gave their pupils little real knowledge or skill – then, when the children entered school, they were far behind. Upon entering the Academy, Menders had been referred to a number of officers who tutored such cadets. Ifor had worked with him on history and languages, sparking his interest in both. He had also coached Menders in playing the strategy game, DeGratz, honing his intuition and logic while making him practice patience and prudence.

"She's so bright," Ifor murmured, smiling. Katrin slept on, clutching the remains of a cookie from the jar Cook had set up on Ifor's bedside table.

Menders smiled to himself. That was typical of Ifor Trantz. Katrin was a very pretty little girl and people always noted it and complimented her. Ifor would see past that surface as most people failed to do, discovering the blossoming mind underneath.

"Very. You'd remember her father, Bernhard Markha," Menders replied.

"Gods, no wonder it's been niggling me. She looks like him."

They were silent. They knew Bernhard Markha was dead and mourned him. His kindness and inclusiveness had eased their ways during times when they were the new pupils, out of place and trying to adjust.

"You're having quite a show tonight," Menders eventually remarked, looking out the window at the northern sky. The aurora was very active, the spectacular arrays of arches and twisting curtains of light the Thrun called The Light At The Top Of The World blotting out the stars. "It's even more brilliant in the winter."

"Thank you for asking me here," Ifor said roughly in his heavy voice that sounded like slabs of lead being knocked together. It trembled a bit and Menders could sense the weakness that had brought this big man so close to tears.

"Thank you for coming. I'm going to need that mind of yours. Now, anything you need before I take this bundle away?"

Ifor shook his head, closing his eyes and turning his face toward the wall.

"Goodnight then," Menders said, lifting Katrin and cuddling her close.

***

Dear Cahrin and Olner,

Thank you for your help in acquiring the men I needed. The response has been overwhelming, but I'm glad for it. Officially we have a new staff of farmers, gamekeepers, crofters and servants. Ifor Trantz and Harcort Menck are Katrin's "tutors". I was stunned by how badly both of them had been injured, particularly Menck's progressive paralysis. They're both lodged comfortably on the ground floor of the house, in an area they insist on calling Cripples' Wing (to my complete disgust). They have hung a sign to that effect.

I'm grateful to you, Olner, for having Gladdas Dalmanthea trace Ifor for me. It seems he loves the outdoor life and has been invaluable by supplying the table with game or fish when his injury is not troubling him. The outside exercise strengthens his back. As you know, his mind is second to none. He has already set up a system for cataloging information and we have begun to extend our circle of contacts.

Lucen Greinholz has located a number of demobilized soldiers, one of whom is an excellent blacksmith, and Cook's son, Tomar, has joined the household in the position of estate tailor. This is a boon as we are all threadbare.

It is repulsive that the Crown and Council provide no pension or assistance for men who have served and been injured in body or mind.

Assassins are started so young and their working life is over by thirty, when the reflexes have slowed too much. These men sacrifice much — their youth, their chances for marriage, social acceptance, health, sometimes their lives, like poor Falk. To think the nation that demands so much demonstrates such a lack of concern for these soldiers — well, my indignation is considerable.

On a happier note, Doctor Franz has declared Ifor's back salvageable, though he's positive that the bullet is too near Ifor's spine to be removed. He has prescribed a regimen of exercise and drinking a great deal of milk. Ifor doesn't mind the exercise but he hates the milk rule, as it goes along with severe limits on his smoking and drinking. However, the improvement he's seen keeps him faithful to the milk diet.

So our ranks have swelled. Cook marvels that such nice fellows, who help in the kitchen according to a roster, could have been employed as they were. Doctor Franz is also boggled, particularly when the men begin bragging about my school days and my prowess.

Unfortunately, Franz is very curious as to the number of kills I have. I've ordered the men not to tell him, as he is a kindly and dedicated soul and I would not want my friendship with him blemished. He is appalled by our profession and if he knew how many people I have eliminated he would be unable to keep it from affecting his regard for me. Hopefully telling the men to stay quiet about it will end the matter.

Your friend,

Menders

It was high summer when Menders received a letter from Commandant Komroff.

My dear "Son" Menders,

I have spoken at great length with Bartan regarding the matter of acquiring specialists to help on your estate. I wish to bring a certain young man to your attention, your first cousin, Baronet Kaymar Shvalz.

Kaymar arrived at the Academy the same winter you were sent to Surelia, so you have not had the opportunity to meet. Against my wishes, he was selected for Special Services training due to his youth, stature and native intelligence — and because there was a massive recruitment of young boys to become assassins at the time. He was a sensitive boy, scarred by unfortunate childhood events and the untimely death of his father. Unfortunately, his ambiguous sexual nature and pretty face made him a prime candidate for the initiative called "The Mordanian Fireboats" by the late Minister of Defense, Deter Varnor.

Minister Varnor conceived the idea of having a large number of expendable assassins who could be trained with little investment of time, money and effort — with the reasoning that they would be no loss to Mordania if they were killed in action and that there would always be more young boys to train quickly and send out on what were, essentially, suicide missions. These young assassins have not been afforded the training and education you were. These young men, including Kaymar, have been cruelly exploited and overworked. Tragically, there are only three of them left alive out of the original number of one hundred and twenty. Two of the three are beyond hope, their minds broken into irreversible madness — and then there is Kaymar, who has nearly reached your record number of kills.

Ceaseless service for more than three years without a leave has taken a physical and mental toll on your cousin, to the point where Bartan interceded with the Queen on his behalf. Kaymar had been working on a deep infiltration that led to a complete breakdown of his health. He has been mustered out of the service by the Queen herself, though this has not been made public, and it is assumed by most that he still works with Bartan. As he, like you, is her cousin, the Queen has made him a Courtier and placed him under her personal protection. He has recovered to a large degree but needs a quiet and peaceful situation, as he finds the bustle of Erdahn disturbing.

I recommend Kaymar for your consideration as a member of the Princess' household. He is unswervingly loyal, diligent, extremely intelligent though not properly educated, has a capacity for ruthlessness that is more than the average and, like you, has never been known to fail at any task set to him, no matter what toll the task may take from him. He would serve you and the Princess well and faithfully.

Be prepared for him to contact you in the near future. Don't be put off by his appearance and mannerisms. He has suffered greatly in the service of his country. I know he is salvageable. Were he not, I would not recommend him to you.

As always, my best wishes for your continued health and happiness and that of your little daughter, the Princess.

Your "Father",

Morschal Komroff, Commandant

Menders sat back in his chair.

He knew of his first cousins, Dorsen and Kaymar, but had never met them. They were the sons of his father's estranged younger brother. The families had never communicated during Menders' lifetime. Kaymar's family lived at Moresby, the southern portion of what had once been the enormous Stettan holdings. The estate had been divided by Menders' grandfather after his eldest son had become a careless reprobate, thus assuring his younger son of an income and home.

There was more story here than the words Sir had set down. Cousin Kaymar damaged by an infiltration assignment, then mustered out in need of a peaceful situation – the Minister of Defense who had conceived the fiendish idea of The Mordanian Fireboats suddenly coming down with a bad case of death... was there a connection? And what was the almost offhand remark, "Don't be put off by his appearance and mannerisms" meant to convey? Menders trusted Sir entirely, but at times Komroff did not enlighten those men he considered "his boys" with every detail he was privy to.

There had been a sudden rash of killings in the Capitol in the last year, spectacularly dubbed The Gutting Murders by the press. Some of the victims were prominent people, others street trash – all were known to have a sexual predilection for children. One had been Hartsen Trentov, the tutor who had victimized Menders and confessed that he had done the same to Menders' cousin. Could Kaymar be involved in this series of killings – and in the death of Minister Varnor?

"Cousin," Menders muttered, "have you been a naughty boy?"

He set the letter on his desk and went to the lounge in the Men's Wing. Bartan's associate who had delivered the letter was there, engaged in a jesting conversation with several of the newly employed group that had taken to calling themselves "Menders' Men". Menders asked him for a word and when they'd walked outside, asked if he knew Kaymar Shvalz.

He saw what he'd expected, a rapid flicker of fear in the man's eyes.

"Of course, everyone in Bartan's network knows Shvalz," he answered, his tone easy, his eyes telling another tale.

"Pleasant young man?" Menders asked innocently, offering a cigar which the rattled fellow took gratefully. Menders didn't smoke very often but always seemed to have a cigar handy for those who did.

"Very much a gentleman," came the careful answer.

"Good at his work?"

"Shvalz has no peer in the present network."

"I was curious because he is my cousin, though we've never met," Menders explained chummily, redirecting the conversation now that he knew what he needed. After some idle chatter and seeing to it that the man was comfortably settled for the night before his return trip to Erdahn, he retreated to his office.

"So the Commandant feels that my cousin should come to The Shadows, even though a seasoned assassin blanches white at the mention of that cousin's name and has no idea that Kaymar is no longer in Special Services. He may be just the man I need," Menders said aloud as he settled himself behind his desk.

***

A large, spreading oak on the south side of the house became known as The Assassin's Tree, as it became the gathering place for those gentlemen at the end of a long summer day. Tables and chairs were taken from unused rooms in the house, DeGratz sets and cards were supplied and "Menders' Men" would sit out in the long, glowing evenings, smoking cigars, tippling wine and talking. Past exploits were bragged about, recent competitions at marksmanship disputed, many lies were told and a lot of laughing went on. A large cork dartboard was nailed to the tree, subjected to many a knife throwing competition. Someone had set up a still in the woodshed, and made a potent lanarfruit brandy that was referred to as 'Liquid Gunpowder'. Menders tolerated such antics as long as the children were not endangered and things didn't get out of hand.

One night Katrin wandered out to the tree in her nightgown. She never slept well during the night-long brightness of high summer. A particularly ribald story had just been told and there was great guffawing and catcalling until one of the assassins looked over and saw her coming across the lawn.

"Behave yourself, gentleman, the Princess is here," he said. There was a general tidying and straightening among the group that made Menders smile. A four year old girl gets out of her bed at night and a group of the most dangerous men in the world start primping, he thought, smiling around Ifor at her.

"You're up late," Menders said.

"I couldn't find you and the sun is still up," she said ingenuously.

"And you very well know why, it's the middle of summer," he laughed as he lifted her onto his lap.

"I heard you all laughing and wanted to know why." She looked around the men with wondering eyes. There was considerable embarrassment.

"We were talking about grown up things that you wouldn't like much," Menders said in a tone that let her know that there would be no more explanation as the men took their seats again.

"What do men talk about?" she asked.

"Oh generally they tell lies and insult each other," Menders answered her. "They talk about women, things they've done, women, war, women, sporting prowess and women."

She looked at him.

"That's silly," she declared.

"Indeed it is, Little Princess." He snuggled her closer, knowing she would be asleep in a few moments. "Continue, gentlemen but tone it down a trifle," he said to the amused gathering.

"There's Mister Spaltz," Katrin said suddenly. Menders looked up.

Indeed, the farmer was approaching across the yard, accompanied by the guard on duty. Menders felt the group of men tighten reflexively as hands went to pistol grips and knife handles. When the sentry signaled to the Man on the roof that all was well, they relaxed. Passing Katrin to Ifor, Menders rose and went to greet Spaltz.

"Evening Mister Menders," Spaltz smiled. "Found myself with a couple of spare hours and thought I would walk over to spend a little time. I have a couple of letters for you from Erdahn – one from our Eiren, the other from her headmistress."

Menders took the letters. "Care to sit with us?" he asked.

"Don't mind if I do. Well, Princess, you have quite a few admirers here," he said, taking a homemade cookie from his pocket and proffering it to her with a little bow.

"Thank you, Mister Spaltz," she said, taking it with a big

smile. "How are you?"

"A bit tired, to be expected at this time of year, but well enough," he answered. "And how are you keeping?"

"Very well, thank you." She bit into the cookie, silencing herself for the moment. Mister Spaltz pulled up a chair.

"Wanted to see if some of you fellows would be interested in teaching a few of the farm lads how to shoot," he said forthrightly. "They're not very good."

"I imagine there are a couple of us skilled enough to do that," Menders said carefully.

"Pish, Mister Menders, I know full well these aren't your everyday farmers, tutors and gamekeepers and I say it's about time too. Lads, when this youngster came out here with that baby he had nothing between her and danger but himself and my girl and another lass, armed with fire pokers."

Ifor started shaking with laughter at Spaltz's words. That set off several of the other assassins.

"Now, your secret is safe with me and no-one around here will twig to it either," Spaltz went on. "Do you know that there's a law in Mordania saying that every man should do a certain amount of shooting practice a week? It's an old one, but it's a law. Now I'm thinking at this point you have this place guarded well, but some of us would like to have the skills to help out if necessary. None of us care for the way things are done in this country. We're the ones who see our boys march away and come back as cripples or not at all. We're the ones who see our daughters lonesome and without a chance of getting married. It would be some comfort to us to know that should danger threaten we could come to help you and protect this child here."

He reached over and gave Katrin's hair a rub. She smiled at him.

"She's being raised in the right way, forward seeing," he continued. "Might just be the salvation of us all one day. We're willing to protect her and to keep our gobs shut about it."

Menders couldn't repress a smile, but he was also glad for the sentiment and for Spaltz's honesty and openness.

"We'll need to make shooting butts and the area will have to be totally off limits to the children. I believe we can arrange something. I want you to understand that there is danger if this is all found out," he explained.

"We know that, the roasting spit for all of us. Raising a private militia is treason. But we won't be like that... just poor peasant farmers improving our shooting skills before hunting season. No-one will talk, Mister Menders. You know yourself this corner of Old Mordania doesn't hold with some of the things that go on elsewhere. We're used to keeping our cards close to our waistcoats here."

"Then it's done," Menders said and Spaltz reached over to give him a crushing handshake.

"And speaking of cards, I see a few decks out," Spaltz remarked suggestively. Before long, an intense game was in progress with the farmer winning almost every hand and the assassins desperate to figure out what he was doing.

Ifor handed a dozing Katrin back to Menders and leaned close to his ear.

"Is it all right?" he asked.

"Absolutely. I'd trust him with my life," Menders murmured back, settling Katrin comfortably and opening the letters that Spaltz had handed him.

Dear Mister Menders,

I have to make a decision soon, and wanted to have your advice.

I have been offered a position at a school in Erdahn, after I graduate. It would be very well paid and a great step up for me.

Mister Menders, I don't want to accept this offer. I know it sounds like I've gone mad but what I really want is to finish here and come home to start my school at The Shadows. This is what I've always dreamed of. I know I won't make much money, if any, doing so but I do so want the children on the estate to begin to learn so that their lives can be better. We're practice teaching now and I see how learning changes the lives of people.

I have missed you all so very much. Please give Katrin a kiss for me. I will hardly know her when I see her again. She must be a very big girl. Please write to me and let me know all she does.

I went to the library today and took out many books, almost more than I could carry. You would have laughed to see me staggering down the street with them. They're on all sorts of subjects and I can't wait to start reading them, so I will close now. Take care of yourself and write soon!

Sincerely,

Eiren

Menders opened the other letter.

Dear Mister Menders,

I am writing to inform you that Eiren Spaltz has been offered a very lucrative post at one of the most exclusive schools in Erdahn upon her graduation from training school. This is an excellent opportunity for Eiren, yet she seems to wish to refuse the offer. I wanted to make sure that she is not making this decision out of a sense of duty because she is being sponsored by you and Doctor Franz. Eiren is an exemplary young woman and if she felt that she was obligated to you in any way, she would turn down even such a wonderful opportunity as this.

Should Eiren decide against taking this position, it is my recommendation that she complete an additional year of training. This advanced training will make her even more capable of starting a school and building it into a successful project. She is most talented and would be well on her way to having the credentials to become the headmistress of a certified school if she undertakes an additional year.

I hope this finds you well. Eiren excels in all her classes and is a

Katrin sighed a bit and snuggled down in his arms. He settled comfortably in his chair, crossed his legs and took a sip of wine. One of the assassins offered a puff on the cigar he'd just lighted and Menders accepted. He actually liked smoking but seldom indulged, wanting to protect his weak lungs. It had been one of those things he'd battled as a boy as he worked to strengthen the indifferent body nature had given him. It was no problem to him now but cigar smoking was not exactly something to venture into. A puff here and there was enough.

Doctor Franz came out of the house, carrying a large brandy snifter and smoking a fat cigar. He sat down next to Menders in an old cane chair that creaked alarmingly.

"What's Spaltz doing?" he asked Menders.

"Fleecing my men at cards."

"Is that wise?" Franz asked with genuine surprise.

"They're assassins, doctor, not murderous madmen," Menders explained wearily. "If you bumped elbows with one in a bar, he wouldn't pull a gun or knife on you."

"Uh, well… perhaps not," Franz conceded. "I do have to admit that I'm glad they're here."

Menders nodded in agreement. "I have to write a couple of letters for Spaltz to post tomorrow," he said, rising with Katrin and going to his study.

Dear Headmistress Dordrein,

Thank you for the wonderful news about Eiren. We have always been convinced of her potential. It is gratifying to know that not only is she doing well, but that you have her best interests at heart.

Eiren is the one who must make this decision. I agree that it is an excellent opportunity for her. I am writing to remind her that at no time has she ever been under any obligation to Doctor Franz or myself.

I can say that Eiren's dream of a school here at The Shadows has been a long-cherished one and I will fully understand if that is what she chooses to do. She must feel free to make her decision without pressure from anyone. As you say, Eiren is an exemplary young woman and is not known for making rash decisions. We must trust in her judgment. Doctor Franz and I will be happy with whatever choice she makes.

Your recommendation of further training for Eiren is welcome news. Please be assured that her tuition will be provided for as long as you and she feel that she would benefit from schooling.

Yours faithfully,

Menders

Dear Eiren,

It was good to hear from you. I am sending this immediately, hoping that it will reach you soon enough to help you. I will write more at leisure to bring you up to date on everything going on here.

At no time have you ever been under obligation to Doctor Franz and me. I want you to bear this in mind when you make your decision about coming home or staying in Erdahn to teach. This is entirely up to you and we will be delighted with whatever you choose. So free your mind and do what you believe is best for you.

Your headmistress has recommended extra training for you, should you decide to continue with your plans to open a school at The Shadows. Doctor and I will be pleased to continue to provide your tuition and board so that you can have whatever education you will need to establish your school.

When you left, the only thing I asked of you was that you make me proud. You have already done so, Eiren. You are free, always. My happiness comes from having helped a remarkable young woman along the way.

Your friend,

Menders

The letters finished, Menders carried Katrin up to her room and put her to bed. Then he stood at her window and watched the comradely group beneath the Assassins' Tree. Men's voices and laughter drifted up to him, as did a whiff of cigar smoke.

It was good knowing The Shadows was secure. He did not have to work so hard now. There were many hands willing to take on the hard tasks. He had time to teach Katrin and had started her on languages and music, not with formal lessons but simply by including her in what he did. She learned so fast! She was playing little tunes on the spinet with both hands and could carry on a simple conversation in Surelian. She was learning to dance and could curtsey on every level of formality as beautifully as the most accomplished court lady. Her manners were excellent, befitting a child much older than five and they came naturally because she had a genuine interest in and compassion for others.

Having some of the burden of running The Shadows lifted meant Menders could turn his mind to other things, particularly danger from the faction seeking to place the Queen's cousin, the Duchess of Ernst, on the Throne by wiping out the present royal line. Of late they had been quiescent, but they would be plotting again soon enough.

Every man who had come to live at The Shadows brought with him many connections, because spies and assassins made it their business to know many people. Information was pouring into The Shadows from all over Mordania and beyond. A clear picture of what was happening in Mordania was forming – at times a very frightening picture that had given Menders some sleepless nights.

But for now, on this lengthy summer evening, with help at hand, pleasant company and the prospect of no longer being the man of all work on the estate, Menders was content.

CHAPTER 22
THE FIREBOAT FINDS SAFE HARBOR

Retired assassin Kaymar Shvalz, eighteen years of age, reined in his horse and sat looking at The Shadows. It reminded him of Moresby, his boyhood home.

Kaymar was a second son. He had no chance of inheriting Moresby, as his older brother had two hearty boys. Though Kaymar was welcome there, it was as a guest in a house that would never be his.

Kaymar could still play a lady's maid for a covert assignment without rousing any suspicions – if he were still a working assassin. He was small, lithe and lean with a pretty face, golden blond hair and eyes as blue as the Sea of Surelia. No-one suspected that he was strong as a borag until it was too late. His specialty had been seductive infiltration prior to assassination, particularly among the nobility and the wealthy. He had the ability to gain the trust of people rapidly. Attracted to both men and women, he used his sexual ambiguity to his advantage when winning the confidence of his targets. This had made him doubly valuable to the Office of Special Services and he had been deliberately trained to exploit his sexual nature.

Kaymar was not cut out to be an assassin, despite his success at the profession. The years between his fifteenth and eighteenth birthdays had seen him becoming progressively unhinged as he plied his trade. He finally encountered a situation that drove him to agonizing depths of self-loathing and self-destruction. His mind gave way completely.

Thoren Bartan brought the young assassin's plight to the Queen's attention in one of her more sober periods and Kaymar was mustered out of Special Services with a pension, unlike many of his peers.

After a period of invalidism, with treatment from Doctor

Franz ordered by the Queen, Kaymar managed to reclaim his traumatized mind and spirit. Bartan and Commandant Komroff told him about Menders' formation of a secret Guard for Princess Katrin. Kaymar had written to Menders, offering his services. Menders had replied immediately.

Kaymar rode up the drive, reveling in the glow of afternoon sun on the walls and turrets of the huge estate house. There was a tang of wood smoke in the air.

Two men walked out onto the steps of the house as he approached. Kaymar realized that one of them was Menders himself, dressed informally for the warmish afternoon in an open collared shirt and casual trousers, his long hair flowing loose. Dark glasses covered his white eyes; his legendary Thrun-style beard and moustache were in evidence.

The other man was tall and massive, with dark shaggy hair and clothing that fitted him awkwardly. He came forward, taking Kaymar's horse while he dismounted. He murmured a deep 'good afternoon' and smiled shyly when Kaymar, sensing the man's proclivities, looked up at him and flirted a bit from habit rather than attraction. Kaymar then turned to Menders, the cousin he had wanted to meet for years.

Menders' handshake was warm and direct but was definitely possessed of the potential to be deadly. His body still exhibited flexibility and grace, though he was taller and heavier than the descriptions Kaymar had heard at the Academy. Kaymar was slightly awed in the presence of the renowned Surelian Solution.

The awe left him once they were in Menders' office. Comfortably appointed, it was neat, orderly and absolutely full of books – Kaymar's sort of room. It reminded him that he and Menders were first cousins. He mentioned the relationship.

"We are indeed," Menders nodded, offering a drink which Kaymar gladly accepted. He noticed Menders took nothing. "I've always been curious about your part of the family. It's a pity that we've never met before, though I guess it was inevitable, considering our fathers' estrangement and being raised in different parts of the country."

After some further light conversation, Menders asked a question.

"Why do you want to come here to The Shadows?" He sat back in his chair, swiveling away from Kaymar, gazing out the window behind his desk.

"As one of the Mordanian Fireboats, I was sent out on missions from the time I was fifteen, without a break. I completed a minimum of five missions a month, usually more," Kaymar began. "It was not a good situation for me. I had no sense of purpose other than following my orders. I became mad, yet they continued to use me. Sir and Thoren Bartan tried to have me suspended or mustered out of the service, but it did no good.

"I was finally sent on a deep covert infiltration, penetrating a faction working to remove our cousin, the Queen, and both Princesses. They planned to replace the Queen with the Duchess of Ernst. I was sent because the man at the head of this group was nancy."

Kaymar's voice broke and he swallowed, hard. Menders, hearing him, turned around.

"To keep things brief, I fell in love with my target," Kaymar continued quietly, his tormented eyes meeting Menders'. "Very much so. He loved me for what I am, not what I could become or what I used to be. I killed him on the same night he asked me to stay with him for the rest of his life."

"You needn't tell me more," Menders responded gently. "This can happen when one works in the way you did, without sufficient maturity and training. Fifteen was far too young to begin sending someone to do seductive infiltration."

"I'm sorry," Kaymar replied, sure that Menders was going to refuse him, desperate to turn things his way. "I know that I don't look my best right now. I felt quite well for a while but the longer I stay in Erdahn, the more I feel that I'm falling back into madness. I need a quiet place and I want work I can believe in. I would also like to see the Princess before deciding whether to ask you to let me stay or not."

"Yes, there are rumors," Menders replied. "It's said that Katrin's as mad as her sister, that she's an idiot and that's why she's been exiled here and not seen in four years. I can assure you that she's neither. It's about time for her to have been brought in and dressed for dinner. I hope you'll join us and meet her."

Kaymar consented gladly.

"Now let me try to make you not want to be here," Menders continued bluntly. "The Shadows is seductive, particularly in the autumn. The winters here are very long and you have never lived in Old Mordania. Anything you've experienced in Erdahn or at your family home in the Southeast is at least twice as difficult here. The cold can be a killer. Two years back we were completely snowed in. Trains could not get through for months.

"We are isolated. There is some society around, but many of the estate owners live in Erdahn almost exclusively, leaving their estates to be run by managers or tenants. Our main company consists of the estate farmers, who are a good lot but not educated or sophisticated. Katrin's Guard are all demobilized soldiers and retired Special Services operatives. They would be your main society. You probably know all or at least most of them." He named a few and Kaymar nodded.

"I don't fear either the winter or the isolation," Kaymar answered. "I'm sick of Court and sick of Erdahn."

"However, I haven't told you what your work would be. It's possible you wouldn't care for it," Menders continued. "I need someone who can shadow two small children, ages four and seven.

"The younger one, of course, is the Princess. She's loving but has a penchant for mischief and will keep you guessing because she learns quickly. The other is a boy, Hemmett

Greinholz. He's the son of Katrin's official guard. He's bright as well, but he won't put you through the mental gymnastics that Katrin can. He's immensely stubborn and can be slow to obey, though he is a genuinely good-hearted boy.

"As the children grow older, they need freedom to roam and play normally, but Katrin must be kept safe. Some of the men who are already here shadow them and do well, but I need someone young enough to be able to think as a child thinks. This is not intended to insult you."

"It isn't taken that way," Kaymar answered.

"There would be other work as well. We all have to take a hand around the place because I can't risk hiring casual servants who might gossip. We are not raising Katrin in the traditional manner, as you will see when you meet her. That could mean a death sentence for me if this information should get back to the Queen. Her orders were that Katrin be raised traditionally."

Kaymar arched an eyebrow and seemed about to speak, then remained reticent.

"So I have assassins here who knead bread, mop floors, chop wood, dig in the garden," Menders continued. "Some have taken over three of the estate farms and are turning out to be good farmers. Two have married already. We have a lot of unattached young women out here, thanks to the male population being taken away every time Mordania is in a war.

"I also need a liaison with the Court and Bartan, someone who can go back and forth quickly and who knows his way around the Palace," Menders went on. "If you wished to stay with us, you would do that as well. I'm buying a small, fast boat to allow us rapid access to the Capitol and back. I think we can vary your assignments sufficiently to keep you from becoming a sort of baby-minder, but your first duty would always be to the Princess."

"I have the Queen's protection and am designated a Courtier," Kaymar volunteered. "That would guarantee me an entrée to Court. It is not common knowledge that I'm no longer in Special Services, so people assume I still work under Bartan's direction. That would definitely work to your advantage."

Menders nodded.

"That brings me to something else," he said. The evening light was now quite low. He removed his glasses suddenly and looked directly at Kaymar.

The effect was startling, even for a young man who had seen a great deal in his eighteen years. Kaymar had never seen eyes like that.

"I must know now, before you so much as meet Katrin, your feelings toward children," Menders said, fixing Kaymar with those eyes. "If you dislike them, I need to know it, because you could not do this job and should not even attempt it. If you like them too much, in an unwholesome way, you had best go your way now or I will have no choice but to kill you."

"I have two young nephews and a niece, whom I love dearly and decently," Kaymar replied, without any heat or taking any offense. It was entirely understandable that Menders would need to know this and Kaymar would have thought less of him if he hadn't brought it up. "You need have no fear on that score."

Menders nodded.

"Should you stay, the only other thing I ask is that you keep your behavior within the bounds of decency around Katrin and Hemmett," he said. "This is what I ask of all of you. The Men have a wing of the house to themselves where the children don't go without permission. I believe men shouldn't have to entirely suppress their behavior. But I do ask that swearing, drinking and romance be controlled when the Princess and her friend are within hearing."

"I'm in complete agreement with that," Kaymar responded firmly.

"I also feel I should let you know that there are no men with your proclivities here with the exception of Ifor Trantz, who joined us some months ago," Menders remarked.

"And your servant, the one who took my horse," Kaymar replied, amused that Menders didn't know what he did about the big, dark, shaggy man. Then he remembered. Menders had told him there were no servants at The Shadows.

"Servant? No - that was Ifor Trantz," Menders answered, his own amusement showing. Kaymar realized with embarrassment that Menders had seen his automatic moment of flirtation. "He has a bullet in his back and was mustered out of the service without a pension. It was unlikely you'd have ever met him at the Academy, he's a few years older than I."

Kaymar was rattled. He'd heard of Trantz – all spies and assassins had. He and his partner had laid the groundwork that made it possible for Menders to end the Surelian Problem. The man was a genius. Kaymar had flirted with him like a rent-boy and almost tipped him for taking his horse! Who would have ever thought that human bear was Ifor Trantz!

"I'm bonded with Mikail Farnov in Erdahn. I would not be seeking intimate companionship here," Kaymar said after an uncomfortable silence.

"Then we have no grounds for disagreement," Menders replied with a smile. "We can manage sufficient time for you to get home to Erdahn often, should I decide you will have the position."

Kaymar's heart sank. He'd thought that he'd talked Menders around.

Menders donned his glasses, then turned his head to listen intently. He held up a hand for quiet and sniffed slightly.

"You're going to meet the Princess," he said, just as the handle of the door turned. Kaymar rose, intensely curious.

The door swung back and a pretty little girl with long, recently brushed golden hair peeped in with a delighted, dimpled smile on her face.

"I'm sorry, Menders, I didn't know anyone was here," she

said.

"Come in, it's all right," Menders replied, rising. Kaymar knew that this child was the center of Menders' universe, just from his voice. Judging from her response, he was the center of hers. She came to stand before Kaymar, giving him a small curtsey.

"Princess Katrin Morghenna, may I present your cousin, Kaymar Shvalz, who is considering coming to live with us."

Kaymar bowed and then took the hand that Princess Katrin extended to him.

"I hope you do," she said, smiling into his eyes. "I'm glad to meet another cousin. Menders is my cousin too. Would you be one of Menders' Men? They have a great time in their part of the house. They're always having games and playing jokes on each other."

"I hope I will be," Kaymar answered, feeling himself warm to her instantly. What a contrast to Princess Aidelia's endless eyerolling and drooling! This child was looking at him with sane and innocent eyes and asking him if he was going to stay for dinner – and she was four years younger than the mad Heiress to the Throne, who could hardly string three coherent words together. Most discernible words spoken by Princess Aidelia were obscenities.

"Come sit with me while I talk with our Cousin Kaymar a bit more," Menders smiled, re-seating himself and holding out his arms to the Princess. She climbed onto his lap and immediately began going through his pockets, smiling when she finally found a wrapped sweet which had obviously been hidden there for her. Menders outlined more of life at The Shadows and answered Kaymar's questions. Then, saying he had to dress for dinner, he turned Kaymar over to the Princess for a short tour of the house.

Within minutes Kaymar was completely charmed by his little kinswoman. They poked their heads into the kitchen and Kaymar had the unique experience of being greeted by assassins of his acquaintance who were wearing dinner dress and aprons. They spoke cheerfully and said that once he'd eaten Cook's meal, he would never want to leave.

By the time the Princess had shown him the other rooms on the ground floor and introduced him to her friend, Hemmett, who announced that he was the Princess' Guard and had been since she was born, Kaymar had lost his heart to her.

She's hope for Mordania, he thought with an unfamiliar surge of happiness. Something worth caring about.

***

In his room, Menders automatically changed into dinner attire while letting his mind reflect on his interview with Kaymar Shvalz.

The young man was unnerving. Though stunningly attractive, his movements were calculated and silent, almost reptilian. His facial expressions were so carefully guarded that he seemed soulless. It was obvious he deliberately assumed a sinister mien, despite his pretty features. His exaggerated upper-class Southern Mordanian drawl was peculiar and took some getting used to.

There had been moments during their meeting where Kaymar's carefully cultivated guard had slipped and Menders, able to watch covertly from behind his dark spectacles, had seen more than the young man probably suspected.

Kaymar Shvalz was hiding a profound sadness beneath his projected exterior of calculation and menace. At first Menders had been put off. He'd decided to dismiss the young man with the coldly blank expression and occasional worrying nervous tics, thinking perhaps he had made a mistake in agreeing to see him.

Watching Kaymar with Katrin had changed his mind. The young man obviously drew hope and perhaps inspiration from her.

Kaymar had not given up on himself. If that was the case, then neither would Menders.

***

Doctor Franz appeared agitated all through dinner. He kept glaring at Kaymar, then giving Menders exasperated looks. When Menders retired to his study after dinner, as was his custom, Franz wasn't long in appearing.

"Menders!" Franz blustered in. "Have you lost your mind?"

"Not yet. I was expecting you, Doctor. Do sit down. Brandy?"

"What? Oh, quite nice of you. But have you gone mad? Do you know who that is? That young man who joined us for dinner?"

"I introduced him, didn't I? Kaymar Shvalz," Menders said, pouring brandies for them both.

"Yes, but... did you know he's..."

"My cousin, yes."

"What?"

"Kaymar is my first cousin."

Franz took a big gulp of brandy, then shook his head. "That's what I thought you said. Do you also know he's mad as a spoon?"

"I know he's had some difficulties."

"Difficulties my spotted pink arse! I attended that young man in Erdhan, on..."

"On at least two occasions."

Franz looked stunned. "But how could you know?"

Menders sat back in his chair. "I make it my business to know what goes on, not just here at The Shadows but elsewhere. When you or anyone leaves here, to go to Erdhan or Erdstrom or anywhere else, I know where you go and what you do."

"You bloody well spy on me?" Franz's face was beginning

to go the color of fine old wine.

"Spy? No. I just know where you are in case anything happens to you. If you were taken ill or injured, I'd have you cared for. If you were suddenly arrested on some mad whim of the Queen, I'd arrange your release. If, gods forbid, you were kidnapped to be used as a bargaining chip by factions bent on attacking us or getting information from you – well, I'd want to know that too."

Franz looked taken aback. "Oh. That's different. I didn't think about it like that."

"Now, getting back to your misgivings about our young friend," Menders prompted, seeing that Franz was sufficiently settled to speak reasonably.

"Cousin!" Franz humphed. "You might have bloody well told a fellow."

"I appoint people to be here on merit, not because of family ties. Kaymar Shvalz being my cousin is a coincidence. Furthermore, he's not in my employ, nor is he in the employ of the Crown. He refuses to take a pennig for his services, says that he wants to be his own man. Now, tell me what you can. Kaymar has already written to me that you treated him in Erdahn when the Queen last sent for you. He's also admitted to me, very openly, that he has been mad in the past. I realize that he's not entirely stable now. It's obvious."

"And you're letting him be responsible for Katrin?" Franz asked incredulously.

"Tell me what I need to know," Menders replied, his patience wearing.

"All right." Franz rose, paced a bit and lit a cigar. "I really shouldn't do this, but I think that Kaymar would allow it. I am absolutely certain that he is the person who killed a number of men in Erdahn, the Gutting Murders. I sat with that young man through several nights of delirium and raving. He gave a pretty good description of his actions."

"I was fairly sure he was the one," Menders responded.

Franz wheeled and glared at him. "Do you know he murdered a lover?" he shot back.

"Yes, he told me. It wasn't murder, it was a mission. He was carrying out a direct order."

"A lover! That's how he treats people he loves?" the astonished doctor protested.

Menders sighed. Franz would never understand how assassins worked – or why.

"Franz, the man he killed was involved in a plot that included, among other things, a very workable plan to kill Katrin, the Queen and Princess Aidelia. Tragically, Kaymar fell in love with him – a terrible thing for an assassin to go through. Even if Kaymar had spared him, his lover was a dead man walking. He would have been executed by roasting spit. Kaymar eliminated him, I'm sure, in a painless manner. It's hard for you to understand, but he had no other choice and was merciful in what he did, at enormous cost to himself."

"Yes, I saw that cost," the doctor said. "He's a very damaged young man, Menders. I can't see him being an adequate guardian for Katrin."

"I can. He has a great capacity for self-sacrifice, as well as a capacity for ruthlessness. His record is exemplary. As for the murders – they're regretful for the damage they have done to him, but none of those men are any loss to anyone. I know why he did it. Frankly, I agree with his actions. Unfortunately he lacked the maturity and detachment that would have saved him considerable pain over what was, essentially, a violation of his own moral code."

Franz threw up his hands in defeat. "Nothing I say is going to change your mind," he fumed.

"I will watch very carefully," Menders assured him. "If I see anything I consider untoward, or if I think he is not prospering here, I will change things immediately. But I believe he's going to be an excellent addition. He needs rest and quiet. He'll get it here. I'm sure he'll repay any kindness we show him a thousand fold."

"From your mouth to the gods' ears," Franz sighed. Then he looked sharply at Menders.

"Just out of curiosity, what would happen if I was kidnapped by someone bent on holding me for ransom?" he asked.

Menders face became unreadable. Franz blanched.

"On second thought, don't answer that. I expect it would go badly for me?"

"You know I could never bargain or give in to such people. Katrin's safety always comes first," Menders replied without inflection.

"Yes, I expected as much. Would have thought less of you had you said anything else."

"There's more than one reason why I want you to carry a pistol with you at all times."

Franz looked away and chewed his lower lip. "I'll think about it. Goodnight."

***

From Doctor Franz's files:
Kaymar, Baronet Shvalz

Patient found to have hidden heart defect after rescuing Katrin, who fell into a deep part of the river while playing with Hemmett. Kaymar was watching the children at the time and dove into water to a depth of some twenty to thirty feet. There was considerable ice melt in the river and both Katrin and Kaymar emerged blue with cold. Katrin was unhurt, but Kaymar was in shock by the time they reached the house.

Upon examination, there is a considerable heart murmur, indicative of a hole between the chambers of the heart. Kaymar says his father died of heart failure at a relatively early age (44). To date he denies any particular heart symptoms, though his past history of injury and severe infection could have a bearing on his heart's condition.

This should not affect Kaymar's ability to perform his usual duties. He is difficult for people to warm to, as his behavior can be off-putting, but the approval and warmth he has been shown since saving Katrin has brought him out of his shell and he's shown the denizens of The Shadows his winsome and charming side.

It is my recommendation that Kaymar be carefully watched, and that he take certain precautions regarding his health. Compliance will undoubtedly be sketchy – his is a wayward nature and his usually submerged madness leads him to occasional episodes of self-injury. It will be necessary to be watchful of the Baronet.

***

The White Beast of winter came, and with it the Thrun. They were fascinated by Kaymar's stunning looks and prowess with any weapon. Tharak, unimpressed by Kaymar's most off-putting glare, cupped the young man's fine chin in his hand, looked into the sea-blue eyes, and told him his Thrun name was Light Behind Clouds. Menders could tell Kaymar was honored, though he shrugged it off with a display of indifference.

Winterfest followed the Thrun carnival. It was the first 'big' Winterfest celebration with all the new Menders' Men and their companions seated at a huge table in the Great Hall, a roaring fire in the massive stone fireplace and decorations hung from the high ceiling beams. It was declared a great success and was set to continue as a Shadows tradition.

***

"So, have you a verdict on Kaymar joining the household?" Menders asked Franz one day while they were taking advantage of an early burst of sunny weather at the end of the winter. They stood on the steps of The Shadows, their overcoats open, hands in pockets.

"Glad to admit that my reservations were unfounded," Franz replied frankly. He rocked on his heels. "Not to say that he's entirely stable – he may never be. He's much improved though, since coming here."

"His heart?" Menders asked quietly.

Franz shrugged. "It will be a weakness for the rest of his life," he admitted. He looked sharply at Menders. "You wouldn't remove him from his position because of it, would you?"

"You have heard of the Mordanian Fireboats by now," Menders said quietly, keeping his back to Franz.

"Of course. I treated Kaymar before you ever laid eyes on him," the doctor responded, his voice growing heated. "I know just what went into making Kaymar what he is. Menders, you can't be thinking of letting him go. You saw how he blossomed when everyone warmed to him after he dove into the river after Katrin. I believe that he will continue to stabilize and heal with time. This is home to him, Menders. He's devoted to protecting Katrin."

"There were over one hundred young boys designated as the Fireboats," Menders continued, as if Franz had not spoken. "There are three of them still alive."

Franz flinched.

"Kaymar is the sanest of the three," Menders continued softly. "The other two are hopelessly mad. They have been moved to my villa in Surelia, where they will be cared for as all Mordania's veteran servicemen should be."

"You can't be thinking of sending Kaymar there!" Franz burst out. "He – I know he covers up with all that sarcasm and hostility, but that boy worships you, Menders! If you sent him away, I couldn't begin to describe what would happen to him. This is a fragile soul we're talking about here. Damn it, man, don't just stand there with your back to me!" Doctor Franz was in full flight.

"I know that," Menders answered. "Kaymar will stay here. He is my cousin, my own flesh and blood. I would never send him away. He has more than proven himself and we will deal with his illness, of body and mind, as need be."

He turned and smiled at Franz.

"Mordania's last Fireboat has found safe harbor," he said.

CHAPTER 23
"I'LL CUT SOME WOOD AND FEED THE DOGS"

As farm work slowed in the autumn, Menders wanted to assure some revelry took place before the bad weather set in. He scheduled the first winter dance earlier than usual. He hoped musically inclined assassins would be interested in joining the farmer's dance band, thereby improving the quality of the music.

Franz watched with amusement and surprise as several of the assassins took a turn playing with the group.

"Musical killers?" he asked.

"Naturally. If you're on a mission disguised as a Court musician, you'd have to be able to play more than Chase My Cat," Menders answered, striking a pose in his new suit. "We all learned to play. I play three instruments myself and was trained to sing as well."

"Aren't we full of ourselves tonight?" Franz said sarcastically, looking around the Great Hall. "These women must have scoured the district to find so many new dresses."

Menders surveyed the room. The estate farmer's daughters were decked out as never before. Requests for bolts of fabric had been coming into his office since midsummer. There were also women present he'd not seen at previous dances, some from the village, some from as far away as Erdstrom.

"It's quite a hen party," Menders remarked. "They must have heard about my new suit."

"Since you're not shopping for a wife, they've probably heard about your pack of single males, you idiot," Franz grinned. "Do you have any idea how many unmarried women there are in Mordania? Bring in a bunch of accomplished young men built like gods and what do you expect? The ladies are lined up and primed and ready to try to catch one of your pretty young knife artists."

Menders laughed. He'd not thought of it, but then he'd blocked out that part of his life completely since sending Ermina away.

"I'd better warn the fellows," he said.

"Leave them alone, they're big boys. Everyone in the world doesn't want to be celibate either, that's your particular aberration. Most of those men would be glad to be caught, mark my words."

"Well, they're free to marry and romance all they want, so long as they're not leaving strings of broken hearts… or other little reminders around," Menders shrugged.

"A great many of these ladies are having a very good look at you too, my boy," Franz said, rocking contentedly on his heels, his hands in his pockets.

"Well they can look all they like. After all, I am stunning," Menders grinned. "And I'm also the best dancer in the place."

"You'll have plenty of partners," Franz answered, knowing it was pointless to go on. Since Ermina had left, Menders had remained staunchly celibate, despite opportunity. He was, as always, polite and deferential to women and he enjoyed their company, but romance was not on his mind. Franz didn't care for the situation. It was simply not normal for young man not twenty-five years of age.

Menders had given up explaining to Franz. Domestic squabbles hit him directly in the gut. He had a long fuse – all assassins did, it was a requirement for the profession – but every fuse has its limit and Ermina had pushed him dangerously close to lashing out a number of times. He was more than content to dance and flirt mildly with the ladies present tonight, and no more.

A valtz was struck up by the makeshift band and Lady Reisa Spartz came to him, curtseying, an invitation to dance.

Elegantly, Menders bowed low, lifted her from the curtsey and swept her out onto the floor.

"You'll have Franz looking out patterns for my wedding gown," he smiled at her, making her laugh.

Reisa was a dear friend of Lady Keel, the widow Franz had been involved with since coming to The Shadows. At one time Franz and Lady Keel were determined that Menders and Reisa, who was recently widowed and the mother of an infant girl, would make a wonderful match. Franz tormented and teased until Menders, to get some peace, agreed to go along with him to a gathering at Lady Keel's home.

He and Reisa enjoyed each other's company, laughed at each other's jokes, played duets on the spinet together, had the same opinions about many things. It was a match made in heaven – except that it would never be anything more than a friendship

"How can you possibly not be attracted to her?" Franz had thundered, absolutely ready to tear his hair out. "She's magnificent!"

"Yes, she is," Menders admitted. And she was, a white blonde with the figure of a goddess and eyes the color of the sea on a sunny day. "But it's not going to happen. She's not ready after her husband's death. Her scars are still fresh. I am not going to commit to anything. Not now, maybe not ever."

"Menders, sometimes I think you're simply not human," Franz had growled, refusing to speak any more on the way home.

Suddenly Menders realized there was a small folded paper in Reisa's hand, and he raised his eyebrows. Passing a note during a dance was a technique used by the more risqué ladies at Court when requesting an assignation with a man – hardly Reisa's style at all.

"It's not that," she said quietly. "It's a message someone has risked much to
send you. A lady you know. I'm sorry that I could not get it to you discreetly before now."

Menders reversed step, thinking. Reisa had returned from Erdahn just today, leaving a Court appointment after only a few weeks. He didn't know many ladies she might have run across unless...

"A lady I knew when I was in school?" he asked.

"Indeed."

Cahrin then. He thought a bit. She must have insisted Reisa give Menders the note in secret, even though the Shadows was secure. As an assassin's wife, Cahrin knew never to take chances when information was vital.

"Is she still enjoying the Court?" Menders asked, forcing himself to smile sociably.

"No. She has gone to her husband's family home in the country. It is not pleasant at Court. It's why I came home."

"I gather you'd rather not talk about it?"

"If you would be so kind." Reisa smiled, but the smile was brittle. Her reticence tied in with the grim rumors he'd heard of the decline in morals and living conditions at Court. They danced on in silence, the folded square of paper burning a hole in his palm.

As soon as propriety allowed, Menders left Reisa, ducked into his office, lit the lamp and opened the note.

Menders,

In great haste — word from G. Dalmanthea to Bartan. Duke Manus is the leader of the faction, and intends to move to assassinate Katrin during the winter months. Olner listening for more information, Bartan also. This is a very serious threat, watch carefully. Enclosing G.D.'s note

Cahrin

Beneath Cahrin's writing was pasted another paper.

My dear Bartan,

I have heard that Sir Slippery Eel, one Menders, is trying, from his country banishment, to find just who is after the Royal Family, particularly the little Princess. Without a doubt it is Manus, who has been in collusion with various parties in Artreya regarding removal of the present Royal Family. He intends to put the Duchess of Ernst on the Throne. Though the present Queen of Mordania is hopeless, Ernst would be worse, as she is a blazing nationalist and bent upon war with Artreya. This would play into the hands of Atreyan munitions barons, thus their interest and support of Manus' plot.

So pass this to my stealthy colleague with my compliments and tell him to let that great idiot, Ifor Trantz, know that those damned shoes he sold me, which he promised would stop pinching once they were broken in, still pinch. I shall get even with him one day. I owe him a hundred flagellations for every blister.

Gladdy D.

Despite the gravity of the matter, Menders couldn't help smiling. His onetime nemesis, Gladdas Dalmanthea, was the first female freelance spy and assassin on Eirdon. She was brilliant and ruthless at her work. He would never doubt her word or her accuracy when it came to information. Gladdas was an odd kettle of fish, to say the least, and the terror of more than one assassin, but Menders had always hugely enjoyed her sardonic, sarcastic sense of humour. He also appreciated her skill, her vast fund of knowledge and her massive network of informants.

Gladdas could be very valuable to him as a source of information. He would write to her, once this matter of Duke Manus was settled.

He went looking for Ifor and found him avoiding the dance in the Men's Lounge.

"Just passed to me," Menders said, handing Ifor the note.

"From Cahrin and Olner, but the information was originally from Gladdas Dalmanthea."

"In that case, it's to be taken seriously," Ifor nodded, scanning the notes. "It would fit. Manus is a longtime champion of the Duchess of Ernst. He has the money and influence to pull off the assassinations."

"Using whom?"

"Possibly Surelian assassins. If they were using any of our people, I like to think I'd know about it."

After a moment Menders said, "Put Kaymar on it with two support agents – yourself and Bertel. I need to know the extent of Manus' involvement and to what degree the Duchess is involved, if she's a player or simply a puppet. I want Kaymar well protected. He'll want to take risks, but you're to prevent that."

"Done," Ifor said quietly, rising and walking toward his office.

Later that evening, Menders unlocked the tall, black iron cabinet in his office and studied the shelves of dossiers within.

Menders had begun to fill in long winter days and nights by compiling all the information he could gather about anyone connected to the Royal Family. He now had over a hundred dossiers on various individuals.

He drew out a folder labeled 'MANUS', sat at his desk, opened the file and began to turn the pages.

***

A few days later Ifor brought a pile of papers to Menders.

"It's Manus for sure," he said, keeping his voice lower than its usual bass rumble. "He's cocky, been talking big, as we guessed he would. The Duchess of Ernst is insistent that the Princesses must be eliminated along with the Queen so there is no obstacle to her inheriting. Manus agrees to the idea."

Menders nodded, showing no emotion.

"Do we have a timetable?" he asked.

"Within the next month," Ifor responded.

Menders' mind was ticking. Was Katrin most secure here, under guard, or better moved to another place, like a safe house? No. A move would expose her and it could be just what their adversary wanted, like flushing gamebirds into the open. Who else was involved, and needed to be eliminated lest they begin another plot later? There could be no survivors among those involved in this venture.

"What other details do we have?" he asked quietly.

"I'm not sure if the Queen's Council and security are aware or not," Ifor replied. "As much as Manus is talking, I can't believe that isn't the case. I can find no indication that any action is being taken."

"Odd," Menders commented.

"Very, unless the Council is tacitly approving the removals. That's difficult to believe, Council heads would roll if Ernst gets on the Throne. It could be that they have a very covert plan of their own, or it could be they've become so lax and incompetent that they're just going to hope nothing happens. It's also possible they're so complacent that they aren't aware of what is going on."

"I bet on the latter, unless they foolishly think Ernst will be someone they can control," Menders said. "Double the guard, standing and mobile patrols on foot and mounted, armed at all times," he said. "If people ask, we'll say they're hunting parties looking to lay up food for the winter. No one is to go about unarmed. Doctor Franz may have to curtail his visits to the village and beyond for a while."

"He won't like that, you know. Cares too much about his patients."

"Then he will have to go armed and escorted."

"He won't like that either. Says he'd rather carry a live snake than a pistol."

"He also won't like my boot up his karzi but it has to be this way. If he complains, tell him to see me."

Ifor nodded and went to his office to set things in motion.

Menders seethed with rage. In a coup it was not uncommon for younger heirs to a throne to be spared. They might be sent into exile or kept very close at hand and in sight. Katrin had only just turned five years old, but her cousin wanted her murdered. Unnecessary and cruel – but then, cruelty was embraced and considered evidence of strength by many members of the Royal Family.

Kaymar, posing as a very young servant fresh from the country, had infiltrated Duke Manus' household, where he had been able to uncover very sensitive information. Duke Manus was an infamous pederast. Menders had ordered Kaymar to play the Duke along, but to avoid his attempts at seduction – not only to preserve his cover, but his fragile sanity as well. Kaymar had the support of Bertel and Ifor Trantz as his contacts in Erdahn. The three of them were proving to be a formidable team.

Unfortunately, the amount of time Menders had to wait for the information they gleaned was frustrating. The train ran once a week, unless a special was arranged. Sending out frequent specials would draw attention. It was possible to send messages from Erdahn to The Shadows more quickly by boat. Ifor was an expert boat pilot and was acting as courier, but at best messages took hours to reach Menders. A situation might alter completely by the time his orders were sent back, and action could not be taken until another agonizingly slow exchange of information took place.

Staring gloomily out at the snow, Menders tried to clear his head. So far he had been unable to come up with a plan to eliminate Manus and the Duchess of Ernst that would not arouse suspicion.

"Menders?" Katrin's voice cut into his thoughts. He

smiled and turned to see her peeping over the edge of his desk.

"Yes, Little Princess?" he answered.

"Why are you angry?"

I will never be able to hide a thing from this child, he thought. We've been together so much that she picks up every nuance. He lifted her onto his lap before turning back to the window.

"I'm angry because there are some people who want to change the way things are, including us living at The Shadows," he said, knowing this was something she could understand. "You don't need to worry about it, because I'm seeing to it that nothing bad happens."

"Then it's all right," she said definitely.

"Very much all right."

"Is that why I've been sleeping in your bed?" she asked.

"Yes, it is, but you always came and got in my bed anyway, didn't you?"

She nodded. "But now you put me to bed in your bed," she observed.

"Just for now. Soon this will all be over and you'll be able to sleep in your own bed again," he said.

"I can still come and get in bed with you then, if the frogmouth comes?" she asked.

"Absolutely. Just like you always have." He had to smile, knowing that most of Katrin's visitations from her particular nightmare monster, a blue-faced frogmouthed creature, were bogus by this time.

"Will you draw a picture for me?" she asked a little plaintively. He had spent so much time on the current threatening situation that he hadn't been able to devote much time to her.

"Absolutely," he responded, turning them toward the desk. "What shall I draw?"

"Wolves."

Menders smiled. Northern Mordanian wolves were the

interest of the moment. Early snowfall meant the wolves were hungry and coming close to the house, sending out lone scouts to sniff around while the pack hung back in the trees, watching with glowing yellow eyes. Menders had no fear of them, as plenty of preventive measures had been taken to bar them from the house. The wolves' nightly serenades of howling caught Katrin's imagination and she listened with delight.

"Wolves it is," Menders declared. Deft strokes of his pencil brought out intense eyes, long sloped down ears, three-toed paws with reptilian claws, mouthfuls of ragged teeth. They were in the classic stance of shoulderpoint high, muzzles held low, hind legs crouched as if ready to pounce. Some rapid cross hatching and texturing brought out fur and long shadows across snow. He handed the page to Katrin to color with the crayons he'd brought her from the village. She sat opposite him at his desk, happily making the wolves even more frightening by coloring their eyes with red centers.

Watching her, his mind returned to the problem of the coming coup attempt and what he could do to stop it. He couldn't get to Erdahn; he couldn't leave Katrin without his protection and Kaymar said Manus and the Duchess of Ernst were closely guarded there. If an assassin got past all the people he had in place now, they would have to get through him before they could reach Katrin. He had not been a working assassin for five years but it would take a very accomplished and brave man to go through Menders.

If he could get Duke Manus and the Duchess anywhere near him, he could eliminate them himself. It would be best to make it look accidental, to avoid uncomfortable questions. Even if a trail did lead back to him, he could expose the plot and claim it was done for the protection of Queen and country. But he would much rather it look as if the plotters had come to an accidental and untimely demise, with their killer remaining safely anonymous.

Katrin was coloring one of the wolves a particularly vibrant shade of blue, making Menders smile. Then the smile faded.

Wolves... now there was something. Yes! Northern Mordanian wolves were fearless and had been known to attack people in buildings, and even railway carriages. His mind began to work on it.

***

My Dear Fahren,

Your correspondence has been greatly appreciated. It gives me a very clear picture of your daily life in Erdahn. I was most impressed to hear of your recent appointment to the service of His Grace, Duke Manus. This is a great opportunity for one so young and I'm certain you will prosper in this new venture.

So far it has been a most delightful winter here in Old Mordania. Snow sports are proving very pleasant and popular, even with me despite the cold I have had. Should your employer be seeking to remove from the Capitol during the next month, you might suggest a holiday at his estate near Erdstrom. Though there is good snow cover, the days have been quite clear and comfortable. The trains are going through regularly.

We are all well here, and look forward to seeing you again. Write as often as you can with all your news.

In friendship,

Your old Headmaster
Mister S

Dear Mister S,

It was with great relief that I had your note of a week ago. I was very glad to hear of your returning health and enjoyment of outdoor activity, even in this cold weather. I gave your recommendation to His Grace and he felt that it would be just the thing for his own constitution, having been fond of winter sport when he was a boy. He has reason to wish to leave Erdahn at present, as he finds the atmosphere during winter stifling, particularly the fogs. He was glad of the reminder of his country estate and the crisp weather that blesses Old Mordania at this time of year.

He and his cousin, Her Grace the Duchess of Ernst, will be travelling with myself and several of their closest companions to His Grace's country home west of Erdstrom on the seventeenth of this month by special train. Since that will bring me near you, I am hoping I will be able to take the opportunity to visit you and your charming daughter. His Grace assures me there will be plenty of time for me to see my parents and brother as well. You know I miss them a great deal, so I'm very excited about this journey.

Closing now, at one, and will post this in the morning.

Sincerely,

Fahren

I have you now, Manus, you bastard, Menders thought as he perused the note from Kaymar, disguised as a chatty letter from an ex-student to a favorite teacher. Knowing Kaymar's style, he read between the lines.

Duke Manus was leaving Erdahn prior to the coup attempt and would go to his estate near Erdstrom to await the outcome. He would be travelling with the Duchess of Ernst and several others by train, and would be in the vicinity of The Shadows at one in the morning on the seventeenth. Kaymar, the Duke's new, trusted employee, would be with them.

He took the note to Franz, who read it and raised his eyebrows.

"Perfect location, the bastard will go right past our door. Just what do you have in mind?" he asked.

"I'll cut some wood and feed the dogs," Menders answered quietly.

***

The Royal Train slowed, then halted on the stretch of track between Rondstein and Erdstrom, twenty miles south of Shadows Halt. There was a particular cutting in the area known to be difficult in the wintertime. A warning lantern hung from a post. Something was blocking the track ahead.

The engine simmered with escaping steam and the air pumps thumped rhythmically. The fireman climbed from the engine and walked away down the track. He returned shortly.

"Tree down on the track," he told the engineer tersely. "We can move it, I think, it's not very big - but not while dragging this lot." He indicated the line of darkened carriages. The engine was fitted with a heavy metal plow for just such situations. Best to work without the weight of the carriages slowing things down and risking derailment – or worse, waking the high and mighty folk sleeping the night away in their berths. It was late, just gone one in the morning.

The men uncoupled the engine and then steamed away to begin the slow and careful process of pushing the tree off the tracks.

As the engine disappeared, a slender shadow separated from the dark forest nearest the carriages, moving across the snow with feline grace. It sprang onto the platform of the last carriage as the door opened silently from within.

Menders nodded to Kaymar. The two men moved into the carriage like oiled shadows, turning toward the curtained sleeping compartments.

Kaymar gestured to one compartment, then drew aside the curtains shrouding another. He stabbed the slumbering Duke Manus directly in the heart, killing him instantly. Menders simultaneously cut the snoring throat of Her Grace, The Duchess of Ernst. Kaymar indicated two other sleeping forms, fellow conspirators of the freshly dispatched pair. It only took a few more seconds to eliminate all the plotters who had wanted Katrin dead.

Kaymar and Menders hefted the limp and leaden form of Duke Manus, dragging it from the carriage and dropping it in the snow beside the railway line. Menders, wielding a small hatchet, hacked at the carriage door and door frame, making deep gouges like claw marks. Then the two men closed the door before shouldering it open again, snapping the lock and shattering the glass window. Menders took a handful of coarse wolf hair from his pocket and dragged it across the broken glass until several tufts snagged there.

Leaving the carriage door open, the cousins jumped from the platform and disappeared into the tree line.

Moments later, the wolves came snaking across the snow, half mad with winter hunger, smelling the blood. They tore at the body of Manus. The bolder ones leapt onto the rear platform of the railway carriage, where the blood smell from within was most tantalizing.

In the trees, Menders watched without emotion.

"Our dinner guests have arrived."

Kaymar shivered with cold as he tore off his bloody clothes. There would be no trace of the young servant who had travelled with the Duke's party other than shredded bloody clothing some distance from the train. He dressed in the garments Menders had brought for him as rapidly as he could.

Menders handed the reins of Franz's gelding to Kaymar and sprang onto Demon's back. Demon circled and snapped, eyes wheeling like fireworks, anxious to get away from the snarling knot of wolves congregated around the body of Duke Manus.

They rode silently away.

Down the line, the engine shuttled forward and back, moving the tree inch by inch. In the carriage, the hungry wolves feasted on fresh meat. Outside, more snowflakes began sifting down, drifting into pools of rapidly cooling blood.

***

In Erdahn, the news of the brutal deaths of His Grace, Duke Manus and Her Grace, The Duchess of Ernst, third in line to the Throne, was greeted with shock. Horribly, they had been killed by wolves when the Royal Train, en route to the Duke's country estate, stopped because of a tree down on the tracks. In the absence of the seasoned engine crew, who would have prevented the Duke leaving the safety of his carriage to ascertain the reason for the delay, ravenous wolves had attacked the Duke before jumping into the open carriage, killing the Duchess and the other members of the party.

People from the city just didn't understand the dangers of country visit in winter. There was far too much danger of being snowed in and not being able to get back to civilization. Really, something should be done about those wild wolves, but they numbered in the millions. It would be like trying to eliminate the Thrun. Such a pity.

At The Shadows, Menders watched Katrin playing in the snow with Hemmett and smiled. A note on his desk from Cahrin had let him know that the assassins employed by Manus to kill the Queen, Princess Aidelia and Katrin had been eliminated. An additional note was enclosed, a response to a rapidly penned missive he'd sent out with Kaymar.

Ah, Menders, the original Slippery Eel,

My congratulations on your masterful work on the Manus situation. Wickedly adept and worthy of you.

I am made aware by your blue-eyed cousin that you are interested in a fair exchange of information and a combining of our networks of sources. I can use your input as to the goings on in Old Mordania and beyond, particularly your Thrun connections. Therefore, consider it done.

I do find it amusing that you are now playing foster papa for a little girl, but you'll make a good job of it. She's a fortunate child. Let's hope she has some worthwhile potential and lacks the less pleasant attributes that have surfaced in her other family members.

Should further threats become known to me, I shall send word immediately.

The best to you,

Gladdy D.

The Duke of Manus' coup was a failure. The Queen was still secure on the Ruby Throne and Menders' network of informants had increased a thousand fold.

Most of all, Katrin was safe – at least for now.

CHAPTER 24
EIREN

A wagon passing The Shadows caught Menders' eye as he peered through the telescope on the roof. It was the Spaltzes, going to the halt. Eiren was coming home today.

Normally he and Katrin would have gone too but Katrin and Hemmett had come down with aching fever, a childish complaint most people endured by the time they were ten. Both children had light cases and spent much of their sickroom time constructing tents from Katrin's bedcovers, in imitation of the Thrun. Unfortunately Lucen had also contracted the disease. In adults it was a grave matter indeed. Menders had gone to the roof for some air after tending the big man, who muttered and tossed in delirium, the fevers climbing very high before they broke.

No-one from the Shadows had gone near the Spaltz farm of late, for fear of spreading aching fever to the Spaltz children and from there to the entire district. Seeing Eiren would have to wait.

It was late spring and the trees were fully leaved. They screened Menders' telescopic view of Shadows Halt. The guard on surveillance duty returned from lunch and Menders went back inside before catching a glimpse of Eiren's return.

She had covered herself with glory in her years at teacher's college, graduating at the head of her class and receiving many honors. She'd been deluged with offers of work, but had turned them all down, determined to come back to The Shadows to start her school.

Mister Spaltz had overhauled and completely painted the little building she intended to use. Franz and Menders supplied the money for it to be stocked with furniture, books and everything else that a small school could need.

Eiren had worked incredibly hard, taking on more studies

than the teachers' college curriculum required. Her letters over the years had reflected the rapid expansion of her intellect. Menders would miss receiving them. They had been a constant source of amusement and amazement, because the young girl had forged ahead so quickly. Over time her letters had grown longer and erudite, no longer chatty missives about weather and classmates. Instead, they became considerable windows into Eiren's views on religion, philosophy, science and the arts — whatever happened to be the topic that engaged her bright and enquiring mind at a particular time.

Menders wended his way to Katrin's room, where whoops of laughter let him know the invalids probably needed to be reined in a bit.

Sheets festooned the room, propped on anything that would hold them up, including Menders' chair from his office. Hemmett was sitting cross-legged in one 'tent', trying to imitate Tharak's impassive mien with little success, while Katrin pranced around on an invisible horse, giving a great show of horsemanship.

"For sick children you certainly make a lot of noise," Menders said, leaning against the doorjamb and grinning.

"We aren't sick!" Hemmett declared. "Time to let us go outside!"

"Oh, you aren't sick? Who was aching and miserable last night and cried and had to be held and rocked?" Menders asked, ducking down and crawling into the 'tent'. "And who said you could take my chair?"

"I did," Katrin said, crawling in behind him. "You weren't sitting in it, so I thought you wouldn't mind if we used it."

"Get your brush, your hair is a mess," Menders told her. When she returned with the requested item, he undid her frowsy braids, and began brushing through the rich golden waves. While she was really sick, her hair got into a horrific tangle, which had taken ages to brush out, an experience neither of them wanted to repeat.

"Rat's nest, rat's nest!" Hemmett chanted teasingly. Katrin made a face at him.

"Enough of that," Menders warned. To keep them distracted, he began on another episode of the fairy tales he constantly spun for Katrin, about the Dark Knight and his beloved Princess, who had all sorts of adventures involving dragons and evil kings. Hemmett nodded off soon, his head pillowed on Menders' thigh. Menders finished with Katrin's hair, braided it neatly and then let her settle back against him as he had the Princess outsmart a terrible wizard and free the Dark Knight from a deep dungeon full of bones.

"That's the best story you've told yet," she sighed rapturously. She loved the fairy tales and would listen as long as Menders spun them out.

"Glad you liked it, Little Princess," he smiled, putting an arm around her. "I saw Eiren coming home when I was on the roof."

"How did she look?" Katrin asked, looking up at him with a delighted smile.

"I didn't actually see her, I just saw her family going past and the smoke from the train. I came down before they went back on their way to the farm."

"Can't we go over there tonight?"

"No. I explained to you that you can't carry this sickness over to them."

"I thought I was better."

"Not that much better. You have to wait a while longer, I'm afraid, at least two weeks."

"Two weeks," she sighed disgustedly.

"I'm afraid so. Work on making them pass quickly, stay busy and you'll be seeing Eiren before you know it."

"I wonder if she got taller and if her hair is as long as mine," Katrin cogitated.

"Very likely. My legs are going to sleep, so let's get out of this Thrun tent and get Hemmett to bed, shall we? You go ahead."

***

Two weeks later, Mister Spaltz dropped in. He sat around with some of Menders' Men for a while, won considerable money from them in card games, then grinned at Menders.

"Now that everyone here is over the aching fever, you should take a jaunt by Eiren's school. The older children are working the farms, of course, but she has the younger ones at school now. They're having a wonderful time and she was saying the other day that she regretted not coming to see the Princess and yourself before now, but didn't want to risk bringing the fever back to the little ones. She lets the children go at a little before three."

"I'll make a point of it," Menders said. "I'm glad to hear it's going well."

"Oh, it is indeed. I want to see about getting a stove in there for them before autumn. We have one up at the farm just sitting in the barn. I might borrow a couple of your men to help with that."

"You're welcome to them." Menders accepted a puff off a newly lit cigar and poured another glass of wine for Mister Spaltz.

He'd intended to go by the school but the usual welter of summer work had sidetracked him. Best not to delay longer or Eiren would think that he might be offended or avoiding her. He was eager to see what she was doing. Demon was itching for a good run, so the next afternoon Menders let him gallop to his heart's content across the estate, coming back by way of the school at three in the afternoon.

As he approached, a knot of children came scuffling and

prancing through the school door. They ran over to him.

"Behave yourself," he admonished Demon, glad he'd let the farlin run off most of his cantankerousness.

"Be careful now," he warned the children, who were gleefully holding up papers and books for him to look at, with a chorus of "Mister Menders, look at my book, look at my paper, Teacher said it was good!" He admired and praised the proffered items and then watched as the children ran away down the road in a bunch, skipping and running, papers flapping and falling to the ground.

He hooked his leg around the pommel of his saddle, making himself more comfortable, and looked over toward the school.

A woman came through the door with an armful of books, turning away from him to fasten the latch. Menders wondered who she could be – Spaltz had not mentioned there being an assistant. Menders made a point of knowing everyone who was on the estate, so his interest was piqued and his senses alerted.

She was, in Franz's parlance, simply magnificent, with beautiful posture and a delectable figure. As she turned toward him, he saw that she had glowing red-gold hair arranged in an elegant upswept style, skin the color of milk with just a blush of pink and naturally pinker lips. As she walked toward him, he could see that she had eyes the color of clear brown agate. Something clicked in Menders' whirling brain – he knew those eyes from a time before, which now seemed a hundred years ago.

"Eiren?" he whispered to himself, knowing he was staring and thankful that his dark glasses hid it. The refinement she'd picked up in Erdahn was exquisite.

Eiren reached Demon's side and smiled up at him.

"Hello, Menders," she said. No 'Mister' – and for good reason. She was entirely grown up now.

"Hello Eiren," he smiled. There was a particular velvety

texture to her skin that made him want to touch it. How could this be that gangly, skinny, awkward young girl with a mouthful of teeth that were too big for her face?

"I'm glad you came by," she said, her voice a vibrant alto, the heavy Old Mordanian accent greatly moderated. "I've meant to get over to The Shadows but there's been so much to do. If everyone is well now I was going to come visiting tomorrow."

"They'll all be glad to see you, Katrin particularly. She's asked after you every day since you came home," he said, still letting his eyes, behind the blessed darkness of his glasses, rove from magnificent hair to deliciously soft lips to tender and touchable skin.

"She must be a big girl by now," Eiren said, casually placing her hand on his knee. He shivered a bit at her touch.

"She is indeed, you'll hardly know her," he said, realizing that he was being extremely rude by sitting on Demon, making her crane her neck to look at him. He slid to the ground quickly.

Eiren was a couple of inches shorter than he was. He saw that without her very elegant boots she would be a bit shorter still, the perfect height for kissing…

Dear Gods, Menders thought, what in the hells are you on about? The girl's only just come home and you're acting like a complete idiot, as if you've never seen a beautiful woman before. She must be wondering what in the world you're staring at.

He took her pile of books, clucking to Demon to follow him.

"I enjoyed your letters, very much," he said.

"I enjoyed writing them. To my surprise, I wasn't homesick after the first few weeks, but I looked on you as my link to home and all that was going on here."

"I expect there was much more happening than you put in your letters?" Of course there was, with a young lady away from home for the first time, growing up, living in a big city. There would have been no end of excitement and adventures.

And suitors, too, Menders thought suddenly.

What was he thinking of? A girl had gone away and three years later, a woman had returned, beautiful and full of grace and elegance and he was goggling at her like a cross between a smitten boy and a lecherous old man. He was old enough to be… to be? To be her big brother. He was twenty-five and she was nineteen. Once he'd seen their age difference as a gulf between a man and a child. But while he had remained static in this pokey backwater of Mordania, she had caught up with him. They were now contemporaries.

When had he begun to think of himself as old? Of course people around The Shadows often referred to him as 'the old man', meaning the man in charge. His responsibilities were those normally assigned to a senior man.

"Oh there was, indeed," Eiren said, answering his question and effectively derailing his train of thought. "All sorts of things to see and do."

"So tell me all about it," he smiled as they started ambling toward her father's house, Demon following behind.

She told him about the college, books she'd read, friends, lectures she'd sat through. Not one to dominate a conversation, she asked questions of him as well, about The Shadows and about Katrin. He began to feel more comfortable. The child he had once known was still there, more mature and enlightened. He could also observe her more carefully without seeming to stare as they walked side by side.

She knew how to dress. She knew how to walk. She wore a perfume that drifted to him and made him sigh covertly. Hands that had been red and raw from scrubbing baby clothing were smooth and white, with perfect oval nails. Hair that had been tightly wrapped in two stiff braids was a shining, glorious pile that he wanted desperately to touch, to pull the pins from and have it come cascading down in soft thick waves.

Demon nudged Menders hard in the small of the back.

When Menders glared in response, the animal rolled its eyes, as if reading his thoughts and warning him to not go making a fool of himself.

Menders was sorry but also relieved when they reached Eiren's home. He suddenly felt awkward.

"I could stop by for you tomorrow and drive you down to The Shadows," he suggested, thankful that his voice sounded confident. "You can see everyone and I'll bring you home so you won't have to walk back in the dark."

"That would be wonderful, thank you," she replied, smiling up at him.

Just then Demon, tired of standing around while people made lip music and gaped at each other, lovingly bit Menders on the left buttock.

Menders yelped and leapt and Eiren burst out laughing. Though he was completely embarrassed and ready to carve the evil little farlin up as dog food, he noticed how pretty she was as she laughed.

"With that, I leave you," he said elegantly, bowing a little to keep up the comedy. It made him too tempting a target for Demon, who nipped again.

Eiren grabbed her books from him and fled, laughing uncontrollably, while Menders, desperately trying not to rub the painfully bruised area, clouted Demon on the head with his open hand. He jumped into his saddle and left precipitously, before the animal doled out any more embarrassing abuse.

The next day Menders drove Eiren to The Shadows. She'd dressed for the occasion in a golden-tan dress that played up her beautiful complexion. Her hair was arranged so it framed her face. Menders found at one point that he had his eyes closed, drawing in a deep breath, trying to smell her perfume. Suddenly he felt her hands close on the reins in front of his. He snapped to attention and looked at her sheepishly.

"You must be tired. I thought you were falling asleep,"

she explained. "You always used to sit up late and work so hard."

"I am a little tired," he replied lamely, chirruping to the horse to trot. "It's a busy time of year."

Over the crest of the road, the dark turrets and forest of chimneys that was the Shadows' roof came into view.

"Can we stop here for a minute?" Eiren asked.

Menders reined in and set the brake.

"I didn't get a good look coming back from the halt. Everyone was talking to me at once." She inhaled deeply, one hand pressed against the lace at the base of her throat.

"It hasn't changed a bit," she sighed, exhaling slowly. "I was so afraid it wouldn't look the way I remembered it."

They smiled at each other. Menders released the brake and set the horse into motion again.

Eiren's reunion with Katrin was touching. Menders watched with delight as they embraced. At first, Katrin was stuck dumb and seemed confused, for she was obviously expecting the same Eiren she had known to return. Being a bright child, she quickly warmed to the idea that this new Eiren was the same one as before, just a grown up version.

"You're big!" Katrin finally cried with delight. Eiren picked her up and looked startled when she found it an effort.

"And you!" Eiren replied.

"And you're pretty!" Katrin added.

"Why thank you. I was starting to wonder if anyone had noticed. No more big teeth."

Behind her Menders groaned inwardly and winced. He'd been so tongue tied, he'd never even said anything! She must think him a complete idiot, rude or blind.

"We've got lots and lots of new people here now and I have a new cousin," Katrin declared. "Let me show you." Katrin took Eiren's hand, determined to introduce her to everyone who was new and reintroduce her to everyone who had known her before.

"Haven't you filled out!" Cook exclaimed, giving Eiren an enormous hug. "It is wonderful to see you again, my girl!"

"I'd forgotten how wonderful this kitchen smells!" Eiren said and was given a ginger spice cookie, just as in times past.

Lucen got very shy, shuffled his feet and nodded, while Zelia gave Eiren a hug and praised her dress. Franz walked in the door, back from his rounds. Eiren smiled and went to him, holding out her hands.

"My gods, it's little Eiren!" he bellowed, swinging her around as if they were dancing the holta. "Look at you! Not so little anymore. Erdahn was good for you, if I say so myself. You won't be single long."

"I'm not getting married but thank you for the compliment," Eiren laughed. Franz spun her around again, more slowly this time, making sure he took in every detail.

"We have dozens of young men living here now, you won't be safe," he chortled. "Why, one look at you and they'll be lined up from here to the post rail, the lucky devils." He glanced at Menders. "What's the matter with you, my lad? You look like you swallowed a toad."

"Nothing," Menders snapped.

"I can't get over how much you've changed," Franz beamed at Eiren.

"Everyone has said so – except for Menders," Eiren said, smiling over to where Menders was standing alone, separate from the others.

"That old long streak of misery? Where're your manners, sir?" Franz jeered. Menders glared over his glasses at him, which provoked raucous laughter on the part of the doctor.

"Your evil Thrun eye doesn't work on me, young man."

"Eiren, I want to show you my new swing," Katrin said, taking Eiren's hand.

"Go on, there's plenty of time before dinner," Cook encouraged. "And Hemmett's running around out there somewhere. You won't believe the size of him. Run and play, and then come back and see the rest of us old folks. Look after her, Katrin, don't let her go running off to Erdahn again."

Franz stalked over to Menders after everyone had scattered.

"You haven't so much as complimented that girl," he said gloatingly. "Now I know your heart is dead." He punched Menders.

"I don't want to seem as if I'm leering," Menders answered.

"You can hardly speak," Franz grinned. "The erudite and eloquent Menders is tongue-tied. Oh, I have lived for this moment."

"Shut up," Menders replied, embarrassed that he sounded more than a little angry. "She's still Eiren! Stop acting like a lecherous old goat!"

"Haven't even told her how beautiful she looks. Shame on you," Franz continued, gloating. "Yes, you belong in here with the rest of what Cook calls 'us old folks'." Franz retreated to the kitchen, jeering like a schoolboy.

Menders went to his office and stared out the window. He must be careful, very careful. In no way could he imply that he was attracted to Eiren. If things had been different... but they weren't. He'd been her patron, he'd sent her to school. Making advances toward her now would look as if he expected her to repay him with sexual favors. He never wanted her to think that. He would see himself burning alive and screaming in all nine hells before he ever behaved like his father.

Then he realized he was remembering the smell of her perfume, the glow of her smile, the golden highlights in her hair. Menders thumped his head on the desk. This was no time to get all foolish in love. Several short months ago, he'd murdered people in order to buy Katrin's safety and he may have to again. Danger was continually present and he must be alert and prepared. There was no time in his life for romance.

He stayed there, forehead pressed against the cool dark wood, until he heard Katrin talking outside. Then he rose and surveyed his reflection in the mirror.

He looked stern and old with his hair tied back, so he released it, then gave his glasses a polish. He wished suddenly that he didn't have to wear them, then called himself ridiculous, put them firmly in place and walked out into the hallway.

Hemmett and Katrin were both holding Eiren's hands. They were chattering away and she was laughing at the resulting gibberish. When she suggested that they give Cook some help with dinner they scampered away. Eiren looked up at Menders, smiling. He went to her.

"Eiren, I'm sorry I haven't complimented you," he said frankly. "I wanted to, but…"

"I was only teasing," she interrupted gently, looking up into his eyes. "I know you're afraid I'll think you're being forward, because you sent me to school. You are far too good a man to do such a thing."

Menders smiled with relief.

"You've come back to us as one of the most beautiful women I've ever seen," he said.

"Thank you." She tried her best to take the compliment gracefully, but then blushed and grinned.

"Oh, hells," she said, patting her reddened cheeks as she went to the dining room to check on the children. Menders watched her go.

***

Menders let the horse walk as he drove Eiren home. Eto, the larger of Eirdon's two moons was already halfway up the sky, while the late summer sunset glowed in the west.

They talked about everything now that an understanding

had been reached. He felt free and easy as she asked him about the establishment of Menders' Men. She laughed when he told her to expect a population explosion soon, because two of the Men had taken wives and were settling down nicely, with one newlywed couple already expecting. She talked about her school and the things she planned to do when the older children began to attend in the autumn. They discussed the unsettled and unhappy atmosphere in Erdahn that had disturbed her. Eiren was amazed at how knowledgeable Menders was about the situation, given his remote location. He explained how his information networks had expanded recently, which impressed her.

"Still working hard to keep everyone safe?" she said, more a statement of admiration than a question.

"It is my primary motivation. As always."

"I have always been so impressed by your ambitions," Eiren said. "But when do you spare time to see to your own happiness?"

Menders glanced at her. "I don't think about it that much."

"You should."

They drew up before the Spaltz farmhouse. He helped her from the phaeton and walked her to the door very properly, taking her hand briefly before she smiled and went inside.

After that night, Menders managed to ride by the school every afternoon at three. When Eiren appeared after her pupils were gone he would dismount, carry her books and walk along with her to her father's house.

Even on the school's two rest days, Menders found he was riding by the Spaltz farm with great frequency. It was amazing how many errands around the estate could be done if you had a fast mount like Demon, even if you made a three mile detour by the Spaltz farm every time.

Once he saw Eiren running to help her father, wearing a spring green dress that floated and swirled around her ankles. The image of her red hair trailing behind her as she ran was locked behind his closed eyes for nights to come. Many times he told himself that this was absurd, that he must stop hanging about the Spaltz farm like a lovesick boy. Eiren was his friend. She liked to talk to him about books and philosophy and she probably did think he was, as Cook had said, 'one of the old folks', not a potential suitor.

Besides, what kind of a life could he offer such a woman? He had forsworn marriage for himself. His personal situation could not come before Katrin's safety. It was best to forget childish notions of romance and keep things no more than friendly.

But he found himself dizzied by her perfume when he was with her. He caught himself staring at trees in bloom and thinking about her and told himself that he was a fool. One day, to his complete and utter embarrassment, he found himself idly staring up into a blossoming apple tree on the front lawn, only to find that Franz was watching and cackling from his window.

"Here, stop daydreaming about that girl and get some work on, you!" Franz called. Flushed with sudden anger and humiliation, Menders raced toward the house, calling out murderous intent to the grinning doctor, who emitted a girlish shriek and slammed the window. Physical abuse was only diverted by the doctor's hastily bolted office door, which he refused to open until Menders retreated to his office.

This has to stop, Menders told himself severely. This delirium – she's nineteen, you're older, soon she'll find a young man her own age. This is simply infatuation. You have heavy responsibilities and you cannot offer her what she should have out of life. So stop it, you fool! Stop it.

He couldn't. That's why they call it delirium.

**

It was a school rest day and Menders had every intention of riding Demon over to Artrim, the village eight miles distant to buy flour and sugar, at Cook's request. He also loved finding something for Katrin when he went to the village, sweets she liked, dolls, toys. Now that she was safely guarded at home without him being constantly present, he took every opportunity to spoil her.

He was cantering by Spaltz's farm when he saw Eiren walking along the side of the road, wearing her spring green dress and carrying a basket. He pulled Demon down to a walk and drew abreast of her.

"Hello," he said, trips to villages suddenly forgotten.

"Hello Menders," she smiled up at him, her expression indicating that seeing him was the best thing that had happened to her today.

"I'm just off to the village for a few things," he said.

"Oh?" Eiren replied in genuine surprise. Then she laughed brightly. "If you are, then you're going the wrong way."

Stunned, Menders turned around in the saddle and looked down the road. So he was. Blast it, he'd been daydreaming again and Demon had chosen to follow the path that had become second nature to him now, toward the Spaltz farm and school.

"Seems I missed the turn off," he said meekly.

"Papa says you're wearing a rut in the road between your place and ours," Eiren laughed.

Menders slid to the ground and let Demon follow him, giving the animal a look that let him know if he did any biting, there would be a reckoning.

"And where are you off to?" he asked her.

"I'm going fishing."

"Fishing?" Gods, he sounded like an echo – or a parrot.

"Yes. It's a wonderful way to rest. When you announce that you're going fishing it sounds like you're planning something productive. In reality you're sitting around doing nothing. If you go home with no fish, you have the perfect excuse. They aren't biting today." She chuckled a little and he had to laugh. He could understand the reasoning. Life on her father's farm was busy and difficult and even though she was now teaching she still did a great deal of work at home. What a perfect way to steal a day to herself!

"In fact, I don't like it when I do get a bite, because I have to bother to pull it in," she went on.

"I don't see any fishing poles," he observed.

"No, I just use a line. Tie it to a branch, throw it in the water and then sit and read or sleep or dream." She rummaged in the basket and held out a coil of string, with a hook flashing at one end.

"Ah – brilliant."

"Would you care to come fishing with me?" she asked, her eyes merry and teasing. "I have lunch here and a blanket so we don't have to sit in the dirt. I even have an extra fishing line. I won't make you put the worms on the hooks if you don't want to."

He could think of a million reasons why he shouldn't go off alone with her, including his iron determination to keep a distance from all women on the estate. Considering his attraction to her, he should not get himself into such a situation.

She was still waiting, looking a little hurt.

"Yes," he said, to his own amazement. "I could do with an afternoon of doing nothing, for a change."

"Good. We go to the river down this way," she said, setting out
along a worn path through the woods. Menders followed with Demon trailing along behind, bemused enough at this new activity not to bite his master's backside. Eiren moved along the path with the ease of familiarity and eventually brought them to a large oak tree on the riverbank. She set down the basket, flung out the blanket and handed him one of the coiled lines.

She baited her hook expertly, flung it into the water and tied the line to a convenient branch. She handed him a worm and laughed as he struggled with it.

"I thought you were an assassin!" she gasped after shrieking with laughter at his attempts to impale the squirming creature. "Do you think it's going to bite you?"

"The problem is that I'm not thinking in the right way," he said with mock seriousness, hardly able to keep from laughing himself. "I must consider this an assassination." With that, he steeled himself and properly baited the hook with the unfortunate worm while Eiren applauded. Once his line was in the water beside hers he settled down on the blanket, where Eiren already had the lunch basket open and was placing various farmhouse delicacies between them. She also took out two books. He picked one up with interest, wanting to see what she would find entertaining.

"Ah, a taste for poetry," he said, mimicking a doddering professor. "And very good taste at that," he continued in his own voice. She'd brought along *Sutremov's Verses*, an old favorite which he hadn't thought of in some years. He opened the book with nostalgia. The poems were deceptively simple but dropped sensual, evocative images into the subconscious.

"I can see you love them too," Eiren said as she bit into a ruddy peach.

"Yes. I haven't read them since I was a boy," he replied, perusing a page at random, letting the word pictures unfold in his mind like night-blooming lanar flowers. Setting the book aside, he examined the other.

He smiled, opening *Essays* by Tatrevich. Philosophy – another passion of his. He and Eiren had discussed the subject at length in their correspondence.

"I took philosophy courses and loved them," Eiren said.

"Your letters reminded me that I loved philosophy when I was at the Academy," Menders replied. "They reawakened my appetite for it."

Eiren smiled and spread soft farmer's cheese on a hearty slice of bread, then handed it to him. "If I know your physical appetite, you're starved."

"Always." He bit into the fragrant slice.

"What else did you read in Erdhan?" he asked.

"Everything," Eiren answered. "Everything I could find. I brought home piles of books. I spent all my rest days at the library. History, philosophy, poetry, novels, astronomy, geography, geology, newssheets, tracts – everything. I couldn't read enough. I don't miss Erdahn, but I miss the library."

He felt delight surge through him. "The library at The Shadows is always open to you," he invited, finishing the bread and cheese. He reached for one of the perfect peaches. "We have a lot of new volumes, between Franz and myself. Menders' Men have contributed too."

He found he was looking at her far too intently. He distracted himself by glancing at their fishing lines while biting into the ripe fruit.

"Do we need to check those?" he asked.

"No. If there's anything on them, the cork floats will go under," she answered, taking a small bottle from the basket, followed by two glasses. "Would you open this, please?" She handed the bottle to him.

"Gods! A bottle of your father's springberry wine! Do you know how hard it is to get one from him?"

"If you're his child, live in his house and are of age, you're free to walk right down into the cellar and get a bottle as often as you like," she laughed. "Otherwise you'll see it once a year, if he likes you and if it's a year in which a comet passes."

Menders laughed and wrenched the cork free. Mister Spaltz's springberry wine was something the gods would weep over. The scent alone was enough to make him want to roll around and sigh. Eiren poured two glasses full and handed him one.

They enjoyed the food heartily, devouring it down to the last crumb.

Menders picked up Eiren's book of poetry again, leafing through the familiar pages, letting stanzas leap out at him with a will of their own, the vivid word pictures piercing his heart.

He read his favorite poem, *Dark of the Year*, to her. She nodded when he was done.

"That's real winter. I read that during what they call winter in Erdahn and had to go hide in the bookshelves at the library until I stopped crying," she said softly. "I wanted to be home so much."

"Did you? I'm sorry you were so homesick," Menders said gently.

"Oh, I enjoyed being there – but on that day, reading that poem, yes, I was homesick. I thought of how The Shadows looked in snow, dark against the white. But I survived and now I'm here, doing what I intended to do."

"And are you happy with your choice?" he asked.

"Very happy." She looked out across the sparkling river and smiled so contentedly that he knew she was being absolutely truthful.

After a moment she turned back to pour out two more measures of wine. They were companionably silent for a time, looking out over the water.

"This is the most peaceful I've been in a very long while," Menders heard himself saying. "I always seem to be going somewhere, doing something. It's the first time I've stopped moving with purpose in months."

"I'm glad," Eiren answered. She finished her wine and put her glass away in the basket. Then she smiled.

"I guess I'm just going to have to throw myself at you," she said, burying her hands in his hair, kissing him gently and passionately on the lips.

He couldn't not respond. Within seconds they were alternately embracing, kissing and undressing each other.

The sun was low when Demon whooshed a big breath in Menders' ear, waking him abruptly. He rolled over and patted the farlin's nose. Satisfied that his master still lived, Demon moved on to munch some grass nearby. Menders turned to see Eiren waking, flushed and beautiful.

"I love you," he whispered, just as she said the same words. They laughed quietly at that, kissed, touched each other's faces, kissed again, then snuggled into each other's arms.

"Did you plan this?" he asked with some amusement.

"Well, I did gamble that you would come down the road," she replied with a wicked smile.

"What if I didn't come along any time soon?"

"I was prepared to wait for hours, if need be. And since your observational skills seemed to have disappeared, I will point out that I had two wineglasses with me, not one. So yes, it was premeditated."

"So you did. I'm a blind fool."

"No – just afraid."

"Afraid?" he asked, making a pillow of his arm so she could rest more comfortably, wrapping the blanket he had folded over them more securely so she would be warm.

"Thinking that I'd believe you were expecting me to make love to you because you sent me to school. Being so very correct and proper, so distant. I'll admit something. I've been in love with you for years. Ever since I first saw you."

"Eiren, you were just a little girl then," he protested.

"Little girls can love and be in love. I have always loved you. I knew what I wanted. I just didn't know how to get it, at least not then."

"I believe you. But I couldn't love you then, not like this, because you were just a little girl."

"Of course," she smiled. "I had to grow up."

"I'm surprised you didn't have lovers in Erdahn," he grinned, nudging the blanket down so he could look at her body again. As Franz would say, it was magnificent.

"Oh, there was some interest, but not on my part. I told them I already had someone," she replied, doing a bit of innocent preening that delighted his eye and touched his heart. "You were worth waiting for."

"I am honored," he said sincerely as she rose on one elbow, leaned over and kissed him, her hair spilling around them both. Delirium.

The light had gone the deep gold of the long northern summer evenings by the time they dressed reluctantly and folded the blanket. Eiren went to untie the fishing lines.

"Menders, you caught a fish!" she cried, laughing aloud.

"Yes, I know, a beautiful, velvety, red haired one," he grinned, picking her up and spinning around with her.

"No, you really did," she protested, pulling the line from the water when he put her down. A long, silvery fish was on his line, gasping and thrashing. Menders removed the hook and returned it to the river.

"We'll leave him for another day," he said, kissing her again.

CHAPTER 25
"THE CLOSEST THING TO MARRIAGE I CAN OFFER YOU"

The summer whirled around Menders and Eiren in a kaleidoscope of colors, sounds and scents.

He would always remember haying time because of the picture Eiren made in an old dress of blue cotton, her skirts held up, her hair caught back simply, helping the other young women trample the hay as the men pitched it into the wagons. He'd deliberately chucked a large forkful of hay right over her and ended up being deluged by armfuls of hay flung down on him by Eiren and all her friends, while the farmers laughed and pretended to scold them for emptying the wagon faster than they could fill it. The annual Haying Dance, held in The Shadows' Great Hall, was full of Eiren for him too. He partnered her in almost every dance and strolled with her in the garden between dance sets.

Dozens of secluded and beautiful spots on the estate would be forever wrapped up in images of her making love to him. He'd never see the river again without remembering the days they spent on its banks or splashing in the deep quiet "swimming place" that Eiren and her siblings called their own.

The Shadows took on new glamour for him as well because she was there so often. His office reminded him of her after she spent a rainy afternoon helping him catalogue and sort a new crate of books that had arrived from Erdahn.

He was very amused when he overheard a conversation between Franz and several of Menders' Men, who had stated their good-natured intention of niggling at Menders about "his little schoolteacher". Franz waxed furious.

"Let me tell you, that man has been through hell the last five years between getting himself mixed up with a ridiculous fool of a woman who didn't know when she had a good thing, and with struggling and working like a peasant to keep this place going almost singlehandedly. Any man who wants to twit him about being in love with a good, bright, loving and wholesome girl can just talk to me first! If anyone deserves some peace and respect, it's Menders!"

"Easy, old man," Kaymar said soothingly. "We won't disturb the courting couple since you put it that way."

Menders smiled. Any of Menders' Men could best Franz in a fistfight within seconds, but they'd heard the genuine concern in his voice and responded. He was grateful to them. He'd made no public proclamation of his love for Eiren but he'd made no secret of it either. He knew the farmers assumed that they were simply another courting couple and that in time they would settle down, marry and have babies. Apparently Menders' Men assumed the same thing.

He and Eiren had discussed their future at some length, at his insistence and to her amusement, while they lay together in their favorite spot under the oak tree by the river.

"My darling, I know you'll never marry," she said when he'd finished a long, sincere speech about his situation. "I was here for years. I've corresponded with you. I heard a lot of the ugly arguments with Ermina as well. You can't marry because the Princess comes first. I've always known and I understand. I agree with it."

He had his mouth open to explain some more, and then comprehended what she'd said.

"You agree?"

"I do. I know how important she is to you and I know how much you love her. I understand why a man with your moral courage can't stand up in front of a priest and swear to love someone exclusively just for a show. I wouldn't want you to do it. I don't have to marry you to love you. I know you aren't one for tomcatting, you never have been. I don't need you swearing to things that you could never do or be."

"You can bear being second with me?" he asked.

"Why worry about who's first and who's second?" she responded. "That's what children do, try to figure out how to stack things in some kind of order of importance."

Menders realized he must be looking like a stunned fish, because Eiren sat up, snuggling the blanket up around her.

"Are you jealous because Katrin loves me and I love her?" she asked.

"Of course not," he said instantly.

"So then why is it so hard for you to understand that I'm happy with what you have to give me?"

He still felt befuddled.

"Try thinking of it as having two loves who are first in your life, but in different ways," Eiren said after a moment.

The light flashed, and he laughed aloud.

"Then, my darling girl, you are my other first love," he said, cuddling her closer under their blanket.

"Of course I am. And if Katrin and I should ever both be drowning, you save her and shove a bit of wood in my direction and I'll be perfectly capable of saving myself," Eiren grinned.

"Gods, you overheard that argument?" he groaned, remembering Ermina shrieking the "what if we were both drowning" question at him.

"They heard that argument in Erdahn. Ermina made me so mad with that nonsense, I just wanted to bite her!"

"Here's a little secret for you – so did I," he laughed, envisioning Eiren jumping out and biting Ermina during one of Ermina's tantrums.

***

A warm autumn let them meet outdoors for many weeks, but one day Menders realized the absurdity of the situation when he felt Eiren shivering. He looked up into the glory of red-gold leaves around them, felt the chilly wind and knew that this couldn't go on.

The woman he loved was enduring discomfort to be with him. The winter would be long. Was he going to expect her to wait for months until they could be intimate outside again? Where could they possibly go? There was no inn within miles. Eiren shared a bedroom with three sisters and her baby brother.

Suddenly Menders could have shaken himself, because the answer was so very obvious and also very much what he wanted.

He pulled her closer to comfort her with his own body warmth, stroking her cheek.

"Eiren, would you come live with me at The Shadows? Be with me – and Katrin? She needs you and it goes without saying that I do. I miss you when we're apart and with winter coming... It's the closest thing to marriage I can offer you. You would be able to continue with the school, I'll get you a horse and governess cart to make it easy to get back and forth. You wouldn't be in that crush at your father's house..."

"Yes," Eiren said.

"We could say that you're Katrin's governess as well and you would be, though you're more like a mother to her – oh."

"I already said yes," Eiren smiled, coiling a strand of his hair around her fingers.

"Should I talk to your father?"

"He's always glad to have a chat," Eiren teased. "It's up to you. I'm of age, he knows I love you, he knows the situation. You don't have to ask his permission."

"I'll talk to him," Menders said.

"You worry too much but I love you for it," Eiren replied, wrapping her leg over his so she could press her cold foot against his calf.

"What do you mean, madam?" he asked, pretending to be insulted.

"You worry for all the right reasons. You don't want

people to be hurt or upset because you really care. But that means that you'll never hurt me casually or deliberately, so I gain from it."

"That's my clever girl," he smiled, kissing her.

Then he looked at his left hand, where a certain ring had been on his little finger for some time, since Eiren had come home.

He'd traded with a Thrun for it last winter. Ornate and delicate, it was not the sort of ring he usually wore – a deep tawny stone flashing with orange fire was embraced in twisting and intertwining strands of gold and silver. It just fit his little finger. He'd put it away for months until it had fallen out of his box of jewelry when he was rummaging for a particular pair of cufflinks. He'd put it on his finger then and it had remained there, despite some twitting from Menders' Men about the ladylike design.

He withdrew it from his finger and turned to her. He slipped off his glasses, the shade under the tree being deep enough. He took Eiren's left hand and poised the ring above her wedding finger – and looked into her eyes, waiting.

"Yes," she whispered. He slid the ring into place and then wrapped himself around her.

***

Despite Eiren's assurances, Menders did go to see Mister Spaltz. It was only right and he wanted to be sure that he retained the farmer's friendship. Spaltz was a bright, even brilliant man and he was the unofficial leader of the estate farmers. They looked up to him. Though Menders could stand ostracism himself, he wanted to be sure that Eiren's situation would be accepted by the families she'd known all her life.

He found Mister Spaltz in his hay barn, loading a cart. Not wanting to be impaled by the farmer's vigorously wielded pitchfork, Menders waited until Spaltz took a breather before speaking.

"Well, hello there young man!" Spaltz grinned and Menders knew everything was all right, even before he started to talk. "Our Eiren told me you'd be by. Asking for her hand then, is it?"

"If I could, I would," Menders said frankly "Has she explained?"

"Of course. Most men would just go to the altar with her and gabble through the words whether they meant them or not and never think one way or another about it. How you treat my girl day to day is what matters to me, not having a priest waving his arms around. You're right by me, youngster."

Spaltz sat down on a bale and indicated for Menders to do the same. He took out a large handkerchief and mopped his forehead.

"I must say it'll be a relief not to be keeping the younger children from spying on you and Eiren. It's been quite a job through the summer. Oh, you thought it was all secret, did you? You should know that papas aren't so blind as all that, having a little one of your own."

Menders laughed. This was going so differently than he had expected.

"Yes, and me having to go over and tell you to go see Eiren. Poor girl, she was heartbroken when you weren't at the halt, though she understood why, of course, she's no fool. But then when you didn't go to see her – well, Papa just put his finger in that little pie a bit. She was that unhappy." Spaltz cackled a bit to himself and shook his head.

"I see. Quite a little scheme," Menders grinned.

"Oh, indeed. I've known Eiren was in love with you since you came here. Mooning about back then, looking at herself in the mirror, very unhappy with being so awkward. She cried like a baby when you took up with that Ermina. Came home all red in the face and bawling. We kept telling her that she was worth a hundred Erminas, to give herself time and get past the awkward stage, but you know youngsters, today is everything, there will never be a tomorrow. All very tragic. It was good for her to go away, see some other places and meet other people. We're grateful to you for that."

"She's made me very proud," Menders answered. "She's polished, brilliant and learned."

"Just the right kind of woman for you," Spaltz nodded sagely. "She's always been different, our Eiren. She'd be wasted as a farmer's wife, but now she's going to do great things with that school."

"She will indeed," Menders agreed. "I am concerned though. Will there be difficulty with the other farm families over Eiren living with me without being married?"

Spaltz shook his head emphatically.

"Half of them are doing the same. You didn't know? Very few of the folks around here can manage the marriage fee, there's always a better use for the money than giving it to a priest to say some words. Sometimes folks here have three or four children on the hoof before they manage to get around to marrying. Some just never bother. No-one will care, my boy, unless you intend to take Eiren as your own and then spend every night at the tavern in the village having to do with the barmaids, in which case they'd think badly of you indeed."

"Well, I haven't done it before and don't think I'll start anytime soon," Menders laughed.

"No, you're not the type. Tell you what. We farmers always have a little send off for new couples, whether they've been to the priest or not. Bit of a party and dance with our brilliant band. It would be a joy to Marjana and me to have one for Eiren and you, if you'd be of a mind to. It's still warm enough during the days, but best to get on with it, the winter's drawing in fast this year."

"Mister Spaltz, it would be an honor," Menders replied. "I

did want to tell you something, though I want it to stay between us. I'm a Lord. I don't use my title. I'm not particularly proud of my immediate family – but I have a Lord's income. Eiren will never be in want and neither will your family, if you ever need help."

"Well then, that's interesting," Spaltz said. "And it's welcome news too, though even if you and Eiren didn't have a pennig between you, the two of you would manage grandly. You're rich in two things, intellect and integrity. You'll find, as you go along, my boy, that you can get by without any of the rest, so long as you have those things and love between you."

He stood up and stretched, picking up his pitchfork.

"Now that's settled, we'll see about that sendoff for you two. Since you've been bending my ear, I'll thank you to help me get this hay loaded, save me a few minutes."

Here I am, the prospective non-son-in-law, in my best shirt, pitching hay with this funny man, Menders thought with great amusement. I wonder if he'd let out what I know is a secret, now that he knows one of mine.

"Mister Spaltz, how is it that you win all those card games against some of the brightest minds in the country?" he asked.

"Ah now, that's easily done. I can keep track of the cards. I know how many are in a deck and how much of each suit and number and I start calculating what has been laid down and what hasn't. I've always been able to do it, no matter what the game. It isn't hard after that to be able to hedge my bets and know who has what in their hand," Spaltz said. "Don't you let your men know that. I took Marjana to Erdstrom two months ago on what I win from them."

**

"Care for some unwanted advice?" Franz said, poking his head through the door of Menders' room while Menders struggled with his neck scarf.

"No, Father Wisdom, I do not," Menders responded, swearing as he jabbed his finger with his stickpin.

"You and she are completely compatible," Franz said, coming across the room and taking the stickpin. "Give me that before you take a finger off – oh yes, a dirk blade instead of a regular pin, no wonder you're killing yourself. Can't you just wear a stickpin like a normal man on his wedding day?"

"I'm not getting married," Menders muttered. "This is not my wedding day."

"Yes, yes, of course. Here, get your hands out of the way. I'll do your cravat or we'll never get there and Kaymar will run off with Eiren. How much of an arsenal are you wearing today? Going to clink and clank as you dance the holta with your fine lady?" Franz rapidly adjusted Menders' scarf and then fixed it gingerly with the stickpin-dirk blade.

"Not as much as usual, if you must know," Menders answered, unable to keep from grinning. Franz loved to jest with him about the knives he wore at all times.

"Ah, the casual touch. Where's your little one?"

"Primping. I'm about to get her now," Menders answered, taking a last look in the mirror. New suit, hair pampered to the point of shining like a raven's wing, glasses gleaming. Waiting for him on the dresser was a hat he'd spent far too much for. It was worth it, a grey silk topper with a sky blue hatband. He picked it up and went to Katrin's room, where she was curtseying in front of her mirror.

"All ready?" he asked. She turned and smiled, holding out the skirts of her new dress to their full width.

"You look so fancy!" she breathed.

"And so do you," he answered, smiling at her in the pink dress he'd brought her from the village dressmaker. Zelia had made a little crown of silk flowers for her hair, which fell to below her waist.

He hadn't belabored the issue with Katrin, simply told her that Eiren was coming to live at The Shadows with them, and that the party today was a celebration of Eiren moving from one household to another. He knew with Katrin that the less lecturing about a situation, the better. She'd shown a little jealousy and confusion at first when Eiren and he were together. Eiren had counseled patience, ignoring Katrin's tentative displays of high-handedness, giving her plenty of attention and affection. Katrin had lots of love to go around, and when she understood that Eiren wasn't trying to replace her in Menders' affections, the jealousy fled.

"Shall we go to the party, my Little Princess?" he smiled. She beamed back at him and took his hand.

***

At the Spaltz farm, Eiren was moving around the yard, putting final touches on the autumn flowers that had been tied to shocks of grain as decoration. Menders held out his arms for Katrin to jump out of the carriage, swung her high and then set her on the ground so she could go to Eiren.

"Isn't your dress beautiful!" Eiren cried, bending to hug Katrin. "Who is your escort today?"

"Hemmett. Is he here yet?" Katrin asked.

"Over with the other children by the tables. It's 'look, don't touch' right now, so no snitching anything to eat," Eiren said.

"Your dress is beautiful too," Katrin said. "I like the leaves."

"All of us worked on them. I thought we would never finish. Go ahead now, find Hemmett and don't let him eat up the feast either," Eiren laughed, knowing that Katrin was desperate to join the other children. Katrin ran off and Eiren turned to Menders.

Her dress for this occasion was a tawny shade and simply styled. Eiren, her sisters and mother had converted it to a thing of beauty by embroidering autumn leaves in every shade of red, gold, yellow, orange and russet around the neckline and over the skirt, as if the leaves were cascading into piles at the hem, which was rich with the mingled colors. Her hair was in the upswept style that made Menders desperately want to take it down and she had laced a few brilliant leaves into it. Excitement touched her face with extra color. She looked radiant.

"Aren't you an autumn sky today," she said softly as he went to her and took her hands. "All grey with a touch of blue."

"And you're the falling leaves," he answered, putting his arms around her and kissing her. Then she put her arm through his and they went to see what needed to be done before their party began.

It was an unlikely gathering, from farmers to assassins to people from the village and some of the gentry from miles around. Reisa Spartz was there, with her little daughter, Lorein, a white-blonde miniature of her lovely mother, at her side. One of the children opened the chicken pen and the guests either sidestepped the invading birds or herded them, according to their inclinations and their familiarity with chickens, back into captivity. A couple of stubborn old hens refused to be captured, and mingled with the festive group for the rest of the day.

There were dances and jokes and such goodwill that any lingering doubts Menders had about the community's acceptance of his liaison with Eiren were completely laid to rest. He let his heart soar, danced with his beloved girl with a will, ate like a horse, drank Mister Spaltz's excellent wine and accepted good wishes and congratulations without reserve.

"She's lovely, just lovely," Reisa Spartz said as Menders accepted her invitation to dance. Hemmett had volunteered to watch out for Lorein, proclaiming his years of experience as 'Katrin's guard'. He sat on the sidelines amusing the delighted little girl with a barrage of funny faces.

"I'm so glad for you, that you found someone who can take what you can give," Reisa said, smiling at him.

"And I hope you will be so fortunate," he smiled.

"I believe I am. I have met someone," she responded. He squeezed her hand a bit. He'd known she was lonely and overwhelmed by the demands of running her estate. The right man would be a wonderful thing for her and for her little daughter.

Franz and Cook pulled him into a three-handed reel with them, and much teasing took place, then they handed him on to Lucen and Zelia for more. Katrin demanded a couple of dances.

"Hemmett let the chickens out," she whispered to him as they valtzed across the dance floor.

"I thought it might have been him," Menders smiled. "Are you having a good time?"

"The best time! Some of the children say Eiren is going to be my mother because she's coming to live with us," Katrin smiled back.

"What do you think of that?" he asked.

She nodded. "I think she'll be like a mother. I'm glad, because now I'll have a mother like Bumpy does."

"That's my girl. Hungry?"

"Yes!"

Eiren saw them coming and had plates ready for them. She found Katrin a place at the little tables for children, then sat beside her while Menders tried to fold himself into one of the diminutive chairs, drawing a cascade of giggles from both of them.

"When you've finished eating, Papa wants us up by him," Eiren said, indicating her father, who was in the midst of calling a figured dance on the wooden floor that had been put down in the barnyard.

"Me too?" Katrin asked.

"I wouldn't be without you," Eiren answered, making Menders smile. He had an inkling of what was going to happen and it was so like Eiren not to exclude Katrin.

"Thank you," he murmured in her ear.

"I love you, I love her," Eiren responded, stealing a tidbit from his plate.

His fifth plate of the day done and Katrin's mouth wiped, they waited by the dance floor until the wild stamping dance was done.

"All right quiet down!" Mister Spaltz bellowed through cupped hands. He called several times for quiet and finally yelled to Hemmett to leave off making hooting noises in the loft of the barn. When there was a semblance of peace, he spoke.

"Now then, we're here today to give Mister Menders and our Eiren a sendoff. They're starting a new life together, and that's something to celebrate. Step up here," he said to them. Menders handed Eiren and Katrin up before climbing the stairs himself.

Mister Spaltz arranged them to his liking and then kissed Eiren, bowed to Katrin and shook Menders' hand which he then joined with Eiren's.

"Our blessings on you both for a long and loving life together," he said distinctly, but with tears in his eyes. "And a special blessing on you, our Princess," he said to Katrin.

Eiren tightened her grip on Menders' hand and he knew that he had the next move. He put his arms around her and kissed her to great cooing and adulation and then lifted Katrin onto his hip so she could kiss Eiren as well. Hemmett, realizing that the solemn moment was over, began hooting wildly in the loft while the haphazard band began a holta.

The sun was drawing low when Menders drove his gig into the barnyard. Preparations were being made to build a great fire, and it was obvious that the party would go on for hours, but he was more than ready to take Eiren home. Her mother had whispered to him that it was time for the formal leavetaking. He was about to put Katrin into the gig when Kaymar intervened, much to Katrin's relief, as she was unwilling to leave now that the party was in full swing. She had been protesting vigorously.

"She'll be all right with me," Kaymar said. "I'm going to stay for a couple more hours and I've deliberately not been drinking so that I could do this for you. We have her furs and coat here, so she won't be cold. You two be on your way. Are you hungry, Katrin? Yes? I am. I'm going to have more of that cake!"

With that, he bore a jubilant Katrin away. Hemmett saw that Katrin was staying and ran across the yard to join the cake eating party.

Eiren came to Menders then, carrying the little box that was symbolic of her possessions. Her belongings had been moved to The Shadows the day before, but this little box had been given to her by her mother, and would contain a few sentimental gifts for them both, as well as two slices of the enormous cake that had been served halfway through the afternoon. Menders stowed it in the gig and then helped Eiren up, before springing into the seat beside her and taking the reins. He made a round of the yard, so that everyone could see them. Then they were headed down the road together, toward The Shadows.

CHAPTER 26
COUSINS' DANCE, WARRIORS' DANCE, WEDDING DANCE

One autumn evening, Menders came out onto the front steps where Kaymar was lighting one of the small, fragrant cigars he favored. He passed the cigar to Menders, then took it back and puffed on it contentedly.

"How are you finding it, after a year?" Menders asked quietly, looking around the grounds.

"It's home. I can think of it as nothing else," Kaymar answered. Menders nodded.

"I'm glad to hear it. I'm making you my second. There is no-one better suited to the task."

Kaymar was pleased, feeling he had passed some final benchmark of acceptance and looked out over the grounds. Much as he had loved his own family home, he had never felt about it as he did about this place. This declaration from Menders made him know that he had found a place where he truly belonged.

He took the hand Menders put out for him to shake.

"Thank you, Cuz," Kaymar said quietly, the endearment slipping out unexpectedly.

"And I thank you, Cousin Kaymar," Menders returned, smiling.

***

Eiren shrieked and dropped the bottle she'd been holding when the enormous Thrun gong sounded. Hemmett and Katrin raced down the hall, making Menders stick his head out of his office to shout, "Put your coats on or there will be a reckoning, you two!" at them. It was very cold, but dry enough to feel warmer.

Menders dashed to the entryway for his greatcoat. Eiren was already there, frantically fastening her furs over her coat and pulling on her hat. He grabbed her hand, then ran out onto the snow covered lawn with her.

She gasped as she saw the Thrun processing up the drive. Katrin and Hemmett were racing toward them.

"That silly little girl! She didn't bother with her furs, that coat won't be enough and she doesn't have her hat either," Eiren cried, turning to retrieve the forgotten items. Menders stopped her.

"Tharak will have her covered in fur by the time they get up here," he laughed. "You don't want to miss this."

Eiren watched as Katrin raced up to Tharak, who stopped the procession and grinned down at her. She gave him an elegant formal curtsey, holding her skirts wide and bowing her head. When she rose, he bowed, caught her up and tossed her high, catching her and whirling on his heels to hold her up where his people could see her.

"Light Of The Winter Sun!" he roared.

His people roared back in response, almost as loudly as the shattering vibrations of the enormous gong.

"They *do* believe it!" Eiren breathed, turning to Menders. "Just like you said."

"Yes they do – and by the end of their visit, so will I, until sanity returns," Menders replied. He pulled her forward as Tharak lifted Katrin onto his shoulder. The music began again, and the Thrun continued their procession up the path to the house.

"Magic In The Eyes!" Tharak roared, grabbing Menders in his usual enormous embrace. "Good to see you!" He looked around at the assembling household and grinned. Then his eye fell on Eiren.

"And who is this, my friend?" he asked, not taking his eyes off her.

"Mine," Menders answered, using a translation of the

Thrun word for beloved wife. Tharak looked at him and then back to Eiren. His huge hand and gently cupped her chin as he gazed into her tawny eyes.

"Yes, it is she," he said to Menders as he perused her. He spoke softly in Thrun, and then translated into Mordanian for Eiren.

"Golden Heart Of Summer," he smiled. Then he was very much the Thrun Highest Chieftain again. "We will show you hospitality, my friends! Come, you will dance with us!"

In Menders' opinion, the only thing better than a Thrun carnival was watching Eiren experience one for the first time. She was fascinated by everything, from the way the tents were pitched to the way Thrun children were raised. She made copious notes and took enormous pleasure in sampling the Thrun's food, playing with their children, trading for garments and trinkets and screaming like a schoolgirl when Menders won a race or contest. It was the third Thrun carnival for The Shadows but the first for her. Menders had the time of his life squiring her around and showing her off.

It was obvious, however, that Tharak was troubled. He came to the house one night to speak privately to Menders. They sat down with a bottle of potent huskberry wine. Eiren whispered to Menders that she would be with Katrin, and left them alone.

"Aylam, my friend, the Mordanians are attacking us again," Tharak said, coming straight to the point as soon as they were alone. "I have lost many people, including women and children."

"Is it the Army?" Menders asked. The Thrun had been targeted by Mordania many times. They were considered less than human, worthy of slaughter.

"It is. Not large numbers, but enough. We need guns, my friend. Will you help us?"

"It must be in secret, because of my connections with the Crown, but I will help you," Menders replied without hesitation.

"We have enough here that you can take some immediately. I will arrange for more. I'll send them to Stettan in care of my tenants, discreetly packaged as farming tools."

"I thank you. We cannot fight guns with bows, no matter how strong our bows are," Tharak sighed. The Thrun compound bow was famous for its devastating power, but was no match for the range and rate of fire of a modern rifle. "No-one will ever know how we got them."

Menders stared into the fire. Centuries ago, the Thrun had indeed raided Mordanian towns. That was something of the distant past and those towns had encroached on traditional Thrun lands. Now they only asked to be left in peace to herd their animals and to go trading in the winter.

From time to time some ass in the Mordanian government would decide that the Thrun's island was actually a part of Mordania. Campaigns to drive them from it or to obliterate them would result. So far the Thrun had survived, but modern guns would give them some parity.

"I can probably get you two, maybe three thousand bolt action rifles over the next few months. I must order them in small lots and through other people to avert suspicion that I'm raising a private army. Can your people learn to use them fast enough?"

Smiling widely, Tharak said, "You forget we are Thrun. Fighting with any weapon comes easy to us. However, enough talk of war."

It was obvious that speaking of the persecution of his people was something Tharak wished to set aside for now.

"Golden Heart, your Eiren – you are wed?"

Menders shook his head. "I cannot marry, because of my duty to Katrin, but in our hearts, she is mine and I am hers."

Tharak nodded.

"That is wed. She loves the child?"

"Like life. She was Katrin's nursemaid when she was a baby."

"I am joyful for you but must assure you that I will beat you in the next farlin race," Tharak grinned, proffering his wine glass for another measure.

"To your long life, my friend!" he said.

"And to yours," Menders replied, raising his glass in salute.

***

Eiren found Menders' Men participating in a Thrun carnival to be a hilarious scene. They traded for huge quantities of the explosively alcoholic kirz, as well as for knives and jewelry. They bought mountains of furs and took part in the contests of skill and speed as if their lives depended on it.

The Men had a betting pool on whether Menders would give in to the ongoing offer Tharak had set up. Tharak considered it great fun to offer trade goods for Eiren to become his seventh wife. Each day the pile of saddles, furs, jewelry and knives grew higher. Menders would make a show of squiring Eiren out to the pile, walking around it perusing the new additions, picking up various bits and pieces, holding up the saddles, testing the knives with his thumb. Then he would make the Thrun wiping-dust-from-hands motion which signified something beneath contempt. He would take Eiren's arm and escort her proudly away while Tharak laughed and pounded his knees with his huge hands before seeking more plunder to add to the pile.

"It's a good thing my father didn't know of this Thrun tradition before now," Eiren joked. "I might have been traded off long ago."

"Not a chance," Menders said, slipping an arm around her waist. "He always knew he had a jewel of rare price. And so do I."

***

Katrin was incredibly happy that the Thrun were back. She was special friends with Thira and loved to ride and play with her. She was given every honor and became so laden with presents that she had to make multiple trips to the house. One day she sought Menders out and climbed on his lap.

"Should I take all these things the Thrun are giving me?" she asked. "Will it make it hard for them not to have them to trade?"

"It would hurt them if you refused their gifts," Menders told her gently.

"I wondered if I should stay away from the carnival sometimes, because every time I'm there, they give me things," she explained.

"I understand, but they come here specifically to see you. I'm sure they've taken what they will be giving you into account, so you don't have to worry about this. I'm proud of you for thinking of it though."

She had made a point of wearing the strand of grey stones around her neck while the Thrun were there. She fingered them now, looking for the flashes of light in the grey depths.

"What is Light Of The Winter Sun?" she asked, turning the stones this way and that.

"It's what Tharak Karak calls you, because of the color of your hair," Menders answered, thinking 'I'm not about to tell you what the Thrun believe, because that is far too great a burden for someone your age.'

"But it means more. I can tell by the way they say it."

"It's because they respect you because you're the Princess."

"I can tell you're lying." She said it quietly, without impudence, just a simple statement of fact.

"Yes, I am. But the reason why they call you that is something that you are simply too young to know," Menders said softly. "I won't tell you now. Sometimes, my Little Princess, there are going to be things that you don't need to be told, and this is one of them."

"Is it something bad?"

"No. It's something good, but it's too difficult for you to understand at the moment. And that's all that we're going to say about it, Katrin."

She wasn't happy with that, slid off his lap and turned to look at him reproachfully.

"If it's about me, I should know about it," she said respectfully and politely, but insistently.

He was about to refuse her outright and send her on her way, but something in her eyes made him hesitate.

"Let me think for a minute," he said.

Could he possibly tell her what the Thrun believed without placing a terrible burden of expectation on her? He did not want her to live according to the expectations of others. Her life would be circumscribed enough because she was a Mordanian Princess, without her feeling pressured to be the prophecy-become-flesh of Thrun legends.

He tried to think of a way to make it into a fairy tale, but the outcome was the same – that Katrin would feel pressured, in one way or another, to live up to an enormous task. No matter how much you want to know, my little one, not this time. Not yet.

He looked back at her standing there, waiting patiently.

"No, my Snowflower," he said softly. "Not now."

She opened her mouth to argue but he lifted a finger and looked at her. She paused.

"I don't like you to tell me no," Katrin said after a minute.

"I don't do it very often but I'm doing it now. I have to draw a line somewhere, sometime."

He could tell she was angry. He watched as several expressions crossed her face in rapid succession. Finally she looked up at him.

"I'm not happy, but I'll do what you say," she sighed.

"Thank you, little one," he smiled, and after a moment she smiled back and came to him for a hug.

"Now then, shall we go out and see what our Thrun friends are up to?" he suggested. "Want to see if I can win another farlin race?"

"With Demon you win every time."

"Maybe I should try the knife throwing contest then."

"You win that every time too."

"Are you saying I should retire from competition?" he asked with mock seriousness.

"No, go win!" She smiled up him again as he escorted her from the office.

***

The last night of the Thrun carnival was, as always, the wildest. Menders' Men were much in evidence, wearing an absurd and motley assortment of Thrun hats bristling with horns, spikes and fur. When they sobered up some of them weren't going to be happy with their trading, but for now, they were jubilant.

No assassin was at a loss on a dance floor, even with Thrun dances they had never seen before. Eiren laughed until she could hardly breathe as Ifor frolicked along in the line of male dancers, tooting on a Thrun horn, wearing an absurd hat with a very big point at the crown.

"He'll be in agony tomorrow!" she groaned. "Poor thing, he'll wreck his back! You should stop him."

"Not me. He's having a wonderful time, and he knows the consequences," Menders laughed in response.

"Tharak was wondering if you'd like to do the Wedding Dance," he continued, when she finally managed to stop gasping with laughter by turning away from the spectacle.

"What? Darling, I don't know their dances."

"I do and this one is easy. All you have to do is mirror exactly what I do."

"In front of everyone?"

"You couldn't look more absurd than that lot," Menders smiled, gesturing at the wildly cavorting Men, then handing her a cup of kirz. She looked at the dance floor, where several of Menders' Men had collided and were in the process of retaliatory thumping. She laughed.

"Do you want to?" she asked.

"Yes."

She smiled.

"Then I'll try. But if I fall over or go the wrong way, you'll have to forgive me. I knew you had Thrun blood but didn't think you grew up with them. How is it that you know their dances?" Eiren asked.

"I grew up – at least to the age of eleven – where the Menders and Tailors made their summer encampments. Tharak is of that tribe. I – life wasn't very pleasant at home, and I spent as much time as I could playing with him and hanging around their camp."

"Poor love. I'm glad he was there for you."

"I love you for that," Menders said and kissed her.

"For what?"

"For not saying you're sorry. People always say they're sorry that my childhood was miserable, when it wasn't their fault."

Franz romped by with a couple of Menders' Men, wearing a Thrun coat and a massive fur hat that made him look as if some maddened animal had jumped on him and was attempting to swallow his head. He was waving a large metal goblet brimming with kirz, splashing a lot of it about in the process. Menders' melancholy moment was shattered.

"It will be interesting to see him tomorrow morning,"

Menders remarked, remembering Franz's Thrun horn solo into Cook's ear.

"This dance you want me to do..." Eiren began.

"Us to do," Menders corrected.

"Kirz makes you nitpicky," she said with a smile. "How is it done?"

"You echo my movements. It's in sequences, presented by the man and then repeated by the woman, so do as I do. I move right, you move right, I stamp my foot, then you stamp your foot, and so on."

"All right," she said with conviction.

"That's my girl." Menders took her hand and began moving through the throng toward the High Chieftain.

"The musicians will play the Wedding Dance whenever you are ready, my friends," Tharak said. "But if you wish, I will say the words as well. It is up to you."

"What are the words?" Eiren asked, surprising Menders. She'd been a bit shy around Tharak, possibly because he kept insisting on bargaining for her to be his seventh wife and she wasn't quite sure that it was entirely a joke. "Are there vows?"

"No, Golden Heart. I bless you and wish you eternal love. Then you dance. Nothing Magic In The Eyes cannot do – but once the dance is finished, in the eyes of the Thrun, you are wed."

"Then yes, please, say the words," Eiren smiled. Tharak roared with laughter.

"Very forward, this one! I shall go and take a few saddles off the pile I'm giving you for her. I would be afraid of such a powerful wife!"

"I didn't think you were man enough," Menders grinned, ducking as Tharak pretended to take a swing at him.

Menders and Eiren watched as the Thrun evicted those Menders' Men who were still standing from the dance floor. Tharak strode onto it, the silver trimmings of his magnificent coat shimmering in the firelight.

He spoke, first in Thrun, then translated his words into Mordanian.

"Tonight we celebrate the union of Magic In The Eyes and Golden Heart Of Summer." He beckoned to them and Menders escorted Eiren onto the floor.

Tharak took their hands, making a circle with them. He spoke again in Thrun, then Mordanian.

"The blessing of Thrun be on you both. From the birth of spring to the death of winter, may your lives be long. May your love be as strong as the sea, as warm as the fire, as lasting as the land, as vital as the air. Now dance, to seal your wedding."

Menders removed his glasses and thrust them into a pocket of his coat, which he shucked off and handed to Tharak. He had enough kirz in him that he would feel no cold.

Eiren removed her hat and shook her hair free. It flamed in the firelight and Menders could hear a palpable murmur of admiration from the crowd. Red hair was prized by the Thrun.

Tharak bowed to them and stepped off the dance floor.

A small gong sounded. A woman's voice began weaving a sultry web of Thrun words, accompanied by a slow, throbbing drum. Menders caught Eiren's eyes with his and stepped out in the slow, seductive dance, weaving his way across the floor from her. Seven hip-swaying steps to the right, then a pause while she did the same. Three definitive foot stamps, another pause as she made the floor ring with the heel of her boot, then a slow, deliberate turn and seven steps in the opposite direction, followed by the stamping again.

It brought man and woman together slowly in a choreographed courtship, zigzagging across the dance floor like brightly colored threads in a loom.

Eventually they met in the middle of the floor. Menders held up a hand. Eiren raised hers to touch it and they circled that way three times, gazing into each other's eyes before, with the final notes of the music, he closed his hand over hers.

The Thrun burst into mad applause, Eiren blinked and Menders laughed, then caught her close and kissed her.

***

Next morning, Menders reminded himself of his rule regarding those who willingly got drunk on kirz not moaning about their hangovers. He got up, made himself eat and was feeling reasonably human by the time the Thrun were ready to leave. Eiren had done the same, refusing his offer for her to stay in bed. She wanted to say goodbye and see them go.

Menders was amused to see that Tharak had left out the pile of goods that he kept offering for Eiren and had added to it, including several beautiful knives, dresses, boots, bags of jewelry, furs and three more saddles.

"It's no good," Menders said as Tharak meandered over. "No trade."

"It is no trade, Magic In The Eyes. I don't have enough in the
world to pay for her," Tharak grinned. "It is a gift. For your wedding."

Eiren gasped and opened her mouth to protest that it was too much. Menders put a hand on her arm.

"We accept with thanks," he said. Tharak grinned more widely. Eiren and Katrin began inspecting the pile while Menders and Tharak walked some distance away.

"You have the guns packed well?" Menders asked quietly. Tharak nodded. Covert messages sent with Kaymar had resulted in the first lot of weaponry arriving by mail train, packed in crates. The rifles were easy enough to disguise; it was the ammunition that was harder to camouflage. Menders finally ordered it shipped in tubs of butter. Casual inspection would reveal a two inch layer of butter, under which were bullets sealed in metal foil.

"Packed away very well. I cannot thank you enough, my

brother."

"I'll send more. Check with my tenants when you return home. More weapons should be there by then. I wish you luck, my friend. I only wish I could do more to help you." Menders looked up at the big Thrun, feeling grief for the losses he'd had, for the people who had been senselessly slaughtered by their own nation.

"You help me every day, Aylam. When things are hard for me, I remember how hard things were for you when you were still a child. I remember how you lived through it and used it to become strong. Then things are not so hard for me. And now, I bid you farewell... until the circle turns again." They embraced and Tharak turned away.

Menders had enough time to gesture to Eiren to put her hands over her ears. Katrin was already covering hers and Menders followed suit as the enormous gong was struck. The drums began, the garzan moaned their deep, almost soundless note and the Thrun began to move away.

Menders found himself alone in the road, watching the figures grow tiny in the distance. Then Eiren was with him, her hand finding and clasping his.

"It's so hard to see them go," Menders said softly.

"Because part of you goes with them?" Eiren asked.

"Yes," Menders replied, almost in a whisper.

Standing together, hands entwined, they watched until Tharak turned and raised his arms in a circle. Then the Thrun were swallowed by the enormous landscape and were gone.

CHAPTER 27
BORSEN

"Mama?" Borsen whispered, leaning close to the mattress on the floor. He knelt and dipped a finger into the gruel he had made. "Mama? I'm going to give you something to eat."

He rubbed his finger, wet with the lukewarm mush, across her lips and tongue. He waited and then stroked her throat gently, trying to get her to swallow. She didn't. She had swallowed yesterday, though she hadn't waked up.

"Please swallow it, Mama," he pleaded. "You need to eat so you'll get well."

Her throat felt cold to his touch. The room was freezing — there was hardly any fire left.

There was not much wood on the Sea Of Grass and what there was got picked up quickly. Mama was very tired and couldn't fight over wood like stronger people could, so she often burned tufts of twisted grass. But now the snow lay thick on the grass and was frozen hard, so she had made a game out of using the furniture. Borsen remembered the day he woke and found the table broken up for firewood. Mama had given him some bread and had him eat it in bed, like she said kings and queens did, since they didn't have the table to eat at now. He had tried to give her some but she said she wasn't hungry.

She had sewed constantly that winter after his father had disappeared one night, but it didn't bring enough money. She'd finally said she'd found work and that he had to be a good boy and wait in the room for her, that he mustn't go out alone. Then she tried to make herself pretty and smiled back at him before she went out the door.

Borsen had waited, listening for rats. He hated killing them. They fought and bit, but they were food. There weren't many rats this hard winter. Too many people were catching them.

He'd heard a Mordanian man say, laughing, how there was not a cat that could match a starving Thrun.

Mama finally came home late, with food. She gave it to Borsen, saying she'd eaten while she was out.

Time had passed, with Mama going out every night to work, always bringing back food and sometimes a few sticks of wood. She slept through more and more of the days. The morning came when she didn't wake up, no matter how Borsen called to her and shook her.

That had been three days ago. The wood was gone except for two chair rung. The only food left was a piece of bread. He got water by collecting snow off the windowsill by the broken pane. Until this morning Mama had swallowed it as he dripped it on her lips, though she'd stayed asleep.

Borsen took off his jacket, the green one with grey trim that Mama had sewn for him last summer, and put it on top of the blanket he'd spread over her. He cuddled close, holding the cup of gruel. He rubbed more of it over her lips at intervals, but she didn't swallow. It was very cold. There was ice on the inside of the windowpanes.

The daylight was brief on this shortest day of the year. The early night was falling when the door of the room opened. Borsen started from a drowse and tried to see who was there.

He knew the footsteps. It was his father. He shrank back against Mama, his skinny hand gripping her arm.

"Come on, boy," his father said roughly. "Time to go."

"No," Borsen cried. "Mama!"

"She's dead. Get up, we have to move on." His father's hand loomed into sight and closed on his shoulder. Borsen flung himself away and pressed his ear to Mama's chest.

Her heart was beating, but he could barely hear it. It was very slow.

"She's not dead! She needs food! Why didn't you bring food?" he shouted, trying to dodge his father's grabbing hands.

"If we give her something to eat, she'll get better!"

His father's hand was gone from his arm but Borsen could hear him going through the pile of folded clothing that Mama had stacked on the floor after she burned the storage box. He was stuffing things in his pack.

"Mama!" Borsen cried, shaking her desperately. "Please wake up!" His eyes filled with tears and spilled over. Now he couldn't see at all.

His father's hand clamped on his arm so hard that he screamed in pain.

"Get up, boy. You're going to earn your keep now. Six years old but you haven't done a thing, kept a baby by her. You'll learn what it is to earn your way now she's gone. You owe me a few years' work."

Borsen fought, but his father was big and strong and heaved him up under one arm. He punched and gouged the fat around his father's waist and screamed for his mother as he was carried away down the stairs of the tenement house.

CHAPTER 28
THE RED BEAST

Dear Cahrin and Olner,

    I've been remiss in my correspondence of late, with all the projects underway here. Not only is springtime a busy season due to all the preparations for planting, but The Shadows is being subjected to a number of construction projects which take a up a great deal of my time and energy.

    We're up to our knees in sawdust. It is high time living conditions at The Shadows were more comfortable, now that we have completed the tunnels and guardhouses and other security measures.

    Franz, Ifor, Menck and I have spent weeks going over this enormous house. Some rooms have been closed up for decades. I must admit I've never managed to go through the entire place. Our exploration has resulted in the following: families living in the main house will now have suites of their own; one for myself, Eiren and Katrin; one for Hemmett and his parents; one for Cook and her Mister Oldstrom. There is plenty of room for more, should any of Menders' Men decide to start families. One enormous bathroom and a number of smaller ones have been devised, so dragging the old tin bathtub around is no more, thank the gods.

    There is ample room for guests or for those of the Men who live in the various outbuildings here, should winter weather become severe. The second floor has been converted into workshops. Cook's son, Tomar, is located up there with his tailor shop, and another room doubles as a planning room for estate business and a potential "battle room", should the occasion arise for us to execute defensive action of any kind. A strongroom has been constructed on the ground floor, with direct access to the network of tunnels which now reach all the outbuildings and other locations on the estate.

    Since the household can swell to twenty-three people during the wintertime, changes have been made to the provision for meals. You were much amused at the notion of Menders' Men being rostered for kitchen duty, but the practice continues, and they consider it easy work. The group "family" dinners now occur only once a month, making Cook's life much easier.

My marathon wood-cutting sessions are a thing of the past, as all the Men turn out for an hour after breakfast and invade the woodlot. This is an enormous relief for me, as you can imagine. It might have kept me fit, but the toll it took in sore muscles and exhaustion was enormous. I am also free of having to hunt for the larder, something I never enjoyed. There are many avid sportsmen among the Men, Ifor Trantz being the most zealous. Ifor organized a boar hunt in the autumn, with the Men setting off with enough spears, crossbows, rifles and knives to successfully invade and subjugate a small nation, their horses armored. They returned with enough pork to keep us all through the winter and to supply the estate farms as well.

Not that I've become a gentleman of leisure. Katrin is growing apace, and her mind grows quickly as well. Eiren is away at her school each day, driving herself in a little governess cart pulled by a chubby mare named Rosie, and Katrin spends much of her time with me. I located a partners' desk in a disused room, and have it in my office, so that Katrin can watch me doing the estate work, or see to her own occupations, like reading, practicing writing, drawing and playing. Eiren devised a curriculum for her, and it is our hope that in time, with proper security measures, she will be able to attend some classes at the school as well.

Katrin is also becoming quite a good young horsewoman, and not only rides her pony, Snowflake, but also the little farlin I got for her three years back. He is aptly named Trouble, but Katrin handles him well. She hugely enjoys our rides, and Hemmett joins us as well on his own pony, Smoke. Katrin was given a lovely boarhound puppy, Dara (the Thrun word for "grace") for her recent fifth birthday, who doubles as a pet and guardian, as boarhounds' protectiveness toward their people is legendary.

Of late, Katrin has begun to be aware of her difference from other children. She plays with Eiren's siblings as well as with other children from the estate. It has always been my intention that she know how to mix with people of all classes and to understand and appreciate their particular customs and problems.

She has expressed a desire to play like the other children at times when the young Spaltzes tell her about their swimming and fishing excursions, where they run down to the river on their own – something that is impossible for a child in Katrin's position. She has begun to chafe at her restrictions, but there is nothing to be done about it. So far, she has not been particularly rebellious, and we hope the trend will continue.

Life here now is pleasant and far from the lonely and somber existence it was for five years. I wish you the happiness that we have.

Your friend,

M

***

Katrin drew back behind the door to the Men's lounge so that she wouldn't be seen.

That afternoon she and Hemmett had been playing in the old nursery while Kaymar read a book nearby. Haakel had brought up a letter for Kaymar with the news that his dear friend in Erdahn had died suddenly from putrid fever.

Kaymar made a soft but terrible noise as he read the letter and then left Katrin and Hemmett in Haakel's care. He disappeared into his rooms for the afternoon. When he came out, he was very drunk and went to the Men's Lounge.

Ifor Trantz had come looking for Menders, telling Eiren that Kaymar was very sick and needed help. Eiren went to find Doctor Franz and Katrin had crept away to see if she could do something to help Kaymar.

She could see him sitting on a sofa while several of the Men tried to get a bottle away from him. His eyes were streaming and red, but he didn't make a sound. His nose was pinched as he drew in rapid, harsh breaths, glaring at the people around him.

Katrin thought about Kaymar's heart and was afraid. His face was red with white patches on his cheeks. He didn't like people crowding him.

Why didn't Eiren or Doctor Franz come? Katrin watched fearfully as Kaymar flushed even darker red and gripped the bottle so hard that his knuckles went pale.

Rapid footsteps startled her and she peeped from behind the door. Menders and Ifor were running down the hallway. They ducked into the Men's lounge.

"All right fellows, thank you for staying with him," Menders said quietly. He turned and looked at the door as if he could see through it.

"Katrin, please go with Ifor. He'll take you upstairs."

"But Kaymar is crying!" she protested, stepping into view. "Can't I help him?"

Kaymar looked up at her blearily, confusion on his face, his enraged expression smoothing away. He reached toward her.

Menders shook his head firmly and indicated for Ifor to take her.

"Not now. Please go with Ifor. I'll help Kaymar," he said.

Ifor scooped her up and bore her away down the hall. She struggled a bit, looking back at the doorway of the lounge.

"Kaymar wanted me to stay," Katrin protested, twisting in Ifor's arms. "He was reaching for my hand. I could help him feel better!"

"I know, I saw," Ifor replied in his rumbly voice that always made Katrin think of big stones. "Don't hurt my back thrashing around like that."

"Please let me go back to the lounge," Katrin pleaded.

"Not now. Let's have a game of DeGratz, and then you can plan to see Kaymar later on, when he's more himself." Ifor swung her down and guided her into the suite. "Perhaps you could take him some flowers. Right now he's not at all well and he needs to be with Menders. That will calm him."

Katrin watched with frustration as Ifor took out the DeGratz board and methodically set up the pieces, ranging kings, queens, assassins, warriors and valets across the painted spaces.

He looked up at her, his deep, dark eyes very kind but stern.

"Go ahead, Princess, sit down. We'll clear our heads with a game. Focus your mind on it and the time will pass."

Katrin sighed and sank down on the chair opposite, looking gloomily at the board. Ifor made his opening gambit, sat back and waited. Katrin considered losing fast on purpose, but she knew that would never fool Ifor. He was going to keep her from going back to the Men's lounge.

She picked up a warrior piece and sighed in exasperation.

"You see, I love Kaymar very much," she said abruptly, looking mutinously at the big man.

To her surprise, Ifor nodded.

"I know you do and that will be a great comfort to Kaymar," he said quietly. "Would you like to know a secret? You have to keep it to yourself."

Her interest piqued, Katrin nodded.

"I love Kaymar very much too," Ifor continued. "I want to go and help him just as you do, but right now it would be too much for him to have us there. So we'll occupy ourselves with a game and wait until a time when being near Kaymar will be good for him again."

Katrin studied his big, heavy, craggy face. He seemed sad and tired.

"You should tell him," she suggested. "It might make him happy again to know he has another friend."

"Not the time for it," Ifor answered. "It might never be the time for it. Right now Katrin, the kindest thing we can do for Kaymar is to leave him to Menders and Doctor Franz. And if you're going to open with the Warrior's Gambit you're sure to lose, so get to thinking and find a better strategy than that."

Katrin sighed again and looked down at the board.

***

From Doctor Franz's files:
Kaymar, Baronet Schvalz

    Patient continues melancholic and restless, a consistent pattern since the death of his bonded. Periods of prolonged gloom followed by episodes of madness. Though patient denies it, I have seen evidence that he is experiencing auditory hallucinations, perhaps visual as well. He has been seen by members of the household speaking aloud to trees, walls and the air. His vocalizations at these times include the words "tainted", "filthy", "worthless". He can become very agitated and when approached or interrupted, barely restrains himself from violence. Guilt is a large factor in his illness because I know that his bonding with Mikail was not the most passionate. There was love and caring there, but it was far from a great romance for Kaymar - more a comfortable and welcome relationship after his past tragedies and hurts.

    Kaymar has been injuring himself deliberately, burning himself with his cigars or cutting himself with various of the arsenal of knives he always has on his person. It is puzzling, but it seems that the pain he inflicts on himself causes a temporary reduction of his madness. Immediately after and for some hours, sometimes days, his symptoms of madness recede. Perhaps during times when he is not suffering from melancholia, this self-injury results in a period of normality, but at present, relief from hallucinations and delusions simply plunges him further into despair.

    I have spoken with Menders regarding my concerns about Kaymar's fitness to continue guarding the Princess. He shares these concerns, but also fears the consequences should Kaymar be removed from duty. Kaymar has a powerful sense of responsibility and fierce protectiveness toward the Princess, as well as a genuine affection for her. I believe this is all that prevents him from taking his life in despair.

    Unfortunately, Kaymar is satisfying his demons by provoking Menders. These men are more alike than they know, both possessed of strong tempers that can tend toward violence should they be pushed far enough. Both have learned extreme self-control because of their assassin's training, but the current situation is telling on them.

    There have been a number of vicious verbal confrontations. It is inevitable that physical confrontation will occur unless Kaymar's condition improves dramatically. Kaymar is secure in Menders' regard and affection for him. He knows that Menders would never reject him or send him away from The Shadows, so he is safe in venting his rage on his cousin. Unfortunately, Menders has his own troubles and his temper is being worn to nothing by Kaymar's continual baiting and challenges.

I see no solution to this dilemma. To send Kaymar away would be the end of him, as he would despair and take his own life. His family is not capable of coping with his illness. His brother is a very normal, placid and unpretentious man, not given to the vicissitudes and emotional storms that plague his younger sibling. His mother is fragile, having barely escaped The Terror in Fambre as a young girl. She has never been truly aware of Kaymar's mental condition, his actual occupation or his sexual proclivities, as she is sheltered and protected by her sons, as she was by her husband before his death.

Kaymar truly has no home but The Shadows and no family who understands him other than Menders. In his illness he is doing everything he can to have his only refuge and ally taken from him.

Kaymar has even been snappish and unreasonable with Katrin, who understandably resents and is confused by this behavior. Where previously he has been strict but kind and done all he could to make the restrictions that are necessary for her safety as innocuous as possible, now he is simply laying down the law and making her very aware of just how fenced in she is. Coming at the time in her life where she's contrasting her situation with those of her peers, this is causing conflict within her as well as anger and resentment over her limitations.

Katrin, while a dear child, can be quite manipulative - as can her mother, and as was her grandmother. What can be an admirable trait in a Queen can be less so in a child. I fear that Katrin, always a quick study, is becoming aware of Kaymar's weaknesses now that his illness is so overtly displayed and will, sooner or later, take advantage of the situation. I have discussed this with Menders with little satisfaction - he feels very strongly toward what little family he has, particularly Kaymar. He is not seeing the situation pragmatically and became very angry with me as a result of our talk.

Shvalz men and their blasted tempers! It is so apt that the Thrun refer to rage and anger as "The Red Beast". It tears at these men. It gives them exaggerated senses of duty and responsibility when they channel it for good, but it also destroys them from within. Worst of all, it makes them blind to the damage they do and the possibilities around them.

Kaymar could find comfort right here at The Shadows if he wasn't absolutely bent on being consumed by sorrow and rage - but I'll say no more about that. All I can do is watch helplessly as Menders, Kaymar, Katrin and another are engaged in what could become a destructive and tragic dance.

***

Lucen appeared in Menders' office doorway, followed by Eiren, who had seen him returning from the halt with the weekly mail.

"Official letter from the Palace here," Lucen said briefly.

Menders took the pile, tore open the heavily sealed envelope and read the document inside, feeling his heart sink.

"Menders! What is it?" Eiren gasped.

"You've just gone dead white," Lucen added, his brow wrinkled in concern.

"No – I'm sorry, it's nothing that bad," Menders answered, handing the letter to Eiren. "I think I can get around it."

It was an official Court summons.

From Her Majesty, Queen Morghenna VIII to Lord Stettan,

Sir,

> *You are commanded by Her Majesty the Queen to bring Princess Katrin Morghenna to Court two weeks from the date of this document, to be presented to Her Majesty.*

> *Morghenna VIII*

"How do you intend to get around it?" Eiren asked, her voice rising with fear. "People don't just say 'no' to the Queen."

"The Princess is sick, don't you know?" Menders said, feeling the color coming back into his face. "Nasty case of putrid fever."

"That'll scare them off," Lucen mused. "Anything else you need?"

"No, Lucen, thank you. Take the afternoon off," Menders grinned.

"I'll go hoe the beans then." He clumped away.

Eiren settled into the chair opposite. "What do you think prompted this?" she asked as she indicated the summons.

"I don't know, I've had no intelligence in that direction," Menders answered. "I'll send Kaymar over to see what's afoot. They won't trifle with putrid fever, that'll put them off right away."

Putrid fever was a common childhood illness. Young patients were not endangered unless neglected, but for some reason the disease was almost invariably fatal in adults. Putrid fever attacked the gut. In adults it caused high fevers and bloody flux before the unfortunate patient died after days of agony. Those few adults who did survive putrid fever lived on as mindless invalids who wasted away in their beds within a year or two. Epidemics of the disease were common in cities. No-one would want it carried into the Royal Court of Mordania.

When Eiren left the room, Menders looked at the letter again and sighed, then picked it up and bearded Ifor's lair.

Where Menders' office tended to be neat and methodical to a fault, Ifor worked happily in a welter of chaos. Just seeing the piles of paper and other materials was enough to make Menders itch.

Ifor looked up as the document was dropped on the desk. He glanced over it and raised his eyebrows.

"What might she be up to? Any ideas?" Menders asked.

"You've just solved a mystery for me, I was wondering what Bartie was on about," Ifor answered, digging in his piles of paper until he came up with a letter from Thoren Bartan.

"Apparently the Queen has had one of her spells of sobriety and has asked some questions as to Katrin's condition and upbringing. I think this summons was written during that time. According to Bartie, she's back to drinking and has probably forgotten all about it."

"Think that a note to the effect that Katrin is sick with putrid fever would settle the matter?" Menders asked.

"Very likely. Do you want to send someone over with it, just to see what's going on?" Ifor leaned back in his chair, reaching around to massage his damaged back and looking up at Menders.

"Yes, send Kaymar. He's the most familiar with the Court."

"Best man for the job," Ifor agreed. "He can smell around and see if there's anything else afoot. As soon as you give me the note, he'll be off. Don't worry, Menders, I don't think this will come to anything. The Queen used to have spells of deciding that Princess Aidelia needed her attention. After an hour of that demented creature she would take to the bottle, but that's understandable. Aidelia would drive anyone to drink, if only to numb their sense of smell."

Menders frowned. "Let's hope this is just another one of the Queen's rare lucid moments," he said.

Back in his office, Menders gave vent to a groan of frustration. Ifor might have thought his words about the Queen taking spasmodic interest in Aidelia would be comforting. They were not. What if, after one of those episodes with her eldest daughter, she thought, 'I have a younger daughter too, who might not be mad' and decided Katrin must live at Court? The last thing Katrin needed was any involvement with her closest relatives. A drunken, slovenly mother and a raving mad sister - no, not for his little girl.

***

Katrin burst out of the heavy underbrush and into the road, nearly running under Demon's feet. Menders hauled on the reins, throwing Demon onto his hindquarters to avoid trampling her. The farlin cried out in anger and pain. Katrin, likewise, stopped so quickly that she fell to her knees in the dust.

"What the hells?" Menders shouted, jumping free of Demon, who was thrashing back onto his feet and snapping at the air. Menders looked around wildly, his hand going to his knife. Katrin knew then that he thought she was being chased by someone.

"Katrin! Damn it, Katrin!" Kaymar shouted in the woods, his voice gaspy and breathless.

Menders turned back to Katrin and snatched off his dark glasses, his eyes filled with fury.

"Did you run away from him?" he asked in a low, terrible voice.

She had.

Kaymar had been snappish all day, refusing to let her go with Olan, Petra and Hemmett when they decided to run down to the river to fish. It was autumn now and one of the last nice days they would have to play by the river. Kaymar had been twitching and muttering to himself all morning. There was a moment when she wanted to join the others at the river more than anything in the world. Kaymar had been talking to a tree like it was a person, paying no attention to her. She'd bolted, running as hard as she could for the river road.

She had not expected Kaymar to snap into action and chase after her as if his feet were on fire. She hadn't even expected to run away - she'd simply run, suddenly and without a plan. She just wanted to go with the other children and be like them.

"Did you?" Menders caught her by the arm, his hand gripping hard. Katrin flinched and stared up at him. He'd never been so angry with her, ever, even when he'd caught her singeing broomstraws in the fire.

She couldn't speak. She tried, but couldn't make the slightest sound. Kaymar could be heard closer, calling for her, his voice becoming desperate and despairing.

"How could you!" Menders nearly shouted. "You know your cousin isn't well! How could you take advantage like that, when we've tried so hard to teach you to care about others?" He turned her around and Katrin realized he was going to strike her.

"Stop it!" Suddenly Kaymar was there, diving at Menders and knocking him away from Katrin. There was a flurry of blows. Demon snorted and tossed his head up and down violently. Katrin backed away in fear – then turned and fled toward the house.

***

My dear cousin Dorsen,

It is with regret that I must inform you of a deterioration in Kaymar's condition. I have hesitated to contact you before now, as I was hoping that time would ameliorate his difficulties, but it is becoming obvious that he is very ill and becoming worse. His mourning over Mikail has plunged him into deep melancholy and overt madness.

Kaymar has deliberately taken to provoking me to the point where we come to blows. I have been sorely tempted to send him away from The Shadows. I have only resisted because I know that doing so would result in catastrophe - that Kaymar would be destroyed by the withdrawal of my affection and support.

As I'm sure you know, Kaymar stays here out of love and loyalty to me and the Princess. He has refused to accept any wage, despite his excellent work and dedication. This is his home and though he is not overt in his appreciation of it, I know that he loves it - and me.

Dorsen, any advice you can give me at this time would be welcome. I am often at my wits' end when dealing with Kaymar as he is now - and I am desperate to find a solution for him. He is losing a great deal of weight and is also displaying the nervous tics that accompany his madness. Casual friendships that he had made with various of my staff have cooled. There was also an incident where he was severely provoked and had to be restrained from attacking one of the other Men (and I don't need to explain that Kaymar is entirely capable, in his present state of mind, of killing.)

I've had no choice but to relieve him of guard duty for Katrin. His episodes of madness make him dangerously inattentive. I know that he cannot help this, but I cannot risk her safety, no matter how dear Kaymar is to me.

Despite this letter being far from full of good news, I hope it finds you and your family well. All are well here and prospering - and I would be entirely happy if I could find some solution for Kaymar.

Your cousin

M

***

Katrin crept down the backstairs and eased over to the door at the bottom. It was ajar and she could see that Kaymar was standing with his back to it. The scent of his cigar smoke had led her to him. She watched with horror as he dropped the butt of the cigar on the floor and trod on it.

That would cause another argument or fight with Menders - she was sure of it, just as she was sure Kaymar was doing things with the intention of making trouble. Ever since he and Menders had fought the day she ran away, he'd been doing things that would make Menders angry. Menders was strict about where the men smoked their cigars because The Shadows was made from wood and would burn to the ground if a fire ever got going.

She watched Kaymar, who was talking to himself.

"You'll never rest, everyone you love dies, dirty disgusting freak. Why don't you kill yourself and save a lot of trouble? You'll never be missed. Afraid? You're worthless. Filthy, tainted. Filthy!"

Katrin gasped as Kaymar tore one of his knives from its sheath and held his arm out in front of him. He slashed it three times, cutting through his shirt sleeve.

"Kaymar!" Katrin jumped out of the stairwell and ran to him, trying to remember what to do when a person was cut and bleeding. She needed cloth, something to stop the blood...

"What the hells are you doing hiding there!" Kaymar shouted, turning toward her. His face was terrifying, contorted with rage.

"Your arm!" Katrin reached out, remembering what Menders had said about bleeding, that even pressing a cut with your hands was better than doing nothing.

"Get away!" Kaymar shouted, turning away from her. "Leave me alone! Let me do what I have to do!"

He had often been strict and sometimes sharp with her but he had never shouted. Though she was hurt and wanted to cry, she could see the blood dripping down as he shoved his knife back in its sheath and then twisted his shirt sleeve, stanching the flow.

"Kaymar?" she ventured in a tiny, frightened voice.

"Go away, Katrin," he replied, his voice low and gravelly. He didn't sound like Kaymar at all.

Katrin wheeled and dashed up the backstairs, bursting out on the second floor right under Menders' nose as he was walking down the hallway.

"Princess, what on Eirdon..." he began.

"You have to come help Kaymar!" Katrin gasped, out of

breath from her run up the steep flight. "He - he cut himself with his knife, three times. He's bleeding! We need to get cloths to stop it!"

To her astonishment, Menders didn't respond. He reached down and took her hand.

"Where did you see this?" he asked.

"At the bottom of the stairs. He threw his cigar on the floor and put it out and then he started talking to himself and then he cut himself." Katrin began to cry. She tugged at Menders' hand, trying to pull him toward the stairs.

She was shocked when Menders held her back.

"Kaymar needs to be left alone," he said. "You can't possibly understand, but he's able to take care of himself. It's very important that you not creep up on him again, Katrin."

"He's bleeding!"

"Yes, I understand. He'll be all right."

Why?" she cried on a rising note.

Menders looked down at her. He took off his glasses and crouched down so they were eye to eye.

"I don't understand certain things about Kaymar any more than you do," he said softly. "He is in a great deal of pain - not in his body, but in his mind. He does some things that most people don't do. He's worked out his own way of dealing with his pain. He's not guarding you at present, so I want you to leave him alone, Little Princess. He needs his privacy. Will you do this?"

"I think we should check to see if he's alright," Katrin ventured.

"He'll be fine. Come on now, I was just looking to see if you would like to go for a ride with me. Go get your things and we'll be on our way." Menders smiled, though it looked as though he didn't mean it. He turned her toward her room, giving her a little push.

She knew he hadn't intended to go riding - he was trying to distract her. Perhaps Kaymar needed privacy, but he'd been hurt. It was the first time she'd known of Menders not helping someone who was hurt.

***

"That's why," Menders concluded as Katrin jogged alongside him on Trouble. Demon tossed his head but calmed when Menders patted his neck absent-mindedly. They were returning from their ride, with the afternoon turned very cold and the weather dreary.

"Why would bad people want to take me away or hurt me?" Katrin asked, feeling anger rising inside her.

It had been a miserable two weeks since she had run away from Kaymar. Menders had a bad black eye from his fight with Kaymar. He had been very quiet and rested in bed a lot. Eiren had explained that the blow to his eye had caused some damage and that he had to allow it to heal. Kaymar talked to himself more than ever and now he had hurt himself – and Menders didn't try to help him.

"It's hard to explain so you can understand, Little Princess," Menders answered. "There are people who want to run Mordania – and they would do terrible things to reach that goal. If your mother were to die, your sister, Aidelia, would take the Throne. If something happened to Aidelia, you would be Queen."

"I don't want to be Queen!" Katrin said abruptly. Trouble shuffled his hind feet in a dancing step and she had to tighten the reins to make him stop.

"And I hope you will never need to be Queen," Menders replied. "It's a heavy burden for anyone, but there are people who long for power, just like some people long for food."

"If it turned out I was going to be Queen, they could have it," Katrin scowled. It was hard enough being a Princess and not having any freedom. What would being Queen be like? Her mother never left the Palace!

"I wish it was that simple, my dearest," Menders sighed, pulling Demon up and reaching out, catching Trouble's reins though Katrin had been mutinously riding on. "You know that I, Eiren, Kaymar and everyone else love you very much, don't you?"

"Of course," Katrin answered, feeling a deep darkness inside her heart as she thought of people who wanted to run the country so badly that they might try to come here and take her... or hurt her.

"Then you must understand that when we forbid something, or restrict you it's because we want you to be safe."

Katrin looked away at the bare trees. The woods were dull and gloomy this time of year, with a heavy grey sky overhead, all the brilliant leaves fallen and brown. She felt frightened and sad – and angry.

"I understand," she sighed.

"Good. Come on, it's cold – let's get back home and have a hot drink." Menders tried to sound hearty but Katrin could tell he didn't feel it. She urged Trouble into a jog again, but there was no fun in the ride. She couldn't stop thinking about people who wanted to take her away and Kaymar cutting himself.

It was as if all the shine was gone from everything and now the world was different and would never be the same again.

***

Dear Cousin Menders,

Thank you for the news regarding Kaymar - it saddens me greatly, of course, having seen his suffering for so many years. He is so changed from the much cherished and lovingly spoiled little boy that he was during my youth, though we found out afterward that even that was not a happy time, as he was being corrupted and exploited by that freak, Hartzen Trentov.

There is little insight that I can give you in dealing with Kaymar when madness is upon him, as he always stayed away from the family during the worst periods of his illness - probably in an attempt to protect our mother. She is a fragile woman who cannot bear much tragedy. I know that Commandant Komroff found taking a firm hand with Kaymar worked well for a time, but eventually that became useless as Kaymar realized his own power and began to respect no authority. His regard for you is very powerful, however, and I believe that he would stop short of provoking you to the point of you sending him away from the only home he accepts.

I will write to Kaymar and suggest that he visit here. I am certain he will decline, as has been his habit when he is ill of mind. I would be more than willing to come and see him and try to speak to him, but I have found in the past that this only worsens his despair.

I was fearful of this when Mikail died so suddenly. He was a stabilizing influence in Kaymar's life. Kaymar is a soul who must have a rock to cling to - if he has that, he is able to withstand no end of adversity and tragedy. When he is adrift, as he is now, he descends rapidly into madness. He is very much like our mother, sensitive and high strung. I am more our father, a rather stolid, calm man who functioned as an anchor not only for our mother, but for Kaymar as well. It was his untimely death when Kaymar was only fourteen that made Kaymar so unstable.

Sadly, because of the difference in years between us, I have never become an anchor for my brother, dearly as I would have liked to. His personality and nature are a mystery to me, and we have so little in common since he declined my offer to live at Moresby and manage the estate with me. The nature of his work requires secrecy and privacy; he confides nothing to me.

Please keep me apprised. In the past I have made arrangements to have Kaymar confined if it became necessary, and will renew them, though I truly hope that such measures will never have to be taken.

My best to you and all your family.

Your affectionate cousin,

Dorsen

Menders set the letter on his desk and closed his eyes.

He was tired. The autumn had been bleak, the winter promised to be a "soft" one, so there would be no visit from the Thrun to break the long dark season. It was Winterfest, but there was tension in the house because of Kaymar's behavior. Katrin had been subdued since he had explained, in a limited way, why she couldn't roam at will. That had been the first rift in her innocence and it was difficult to see. Inevitable, of course – but painful to watch her struggle with it.

Kaymar was closed away in his room. Three weeks back he had gone after a new Menders' Man who had referred to him as a pederast. It had led to a violent scene. Kaymar was barely restrained, the new Man immediately dismissed. Kaymar's previous behavior had already made the Men wary of him and now the group was divided, with some fiercely offended by Kaymar's actions, others sympathetic but scornful of his inability to control his temper.

Not the atmosphere to have around a Winterfest table. Kaymar would likely not appear, but his absence would make the situation even more uncomfortable.

Menders glanced at the letter again and then tossed it into the fire. He couldn't bear the thought of Kaymar coming across it. The thought of his young cousin being confined was as painful as seeing a rare wild animal in a small cage. People like Dorsen, well meaning, would think it a kindness. Kaymar would be better off dead than locked up.

Which left it to Menders to attempt to reach him. If Kaymar could be brought out of his present misery, if he could begin to break free of the pain that dogged him, he might gain a foothold on health.

Menders left his office, passing through the dining hall where a committee of the Men were engaged in hammering up greenery and laying the table.

"Is Shvalz going to be here tonight?" one of them asked,

his voice genuinely concerned.

"Yes, there's been no sign of him," Menck, crowned with a wreath and holding three others for Haakel, who was tapping at a tack, chimed in.

"I'm going to talk to him now," Menders responded.

"Good, we need him for the descants," Haakel said. "He's the only one can sing the falsetto lines in the carols."

"Thank you, brothers," Menders said with a sudden smile, feeling his spirits lift. The Men were going to forgive – now to speak with Kaymar.

He passed Ifor in the hallway of the Men's Wing, just as he was preparing to tap at Kaymar's door.

"Best of luck," the big man murmured.

"Yes, I'll need it," Menders whispered to himself as he knocked and, after a considerable silence, heard Kaymar's permission to enter.

***

My darling son, Kaymar,

    I wanted very much to send you greetings at this Winterfest, as I know you are still mourning your dear Mikail. I am much concerned for you, little Kip. I have it from Dorsen that Cousin Menders has written to him about your melancholia and madness.

    Kip, I am knowing that your dear Papa and you boys have always protected me, but I understand more than you might suspect. You are the child who is most like me. You have inherited my fragility as well as your Papa's mother's tendency to melancholia. Mikail's death is a terrible blow, but you are young and you must continue, though that is probably hard for you to believe. Though the heart is broken, we keep on living. It is what you make your living into that matters.

    You protect your cousin, the little Princess Katrin. You know well how sick this country is at heart. Having come from Fambre where revolution tore the country apart, I know how important it is that this child be kept safe. She may be the salvation of Mordania. I know more of your work than you might think, Kip. You were meant to protect and preserve this royal child.

Though your heart is broken and your mind is in turmoil, it is time to watch for your opportunities. Comfort will come if you will grant it entrance. You must take steps to accept that comfort when it presents itself.

Now then, Mahmay has lectured enough. I have Winterfest preparations to make. Know that I think of you often, my youngest.

Your loving mother,

Dorlane Cheval-Shvalz
Princess of Fambre

Kaymar had read his letter over twice and was sitting on his bed, thinking of his lovely mother, a true Fambrian Princess who gave lie to the many women who claimed to be such. She was frail and high strung, but she had an inner core of steel and truly ruled the roost at Moresby in an elegant and loving way.

A tap on his door startled him. He had been drifting in thoughts of Mahmay, as the Fambrians lovingly called their mothers. He considered not answering, not being in the mood to be dutifully invited to join the Winterfest gathering. Then his eyes fell upon his mother's exquisite handwriting.

"Enter," Kaymar said quietly and waited for his cousin to come in.

CHAPTER 29
KATRIN'S BIRTHDAY

Dear Aylam,

The tools you sent have been very helpful and the trouble we've had from the pests I told you about is much less. Hopefully the pests will go back to their old haunts soon and leave us in peace.

The ice bridge is not forming this year, with the soft winter, so we will not be able to see you. Please pass my greetings on to Katrin. Tell Golden Heart not to be despondent, as the time I will spend here will give me a chance to accumulate enough bride goods to buy her for my seventh wife.

We are all well and I have a new son to occupy the winter months. It is as well we cannot travel, as there have been many new babies this summer. Thira is clamoring for me to send her best greetings to Katrin. I will spend some time this winter teaching her to read and write Mordanian, as she is very keen. Then she can write her own letters and stop commanding her old father to her will.

You may send a return letter through your tenants at Stettan. The warrior who is carrying this letter is leaving us to live in Erdstrom, which is something that saddens me greatly, as you know too well the fate of so many of our people who try this. Perhaps a well placed word from you will dissuade him, or at least guide him away from harm.

Let me know all your news. I think of you often, my brother.

Tharak

Menders rolled the thin, animal hide parchment into its delivery tube and put it aside. He began to write a response.

Dear Tharak,

I had suspected the ice bridge would not form, as the winter here is mild compared to previous years. Eiren has been able to keep school open with the exception of a few very nasty days. She was dejected over not seeing you this winter, and wanted to let you know that she's practiced chewing hides to soften them all summer, in preparation for becoming your seventh wife. I doubt, however, that the entire Thrun nation could come up with enough bride goods to make me trade her to you!

Though a soft winter is drab, it does make a lot of social visiting possible and we've been quite busy with a round of dances held here at The Shadows, as well as a visit from my old friends, Cahrin and Olner, who brought their two lively boys along with them, providing welcome company for Katrin and Hemmett. Things have seemed a bit flat since they returned to Erdahn.

We've been hard pressed to find sufficient occupation for Katrin. Winter coming on has helped, as everyone's freedom is restricted and it isn't possible for her to run down to the river or into the woods. After one good snowfall, Eiren and I took her for a sleigh ride to the village, which was an enormous success, as she has never been anywhere but The Shadows. We hoped to stay overnight, but the weather threatened to turn and we had to hurry home.

Katrin is learning quickly and is ahead of her age in reading and other subjects. She is becoming quite skilled at the spinet, and loves to dance. I have not made much of it, but she is also acquiring some of the skills of an apprentice assassin. If nothing else, the exercises will challenge her mind and give her good balance. They could also be lifesaving, if certain circumstances arise.

I am enclosing a little letter from Katrin to Thira. Let's encourage this correspondence, as it will be good practice for them both.

I have children making a great deal of noise upstairs with the new toy soldiers that Lucen carved for Hemmett as a Winterfest gift, so I shall go and quell the insurrection. I think of you often, my brother.

Aylam

After quieting the children, Menders stopped by the

kitchen to raid the cookie jar and began one of his frequent winter occupations, walking up and down the first floor hallway. His steps fell into time with the ticking of the great clock in the entryway below.

Katrin's birthday was next week. When he'd suggested that receiving gifts from the nine members of the household and all fifteen of Menders' Men, to say nothing of Eiren's family, various estate farmers and other people who knew her would swamp the playroom and her wardrobe, he'd been vigorously shouted down. The village shops had started to keep lists so that no-one would commit the gaffe of giving the Princess the same present someone else had.

Eiren had chosen to make a dress for Katrin as her gift. It was a work of art, white with gold embroidered snowflakes scattered over it. Eiren was running short of time and pressed Menders into service, laughing with delight when she found that he was able to embroider the snowflakes skillfully once she demonstrated the technique.

"How on Eirdon?" she laughed.

"What if I had to pose as a tailor on a mission?" he reminded her. "All assassins and spies learn to sew, most out of necessity because they're infamous clothes-horses and have to alter their clothing to conceal weapons. You can't go to the local tailor and tell him to sew hidden pockets in your coat that will hold a set of throwing knives or a pistol."

"I'll let you mend your own socks then," she teased.

"I can and have for years. I'd be glad to, you have enough to do."

"Faw. I can manage to mend my own man's socks," she said, finishing off another golden snowflake.

"She's going to be thrilled with this," Menders said, spreading the skirt of the little dress. "And I see you were very clever and made it to let out when she gets bigger."

"A trick all farmers' daughters know," Eiren smiled. "We

could make a dress last for four years, if we were clever, and we got into the habit of wearing them plain for a year, embroidering designs on them for the next year, adding new cuffs and collars the third year and then piecing them with contrasting fabrics the last year before they were cut up for other projects. That pillow is covered with the skirt of one of my old dresses," she said, pointing to a tawny beige cushion embroidered with stars. "We wasted nothing."

Menders took another turn down the hallway, considering what to give Katrin himself as well as what might be done to change the usual winter routine and to replace the Thrun carnival. Getting up competitions wasn't very appealing, because they went on all the time at The Shadows now. Marksmanship, footraces, horse races and wrestling were very popular with Menders' Men. It helped them keep their skills sharp and worked off energy, of which they all had a plentitude. Organizing more wouldn't have any particular glamour or novelty.

He stopped pacing and looked out the window. Sunlight reflected from the frozen surface of the stone lions that flanked the front door.

The idea dawned suddenly and was so exquisite that he grabbed his coat and hat and headed for the woodlot.

A quick inventory yielded everything he would need. He made some sketches and detoured by the toolshed to be sure that there was plenty of twine available. Then he took a trek into the woods, studied the sky for a while, spat on several branches and watched how long the spittle took to freeze. Thoroughly chilled, he made his way back to the house.

Later that evening Eiren was going over school papers when Menders told her he was going outside for a while.

She glanced quizzically at the frozen window and then at him.

"Ah me, another woman," she joked.

"Yes, a liaison in the toolshed. I so enjoy being naked in

the freezing cold," he grinned, bending to kiss her. "It's a secret, but you'll like it. I'll be late."

Outside he followed his earlier footprints into the woods. Once there, he built a fire, then began trudging back and forth to the woodlot for long flexible saplings that had been cut during the summer. Journeys to the toolshed produced huge balls of twine, wire, a bucket, a ladder, the sledgehammer and several saws as well as a pair of work gloves to wear over his own elegant leather ones.

A frenetic hour and a half of sawing, bending, tugging and wrapping rendered a skeletal armature of a grundar, the giant elk of the northern Mordanian forests, eighteen feet high at the shoulder. He'd secured it to the ground, driving metal pegs into the earth with a sledgehammer. After warming his numbed hands at the fire, he returned to the armature and packed it with snow. He flung water over the structure. It froze immediately.

Pleased with the success of his plan, he began to flesh out the sculpture with more snow, followed by deluges of instantly freezing water.

Many hours' work left him aching muscles, a sheen of sweat under his clothes and a colossal grundar sculpture made of ice and snow. The firelight made it sparkle – when the sun touched it, it would be incredible. Menders dragged himself into the house and checked on Katrin.

She was sound asleep in her bed, her arms around a stuffed walrus toy that had been a Winterfest gift from Franz. He made sure the fire was burning well, kissed her and whispered, "Everything is all right, sleep well, Little Princess." Then he went thankfully to Eiren's room, stripped in front of the warm stove and washed with the hot water she had left simmering. When dry and suitably warmed, Menders crawled beneath the bed covers. Eiren murmured and snuggled against him. He fell asleep almost immediately.

The next night he repeated the process, first taking time

to set several telltale traps that would make noise if anything approached. He didn't want wolves or a real grundar, for that matter, creeping up on him. Such animals did not fear fire and also had notoriously bad tempers. The first night he hadn't bothered, but the idea of making one ice sculpture had expanded in his mind. He had a grand plan.

That night yielded another enormous grundar. He had a system now and the work went faster. If the weather held and he didn't collapse from lack of sleep, Katrin's birthday would be full of wonder.

Crawling into bed, shivering, he woke Eiren, who wrapped herself around him.

"You're so cold!" she exclaimed. "Your poor hands! What on Eirdon are you doing out there all night long?"

"Something wonderful. Don't make me tell, you'll see in a few days."

"If you don't freeze first. Here, get closer. If you're going to go gallivanting around in the snow in the middle of the night, at least wear double socks. Poor darling."

He was creating an enormous boar the next night when one of the telltales rattled, then clanged and Franz's voice rang out.

"Who the hells put a string full of saw blades across there!" Menders disappeared into the trees as several members of Menders' Men hissed at Franz to shut up. He ghosted up behind Franz and said, "May I help you?"

Franz jumped and shrieked, turning around so fast he fell over the telltale again. Once extracted from the snow, he stood there glowering.

"What in hells are you doing out here all night long?" he asked.

"Swimming and chasing women. What the hells does it look like?" Menders pointed to the two huge ice grundar, which were even more spectacular after melting slightly in the daytime, then refreezing at night. Menders had flung buckets of water over them nightly and they were now something out of a fairy tale, glistening and sparkling in the firelight.

Menders' Men came out of the shadows and stood there staring, openmouthed.

"You made these?" Haakel asked.

"No, they followed me home. Of course I made them. They're for Katrin's birthday."

"You've been out here most of three nights in the cold doing this?"

Menders didn't even bother to answer, just went back to his boar. Within seconds he had an audience. They didn't ask many questions, but studied what he'd done.

"Can we make some?" Haakel asked.

"Saplings there, snow all over the place, melt down snow and ice in the bucket. But get your own buckets, that one's mine." He hauled two ends of saplings together and lashed them firmly with twine.

There was a general exodus in the direction of the shed and house. Soon they were back, carting tools, more ladders, buckets and several jugs of cider that they set to warm by the fire, a box of metal cups and a basket of food. They set to work with a will, sawing, lashing, staking and packing snow on several structures that, after some hours, became a borag, a langur, a horse and a leaping fish. Menders watched with satisfaction as a cheerful Kaymar helped Ifor Trantz build a giant wolf with icicles for teeth and red firestone gems for eyes. Winterfest had brought his troubled cousin the comfort he needed in the form of Ifor's devotion. It was good - and droll - to see warmth-loving Kaymar braving the bitter cold to work beside his new bonded.

Menders' project was much easier with company and help, and a small idea snowballed into a huge one. Each night, the men of The Shadows trekked into the snowy woods, spending hours hauling and sawing saplings, building frames and packing them with snow. A system had been developed and they were turning out several animals a night, ranging them throughout the woods in a breathtaking display.

Lucen joined them after tromping out one night with a shotgun to see just who was making such noise. He constructed an archway in the form of a huge heart as the entrance to the world of ice animals. The crown jewel of the collection was a thirty foot giraffe. It towered above the frozen menagerie and turned out fine after Menders insisted that someone go refer to a book on animals, for it became obvious that the Men had conflicting ideas as to what a giraffe looked like. The real things were a very long way away on the grassy sunlit plains of Surytam. No-one at The Shadows had ever laid eyes on one.

Exhausted on the night before Katrin's birthday, the sculptors flung the final buckets of water over their creations, cleared up all the tools and spent considerable time erasing their footprints and shoveling snow over the trampled areas around the animals.

A couple of hours later, at sunrise, Menders was up again, wanting to wake Katrin before everyone else rose. He always spent a little time alone with her on her birthday, before the rest of the household began to celebrate.

She woke quickly, looking rosy and excited. Menders felt bleary and weary but the bright expectant look on her face helped erase the ache in his bones.

"Happy birthday, Little Princess," he whispered conspiratorially. "Something wonderful happened in the night. Get dressed and come outside to see."

They crept down the stairs and out of the house without a sound.

"What is it?" she asked has he led her away from the house.

"It's something that only happens for special birthdays," he said. "You have to be quiet or they'll run away."

He could tell she was about to burst with questions. He led her onward into the woods, which were glistening with the first light of the sun.

She stopped short in amazement when she saw Lucen's heart archway, glowing gold and sparkling like a million diamonds. Menders urged her on.

"Once you walk under that magical archway, they won't be able to run away and they'll be here with us the rest of the winter," he whispered. She took his hand, her bright blue eyes crackling with curiosity. They stepped under the archway.

The huge grundar were first, towering high above her, brilliant colors glistening from their depths. Great antlers thrust up against the sky, transparent in places, dripping with long pointed icicles. Behind them stood colossal boars, their tusks winking in the sunlight.

Menders leaned against a tree, delighting in Katrin's wonder as she moved from one enormous sculpture to the next. She gazed up at a giant manquar in awe, slowly reaching up to touch one of its long, sharp claws. The wolf and his mad red eyes made her shrink back a little at first, but then she patted its frosty muzzle. She finally came to the giraffe, and turned back to Menders, her eyes huge.

"Where did they come from?"

"They come from The Light At The Top Of The World," he said. "From farther north than the Thrun live, from a place where it is always winter and there is always ice and snow. These animals are born from the breath of the first winter wind and they live, even though they are made from snow and ice. They blow down on the wind, circling Eirdon until they find a place where they feel the people are worthy. Then they come to the ground to play. If just the right person walks under the magical archway to their kingdom, they freeze in place, just like this, and make their home there for the rest of the winter."

"Can they move around?" she asked, turning to stare at

the animals again.

"Only when it's dark and there is no-one looking."

She walked farther into the woods, finding farlins, the borag, horses, fantastical birds and fish, a greenback whale and more wolves. Menders could feel every muscle in his body aching, but it was worth it, just for the look in her eyes. She came running back to him, arms outstretched, He caught her up and spun her around.

"Did you make the magic happen?" she asked, hugging him and then bending back so she could look into his face.

"I might have had something to do with it," he grinned. "I'm a wizard, you know."

"No, you're the Dark Knight and you can do anything!"

He felt a lump in his throat. She'd listened to scores of stories about the Princess and the Dark Knight, but had never mentioned seeing a connection. It touched him to know that she understood.

"I had a word with the winter wind as to where those animals should come," he said. "What do you think?"

"They're beautiful. And they're so big! Will everyone be able to see them, or just you and me?"

"The magic is for everyone, but you're the very first person to see them, my Little Princess."

They tramped back to the house where Eiren stood in the door as they came up the steps, smiling, bending to give Katrin a kiss. Menders slipped past them to where Franz was grinning like a bear with a fresh beehive.

"I kept everyone back so you could take her out there alone," he said softly. "How did she like it?"

"It was… I'll remember it when I'm very old," Menders said rapidly, not wanting to let his emotions get away from him. Franz gripped his forearm for a moment and then turned to wish Katrin a happy birthday. The congratulations began, while she told everyone about the magical animals that had come to live in the woods. A mad exodus followed as people went to see. Cook came back with tears in her eyes. She hugged Menders then kissed his cheek.

"What you dear men will do for that child warms my heart." Breakfast was an especially lavish affair.

Later, Menders strolled through the acres of sculpted animals with Eiren, enjoying for the second time a dear one's delight. She was amazed.

"Tell me you didn't do all of this," she gasped, staring up at the giraffe.

"I never could have. The fellows all came out the third night and helped. We were out here for six nights building them."

"I'll have to bring the school children and my family here," Eiren breathed, looking up at the giraffe. "They'd think I'd gone winter-mad if they didn't see this with their own eyes."

"Bring anyone you like," Menders smiled. "But give me a night's sleep first."

She smiled up at him and touched his face.

"Remarkable man," she whispered.

CHAPTER 30
PUZZLES WITH NO SOLUTIONS

Katrin and Hemmett burst out of the woods and leapt onto the big rock by the river. It was a fine, sunny morning and they had managed to give Haakel the slip.

"Nobody following us," Hemmett panted, looking down the path.

"Nobody spying on us!" Katrin said jubilantly.

With summer come again, Katrin had become restless about being watched. It wasn't that she wanted to do anything that was wrong – she didn't. She just wanted to be like the Spaltz children, who ran down to the river on their own and played for hours unattended.

"Still don't see Haakel," Hemmett said more calmly now. "He thinks we went on into the woodlot, I'll bet. Faw!" He looked very pleased for a moment. Then his smile began to fade.

"Willow, there's going to be a row from Menders for this," he said dubiously. "There was enough trouble last autumn when you ran away from Kaymar."

"We'll say we were just playing and didn't know we'd left Haakel behind," Katrin answered cooly.

"You're getting to be the worst liar," Hemmett sighed. "Menders would never fall for that anyway. Let's go back."

"Not after all that running. I thought you wanted to get away from them too. Are you really afraid of a little trouble?"

"I'm supposed to take care of you," Hemmett said, grabbing for her hand. "We're going back to the house."

"No!" Katrin jerked her hand from his grasp. She ran to the edge of the rock and looked out over the river. Hemmett followed her, trying to catch her hand.

They froze in place, staring at Kaymar swimming in the river, fifteen feet below. As they watched, he turned on his back to float, saw them and began treading water, flinging his long blond hair out of his face with a splash.

"Who is with you children?" he called.

"Haakel," Katrin responded quickly.

Kaymar's blue eyes drilled into hers.

"Tell him to come up by you and speak with me," he said quietly. Katrin gulped and tried to answer, then looked away.

"He isn't with us," Hemmett blurted. Katrin looked up at him and saw his face was bright red.

"I thought so. You come down here on the beach. If you run off, believe me, I will catch you," Kaymar said coldly, starting to swim toward the shore.

They looked at each other and Katrin felt real fear. Hemmett took her hand and helped her off the rock.

Kaymar was close to shore. "Turn around, Katrin," he said briskly. She did and she could hear him hoisting himself out of the water onto the rocks. Hemmett gasped softly. Katrin turned around at the sound.

She heard her own sharp intake of breath as she stared at Kaymar's bare back as he stepped into his trousers.

It was crosshatched with terrible scars. Some of them were huge, the size of a big man's hand. Others looked so deep that she expected to see Kaymar's bones.

Kaymar had heard her and turned as he finished buttoning up.

His chest and belly were as bad as his back. In places the scars were so thick they looked as if they had been plowed into his skin. The insides of his arms were corded with even more scars, deeply crosshatched. Some looked very new, red lines on top of older, silvery scars.

"Did you..." Katrin began. Kaymar cut her off.

"I told you to turn your back. Obviously you're not doing what you're told today." He jerked his shirt on and buttoned it swiftly. Then he was right in front of them, his hands gripping their shoulders.

"I know whose idea it was to run away from Haakel," he said, his nose only inches from Katrin's. "You've gotten altogether above yourself, Your Highness. Now, I have been in Erdahn for a week, working for Menders and meeting with your mother, the Queen. I had to come back on the train and just got in. I've been ages getting here and I was really looking forward to having a swim and a rest – and now I have to walk you two back to the house. That's the end of my rest day, isn't it?"

"We can walk back on our own," Hemmett offered in a very small voice. Katrin couldn't have said a word with Kaymar's blazing blue eyes right in front of her.

"You've shown that you're not to be trusted." He turned away to pull on his socks and shoes, then picked up a small satchel he'd obviously left nearby. Katrin felt terrible. Kaymar looked very tired. She knew that he hated the long train ride because the noise made it impossible for him to sleep.

"Let's go." He gestured for them to walk ahead of him. Katrin turned and stumbled toward the path. Hemmett reached out and took her hand. She held on tightly, suddenly afraid of what they would face at the house.

As they emerged from the woods, they could see Men moving briskly about, obviously looking for them. Menders was on the front steps, sending people in different directions. Katrin could see Haakel. He was pale, looked sick and was pointing toward the place where she and Hemmett had given him the slip.

Ifor was standing by Menders, looking out over the lawns. As they walked closer, he saw them.

"Kip has them," he said. He ran down the steps and over to Kaymar, giving Katrin and Hemmett an angry look. "Kip, you look terrible."

"Many thanks," Kaymar said sharply. "I stopped on my way from the halt to have a swim and rest a bit. The damned train was held over for hours, I've been on it the better part of three days. They came running up to the river, so what could I do?"

"Come on in the house," Ifor said gently. "We'll get you comfortable." He put an arm around Kaymar's shoulders. "You children go on."

Katrin clung tightly to Hemmett's hand as they walked reluctantly toward the steps. She could see Menders watching them. His face was white with anger. They were in for it – but she couldn't stop thinking of those terrible scars on Kaymar's body.

"Bumpy, what happened to Kaymar? I saw him cut his arm once but how could he cut his back?"

"Don't know. Oh Willow, why the hells do you always want to run away?"

"Both of you, go to your rooms," Menders said fiercely when they got to the bottom of the steps. "Don't leave them until I've spoken to you."

They walked numbly up to the door. Katrin could feel Menders' eyes on them every inch of the way. Hemmett released her hand at his suite and went in. She could hear him sniffling and sniffled herself as she went on toward her own room.

***

Katrin tapped softly on the door to the new suite Kaymar and Ifor shared. She almost hoped they couldn't hear her.

Menders had given her a terrible lecture. He had been furious and took her to apologize to Haakel. Then he had sent her up here to apologize to Kaymar – alone.

Haakel had been kind and accepted her apology right away, though he told her that if she ran away from him again, he would no longer be her guard. He had been very grave as he told her this and Katrin had wanted to cry.

But Haakel was easy to apologize to. He was jolly. Kaymar wasn't.

Ifor opened the door and stood there looking down at

her. With the light behind him, he seemed to fill the entire doorway with darkness.

"May I talk to Kaymar?" Katrin asked softly.

"Come in." Ifor stood aside.

This suite was one of her favorite places at The Shadows. Menders had given it to Kaymar and Ifor at Winterfest. They had spent much of the winter and spring painting and getting furniture for it. Ifor had beautiful paintings and statues and they made the rooms interesting. There was always something new to see because Ifor changed the art around all the time.

"Kaymar's in bed. I'll have a look to see if he's sleeping," Ifor said.

"Is he sick?" Katrin asked fearfully.

"Tired. Doctor Franz says he needs to rest in bed for a day or two, his heart is stressed," Ifor answered levelly.

"Because of what we did?" Katrin whispered.

"More being on the train for three days and not getting any sleep – and he had a rough time in Erdahn. What you did today was the icing on the cake, however," Ifor replied, going to the bedroom door and peering in. He said something Katrin couldn't discern, then turned to her.

"Go on in." He held the door open, then closed it behind her.

Kaymar turned in the bed and stared at her. He looked weary and angry. He said nothing, only raised his eyebrows.

"I'm sorry, Kaymar," Katrin ventured. "I shouldn't have run away and I'm sorry I spoiled your rest time. I hope I didn't make your heart worse."

"I thought better of you, Katrin," Kaymar said coldly. "You're a bright child. You know the rules are in place to protect you, yet you still do stupid things like running away. Anyone could be out there. I know you've been told this. Worse still, you get Hemmett to do wrong as well as yourself. He'll go along because he'll do whatever you want and he also thinks he has to go along to protect you."

"I don't mean to. It just seems like fun," Katrin stammered.

"Of course you mean to. You think you're clever to get away from your guards and you're pigheadedly determined to get your own way. I never thought you would act a spoiled brat, Katrin, but you have been this year, and I, for one, am sick of it!" Kaymar snapped.

Katrin felt her throat stretch tight and turned away, bumbling toward the door. Tears flooded her eyes and burned the back of her nose as she turned the door handle. She bumped into Ifor and swiped at her eyes with her sleeve, looking for the front door.

"Oh hells," Kaymar's voice came from the bedroom. "Catch her, Bear."

Ifor's big hand stopped her and turned her around. "Now then, don't cry," he said kindly.

Suddenly Kaymar was there on his knees in front of her, putting his hands on her arms and then hugging her.

"There now – oh Katrin, don't you know that we're all trying to keep you safe?" Kaymar asked. "We don't restrict you to spoil your fun, we do it to keep you safe. That's what this – The Shadows, Menders' Men, me – that's what it's all about, child."

Katrin leaned back and looked at him. He was in his nightshirt. There on his knees he looked like a boy not much older than her. There were dark circles beneath his eyes. She could smell the Hetzophian oilwood perfume he used.

"I'm sorry," she said, far more genuinely than she had said it to Haakel. Kaymar smiled – and the smile hurt her heart, because it made him look even more tired and sick.

"All right then," he answered.

His nightshirt sleeve had fallen back from his right wrist and she could see not only the thick network of scars on the inside of his arm, but cuts that looked like they were brand new.

She opened her mouth to ask what had happened but something in her mind told her that no matter what the answer, this was something beyond what she could understand. All she knew was that Kaymar had been hurt – many, many times.

She looked at his eyes and knew that he saw her curiosity. He was not going to tell her anything. She leaned forward and kissed his cheek.

"Menders told me to come right back," she said. "I hope you feel better soon."

"Goodnight," Kaymar said quietly, rising to his feet. He turned and went back to the bedroom and Ifor saw her back to her own suite, where Menders was waiting.

"I apologized to Kaymar," she said, going to stand before him. "He looks sick. And he has – Menders, why does Kaymar have scars all over him? What happened to him?"

Menders said nothing for quite some time while Katrin waited.

"Kaymar struggles with many things, but that is his business," he finally answered. "It isn't for you to ask or even to wonder about. Now, this has been a hard day for everyone, thanks to you, and I think we'd all like to have an early bedtime. Off you go."

She went, wondering how she could stop wondering about those terrible scars.

***

From Menders' Journal:

Difficulties with Katrin today. She's been teasing Hemmett for being slow to read. Though I am well acquainted with Katrin's faults, they never fail to disappoint me.

Hemmett has progressed with reading through immense determination on his part. He only learned the alphabet after Ifor Trantz carved the letters out of wood, so that he could hold and feel them. Every other method of teaching him failed utterly. I fear this has been damaging to him, as it is becoming obvious that Hemmett feels inferior to others. Much of his clowning is a cover for his insecurity.

The incident today stemmed from an ill-considered attempt to have the children share lesson time now that my eyes are infected again and I am confined to bed much of the time. Eiren normally tutors Hemmett and sets lessons for him to complete; this method has never been ideal for Katrin, but she has joined them the last few days.

Admittedly, it is taxing and even infuriating listening to Hemmett trying to read, and it is only his own frustration and sincere effort that keeps Eiren and me from losing patience with him. There is some quirk in his mind that makes it difficult for him to recognize the letters and remember words. He often complains that the letters change shape or change their order within a word. It must be horrible for him. Sometimes he goes bright red with frustration and the sounds he makes trying to work out the words are absolutely tortured.

Unfortunately, Katrin has no recollection of learning to read, as she has done so since she was tiny. She is too young to understand that Hemmett simply cannot "just try harder", that he is trying as hard as he can to surmount a nearly insurmountable problem. She has shown impatience before, but today burst out telling Hemmett that if he would only concentrate, he could read, and that the book he was struggling with was one she read when she was four – which is the truth.

Poor Hemmett fled. Eiren gave Katrin a well deserved dressing down, the first one she's ever delivered to the Princess. I rose from my dreary sickbed and had Katrin, who needed to be taken down a peg, attempt to translate some sentences in Surelian to demonstrate her own brilliance, deliberately writing them so she couldn't possibly accomplish the task.

At first she was very cocksure but after a few minutes realized she didn't know most of the words. She asked for help. I told her I could translate those sentences when I was four (a lie) and that if she just tried hard enough, she would be able to do it.

Katrin can be high-handed but she caught on immediately and was *very remorseful. She went to find "Bumpy" to make things up with him.*

We shall not continue to have Katrin take formal lessons. It simply does not work, as she becomes bored quickly and indulges in displays of irritation and temper. Time enough for formal schooling later. Hemmett also does not need her around when he's struggling, as her quickness only increases his feelings of inadequacy. Until I am back on my feet, Ifor will have her help him in his office or have her tend to Menck's room. Sadly, Menck's condition is worsening, and he is often bedbound or has to use his invalid chair. It will be a good thing for Katrin to do things for someone who cannot do them for himself.

***

Katrin ran out of the house after lessons. Bumpy had stayed behind for special tutoring from Menders. Ever since she'd hurt his feelings about his reading, she left him and Menders alone. She ran into the woodlot, looking at the colored leaves and finding acorns.

After a while she felt restless. Ever since she and Bumpy had run away to the river it had been forbidden to them. It was autumn now and soon they wouldn't be able to get down to the river rock until winter was over. That would be months away.

She suddenly wanted to go down to the river more than anything. She gave a quick look around, saw no-one watching and began to bolt for the thicker woods surrounding the woodlot.

"Don't try it," Kaymar said sternly, right behind her. Katrin jumped in surprise and turned toward him. He said nothing more. Kaymar didn't waste his time. She knew the rules.

She turned and walked further into the woodlot, with Kaymar fading into the trees nearby. Then she stopped and turned back, looking for him.

"Here," he said, stepping out of the underbrush, his eyebrows raised inquisitively. Katrin took his hand – something she hardly ever did.

"Want company, Cuz?" Kaymar smiled, giving her hand a squeeze.

They walked far into the forest, farther than Katrin could ever remember going before. She was wearing some of Bumpy's old clothes, which Eiren let her do whenever she was going to do something that might ruin her dresses. For a time she pretended that they were heroes going on a quest. Then they just walked, looking at odd mushrooms, collecting leaves and talking about different animals. They sang a round together, Katrin's treble and Kaymar's high tenor chiming together in harmony.

As the song wound to a finish, Katrin sat down on a fallen log. They had walked a long way. Kaymar settled beside her and grinned, something he didn't often do. He had been much happier since he and Ifor had started living in a suite together. She could remember the year after Kaymar's friend died, when he hadn't smiled once, at least not that she had seen.

"I see riding one little cousin home on my shoulders in my future," he said. "We've had quite a walk, my dear."

"I've never been this far into the forest," Katrin said. "I would like to build a house right here. A secret house only I know about."

"When I was your age, I wanted to build a house in a tree – in fact, I would still like to," Kaymar answered.

"What if the wind blew?" Katrin scoffed.

"It would have to be a big tree. There are trees in Surytam the size of The Shadows. They wouldn't sway too much," Kaymar said. "Imagine a little house in a tree like that."

"You should find a big tree and build that house here!" Katrin cried, excited at the idea.

"Your handsome cousin is far too lazy to do that much hard work," Kaymar laughed, pulling a small tin from his pocket and offering her a piece of candy from it.

"You work all the time," Katrin protested. "You're always

watching me or going to Erdahn for Menders or making things in your shed. You aren't lazy."

"Oh, by nature I'm lazy indeed," Kaymar replied, reclining against a branch that stuck straight up from the log. "Things like building houses are not for me. Perhaps one day I will hire someone to design and build a tree house for me, while I watch and tell them what to do."

Katrin laughed at that. Kaymar could be bossy and she should know. He watched her more than any other guard.

"We should start back," Kaymar went on. "Don't want to be late for dinner. Want a ride, or are you up for more walking?"

"I'll walk," Katrin said, jumping up and taking his hand as they turned back toward The Shadows. She asked him questions about Surytam for a while. Kaymar had been there and could tell about all sorts of strange and interesting things.

She stopped in her tracks suddenly, sniffing, wrinkling her nose in dismay.

"A felschat!" she said in horror. Suddenly the air was laced with the pungent odor of the forest dwelling animal, known for marking territory with its scent glands – and for spitting the terrible scent at anything that threatened it. Grey and pudgy, they waddled around the forests and feared nothing, because nothing could stand the way they smelled.

Kaymar tightened his grip on her hand and hurried. "Yes, and we don't want to meet up with him," he said, his voice tense. He pulled his handkerchief out of his pocket and held it over his nose. Katrin pinched her own nose shut and trotted along with him, though she looked around curiously, to see if the felschat was nearby. She had only seen one at a distance, when Menders and Eiren had taken her to the river to swim last summer.

The smell got worse. Kaymar stopped, pressing the handkerchief to his nose and mouth. His face was turning dark pink and Katrin realized he was trying to hold his breath. He looked around, his face growing redder by the second.

"There he is," Katrin gasped, pointing to the left. A lumpy, bristly, grey creature with an undershot jaw rustled out from behind a bush, its squinted, reddish eyes roving over them.

Kaymar took a great gulp of air through his mouth. He thrust Katrin behind him and backed away from the felschat.

The animal grunted and charged toward them, pumping its jaws as it spewed the foul fluid from its mouth. Katrin began to run but was almost pulled off her feet as Kaymar fell to the ground and lay motionless.

Katrin looked around for a stone to throw at the felschat but suddenly remembered Menders' words.

"If you're ever threatened by an animal and know you can't outrun it, make yourself small. Get down on the ground and curl up in a ball with your hands on the back of your neck and don't move. Even if the animal comes right up to you, don't move or make a sound. The animal will think you've decided not to fight or hurt them and will go away."

She crouched down against Kaymar's side, tucking her head against her bent knees, clenching her hands on the back of her neck.

She could hear the felschat snuffling around, grunting and waddling through the leaves. The smell was horrible because it was so close. Tears streamed out of her eyes and she huddled closer to Kaymar, pressing her ear against his side, trying to hear his heart beating.

After a while, she could hear the felschat moving away. She peeked over Kaymar's shoulder and saw it shuffling through the trees, its clublike tail dragging behind it.

"Kaymar?" Katrin sat up and tried to shake him. She could see him breathing. He couldn't have held his breath until he fainted, it was impossible to do. She knew that from the time she and Bumpy tried it. "Kaymar!"

She kept shaking him until his eyes opened slowly. They looked sleepy, and Kaymar didn't make a sound, or seem to see anything. Then his eyes snapped wide and he sat up, staring around him. He slapped his handkerchief over his face and started trying to rise.

"Katrin!" he choked.

"I'm here!" she cried, tugging at his arm. Kaymar turned, his eyes wild. He caught her close to him, squeezing her tight.

"Thank the gods," he gasped. "How long?"

Katrin pulled back. He was squeezing so hard she could hardly breathe.

"A few minutes. The felschat went away. I hid behind you and stayed still."

Kaymar scrambled to his feet, pulling her up with him.

"Come on, let's get away, it's still thick here, I don't want to…" he mumbled as they rushed on through the trees. Katrin was busy watching out for roots so she didn't trip and didn't notice that they had come to the woodlot.

Kaymar sank down on a log and wiped his face with his handkerchief. He looked terrible, pale with red splotches on his cheeks. He caught his breath for a moment and then looked at her.

Katrin was used to Kaymar being what Menders called "flippant" and she was also used to him looking creepy or scary. It never bothered her, because she knew he was good. She had never seen him looking frightened before. She went to stand right next to him, her hand on his shoulder.

"Did you faint?" she asked softly.

"Sweetheart…" he began. He looked around as if he was trying to find something. Then he looked into her eyes.

"You know the boarhound puppy that has fits?" he asked, his voice gentle.

"Yes. He falls down sometimes and thrashes around and Menders said he shouldn't be bred. That's why Haakel is keeping him as a pet," Katrin answered.

"Sometimes when I smell something bad enough, I have a

sort of fit," Kaymar said slowly. "That's what happened when that felschat spat at us. That's why I fell down."

"I thought you'd tripped at first and knocked yourself out," Katrin mused. "Then I knew you had fainted. It was like you were asleep. Why does a bad smell do that?"

Kaymar shrugged. "I don't know. Neither do the doctors I've seen. It's not just any bad smell. I can walk by a rubbish heap and feel fine. It has to be something like that felschat."

"It was so horrible it made me feel dizzy. And as if I was going to be sick."

"It makes me feel that way too, but then I faint." Kaymar put his elbows on his knees and rested his chin on his hands. "I never expected to have a fit when guarding you, Katrin. It doesn't happen often, and you did the right thing in this case. You do know what to do if anything ever happened to me when I'm guarding you…"

"Get away and out of sight if it's a person who's attacked you. Get up a tree or under something heavy if it's an animal. Run right back to The Shadows if you've been hurt and get help," Katrin recited firmly. "I've known that since I was little."

Kaymar looked up at her, looking like himself for the first time since he'd had the fit. His eyes were twinkling with amusement. "As if you weren't little now, grown up seven year old," he teased. Then his face grew grave.

"Katrin, we can't let Menders know that this happened," he said softly.

Katrin felt a terrible cold chill go down her back. This was an important thing, something that Menders had to know. There had been danger and Kaymar had been ill.

"That would be wrong," Katrin said. "Menders has to know when things happen."

Kaymar closed his eyes.

"Child, if we let him know I have fits, he won't let me guard you anymore," he said very quickly. Katrin gasped and felt sick.

He was her favorite guard – and her cousin. He didn't play with her like Haakel and Bertel, but she knew he would defend her with his life. And he always told her the truth. Even when it was something she didn't like. He didn't think anything of scolding or punishing her if she did wrong. Bumpy too. Kaymar was fair and he understood how children thought and felt. Even though he was very grown up, sometimes she felt as if he was also a child.

But she should tell Menders. If Kaymar had a fit when he was guarding her, it would be dangerous. Today the threat was only a felschat that couldn't have done much harm, but if Kaymar fainted some other time…

"It's too big for you, isn't it?" Kaymar asked her, reaching out and touching her cheek. "Not fair of me to put it in your hands. Katrin, I haven't had such a fit in years. I thought I had outgrown it altogether. Unless a bad man comes here with a felschat that spits at me, I don't think I'll be fainting again anytime soon."

Katrin laughed out loud. The horrible tingly feeling down her spine went away. Then she thought about Kaymar not being her guard.

"Would you leave The Shadows if you couldn't be my guard anymore?" she asked.

"No, Menders would find plenty of things for me to do," Kaymar answered. "But he wouldn't want me to guard you, because he would think it too risky. Menders would make a mistake, thinking that he was doing the safest thing, but he would end up taking away the best protection you could ever have."

Katrin stood there, leaning against his shoulder. Kaymar put his arm around her waist and gave her a little squeeze. He said nothing, letting her think.

Something in her mind said, "He is your protector." It was as if someone had spoken to her.

She blinked and then looked at him.

"I won't tell Menders," she said. "I hope that isn't a lie, but I want you for my guard, just like you have been."

Kaymar sighed a little and then looked at her.

"You're a bit young to understand this, but I'm going to tell you anyway," he said firmly. "As you grow older, you are not going to want to tell Menders everything, and it won't be necessary for him to know everything about you. I consider him as close as a brother to me. He knows more about me than my own brother does. That doesn't mean that I tell him every little thing I do. If I thought that there was truly a risk to you because of my fits, I would tell him myself."

"And you want to be my guard," Katrin added.

Kaymar looked right at her. "Yes, Princess Katrin, I do," he answered. "I consider it my duty and privilege."

"Then we'll go on just like we have," Katrin said.

"It's agreed," Kaymar answered, looking very stern. "And while we're talking, it's time to discuss something else. It's high time you stopped trying to run off on your own, Katrin. You've caused a great deal of trouble, yet you were about to run off again today. You know all the reasons why you shouldn't do it."

Katrin felt her face contorting into a scowl.

"I want to be like other children," she said angrily.

"I know. You aren't like other children. This has been explained many times. I know you understand. Time to accept reality, Katrin."

She felt hot tears close and gulped.

"I know it's hard," Kaymar continued.

"I hate being the Princess," she said angrily.

"I think we all hate something about ourselves," he answered. "We learn to work around it."

"Do you hate anything about yourself?" Katrin shot back mutinously. Kaymar laughed, a short, mirthless sound. Then he looked at her for a long time.

"I think you can understand," he said softly. "Yes, sweetheart, I do hate something about myself. I'm mad, Katrin. Do you know what that means?"

Katrin didn't know what to say. She had heard some of the Men saying Kaymar was mad.

Kaymar often talked to himself but not like other people, who might wonder aloud or swear if they dropped something. He talked as if he was talking to someone who wasn't there. He didn't do it all the time but when he did, it was very strange. Sometimes he looked like he was afraid of something, or very angry. Once in a while he would laugh when there wasn't anything to laugh at.

And the scars. Could they be part of being mad?

"I think so," she ventured.

"It's an illness, but it doesn't make my body sick. My mind is sick. Sometimes I'm sad for no reason, so sad that you can't imagine it. Other times I feel afraid or angry. I have frightening dreams, sometimes when I'm awake. Sometimes I hear voices in my head," Kaymar said quietly. "It can be terrible, but I've learned how to control it. I learned how not to listen to the voices and how to work my way out of the sadness and the anger. It's hard. Sometimes I want to give up, but I have a lot of things to live for. So I have to accept it, know that I am not like other people, and work with that."

"Why are you mad?" Katrin asked.

"Some very bad things happened to me when I was younger," Kaymar answered. "A mind can break just like a body can, if enough happens to a person. Once a mind is broken, it's never quite the same."

"Is that why you have scars all over you?" Katrin blurted.

"It's part of it, yes," Kaymar replied. "We're not going to talk about that, because it's nothing you need to know. My life has been far from easy, Katrin, and I had to grow up far too young, just as you will have to do in some ways. If I could have changed it, I would have, but I had to learn to accept a lot of very unhappy things about life – and about myself."

Katrin thought of Kaymar's scarred body and of him being mad. 'My life has been far from easy.' He seemed happy much of the time now. Whatever put those scars on him had to have hurt terribly, but he had a nice life now.

"I won't do it anymore, Kaymar," she said suddenly, lifting her head and looking at him.

"Thank you," he answered. He gave her a little hug and then stood.

"Would you spend more time with me like today?" Katrin asked, looking up at him. Kaymar blinked in surprise.

"If you'd like. We had a good time before that felschat turned up," he answered. "I don't have to be hidden all the time. Think of something you'd like to do tomorrow and we'll see to it," he answered.

Katrin took his hand as they walked out of the woodlot and toward the house.

***

"Bear?"

"Yes, Kip, I'm right here." Ifor looked around his book at Kaymar, who was lounging on the sofa opposite.

"Ran across a felschat when I was walking with Katrin today."

Ifor tapped his nose. "I can still smell, Kip."

"Come on, I've had a bath and burnt everything I wore," Kaymar snorted. "That damned animal didn't hit me directly, it wasn't like I was reeking when I got back here."

"You're a veritable rose now. Stop pouting and tell me what you want to say," Ifor said good-naturedly, smiling at the beautiful young man across the room.

"I had a fit. Fell down in a dead faint while I was trying to get her away from the thing," Kaymar said abruptly. "The stink did it."

"Yes, you've told me about that trouble," Ifor responded, putting the book down. "You haven't had it in years, you said."

"That's true and I haven't thought of it for years. But it left Katrin completely unprotected today."

"How long were you in the fit?" Ifor asked.

"Katrin said not more than a few minutes. But during that few minutes, she was alone."

Ifor cogitated in silence for a while.

"I'm sure you've calculated the chances of something like this happening again," he finally said. "There is no right answer here, Kip. Only the best one you can find." With that, he got up and went off to bed.

Kaymar couldn't help laughing to himself. Ifor put it in a nutshell and left the stage. Infuriating, sensible and incredibly typical.

His laughter faded as he remembered the last time he'd fallen unconscious over a stench.

He had gutted a man – not in the course of an official assassination order, but during his years of continual madness, when he tracked down and removed men who preyed on children. The moment this particular pederast's guts were cut open, a wave of reek had knocked Kaymar cold.

He'd wakened from the faint lying in the alleyway right next to his dead victim. He'd been as thoroughly terrified by his vulnerability then as he was terrified by what had happened today. When he'd regained consciousness and realized that Katrin had been unprotected, during that moment of not being sure just where he was or where she was, he'd experienced fear that he'd never known.

Even so, he was her best defense against the dangers that threatened her. He had the advantage of being years younger than Hake and Bertie. He had the advantage of being able to contend with Katrin's occasional rebellions directly and without sweet-talking or cajoling her. He had her respect – she had his devotion.

He'd found that best answer Ifor had told him to search for.

As he got into bed and snuggled against his bonded's broad back, Ifor's heavy voice came out of the darkness.

"Stay out of the woods with the littlies for a day or so, give me a chance to shoot any felschats I see. They're damn pests, could do with a little thinning out. That'll fend off any more fainting fits."

Kaymar smiled in the darkness and went to sleep.

***

Kaymar was roaming the perimeter of The Shadows' lawn, something he did frequently. He was not officially on duty, as both children were inside the house and weren't expected to go outside for the rest of the day – but Kaymar was never off duty. He tended to prowl. It was one of the things about him that people found disturbing. Prowling gave him time to think.

It was hard to believe he'd been at The Shadows for three years. One year had been dulled by the deep grief and madness that had overtaken him after the death of his bonded lover, Mikail. Kaymar could barely recall details of that year. The time stretched from early winter to early winter as a grey, dreary fog. As happened when his melancholia became severe, his vision had altered, the colors of the world fading to monochrome shades of grey. The only variation from this numb withdrawal had been violent episodes of anger that had led to Menders' Men shunning him during that year.

Then Menders had persuaded him to come to Winterfest dinner, appearing at his door and sincerely asking him to join the rest of the household. Kaymar couldn't say no. He'd been made welcome at dinner, Menders' Men obviously ready to forgive his lack of control. The wine flowed very freely, particularly as the night wore on, and the traditional songs had been sung, the customary jokes made. But Kaymar felt absolutely no joy in the occasion and excused himself fairly early, having been polite and cordial while drinking far too much. He wanted nothing more than the escape of sleep in the silence of his rooms.

When he entered the hall that ran the length of the Men's Wing he saw Ifor Trantz drunkenly trying open his door, swearing incoherently to himself as he scraped at the lock with his key. Kaymar walked silently toward his own apartment across the hallway from Ifor's, loathe to startle the big man, who was known to react violently when surprised in a drunken state. Then he thought better of trying to pass Ifor undetected. Though Kaymar was far more skilled at fighting and was not handicapped by a damaged back as Ifor was, he was more than a foot shorter than the older man. He had no desire to be lashed out at by an inebriated giant.

"Can I help you with that, Ifor?" Kaymar asked from a safe distance.

The door came open and Ifor turned toward him simultaneously. Kaymar was frozen in his tracks by the loneliness and hunger in the other man's eyes, then gaped as Ifor took two huge steps across the hall to him and started stammering out a bumbling proclamation of love. He finally put his hands on either side of Kaymar's astonished face and kissed him with all the finesse of a bear trying to embroider a handkerchief.

What Ifor lacked in subtlety, he more than made up for in passion. Within seconds, Kaymar found himself in the big man's bed, being made love to with a will, without all the subtleties and sophistication that had earmarked his previous love life. He would have laughed if he hadn't been caught up in the tide of Ifor's passion – the first emotion, other than rage and sorrow, that he'd felt in over a year.

The next morning he woke before Ifor, who was snuggled

up against him, for once not snoring deafeningly. He had a gentle smile on his face. Kaymar felt himself smiling in response, the muscles of his face actually protesting a little. Had it been that long since he'd smiled?

Not my type at all, he thought, surveying his huge bedfellow. Though he found women attractive and liked their company, Kaymar always made his strong emotional attachments with men. So far his lovers had been older, sophisticated men around his size.

Ifor was more than twice the bulk of Kaymar, with enormous hands that spanned Kaymar's waist with ease, something the big man had marveled at repeatedly the night before with such touching, drunken naïveté that Kaymar hadn't been able to laugh over it. Ifor had all the sophistication of a grundar, though he was intellectually brilliant. Socially, he was shy, introverted, awkward and bumbling.

Not at all Kaymar's cup of tea.

Ifor opened his eyes. For the first time Kaymar saw that they were nearly black and quite attractive, though most people never saw them because Ifor kept them cast down and let his hair hang over his face.

"Did I hurt you?" Ifor mumbled, looking fixedly at the wall behind Kaymar.

"Of course not," Kaymar answered quietly. "Why would you think you did?"

"I'm a clump," Ifor muttered. "I don't know the softer ways and I know you're used to them." He started to turn away, his face brick red with embarrassment.

"Yes, it was a bit sailor-style but the softer ways are nothing you can't learn," Kaymar replied, putting a hand out to keep Ifor from rolling over. The big man was surprised and looked directly at him.

"Learn?" he said roughly.

Kaymar's mind, quicksilver fast at any time, was flashing

like summer lightning, dozens of thoughts crowding and tumbling over each other.

So he's not my cup of tea. This man loves me. While he was drunk he told me all of it. He's been in love with me since the first time he saw me. He's waited and had no hope for a long time because I was bonded to Mikail. Then he stayed silent for a year, let me mourn and never so much as approached me. He wouldn't have last night if he hadn't been blind drunk. Yes, he's rough and unkempt, his clothes look like an unmade bed and he has all the sexual finesse of a goat in rut, but all I have to do is look in his eyes and know that he'll love me for all time.

Only an idiot would turn down love like that. Do I love him? Not yet, no, but I will, and I'll love him better than anyone else ever could. It takes a while for my heart to hitch to someone, but when it does, it holds. He's good and kind and he'll never stray. And short of wanting him to take it more slowly and gently in bed, I wouldn't

change a damn thing about him, ever. Not from his scuffed shoes to that nest of impossible hair that he can't control without a gallon of hair oil.

"I mean if you're offering, I'm accepting," Kaymar said a little archly.

Ifor stared at him.

"But I'm such a big damn fool and you're…"

"No matter."

Ifor grinned, the first time Kaymar had seen him do so. It changed his face, lifting the heavy contours, smoothing away the perpetual scowl lines. I've been able to make someone that happy, Kaymar thought, grinning back.

And suddenly, color had flooded back into his vision and his world.

Now it was the following autumn and he'd learned to love Ifor. They were inseparable and worked well as a team. Menders sent them on missions together and had also given them a suite of rooms in the Family Wing so that they didn't have to try to live as a couple in apartments separated by a hallway they shared with a bunch of men who weren't nancy.

Best of all, light and laughter had come back into Kaymar's life. If it had taken a "big damn fool" to do that, good enough.

On this early autumn evening, Kaymar's prowling was a good way to kill time until Ifor returned from hunting, one of the few things they didn't share. Kaymar was about as outdoorsy as a crystal vase and could do without hunting and fishing, which were the breath of life to Ifor.

Kaymar put his hands in his pockets and shuffled a bit in the autumn leaves carpeting the ground in a mosaic of color, smelling a drift of cigar smoke from the house, delighting in the crisp chill that was setting in with the dropping of the sun.

A man sprang up out of the bushes, brandishing a knife. He lunged at Kaymar, who instantly drew the dagger attached to his belt, hammering it into his attacker's heart.

He stared at the fallen body of the man at his feet, and then at the dagger in his hand. He hadn't thought. He'd reacted automatically and with lightning speed. Now a man lay dead, and Kaymar had no idea who he had just killed.

***

Menders, pulling on his good jacket in preparation for dinner, heard three shots in rapid succession outside, very near the house. He dashed from his room, glanced in to make eye contact with Eiren who was helping Katrin with her hair and indicated with a slight head motion that he was going to investigate. Eiren, knowing the signal meant that an intruder had been found, nodded ever so slightly and said, "I hope that was someone getting a deer, Cook said we need some more meat."

"I don't think so," Katrin said knowingly but without

concern. "No-one here needs to shoot a deer more than once."

Menders ran out onto the front steps and saw Kaymar in the dimness, bending over a figure on the ground. He hastened in that direction. Seeing Menders, Kaymar stood, obviously rattled.

Menders put his hands on his younger cousin's shoulders. "All right?" he asked.

Kaymar nodded.

"I'm sorry, Menders – he surprised me and I killed him outright," he said frankly.

"Do you know who it is?" Menders asked.

"No, it's very odd." Kaymar handed Menders a knife any self-respecting assassin wouldn't use to scrape a carrot. "He was armed with this. He has no papers, no identification, no purse or wallet. Only this around his neck." He held out a medallion. Someone extended a lantern, as the light was fading fast. Several of Menders' Men had arrived on the scene. They peered at the medallion in the flickering light.

"Ephraemite," Haakel said shortly.

"What the hells?" Menders asked aloud, staring at the body,

The shoddy piece of jewelry was formed into the symbol of the prophet Ephraem, whose followers were obsessively unhappy and guilt ridden, considering anything outside their rigid faith "an abomination". Because of their fondness for preaching loudly in the streets, decrying and abusing all and sundry, they had been driven from Mordania years ago by Katrin's grandmother, Morghenna the Terrible. They had colonized an arid island near Surytam where they indulged their penchant for being miserable without stint.

The man was gaunt to the point of emaciation and wore the roughest of clothing, not at all sufficient for the cold autumn weather.

"Spread out," Menders said to the men gathered round. "I want the entire area searched, outbuildings, everything. Let's make sure he has no friends about. Check with Lucen, cover what he and his men haven't seen to already. Hurry. I don't want to have Katrin wondering why we're not at dinner."

"Ifor's going to be coming back from hunting, so don't shoot him," Kaymar added, ghosting off into the darkening woods.

They scattered, leaving Menders by the body.

Menders knew of six or seven potential plots that might involve danger to Katrin and felt little fear of any of them. Plots were all too easy to find out. People didn't know when to be silent. The moment you had a plot that involved more than one person, the possibility of someone saying something to someone else became exponential. With his connections he knew about any plot almost before the plotters did.

It was the lone lunatic who frightened him. Perhaps that was what this was. The jarring note was the man's Ephraemite medallion and emaciation. Ephraemites were known to starve themselves. They thought it made them pure. If the Ephraemites had somehow found out where Katrin was and had decided that she, like everything else in the world, was "an abomination", that could be a problem.

To Menders' way of thinking, Ephraemites were barking mad. That could mean an entire religious sect of potential lone lunatics – all of them with a longstanding grudge against Mordania – out there, posing a threat to the Royal Family.

He heard someone approaching and looked up.

It was Franz, coming from the house.

"Just in from calls," he said, coming over to Menders. "Eiren suggested I come up and have a look at the cause of all the rumpus."

He squatted by the body and moved the lantern closer.

"Nothing much to him," he said. "Let's get him moved where Katrin can't see from a window and examine him later. I doubt I'll be able to tell you much."

Kaymar walked up to them, deliberately shuffling his feet in the fallen leaves to herald his arrival.

"Menders, this is a long shot and probably worth nothing," he said. "It could be possible that I was the target, if this man was here to kill anyone at all. If anyone on the place would be considered an abomination by the Ephraemites, it would be a nancyboy. An Ephraemite woman called me an abomination in Surelia once."

Menders hadn't even considered such a possibility. Franz put his hands in his pockets, obviously pondering it. Both then shook their heads simultaneously.

"We're all thinking like assassins and we're assuming he is an Ephraemite," Menders said. "There could have been other motivations. He could have been mad or ill. He could have been intending to rob someone. It's possible that this medallion is something he picked up somewhere, from someone he might have robbed. Kaymar, have someone go around to the farms and cottages tomorrow, see if anyone is missing that knife. See if anyone has seen him around. He could have come in on one of the trains. Let's stop assuming he was here to kill Katrin or anyone else and see what we can find. I want the truth, not speculation."

Just then Ifor rode up on his big horse, a deer carcass behind his saddle. Uncharacteristically, Kaymar rushed to him and embraced his leg while he was still on his horse, regardless of the obvious discomfort of some of the Men. Menders noticed the desperate relief on Ifor's face as he saw Kaymar unharmed. The expression was wiped out by fury a moment later when he heard the dead man had gone after his bonded.

Cook yelled from the house, declaring that if they didn't get in to dinner she would feed it to the chickens. They laughed, grateful for the distraction. Menders left them to sort through the story and went to the dinner table, where the subject of dead emaciated men was as buried as The Giants.

Later that night, Menders turned in bed for the hundredth time, making Eiren stir. He decided he might as well get up for a while, or risk waking her. He dressed and went to the hay barn.

The body was laid out on a row of hay bales. Menders sat on another bale and sighed.

Who the hells are you, he thought. Why did you come here? I can't believe that it was for Kaymar. That's even more unlikely than you coming after Katrin. Were you desperate for money or food, ready to rob anyone who came along? How long were you out there? Katrin was playing near there only an hour before you jumped out at Kaymar. Why have you come into my world?

He sat there for a long time before he went back to bed. One thing he hated was questions without answers.

Franz went over the body the next day, and as he had predicted, came up with little.

"The obvious," he told Menders. "Skeletal, hasn't eaten in a while. No overt signs of illness, but that doesn't mean he couldn't have had some internal problem, a brain fever or growth. That can emaciate people and it can send them mad as well. The Ephraemites tend to be
covered with scars from their hobby of beating and torturing each other. This man didn't have a mark on him. Short of carving him up to see if he was seriously ill, that's all I can let you know."

A canvassing of the estate farms and cottages had turned up nothing. No-one recognized the knife or was missing one, no-one had seen a man answering to the description of the body. The stationmaster from the halt had seen no-one. No Ephraemites had been seen around the district in years.

Two weeks later, Menders still knew nothing. He'd sent Kaymar to Erdahn, to try to roust out what he could about Ephraemites. Ifor had contributed what he could find, but it was not much more, just the known facts about the religious sect. They worshipped a single entity, The Sun, and unquestioningly followed a creed set out by the Prophet Ephraem, based on a conviction that everyone was inherently sinful and in need of chastisement. Little was known of how their society and religion were organized. They were extremely secretive since fleeing to their island refuge – and no-one cared enough about them to approach or contact them.

The body of the man was consigned to a grave next to Madame Holz and his reasons for being at The Shadows with his blunt knife were buried with him. Ifor arranged a gravestone for him, the name Mister Enigma carved into the stone.

Mister Enigma lived on in Menders' mind, a puzzle with no solution.

CHAPTER 31
"ONE DAY I'LL MARRY A FIREBREATHER"

From Menders' Journal:

> *We have found that giving Katrin tasks to do for Menck has done a great deal to give her a sense of purpose and to keep her busy. It was my original intention to work off some of the brattish behavior that began to appear at age seven, a time that Eiren assures me can be difficult for girls, but Katrin has taken her work to heart. She not only dusts and uses the carpet sweeper in Menck's room, she also keeps him supplied with water to drink and wash in and supplies fresh flowers as well. She has established a cookie jar on his desk (though she is its best customer) and Menck himself stopped her trying to clean the privy.*

> *In return, he is tutoring her gently and carefully in mathematics. She is learning quickly. She does not grasp that subject as easily as she does language based disciplines and was not prospering with me in this regard, so I am glad to have him take over. It keeps his mind off his condition, which continues to worsen. It is becoming painfully obvious that it will not be long before he is completely paralyzed from the waist down. No amount of traction, massage or other treatment has made much difference.*

> *I've offered once again to send Menck to Erdahn to consult with specialists and have some treatment, but he has turned me down, reminding me that such measures have never done anything before, and have even worsened his condition. I take this as meaning that he has come to grips with the situation and is content to stay where he is. It is difficult for those of us who went to school with him and remember him being so very athletic and active. Even harder for him, I imagine.*

Menders looked up from his journal as the front door banged open. He would wager everything in his pockets that Hemmett had just come home from his journey to Erdstrom. He'd been away with his father overnight.

"Willow! Where are you?" Hemmett began clattering up the stairs, shouting for Katrin. Menders smiled and shook his head. The little boy was still entirely devoted to her and told her everything. Listening in on his tales of Erdstrom would be amusing. Hemmett filtered things through his unique mind and the retelling was often hilarious.

"I'm here," Katrin called from the library. A moment later she ran past Menders' office door and from the sound of things, was being enthusiastically hugged by the overnight wayfarer.

"I brought you a present but it's in Papa's bag," Hemmett blurted. "And guess what there was on the way back? A fair! We stopped at it and there were so many things to see! Papa won a knife for me at one of the games!"

Katrin duly admired the knife and Hemmett's travelogue went on.

"There were stilt walkers and a lady dancing and there was a man who could breathe fire, just like a dragon!" Hemmett exclaimed. "Like this!" From the sound of things he exhaled violently, probably directly into Katrin's face. She shrieked.

"People can't breathe fire, they would burn up!" she protested.

"This man did. He had a torch all lit and he would put it up to his mouth and whoosh! Big flames leaping out. Papa said that he does it by taking some very strong drink in his mouth and lighting that on fire as he blows it out."

"It couldn't have been real flame, he would burn his lips off," Katrin said dubiously.

"Papa says he knows just how to do it. He could send those flames out so far, I'll bet it was twenty feet." Hemmett imitated the fire breather audibly again and Katrin followed suit.

"I would truly like to see that," she said with a note of longing in her voice that made Menders sigh.

She had asked to go to Erdstrom with Lucen and Hemmett. He'd had to explain that was something she simply couldn't do because of the risks involved.

"It's because I'm the Princess, isn't it?" she'd asked, almost rhetorically.

"Yes, it is," Menders had replied. He wasn't about to start telling her comfortable lies.

She'd only nodded and said nothing more about going to Erdstrom. She didn't know that he observed as she watched the wagon going away up the road when Lucen and Hemmett began their trip, and that he saw her looking at the map of Mordania sometimes, drawing lines with her finger between The Shadows and Erdstrom or sometimes between The Shadows and Erdahn.

"Why don't you ask Menders? It isn't that far. It's nearer to here than to Erdstrom. You could be up there in an hour and you're old enough to ride that far," Hemmett suggested.

"No, I can't ask," Katrin answered quietly.

"Why not?"

"Because I won't be able to go. You can do things that I can't do because I'm the Princess. It hurts Menders' feelings too, because he'd like to take me but he can't."

There was a silence.

"I'm sorry," Hemmett said. "I won't talk about it anymore if you want."

"No, I like to hear. I just can't go, that's all."

Damn, Menders thought, swiveling his chair around and glaring through the window.

Katrin was squelching her very understandable desire to rebel to protect his feelings. Seven years old. Damn. Damn, damn, damn.

Katrin was laughing as Hemmett continued regaling her with tales of the fair and Erdstrom, so she was content for now. He would

go and take a look at the tunnel leading to the stables. Lucen had mentioned that one of the timbers looked stressed, and Menders would rather it was seen to before the winter set in. Best to stop brooding and get busy.

He went to the strong room, locking the door behind him before he lifted up the trap that led to the tunnel system. He lit a lantern and, leaving the trap open, stepped down the stairs into the darkness.

The tunnels had held up well through the last winter and had saved infinite trouble and discomfort, though there had not been any blizzards or extremely heavy snowfalls due to the mildness of the season. But it was far more comfortable to move from the stables to the house in the quiet of an underground tunnel than it was to struggle against the wind, slipping on snow and ice. And soon enough there would be another hard winter, where the tunnels would be lifesavers.

Menders took his time, inspecting each beam and support thoroughly. They were holding well, for the most part, though he saw a couple that could use work or replacement. Close to the stables he found the beam that Lucen had mentioned. It definitely needed replacing, it was cracking lengthwise. Probably a defect in the wood. Good thing Lucen had caught it.

Menders walked on until he was under the trap door in the tack room. He was about to open it when he heard a quick light step on the floor above – Eiren, home from her school, putting away her mare's harness.

He opened the trap a crack and cackled wickedly. He had satisfaction of seeing her feet turn around quickly.

"Klaas, there must be a big rat in that tunnel," she said loudly, putting a foot on the trap and pressing it down gently.

"No rats in here, Eiren," Klaas, the stablemaster answered, coming close from his office. "I can't take the chance with the children playing around so I keep traps and such – oh, I see. That kind of rat. I'll leave you to deal with him." He went back toward his office, chuckling. Eiren took her foot off the trap door and Menders pushed it up.

"Come down into the underworld with me," he intoned,

looking up at her with the lantern held below his chin so it would cast eerie shadows on his face.

"Nothing doing, sir," she said, turning and finishing with the harness.

"Then I'll just come up there," he replied, doing so and kicking the trap shut. After a kiss, she linked arms with him as they walked out of the stables.

The walls of The Shadows were glowing gold in the late afternoon light, their color mirrored by the vibrant autumn leaves. As he and Eiren walked along the drive, not speaking, the front door flew open and Katrin and Hemmett raced out, laughing as they ran toward the pond. A moment later they were followed by Haakel, who had the task of shadowing them during Kaymar's absence. His shadow and those of the children were long and blue on the still-green grass. There was a distinct tang of leaf smoke on the air.

"I want to take Katrin up to that tawdry little fair that sets up between here and Erdstrom every year," Menders heard himself saying.

"Is it safe?" Eiren asked gently.

"No. But I want to all the same."

"The fair is leaving the district after tomorrow, according to the children at school," Eiren sighed. She empathized with his frustration; it mirrored her own when trying to provide a normal life for Katrin.

"Grundar shit," Menders muttered.

They stood for a while, watching the children, who were having a rock skipping competition. Hemmett was spectacularly good at it, Katrin not so much, but she made up in enthusiasm for what she lacked in prowess. Haakel, not as unwilling to join in the children's games as Kaymar could be, was giving a good show himself. Menders couldn't help smiling.

After dinner, Eiren came into her room where Menders was resting after being dosed with the eye drops that he used twice daily. She carried a pile of clothing from the stores of castoffs kept for times when someone on the estate would need a garment. Menders blinked his eyes clear and sat up, pushing his glasses onto his nose.

Eiren held up a little girl's dress in a plain broadcloth, then rough garments for a man.

"Perhaps…" she said, and then stopped.

"Brilliant!" he exploded, looking at the little dress. There was also a scarf to cover Katrin's golden hair.

"This was my sister Sana's until she outgrew it. I see she got rid of it before letting the last tuck down," Eiren said, spreading the skirt of the little dress. "It's worn enough that no-one would ever suspect that Katrin is a Princess."

"This suit of clothes will make everyone think that I'm a scarecrow," Menders grinned, looking at the rough garments.

"You can sacrifice elegance for a day, my dear," Eiren said, much amused.

"I have to go talk to the fellows," Menders replied, getting up, kissing her and heading out the door.

***

Katrin woke much earlier than usual.

There was a man standing by her bed, slouched over, wearing an awful old jacket that looked like a horse blanket.

Her breath hitched in her chest and she began to squirm across the bed away from him, trying to scream, remembering how Menders had always told her to scream long and loud if there was any danger and to get away as fast as she could.

The man looked over his coat collar at her – and was Menders. He waggled his eyebrows at her.

"What are you doing?" she cried, her fear turning to laughter. "Where did you get those horrible clothes?"

"'Ere now, me proud princess," he said in a funny voice,

bowing to her like someone who'd never done it before, "What you say you put on this 'ere fancy ballgown and we go an' 'ave a look at the fair?" He held out a worn old dress.

She jumped right out of the bed, hugging him with all her might.

"How did you know I wanted to go?" she cried. "I never said a single word! I knew I couldn't go!"

"I'm magic," he smiled.

He helped her with the dress, which was skimpy and too tight under the arms. He showed her how to tie the scarf to cover her hair, like some of the little farm girls did when they worked in the fields.

Katrin was so excited that, for once, she had trouble eating. Eiren packed up the food, saying they'd get hungry enough on the way. She laughed as Menders tucked his hair up under a horrible old hat that looked like a horse had stepped on it and she said he looked like a proper country bumpkin going courting before kissing them both and sending them on their way.

There was a wagon and dray horse waiting outside. Menders tossed Katrin up into the wagon, took up the reins and clucked to the big horse.

Katrin felt that she could never look enough or see enough of the new things that went by on either side of the wagon. She had never seen these woods and mountains before, and was transported when they drove by a waterfall that cascaded under a wooden bridge in a foamy rush.

Sometimes they passed people on the road. Katrin waved and smiled every time, fascinated by the unfamiliar faces. She could tell when they were getting near the fair, because there were more carts going in the same direction. All of them had children in them. They called out to one another and boasted about the things they were going to do. Katrin had never seen so many carts. She could barely stand it and held onto Menders' arm, hugging it hard and smiling until her cheeks hurt.

"Look down the road," Menders said. She did. There were tents and flags and people. She'd never seen so many people!

Menders found a good place for the horse under a tree, and handed some coins to a man standing nearby to watch it for him. Then he held out his arms for Katrin to jump down, straightened her scarf, took her hand - and they walked into the fair.

There was so much at first that she couldn't even see it. She told Menders and he suggested that they wait a while, until she got used to things and then they would decide what to do next. Katrin looked around until she was more used to all the people and tents and noise and her heart wasn't hammering so hard from excitement.

"What's that?" she asked, seeing people tossing little circles of rope over sticks set in a board.

"It's a contest," Menders said. "If you can get three of those loops over three of the sticks, you win a prize."

"That would be easy," she said. She wanted to try it.

"But the man who runs the game is very clever, and he's fixed it so it isn't as easy as it looks," Menders explained. "Watch for a minute."

She did and saw that people managed to get the first two loops easily, but then they always missed the last one that was the furthest to throw.

"I don't think I could do it then," she said.

"Oh, we'll give it a try," Menders said, moving her over to the game. They stood next to a young man who had just bought several tries. Menders put down some coins and handed her the loops.

Yes, he was right – the first two were easy, the last one she couldn't get on the right stick.

"Faw! I didn't win anything but it was fun anyway," she grinned.

"Oh, it's my turn," Menders said in her ear, "and I just happen to know a trick or two. Watch."

He put down another coin and picked up the loops. He tossed the first two, then took careful aim and got the third one to go where it was supposed to! Katrin squealed and jumped up and down. The man who owned the game gave Menders a little doll that he immediately handed to Katrin. She grinned at the man, who managed to grin back. He looked upset.

Katrin looked where he was looking and saw that it wasn't because they had won something but because the young man next to them was throwing loop after loop and winning every single time. He had a pile of prizes on the counter beside him. He kept trading them back to the man who ran the game for bigger and bigger things. He finally stopped throwing the loops, pushed all the prizes across the counter and said, "Give me yer best then, friend." The man grunted unhappily, handing over a pretty bracelet, just right for a little girl.

Just then a scary looking fellow walked up behind the young man and said softly that he could move on now.

"Oh aye, right, shall do," the young man said. He looked at the bracelet.

"T'won't never fit me wrist," he said, holding it up to the light. He turned, bent down and handed it to Katrin. He tilted his hat brim up a bit so she could see his bright blue eyes, so like her own.

"Care to 'ave this trinket, little girl?" he asked. It was Kaymar! He put a finger to his lips and winked. Then he was gone in the crowd and she had the bracelet in her hand.

Menders laughed and helped her put the bracelet on before he took her hand and walked her away from the crowd.

"That was Kaymar!" she whispered in his ear.

"I know. There are more than just me watching out for you today, so if you see any of the Men, just smile, but don't say anything. They wanted to come to the fair too. Now, don't miss everything watching for them; you see that lot every day."

The smells of food were wonderful and they ate everything there was, cakes, cookies, sausages, apples coated with soft taffy. They looked at every single display of fruit and vegetables, comparing them with the ones grown at The Shadows.

"We should have brought some to show off," Katrin told Menders.

"Perhaps so – maybe next year," he replied. "Look over there at the fellow swinging the hammer." He explained to her that the hammer hit a button and sent a weight flying up a pole. It you hit it just right with the right amount of weight, it would make a bell at the top of the pole ring and you won a prize.

"Can you win that one?" she asked.

"That I can't say, but I'll give it a try once this fellow gets finished making a fool of himself," he grinned. That made her curious. She looked closer.

"It's Haakel," she laughed in a whisper. And it was – and he was not doing very well. The man who ran the game kept convincing him to try again and again. He must have finally gotten the hang of it, because he suddenly started making the bell ring every time, until the man told him that was enough, gave him a bunch of cigars and sent him away.

"He fooled that man," Katrin said. "You try."

"Watch this." Menders set her up on some hay bales so she could see, then went slouching up to the man, looking like he was about to fall down from tiredness or hunger, and gave him a coin.

"Watch the little man, ladies and gentleman, he's going to step right up and have a try!" the game man yelled. "He probably don't weigh more than that hammer, but he's a gamecock, he's ready to show us what he's made of! Pick it up there and give it a try, little fellow!"

Is he ever going to be sorry, Katrin thought, jigging up and down in excitement on the hay bales. She'd seen Menders work in the woodlot since she was born. When he swung a sledgehammer, he did it from the ground up, so fast and hard that big logs flew all to pieces.

Once there was a good crowd standing around, laughing about how he was going to faint when he tried to pick up the hammer, Menders grabbed the handle and swung it around so fast you could hardly see it. The weight whizzed up the pole so hard and fast it nearly knocked the bell off. The game man gave him a cigar and told him to go away. He came back to Katrin with it, laughing.

"Care for a cigar, my dear?" he asked. She opened her mouth as if she was ready to have a smoke, but he handed it behind her. She craned around and saw Haakel wink and walk off, putting the cigar in his pocket.

"He was there behind me all the time?" she asked.

"I wouldn't go off and leave you alone in this crowd if someone hadn't been with you," Menders explained.

They saw everything. There was a beautiful lady who danced to very strange and exciting music, though for some reason Menders kept giggling. Katrin thought it was thrilling, especially the way the lady kept looking like she was going to take her clothes off, but never really showed anything. There was a carousel that Menders let her get on alone, but the moment she chose a beautiful white horse Kaymar was there, lifting her on and standing next to her while the carousel went around. She asked him how he liked the fair and he showed her his pockets full of prizes and cigars.

They played every game they came to. Katrin won a couple of them, pushing the little handkerchief and toy puppy that were the prizes into her pockets. Menders won a cage with two little birds at the shooting gallery, with lots of targets moving around fast. She was worried about the birds in the crowd, but

Kaymar came up to them, took the cage and walked off toward the wagon. She saw that Ifor was playing the shooting gallery. He had a pile of prizes, just like Kaymar had at the ring toss game.

They ate sausages in buns while sitting on hay bales. Katrin looked up to see Doctor Franz, dressed like a farmer, going by with two ladies, one on each arm. He looked over at her and winked. Then they were gone in the crowd.

"Did you see? He had two!" she whispered to Menders, who was having a sort of coughing fit. He nodded, and managed to swallow his bite of sausage. It must have tried to go down the wrong way.

"Yes, well they were both rather small," Menders smiled.

"What will he do with two ladies?" she asked.

"Probably lie a lot and spend too much money," Menders said. That didn't make much sense.

"He might get tired of kissing them because he would have to kiss twice as much," she observed. Menders nearly swallowed another bite the wrong way. "That sausage doesn't agree with you," she worried as he managed to stop choking and stood up.

"Oh, I'll take it with me," he said. "Why don't we go find that fire breather Hemmett was telling you about?"

They saw the strong man, who lifted huge weights, and a bunch of men who were doing tricks on horses. They weren't a patch on the Thrun and Katrin said so.

"You're right there," Menders replied. "Listen. If that isn't the sound of someone breathing fire, I'll be very surprised."

And it was. Katrin sat on Menders' shoulders, staring at the fire breather. Hemmett hadn't been making it up – the man really did breathe fire like a dragon. He made it go in all sorts of ways, in curves and bursts. It was like something out of a dream. She could have watched forever.

Finally she let Menders move on. She was really tired and felt sort of sick from all the things she'd eaten. The sun was low when they got back to the wagon.

Once they were away from the fair, she heard hoofbeats behind them. Kaymar drew even with them while Menders stopped the wagon. Kaymar got off his horse and hitched it to the tailgate, then climbed up and sat next to Katrin, putting his arm around her.

"You look pretty tired, Cuz," he smiled as she snuggled against him and closed her eyes. "I think you had quite a fair."

She nodded.

"I think when I grow up, I'll marry a firebreather," she said. She felt Kaymar laughing where she leaned against him. Menders was laughing too but she didn't care. She'd seen the fair, had gone and had fun just like regular children, not like a princess at all. At that moment, that was all that mattered.

Katrin went to sleep.

***

Menders groaned and collapsed on Eiren's bed. She tugged off the big boots he'd worn all day and he wiggled his toes in ecstasy.

"You look like you had a day of it," she laughed, peeling off his socks and blowing on his hot and aching feet.

"My darling, I have eaten so much stuff that even my stomach is protesting," he sighed.

"Impossible!" Eiren laughed.

"I must warn you that you will be presented with several ghastly pieces of cheap jewelry tomorrow by Princess Katrin, who is convinced they are the Crown Jewels," he smiled.

"I'll be delighted to receive them," she smiled, folding the rough jacket and setting it aside with the bucketlike hat. "How did our little one enjoy her day?"

"It was worth every aching step, every sore muscle, every suppressed laugh," Menders answered, sitting up against the headboard and grinning at her. "She was transported. She had the best time! I only wish you could have been there."

"I've seen many a country fair. I think this was something for you and Katrin to do together. It's the stuff of wonderful memories." She carefully covered Katrin's caged birds for the night.

"Wait until the Men realize that they have a million gewgaws. They'll be giving it all to her in a day or two," Menders warned, rising and shucking off the wretchedly fitting trousers and shirt with relief. He hefted the pot of water Eiren had kept warming on her little stove, poured some out at the washstand and began sponging himself down, feeling as if he'd picked up the dust of the entire district.

He told Eiren about Franz going by with the two women and what Katrin had said about him getting tired from kissing two at once while he scrubbed his hair.

"Dear Gods, say he didn't bring them home with him," she laughed. "We can't hang them on a hook like the birds!"

"No, he abandoned them at some point – or they abandoned him. He rode home in the wagon, unconscious after far too much hard cider. Katrin was so exhausted she never even noticed him wedged in between all the junk in the back. For all I know, he's there still." He toweled his hair and gratefully shrugged on his dressing gown.

"Back to civilization," he sighed. Then he grinned, looking over at Eiren.

"Katrin's announced that she intends to marry a firebreather," he said, "and you'd best prepare yourself for a little girl imitating the amazing exotic dance style of the very aged and unattractive 'Surelian' dancer, who looked as if she probably grew up in the less desirable part of Erdahn. Katrin thought she was wonderful."

Eiren sat down and laughed. She could give herself over to laughter like no woman he'd ever met. He drank it in. Two years and he was still completely enchanted with her.

"I suppose we'll have a few days of attempted firebreathing and gyrations," she finally gasped, looking up at him.

"Gods, I never thought of that. Better hide the matches. I'll prepare myself to deliver a fatherly cautionary speech tomorrow morning, first thing," he groaned, going to the bed and stretching out. He was rapidly falling asleep – and sure enough, before long, he felt Eiren gently untying the sash of his dressing gown. He let her help him under the covers and smiled.

His Katrin had seen the fair.

CHAPTER 32
A FORCE OF NATURE

From Her Majesty, Queen Morghenna VIII to Lord Stettan,
Sir,

You are commanded by Her Majesty the Queen to accompany Her Royal Highness, Princess Katrin Morghenna, to Court three weeks from the date of this document, to be presented to Her Majesty upon the occasion of Winterfest. The Royal Train will be sent in sufficient time to accommodate you.

Morghenna VIII, Queen of Mordania

"Here we go again. At least there's been warning this time," Menders growled, flinging the document down on his desk and looking up at Kaymar. They'd had word from Bartan that the Queen was going to command Katrin to Court.

"So what do we do?" Kaymar asked. He perched on the corner of the desk and lit a cigar, then proffered it to Menders, who took it gratefully. "Can't say she's sick again, they'd be getting wise to that dodge." Menders had used the excuse of illness when a similar summons had come last year.

"We hope for lots of snow. If that doesn't work, we do something else," Menders answered, taking the first puff and handing the cigar back, though he was rattled enough to want to keep it and smoke the entire thing.

"Would they expect you to take her by boat if the train can't get through?" Kaymar asked. Menders shook his head.

"I'm forbidden to travel with her by boat. If we can stop the train getting through, that will be sufficient," he answered. "I need you back there to keep an eye on the Queen."

"She's already drinking again. This message was dated and

sent before we left to come back here," Kaymar answered. "I saw her myself. She tried spending some time with Princess Aidelia because she's desperate to find some way for her to be helped or treated. Thirty minutes with Aidelia and she hit the bottle hard. She hadn't stopped when I left. That was three days after this message was sent. I'll go back if you want me to, but I might be of more use to you here if we're to see to it that the train can't get through."

After a thoughtful moment, Menders nodded his agreement. "We've only a week and a half left since this was so long getting here. Did you talk to the driver when you picked up the mail today?" he asked. When Kaymar nodded, he continued, "How are the tracks between here and Erdhan?"

"Bad for a good twenty miles either side of Rondstein, the driver said. Slowed them up by three days."

"Gods and she wants me to risk taking Katrin there with the possibility of getting snowed in and sitting on the track for days at a time?" Menders muttered to himself.

"Cuz, the Queen never comes out of the Palace and is unaware of the world," Kaymar said quietly. "Some flunky got the job of writing this. It isn't her handwriting. She hasn't even signed it, they just used the stamp. By the time she needed to sign it, she was probably beyond being able to hold a pen."

"I know. Let's plan what we'll do about this train," Menders said, knowing that being emotional about this issue was not the answer.

Menders unfolded a map detailing the railway in eastern Mordania. There was one line with a terminus in Erdstrom, where the train was turned back toward Erdahn.

"This is where the heavy snow has been this winter, according to the driver," Kaymar said, indicating a stretch of track around the small town of Rondstein, some twenty miles south of The Shadows.

"Hmm – frost heaves do damage to tracks," Menders

mused, studying the area. "It's early enough in the winter for that."

"I was thinking of setting charges," Kaymar suggested. He rather enjoyed explosions and other incendiary mischief. He'd taken over a neglected shed at The Shadows and spent a great deal of his free time concocting various explosive devices – small charges for removing stumps, fireworks for different holidays and birthdays and other menaces that sometimes exploded violently when they weren't supposed to, leaving Kaymar with singed eyebrows and frizzled hair.

Ifor had dragged a huge horse trough to Kaymar's shed and filled it with water so the pyrotechnician could douse himself when his clothing caught fire. He also patiently replaced roof sections that were removed by unexpected detonations of unruly rockets.

"I can't have it looking as if something has been done deliberately. I have to be able to blame nature for it," Menders answered. Kaymar nodded, though Menders could see he would have loved to have made enough bombs to blow the track to atoms.

"You can make some fireworks for Winterfest," he said cajolingly, earning himself a punch on the arm, which made him laugh. Kaymar amused him no end and Menders didn't mind letting him know it. "We'll see if nature is going to help us along this time. If it doesn't, then you and I and several other hearty gentlemen are going to take a little trip to Rondstein," he continued, looking back at the map.

Menders watched the sky and was rewarded with two heavy, but not massive snowfalls. The trains were still coming through, though much delayed. The weather was warming enough that some of the snowfall was melting and then refreezing, making it difficult, but not impossible for the trains to cut through the accumulation.

"One thing I haven't wanted to contemplate," he said as

he and Kaymar stood in the war room, watching snowflakes cascade from an iron grey sky. "What is the situation at Court if I do end up having to take her there?"

Kaymar shook his head.

"Don't," he said. "Any decent person has fled. The Queen is almost entirely out of things and stays to herself most of the time. Now that Aidelia is almost thirteen years old she has her own hangers-on. They're an entirely different kettle of fish than the drunkards who used to pander to the Queen. They are… a polluting influence. If the Queen were sober, she would keep Katrin away from it, I believe – but you can't count on her condition from hour to hour."

Menders waited. Kaymar didn't care for long silences and he would fill in the gaps. He tried to resist, walking across the room and looking out at the sledding slope where Katrin and Hemmett were sliding downhill, accompanied by Eiren and Franz. He finally sighed and spoke.

"Aidelia's perverted," Kaymar continued. "She's already sleeping with men and has been for some time and she isn't even having cycles yet. She maims and kills animals. She's attracted some people who – they sicken me. I've seen and experienced a lot of things but the freaks around Aidelia are beyond anything I would ever be able to stomach. The idea of Katrin being anywhere around it…" His voice trailed off.

Menders waited patiently.

"She knows about Katrin. Aidelia knows about her," Kaymar finally continued, his eyes riveted on the snow covered landscape. "She raves about hating her – and about killing her."

"Thank you for telling me this. I need to know and I don't need to be sheltered from anything. It's obvious that Katrin will not be going to Court."

Menders paced across the room, a plan crystalizing in his mind.

"I need at least six men, all with good backs. Lucen, Klaas

and several of Lucen's Men as well. We're going to go to Rondstein. We'll take farlins, the weather is too much for horses. The Royal Train is being sent out in three days, which gives us plenty of time. I'll make up a list of things I want brought with us, including your explosive charges, so smile and run along." Kaymar snickered and complied.

Menders looked over the map again, trying to banish Kaymar's description of Aidelia from his mind. He was no shrinking violet and Kaymar was even less so. Kaymar was now bonded to Ifor and completely faithful and devoted, but Menders knew through his network that Kaymar's amorous experience had begun very early and at one time had spanned a great variety of activity, much of it less than savory. If Kaymar said Court was no place for Katrin to be, Menders needed no more to be said.

Now, to appear to be a force of nature.

***

Men mounted on farlins rode along the snow clogged railway line in the dark, stopping ten miles from Rondstein. It was early in the evening, but the long winter night meant that full darkness came early.

They dismounted and gathered in a knot, their backs to the wind.

"It might be deep enough to keep the train getting through," Menders said, "but I don't want to risk it. We'll break the track here."

They set to work with shovels, clearing the rails and loosening the plates holding the steel rails together, fumbling with painfully cold hands. To give the effect of the ground having heaved up, a small explosive charge was dug into the track bed and set off, displacing and warping the rails beyond repair.

The process was faster now, as they had done the same thing some ten miles back. It would be done two more times, closer to Rondstein and on the other side of the town as well. It could be weeks before the railway crews could get through to repair the track and there was a chance it would be buried by snow for months to come.

"I'm going back," Menders said, once he was certain all was going well. The weather was so cold that no engine driver was going to spend long investigating while wading around in snow up to his knees, with the possibility of winter-starved wolves taking an interest. So sorry, Your Majesty, the frost heaves wrecked the train track. Can't get through until the snow melts a bit and repairs can be made. Such a shame. You don't get to see the child you've ignored for almost eight years.

He didn't want to be away from The Shadows any longer than necessary.

"Carry on with the rest of it," he said to Kaymar, walking him a little distance from the rest, who were carefully spreading the snow over the area they had dug out. "Don't forget warning lanterns, I don't want that train derailing. Stay in Rondstein overnight to let the farlins rest."

Snow began to fall.

"It could be that we've gone through a lot of effort for nothing," Kaymar said. "The snow just might take care of it after all."

Menders swung up on Demon and turned back toward The Shadows. It had already been a night's hard ride, but Demon was ready to go. He jogged on in the half trot that farlins could maintain for hours. The snow fell in large, fat flakes, but they followed the railway line, Menders occasionally forcing Demon down to a walk for a rest before letting him jog again.

Menders was near frozen when he reached The Shadows. He shuddered and shivered his way through the tunnel from the stables to the house, thinking about Kaymar and the others out there in the dark. He made his way up the stairs to the suite.

Katrin never stirred as he put another log on the fire and

then bent to kiss her forehead.

"Everything is all right – sleep well, Little Princess," he whispered.

***

The "frost heaves" and snow guaranteed that the train didn't get through at all. Kaymar went to Erdahn by boat to see what impact, if any, was made by Katrin's inability to appear at Court.

A message arrived from him for Menders.

Dear Sir,

The parcel that failed to arrive has not been missed by the party it was addressed to, and no further attempts to have it delivered will be entered into for the time being.

Your servant,

Karschal

Menders laughed aloud and took it in for Eiren to see. She was dressing for the big Winterfest dance that evening. She smelled divine, having used the exquisite and expensive perfume he'd given her as a gift that morning.

She read Kaymar's note and threw her arms around him.

"Thank the Gods," she said. "I was terrified you'd have to take her there."

He kissed her and then lifted her and spun her around.

"I have a few tricks to stay ahead of them – at least for now," he laughed.

CHAPTER 33
KATRIN CATCHES MENDERS OFF GUARD

Eiren whirled to face her attacker and made a lightning lunge, her knife held at throat level. He jumped back, bent, caught her skirt and pulled her off balance. He ended up holding her from behind, his knife across her throat.

"Damn!" Eiren said in disgust. "Blasted skirt!"

Menders released her with a laugh.

"I will have you observe, my dear, that I am sweating like a pig and panting like a grundar in rut. Very, very few people on this planet can do that to me in a fight. I'm proud of you. I'm a better fighter because I have more experience, but you have aptitude and fight well." He wiped his forehead with his sleeve.

"Good enough to take Katrin to school with me alone?" she asked, collapsing on a chair in relief.

"You're good enough," he said, wiping his forehead again. "You're more than good enough. Better than some of the Men – and that's saying a great deal."

Eiren had worked for almost three years to become truly proficient with a knife. She was skilled with firearms as well. She couldn't best him but he wouldn't want to fight her seriously either. As it was, she'd inflicted a nice welt across his belly while they were practicing a couple of weeks ago. She'd been horrified; he'd been delighted.

As Katrin grew older, she would need competent women who could guard her. It wouldn't do to have men shadowing her everywhere. He and Eiren had agreed it was time for Katrin to be exposed to formal schooling and Eiren was now skilled enough to function as a bodyguard for her. By nature, Eiren did not have an aggressive personality, but years on a farm had given her the ability to be ruthless when necessary.

At nine, Katrin was tall for her age and beyond her years intellectually. She was possessed of a willful, high-handed streak that would have been infuriating if she hadn't also been sweet-natured and compassionate. She frequently went by contraries and punitive measures seldom worked with her. Menders had found that it was best to let her take the consequences of her actions when practical and to keep her occupied so that she couldn't get into mischief.

Eiren had asked Menders to teach drawing at the school twice a week earlier in the term. He took Katrin along with him. She needed to appreciate that for many people, learning was work and not always easy, as it was for her. For similar reasons he'd had her take on household tasks and farm chores so that she would know what other people had to do to earn a living.

"It will be good to have a helper now that Sana is in Erdahn," Eiren smiled, carefully polishing the knife before putting it away. Even the blunt practice knives were treated with care and respect when Menders was in charge. "Two days a week would be enough to begin with."

Sana, Eiren's fourteen year old sister, had been sent to teachers' training college as Eiren had been. This left Eiren coping singlehandedly with the forty-three children who attended her flourishing school.

The students came from farms on The Shadows, the village of Artrim eight miles distant and several nearby estates. Reisa Spartz had enrolled her daughter, Lorein, setting a fashion among the nobility nearby. A brother and sister came by train from Rondstein once a week, boarded with Eiren's parents and rode back for the weekly rest days before repeating the cycle. Once word was out that schooling was available, Eiren hadn't lacked for pupils. She was now able to charge a nominal tuition to those who could afford it, though she never denied any child who wished to learn.

Eiren recruited anyone she felt could help her pupils gain knowledge. Menders was amused to find that she had press-ganged reticent Ifor to give talks on history. Liking children, the reason why he'd been one of the Military Academy tutors, he left his shyness at the school door and made his topics come alive as stories the children clamored for. Menck came down on some of his good days to tutor in basic mathematics and Eiren had even convinced Kaymar to teach the older pupils the branches of advanced mathematics that were his particular passion.

While Menders guided the schoolchildren through the rudiments of drawing, Katrin went from desk to desk, helping the students when frustration set in. She drew beautifully herself, as Menders had taught her since she could hold a pencil. She had an instinctive ability to help the other children without seeming to patronize them.

Eiren's pupils soon forgot that Katrin was a princess and treated her as an equal, which Menders heartily approved. Having her do nothing but amuse herself and run wild with Hemmett was not his plan for her. Any challenge was welcome.

Menders also needed time to tutor Hemmett without Katrin present. The boy was wild to attend the Military Academy in Erdahn when he was older. Sheer doggedness on Hemmett's part had resulted in him learning to read, though reading would never be a pleasure to him. He'd also managed to master the ability to do mathematics on paper as well as in his head. He diligently read everything Menders set for him and attended Eiren's school on the days Kaymar taught the advanced mathematics class. In another three years, Menders felt that he would be ready for the Academy. With his own recommendation as well as those of some of Menders' Men, who were Academy graduates, Hemmett would have no difficulty being accepted.

It was Hemmett's ambition to be the head of Katrin's official Guard, which would be assigned to her by the Queen when she turned sixteen, the age of majority for members of the Royal Family. He was utterly devoted to her and it was only through gentle and unsuspected machinations of the adults that they weren't continually in each other's company, as they had been when they were smaller.

Franz occasionally had something to say about the way Katrin was raised and Menders always listened. Most of the time he agreed with the doctor, as he did in the case of Katrin and Hemmett.

"He's a growing boy and physically mature for his years," Franz had said bluntly when he came to Menders about his concerns. "He's in love with her. At this point it's still a childish sentiment, but it's something to watch or there will be trouble in the future. He should go to school now, if he's ready."

"He's not ready. He would fail if he was sent now," Menders answered. "Twelve is simply too young. I will watch him and speak to him if need be."

"That would put the idea into his head," Franz replied. "So far, he hasn't put a name on his feelings for her, but they're there. And with her looking so much older than she is …" He didn't go on. He didn't have to.

"I know," Menders answered. He'd always encouraged chivalry on Hemmett's part where Katrin was concerned, originally because Hemmett was so much larger than she that he could hurt her without intending to. Now that tutelage served him well, because Hemmett channeled his affection into protectiveness and concern.

"I would keep a sharp eye out," Franz said quietly. "I'm not being salacious, Menders."

"I know it," Menders replied. "Let me know if you see anything you consider untoward. It'll be like the old days when we had to try to keep them in their clothes on hot summer days."

Franz laughed a little, remembering. Katrin had been a devoted summertime nudist at the age of three and Hemmett was always ready to follow her lead. More than once they'd been caught wading naked in the pond, intent on capturing tadpoles. Thankfully the fad for nude tadpole hunting had finally passed before a decree had to be handed down from on high. Menders was devoted to the notion of benign neglect in certain matters, and that had been one of them.

Now, however, was not the time for benign neglect. Having Katrin go to the school with Eiren would be a help, providing her with a new interest at the same time it would create distance between her and Hemmett.

The door to the Great Hall opened and Katrin peered in.

"There you are!" she exclaimed, coming toward them. "Cook wanted to know if we're eating here or if we want a basket lunch."

"Well, I don't know, what do you think, Eiren?" Menders asked teasingly. He could tell that Katrin was more than ready to go on a picnic, but wouldn't ask directly.

"It sounds like a wonderful idea to me," Eiren smiled. "Since it's a rest day we can drive out to the village and do a bit of shopping if you'd like and we might even be able to convince Menders to tear himself from work to come with us." She flirted with him through her eyelashes.

"Maddened farlins couldn't keep me away," he grinned.

"Oh!" Katrin cried, "Could we stay overnight? At the inn?"

Menders was about to say they couldn't, but Eiren put her hand on his knee.

Katrin had been desperate to go to the village and stay overnight since the winter day when he and Eiren had taken her there two years ago. He'd intended to stay overnight then but a sudden shift in the weather had forced them to return to The Shadows. They couldn't risk being snowed in at the village for days or even weeks. But now it was midsummer, the weather was dreamily perfect.

The rest of the household needed a rest from the norm of eternal vigilance. Menders himself would not rest, of course, but the others would appreciate a break. There had been two plots against Katrin's life in the past year. One was part of an amateurish coup attempt. The other, far more serious, arose from a faction that sought to eliminate Katrin as a potential threat to Princess Aidelia, whose bizarre behavior had finally motivated the Queen's Council into questioning her fitness to become Queen. Menders learned of both plots long before anyone had a chance to get near Katrin. Kaymar had eliminated the perpetrators.

But the threats meant that the late winter and springtime at The Shadows had passed in a state of high alert. Menders' Men were tired and on edge. Menders had scheduled more rest days and sent a number of the Men on holiday altogether, but an overnight without the Princess in the house would be a novel situation. It would make a nine year old girl incredibly happy as well.

"I think we could manage that, particularly since Eiren has just passed her test to act as a guard for you," Menders smiled.

"You did!" Katrin threw her arms around Eiren's neck. "That means we can go to the school together without Kaymar!"

"Poor Kaymar," Menders teased.

"He won't mind and you know it," Katrin laughed. "And some of the children are afraid of him, though I don't know why."

No, she wouldn't, Menders thought. Fond as he was of Kaymar, he would be the first to admit that his second in command was eerie at best. At times, when he was feeling contrary, Kaymar delighted in presenting a sinister mien. Even some of the Men gave Kaymar a wide berth.

"May I see your knife?" Katrin asked Eiren, who was still holding the sheathed practice weapon.

"This is only for practice," Eiren explained, setting the practice knife aside. "This is my proper knife." She unsheathed her knife carefully, silver blue light shimmering along the cutting edge. She handed it to Katrin handle first. Katrin turned it over in her hands.

It was a thing of beauty, Menders thought proudly. He'd made it for Eiren himself, showing her each step in the process as he formed and tempered the blade, balanced the knife specifically for her hand. He'd carved the bone handle into the shape of a large-eyed falcon, carefully setting a number of his Thrun gems into the finished weapon. Learning knife making had been required in Special Services training and it was a particular hobby of his, as his enormous knife collection testified. Sharing it with Eiren, who had become very interested in the craft during the process of creation, had been a joy.

"Isn't it time for me to have a knife of my own?" Katrin asked suddenly, looking at him, her fingers stroking the falcon handle. "Hemmett had one at my age. I *am* half grown now, Menders."

He looked at her, as if seeing her anew.

The years go so fast, he thought. He'd taught her some defensive techniques already, but they emphasized escape, how to elude danger. He'd known the day would come when she needed to learn more but he'd blinkered himself about it. There was a certain loss of innocence when someone learned to use a weapon.

"Yes, it is time," he said softly. "I'll make one especially for you, like I did for Eiren, and you can help with it. But we can't bother with it today if you want to go to the village and stay overnight. Now, go pack a bag with what you need while I make arrangements to be away."

Katrin handed the knife back to Eiren, scampering away in high glee.

Eiren smiled at the unguarded expression he let come onto his face once Katrin was gone, stood, kissed him and stroked his hair.

"She certainly caught you off guard," she said. "What would you like to take for our mad jaunt to the village?"

He told her what shirt he wanted and left the rest to her, then went to let Kaymar know that he would be away.

He was on his way the stable to get the carriage when Katrin came running down with a case, wearing her best dress. She ran past him, saying giddily that she would go and help Klaas get the gig hitched up. She raced out the door and down the drive, while he couldn't help laughing. He almost felt superfluous, with such a capable nine year old around.

CHAPTER 34
TRUE COURAGE

Katrin looked over her shoulder as Eiren built up the fire in the school stove. It was getting colder. The schoolhouse windows were cloudy with frozen condensation.

Katrin had been helping a little girl write her letters, but Eiren turned and beckoned to her to come to the front of the room.

"It's getting so cold, I think I'd better let them go home early," she said softly. She always talked to Katrin as if she was another teacher, not nine years old. "Could you help the little ones get into their coats and other things?"

Katrin went to the entryway where the coats were hung, collecting the smallest ones. It was easier to bring them out to the children than have the little ones struggle in the crush at the door.

Eiren clapped her hands for attention.

"It's growing very cold so I am going to send you home early today," she announced. "I want all of you larger children to watch out for the little ones, please. Don't stop or dawdle on the way. Go straight home."

The children nodded quietly. They all knew how dangerous the weather could be in Old Mordania. It was late autumn and the profound cold was a good sign that winter was about to appear.

Katrin bundled one small child after another into coats, made sure mittens were firmly on hands, wound scarves around throats and tugged caps down snugly. She admonished each one to go home quickly. They all promised and some of them hugged and kissed her. They really liked her, the little ones, and were always happy on the days she came to the school.

Eiren went outside and looked to the west. Katrin knew she was watching for storm clouds. By the time she came in her face was red with cold and she was shivering.

"It's still clear to the west," she told the children. "I want those of you who come on foot to run home as fast as you can if that's closer than a mile. Those of you who ride or drive, please take the ones who have to walk more than a mile and move those horses along. I think there's a storm coming."

The children didn't have to be told twice. They raced away from the schoolyard.

"Thank the gods they all go east. We're the only ones who have to travel west," Eiren said, looking out the western window of the school. "We'll need to put the shutters up. Best to put our things on first, we'll leave right after we see to the shutters."

They hurried into their coats. Eiren found extra pairs of gloves for them to tug on over their regular ones as well as some extra heavy stockings she kept in her desk. They had no furs with them. It was usually too warm for furs this time of year.

They had to struggle with the shutters because their hands went cold so quickly. The shutters had not been put up yet this season, so they had to lift them into place and then work the latches. After they had the two up on the west side of the school, Katrin felt frozen clear through and Eiren said, "That's enough, we can't stay out here any longer." They hurried inside and stood by the stove.

"Gods," Eiren shivered. "I can't remember anything like this. Unbutton your coat, Katrin, I want you to bundle up more." She wrapped a couple of shawls around Katrin and together they managed to button her coat over them. Then Eiren found a couple of heavy veils and wrapped one around Katrin's head and one around her own.

"I don't know whether to go to Papa's for the night or head for The Shadows," Eiren said. She looked out the window again. Katrin followed her gaze.

There were no clouds coming. She thought that very strange, for usually such rapid drops in temperature saw the arrival of great banks of grey, wooly clouds.

"Let's go home," Katrin said. Eiren nodded.

"Yes, with this intense cold, I don't want Menders thinking we're caught out in it and there's no way to let him know we went to Papa's," she agreed. "I wouldn't want him coming out into this looking for us. Warmed up? Let's hurry."

The cold was terrible, sharp like knives. Together they got Eiren's mare, Rosie, harnessed to the governess cart and climbed in. Katrin pulled the lap rug out as Eiren shouted to Rosie to get home. The horse set out at a fast trot in the direction of The Shadows.

Katrin found it was hard to breathe. She snuggled up to Eiren, who held the reins with one hand and put her other arm around Katrin. After a moment or two, she changed hands, putting one in the pocket of her coat. Katrin was holding both her hands under the rug but they were already so cold she could hardly feel them.

Suddenly Rosie slowed and tossed her head. Eiren handed the reins to Katrin and got out of the cart. She covered Rosie's eyes with her hands for a moment, then went around to the back of the cart, took out the horse blanket and put it on over the little mare's harness. She came back to the cart, took the reins and Rosie started out again.

"Her eyes and nose are getting frost around them and her sweat is freezing on her," Eiren said calmly into Katrin's ear. "This is a terrible cold snap. Are you all right?"

Katrin nodded. She was cold, horribly so, but not so cold that she couldn't bear it. She and Eiren huddled together on the seat. Eiren pulled the lap rug higher around them and slapped Rosie's back with the reins.

They hadn't gone much further before Rosie slowed again.

"I'll do it this time," Katrin said. She got out of the cart, ran to Rosie and removed the ice from her eyes and nostrils.

Katrin scrambled back in as the cart started to move. Moving about had warmed her but the instant she sat down the cold was back, tearing at her like a wolf.

Suddenly a wind hit them, so strong it rocked the cart. It nearly blew Katrin over backwards. Eiren looked up at the sky. Even through the thick veil Katrin could see that she had gone white.

Katrin looked up and gasped in horror.

She'd never seen a cloud like that before. She'd never seen a cloud moving so fast - and she'd seen hundreds of storms sweep out of the west.

It was pitch black, boiling and climbing high into the sky so fast that it made her feel sick to watch it.

Eiren grabbed the whip from its socket and cracked it over Rosie's head, yelling for her to get home. The wind whipped her words away so that Katrin couldn't even hear her. The horse ran for a minute or two, then slowed, her sides heaving. Eiren had to get out to clear Rosie's face while Katrin held the reins. They started out again, making little headway before Rosie began to stagger and Eiren had to repeat the procedure.

Katrin looked around. They were only halfway from the school and they had been struggling against the cold for ages!

Just as Eiren reached the cart, a huge gust of wind nearly blew her off her feet. With it came snow, so much that Katrin could barely see Eiren beside the cart. Katrin leaned over, her hand out. Eiren caught it and climbed in, putting an arm around her.

They started again, but within moments the snow was up to the axles of the cart. It bogged.

Eiren put her mouth to Katrin's ear.

"We'll have to walk," she shouted. The wind was so strong that Katrin could barely hear her.

Eiren pulled two coils of rope from beneath the seat. She tied the end of one coil around Katrin's waist, paid out about fifteen feet of rope, and tied it again around her own. Then she helped Katrin from the cart and around to where Rosie was standing, shivering and frightened.

Their hands were so cold they couldn't remove the horseblanket to unbuckle Rosie's harness. Eiren drew her knife and sliced through the thick leather. She tied the end of the second rope to the cart, then walked to the horse's head. Katrin took hold of the harness near Rosie's rump and they began to walk into the wind and blinding snow.

After they'd walked about twenty steps, Eiren took the coil of the rope that was tied to the cart and walked off the side of the road, wrapping it around the closest tree. She struggled back up to Katrin, cleared Rosie's nose and led on. After another twenty steps, she did the same thing. Katrin realized she was making a trail with the rope, so that they would not get lost, so that they could get back to the cart if they had to.

The third time Eiren started to walk to the trees, Katrin groped her way up from the horse's rump. She put her face close to Eiren's and saw that Eiren was panting and exhausted.

"I'll do it," Katrin said, taking the coil. She waded through the snow until she bumped into a tree, went around it with the coil and then fought her way back to the road against the wind, snow and cold. She caught hold of Eiren. They both clung to the horse and continued forward another twenty steps. This time Eiren took the rope to the trees, and came back, while Katrin cleared the ice off Rosie's nose and eyes, patting the little mare and trying to calm her. The poor creature was trembling with fear and fatigue but she went on when Eiren came back and spoke to her.

The wind strengthened and blew Katrin off her feet. When she fell the snow was all around her, above her head. Eiren helped her up. Eiren stomped her own feet, and made Katrin stomp hers. They were like wood blocks, but she could just feel them. They struggled on, Katrin counting the steps in her mind.

When twenty were taken, she tried to take the coil of rope from Eiren, but Eiren shook her head.

Katrin didn't try to argue with her. She clung to Rosie's bridle, shielding the trembling animal from the terrible wind with her own body.

Eiren took a long time getting the rope around the tree and could barely struggle back through the deepening snow, which was now up above her knees. Katrin grabbed Eiren's hands, hauling as hard as she could, helping her back to the horse.

To Katrin's amazement, Eiren lifted her veil a little, smiled and yelled against the wind,

"We look like snowmen!"

They did indeed. Katrin had to laugh, even though she was so cold it hurt.

"Come on," Eiren yelled, covering her face and putting an arm around Katrin. Rosie started forward. The snow was drifting so deeply that they were struggling to walk.

Twenty more steps. Katrin looked at the coil of rope in Eiren's hand. It was terribly thin, it wouldn't last another twenty steps!

"If it runs out we'll go from tree to tree," Eiren shouted to her. Katrin tried to take the coil but Eiren shook her head. She struggled to the trees, looped the rope around. She fell heavily as she struggled toward the road.

Katrin was about to go to her but Eiren rose on her knees and motioned her back. She got to her feet and staggered to Katrin, holding her side and panting heavily. They struggled forward for another twenty steps.

Katrin's legs were shaking as if she no longer had any bones at all. She took the rope from Eiren and waded through the snow to the trees, looping round, wading back. She tried not to be afraid when she turned back to the road. The snow in the air was so thick that she couldn't even see Eiren. The wind was blowing the snow sideways, clogging her veil and driving icy flakes under the collar of her coat.

Eiren grabbed her, pushing Katrin's hand under part of Rosie's harness. She struggled to the little horse's head and hauled on the bridle.

Rosie wouldn't move. She was cold and exhausted. Eiren coaxed her, tugged at the bridle and then slapped her neck. The mare still balked. Katrin slapped Rosie's rump, trying to ignore the pain that exploded in her icy hand as Eiren leaned on the reins. Rosie was as still as if she was carved from stone. She would not budge.

Eiren drew her knife and poked Rosie's rump with it. That got her moving, fast. They held on with all their might as the horse plowed along.

Rosie finally slowed, her nose and eyes encrusted with ice. Eiren was starting toward the trees with the last of the rope when a gust of wind made the snow swirl upward. Katrin thought she saw something dark up ahead. She lunged at Eiren and caught her arm.

She was too tired to speak and the wind would have torn her words away, so she pointed. Eiren turned to look.

The air was thick with snowflakes but then another cruel gust tore at them, cutting straight through their coats. The snow swirled upward.

A dark form was advancing toward them. They yelled and waved their arms. Eiren caught Katrin close. They walked toward the dark figure, which had been blotted out by faster driving snow.

It was impossible for Katrin to tell which direction they were moving in. She looked down and saw that Eiren had one foot in the rut along the side of the road and that she didn't take a step until she found the rut again. Katrin kept peering ahead, trying to see the dark form, but the wind kept driving snow into her veil.

Another upward gust of wind revealed Demon, eyes

rolling with rage, snorting and biting at the snowflakes. Beside him was a man. A glint of spectacles between a heavy muffler and fur hat let Katrin know it was Menders.

He grabbed them both to him, kissed them through their veils, then pulled furs from the pack on Demon's back. He enveloped them in the warm softness. Drawing a pistol from his pocket, he fired into the air twice. After a moment they heard distant answering shots.

Menders didn't waste time trying to talk against the howling wind. He tied Rosie's reins to the pack on Demon's back and began to put his arm around Katrin.

She shook her head, and pointed to Eiren, because she knew Eiren was completely exhausted. Menders began to protest. Katrin drew herself up and stepped back.

She was the Princess. Eiren needed help more than she did.

Menders nodded and pushed her hand under the belt of his greatcoat. She held on tight. Menders put his arm around Eiren, grabbed Demon's tail and yelled to the farlin to go home.

Demon put his head down and hauled along like a machine. When Rosie tried to balk he just dragged her behind him until she understood that she had no choice in the matter and walked on.

Suddenly dark figures appeared all around them, looming up through the snow. One reached out to Katrin, helping her along, lifting his fur hat long enough for her to see Kaymar's blue eyes. Another, bigger than the others so she knew it was Ifor, put his arm around Eiren's waist, helping Menders lift her and carry her along. The rest of the Men linked their arms and walked in front, blocking the snow and wind.

Soon they reached the stable, stumbling through the door into the warmth and wonderful smell of horses and hay.

Outside the storm was howling and tearing at the stable like a maddened animal. For the first time in her life, Katrin understood just why the Thrun called it 'the White Beast.'

Menders, looking like a snow monster, removed Katrin's hat and veil.

"Are you all right?" he asked.

She nodded. Her throat was raw from screaming against the wind.

"Can you feel your hands and feet?" he asked.

"Yes – they hurt," she rasped.

"Good," he said and she knew he meant that they weren't frozen.

Franz had pulled off Eiren's snowy furs, hat and veil and she looked over at Katrin.

"That was a scrape," she smiled, and Katrin had to laugh.

Klaas brought them warm cups of tea. Katrin drained hers in one gulp. She couldn't believe how thirsty she was. Menders was helping Eiren out of her coat. Kaymar was doing the same for Katrin.

Hemmett popped up out of the hatch in the tack room, grinned and crossed his eyes at Katrin, then yelled down the hatch that they were there and all right. He came over to her.

"Sit down, Willow," he ordered. He knelt at her feet, unlacing her boots and tugging them off her feet along with her stockings. He sighed in relief when he saw her feet were red.

"Big red feet," he teased as Kaymar gently removed Katrin's gloves and revealed that her hands were red too.

"We didn't have time to freeze, we thrashing around so much," Katrin shivered, reaching out for another mug of tea. "Eiren had to prod poor Rosie with her knife to make her go."

She looked over at Eiren, who was gulping more hot tea. She was shivering. Franz had her boots and stockings off. Menders was warming her hands in his.

"Is she all right?" Katrin whispered to Kaymar, who was stripping off his own snowy coat.

"She's not as young as you are, your circulation is better," he murmured. "She'll be fine, no real damage."

"You wouldn't believe how brave she is," she told him. "She had to be scared to death, but you'd never know it. She just went on and on and acted like it was all just an adventure - but I know she was scared."

"That's what true courage is," Kaymar smiled, giving her nose a tweak.

Later, when all the excitement had died down and Katrin was tired of lying in bed, she got up and padded through the suite. She wanted to see Eiren. Franz had found she had a broken rib and mild frostbite. She would be in bed for a while.

The door to Eiren's room was slightly open, which meant it was all right to go in. Katrin hesitated when she heard Eiren speaking, sounding miserable.

"I'm so sorry that I didn't just go to Papa's," she was saying. "I had no idea that storm would come up so quickly, but the cold should have warned me. I'm sorry I put her at such risk, my dear."

"Don't blame yourself," Menders answered her. "You did exactly what I would have done under the circumstances. I would have gone mad if you'd gone to your father's, because there is no way to get word here. I've never seen weather change so fast. There was no way you could have predicted that blizzard. You did splendidly and you know you saved her life."

"I poked poor Rosie with my knife!" Eiren said, her voice high and harsh. Katrin knew she was crying.

"You know your only hope was to have Rosie pull you along," Menders said gently. "You did what you had to do. We try to give Katrin a normal life in an abnormal situation. That means that at times there are going to be risks, like when she fell in the river and Kaymar damaged his heart getting her out. The alternative is to mew her up in the house doing needlework. That would be the worst thing in the world for her. So once in a while we come a cropper. We're through this one. Don't cry any more, my love. All is well."

Katrin couldn't bear the idea that Eiren was upset and crying. She poked her head around the door.

"She went on even when she could hardly walk," she stated fiercely, startling both of them. Menders was sitting on the side of the bed with his arms around Eiren, who was, indeed, in tears. "Sometimes I just wanted to lie down in the snow and give up, but I saw how she kept going even when she fell hard. Kaymar says that's what courage really is."

Eiren started to laugh and held out her arms to Katrin.

"Come here, darling," she smiled. Katrin climbed up on the bed to her, hugging her carefully, not wanting to hurt her broken rib.

Eiren fell asleep very soon. Menders told Katrin she needed to go to bed as well. Before she did, he hugged her and then smiled down at her.

"Eiren was telling me about how you helped her and took the rope into the trees," he said. "And I appreciated the way you wanted me to take care of her when we were out there. I'm proud of you, my Little Princess – proud of both my girls."

CHAPTER 35
THE QUEEN OF MORDANIA –
AND ANOTHER PRINCESS

To Lord Stettan:

Sir,

> *You are commanded to present Princess Katrin Morghenna to Her Majesty, Queen Morghenna VIII at Court within one week of the date of this document. You are to transport her by whatever means necessary. Failure to present the Princess will result in the Queen's most severe displeasure.*

> *Morghenna VIII*
> *Queen of Mordania*

Menders showed no emotion as he read the Royal Command. He nodded to the courier who had brought it on this beautiful late spring day, directing the man to the kitchen for food and drink. Once left in solitude, he eased the door of his office shut and proceeded, silently, deliberately, to tear the letter into small strips.

There was no getting around it this time. The wording of the document let him know that it was suspected that he made it impossible to take Katrin to Court in defiance of previous commands.

He couldn't have the excuse of the train not getting through, as it was springtime – and the letter stipulated that he should use any means of transport necessary to get Katrin there. He had only a week. No mention was made of the Royal Train, so his options were extremely limited.

He went to Franz's office. Franz looked up in surprise as

Menders announced the latest summons.

"Hmm," Franz mused. "We've used the excuse of sickness twice and you tore up the train tracks once. Making another excuse could end up being worse than taking her to Court would be. If I say she's ill again, they'll start thinking that she's weak and demand to know why she isn't being toughened."

"I know," Menders responded quietly, sitting in the armchair opposite Franz. He had managed to subvert a summons to Court when Katrin was ten, claiming that she was ill and that the winter weather would worsen her condition.

"Tell me," he said after a moment, "what would you say Katrin's intellectual age is at the moment?"

"Thirteen or fourteen," Franz answered immediately. "In some ways, even older."

"How do I prepare her for this?" Menders asked. He was startled to hear that his voice sounded very small.

Franz sat back in his chair and thought for a moment.

"You'll need to talk to her, and tell her the damn truth," he said finally. "You know best how to approach her without frightening her. Don't let her get some romantic notion that she's going to see her mother because of some spasm of maternal sentiment. Don't give her the idea that this is a pleasure trip. The Queen has probably gotten a craw full of Aidelia again and is wondering how the spare is coming along."

Menders nodded. After a moment, Franz spoke again.

"Tell her that her mother is a drunkard, her sister is mad. Tell her that you keep her away from them for good reason, and that she has a fine life here among people who love and value her. She's not a fool – she's figured a lot out for herself."

Menders nodded again. After a moment, he stood slowly and turned toward the office door.

"You do realize that I might be a dead man," he said softly, not looking at Franz. "Once the Queen sees her, she'll know I have not followed her commands regarding Katrin."

"Yes, my friend, I do," Franz replied. His voice was grave and dull.

***

Kaymar hurried from the stable to the house and went to Menders' office immediately.

"I know I didn't beat the letter here," he said breathlessly, "but I know the circumstances behind it. Aidelia went after another governess and this time she killed the poor woman – more by accident in a tantrum than by design. She knocked her down the stairs. The Queen was shocked sober and actually spoke to a couple of doctors. Apparently they have suggested she take a look at Katrin."

Menders motioned for Kaymar to sit down.

"That means she'll have a vested interest in Katrin being kept safe," he mused.

"Yes and after what she sees with Aidelia all the time, Katrin is going to be very attractive. If you play your cards right, you should be secure," Kaymar said encouragingly.

Menders drew a deep breath, and wondered just what the right cards might be.

"All right," he said, beginning to feel more sure of himself than he had since the Queen's letter arrived. "We need to form a plan for taking her there. I'd rather take her on the boat. That way we don't have to wait for and depend on the train. Too many places a train can be stopped."

"I thought you weren't allowed to take Katrin on the boat," Kaymar remarked.

"The Queen's own words are 'any available means.' So it's the boat. The trip will be shorter, completely in our control and we'll be able to leave as soon as we're able without waiting on the train. If things get out of hand I want to be away from there as fast as possible."

"Makes sense. The boat is fit and ready to go," Kaymar

told him. "I gave orders to have it completely refueled and checked over when I left the pier."

The small steam cabin cruiser that Kaymar used to travel between The Shadows and Erdahn quickly and secretly was deep hulled, very seaworthy and Ifor declared it capable of a good turn of speed. It was also part of a larger plan – to get Katrin out of Mordania entirely if it became necessary.

Menders had considered of doing just that when the Queen's command came. But if he did, Katrin would spend the rest of her life being hunted by the Queen's agents, or by one faction or another seeking to use her as a puppet or to kill her. Menders would have an official death sentence hanging over his head, a bounty making his demise even more desirable. If he could preserve Katrin's way of life by taking her to Court and somehow working the Queen around, he would do so before subjecting her to life in exile.

"The sooner you go, the better," Kaymar told him. "When I left she was still off the drink, but she'll go back to it sooner or later. At this point it's more than a craving. It's a way of life, and she can't stop for any length of time. You'd be better off seeing her when she's sober. When sober she's truly not a terrible person, Menders."

Menders blatantly refrained from comment and Kaymar couldn't help grinning.

"Yes, I know it's hard to believe," he added. Menders shook his head.

Kaymar habitually defended the Queen against Menders' fierce disapproval. Menders was boggled by that. Kaymar was a man of exquisite taste and immaculate habits. The idea that he could tolerate and even seemed fond of their unwashed, reeking royal cousin was more than Menders could comprehend.

"I want you and Ifor to come with us. I need you with us at the Palace. You know the terrain there," Menders said after some thought. "The fewer of us that go, the better, and the easier to move quickly if need be. No matter what happens, do not leave Katrin alone for a moment."

Kaymar began to speak, but Menders motioned for him to wait.

"Kaymar – if something should happen to me, you are to take Katrin. Don't come back here. Send word to Franz and go to my house in Surelia with her. Keep her safe until Franz gets there."

"If it comes to that, I will stay with her the rest of my life," Kaymar said quietly. "Ifor as well. Where I go, he goes."

Menders rose and put a hand on his cousin's shoulder.

"Get something to eat and have a rest. I think we should leave tonight, after dark," he said, his voice tight with tension.

"Shall do," Kaymar replied. "Cuz – I know this seems very serious, but I truly believe after the Queen sees Katrin that we'll all return here and take up where we left off."

"I hope you're right. What bothers me more than anything… what if the Queen decides that Katrin must stay at Court?"

Kaymar blinked. He clearly hadn't considered the option. "She hasn't told me… there's been no indication that she…"

Menders stared at him. Kaymar suddenly became distant, his eyes focused as if he was looking at something far away. Suddenly he snapped back and smiled with his lips but not his eyes.

"Well, you'll just have to talk her around that point," he said firmly. "Use your natural persuasive talent, cousin of mine. It works like a charm." He left the room abruptly.

***

Eiren was in her room, trying to go over school papers. She knew about the Royal Command and had been quiet and tense since it arrived.

She looked up at Menders when he walked in, her face quivering, barely controlling tears.

"Yes, I have to go tonight," he whispered, going to her, holding her against him. "Kaymar has given me good reason to expect that all will be well – but my darling, if it isn't, if for any reason I don't come back, you know that I've provided for you. You are safe from them because your association with me doesn't matter to them. So you are free to stay here and continue with what you do now, or to go to Surelia with Franz to live with Katrin there. I am sure that Katrin is not in danger, no matter what becomes of me."

"Don't talk of such things. You know I'll go with her," Eiren choked. "But you must come back."

"I will do everything I can," he promised. Kneeling, he kissed her sweet face and tried to wipe away her tears, but they flowed down faster than he could staunch them.

***

Menders went to find Katrin.

She was sitting up on a limb of one of the lanar trees in the orchard, reading a book. There were numerous chocolate wrappers littering the grass beneath the tree. Menders couldn't help smiling. Katrin had a powerful sweet tooth, and loved to read – interests that often coincided.

With a couple of steps, he was up in the tree with her. He straddled an adjacent limb while she smiled at him.

At eleven, she looked more like a thirteen year old, with long legs and truly beautiful hair that reached almost to her ankles. She was very tall for her age, almost as tall as Menders. There was no sign of her body blooming as of yet, but it was graceful and strong thanks to years of work and play around The Shadows. Her overall mien was of a much beloved girl who was comfortable in her skin.

"I need to talk to you, Little Princess," Menders said, taking the book from her and putting it in his pocket. She so loved books that she tended to keep peeping into them if he didn't do this, not out of rudeness but from sheer curiosity.

"Is something wrong?" she asked, instantly alert, her eyes scanning his face rapidly.

"Yes, my dear. Nothing you've done. I've received a command from your mother, the Queen, to take you to Court in Erdahn as soon as possible."

He was gratified that she only seemed surprised. He had deliberately avoided making her mother a bogey in her life. He'd responded truthfully and simply to the questions Katrin had asked, giving her no more information than she needed. So now she wasn't fearful, only curious.

"Why is this?" Katrin asked.

"I'm not entirely sure," he replied. "There has been some trouble with your sister, Princess Aidelia and it's very likely your mother wishes to see how you've progressed. It's likely your sister will not be fit to inherit the Throne."

Katrin frowned.

"Why? What has she done?" she asked.

This I won't tell her, Menders thought forcefully.

"They say she's mad." Katrin spoke firmly.

"They?" Menders asked, his eyebrows shooting up. "Who is 'they'?" For a fleeting moment he wondered what Kaymar might have been telling her.

"People."

"Which people?"

"I hear people talk, Menders, all the time. They say Aidelia is mad. Is she?"

Menders considered his response, hearing Franz's words echo in his head.

"Katrin, it's time I told you things about your family that I have kept from you. You were too young to know about this before and I preferred not to burden you with it. Now my hand has been forced. You need to know before we go to Erdahn.

"Your mother, the Queen, drinks to excess all the time. When people do that, they develop a dependency on drink that is almost impossible to break. Your mother has this problem and the amount that she drinks impairs her judgment. It has adversely affected her reign.

"And yes, your sister, Princess Aidelia, is mad. She is irrational and frequently violent."

"If she is, does that mean that I might..." Katrin went pale.

"No, my dear. If you were mad, we'd know about it. You and your sister have different fathers. You are only half-sisters. Aidelia's father was mad, and she has it from him. Your father was absolutely sane – as you are."

"I see," Katrin said slowly, drawing her feet up to rest them on the large branch she was seated on. She leaned back against the trunk of the tree. "Not a good situation to walk into."

"No, it isn't. I wish I could make it otherwise, but I have no choice but to take you."

She was quiet for a moment, looking over at the house.

"You didn't take me those other times," Katrin announced. "You always made up some story or another."

Menders looked at her in astonishment.

"Yes I knew, sometimes. I used to wonder why we didn't go. Then one day I understood. You're in danger, aren't you?" she asked. "I can tell by your voice."

"Yes my dear, there is some danger because I have not raised you according to the way royal children are supposed to be raised, because that is a brutal regimen and I would not inflict it on you."

Katrin nodded. He had told her about toughening. The very idea sickened her.

"You, Kaymar, Ifor and I will leave tonight," he told her,

wanting to get away from the topic of danger to himself. "We'll take the boat. The crossing is fast and easy this time of year. I'm hoping that we will finish our business at the Palace quickly and be back here before long."

She nodded, taking a deep breath.

"Try not to be afraid, Katrin," Menders said. "There is no danger to you, I'm sure." Except for the danger that your drunkard mother will decide you have to stay at Court with your murderous sister, he thought. I can't tell you that and I won't let that happen, if I have to kill the Queen herself. Even if they put me on the spit for it.

"I'm not afraid for myself," she said softly.

"Katrin – if I am called away from you at any time while we're there, you are in Kaymar's care. If he tells you to do something, you must do it, without question, and without hesitation. Do you understand? He will have direct orders from me, so anything he says you must consider to be coming from me." He reached out and took her hand. She gripped his hand hard in response.

"I understand," she said, looking at him with those brilliant blue eyes that had mesmerized him from the moment she had been put in his arms.

***

Menders squeezed Katrin's hand as they stood outside the doors to the Queen's Throne Room. It was late afternoon. They had arrived the previous night. Menders was infuriated that after all the fuss and drama of obeying the command to bring Katrin to Court, they had been allowed to linger until now before being presented.

Upon their arrival they had been shown to a small room where Katrin, exhausted by the late hour and the excitement of the boat trip, had fallen asleep. Menders and Kaymar spelled each other keeping watch until dawn - and then they had cooled their heels the rest of the day. They had been given nothing to eat and were hungry to the point of being faint.

Menders didn't dare speak to Katrin now but when she squeezed his hand in return he knew that she was as calm as she could be under the circumstances.

She looked wonderful in a white dress embroidered with golden snowflowers. It had been her Winterfest present from Eiren. It suited Katrin's pink and gold coloring and made the most of her tall, graceful figure. Her posture was perfect because he'd taught her to hold herself well. Her hair hung in a shimmering fall down her back, held back with two golden combs that had been his Winterfest gift.

He and Kaymar stood on either side of her, waiting.

Finally, the door swung open and the Queen's Chamberlain stood before them.

"Princess Katrin Morghenna of Mordania and her guardian, enter. The bodyguard will remain outside," he proclaimed.

Pretentious ass, Menders thought, hearing Kaymar's soft snort of disgust. He released Katrin's hand and stepped behind her, trying with all his might to project confidence and strength into her.

He need not have worried. Katrin walked forward as if she entered this room every day of her life. She sank down into a formal curtsey while Menders simultaneously executed a formal bow. She held the curtsey effortlessly at its lowest point, waiting for the Queen's bidding.

"Rise," the Queen said sharply, her voice scarred and hoarse from years of drinking.

As Menders straightened, he looked at her.

The lighting in the chamber was low, the corners all but in darkness. The Throne was centered in a pool of yellow light cast by a ring of sputtering gaslamps hanging from the ceiling.

The wretched woman, Menders thought. What a visage to present to your daughter on your first meeting!

She was wearing the entire regalia of The Queen of Mordania - the heavy jeweled, armored, blood-red formal gown, the hideous red wig and worst of all – the teeth. Her pale, heavily beringed hand gripped the black iron staff that was the symbol of her authority.

The Queen's grandmother had gone through the painful process of having her teeth filed, as legend insisted the early Queens of Mordania had, to present a fearsome appearance. Since then, Katrin's grandmother and mother had resorted to a set of false teeth clipped over their natural dentition, but the effect was still horrifying. Her mouth looked like a demonfish's, jagged teeth yellow-white against the dark interior as she sat, gap-mouthed, staring at the thing of beauty that was her second daughter.

Katrin raised her eyes from the floor to look at her mother, and Menders felt a rush of admiration. An older child than Katrin would have flinched or even cried out upon being faced with such a horrible apparition, but Katrin remained calm, waiting for the Queen to address her.

"You are Katrin?" the Queen asked, her voice hissing and whistling through her pointed false teeth. Menders thought it an absurd question. Had the Queen slipped further into alcoholic madness than he had imagined?

"Yes, Your Majesty," Katrin said quietly, but firmly.

"How old are you now?" the Queen asked, looking confused.

"I am eleven years of age, Madame," Katrin answered.

The Queen's eyes shifted to Menders and he saw that she was rattled. Good!

"She looks older," the Queen said.

"Princess Katrin has always been tall for her age, Your Majesty," he responded.

"Come closer," the Queen said to Katrin, who obeyed

until her mother's hand went up, stopping her short about ten feet from the Throne. The Queen's motion sent a wave of stench toward Menders that nearly made him lose countenance. Where Katrin stood it must have been appalling, but she made no sign.

"Turn around," the Queen commanded. Katrin did so gracefully, her eyes dutifully downcast. The Queen stared at her, then looked at Menders again.

"She resembles her father," she said sharply.

"Yes, Madame," Menders responded. He sighed slightly with relief. She'd acknowledged, in that statement, that Katrin was her child. Indeed, Katrin's resemblance to Bernhard Markha was marked, particularly now that she was in this tall, leggy stage. The color of her eyes was his, not the Queen's aqua, which had once been beautiful, but was now bleared and bloodshot. Katrin's hair was Markha's, as was her tall, strong body. The Queen was tall, but corpulent. Flesh bulged over the top of the formal gown and ringed her neck thickly.

"What have you achieved in your schooling?" the Queen asked, staring at Katrin.

"Madame, I have been reading Gerhalt's *History of Mordania* and Erenson's *Moral Philosophy*," she answered. "I am learning geometry and have also done algebra. I am studying astronomy and the geography of Eirdon. I play the spinet, the cromar and am learning the viol. This spring I have been working on my penmanship, because it isn't as good as it can be. I study Surelian and Samorsan. I ride both Artreyan and Mordanian style and own a pony named Snowflake and a farlin named Trouble. I have learned all the formal dances of the Mordanian Court. I have recently read all about electricity."

"Impressive," the Queen replied slowly. "Who are your teachers?"

"I have two tutors, Madame, Mister Trantz and Mister Menck. I also have a governess." Katrin responded so easily that Menders was stunned. He had not coached her this far. He'd had no idea that the Queen would ask anything beyond a few basic questions.

"Are they pleased with you?" came the hissing voice.

"Very often they are, though at times I fail to do so – so I try harder," Katrin answered softly, with a hitch of regret in her voice.

A brief, carnivorous smile passed across the Queen's face.

"I am pleased," she said. "Your ward is most satisfactory." Her eyes flicked over Menders' face, but showed no emotion. "You may go," she said to both of them.

Menders delayed his own bow by a second so he could observe the Queen's expression as Katrin sank down into her formal curtsey again, her head touching her knee, her skirt billowing out around her in a field of white and gold. In parting, according to etiquette she rose in her own time and backed gracefully to the door. It swung open and she and Menders backed into the hallway.

With a last look into the Audience Chamber, Menders saw a single human emotion flicker across the Queen's face.

Regret.

***

Thoren Bartan, the Court Assassin, knocked gently on the door of the room where Menders, Katrin and Kaymar were waiting – waiting for anything, a meal, word that they could go, word that they had to stay. It had been hours since Katrin's interview with the Queen. Menders could tell she was faint with hunger. His own stomach was a roiling vat of acid. He dared not send Kaymar out, he wanted him close by. Menders paced and fumed despite Kaymar's assurances that all would be well.

Bartan was a welcome sight. He shook hands heartily and then bowed with great respect to Katrin, his dark eyes taking her in with one glance.

"It went well," he said in lowered tones, opening a bag he carried and removing packets that smelled wonderful. "You can forget about regular meals in this place. These are safe, they aren't from the kitchens. My wife made them in our suite."

Katrin opened her packet and began to eat. Kaymar and Menders did likewise.

"I think they're about to let you go. The Queen was very impressed with the Princess," Bartan continued. "I'm sorry I couldn't get to you before now but one must be careful. Once you're released, I'll let you into a passage that leads directly to the docks. Kaymar knows the way. Believe me, no-one will notice or care, now that the Queen has had her way."

They finished the food with small talk, though Menders noticed that Katrin kept her counsel. She had been very quiet since the interview with her mother. He'd also told her that it wasn't safe to speak much. She'd spent some of the afternoon resting on the bed and reading a book she'd brought along with her. He knew she had questions, but didn't want to speak before Kaymar and certainly not before Bartan.

Bartan was just gathering himself up to go when there was an abrupt knock on the door. Menders motioned to Katrin for silence before opening it.

The Queen's Chamberlain stood in the doorway. He gestured to Menders

"You are to attend the Queen immediately, my Lord."

Bartan cast a look of complete bewilderment at Menders. Menders turned to Kaymar. Katrin realized he was confused, while Kaymar looked ill.

"I'll see you in a while," he said, smiling at Katrin. When he turned back, he saw that the Chamberlain had stalked on down the hallway, confident that Menders would be right behind. With two rapid steps, Menders was at Kaymar's side.

"Get her to the boat. If I'm not there by midnight, sail."

Kaymar nodded silently. Menders turned to Katrin,

cupped her chin in his hand and kissed her quickly on the cheek.

"Kaymar speaks with my voice," he reminded her, smiling.

As he went out the door, he whispered to Bartan, "Help them."

"I will, brother," Bartan answered.

***

For the second time that day, Menders stood before the door to the Queen's Audience Chamber. This time he was sickened, pleading with fate that Bartan would get Katrin and Kaymar out of the Palace. Somehow he must buy them time by keeping the Queen busy, however he had to do it.

He was sure he was already a dead man. If he could stay alive long enough, Kaymar would get Katrin away to safety.

He took out his watch with a minimum of movement. Half past eleven.

The door swung open. Menders walked forward, going through the entire bowing and waiting routine.

"Rise," the Queen said.

When he did, he saw she was seated on the Throne, no longer in her armored gown, the teeth not in evidence. Her stench reached him, making the food he'd just eaten churn in his stomach. He mentally turned off his nose or he would vomit all over the floor, though it was so grimy that no-one would notice.

"Come forward," she commanded.

***

Katrin followed Kaymar from the room they'd waited in all day. She was terrified for Menders.

The corridor was long and dim. Suddenly Bartan shrank back into the shadows of the room and Kaymar stepped in front of Katrin.

There was a girl standing in the corridor. Katrin smelled her before she saw her. It was the same filthy reek that had come from the Queen earlier, as if she had never had a bath in her life. It made Katrin's eyes water. Her stomach tossed at the thought of someone being that dirty.

The girl came forward into a small pool of light cast by a nearby lantern. Katrin drew back involuntarily.

The girl's eyes rolled, roving from Kaymar to Katrin and back to Kaymar again. She had red hair, like the Queen and her mouth gaped open. She was drooling, a thick stream that slimed her lips and dripped onto the floor.

"So it's you," she hissed, trying to duck past Kaymar toward Katrin. Kaymar kept himself between Katrin and the disgusting creature. Katrin realized this was her half-sister, Princess Aidelia.

"Country cow, country pig," Aidelia chanted, clawing at Katrin, reaching around Kaymar. Katrin could see her fingernails black to the quick and stayed tight behind Kaymar's back. "Fat little bitch! You'll never be Queen!"

Suddenly Kaymar's hand descended on Aidelia's wrist as she lunged at Katrin, her jagged fingernails raking through the air.

"You've laid hands on me!" Aidelia growled at him, her eyes slewing in his direction as she tried to bite him. "You laid hands on a royal person! That's treason, you're a traitor!"

"I'm your cousin and a royal person as well. I can touch you, Aidelia, and you know it," Kaymar answered calmly, holding her fast. "Who will believe you when you carry on this way?"

Aidelia thrashed until she was free of his grip and stepped back.

"I'll kill you one day, country pig," she slobbered. Katrin could see a terrible network of scars on her arms, as if someone had taken a razor and slashed her again and again. "Just as I killed that governess. No-one will ever stop me! They're afraid of me and I will be Queen!" With that she turned and ran away down the corridor, weaving from side to side, finally turning off to the right and out of sight.

Kaymar held tight to Katrin's hand as Bartan hurried them down the corridor and along a long, dank passage. She clung to the small case that held her best dress and shoes and tried not to give way to tears.

Suddenly they burst out into the night and were in a darkened garden. Bartan led them down a path between dense and overgrown bushes, then keyed open a small gate, standing aside for them.

"I'll get him out to you if I can," he said to Kaymar. "Take care of her, she's precious." With that, he was gone, back into the shadows.

Kaymar tugged at Katrin's hand. They ran down the darkest side of the street. They ran to a corner, turned left, then ran further.

They turned down street after street, people scattering out of the way when they saw Kaymar coming. Katrin saw light reflecting on water. A moment later they were running down the dock to the boat. Kaymar helped her into the cabin.

"Stay there, Cuz," he said gently. "I have to talk to Ifor. I'll be right back."

She listened as he went up on deck and spoke in hushed tones to Ifor. Kaymar's voice was low but she heard him say Surelia.

Surelia! Go to Surelia! What could he mean? That was mad! What would happen to Menders?

Menders had said that Kaymar spoke with his voice, that his words were Menders' words. For some reason, Menders wanted her taken to Surelia. Something had gone terribly wrong.

Menders – where was he? She should have talked to her mother! She should have done something to save him!

Katrin began to cry and didn't realize that Kaymar was

back in the cabin until he sat beside her and put his arm around her shoulders.

"Go ahead, Cuz, let it out," he said gently. "But it isn't time to be so worried just yet. I know Menders well, and I know the Queen too. He'll be along, I think."

Katrin put her head on his shoulder and wept.

***

"Is the child intelligent?" the Queen asked, looking blearily at Menders.

You saw her with your own eyes, what did they tell you, he wanted to say.

"Yes, Your Majesty, she's very intelligent," he answered. "She has always been very advanced for her age."

The Queen cogitated on that for a moment or two.

"Is she mad?" she asked, very quietly, staring at Menders.

He took off his glasses – the light was low enough – and looked directly into her eyes, so there could be no question of his sincerity.

"No," he answered.

She didn't look away from his eyes, as most people did.

"How did you raise her to be as she is?" she asked. "I understand you have taken liberties with her."

Menders bristled with rage and barely managed to stop himself from lunging at her.

"I meant with her upbringing," The Queen added, sensing his coiling anger. "Your father's proclivities for treating people as objects were well known, but I would not have consigned this child to your care had you been like him. But it is obvious her training has not been… shall we say, usual? Don't lie to me, because I know that she has not been raised according to the custom for royal children. "

I'm dead, Menders thought, but at least I'll have the

pleasure of seeing you flinch with pain for everything you've missed of your beautiful daughter, to whom you've never so much as bothered to send a birthday gift.

"Madame, I have reared her as a loving parent would," he answered. "She is my paramount concern. I have devoted the last eleven years to raising her with kindness, tenderness and love."

She did flinch. But his satisfaction was short-lived, because he thought of Katrin, who would be terrified and confused at this moment, and of Eiren, doubtless weeping helplessly at The Shadows. He would not see them again because the world was mad and he was at the mercy of one of the maddest parts of it.

"That is all well and good, but it is not what was commanded of you. It is treason," the Queen said softly. "However…"

She paused and let the word hang in space, like silence before a storm.

"You will find no objection coming from me," she continued. "Given the results, I will not question your methods. The child is a credit to you. You are safe from any interference – from *me*."

Suddenly Menders knew the threat of a traitor's death, the threat that had hung over his head for so long, had suddenly and inexplicably been taken away.

"Go, white-eyed Lord Stettan. Take my daughter back to the country and keep her safe there," the Queen said abruptly, standing. "I now know what I needed to know. Teach her well and watch over her diligently. Go."

He bowed and escaped as quickly as he could. In the corridor, he came face to face with what had to be Princess Aidelia.

She smelled like a zoo, slobbered and drooled, her eyes roving in their sockets. Her red hair was greasy and foul. He could smell the decaying food caught between her scummy teeth.

"I'll kill the country pig," she raved, digging her nails into his coat sleeves. She hissed and rolled her eyes at him.

Menders backed her against the wall, glaring at her with his unshielded eyes until she quailed and flinched away from him.

"I see exactly what you are," he said with a tone of steel edged malevolence that had been known to make grown men flinch. "I could kill you in an instant and no-one would grieve. Get out of my sight."

"Freak – freak!" she cried in a panic, breaking free and running away down the hall.

As soon as was she gone, Bartan stepped from the darkness.

"There's still time, hurry!" he whispered, showing Menders his watch. Ten minutes to midnight.

They raced down corridors, ducked into a passage and then tore through the Palace garden. Bartan led the way, running directly toward the Harbor.

The boat was just pulling away. Menders ran headlong down the dock and leapt over the water, landing hard on the deck.

***

Katrin collapsed on the bunk, crying into a pillow. Kaymar had gone up on deck to talk to Ifor at midnight. He'd tried to encourage her up until the last moment that Menders would come. Now it was obvious that he couldn't. She had never known a day in her life without him.

There was a chorus of shouts up on deck followed by an enormous thump. She sat upright, then fell over as the boat roared into life and tore away from the dock.

Suddenly Kaymar was on the stairs, looking through the cabin door.

"Come up on deck," he said, grinning widely.

She pushed past him.

Menders was sitting on the deck, swearing as hard as he could, holding his head.

"Menders!" she shrieked and ran to him. He pulled her close and kissed her cheek. Then he rubbed his head again.

"What happened?" she cried.

"I thumped my blasted head," he groaned. Then he grinned at her. "But we're going home, my Little Princess – and your mother, the Queen, has said she will not interfere with the way I'm raising you!"

"Certainly news worth making a grand entrance over, old man," Kaymar said. "Come on, let's get you patched up."

***

Katrin slipped into Eiren's room, where Menders was lying in bed. He heard her and smiled.

"And how is my patient today?" Katrin asked, mimicking Franz.

"Oh, achy and grouchy as the day is long," he answered. Menders had been confined to bed by Franz because he was dizzy and ill from the injury to his head, and he wasn't happy about it. Unable to read because of a terrific headache, he was restive and bored.

"I've also had a letter from the Palace and I've managed to read most of it," Menders said, holding up a heavy piece of paper. "The Queen has formally decreed that I may raise you as I see fit. That is a terrible load off more than one mind, my dear Little Princess. She's even signed it, so it's official." He held the letter out at arm's length and admired it for a moment before blinking in pain and putting it down again. "I might have this framed and hang it over my desk."

"Good," Katrin said, sitting carefully on the bed beside him.

Menders gave her a look and settled himself more comfortably, flinching as he moved.

"All right, I know you need to ask me questions," he said quietly, taking her hand.

She tried to gather her thoughts.

"My mother - why is she so dirty? I mean she smells, like... even animals don't smell like that!"

"Probably for several reasons. When people drink as much as your mother does, they lose all comprehension of the real world. They can fall into states of melancholy, a deep sadness where they don't care how they look and don't even perceive how they smell or appear. And since she's the Queen, people will take her lead, no matter how she keeps herself or chooses to live."

It made a sort of sense, though the memory of that stench was still nauseating.

"Why does she drink like that?" Katrin asked next.

"The story is that your mother was quite an intelligent and talented girl, but her upbringing broke her spirit to the point where she had no ambition left to do anything but deaden herself with drink. Once a person reaches that point, it becomes a vicious cycle. They need more and more drink over time to get the effect that they seek."

Menders looked very grave and Katrin flushed, remembering the time she and Hemmett had snuck half a bottle of wine out of the kitchen. They'd felt wonderful for a while after drinking it, giggling and howling like monkeys until they both suddenly vomited horribly all over themselves. Just then Menders came and caught them with the empty bottle. He'd said it served them right and gave them a stern lecture about not being allowed to drink until they were eighteen. After that, Katrin didn't think she'd ever want to drink wine again. She'd felt awful for three days.

Menders gave her hand a squeeze and she realized she'd been sitting there silently for a while.

"My sister," she said, and shuddered. The horror of that drooling, raving girl was soul chilling.

"Yes, I saw her," Menders replied.

"So did I. Could I end up that way?" Katrin could barely make the question come out.

"You haven't so far, Little Princess." Menders didn't smile. She looked at him and he pulled her closer.

"Do you remember how often I say that something is all right for now?" he asked. She leaned her head against his chest, hearing his heart beating, and nodded.

"That's all we ever have at any one time, Katrin," he continued gently. "We can plan for the future and it's good to do that, but the only thing we can be certain of is what we have at any given moment. At this moment in time, you are not mad. You're a healthy, intelligent and much loved girl. Your life is a happy and productive one. Live with that, Katrin, always. It's now that matters most."

Katrin smiled and sat up, thinking. Menders waited patiently.

"What else troubles you?" he finally asked gently.

"Why did Kaymar tell Ifor to go to Surelia when we got on the boat?" she asked.

Menders sighed.

"I wish I'd been able to keep this from you until you're older," he said. "But I couldn't keep you from having to go to Court this time. Since you were tiny there has been a plan to take you out of Mordania if something happened to me, because I don't want you ending up living at Court or put in the care of someone who would be cruel to you. Should something happen to me, you would go with Franz to a house that I own in Surelia, where you would be raised as his daughter. Eiren would go too."

Katrin felt a sickening twist inside her at the idea of something happening to Menders. He knew it, and took her hand.

"I'm not counting on dying soon." he said, smiling, "but it

would be criminally careless not to have a plan, just in case. Kaymar and Ifor have also said that if you did have to go to Surelia, they would go with you. You would never be alone in the world and you will never end up at Court against your will. It's only good sense to have such a plan, Katrin. Don't dwell on it, because there's no point in fretting about things that will probably never come to be."

Katrin nodded. Behind the sick feeling was warmth and gladness that the people she loved best were willing to go with her to another country if need be.

She had one more question.

"Why do you think my mother wanted to see me?" she asked. "I don't think she loves me or wants me with her."

"Curiosity, to see if you are turning out better than your sister is," he answered immediately. "If Aidelia were my heir, I'd want to see my second daughter too. She was impressed with you – very much so."

That didn't make Katrin feel any better. She was not happy about her mother and sister and she didn't particularly care whether her mother was pleased with her or not.

"I don't feel very proud of them," she blurted.

"Understandable, little one," Menders replied. "They're nothing to be proud of. Perhaps now that we've talked, you'll understand why things are as they are. I've done all I could to shield you from them, but now that you're growing up, I can't do that so much anymore."

Katrin looked at the floor. It was so much to know, and a lot of it was disturbing. She was glad she lived far away. She was glad that she had never known her mother and sister – and she was glad that she had Menders. She would have to think about all this, but she was sure of one thing.

"Menders – I don't want to be Queen," she said, looking up at him.

"I hope, my dear, that you never have to be," he

answered, patting her hand where it lay on the blanket. Queens of Mordania no longer ruled. Instead, they were used, by a self-serving and corrupt Council. The mantle of responsibility extracted a high toll – one he never wanted visited on Katrin.

CHAPTER 36
BORSEN BOUND NORTH

Borsen huddled against the wall next to the mattress he had to share with two of his half-brothers. His father had just come in.

"Time to move on," his father said abruptly to his woman. "Get them out of bed, or they get left behind."

Borsen fished his secret packet of food, collected from a rubbish bin behind a restaurant, from beneath his folded jacket. He tucked it carefully into one of the jacket's inner pockets so no-one would find it. It would last him several days.

His father's woman gave him little enough of the food she made, giving most of it to her own children, but he'd learned to make do. He didn't get much because he refused to help his father rob people. His father had found years ago that he couldn't see well. He'd declared Borsen useless, saying useless blind brats couldn't expect much. The woman had been glad to see to it that Borsen had the scrag end from that day on.

In cities it wasn't bad, because he could find food thrown away behind the cafes and restaurants, perfectly good and better tasting than anything he'd ever had before. When they went to the country, he starved, having to depend on the woman for whatever she would give him.

He snaked his hand under the mattress during the flurry of the woman getting her children to wake and dress. His thin fingers found his drawings. When no-one was near, he pulled them out and pressed them into another pocket.

Minutes later he was walking wearily along with the rest of them, carrying the small box that held his clothing. Then he remembered.

He hadn't taken his scraps! His scraps of cloth from his mother's sewing, which she'd given him to play with when he was little. He'd found them bundled into the clothing his father gathered up the night he'd taken Borsen away with him, the night his mother died. He'd taken care of them all these years and comforted himself by holding them against his face when he couldn't sleep for being hungry – and now he'd forgotten them.

Hot tears flooded his eyes and ran down his cheeks, but he didn't dare run back to get his scraps. He would be left behind and he had no way to make a living. He was ten, or maybe eleven. He couldn't remember. It had been years since he'd been reminded of his birthday, not since his mother had died. No-one would apprentice a boy so young. He had to hold on until he was older and could find a tailor who would take him on.

They boarded a train bound north. Borsen tried to stay out of his father's sight, making himself small and quiet.

"Once I fence this lot we'll have plenty of food and drink," his father said to his woman. "It'll be easy living for us."

Suddenly Borsen knew his father was looking right at him. He kept his eyes down and tried to disappear.

"Except for you," his father said, his voice dripping with hatred. "Useless brats don't get to stuff their faces. Gods, why didn't you die when your worthless mother did?"

Borsen kept his head down and tried to remember his mother, the Giants beneath the soil and where the statue with the shining stone was.

CHAPTER 37
HEMMETT GOES TO SCHOOL

"Who am I going to play with now?" Katrin cried, glaring at Menders, her eyes brimming with tears.

Menders looked at her with a mixture of commiseration and frustration. She'd already pulled away when he tried to put his arms around her. He could understand why.

Hemmett was leaving for military school in the morning. A difficult situation between Katrin and Hemmett had been narrowly averted. Katrin was unaware of it and only knew that her sole contemporary and playmate at The Shadows was suddenly going across the country and would be away for months. At the moment Hemmett was overjoyed at being admitted to the school he'd worked so long and hard to be ready for and wasn't considering the ramifications of this change in his life.

At nearly fourteen, Hemmett was already the size of a grown man. During the summer just past his voice had broken, and it was obvious that he was very physically mature for his age.

Within a week's time, Kaymar, Eiren and Franz had all come to Menders and brought up the same subject.

Though perfectly respectful and decent, it was painfully clear to any adult that Hemmett was in love with Katrin. He gazed at her, sighed over her and fell all over himself trying to do things for her. Katrin, eleven years of age and with maturity nowhere in sight, was oblivious. She still saw Hemmett as her playmate and constant companion and that was all.

Finally Lucen asked if Menders thought that it would be possible for Hemmett to begin at the military academy this year. He was anxious and uncomfortable. His relief when Menders smiled was pitiful to see.

"He's ready," Menders told him. "If you and Zelia are

agreeable, we can certainly send him this year. He's been mad to go, so there'll be no argument from him."

"We'll miss him, of course, but… Menders, I'm sorry about all this," Lucen said, not one to mince words.

Menders shook his head.

"Don't apologize. I've seen it coming for years. It's just that we've been caught out because he decided to do two years' growing in one summer. He's done nothing wrong and he would do nothing wrong. I don't want him thinking that he's being separated from Katrin as a punishment. He's worked very hard to be able to go to the Academy and it should be treated as a great accomplishment on his part."

So arrangements were made quickly – perhaps a little too quickly, because Katrin was genuinely shocked when she was told Hemmett was leaving.

There had been no time to lose, as the academic year was about to begin. Menders realized that he had been so determined to get Hemmett ready to go and away from Katrin that he hadn't given enough thought to the impact such a sudden change would have on her.

Now it was obvious that he'd miscalculated. She was heartbroken and angry.

"He was supposed to go next year!" she wailed, covering her face with her hands.

Menders was at a loss. Her grief and dismay were very real and for once she refused to let him comfort her. Worst of all, the intensity of her reaction let him know that the right decision was being made. Katrin wasn't in love with Hemmett, but much more time together would create a bond so strong there would be enormous trouble in the future.

"Little one, I'm sorry," was all he could say. His voice shook.

That did it. She looked up, someone else's misery making her forget her own. Menders managed a smile. He wrapped his arms around her.

"I'm sorry, Little Princess," he said again. "It's a wonderful thing for him. You know how hard he's worked. Since there's room at the Academy this year, we thought it was best for him to go. Please don't cry like this, because he'll see. That would ruin everything for him."

"Oh, but Menders," she wept, "What am I going to do? I'll be the only child here!"

"Yes, I know that," he sighed. "It won't be easy, but I was thinking of a solution for you. Once you're calmer, we'll talk about it."

That caught her attention but she still cried for a while. Menders let her. He didn't believe in telling a crying child to stop, particularly Katrin, because she cried so seldom. When she did cry it was for damned good reason.

Finally she sat up and he gave her a clean handkerchief. As she used it, he began to speak.

"Since Hemmett is beginning his life as an adult, I thought you might like doing the same thing here," he said. "Would you be interested in learning how to run your estate? That would be something to brag about when Hemmett comes home during recesses to boast about what he's been doing."

She looked at him over the handkerchief, intrigued.

"But I already ride around with you," she said.

"Yes, but you don't run The Shadows, I do. I am willing to teach you how to run The Shadows, if you are interested."

She gulped and nodded.

"There's a lot to it. You won't learn it in a week, but I think that it's time you started to know what is involved," Menders continued.

"What am I going to do when I'm grown?" she asked.

That was the question Menders had no answer for.

"Hemmett is going to be a soldier. Eiren's a teacher and her sister Sana is going to be too. Everyone goes away to school, except for me," Katrin went on.

"Do you want to go away to school?" Menders asked, not wanting to face the question about what her adult life would hold, because he absolutely did not know.

Katrin looked frightened. Despite her jealousy of other people's travels, the thought of leaving The Shadows gave her some pause.

"No," she said in a small voice.

"That isn't a threat. I honestly want to know," he explained. "If you truly want to go away to school, it could probably be done, one way or another."

Katrin shook her head immediately.

"I want to stay here with you," she answered quietly. "But sometimes I wonder what it is I'm supposed to get ready to do when I grow up."

Menders leaned back and crossed his legs in front of him.

"This is a problem for Princesses who aren't the Heiress," he said after some thought. "There is no sense of purpose. Unfortunately, very often such people spend their time idly amusing themselves. That leads to boredom and discontent."

"What do princesses do?" Katrin asked.

"Those who don't become Queen tend to marry and have children," Menders answered. Katrin looked dubious and he smiled. "You're a little young to worry about that yet. But being a Princess with land means that you run that land just as a Queen would run a country. The Shadows belongs to you, Katrin, not the Queen. It was ceded to you when you were born. The income from it will eventually be yours."

"There's an income?" she asked, looking thunderstruck.

"Of course. The tenant farmers, like Mister Spaltz, pay rent and The Shadows produces crops that are sold. All of this is the income from the estate. Once we modernize a bit more, I expect we will have surplus timber to market as well."

"What happens to this income?" Katrin was curious, her

upset and tears forgotten.

"At present I put most of it back into the estate for improvements. Things like new types of crops, new strains of plants, farm machinery. Improvements to the house. Money set aside for emergencies, both at The Shadows and for the estate farmers. Things that will make The Shadows produce more and make more money in the future. We'll have steam power soon and mechanized farming. Managing all this took me years to learn, so it's not something you're going to pick up overnight. You might as well get started now."

"If I have an idea about how things should be done, will you listen to me?" she asked eagerly.

"Princess, when I have ever refused to listen to you?" Menders returned. "Of course I would listen, and we would make a decision together as to what to do."

She smiled.

"Fair warning," Menders added, not wanting her to be carried away on a tide of enthusiasm, only to have it dashed on the rocks of things like bookkeeping, "some parts of running an estate aren't particularly fun and can be frustrating and boring."

"I still want to try," Katrin said with determination.

"And so you shall. Now, you need to wash your face and look presentable. We're having a celebration dinner for Hemmett tonight and it would be dreadful if you sat there being the specter at the feast. Can you try to be cheerful for his sake? If you act as if you're upset and sad, it will ruin what should be a very special time for him."

Katrin sat up, swallowed hard and then nodded.

"I'll change my dress too," she said. "I won't ruin things for Bumpy but I'm going to miss him."

"Eiren's suggested that she could use some more help at the school, if you'd like to go another day each week," Menders tempted. She smiled immediately. She was a true help to Eiren and it gave her contact with other youngsters.

"All right then, we'll talk to her about it," Menders said, rising. "It will give you more time to be with Petra Gunter and your other friends at school – and remember, they are always welcome to come visit you here."

Katrin stood and put her arms around him.

"I know it will be hard not having your best friend here all the time," he said gently, knowing she was still upset and really wanted to continue to cry. "I'll do all I can to fill in for you."

"You more than fill in," Katrin answered, looking up at him. "You're Menders."

"Thank you, my Little Princess," he smiled.

***

"I'll write lots of letters, Willow," Hemmett promised, looking down at Katrin as they stood on the front steps of The Shadows. "And it won't be that long before I'm home for Winterfest. I'll bring you something really nice as a present from Erdahn."

Katrin smiled and nodded, all the time feeling like crying. She was glad Kaymar was down at the stable getting the phaeton and horse, and that Menders had kindly walked over to the side of the steps, so he wasn't standing close. Lucen and Zelia and everybody else were still in the house, which was nice too.

Hemmett saw through her bravado. "And you write back as soon as you get them. That'll keep you busy and you'll be so occupied running The Shadows that you'll lose track of the time." He looked encouraging but she didn't dare say anything. If she did, she would start howling, she just knew it. She had her jaw locked tight shut.

Hemmett looked over at Menders, who sighed and shook his head. Then he looked back down at Katrin.

"You know, I'm glad you're not acting like you're happy that I'm going," he said. "It doesn't bother me if you cry. I'll miss you a lot."

That finished Katrin's resolve and she melted into torrents of tears. She tried to cover her face, but Hemmett bent and picked her up into a big hug, lifting her as if she weighed nothing. She put his arms around his neck and wailed while he patted her back.

"All right now, I have to go," he said. She could hear Kaymar pulling up in the carriage. "I'll write just as soon as I get there, so you know that I'm fine. You look after Smoke for me, make sure he gets ridden. Don't cry until you dry up now, Willow. Remember, I love you." Hemmett's voice was shaking. Katrin gulped and gulped, determined to control her tears.

"Come on, Little Princess," Menders said behind her. Hemmett put her down. She held onto Menders. He gave her a handkerchief and kept an arm around her as she stepped back so that Lucen and Zelia could say goodbye.

Hemmett hugged them both hard, Zelia twice, then turned to Menders. Menders put a hand out, but Hemmett shook his head and hugged him too. Menders laughed, and hugged back.

"Make me proud," Menders grinned, standing back and putting a hand on either side of Hemmett's face. "Stand tall, work hard."

Hemmet snapped to attention and fired off a parade-ground-perfect salute. Menders returned it.

"Remember, soldier," Menders said, with a slight tremor, "I expect your name to shine."

"Yes sir!"

Hemmett grabbed his case, swung it up into the phaeton, hugged and kissed his parents again, and then jumped up beside Kaymar. He waved as they went down the driveway, occasionally wiping at his eyes and nose with his sleeve.

***

Dear Willow,

This is my first free time since getting to school and see, just like I said, I'm writing!

The boat ride over here was great fun. Kaymar told Ifor to really let it rip and we tore right along. I wouldn't want to do it if the water was rough though. I felt a little sick as it was.

School has been good. They give us lots of food but it isn't a patch on Cook's meals. You can tell her that, it'll make her happy. The classes are easy for me! Menders had me doing things that were two years ahead of what I would be doing here, so I'm going to be fine, and having these classes now is going to be good review for me.

Military drill is fun. Yesterday we were stabbing dummies with bayonets. I'm the best because of all the practice I've had with Menders' Men. I'm so big that nobody tries to haze me and when they haze the other fellows, I knock heads together. If they'd just put me in charge here, I would straighten this place right out! They say that the Commandant reads all our letters, though I can't think why he would, it would be some boring, but let him take the hint about me taking over. Faw, that would be something!

Tell me all about everything and give my love to everybody, especially Menders and Eiren. I will write to them, of course, but you were first. You know how long it takes for me to write too.

I'll look for a letter from you. Remember, you promised to write back right away!

Love,

Bumpy (Hemmett)

Dear Menders and Eiren,

I've already written to Katrin, but I wanted to get a letter off to you before they make me march around some more. Things are really good and I'm happy to be here. A couple of the older fellows tried to push my head in *the privy and they found out that was a big mistake. All those years of training with the Men? Faw, I twisted them around and dipped their own heads in like they were prawns going into a sauce. Nobody bothers me now.*

They say the Commandant reads all the letters going out. Is that true, Menders? He showed me your records and awards and things. Told me if I strove to be as good as you I couldn't do better. He's a nice fellow, but can't half yell. Everyone yells and when I have to yell in class, I'm the loudest. Scared the sergeant to death the other day.

I will be writing to Mama and Papa in this same post but everyone else will have to wait, as I am running out of time and have to go off and stab more dummies with my bayonet. It's so dull Menders would throw a fit and take it off to the forge to hammer it and work it over the whetstone.

Keep my letters, because when I'm a famous soldier they'll be valuable. Write to me soon!

Your friend,

Hemmett

Menders finished laughing over this missive and handed it to Eiren. She began to giggle.

"That final admonition to keep his letters is too rich," Menders snickered. "I'd say our lad has found his element, yelling and stabbing dummies with his dull bayonet."

Katrin darted in and absconded with paper and a pen, grinning.

"Where are your own papers and pens?" Eiren called after her, still smiling over the mighty Hemmett dunking the upperclassmen in the privy.

"I've run out," Katrin replied with transparent innocence. Most likely she'd used up all the paper and had lost her pen. Eiren shook her head and carefully refolded the letter, putting it back in its envelope.

"We'd best take his advice about saving his letters," she

smiled, slipping the envelope into her desk drawer.

Dear Bumpy,

I was so glad to get your letter! That boat ride is really exciting but I would like to do it in the daylight sometime. Both times I went across it was pitch black. On the way back we went really fast because Menders banged his head.

I don't know why the Commandant would read all the letters. Menders says there are over a hundred boys there. It would take him all week to read them! I don't think you need to worry about it.

I told Cook what you said about her cooking. She was very proud and said that she will send you some cookies next time Kaymar goes over. Knowing Kaymar, you will never see them. He's so bad. The other day he set off a stink bomb in Franz's office because Franz had been teasing him with my old stuffed walrus and threw it down the hall like a hopfootle ball and hit him on the back of the head. So Kaymar went off to his shed and made up this stink bomb that smelled like cabbage burning. He put it under Franz's desk. Menders thought the house was on fire and then Franz came staggering out all red in the face and choking. It was hilarious.

I have been learning about the estate. Some of it is boring, like doing accounts, but most of it is really interesting. I'm also learning how to make soap. I tried making a batch using ground cloves instead of lemon and put in the same amount of cloves as you would lemon. It smelled as bad as that stink bomb did. Cook yelled and yelled, when she wasn't laughing. I didn't use up all the cloves, but almost. Menders had to go over to the village for more, and took me and bought me a new dress. We had to bury that batch of soap in the woods. Your father says he can smell it when he goes into the woodlot.

I go out with Franz on some of his calls too and I really like it. We see some of the old people. I've already had ramps put on the house steps for two of them who have bad rheumatism. Franz just hit his head when I suggested it, and said, "Why didn't I think of that!" Menders says to keep on coming up with ideas. He doesn't know what he's letting himself in for.

Let me know everything you do. What will you do on your rest days? Tell me all about Erdahn. I've been there, but it was night and I didn't see a thing.

I miss you.

Love,

Willow

Dear Hemmett,

Eiren and I were delighted to read your letter and to know that you haven't allowed anyone to haze you. You'll find, if you continue to make prawns of the potential hazers, that they will leave off. Protecting the other boys from hazing will win you a lot of friends.

It would take your Commandant hours to read all the outgoing letters. That is a rumor that goes around the Academy all the time. Do give him my regards when you speak to him next. He is a very good and fair man, and if you ever have any troubles, he is the person to see.

All has been going well here. We are getting ready for winter, as usual. It looks like it will be a hard one, so we're hoping that the Thrun will get through this year. Katrin has been working hard at learning how The Shadows is run, and has given Doctor Franz and me some good suggestions. She also did a bit of experimenting with clove soap, which was an unmitigated disaster. It required a rapid burial far from the house.

Katrin has exercised your pony a great deal and Kaymar has ridden him a bit too, as he's small enough. Everyone is well, and sends their love.

In friendship,

Menders and Eiren

Dear Willow,

Well, I've had my first rest day. My friend Villison and I went out into Erdahn to have a look around. I can't half begin describing it to you — more houses and people than you can imagine. The houses once were all different colors and are very close together, but the colors have faded now and there's lots of grey, because of all the smoke from the factories. They call Erdahn the 'Iron City'. Some streets don't have a tree anywhere in sight. It's very different to The Shadows.

We looked in all the shops and I spent some of my pocket money on some new shoes and chocolate. I've already outgrown my old shoes. Sometimes I wonder if my feet will ever stop growing.

Villison and I rode on the trams. They are like a single railroad carriage car, but run by steam. You pay a pennig and ride all you want until you get off. Then you have to pay another pennig when you get back on. It seemed really odd to be moving along without a horse in the equation somewhere.

There are quite a few parks in the nicer parts of Erdahn, and lots of places where you can get food. Villison and I ate a lot. He's a good fellow, but awfully silly, and is always in trouble of some kind or another. Even though he's been at the academy a year more than I have, he's in my class. He'll never make officer and says he doesn't want to be, so I wonder why he's even here? But he's good fun. He hates to wash, so I was wondering if you would send him some of your famous clove soap, to encourage him in cleanliness.

The Palace is huge, right in the middle of Erdahn. We went up to the gate and looked at it. It's really grimy, like nobody has painted or taken care of it and the garden is all overgrown. The gates are rusty. Not a patch on The Shadows. I didn't see the Queen, but there was a sentry standing around who looked a right lout. I wanted to clip him on the ear and make him stand up straight. I should have yelled like I do in class. That would have waked him up.

I don't mind telling you that I've been homesick. I started bawling when I went to bed the other night. It'll pass though, once I get used to being away.

I really miss the swing at The Shadows. It has such nice memories. And I miss you, Willow.

Love,

Bumpy (Hemmett)

Dear Menders and Eiren,

You were right, all the hazing has stopped and now everybody gets along. I have a new friend, Villison. He's been here a year more than I have, but is in my class. He's not one for studying but he's a good mate. We went out into Erdahn on our rest day and he showed me around. It's a huge place, and I don't think that I'll ever get to know my way around it.

I gave your regards to the Commandant, and he was very pleased. Told me even more stories about you, how you were one of the youngest and smallest boys he'd ever seen come into the academy and how hard you worked to get strong. I told him about how you punch nails into trees with your hands to mark them in the woodlot, and he laughed fit to die. I don't know what he found so funny. He said he will write to you about how I'm doing.

I'm really glad you worked me as hard as you did, because I'm having no trouble in classes. I still make sure I do every scrap of work, because the time will come when I have to start doing things I haven't learned yet. I've already contacted those tutors you recommended so I can get a head start on the things I'll need to know in third year. You've got me prepared for the first two years, no problem.

Tell Kaymar that several of the fellows would like his recipe for the stink bomb. It would come in handy around here on bath night.

Tell everyone hello and give them my love. Have to get ready for a mathematics quiz tomorrow.

Your friend,

Hemmett

Dear Son Menders,

I just wanted to drop a line to let you know that your protégé, Hemmett Greinholz, is doing very well at the academy. He shows a great deal of enthusiasm and is more than willing to work to overcome his difficulties with formal studies. He excels at military training, and will definitely graduate as an officer.

He is greatly inspired by your past prowess, but shows no interest in or aptitude for Special Services training, so will remain at the Academy in the officers' training school. I know this has been a matter of some concern for you, so I'm sure this news will come as a relief.

It has been a great pleasure to learn that you are well, as are the graduates of this institution you have given work and hope.

Your affectionate "father",

Morschal Komroff, Commandant

CHAPTER 38
AN ESSAY

Eiren looked up from the papers she was grading, and held out a page to Menders.

"Look at this little essay," she said. "It's remarkable. I was wondering if you might be able to place the statue the child is writing about."

Menders took the paper, raising his eyebrows at the truly terrible handwriting that tipped crookedly down the page.

"Not typical of your students," he said quietly.

"He's a new boy, an odd little thing. He doesn't speak much and he struggles with the work. His education has been spotty. The most I've gotten out of him is that his family moves frequently, but he's attended school wherever there is charitable tuition available. Don't worry about the writing and spelling, read what he says."

Menders frowned, trying to place the family in his mind. He kept tabs on who came and went from the area, but could not possibly be aware of everyone all the time.

An Important Moment

When I was verry small about four years old my famly was in a town where my father was lokking for work. We were verry pore and it was raneing hard. My mother and I had no place to get out of the rane and we sheltred under a big stachue. The sides of the stachue had lady heros carved on them and my mother tol me storys about a lady hero who was a quene. The stachue was made of wite stone with green lines and when I lokked close I could see it was all shiney bits very close together. My mother held her cloke over me like a roof and I kept putting my hands on the stachue all wet with rane it was smooth and cold. She told me a pome about stachues where she was a girl called giunts and how they sleep in the ground. That day is my important moment becuz I was happy and my mother was happy and that wasnt ofen as we were always cold and hungry. I wish I new the name of the stone of the stachue and where it is. My mother died when I was six years old and if I could get back to the stachue I mite rememer her better. I try hard to rememer but it fades away. I dont want her to fade my luvly mother.

"It sounds like the plinth of the statue of Queen Glorantha in Erdahn," Menders mused, perusing the wavering lines of writing. "It's the only large statue I know of that has a female hero in the carvings. Has this boy lived there?"

"He hasn't told me," Eiren answered, taking back the paper. "But he must have if that's the statue he saw. I had guessed the stone is marble, from his description. I'll tell him about the statue in Erdahn. I hadn't thought of it, but it sounds right."

"I don't want her to fade, my lovely mother," Menders said softly. "That's haunting."

"He's a haunting little boy," Eiren said with regret.

"I wondered why you were taking such enormous lunches to school lately," Menders smiled, looking at her. He knew she supplied several of her students with at least one proper meal a day. He could see to it that all people living on The Shadows had adequate food, but the school drew children from the entire district and poverty was rife.

"He's one of my best customers, though he takes the food away to a corner to eat," Eiren sighed. "I just hope knowing about the statue will take some of that longing out of his eyes."

Menders thought of the badly spelled essay and ground his teeth slightly, thinking of a hungry child at the school. He no longer led the art classes. A young tutor on one of the neighboring estates who had taken over once Menders' workload at The Shadows became too demanding. He was simply not familiar with many of the schoolchildren now.

"What's his name?" he asked suddenly.

Eiren looked up from her papers.

"Borsen," she replied.

CHAPTER 39
LETTERS FROM ERDSTROM

Dear Petra,

I'm hurrying to write to you so that the letter can make it back on the train. I know you've been to Erdstrom before, but it being my first trip, I'm just about to die of excitement. I know I'm driving everyone here crazy gooing over everything, but I didn't think you'd mind hearing about my great journey!

The hotel we're staying in, the Metropolitan, is astonishing. I don't tend to think of The Shadows as grand, partly because it's home and partly because it's old-fashioned now, though I love it, but this place! Marble and gilt everywhere, rich wood, gold faucets in the bathrooms! My room is incredible, all pink and gold with pink roses on the carpet and a bed that has a six step stair just to get into it. Gods help me if I fall out. It would probably kill me. Menders says the room is so frilly it makes him itch, but I love it. I could spend the entire two weeks there and not get tired of it.

It has been decided that we are going to present ourselves as a family, so Menders is now my father, Eiren my mother (which means she would have been thirteen when she had me, but Menders says that people usually don't do the arithmetic) and Kaymar is my uncle. He's put some dreadful stuff in his hair to make it look black and is wearing dark spectacles like Menders, so he'll pass for his brother! It's killing. Hemmett is to be my brother.

Hemmett was already at the hotel and here's another huge surprise – he's grown a moustache! I was amazed, but he says the cadets are allowed to have one if they can grow a decent one and keep it within regulations. He looks so much older. But he's the same old Hemmett under his grandness and uniform, claims he's so manly now that he has to shave six times a day. Well, his face is scratchy enough, I yelled when he hugged me hello.

Right away Eiren took me to a dressmaker. Everything I have is so tight since my cycles started and everything decided to grow at once. Kaymar calls the woman who owns the place Madame Intimidation but she's really very kind and understanding under all the grandeur. I'm to have an evening dress to go to the ballet, even though I thought I would just wear my blue and gold Thrun dress. Eiren ordered several more things for me, including all new underwear, and it was all I could do not to want some of everything, all the laces and ribbons, on it. Eiren just laughed and says that's typical of women in dressmaker's shops.

Then we went to a shoemaker. The moment he saw how tight my shoes were, he took them off and wouldn't let me have them back. So I have some new ready-made ones, and four more pairs and a pair of evening slippers are being made for me, including a pair in spring green! I wanted them so much because I am having a spring green dress made, but how practical would shoes like that be when I make soap and weed the carrots? Eiren knew I longed for that color though and ordered the shoes, and gloves to match. I thought it was a terrible waste, since I'm just going home after our two weeks here, but Menders has said we'll see to it that I get a chance to wear these grand things beyond this trip! That means more jollifications!

We went to lunch after the trip to Madame Intimidation. Petra, you are absolutely coming with us next time, whether your father needs help on the farm or not! The restaurant was so grand – and everyone in it was looking at me, or seemed like. I balked going in because there were so many eyes, but Kaymar, who was escorting me, just whispered that I'd better get used to it, that people tend to look at beautiful women. Me? I know good and well that my mouth is too wide and my nose is far too definite, but Kaymar doesn't flatter.

I ate everything on the menu and it was so good I was tempted to sneak some back to the hotel in my pocket, but didn't, of course. While we were eating, Menders told us about his trip to the oculist. Thankfully his eyes are not doing too badly, but he needs new eyeglasses and will have to have both dark and clear pairs and pairs for reading. I told him he'll rattle when he walks with all those pairs, but he just laughed and said he would get Tomar to make him a special waistcoat with lots of pockets.

Menders is so much more relaxed here. With Kaymar, Ifor, Haakel and Bertel with us, as well as Hemmett and Doctor Franz we have plenty of security, and the hotel has security as well. Nobody knows who I am. So now Menders is laughing more and not looking so serious. I'm having lots of memories of when I was little and he was so young and carried me around everywhere with him and tossed me in the air all the time. Do you remember how he would get down on the floor and play with us in the nursery when you visited, when we were just little things? He laughed so much then! I hate to think that because I'm the Princess he's gotten so much more somber. I have to find a way to do something about it, because Menders does so much for me, and he should be happier.

I have to close, because Bumpy is going up to the train station to post my letters along with some letters Menders is sending back.

Your friend,

Katrin

Dear Sana,

I wanted to write to you separately from the letter that I've sent to the family, to encourage you in your first adventure of teaching the school on your own. I'm proud of you for offering and I'm sure that you're doing a wonderful job.

I am just back from taking Katrin to the dressmaker. There were the usual spoiled girls there, complete with pouting and tantrums. Katrin was so entranced by everything that she didn't even notice them, but the blushing mammas contrasting our girl to their brats were many.

So now Katrin has a young lady wardrobe on the way. I'm thankful that I no longer have to pretend not to notice how she was splitting the seams of her old clothing! We didn't want to tell her about the trip here too soon for fear that it would be necessary to postpone or cancel. Menders has plans to take Katrin to buy her first adult jewelry to go with her new evening dress, so she can wear it to the theatre.

Katrin is wild to go to the ballet and as you know, in the last two years she's dreamed of becoming a dancer. I look forward to our theatre evening with mixed emotions – Katrin has grown far too tall to be a dancer, even if her position as Princess would permit such a thing. I fear that what should be a wonderful experience could be a disappointment. She loves dancing and has true talent. *Well, I shall not borrow trouble. She is so excited to be here in Erdstrom and enjoys all these new experiences so much that it might ease her realization that dance as a profession is something that will be denied her. If it were possible, Menders would move the planet to make it so. I believe he would even confront the Queen herself if it was something that would be possible – but nothing can make Katrin smaller.*

Enough on that gloomy theme. We are all well and having a wonderful time. If you have any urgent questions or problems, send to The Shadows and someone will be dispatched to us immediately.

Your loving sister,

Eiren

Ho, Villison!

Only a short note, as I'm not about to take too much time from jollifications to write to an old wastrel like yourself. Know that while you're bored to tears on your mamma's estate, I am having the time of my life here at the Metropolitan, squiring a gorgeous Princess around. She got some proper clothes the first thing, so no longer looks like a country schoolgirl. We get tons of attention when I lead her out to dance at the hotel in my dress uniform. After all, we are a most devastating couple.

So what is happening down there in the southern land? Finding plenty of mischief to keep your mamma in fits? Did they let you pass on to next class, or are you held back again?

Wish I'd thought to get you invited on this junket. Menders has Katrin off buying some jewelry and I'm at loose ends until we go for lunch at one. I could do with some rambling around the shops and a beer or two!

Let me know if we can get together before school starts up again. I'll write you again when we get back to The Shadows.

Your best mate,

Hemmett

My dearest Mahmay,

Ifor and I are in Erdstrom with the rest of the family – I realized that I hadn't responded to your latest letter and didn't want to wait until we were back home, lest you worry that something had happened.

Though we are very preoccupied with providing Cousin Katrin with security, everyone is enjoying this visit to the city. Erdstrom has grown and is now called The Second Capitol, very sophisticated with theatres, many shops and other entertainments.

I hope that when Dorsen and his family come to visit in the summer you will come as well. We have every comfort at The Shadows, now that we've survived several summers of construction, sawdust and Cousin Menders having the time of his life amid the chaos. We could take a jaunt to Erdstrom and spoil you with the pleasures of the city!

I would like very much for everyone in the family to get to know Katrin. Though surrounded by loving people, she is, by the very nature of her station, isolated. Menders is an excellent father for her as well as her cousin, and Eiren is very much her mother, but she is curious about her own family.

She has grown close to me over the years and often asks about all of you. I believe you and she would get along famously. It would be good for her to have your influence. Katrin is among men too much because of her situation and needs the guidance and friendship of older women.

And now my dear Mahmay will scold me for calling her an older woman, yes, I know. Fuss, fuss.

Must close, Ifor is pawing the floor with his hoof, wild to get out to the opera. The things I tolerate for love.

Many kisses, your loving son,

Kip

From Katrin's journal

I couldn't resist this beautiful little book and I've often wondered what it would be like to keep a journal as Menders does — so I shall try.

I have the sapphire set Menders bought for me beside me on the desk and I can't bear to close the lid of box. It twinkles so and the color is so rich! I nearly fainted when Menders bought it, even though it was the most expensive set in the store. I had no idea when he asked me to choose between five sets. It was like that night long ago when Tharan-Tul had me choose a strand of gems. I was about to take a more elaborate set, but then I saw the deep green flash in the blue sapphires of the simpler set that I chose. It seemed more "true" if such a thing is possible of stones, just as my grey strand of cloudstones I chose when I was five seemed more "true" than all the brightly colored strands it was jumbled in with.

When I picked the set, the sales clerk went the color of milk and was like to fall down. He muttered something to Menders about the set being the most expensive in the place, that he'd only put it out for comparison, but Menders was most lordly and told him to bring the matching ring. He sent me aside to look at other things, but I listened (Menders taught me how to hear everything years ago, which now comes back on him when he'd rather I was deaf!)

When I heard the price, I just stood there with my mouth hanging open. A fortune. I wore a fortune of stones to the ballet tonight, necklace, earrings, brooch and ring. With my hair fully up and a blue satin evening gown with a train the same color as the stones.

I'm still breathless. The ballet was beautiful and Menders took me backstage afterward so I could meet the dancers.

The moment I saw them I knew I could never be one. They are the size of children and I'm big enough to pick them up! And their feet! I saw the star, Madame Millenvue's feet when we went to her dressing room to congratulate her. Blisters, bruises, calluses, crooked toes, missing toenails — gods! And Madame said there is always pain, but the dedicated dancer transcends it.

I love to dance but I thought being a dancer would be — well that it wouldn't be a trial of pain, with damaged feet sure to become crippled with age. When we left the theatre, I said something about their feet to Menders. He stopped and looked at me and said that the larger a person was, the more toll dancing took on the body — and then he looked so sad and said "I'm sorry, my Little Princess, I couldn't bear to tell you."

I wasn't sad. Once I saw what it took to be a dancer — I didn't want to be one anymore. That doesn't mean I can't dance and take lessons, which I will continue to do, but I don't want to have that sort of pain. I'm afraid of pain. I could tell Menders admired the dancers for what he called "their sacrifice", meaning they endure all that pain to dance — but that isn't anything I want. So that settles that.

Another moment with Menders today — when I chose the diamond set that he eventually bought for Eiren. I was terrified to even consider it, but he said my choice wasn't written in stone, he was just curious as to what I would pick for her. So I thought of Eiren, of her running to meet Menders when she comes home from the school, of that time she and I were caught in the blizzard and she was so brave — and I chose a set with a simple necklace that was a half circle of diamonds. They were like autumn stars on a frosty night.

Menders said, "Yes, that's the one that said her name to me as well." Then he said more softly, "Blood from my blood, body from my body." He bought them, and gave them to Eiren later. She was speechless and cried, but was so happy. Menders was so proud when she wore those diamonds to the ballet. I so want what they have! Someday.

On our way back from the jewelry store, I asked Menders about "blood from my blood, body from my body." It seemed so very intense and strange.

He didn't say anything for a while, but I waited. He sometimes takes his time sorting out what he's going to say. Then he said,

"It's a saying that describes how parents feel about their children, who are literally made from their own blood and flesh. It is the way that I feel about you, though I didn't make you — well, in a way, in the most important way I did, because I've raised you. When you chose the very same necklace that I had as a gift for Eiren, I was reminded of how much you are like me, and how I feel that you are as much mine as you would be if I had truly been your father."

That's the best I remember it. Then he took out a small box and *gave it to me. He'd bought it on the sly in the jewelry store. It had a little brooch in it in the shape of a snowflower with diamond dewdrops on the petals.*

I remembered when I was tiny he used to call me Snowflower, before Menders' Men and so many people about. He's always used Little Princess as a name for me, but when he gave me the brooch, I knew he'd never forgotten those days when he was just a boy and I was Snowflower.

I am a lucky girl and Menders is calling through the door for me to put out the lamp and go to sleep. I like this journal!

Perhaps I'll be a writer!

CHAPTER 40
A LOST BIRD FLIES HOME

Katrin watched as the little boy called Borsen slowly edged his way toward Eiren's desk at lunchtime, as he did every day. Eiren was ready for him and handed him a wrapped packet of food with a smile. Borsen didn't smile back. He whispered a thank-you and then retreated quickly to a corner of the schoolroom. He huddled in a chair turned toward the wall and began unwrapping the packet.

Katrin and her friend Petra Gunter exchanged glances. Katrin had already asked Eiren why she didn't inform someone in authority of how thin Borsen was.

"I'm afraid if I did, his family would simply pick up and leave," Eiren answered frankly. "At least this way I know he's getting one big meal a day and I give him food to get him through rest days as well. I don't know his family. It may be that they're simply poor and can do no better. It's not a crime to be poor. And if anyone in authority did bother to take an interest, which isn't likely, he would be taken to an orphanage. A child like Borsen wouldn't last a week in one of those places."

Katrin thought it was a crime for anyone to be as thin as Borsen, though his stomach stuck out as if it was fat. Eiren said that was a sign of malnourishment. He often had sores around his mouth and his hair was dull and dry.

Olan Spartz, Eiren's brother closest to Katrin's age, muttered, "Poor little bugger." Varnia Polzen, one of the big girls in the top class, clenched her jaw tightly but said nothing, her piercing grey eyes fixed on Borsen as he crouched in his corner.

"Would you mind if I ask him to sit with us?" Katrin asked, suddenly ashamed that she'd never thought of it before. She helped at the school four days a week now and had seen Borsen huddled over the food Eiren gave him many times, but it had never occurred to her to invite him to sit with her and her school friends.

Petra and Olan both looked ashamed as well and shook their heads. Varnia said nothing and made no sign, but Katrin could hear her draw in a quiet breath. Katrin rose and went over to Borsen.

He started, having been intent on his food, and drew away from her until she was very close. Then he stared at the floor.

"Borsen, why don't you come and sit with us?" Katrin smiled, putting a hand on his arm. "We'd like you to."

He shivered but Katrin waited patiently. After a moment, he rose and followed her back to the table where she and her friends sat. She settled him in a chair next to her and started talking animatedly to the others, who followed her lead. They let Borsen get on with his lunch, but Katrin could tell he was listening intently.

"I don't want any more of this," Olan said, putting some cheese out in front of all of them. "It won't keep, so take whatever you want."

After a moment, Borsen's bird-claw hand crept out and took a piece. A few moments later he took another one. Katrin had an extra apple and put it out as well, offering it to the table at large. When the lunch period was ending, Borsen slowly reached out, pushing it into the tattered pocket of his ragged little jacket. He whispered a nearly inaudible thank-you and crept back to his desk.

After that, Katrin and Olan always made a point of bringing extra food and made lunch a shared meal. Petra's father, Mister Gunter, was the least successful farmer on The Shadows, so there was nothing extra for her to bring. The Polzen farm, Varnia's home, was known for its sparse harvests, but Mister Spaltz more than made up for it when Olan explained Borsen's situation. He sent great slabs of cheese, bottles of milk, meat and extra slices of bread. Katrin brought extra sandwiches, stew and fruit. On the days that Katrin wasn't at the school, the others continued to have Borsen sit with them. It took weeks, but he would finally speak if you addressed him directly. One day he even managed a shy smile.

Once you got Borsen to talk, he was interesting. Though his schoolwork was below average and he sometimes didn't do assignments at all, he was very bright.

He was also able to draw and finding someone else who could draw well always intrigued Katrin. That was often the reason for his forgotten assignments; he would be caught up in drawing something, usually men in elegant clothing. Katrin found that out by accident when she was going from desk to desk helping with an art class, and looked over Borsen's shoulder. He wasn't drawing the still life set out by the art teacher, but a fashion sketch of a man in a tailcoat, full-cut trousers and a top hat.

"That's beautiful!" Katrin whispered, bending over the sketch.

Borsen immediately covered it with his hands and kept his eyes down. Katrin put a hand on his arm and then went on to the next student.

That day at lunch, Petra, Varnia and Olan were absent, as it was a busy time on their farms. Borsen came over and sat quietly beside Katrin. He took a pile of papers from his pocket and placed it in front of her.

Katrin leafed through it to find page after page of drawings similar to the one she'd seen during art class. They were fashion drawings of men's clothing. Some were carefully colored with what looked like chalk. Some were just parts of clothes, little details but expertly done; a man's turnback cuff and button, elaborately stitched decoration, piping on a shoulder epaulette.

"These are excellent," she told him. "Who taught you?"

"Nobody," Borsen whispered.

"Really? I can't draw like this, and I've been studying for

years," Katrin smiled. "What did you color these with?"

"Soft rocks I found." Borsen snuck a look at her.

"How smart!" Katrin looked through the pile again. "Why do you just draw clothes?"

Borsen looked down, and she thought he wasn't going to answer.

"I want to be a tailor," he finally whispered. "I was hoping I could find a tailor here to apprentice to but there isn't one. I'll have to wait until we move to a city, but I doubt I'll find one who'll take me because I'm Thrun."

Katrin started.

"What's wrong with being Thrun?" she asked. "The Thrun come here almost every winter for a carnival. They're wonderful people!"

Borsen turned his brown eyes on her again and stopped taking little bites off the sandwich she'd given him.

"You don't know about City Thrun then. That's what I am," he said, his voice with the lilting Thrun accent soft and sorrowful. "In the cities they consider us scum because most City Thrun are beggars and thieves. It's almost impossible for Thrun to get work in the cities. That's why I hoped there would be a tailor here. It's better in the country." Borsen turned his attention back to the sandwich, but not before Katrin saw tears in his eyes.

As the autumn came, Borsen continued to join Katrin and her friends at lunch. Once in a great while he would smile. He never spoke as freely as he had to her alone, but he listened happily. The food he was getting had made a difference, though he was still painfully thin and his belly was still too large.

When harvest began, a number of pupils of the type Eiren called "busy time scholars" turned up at the school. These were older boys who decided they wanted to go to school around the time the heavy work of harvest on their fathers' farms began. They would turn up for several weeks, do nothing, disrupt classes and harass younger students. When Eiren confronted them about their behavior, they would beg pardon and promise to behave, but that only meant their tactics became more underhanded. Worst of all, they had chosen Borsen as their victim this year.

Suddenly they always seemed to be where Borsen was walking. They would bump him, trip him, send him flying into a wall. Then they would sneeringly apologize and do the same again as soon as they could.

Eiren sent them home for several days. Katrin was shocked that she allowed them back.

"It's a difficult situation, darling," Eiren sighed as they rode home in the governess cart. "If I deny those boys access to the school, their parents can point out other children who attend who don't work particularly hard. Some of those children might just begin to do better one day, and they all benefit from being in school. Some of them are simply not capable of doing better, but do what they can."

"Like Borsen?" Katrin asked. "He doesn't do all the assignments."

Eiren nodded. "School is a haven for Borsen," she said quietly. "I believe he does what he can. So you see, if I sent those boys away that could endanger Borsen's ability to come to school."

"I don't like them," Katrin said after a minute.

"I don't either, but I have to be careful when I exclude someone. Education should be available to all." Eiren answered. "Yes, even those who don't want it, like those louts," she added, catching Katrin's look.

A few days later, Katrin was helping a girl with a writing exercise. One of the "busy time scholars" went to the front of the schoolroom to ask Eiren a foolish question. He was given a brisk dismissal and sent back to his seat. As Eiren responded to another student, the boy detoured by Borsen's desk, pouring the contents of a bottle of ink over the paper Borsen was drawing on.

"That's for you, you little nancy trash," the big boy

sneered, sauntering to his seat and slumping into it.

Katrin snatched up a sheet of blotting paper and began mopping the pool of ink. Borsen was staring at his inky shirt with horror. It was the only one he owned.

"Milk will take that out," Katrin said quietly.

He looked at her and she flinched. Where was Borsen going to get milk to take ink out of a shirt when it was obvious he didn't ever get any to drink? His shirt wouldn't take much scrubbing either, it was threadbare and frayed already.

Katrin started toward the front of the room to tell Eiren what had happened, but felt a tug on her skirt. She turned. Borsen shook his head, crumpling the damp, blackened sketch he'd been working on.

Later as they sat together at lunch she asked him why.

"It would make it worse," he whispered, looking at the floor.

"Mistress Menders wouldn't want them picking on you like this," Katrin protested. "They shouldn't be calling you names either."

"If she tries to stop them, it will be worse," he repeated. "And I am a nancy." He flicked his eyes up to look at her.

"That's still no reason for them to bother you," Katrin replied.

"Thank you." After that he wouldn't speak again. He kept fingering his ink-stained shirt nervously.

One morning two days later, little Lorein Spartz came galloping up to the school on her pony. She jumped down and went puffing up to Eiren.

"Mistress Menders, those big boys are following Borsen! They keep hitting him and kicking him!"

Eiren caught up her skirts and ran down the steps and into the road. Katrin followed and was rapidly joined by Varnia and Olan.

Borsen was plodding toward the school, with the three

big boys behind him. They were pushing him and kicking at his spindly legs. Varnia began to hurry toward them with long purposeful strides and clenched fists but Olan ran ahead of her, motioning for her to stay back.

When the big boys saw strong, wiry Olan coming toward them they dropped back, trying to look innocent. Borsen was covered with dust from the road, the knees of his trousers were torn and there were bruises showing on his hands and arms.

Varnia put an arm around Borsen and hustled him into the school while Eiren confronted the three loutish boys. In a moment they were on their way home again and Eiren ran inside to Borsen. Katrin saw her speaking to him earnestly but he kept shaking his head. Eiren finally put an arm around him in a little hug and he went off to his desk, where he sat quietly, his eyes down. Varnia, her face white with rage, dipped a handkerchief in the water bucket and began wiping the dust from Borsen's face and hands.

Katrin felt a burning in her chest while she stood on the schoolhouse steps, watching the three big boys laughing as they walked away. They were very pleased with themselves.

If something didn't change, they were going to end up hurting Borsen. There must be something she could do!

***

"Menders?"

"Yes, my dear?" Menders looked up and had to smile. Katrin was wearing a very old, outworn dress and had a scarf wrapped around her head, her official soapmaking outfit.

"I was wondering if we could get an apprentice for Tomar." She stood in the doorway, looking at him intently.

Menders' eyebrows went up. An apprentice for the tailor would be an excellent thing indeed. Tomar was severely overworked and had recently moved from his cramped little workroom into what had been the old nursery, which had plenty of space and excellent light. Tomar's worktable was groaning under the weight of mending and clothing in all stages of construction. Though he stitched continuously for eight hours and more a day, there was no way he could ever keep up with the workload.

Menders already planned to hire two young secretaries into the household, Eiren's younger brother, Olan Spaltz and Katrin's friend, Petra Gunter. Both young people were finishing school and had few prospects for the future. Olan had not cared for school and had no desire to continue further. Petra was doomed to spinsterhood on her father's very primitive farm, as he insisted that she was needed to help work it. Marrying at fifteen would be her only possible escape.

Menders had been glad to offer a secretarial position to Olan once that young man realised that he didn't want to be a farmer, and several improvements made to Gunter's place freed Petra from being needed at home for long days of hauling water and milking cows.

Having the young people take over much of the endless copy work that went into maintaining correspondence and records for the estate would relieve a lot of the strain on Menders' eyes. He was more than willing, if an amenable young person could be found, to ease Tomar's staggering workload.

"An apprentice tailor would be very useful," Menders said. "It was something I was meaning to attend to... at some time or another." He indicated his desk, layered with papers. "I'm glad you thought of it."

Katrin smiled and came to sit across from him.

"There's a boy at school, Borsen Carvers. He... he likes clothes, a lot." Katrin suddenly seemed reticent. Menders waited for her to continue. She looked up at him and squared her shoulders.

"He's very gentle and quiet, and he wants to apprentice to

a tailor but there isn't one anywhere around. He doesn't know about our tailor," she went on. "He's like Ifor and Kaymar. Some of the older boys torment him. Would his being a nancyboy be a problem?"

"No, of course not," Menders answered. "So long as he wants to do the work and learns, whether he's a nancyboy or not is completely immaterial. How do you know this, Katrin?"

"He told me. He's very lonely – and he's so thin! He doesn't say much about his life at home but I can tell he's not happy. He draws beautiful clothing designs and he's desperate to learn tailoring. I'm sure he would work very hard."

Menders nodded. So far, so good.

"How long have you known young Borsen?"

"A year now, since he started coming to school. He thinks he's twelve, but he's not sure. He's tiny, even though he's Thrun, more the size of the eight year olds. He's very quiet and good and never gets in trouble. He's smart but has trouble with schoolwork."

Suddenly Menders remembered the essay Eiren had shown him.

"The boy who wrote the essay about the marble statue?" he asked.

"Yes, he's the one."

Menders nodded, thinking. The boy had an original turn of mind. No dullard could have written that touching little essay.

"Do you know anything about his parents?" he asked.

Katrin shook her head. "Borsen doesn't talk much," she explained.

"Well then, change out of your beautiful ballgown and we'll ride over to the school and have a word with your friend. If he wants to be apprenticed, I can speak to his parents and see what can be done," Menders smiled. Katrin jumped up, hugged him hard and fled upstairs, where she could be heard banging her wardrobe door around and pulling on her riding boots.

As they rode up to the school, the door opened and waves of children poured out, as the school now served over sixty pupils from the ages of five to sixteen.

Menders saw a group of large boys clustered at the side of the steps leading down from the main door. He watched idly but then sprang off Demon's back as he saw them deliberately thrusting a stick under the feet of a small boy. The child tumbled down the flight of four stone steps, landing face down in the dirt.

Katrin bounded off of her farlin and raced over to the big boys. Their nasty glee over the injury they'd done to their victim dissipated as the Princess of Mordania confronted them.

"I know each and every one of you!" she roared. "Don't you dare try to run away! You think you're so brave, hurting someone smaller than you, so just stand there now and take what's coming! Menders is Master of The Shadows and he will deal with you!"

One of the boys, the oldest and tallest, raised a hand as if to strike Katrin. She glared at him defiantly.

"Goren, no!" hissed another boy, grabbing at the first boy's sleeve. "She's the Princess! White Eyes will kill us!"

Eiren ran out of the schoolhouse door, followed by a rawboned, thin young woman Menders recognized as the daughter from the Polzen freeholding. Eiren dropped to her knees in the dust by the fallen child.

"Borsen, are you hurt?" Eiren asked. Menders saw that Katrin had the instigators of the incident cornered, cowering and obviously going nowhere, so he knelt by the child as well.

He lifted the boy's face to his.

My Gods, it's me, he thought, taking in the frail form, pale face and large Thrun eyes. Aylam Josirus all over again, small, weak and tormented. There were tears in the boy's eyes but he swallowed repeatedly, refusing to let them fall. How well Menders remembered doing that.

"Don't try to sit up yet," Menders said quietly. "Not until

I've seen if you have anything broken. Can you feel your feet? Move them – good. Now, can you feel your hands? Wiggle your fingers for me. Good boy. Anything hurt?"

"All over," Borsen said softly. "No one place."

The Polzen girl, who had been quivering with rage as she knelt beside Borsen, stood abruptly, eyes blazing and began striding the direction of the three louts. Menders caught her wrist, shaking his head when she turned to glare at him. She knelt by the Borsen again.

"After a fall like that, you'll be very sore," Menders said kindly. "Now, Eiren and I are going to help you roll onto your back. You just lie there for a while. Would you bring some water, please?" he said to the Polzen girl and then nodded to Eiren. Together they turned the little body.

Borsen winced but did not cry out. Menders was relieved. There was no serious damage, though Borsen's hands were deeply scraped from his attempt to break the fall. He settled the small dark head against Eiren's thigh, rose and strode over to where Katrin was holding the three big boys at bay.

"You miserable bastards," he said quietly, glaring at them over his glasses. "It takes a true coward to hurt someone that small and frail." He called to Eiren, never taking his eyes off his quarry.

"Do any of these boys pay tuition?"

"No. All of them are here through your patronage," Eiren answered. "I expelled them yesterday. They're banned from school grounds."

Menders' turned back to the cowering boys. "I don't want people like you around the children who come here. Your parents will hear from me, and they will know exactly why you have been expelled. I hope your fun was worth losing the chance for schooling. You probably won't enjoy spending the rest of your lives shoveling shit. Perhaps I'll tell your parents I've gotten you commissions in the 35th Infantry. Mordania needs cowards. After all, we have to give the enemy something to shoot at. Now, get out of here and don't come back."

They fled. Menders put an arm around Katrin's shoulders.

"I'm proud of you, Little Princess. Now, let's go see to your friend."

"One of them was going to hit me but the others stopped him. I was going to let him. I wasn't afraid."

"Oh did he?" Menders said, glancing at the fleeing boys and filing the information away for later reference.

Borsen was sitting upright now, still very rattled. Katrin crouched beside him. Eiren had bathed the scrapes on his hands and Varnia Polzen had gathered his scattered books and papers.

"Now then, how to get you home?" Menders said, bending over him. "Where do you live?"

"About two miles from here," Borsen whispered. "I can walk home now."

"No, my boy," Menders said firmly. "Perhaps you could, but I shan't let you, not after a fall like that." He looked up at Eiren.

"I want to speak to his mother," she said. He could see she was trembling and shaken. Katrin was still furious. The Polzen girl drew in quick little breaths through nostrils that were tightly pinched with tension and rage. Menders understood why they were upset but the last thing Borsen needed was more emotion flying around. He was desperately trying not to cry.

Menders beckoned to Eiren and walked her away from the young people.

"Why don't you let me drive him in the cart?" he suggested. "You ride Trouble home. Katrin can manage Demon. I'll explain things to his mother. He's already overwrought and Katrin's so angry she'll just upset him further."

Eiren began to protest, but he laid a finger on her lips.

"I want to see if this boy would like to be apprenticed to Tomar," he explained. "It would be a good situation for him. If he's amenable, I'll bring it up to his parents."

"It would be salvation for him," Eiren said. "All right, I'll leave him to you."

They returned to the youngsters.

"Borsen, Menders is the Master at The Shadows," Eiren said gently. "He'll drive you home in my cart. He'd like to assure your parents that no more harm will come to you here. Is that all right with you?"

"Yes." Menders saw that Borsen seemed relieved. He'd been right in assuming the overwhelmed boy needed no more emotional display, no matter how heartfelt.

Katrin began to protest but Menders looked at her and shook his head. She didn't understand, but nodded silently.

"Now then," Menders said, helping Borsen up, "let's get you home."

Menders didn't press the child for conversation for the first half mile, letting Rosie jog along lazily. By the end of the next half mile, he knew that being companionably quiet was doing what he expected. Borsen suddenly put his head down on his knees and began to cry. Menders could hear that there was relief in the outburst.

When the worst of it passed, Menders drew up under a shady tree and waited for Borsen to look up.

"You know, when I was your age, I was just as small as you are," he said conversationally. "I also had a very difficult time when I was a boy."

That did it. Borsen slid across to him, burying his face in Menders' shirt front. Menders put his arms around the fragile child and let him cry, remembering how Tharan-Tul had done just this, letting Aylam Josirus cry out all the pain and fear in his heart without chiding him to stop. Menders could still remember how clean and clear his mind had felt afterward.

Soon the sobbing quieted and Borsen was still. Menders patted his shoulder gently and supplied a clean handkerchief.

Though tear streaked and weary, Borsen's face no longer had that pinched look of a child trying to stay in control of himself.

"Katrin and I came to the school to speak to you," Menders said. "She told me you'd like to be apprenticed to a tailor."

The boy nodded slowly, his huge dark eyes riveted on Menders.

"Well, we have a tailor at The Shadows who's about to die of overwork," Menders continued. "Would you be interested in being apprenticed to him? His name is Tomar Fersten. He's very skilled and he's a most kindly man, with a family of his own."

"Yes, please," Borsen whispered. His small hands were shaking and he began to wring them nervously. They were thin as bird's claws. His arms were emaciated. Menders could feel the jut of a swollen belly against his side where the little fellow was leaning against him, and ground his teeth in rage. The child was starved.

"All right then, but we must ask your parents," Menders said, keeping his voice measured and calm. Borsen nodded. Menders took up the reins again and clucked to Rosie, who started out once more.

After another quarter mile, Borsen spoke abruptly. "My parents won't care. My father hates me. He'll be glad to see me gone."

"I see," Menders answered unemotionally, as if they were discussing the weather. "Well, if that's how things are, it's just as well you get started on your own life. My own father hated me, so I know what it's like. I went to military school when I was eleven and that's when my life started to be good."

He heard a little sigh of relief beside him and smiled.

Half an hour later, Borsen's pitifully small box of belongings was in the cart with them as they drove back toward The Shadows. Menders was furious, but showed nothing to Borsen, who seemed unaffected by his parents' immediate acceptance of Menders' offer and their insistence that he take Borsen with him immediately. They showed no concern over where he was going or what sort of people he would be living among. It was obvious that Borsen's father, a large, fullblood Thrun who certainly didn't share the emaciation of his eldest son, despised the boy. The woman with him only shrugged, looking at the floor.

Menders offered to bring Borsen home for his rest days and made it clear his family was welcome to visit him at The Shadows. In response the father turned away, opening a bottle of wine, while the woman picked up a grubby baby and began to nurse it. Borsen got his things and left without a word.

Katrin met them as they drove up in front of The Shadows.

"I fixed up an apartment for you," Katrin said to Borsen, showing him two rooms on the first floor near the Family Wing. When she went for water for the washstand, Menders took the opportunity to speak privately to the boy, who seemed completely flabbergasted and kept touching the bed hangings with wonder.

"Borsen, I want you to understand that you are under my protection," Menders told him gently. "You will come to no harm here. If anyone ever tries to hurt you again, you are to come to me, and I will help you. This is your home. Do you understand?"

"Yes, Mister Menders."

"Just Menders. We're very informal here. The Princess is Katrin, my wife is Eiren. Now, let Katrin get you settled and show you around, and then later I'll introduce you to Tomar. You can get started tomorrow, if you like."

Borsen grinned suddenly. His face changed from pinched to elfin in an instant. Menders couldn't help grinning back.

"I'm glad to have you here, Borsen," Menders said, extending a hand for the boy to shake. "Tonight you're getting thrown in at the deep end because it's family dinner, which means that there will be thirty-eight people in the dining room at once.

Do you think you will be comfortable with that?"

After a moment's thought, the little boy smiled and nodded.

Katrin came back with the water and asked Borsen if he wanted to see the rest of the house. He nodded and grinned again, and the two of them rushed out eagerly.

***

If a hawk turned into a woman it would look like Varnia Polzen, Menders thought as he studied the young woman standing stiffly before him. She was sharp featured and dark, with large grey eyes that could only be described as piercing. It was obvious that she seldom, if ever, smiled. Tall and thinner than she could be, she possessed a wiriness that indicated strength most people would not expect.

The Polzen farm was grimly familiar to Menders – a freehold, rare in the district where most were tenant farmers on The Shadows and other estates. It was bleak, windswept and unfruitful. Mister Polzen, the owner, was a dour and callous man, rendered uncaring by years of failure. Indifferent to the suffering of others, he was uncaring toward his livestock and family.

There were a number of sons who worked the farm, all unschooled, near-savage boys, and the one girl, Varnia. Polzen's wife had died some years back, leaving then ten-year old Varnia to do all the woman's work on the place, toiling endlessly and desperately to keep up with the heavy chores. She rose hours before sunrise to have the work finished so she could attend Eiren's school, where she was an average but diligent student.

She had just completed her final school year and would be doomed to a miserable spinsterhood on the grim landholding unless she married. Her looks were not the type to catch a man's eye quickly. Or, perhaps, at all, Menders thought regretfully.

Varnia had been protective toward Borsen when he began attending school. More than once Eiren had barely averted an outright brawl when Borsen was harassed and Varnia would rise, fists clenched, ready to hurl herself at his tormentors. Though fierce and taciturn, the young woman was tender and kindly toward the little boy.

Now, a week after Borsen was apprenticed at The Shadows, Varnia had appeared and asked to speak to Menders. Attired in a severe grey dress, her hair tightly coiled in a knot at the nape of her neck, she initially refused a chair and only consented to be seated after handing Menders several letters of recommendation.

"I'm here to apply for employment, Mister Menders" she said crisply. "I've had seven years' experience running a household. I will be willing to accept any form of domestic work."

Menders leafed through the letters. They were from various people in the district who apparently knew Varnia Polzen and could attest to her diligence and character. He let his mind whirl into action as he scanned the letters.

"What of your own family?" he inquired.

"They'll manage," Varnia replied, without longing or regret.

Menders made a point of keeping household duties within The Shadows' residents, sharing out the work between the Men, occasionally hiring some of the tenant farmers' wives and daughters for seasonal cleaning. Katrin's security was the compelling reason for this. The fewer people privy to the workings of the house, the better.

He didn't know the Polzens well and didn't want to. He had exchanged some rough words with Mister Polzen about a cow left lying in his farmyard after a difficult calving. When Menders happened along, the suffering animal had been out in all weathers for several days and was in agony from infection. When he confronted Polzen, he was told that the cow was being left to "take her chance" and that a bullet wasn't going to be wasted on her. Menders offered to shoot the cow himself and did so after the farmer shrugged indifferently. He'd avoided the place ever since, thankful it was not one of The Shadows' tenancies.

Young Varnia seemed cut from a different bolt of cloth than her sullen father and slovenly brothers, whom Menders had seen loitering in the village from time to time. Still, he wanted to know why she had chosen The Shadows when she had already worked for some of the people who had given her references.

He looked at her over his glasses. She met his gaze.

"Borsen is a dear little boy, isn't he?" Menders asked gently, going with his instincts as to why this young woman was here.

"Yes," she answered, never wavering. "That is the main reason why I have applied to you, Mister Menders. I would like to see to it that Borsen is looked after."

"We fully intend to do that," Menders said with some amusement.

"Yes, and I mean no insult, but he is very frail and I could provide whatever extra care might be necessary. I would also perform any other sort of domestic work you might require."

Menders waited.

"My eldest brother has just married, Mister Menders," Varnia continued coolly. "I was not happy doing all the woman's work on the farm, but I am certainly not going to stay and do the bidding of some other woman. I wish to be here not only because of Borsen, but because I am a friend of the Princess. From the way she has been raised, I can tell that this is a decent and loving home. But I am not afraid of hard work and hard situations. If I do not find work here, I will find it elsewhere."

Menders nodded, leaning back in his chair. He thought for a moment while Varnia waited with no sign of discomfort or impatience. She gave the impression that she was as comfortable with silence as Menders was.

"I would like to speak to Eiren for a moment," he finally

said. "I can give you an answer today, if you would like to wait."

She nodded.

"There are plenty of books to browse. I'll be back in a few minutes." He rose and left her there. He hurried upstairs, finding Eiren in their suite.

"Hire her," Eiren said succinctly as soon as he finished sketching out the situation. "She's a fine young woman and you can trust her. We could certainly use the help and she could use the freedom from that terrible place she's had to live in."

"I need no other recommendation," Menders smiled, kissing her swiftly.

Back in his office, he nodded to Varnia.

"If you wish to work here, we would be glad to have you," he said, eliciting the slightest smile from the solemn faced young woman. "I'll need to speak with your father, of course."

"I speak for myself, Mister Menders," Varnia said firmly. "I am of age and do not need my father's permission to take employment."

Menders nodded. "Very well. When can you move in?"

"Now. I have my things with me." She rose and picked up a small bag that she'd carried in with her. Varnia Polzen traveled light.

***

From Doctor Franz's files:
Borsen Carvers, initial examination:

Patient is male, approximately thirteen years of age (he is uncertain of his birth date and year.) This child is chronically undernourished and presents the appearance of a nine year old. He demonstrates the fragility of bone and swollen belly associated with ongoing lack of sufficient meat and milk. There are multiple scars on his hands and fingers, some of them quite recent. He states that these are from rat bites, resulting from catching rats for food. There are bruises from a recent fall (incident at school) and also from what appears to be physical abuse.

Borsen is not forthcoming about whatever abuse caused his bruises and is quite reticent about himself. Makes the statement "we go on from here," when questioned about his recent life with his father and stepmother. He is cautious, but obviously craves attention and affection. His is a gentle and retiring nature upon first meeting, but he responds well to Katrin as a peer, has a good sense of humor and in time will probably shed a great deal of his shyness and reserve. He has hugely enjoyed the attention given him by members of the household and holds Menders in absolute awe.

I fear, however, that this child will always be undersized and frail. Once the swollen belly appears in a patient's symptomatology, growth is forever stunted. There is also the distinct possibility of brittle bones. A diet of high nutrition has been recommended, supplemented with goat's milk, meat extracts and supplements. Borsen has a voracious appetite and will make up some lost ground. However, I doubt he will ever reach average height. He will need careful handling and attention and will always need to be mindful of his health.

***

Menders looked up from the estate account book with a smile. From the sounds reaching him, Mister Spaltz had just breezed into the house.

"Hello there!" the farmer said to Kaymar, who was lounging around the front door, taking advantage of one of the last warmish days that The Shadows would see for months. "Been keeping yourself out of trouble?"

"As best I can, considering all the temptation around me," Kaymar answered, making Mister Spaltz explode in his characteristic cackling "hee hee". He considered Kaymar hilarious and referred to him as The Mordanian Wildcat, impressed by the dichotomy between Kaymar's diminutive size and impressive strength. Spaltz could watch Kaymar chuck hay bales about and cackle endlessly.

"And there's our Kat! Give us a kiss there, my girl!" Katrin had come down the stairs to the foyer. "How's your lovely mama? Keeping well? I didn't stop by the school on my way down, though I'll look in on her when I go home. Where's your pa?"

Menders couldn't help grinning. Mister Spaltz simply considered Katrin Menders' and Eiren's child and, therefore, his granddaughter. He caused varying levels of local confusion by referring to himself as the Princess' granddad and Menders never bothered to enlighten anyone. It was far more amusing to let people puzzle the conundrum.

"Thanks, m'love, no need for you to show me the way," Spaltz was saying. "Get on with whatever you're doing decked out in your regal robes." A giggle from Katrin echoed a snort of amusement from Menders. Katrin was embroiled in changing the bed hangings in the suite, suitably attired for the task in an ancient smock and a dreadful old cap she'd dug out somewhere. At this point she was probably entirely grey with dust.

A moment later, Spaltz appeared at Menders' door, his expression belying the lighthearted exchanges that Menders had overheard.

"A word, son?" he asked, easing the door shut behind him.

"Of course, always," Menders said. "Care for a drink?"

"Yes, I would. How is your new apprentice, young Borsen, getting along?"

Menders' eyebrows went up. Spaltz was a man who told a tale in his own way, so it was pointless to press him.

"Very well. Thriving with Tomar and settling in nicely."

And so Borsen was. It was like watching a plant that had been moved from dry shade to watered sunlight. His pinched face was rapidly plumping out, pounds were piling on his fragile frame and the bloated belly had shrunk to normal size after medication from Franz and plenty of food. Smiles were often seen and Borsen was even beginning to speak spontaneously rather than only when spoken to. Once it became obvious that Borsen was not likely to set fire to the place or steal from anyone, Menders relaxed his watchfulness and the boy slipped easily into the routine of the household.

Mister Spaltz gratefully accepted the brandy Menders had poured for him. He flopped into one of the armchairs and sighed, crossing his legs.

"Well, it's good he's settled in. That lot, his family, have scarpered."

"They're gone?"

"Aye. Gone in the night, unpaid bills and rent, who knows what else. Went by there yesterday on my way to the village to let them know the boy was getting on famously here. The place is deserted and no-one with an idea where they've lit out to."

"Grundar shit!" Menders growled. Borsen had been doing so well, and now this, abandoned like a worn out shoe?

"It's a scandal," Mister Spaltz agreed. "Worse, there were some robberies in the neighborhood just before they went. I always wondered how they were surviving, with the man obviously not working, but I think we know now. Whoever did the stealing knew what he was doing. Took things that will fence easily and can't be traced. No sign of such doings with young Borsen?"

"No, he's scrupulously honest," Menders answered, raising his eyebrows. "Tells the truth no matter what. Found six florins in the pocket of a jacket he was mending the other day and gave it back right away."

"Hard to believe he's from a bunch of thieves."

"I've been very careful to watch him. Eiren never saw any sign of trouble with him at the school. He was there for almost a year."

"Well then, he's landed on his feet, ending up here," Spaltz ruminated. "Still, to think of folks just walking away and leaving him without a word – sad. I wouldn't do that to a sick stray dog."

Menders was suddenly reminded of Tharak's words. It can take seconds to father a child, but it takes a lifetime to be a father. He repeated them to Spaltz.

"Now then, that's the truth," the farmer agreed quietly. "Eiren was our firstborn, as you know, and when they handed her to me I knew that it wasn't the bedsport nine months before that made me her father but the determination I felt when I looked at her, all red and screaming. I knew I'd fight off wolves to keep that little girl safe. I'd fight them with my teeth if need be. I was younger than you were when you had your Katrin, only sixteen. Marjana and I married young but I was a father at that moment, and I'm still working at it. I doubt young Borsen has ever really had a father."

"No." Menders sat back in his chair, thinking.

"I'll let him know what has happened," he finally said. "I don't know how he'll take it. There wasn't any love shown by either his father or stepmother."

"I'll leave it with you then." Spaltz finished his brandy. "I'll step across the hall and see our Olan before moving on."

Menders stopped by the kitchen for a couple of sandwiches. Then he mounted the stairs to Tomar's workroom. It would be best to let Borsen know what had happened without delay, in case he wanted to try tracing his family.

Despite his anger, Menders had to smile when he looked into the nursery-turned-tailor shop. The contrast to the tailor's old cluttered workroom was stunning. Natural light flowed from the bank of windows. Everything was neat and orderly. Tomar and Borsen sat tailor-fashion on opposite ends of the big worktable, crosslegged with their backs against the wall, their work on their laps. They were chatting back and forth companionably. Menders noticed that Borsen was bent double over the work on his lap, unlike Tomar, who sat upright against the wall. It was the only trick of the trade that Tomar said the boy simply couldn't seem to pick up. Menders had a flash of intuition about Borsen's hunched posture.

He spoke from the doorway and watched closely as Borsen and Tomar looked up to greet him. Borsen squinted rapidly, then allowed his eyes to return to an unnarrowed state.

"A letter came from Hemmett this morning," Menders said. "He's wondering if you could manage some trousers for him to have when he comes home for Winterfest recess. I was going to take Eiren and Katrin to Erdstrom and he'll come along too. Apparently he's outgrown everything he owns - again. He sent the measurements."

Menders handed the letter to Borsen, who hunched over it just as he did over his sewing, squinting. Then he sat up, having taken in the information, and acted as if he was still reading it, though Menders was certain his eyes perceived nothing at a normal reading distance.

You hide it well, my boy, but your eyes are worse than mine, Menders thought, as Borsen pretended to read out the figures to Tomar.

"He must be huge," Borsen said softly when he finished. "How old is he?"

"He'll be fifteen this winter."

Borsen looked dubious. Of course, the idea of a fifteen year old giant being at his haven for two months must be daunting, considering his past experiences.

Menders explained. "He's a very nice fellow, no bullying there." He smiled as Borsen breathed a sigh of relief and returned to his work.

"We can get on them right away. I have Hemmett's patterns, and it will be good experience for Borsen to alter them," Tomar said, laying his own work aside. "It's time to have lunch,

Borsen."

"I've not finished this," the boy murmured.

"It'll wait until you're back," Tomar grinned.

"I'd like to finish. I'll eat as soon as I do," Borsen replied, intent on his seam. Of course, Menders thought. If he puts it down, he'll have a time finding the needle again, with those eyes.

"That's all right. I need a word with this young man and I've brought along something to keep him from fainting from hunger," he intervened, setting the sandwiches out on the table. He'd noticed that Borsen was eternally hungry, entirely in keeping with his age and the fact that he'd been severely malnourished in the past. He still wasn't confident enough to raid the kitchen when necessary.

Tomar took himself off. Menders waited until Borsen reached the end of his seam, backstitched four times and then knotted the thread, cutting it neatly before he meticulously positioned his needle in his pincushion.

"Well done," he said, handing the boy a sandwich. "Borsen, I've had word of something that you need to know. It seems that your family has gone. Mister Spaltz went there yesterday to let them know how you're doing and found the house empty."

Menders watched closely. No real emotion, other than a weary acceptance. The boy nodded, concentrating on his sandwich.

"I thought they probably would, with me gone," he said softly. "I make money now, so I'll pay the rent that they didn't pay."

"That house isn't part of The Shadows," Menders said.

"No, to the white haired lady. She owns it."

Menders frowned. White haired lady? Then he knew.

"Lady Spartz?" Indeed, it probably was one of Reisa's tenancies.

"Yes, Lorein's mother. I'll pay her. I know they didn't pay

the rent."

"I'll see to it Borsen and we'll work something out," Menders offered, relieved that he wasn't coping with weeping or upset. "Now, I think we need to sort out a few things. In time you would have told me, I'm sure, but if we're to find your family for you, I'll need to know now. Where did you and your family come from?"

"Rondstein, for a little while. We moved all the time," the boy said quietly, putting his sandwich down. He stared at the tabletop for a minute and then looked up at Menders, who had made a point of sitting fairly close so Borsen could see him.

"Should I want you to find them? Because I don't," he said with a finality that Menders knew would never be shaken.

"No, you don't have to want that," Menders replied. "I can understand why you feel that way."

"She's not my mother. My mother died when I was six." Borsen spoke flatly.

Menders waited.

"He's my father but he never had any use for me, because I was always so little. I wasn't any good at helping him. I didn't want to," Borsen continued. "He's a thief, but I'm not. He used to have me watch for him while he stole but I... didn't do it right and I didn't want to help him steal. I can remember my real mother. She used to say it was wrong, stealing."

"So you were born in Rondstein?" Menders asked.

"No, I was born on the Sea of Grass."

"That's interesting, so was I," Menders said companionably. "Do you know which area?" The Sea of Grass was a very big place.

Menders looked at Borsen more closely. He could tell the boy was almost entirely Thrun. His father was a fullblood and considering Borsen's looks, his mother had been a good part Thrun as well. It wasn't unusual in this part of Mordania. It was even more common on the Sea of Grass, where intermixing of

Mordanians with Thrun was common. Borsen's speech, with the singsonging intonation and emphases used by the Thrun, was more singular, but not unheard of.

"Mama did say, but it's so long ago now. She was part Thrun."

"I can see that," Menders smiled. "I'm part Thrun too, one quarter."

"I'm almost all Thrun. My mother said I'm a quarter Mordanian," Borsen grinned. "Both of us added together make one Thrun and one Mordanian." Then he looked pensive.

"She told me the name of the place she came from but I can't remember it. I'm trying to hear her voice." He closed his eyes, obviously concentrating. Then he shook his head.

"Do you know your mother's name, before she married your father?" Menders asked. He could place the origin of Borsen's mother from the family name.

"That's easy. It was Tailors. Maybe that's what gave me the idea to be one. And her first name was Thara," Borsen replied eagerly, glad to be able to give Menders a definite answer.

Menders felt as if he'd been slapped.

Tailors? The Thrun used Mordanian surnames that were literal translations of their tribal names, which were simply a description of the occupation of that clan. Thus the name Menders, a rough translation of the Thrun word that meant 'weaving man', and carried the deeper meaning of one who repaired things and made them whole.

The Tailors were a clan who made clothing. They were a settled, rather than nomadic group, and had joined with the Menders through marriage for centuries. This combined tribe lived in the region of the Sea of Grass that encompassed Stettan. Much of the work force on Stettan had been Tailors and Menders. Tharak Karak was of the Tailors clan – as Menders' maternal grandmother, who married a man of the Menders clan, had been.

Menders looked at Borsen again, closely. He'd avoided doing so up until now, because of the boy's shyness. It couldn't be, surely?

Suddenly Borsen's face lit up.

"Starten. That's it. She was born at a place called Starten... or Sterten... or Settan?"

"Stettan?" Menders suggested.

"That's it! I can hear her saying it, that's the very word! Stettan. She used to tell me that there was a big house there, with four round towers and many Giants nearby."

Borsen seemed quite pleased and Menders smiled at him, though he was stunned. From half way across the country – how did this little bird manage to find his way home? He was of the Tailors from Stettan. He was Menders' own kin in some degree or another.

"I was never there. I was born further west," Borsen chattered on, his tongue loosened by his successful recollection. "My father moved us all the time, running from the law. It was always a new place, never paid the rent, then running out in the middle of the night after he'd rob a bunch of houses... oh! Did he rob people around here?" Borsen looked up at Menders, horrified.

"There were some robberies right before they left," Menders answered truthfully.

Borsen's eyes filled with tears.

"That bastard!" he said roughly, his face flushing. "I'll pay everyone who was robbed, Menders. I don't want people hating me here."

"They won't know. It's our secret," Menders countered immediately, realizing that attempting to pursue Borsen's father was pointless. The man was probably miles away, untraceable, an old hand at his game. "It isn't your fault, Borsen, so don't take the blame upon yourself. Now then, how many fingers am I holding up – and don't squint." He held up his hand about three feet from Borsen's face.

The boy turned bright red.

"I can't see them at all," he muttered.

"All right, that's what I thought. Bad vision can be corrected you know," Menders smiled, indicating his own glasses. "Would you like to come with me to Erdstrom in a few weeks? My oculist is there. We'll have you fitted with glasses so you can see properly and you won't have to be bent over your sewing."

Borsen looked as though he'd been invited to commune with the gods.

"Now then," Menders said, standing up, "I suggest we go and have something more to eat. I'm hungry all the time. I know you are too and it's important you eat whenever you want to. There's always food to be had in the kitchen. You're free to go there anytime. No-one in this house ever goes hungry, understand? Now, slide off that table and come on."

The little boy beamed delightedly, jumped down and took Menders' hand as if it was the most natural thing in the world.

***

"Your nephew!" Franz stared at Menders. "There is a resemblance, yes, but it could be between any two dark-haired, puny, Thrunnish types. You have to be jumping to conclusions!"

"If you'd seen me at his age, you'd have no doubt," Menders answered. "There is no other place on the Sea of Grass called anything sounding like Stettan, nothing beginning with an 's' at all. The Tailors clan lives only in that area. And if you knew my father," Menders grimaced. "He used those Thrun women. Not a female servant in the house was safe and it didn't matter if they were only girls ..."

"You needn't spell it out. I know," Franz said gently.

Menders shook his head, trying to dispel the childhood memories, the sounds of young servant girls being forcibly deflowered, the cries of pain and grunts of lust.

"You know about Thahlia being my half-sister and Thira being my niece," he continued roughly. "Several more of Tharak's people are also my close relatives. They were always taken in by the clan, half Mordanian or not. But some of those poor girls were ashamed that they had my father's bastard in their bellies. They became targets for unscrupulous Thrun men who wanted to live in the towns. The girls would go away from the clan with them, believing that life would be easy in the city with plenty of money to be made. They'd end up as City Thrun, petty criminals, prostitutes.

"One girl finally put her knife through my father's eye when he tried to rape her and finished him off. Once he was gone, I tried to track some of his illegitimate children down, to make amends. It was like trying to reweave a broken spiderweb – there were so many, but they left no trace."

Franz was silent for a while.

"I still find it an enormous leap for you to decide that Borsen is your nephew," he finally said. "His mother could have been from Stettan but conceived with someone else. Your father couldn't have been the only Mordanian man in the area."

"That's true, but Borsen told me part of her name. Thara."

"And?"

"It's a Thrun word. One of its meanings is 'eyes. Thara is the feminine form. The masculine form has a 'k' at the end of it." Menders looked away out the window.

"This is like pulling hen's teeth," Franz sighed.

"Sorry." Menders shook himself and looked directly at Franz. "I assure you her other name was Borgela, which means 'white'. My Thrun name is Thartan a'a' Tharak, 'Magic In The Eyes'. Tharak Karak means 'Eyes That See Forward'. I'm positive Borsen's mother's name was Thara Borgela – 'White Eyes'."

"Why do you make this assumption about her name?"

Franz asked, his voice edged with frustration.

"All people with my eye condition don't have the white eyes. That's a very extreme form of the disease," Menders explained. "Most people have the visual problems though their eyes appear normal. It doesn't come from my Thrun side, but from my father. He had the same condition I do, though his eyes were brown. Stettan is the last bastion of Mordania on the Sea of Grass and there is no other settlement or estate near there. My father was the only man in the entire district with this eye disease. Even his full brother, Kaymar's father, didn't have the white eyes, or pass the condition on."

"And?" Franz urged. He turned his hands palms up and shrugged in irritation and impatience.

"Franz, Borsen is nearly blind and he's sensitive to light. If you look in his eyes, I know you will see the same abnormalities you see in mine. And his name, Borsen – the Old Mordanian custom of naming a boy by putting 'sen' behind the first syllable of the mother's name. Borsen, son of Borgela."

Franz sat back slowly and lit a cigar. After a moment he raised his eyebrows and shook his head wonderingly. "Impressive deductive reasoning, my friend. Borsen hides his poor eyesight well but being nearly blind is a weakness that can be exploited, so I understand why he did so. I can have a look at his eyes if you wish."

"Please. I'll take him to Erdstrom for glasses when we go up next month." Menders accepted the cigar for a puff and handed it back.

"So it seems you've happened upon a little kinsman," Franz mused.

"It seems incredible, but I believe I have," Menders said. "It's a part of life I thought I'd put behind me. Stettan, and all that. I've never even been back there, you know. Not once."

"Pasts have a way of turning up," Franz philosophized, "and that boy has just lost everything he had. From what you've told me, it wasn't much. You can give him a family, Menders, just as you've given him a future and a home. What greater gift could you give him than to let him know that he's not entirely alone in the world? If I was related to you, I would want to know."

Menders was relieved to feel himself smiling. He drew a deep breath.

"Thank you. It just seems so impossible, of all places in the world this boy washes up here," he said. "Something out of a novel."

"Singular things happen around you," Franz replied. "To you, it's just everyday life, but to someone observing, it's much more."

"Like what?" Menders scoffed, looking at Franz as if he'd gone mad.

Oh – take your cousin, Kaymar as an example. I'd have staked everything I have on him having become a victim of his own urges and past. He ends up coming to The Shadows because you're here. He had some troubles and still does, but he settles down with a very nice fellow and for the most part, has quite a happy life. Crippled and injured servicemen like Ifor and Menck came here where they can lead productive lives instead of becoming destitute beggars – and that is entirely because you're here. Against all tradition and expectation, a Princess of Mordania is being protected from the cycle of destruction that is the Royal Family, and is becoming a kind and loving young woman. And while I'm blathering, let's not forget a doctor who runs to fat, who was lonely and drinking himself to death after losing his wife and baby, a man who never admired anyone in his entire life, who comes to admire a boy still wet behind the ears, simply because that boy was you – and I learned to live again and love life.

"Extraordinary things happen around you, Menders. I've long since stopped trying to convince myself it's all coincidence. These things are happening for a reason, which has yet to be made clear - and the catalyst is you."

Menders stared at him. Franz was so often flip and cynical that this impassioned, sincere speech was shattering.

"Next you'll be spouting Thrun prophesies, Doctor," he managed with weak sarcasm.

"This child has been sent into your care," Franz insisted. "Just as Katrin was. Have you ever wondered at someone handing a newborn baby to an assassin – *the* assassin? What are the chances of that? Some old fart being put out to pasture should have been assigned as a guardian for Katrin, not a boy who happened to be the most lethal person on the planet. Has it never struck you as a bit unexpected?"

"Of course it has," Menders answered.

"You managed that peculiar situation, as you manage everything that comes your way. Strange things fall into your lap and you pick them up and weave them together to make something coherent out of them. To you, it's routine, but to the rest of us, it's much more."

Menders didn't know what to say, so said nothing. Praise was not something he sought from others and he was inwardly embarrassed by it.

"Look at Borsen as a way to make right some of those past wrongs, Franz continued when he realized Menders was not going to speak. "You said you tried to find some of your father's byblows. It's taken a long time, but one has just fallen into your lap. You can't help Borsen's mother. You'll probably never be able to help the others - but Borsen is here, and he's yours. He needs you, Menders – and you need him."

"How so?" Menders scowled, but Franz was immune to his repertoire of menacing expressions.

"He's a child who can't be taken from you by the Queen," Franz answered bluntly. "You've been granted a little son, Menders. If ever a boy needed a father, it's Borsen."

"I'll tell Eiren first," Menders said after a moment. Then he smiled.

"Ah, I know that look," Franz grinned back. "Menders has just talked himself into rising to yet another challenge."

***

"Was your mother's full name Thara Borgela Tailors?" Menders asked Borsen, who was sitting beside him on the sofa in the family suite.

Borsen nodded slowly.

"Yes," he said, looking startled. "That's where my name came from – Borsen. Mama said she didn't think that Tharsen was a pretty name, so she used Borgela to make my name instead of Thara. How did you know that?"

While omitting certain unsuitable details, Menders carefully explained about his father's illegitimate children and that his father had been Lord Stettan, making Borsen's mother Menders' half-sister.

Suddenly Borsen sat bolt upright and stared at him.

"Are your eyes brown?" he asked excitedly. Menders shook his head.

"If you would let me see your eyes," Borsen continued, "I'll be able to tell you right away."

Menders dimmed the lamp. He hadn't realized that Borsen hadn't seen his eyes, but given the child's poor vision it was unlikely that he had caught so much as a glimpse.

He removed his glasses.

"Mama!" The cry came from Borsen's heart. He was staring at Menders' eyes, wringing his small hands, looking as if he didn't know whether to laugh or cry.

"Her eyes," he choked in Thrun. "You have her eyes."

Menders waited as Borsen wiped at tears with his sleeve and then squinted at him again.

"She had white eyes, just like yours," he finally said, switching back to his heavily accented, often halting Mordanian.

"It's like she's looking at me. The light hurt her eyes very much. She didn't see well, just like me, but my eyes are dark and the light doesn't hurt them so much."

"That's right," Menders said gently.

"So it's true, what you said." The uptilted brown eyes were filled with wonder as they focused imperfectly on Menders' own.

"I have no doubt, Borsen. You are my nephew."

Menders felt his heart opening, as it had when he'd first held Katrin in his arms; when he first saw Eiren as a grown woman, walking down the steps of her schoolhouse. It had opened again for this frail nephew. He put his arms out to the boy, who flung himself into them.

"You have a family," Menders said fiercely in Thrun, hugging the little body close. "You are loved and you are part of us now, Little Man."

"My mama called me Little Man. Please, may I call you Uncle?" Borsen whispered against Menders' neck in the same language, his thin little arms squeezing tighter.

"Of course." Menders gave Borsen's back a rub and then released him.

Borsen sat back on his heels, looking as if he didn't know whether to jump around or turn cartwheels. Instead, he snatched up a little pile of papers he'd brought to the suite with him and handed them to Menders.

"Katrin said I should show you these," he chattered, the Thrun words tumbling out giddily. "They're my drawings. She says you're a great artist and can teach me."

Menders replaced his glasses and looked – then looked again.

I didn't need to do all that detective work, he thought. All I had to do was see my own style drawn by your hand.

The drawings were designs for men's clothing, all beautifully rendered, the body proportions correct. The level of detail was amazing for a young boy who was virtually blind. The clothing styles were original and exquisite and the male body was lovingly worshipped in the drawings.

"These are very fine," Menders said admiringly. "I can certainly help you with your drawing. We'll get you some proper drawing pencils and colors and you'll improve very quickly."

"I'm glad you like them, Uncle," Borsen replied. "I looked at magazine drawings when I could find them and tried to do the same things with my sketches. My father used to make fun and tear them up, so I hid them and didn't show them to anyone."

"Make some of these clothes and no-one will ever make fun again. Show these to Tomar," Menders said honestly. "I'd give my left foot to have that dark green jacket with the grey trim."

"Mama used to make clothes and I had a little suit in just those colors when I was tiny," Borsen reminisced. "I used to have a pile of scraps that she gave me but they got left behind once when we moved. Uncle – can I still be a tailor? Now that I'm your nephew I don't have to take over from you here, do I?" The boy looked fearful at the thought.

"No. If you want to be a tailor, a tailor you shall be," Menders replied firmly. "This is not my estate, it's Katrin's. I only run it. There's no nonsense like following in my footsteps, so don't panic."

"And you don't mind that I'm a nancyboy?" Borsen asked the question quickly.

How effectively he uses my own technique, probably without realizing it, Menders thought. Borsen had perfected the trick of getting people talking, only to throw in an important question fast, to catch them off guard. There's no doubt you are mine, body from my body, blood from my blood.

"Not in the least," he answered.

"Thank you, Uncle," Borsen said softly. "Some people have minded."

To me you are a gift, my little son," Menders responded, putting a hand on Borsen's fragile shoulder.

***

"That means I'm your cousin," Katrin said excitedly. They had gone up after dinner to see the new sewing machines that had just been installed in the tailor shop, and Borsen had told her about his conversation with Menders "And Kaymar is also your cousin."

"Really?" Borsen looked stunned.

"Yes, if you're related to Menders, you're related to Kaymar and me. You have cousins among the Thrun as well. It means you're a member of the Royal Family. You're also cousin to the Queen."

Borsen squinted at her, for once not bothering to hide the fact that he could hardly see. "How can that be with me Thrun and a bastard?"

"That doesn't matter – Royal Family is Royal Family – and the Royal Family has plenty of bastards. Menders told me that long ago." Katrin grinned at him.

Borsen goggled at her and then started to whoop with laughter.

"If my father knew that!" he howled. "He's a common thief and I'm part of the Royal Family! Oh, that's too funny! Maybe I could have his head cut off."

They giggled and then bent over the sewing machine together.

***

Hemmett always refused to be picked up at the halt when he came home by train. He insisted on marching to the house, raucously singing soldiers' cadences as he tromped the two miles.

Menders could hear him coming up the road, roaring deafeningly about how he was the best marching man in Mordania. He rounded the corner of the drive, duffel balanced on his head with one hand, striding along like a legendary hero, his uniform perfect.

"Good Gods, he's even taller," Menders remarked to Eiren, who was watching from a second floor window with him. They were taking a break from helping with Lucen's latest construction project, a dumbwaiter, which was going on apace.

"I think he's bigger than Lucen now," she replied, laughing as Hemmett began to incorporate a capering dance step into his march. Katrin had come out onto the steps to meet him, followed by Borsen, who was taking his lunch break.

"Ho there, yer bleedin' Royal Highness," Hemmett grinned when he reached the bottom of the steps, dumping his duffel in the dirt. "Proper respect shall now be paid." He performed a slight curtsy, tugging at the legs of his trousers and then pretending to remove his drawers from his backside. Menders snickered and Eiren covered her mouth to hold back laughter. Obviously, Hemmett had no idea they were watching, or he'd never be so playfully disrespectful.

Katrin leapt at him and he spun round with her.

"Ooof! Hello there, Willow! Gods, I've missed you, life's been dull as a wake lately!"

"What, with all those exploding pillows and such?" she laughed back.

"Faw, it's been really quiet. We got pretty wild at midterm and Sir came down on us and told us to pull it in, so we did."

"What did you do at midterm?"

"Well, let's just say it led to some flooding of the second floor after the fire got going and that idiot Villison chopped through the water pipes with the fire axe to try to put it out," Hemmett grinned.

"Oh, Hemmett!"

"Now then, don't nag. I didn't do it, though I enjoyed the show," he replied, putting her down. He looked over at Borsen, who was studying him warily.

"Is this the new cousin?" Hemmett asked, making his voice gentle.

"Yes, this is Borsen," Katrin said proudly, climbing the steps. "Borsen, this is Hemmett."

Hemmett put out an enormous paw, engulfing Borsen's little hand with a friendly handshake. Suddenly Borsen grinned and Hemmett gave out a great haw-haw that shook the house.

"I'd know in a second you were Menders' nevvy, you look just like him," he announced. Menders was amused to see Borsen draw upright with pride. He'd already announced to Katrin that he intended to stop cutting his hair and was going to try to grow a beard, in imitation of Menders. The hair was coming on apace, but the beard had, so far, been a failure.

"This is all the welcoming committee I get?" Hemmett said, looking around.

"Everyone's been working on the new dumbwaiter and they're taking lunch," Borsen said suddenly.

"He talks too," Hemmett said in mock amazement to Katrin.

"Don't tease, he's the one making your new trousers, and he'll leave a pin in the backside seam if you're rude," she retorted.

Menders was pleased to see camaraderie bloom between Hemmet and Borsen during Hemmett's holiday. Hemmett, despite his madcap ways and tendency toward irreverence, had a warm heart and was intensely protective.

Hemmett always rejoiced in returning to The Shadows. He adored the country life and stepped right back into his role there as if he had never been away. If there was a hunting party or dance, Hemmett was in the midst of it, cracking jokes and laughing. His toil in the woodlot was something to see, as he hurled logs around and made chips fly like bullets. He was now an enormous youth, with big muscles and a deep baritone voice.

Menders could see Hemmett was still in love with Katrin, but he also mentioned girls he admired in Erdahn, as he and the other cadets were now of an age to be introduced into society. His manners, when he chose to use them, were impressive and polished. He was capable of disciplining his naturally raucous nature into a controlled bearing that was awe inspiring. He'd had the highest recommendations for his work and was considered one of the up and coming men at the Academy.

Commandant Komroff mourned that Hemmett consistently turned down opportunities that would groom him for a senior position in the Army, but Hemmett always insisted that his ambition was to captain Katrin's Guard. Although that in itself was a worthy and noble posting, the Commandant argued that it would not sufficiently task Hemmett's natural abilities for leadership and military organization.

Menders, despite his considerable regard for the Commandant, backed Hemmett unswervingly. Hemmett would not be cannon fodder, not even high ranking cannon fodder, if Menders had anything to say about it.

***

While in Erdstrom the week after Hemmett's homecoming, Menders took Borsen to visit his oculist. The man marveled that Borsen could manage at all with such limited vision. After his examination of the boy's eyes, he confirmed that Borsen and Menders suffered from the same condition.

"Your nephew, you say? Well, you both have the same ailment, though this young man's problem is not as advanced or as severe. If you begin to wear spectacles and guard your eyes from bright light, young man, you should avoid some of the complications your uncle has had," the oculist told Borsen. "Now, let's see what sort of spectacles you'll need."

After considerable fiddling and switching lenses, the oculist found a formula that would correct Borsen's vision a great deal, though he warned Borsen he could not expect perfection. He recommended not only clear spectacles, but dark ones for bright light as well.

Excited by the prospect of restoring sight to the near blind, the oculist ground Borsen's lenses right away and the glasses were ready within a few days. After a brief period of dizziness that quickly passed, a new world opened before Borsen's eyes. Colors, shapes, details he'd never seen before leapt at him from every angle. By the time he and Menders left the oculist's office, he was skipping around in excitement, crying out about things that he was seeing and tugging on Menders' hand to get his attention every few seconds.

"Look Uncle! What is that?" he would shout in Thrun, pointing at a street lamp or clothesline. Menders would tell him, trying not to laugh. He walked Borsen down to the ocean, where the boy gazed open-mouthed and then watched the seagulls, brown eyes moving rapidly, trying to take everything in at once.

"I must draw this," Borsen breathed. Menders handed him a pocket sketchbook and pencil he'd carried along. He waited patiently, strolling the boardwalk while the boy drew frenetically, unaware that he was attracting a crowd of the curious and admiring. He sketched with such furious energy that smoke curling from the paper would not have been surprising.

His drawing completed, Borsen looked up and found himself surrounded by people. For a moment he looked panicked, but when he saw Menders coming toward him he breathed a sigh of relief. People were asking to see his work. He held it out for perusal.

"I quite fancy that sketch," a man said. "Would you take ten florins for it, young man?"

Menders looked at the page and blinked. Now that Borsen could see, his drawing was phenomenal. The sketch was the sea, sky and wheeling gulls. The perspective was slightly wobbly but that could be overlooked because of the sheer emotion that the boy had infused into his pencil strokes.

"Should I sell it, Uncle?" Borsen asked.

"That's up to you," Menders told him. Borsen considered the question, and then carefully tore the sketch from the book and held it out toward the man who wanted it.

"Oh, but you must sign it," the man told him, taking out the money.

Menders was greatly amused to see the boy sign it with a large 'B' in the corner, in imitation of Menders' own way of signing things quickly with a large initial 'M'.

"You're a sold artist," Menders told Borsen with admiration. "Some artists wait their entire lives to sell a work."

"I can't wait to tell Katrin and Hemmett!"

"We'll make our triumphant return to the hotel then," Menders said grandly, gesturing up the street.

Smiling people nodded as they passed, their attention drawn by the little boy's obvious happiness. Borsen was far from filled out, still very small for his age, but he bore little resemblance to the pitiful child who had come to the Shadows. He was a winsome picture as he hopped and skipped along, clinging to Menders' hand.

***

On the last night of their stay in Erdstrom, Menders sat up late with Eiren.

It had been a delightful trip all round. Katrin's security network had functioned marvelously and having Borsen along had been enjoyable for all. His enthusiasm was infectious. He'd been thrilled by the ballet and sketched the costumes frantically until he fell asleep against Hemmett's shoulder, his soft snores occasionally making an obligato to music.

"I almost hate to leave for home tomorrow," Menders said, curling a lock of Eiren's hair around his finger as she snuggled against him on the sofa.

"Until you get in sight of The Shadows and think of a million things to do," Eiren smiled. "Or see Demon in the pasture and decide to let him try to break your neck."

"Ah, a nagging wife, there's nothing quite like it," Menders teased, then cocked an ear and listened closely to sounds from the corridor.

"Little boy about to appear," he said to her. She laughed aloud.

Borsen wandered into the lounge from the room he shared with Hemmett, blinking through his spectacles at the light.

"I'm sorry to interrupt, Uncle and Auntie," he said politely, "but I just thought of something important and wanted to ask you about it."

"No apologies needed, son," Menders answered. "What thought troubles you?"

"How would I go about changing my last name? I hate it and I don't want it. Carvers is my father's name and since he left me behind, why should I use it?"

Years ago, when he was eleven, Menders had gone to the Commandant of the Royal Military Academy and asked a similar question, wanting to drop his father's family name in favor of his mother's.

"If you don't have a birth certificate, which I doubt you do, it's a matter of simply using the name you prefer until you're of age and can change it legally," Menders said. "I did the same when I was younger than you and took my mother's maiden name."

"That's the name I want too."

"Your mother's maiden name? Just start using it, drop Carvers."

"No, not Tailors. I have a plan. When I have my great

establishment, I'll call it Borsen's. That will honor my mother, since she made my name after hers," Borsen said with such sincerity that Menders couldn't laugh. "I want my last name to be Menders."

"I'm honored, Borsen," Menders replied. "Please feel free to do so."

"I'll be sure to sign things with my first initial, so that there isn't confusion. People might think I'm you," the boy said, turning and shambling off to bed.

No, you'll never be mistaken for me, Menders thought as he watched the small figure retreat. You will become someone wholly remarkable in your own right, your own person, not the shadow of another.

Menders and Eiren held their breath until they heard him get back into bed, and then dissolved in silent laughter. Eiren finally caught her breath.

"Oh dear, oh dear," she whispered. "How to keep from laughing? He's adorable, but he's also so funny!"

"He's a joy," Menders answered. "All three of them are, from the military man to the Princess to the diminutive future owner of a great establishment. He's welcome to my name and anything else he wants or needs."

"You know he worships you," Eiren said, going quiet.

"Yes," Menders replied, suddenly equally serious. "At first that bothered me, until I realized that even at his age, his personality is powerful. He thinks he wants to be like me but in time, he will be his own man."

"Still, he worships you," Eiren repeated, her eyes gleaming in the soft light. "He's not the only one." She reached up and kissed him.

***

From Menders' Journal:

The great house is asleep. Winterfest night, another year gone by, its passage duly marked and celebrated. The revelers are all abed, with one exception - myself.

I cherish these solitary hours when I can feel the house around me, the weight of the great beams that make this building a fortress, the heartbeat of the tall clock in the entryway.

Although alone, I am not lonely. All I hold dear surrounds me. I keep my solitary enjoyment close, hidden from those I love. I fear they might be hurt, thinking that I wish to shun their company.

On this night it seems I was not alone after all. Long after midnight, I heard a boy's high treble, clear and true, one that could have been my own in the days when I was Aylam Josirus, filtering down from above. It seemed to be the spirit of Winterfest itself and was filled with the mystery of the falling star that brought men to Eirdon. It sang an ancient Thrun lullaby that I have not heard since I was a boy, more years ago than I care to calculate.

Climbing the stairs, I traced the sound to its source – Borsen, sitting alone in the dark tailor's shop, watching the dazzling pageant of stars through the high windows. He sang with the freedom of one who believes himself alone and unheard, perhaps communing with the mother he loves so much and misses still. The purity of it was heart aching.

I sensed Borsen's desire for solitude and chose not to announce myself to him. Presently he went to bed. After a while I looked in to find him peacefully asleep.

This child catches at my heart. So like me, yet so blessedly unlike me as well. My Little Man, the son I never had.

CHAPTER 41
"THE THREE CHOSEN CHILDREN"

Icicles crashed from the eaves of The Shadows at the shattering sound of the great Thrun gong. Ifor, nursing a severe head cold, bellowed from his suite as the vibrations rattled his aching skull.

Katrin ran toward the front door, pausing only as Menders shouted from his office for her to wear her coat.

Hemmett gave a great whoop and dropped a sheaf of coded messages he'd been filing with Kaymar. He ran down the hall, ignoring Kaymar's amused scolding.

Borsen leapt from the tailor's table, scattering pins far and wide. Tomar watched his fleeing apprentice and was thankful that he owned a magnet.

The three young people scrambled for coats, hats and furs, then boiled out of the front door in a knot of flailing youthful exuberance. They raced down the drive toward the advancing Thrun.

Borsen slowed as they drew close.

"Whoa, look at them!" he gasped.

"Come on, you'll miss it!" Hemmett yelled, backtracking. He hoisted Borsen onto his back and ran effortlessly along.

"Miss what?" came Borsen's voice, distorted by all the bouncing as Hemmett pelted across the snow.

"Miss the part where Tharak picks Katrin up and tosses her in the air like she's a tiny baby," Hemmett replied, racing onward. Katrin was leading them by several paces. She had become leggy of late and ran like the wind.

"That's not possible, she's a big girl!" Borsen protested.

"And Tharak's bigger!"

As they reached the Thrun, Hemmett slid Borsen to the ground as Katrin ran up to the huge man leading the column of people and animals. The giant swung her up off the ground and flung her into the air, then laughed as he caught her and held her high. Katrin's hair flashed gold in the thin winter sunlight. The huge man turned, still holding her up and shouted words in Thrun, then repeated himself in Mordanian.

"Light Of The Winter Sun!"

"What does he mean?" Borsen asked Hemmett.

"The color of her hair – and something else that nobody will tell us about."

"Why not?"

"Don't know," Hemmett answered. "That's Tharak. He's the high chieftain. You watch, he'll be giving Katrin presents constantly. She'll make out like a thief while they're here."

"Presents?"

"Furs, jewelry, gems. You wait and see. Wait till you see their clothes, tailor boy."

Someone pulled off Borsen's fur hat and ruffled his hair. Borsen looked around at Menders, who had come up behind him.

"How do you like the show so far?" Menders smiled. Borsen grinned up at his uncle, then turned abruptly as a shadow fell over him.

He looked up, to a great silver and gold belt buckle the size of a plate. Then up some more, across a broad chest criss-crossed by silver studded straps, then up further into a huge grinning Thrun face, topped by an enormous horned hat. Borsen shrank back against Menders.

The man stopped grinning and crouched down to his level.

"I see my childhood friend in you, Little Man," he said kindly, putting out a hand for Borsen to take. "Who might you be?"

"I'm Borsen Menders," Borsen squeaked. He felt Menders' hand tighten comfortingly on his shoulder and felt less afraid. "My mother's name was Tailors."

"I've found a nephew," Menders added.

The big Thrun cupped Borsen's chin in his hand and looked deep into his eyes.

"I see your Thrun name is Tharkul a' Thrunar," the huge man said. "Reflection Of My Friend. I am Tharak Karak a'a' Thrun, High Chieftain of the Thrun and of the Tailors clan. Since my first wife is the half-sister of Menders, I am also your uncle as well as your cousin, little nephew. That makes you a Chieftain among us," With that he pulled Borsen into a huge embrace and Borsen was no longer afraid.

Tharak Karak rose and threw his arms around Menders, laughing, then picked Borsen up as though he weighed nothing and set him on his shoulder. The enormous gong crashed again, low horns started to play, and the procession swaggered toward the house. Borsen was wildly elated, and exchanged grins with Katrin, who was holding Tharak's hand as they walked along.

**

Later Tharak and Menders strolled through the camp, as was their habit on the first day of the Thrun's usual winter visit. The children were moving along ahead of them happily, Hemmett occasionally lifting Borsen so he could see things more easily.

"Your family has grown, Aylam," Tharak said. "Katrin has become a woman, I see."

"In many ways, yes she has," Menders answered. "Then Borsen appeared out of nowhere." He outlined Borsen's past and the events of the last few months. Tharak listened closely as he explained the relationship between himself and the boy.

"The mother was called Thara Borgela, you say" Tharak mused. He stood still, furrowing his forehead.

"I know these people. You are correct, my friend," Tharak continued. "Borsen's mother was your father's child. Her mother stayed with the Thrun for a while, but then left for the cities as so many of the women who had half-Mordanian children did. She was not seen again, but I remember the white-eyed baby, Thara Borgela. She was older than you, Aylam, you would not remember. You came to us later."

Menders nodded, seeing vague shadowy outlines of people's faces in his mind's eye – people he had never met, yet felt drawn to.

"So your child has found you." Tharak spoke solemnly, watching Katrin, Hemmett and Borsen perusing a pile of furs. "I thought it would be a child of your body and Golden Heart's, but the time for that is past. Such a child would not be the right age if born now. There they are, Aylam – Light Of The Winter Sun, Light Brighter Than The Sun, and Reflection Of My Friend, the three chosen children. The prophecy is coming to pass. Perhaps this time it will play out to completion and the Circle will turn. It has not before, though the opportunity has been there."

Menders backed away from Tharak, cutting the air sharply with a slash of his hand, a Thrun gesture that indicated no more was to be said.

"Don't tell me," he said abruptly. "Don't start going on about that. Prophecies make people try to force them into being. If something is going to happen, it will."

Tharak shook his head and then caught Menders around the shoulders.

"Your reservations are known and noted my friend. However they do not change that which is and the choices that are to come. I will only say this. The threads are coming together in your hands, Weaving Man. Now, let's go and find your lovely Golden Heart, so I can begin to barter for her to be my seventh wife!"

"You still don't have number seven?" Menders asked, deliberately putting references to prophecies, threads and weaving men out of his mind. He knew the Thrun called him Weaving Man, a name from their ancient sagas, as well as Magic In The

Eyes, but he wasn't going to become a slave to anything mystical, regardless of what Tharak might say.

"Number seven must be very special," Tharak laughed. "I am still waiting for her."

CHAPTER 42
SECRETS AND LETTERS

A cry rang through the Family Wing. Kaymar, who had been stalking up and down the corridors of the first floor, started and moved swiftly in the direction of the sound.

In his study, Menders dropped his book and rose, going to the door of Borsen's apartment.

Kaymar was already there, bending over Borsen, who was weeping aloud though his eyes were shut. Another nightmare – these night disturbances had become frequent during the winter months.

"Come on now, Little Man," Kaymar was saying, his voice so unaccustomedly tender that Menders blinked. "Wake up. You're safe at home. It's Kaymar, Borsen."

Menders moved to the other side of the bed and boosted himself up to sit on the mattress. Borsen, in the talons of whatever dream tormented him, thrashed away, fighting, tangling himself in the covers.

Menders' and Kaymar's eyes met. They knew what would happen the moment either of them touched the child – and wanted to avoid it.

"Borsen, it's Uncle," Menders said, keeping his voice low and calm. "Wake up, Borsen. You're having a dream."

"The room's damned cold," Ifor said from the doorway. "Every time he has a nightmare, the room is cold." He lumbered over to the stove and opened the damper, bending to heave in a log.

Borsen's eyes were clenched shut, his entire body shuddering with emotion.

"Best go ahead and shake him out of it, Cuz," Kaymar sighed. "I'll catch his legs if he starts kicking."

Menders reached out and put his hands on Borsen's

shoulders.

The child began to shriek and fought with all his strength, his eyes going wide in a waking nightmare.

"Mama! Mama! Don't let him take me! Wake up, Mama!" Before Kaymar could react, he kneed Menders painfully in the ribs.

Menders never flinched, pulling him into his arms, taking the blows and kicks as he rocked the boy back and forth, speaking to him gently. Kaymar came across the bed and put his arms around Borsen as well, preventing him from flailing against Menders.

"Dear gods," Ifor murmured as they struggled with Borsen. "What in the name of Grahl torments him like this?"

It was a rhetorical question. This drama had played itself out many times now and so far, no-one had been able to find what Borsen's nightmares were about. Something was locked deep inside Borsen's mind and he was refusing to let it surface.

"Now you're waking up. It's Papa, Borsen. Don't be afraid, it's Papa," Menders whispered, so intent upon comforting the little boy that he failed to guard his words. He didn't see Kaymar's jealous glance or Ifor's raised eyebrows.

Suddenly Borsen gasped, became aware of them and began to cry.

"All right now. It's all right. See, Kaymar is here, so is Ifor. You're at home and you're safe," Menders said firmly. He held out his hand for Borsen's glasses, which Kaymar, with one lithe movement, swept up from the bedside table. Now that his eyesight was corrected by his spectacles, Borsen panicked when he was without them. Menders slid them into place on the boy's nose and then rose, holding Borsen close.

"I'll take him to my office," he said. "Thank you both." He turned and walked out of the room, murmuring softly to Borsen.

Kaymar began making up Borsen's bed without a word,

tugging viciously at the twisted sheets and blankets. Ifor opened the door of the stove and put in another log.

"The boy would be better with lignus burned in here. It wouldn't go cold in the middle of the night," he said as if Kaymar wasn't glowering with jealousy. He waited until the smaller man was finished with the bed and then went to him.

"My dear, we all love that boy," he said. "Right now, he needs Menders. You'll have your chance to be of help to him. He'll need you a great deal as he grows up, because Menders can't begin to understand many things about him."

Kaymar said nothing, but nodded. Ifor watched as he stalked away down the corridor, flicking his knife from its scabbard at his waist. Then Ifor sighed, deliberately cleared his mind of the burdens of everyone and went back to bed.

Later, Hemmett moved silently through the house on his way to the kitchen for a glass of milk. Just as he was reaching for a glass, he heard Borsen's tearful voice coming from Menders' office. He moved toward the sound. He listened.

Some minutes later he turned away, stricken by what he'd heard Borsen telling Menders. He no longer wanted anything to drink – or to eat. Heart heavy, he retraced his steps up to his room.

***

Dear Cahrin and Olner,

It was wonderful to have you and the children here in my quiet part of Mordania, although as you saw from the Thrun carnival, it is sometimes far from quiet.

With the winter past, work on the new boarding school has begun. Our previous arrangement of having children travel in to board with local families was a strain for all concerned, and my suggestion to have the children board at The Shadows was wisely turned down by Eiren, who correctly said it would undermine her authority with them. So the new school will fulfill all our needs — although at some considerable expense. I shan't bore you both with what it costs to have bricks shipped out here.

Katrin has shown great interest in being one of the school's patrons. She showed me the accounts she has kept from her soap making enterprises — quite a tidy sum, which was combined with a small amount from her royal income and invested in the school. She has made some useful suggestions for the building such as a separate entrance for little ones so they don't get trampled. As you saw for yourselves, she is a clever, thoughtful girl who is mindful of others. I am immensely proud of her.

Not to be outdone, Borsen and Hemmett both contributed their own ideas. Borsen insists I tell you of his idea for a trade school — a first class idea, for as he explained, not everyone is capable of, or should be forced into pure academia. Hemmet took a page from his military training to suggest physical exercise classes in order to, as he put it, 'wear the cussedness out of the students'. Hemmett is back at the Academy now, having his own youthful cussedness worked on by Sir, no doubt.

And now that a certain young apprentice tailor has run along and is not looking over my shoulder... thank you, Olner, for ordering the jacket from Borsen. It meant the world to him to have his first 'foreign order' as he calls it. When I reminded him that you are in Erdahn, which is in Mordania, he simply replied that it might as well be another world away.

Sometimes I feel that isolated here, too. Borsen is an insightful lad and as you remarked, he has come a long way from the waif we took in, though there are still troubles that plague him. Of late we realized that his room going cold at night can lead to him having nightmares. I believe I mentioned he had been left in terrible circumstances when he was only six years of age, abandoned by an uncaring father as his mother starved and froze to death in front him.

Given such horrors and hardships, it is easy to see why the little lad craves our love and affection so much. He does his best to rise above the memories of such things but I fear that these are scars that he will bear for life. I am thankful that he can confide his fears to me, but cannot press him for confidences — those have to come when he is ready.

It's high time I was at the school building site. Eiren teases me that

I should become the headmaster… can you see such a thing, my friends? Me, in a stiff black top hat and severe sideburns, books under my arm, face set in a stern grimace… yes, I know you're laughing at the imagery. As am I.

Affectionately,

M

Dear Cahrin,

I write to you, feeling you may be the only person who would understand my fears. There was an incident here yesterday at the school building site, involving Menders and one of the workmen.

With Katrin now a keen patron of the school, we all go to view the progress frequently. Katrin takes great pleasure in this and dresses beautifully for each occasion.

The men on the site are carefully selected and their references closely examined, but there was a new man brought in on short notice to replace someone who was injured. To come straight to the point, this new man made a loathsome and insulting remark about Katrin – and Menders overheard him.

Suddenly my calm, reassuring man of reason and intellect was transformed into a… thing, a raging beast that tore into the workman with horrifying fury and speed. Cahrin, I say this with no exaggeration, drama or hysteria. I believe that Menders meant to kill the man and was capable of doing so with his bare hands.

Kaymar and some other men tried to pull Menders off but he shrugged them away with the strength of a giant. He laughed, as if he was enjoying himself while he throttled the workman! I think that was worst of all. It took all Kaymar's wiry strength as well as the efforts of several others to subdue him.

As quickly as the rage appeared, it subsided. Menders stalked away without a word. I ushered a shocked and stunned Princess from the scene as rapidly as possible. Kaymar stayed behind to mete out whatever further disciplinary action he felt was warranted.

Although what was said was obscene, loathsome and crude and cannot be excused under any circumstances, I do not believe that it warranted such a violent response. Like Katrin, I was horrified by the fury of Menders' reaction.

I realize Menders has not gone mad, or taken some turn, but that what welled up in him was some inner darkness that must always be there, something he strives to control at all times – and usually does. I know very little of his past, small details at most, and I also know there are things he does not wish to discuss. I have my suspicions of what might have happened to him in his childhood, but know that he will never confide those experiences to me.

You are the daughter of an assassin and the wife of another. You are the only person I can turn to now for advice and guidance as to how to help him.

While I do not fear for my own safety or that of anyone Menders holds dear, I am at a loss to explain or understand the inner complexities of my most beloved husband and friend.

Sincerely,

Eiren

Finished with her letter, Eiren went to bed but could not sleep. From her window, she could see the lamp in Menders' office casting a long rectangle of light on the ground outside. He had been pleasant but abstracted and distant during dinner, then returned to his office where he had already spent the entire afternoon.

It wasn't unusual for him to get caught up in work, but she knew he wasn't working tonight. He was angry with himself.

She'd known almost from the beginning that Menders had a very dark side, and though she knew he would never harm her, she had made it a point never to provoke that darkness.

Eiren sighed. She truly hated it when Menders was this

distressed because she wanted to comfort him and let him know that he was human after all, and that no-one else expected him to be as perfect as he expected himself to be. That would be no consolation to a man like Menders. He expected too much of himself, and she knew from experience that trying to convince him otherwise would guarantee his going into a cold, silent anger.

You wanted him, so you take the bad with the good, she scolded herself. Almost all of life with him is pleasant and full of joy. Let him have his time alone. Things will get back to normal soon.

She woke when he came into her room. She always knew when he was near, even though he moved silently. He put a log on the fire, undressed quickly and crawled into the bed with her without a nightshirt, despite the cold.

She held her arms out. He said nothing, resting his head on her breast and wrapping his arms around her in turn.

He shivered silently for a very long time before he fell asleep. Sleep eluded Eiren, so she just held her beloved man and waited for morning.

My dear Eiren,

The assassin's lot is not a happy one. You may think that a terrible, callous thing to say given your recent circumstances, but sadly, when such things happen, those words come to mind. You are correct. I am probably the only person you know who understands your grief and anxiety. Being born into the business, I was sought after by young men of the Special Services for my assumed ability to tolerate some of the more dire aspects of their natures, which all of them have, your Menders and my Olner included.

These are exceptional men. They are also surely the last of their breed, as modern-day assassins are not so rigorously trained in the more subtle arts, or taught such levels of control and self discipline – and the result is men like poor Kaymar, who was given no more education than a thug and was only intended to be dispensable.

I do know that Menders was cruelly treated as a boy, by family and others, and was subject to the old ways of 'toughening' children. As a young man he was very prone to outbursts such as you described and sometimes instigated them. I saw this several times when we were courting. It was the reason I chose not to pursue marriage with him, although his long mission away in Surelia helped further the separation. I always let him believe that was the reason I rejected his suit. I know I can trust you, my dear friend, not to reveal this to him.

You might be asking yourself what you can do at times like this. I know I have, many times, when Olner's own darkness rises like a bitter tide. Sadly, the answer is nothing, damnably frustrating as that may be. Such men mature with time and take on new lives for themselves as they leave their careers as assassins behind — but the fact that they were trained to violate one of society's deepest taboos remains. If Menders holds himself in more rigid control now than ever before, it is because of his love for you and the Princess, and the two young men he lovingly calls 'his boys'. The incident you described is an exception to your usual life, and dwelling on it will only cause you unnecessary pain and worry. Let it pass and your happy life will return.

Write again soon and let us know all your doings and the children's. How is your Borsen getting along? He is such a darling little man!

With love,

Cahrin

CHAPTER 43
KATRIN'S RED BEAST

"I'm driving into the village," Menders said from the doorway of the suite. "Would anyone like to come along?"

Katrin and Eiren were collapsed on sofas. Although it was early spring, a prelude of summer's brief fiery heat had produced an unseasonably warm day. The ladies were feeling it after a morning of housecleaning.

"Oh, I'm exhausted, darling," Eiren puffed. "Another time, surely."

Menders laughed a little at her flushed face and went to kiss her.

"What about you, my Little Princess?" he asked.

"It's too hot," Katrin groaned. "Can't you put off until tomorrow?"

"I need finishing nails today," Menders chuckled. "I'll squire you ladies over another day then."

"Wonderful!" Katrin replied, fanning herself. "Perhaps the weather will change."

"Depend on it," Menders grinned. "Far too early for it to stay this warm, my dear. I'll be back soon." He walked away down the hall.

Katrin collapsed back onto the cushions, fanning herself again.

"I can't remember such a warm day this early," Eiren sighed after a few minutes. "I let the stove go out and I think we'll just have cold food tonight."

"That sounds fine to me. The idea of a fire right now is agony," Katrin groaned.

"Uncle! Uncle!" Borsen shouted outside. He could be heard running across the drive. Katrin sat up and looked out the window.

"How can he run around in this heat," Katrin wondered aloud. "And in that dark suit he always wears."

"Youth is invincible," Eiren smiled.

As Katrin watched, Menders caught Borsen up in a huge hug. Borsen chattered excitedly. Menders laughed and nodded, then they went into the stable together. A few minutes later, they drove out in the phaeton, Borsen grinning as Menders handed him the reins once they were on the road.

"He just took Borsen with him," Katrin said darkly.

"So? You just turned down an invitation to go," Eiren said in surprise. "Why would you mind if Borsen goes along? He wants to buy some fabric he's been saving for and it's a good chance for him to get it before it's all sold."

Katrin felt herself flush with embarrassment. "It just seems strange, is all," she said lamely, remembering a time not so long ago when Menders would have either taken her or gone alone.

"You're overheated," Eiren smiled. "Go and put on a lighter dress and I'll help pin your hair up off your neck. You'll feel better then."

Katrin did as Eiren suggested and felt cooler, but there was a nasty burning in her chest that didn't fade as she thought about Borsen. It seemed that every time she turned around these days, there he was, in his little dark suit and dark glasses that matched Menders' own. Standing right beside Menders… where she had always been.

Borsen was the absolute favorite of everyone at The Shadows. People seemed compelled to pick him up, to hug him, to hold his hand, to have him sit on their laps. Cook doted on him, the Men adored him, Tomar idolized him. Everyone had picked up on Menders' calling him Little Man. Even Kaymar, who was undemonstrative with children, hugged him like a lost brother. Ifor carried him around on his shoulder. Mister Spaltz called him his grandson, just as he called her his granddaughter. It was nice that people cared, of course, but it was also irritating in some way that Katrin couldn't explain.

Worst of all was Menders. Borsen gravitated to him ever since he'd been told Menders was his uncle and was always holding his hand, chattering away, perched on his knee or sitting beside him. They sketched together. Menders got Borsen interested in reading once his vision was corrected and they talked over the books for hours. They spoke Thrun together constantly. Menders was teaching him to drive – Menders was just smitten with Borsen.

"Well, you brought him here," Katrin muttered to herself, her lighter side trying to reason with her darker self. Katrin had found him, saved him and befriended him. She'd loved helping him, but now everyone else was putting their fingers in the pie. Borsen had love and adoration from all sides and didn't need Katrin so much anymore.

She'd always been loved and cared for, of course, but nothing like the way people doted on Borsen. That was probably because she was the Princes. People didn't get as close. Well, everyone couldn't be a pretty little Thrun boy people just itched to pick up and cuddle. Some people were big for their ages and stuck being princesses! It was hardly fair.

Katrin had worked herself into a black mood by the time Menders and Borsen returned. The day had continued miserably sultry and humid, the kind of weather that always made her feel sick, and she had a headache from it. Sprawled on her bed and looking at a book she wasn't reading, Katrin was not pleased when she heard Borsen making his way up toward the suite. His progress was marked by enthusiastic greetings from everyone he encountered.

"There's my Little Man!" That was Franz, guaranteed to be swinging Borsen around by the hand.

"Whoops, little Cuz!" That was Kaymar. "We're cooking outside tonight, all the Men. Does that sound good for dinner? It keeps from heating the place up. Good, we'll count you in."

"Hello darling! Did you have fun at the village?" That was Eiren, of course. She was as soppy about Borsen as Menders was. Always giving him a kiss, having him sit next to her to hear him read or help him with his lessons.

"Hello, Cuz!" Borsen said from Katrin's doorway, his voice joyous.

Katrin looked up without a word. He was holding a wrapped parcel and beaming at her. "Wait until you see what I got!" he said excitedly.

"I really don't care," Katrin snapped. Borsen looked shocked and stepped closer.

"Why? What's the matter?" he asked.

"Do you think you can just walk into my room without knocking?" Katrin asked, her voice rigid with resentment.

Borsen blinked.

"I… I'm sorry," he stammered. "I always have just come in if the door is open. I just wanted to show you…"

"I don't care to see. Who do you think you are, anyway? This is my estate, you know, and I can have you off of it anytime I decide we don't need a tailor's apprentice, just like I decided we needed one. You wouldn't even be here if it wasn't for me!"

As she saw the horror that flooded Borsen's face, part of her was ashamed even while another part of her was gloating. Something tingled and crackled in her blood. For an instant she thought she heard a rustling of whispered voices from the corners of the room – or perhaps from inside her head.

A moment later she was alone in her room, Borsen's parcel lying on the floor, the paper broken open. Eiren was standing in the doorway, glaring at Katrin, rigid with anger.

"I overheard that exchange, young lady! How could you be so cruel?" Eiren seethed. She continued upbraiding Katrin, but the words fell without effect, for something worse than words lay on the floor.

Katrin stared at the cloth spilling from the torn paper. It was a light cotton, white with a beautiful print of spring flowers – not the men's suit fabric that Borsen had been coveting. It was cloth she had admired but been unable to pay for the last time they were in the village together.

He had bought it for her, with love.

Oh no.

***

Piteous wailing made Menders look out his office window. He saw Borsen rush from the back kitchen door, blundering along, blinded by tears. Kaymar and Ifor were loitering in a shady spot, but turned and then ran toward the boy, who collided with a tree and then rushed unsteadily onward.

"What is it, Little Man?" Kaymar asked, catching Borsen. Ifor crouched and took Borsen's glasses, cleaning them on his shirt, then swabbing at the boy's eyes with his handkerchief. Menders vaulted over the windowsill and ran to them.

Borsen hurled himself in Menders' direction the moment he heard his voice. A quick grab kept him from falling over a tree root. Then Borsen was held close in Menders' arms, his arms tight around Menders' neck, sobbing brokenheartedly.

"What the hells happened?" Menders asked the other men, who looked at each other in confusion.

"Can't get a word out of him," Kaymar said.

"Doesn't seem to be injured, as far as I can see," Ifor added.

"Now then, what is it?" Menders murmured to Borsen, knowing that the best way to calm a crying child was to remain calm yourself. It took a long time before a response came.

Once Borsen related what Katrin had said to him, it was all Menders could do to remain calm. Seeing Kaymar's enraged expression brought him back to reason, knowing he must look like that himself, or worse. With the recent incident at the building site still fresh in his mind, Menders steeled himself to remain in control of his emotions.

"I should probably be apprenticed somewhere else," Borsen wept, unable to stop sobbing.

"No, that isn't going to happen, this is your home now," Menders answered. "You're my boy. Katrin doesn't make the decisions about the estate. It's her estate, but I run it."

"Why did she say it? I thought she was my friend! I love her!" Borsen wept.

"She said it because she's thirteen," Menders sighed. "She is your friend and she loves you too, but at thirteen… even nice girls sometimes grow fangs."

Kaymar, who was still standing by, snorted sarcastically. Menders looked over Borsen's shoulder at him.

"I'd like you gentlemen to leave this to me," he said quietly. "I'll deal with Katrin. Everyone else needs to get back to business."

Kaymar looked ready to protest but then sighed and walked away with Ifor, much to Menders' relief. Kaymar was very fond of Borsen and intensely protective as well, but he had a vicious temper that dwarfed Menders' own.

It quickly became obvious that Borsen was too heartbroken to calm down. He tried, but then would burst into new wails of grief, clinging to Menders with all his might.

"All right, Little Man, I know. I understand. Fresh wounds hurt old scars, don't they?" Menders whispered, patting his back. "We're going to go see Doctor Franz so he can give you something to help you calm down. Then I think you need to go to bed because you've managed to cry yourself into a fever." He carried Borsen back into the house, put him to bed and then went for Franz.

"He might quiet a bit faster if you weren't here," Franz whispered to Menders after a small dose of ramplane failed to help Borsen stop crying. "It comforts him to have you with him but it also reminds him of what upset him in the first place. I'll sit with him. Once you're not here, I'm certain he'll drop off."

Menders nodded, bent over Borsen and said, "Now remember, this is your home and you're my boy." Borsen smiled weakly, and began to fall asleep.

Menders went to a particular bench in the rose garden, knowing that Katrin would be looking for him sooner or later. He wanted very much for her to come to him, so that he didn't have to seek her out and confront her like some vengeful disciplinarian. He was trusting in Katrin's own nature and upbringing to make her know she had done the wrong thing.

He took calm, deep breaths, clenched and unclenched his hands, then seated himself.

Nearby The Men were preparing their outdoor cooking, and called for him to bring Katrin and Eiren to dine with them later, to which he nodded a smiling acceptance.

Then he waited.

***

Katrin fled from Eiren's savage scolding. She knew it was well deserved, but she couldn't bear it, not from Eiren. Seeing her so angry was frightening; she was always soft-spoken and gentle. The cruel words Katrin had flung at Borsen seemed to be burning away somewhere on the back of her tongue. It was as if some vicious other-Katrin had risen up and said them.

She crept down the hall and peeped through the door to Borsen's room. He was in bed, with Doctor Franz sitting beside him. She could smell ramplane and watched silently as Doctor Franz reached over to feel Borsen's forehead, looking concerned.

Oh Gods, I've made him sick, she thought, guilt stricken. He wants to be a strong man but he's such a frail little thing! Franz says he's made of silk and toothpicks, that all those years of not enough food have undermined his entire constitution.

Why did I do it? Why?

Because you wanted to. The thought was so much like a whispered voice that Katrin whirled around, fully expecting there to be someone behind her.

She wanted Menders suddenly, even if he was furious and would tear strips off her. She deserved it. She tiptoed past Borsen's door to the glass door at the end of the hallway and looked into the rose garden.

Menders was sitting on a bench, not far from where the Men were building up wood for a big fire. For once he wasn't reading or writing in a notebook. He was just sitting. She knew he was waiting for her.

Katrin swallowed a couple of times and went to him, a dark knot in her stomach making her feel sick. Menders looked up and patted the seat next to him.

Katrin sat down.

"What's wrong with Borsen?" she asked fearfully.

"He was heartbroken over what you said to him and cried himself into a fever," Menders answered. "Did you really say that you could send him away from here, Katrin?"

She looked at the ground, unable to admit it in words. She could only acknowledge her guilt with a nod. Menders sighed.

"You know that isn't true," he said softly.

"I don't know why I said it!" Katrin cried in a whisper, knowing it was a lie. Despite feeling bad about hurting Borsen, there was a thorn of resentment lodged in her heart.

"You're a bright child. I like to think you've been well brought up. If you examine your feelings, I think you'll know why you did what you did."

Katrin nodded. "I… was jealous and I took it out on him. I'm sorry. I was wrong."

"It's true that everyone here has been very taken up with Borsen. I can understand why you'd be that angry," Menders said, his voice very controlled, but kind.

"Well, you're the worst of all," Katrin replied irritably – startling herself. She hadn't meant it to come out like that, even if it was how she felt.

"Oh yes, and just how is that?" Menders tone cooled.

"I… you positively dote on him, day and night! More than you ever did with me!" Katrin's temper flared.

"Oh, what nonsense! And what if I do?" Menders said. "My affections are mine, to give as I wish to whomever I wish – and, may I add, I certainly have doted over you for many years and still do." His voice was level and frighteningly cold.

Katrin stood up suddenly, to her own surprise. "But he's not your child!" she protested before she could stop herself.

Menders rose also, so quickly, so effortlessly that she could not have been more surprised if he'd drawn back to strike her. His face was a mask, hard and unreadable. For the first time in her life Katrin understood why some people were afraid of Menders.

"No, he is not my child," Menders said with terrible calmness. "Might I remind you, young lady, neither are you."

Katrin gasped.

"Yes, that's right. My life has been given over to the care of other people's children," Menders went on. "The fact that I choose to love them and care for them as my own is something I consider a blessing, not a detriment. It would serve you well to remember that, Katrin."

Katrin felt sick and light headed. Why had she said that to Menders? A voice inside her head seemed to be screaming for her to stop, to remind her that she was not like this, but her blood was on fire and she felt a terrible urge to fire cruel words back at Menders, to hurt him as she had hurt Borsen. She fought the urge. Desperate to regain something of herself, she could think of only one thing to do.

Stepping back, she made a full formal curtsy to Menders

and said, her voice shaking,

"I have insulted and angered you and hurt my brother deeply. I am truly sorry and apologize. I am ashamed of myself and beg your forgiveness, Father."

When she rose, Menders just looked at her for a moment. Then he stepped forward, took her hands and drew her into a hug. Katrin sighed in relief and fought back tears. Anything Menders said or did could not be more frightening to her than hearing his heart hammering chest beneath her ear, like the pounding hoofbeats of a running horse.

She'd seen Menders this angry only once before, when he'd torn up that carpenter who'd said vulgar things about her at the school worksite.

"My child - my beloved daughter, I also must apologize to you," he said. "I've been very taken up with Borsen, because he craves attention and needs it desperately. You're so very grown up now that it's easy to forget you're thirteen and still a girl. I never meant to exclude you, Katrin. I'm man enough to admit that I have been quite enamored of having a little son and I have neglected you. That was unfair and it won't continue."

"But you can't stop now that you've started, it would hurt Borsen so," Katrin said into his shoulder.

Menders chuckled, a welcome sound. "No and I won't, but I can be more balanced with my attentions."

"Do you like him more because he's a boy?" Katrin asked, drawing back and looking at Menders fearfully. "And because he's your nephew?"

"No. A son is a son, and a daughter a daughter," Menders answered seriously. "Each delightful and enjoyable in their own ways. Katrin, no-one can take your place in my heart but there is room for Borsen as well, just as there is for Eiren and Hemmett. Borsen needs us all right now. People are responding to that need, which is why they're making much of him."

"I knew that. When I said it – it was like some horrible

thing rose up and talked with my mouth," Katrin said.

"Ah. You've met your personal version of the Red Beast," Menders replied, seating her on the bench, then sitting beside her.

"Red Beast?"

"It's what the Thrun call it, that part of yourself that contains anger, jealousy, rage, all the things that we as civilized people tell ourselves we control. You've seen mine."

Katrin nodded. She had indeed.

"You can learn to control the Red Beast," Menders went on. "You can even use it when you need it. But sometimes it gets away from the best of us - and then there's little we can do other than try to contain and mend the damage."

"I was afraid you would be mad at me forever," she ventured.

Menders smiled and shook his head.

"I was very disappointed in you, yet I trusted you to know you did wrong. You've proved my trust. I also knew that what hurt I felt would pass. But you're going to have to gain Borsen's trust again. You shattered his confidence about being here, you see. He thinks that you hate him. Please, remember that he's frail, Katrin. It will be a long time before a shock like this won't make him ill. If ever."

"Silk and toothpicks," Katrin muttered.

"Doctor Franz's apt description."

Katrin nodded. Then she remembered that torn parcel that was still on the floor of her room.

"He... he brought me a present," she choked.

"Yes, I know," Menders replied. "I was there. He went on about it all the way home. He loves you, Katrin."

Katrin blinked at tears. Menders laughed a little and handed her his spare handkerchief.

"Now then, that's enough emotional turmoil for one day," he said firmly. "Borsen should be waking up in a little while. It would be good to make this up right away and start out fresh.

Go on inside now."

Katrin, suddenly feeling light, got up and ran across the yard to the front doors. Eiren was there, looking weary and hot, but she came to Katrin and gave her a kiss. They went inside together as Menders watched.

No doubt they would have a talk and sort things out. All would be well, and as before.

Perhaps not quite as before, Menders thought after a moment. Such happenings inevitably left permanent change in their wake, and likely that change would be in Borsen, who did not need his fragile confidence shaken or his frail health compromised.

Menders went to his office, locked the door, then washed his face and hands in the washbasin on the stand by the window. He looked closely at himself in the mirror.

Keeping his temper under control when provoked always took a toll. His face looked pinched and drawn, flushed in places, his eyes red around the edges behind his dark glasses. He combed back his hair, thinking of the exchange between himself and the Princess.

She had never spoken to him like that before. For just a moment as she faced him down, her face hard and furious, he'd thought he seen the shade of Katrin's grandmother, Morghenna the Terrible. He'd believed careful upbringing, love and attention could rid a child of inborn influences, but Katrin had just shown the sort of cruelty and jealousy that had made her grandmother infamous. Despite all the love and nurturing she had been given, it was there.

There was a slight rattling at the doorknob, then Kaymar let himself into the office, pocketing the lock pick he'd just used to gain entrance. Menders groaned in exasperation as his cousin settled to lounge in a chair.

"Weary of fatherhood?" Kaymar asked fliply.

"Weary of you ignoring locks," Menders snapped.

"You need someone to listen to you," Kaymar said, unimpressed. "I saw you talking to her. It did not go well."

"No." Menders voiced his impression of Katrin resembling her grandmother while Kaymar listened silently. "What I most fear is that those influences I've tried so hard to eliminate in her will come to the fore no matter what," Menders finally sighed.

"You misjudge the Queen, whom you have never had a chance to get to know," Kaymar replied, lighting a cigar. "You can glare at me all you like, Cuz. There is a lot of good in the Queen and there was a lot of good in The Terrible. I didn't know her, but I know our royal cousin well enough. Katrin has just had an attack of jealousy that wasn't entirely unwarranted. She's young, so it was childish and cruel. Don't read so much into it."

"Let's not discuss the Queen," Menders responded shortly, sitting on the edge of the desk. "Do you find, as you get older, that you no longer see things in black and white? When I was younger, I decided that I would never have children, because they would take away from my devotion to Katrin. Now that Borsen is here, I know that was a foolish choice. Black and white shifts to shades of grey."

Kaymar barked a short sardonic laugh.

"Cousin, I have never seen things in black and white," he drawled, leaning back in the chair and raising his eyebrows at Menders. "I have always seen all shades of grey and all sides of every question. There are few evil and few good people. The Queen is not evil, you aren't good. It isn't that easy. I live with shades of grey – and when I'm having melancholia, I even see in shades of grey. We all make choices we regret with the passage of time. We go on from here, as Borsen says."

Menders looked at the handsome young man.

"What would you have done differently?" he asked.

"Knowing what I know now, that I would have ended up here, with Ifor?" Kaymar responded. Menders nodded.

"Not a damn thing, Cuz," Kaymar smiled. "Not a damn thing. Let's go get dinner, shall we?"

Dear Bumpy,

I don't know if Borsen has written you about something that happened, but it's really bothering me. Everyone, including Borsen, keeps saying that it's all right and that things are all ironed out, but I still have moments of feeling horrible about what happened.

Basically, I got jealous of all the attention Borsen gets. I said some terrible things to him, including that I could have him sent away from The Shadows. It scared him to death and he had a crying fit that made him sick.

Then Menders and I had a set-to. Can you believe it? It was over fast and we ended up apologizing to each other but I think I really would have felt better if he'd scolded me properly. I was so cruel to Borsen, and one part of me was horrified even when I did it, while another part was really enjoying hurting him. Just as when I talked back to Menders – it was like someone who wasn't me was trying to cause trouble.

Borsen and I talked about it. He said it was what Menders calls 'the Red Beast' – uncontrolled emotion that affects us all from time to time. But knowing and having everyone else being so understanding doesn't seem to help.

I knew Borsen didn't have an easy life before coming here, but I had no idea he had lived on the streets. He said he was what they call City Thrun, but I'm not entirely sure what that means. To me the Thrun have always been Tharak's people, but from what I've been able to find out, the Thrun who go to live in the cities are different. Borsen mentioned sleeping on the streets when we had dinner outside the other night, but he won't say much, just says 'we go on from here'. He talks about his mother telling him to always 'follow the way of light'. It sounds strange and mystical.

Do you know more?

I know I should just let the whole thing go, but I think I would feel better if someone scolded me just a little. Even Kaymar has been sweet about it, like I was the one who was hurt instead of Borsen, although right after it happened I am told he looked about ready to chew the handle off his dagger.

I hope everything is going well for you there, and exams are easy. I'll be so glad when you get home! Perhaps I need my big brother to kick some sense into me — gently, of course!

Love,

Katrin

Dear Self-Reproaching One,

I'm flogging away studying for a tactics exam, but I wanted to answer your cry for someone to scold you. The gentle kicking can come later, given that no boot can reach several hundred miles. And no, I cannot imagine you having a set-to with Menders. The less said of that, the better, I think.

Borsen did mention the incident in passing, but he wasn't making anything much of it. He's a very accepting little fellow. The important thing to remember is that all this is new to him. He's really not feeling secure yet. It isn't like us, who have both been there at The Shadows with the family all our lives.

As for your question about City Thrun, yes there is such a thing. They aren't like the Thrun you know. City Thrun are the ones who leave their tribes and go to the cities, thinking that they're going to get rich. Instead, people in the cities don't want anything to do with them, won't hire them, won't even give them money if they beg. So they start picking pockets and shoplifting. The children rummage through rubbish bins behind stores and restaurants. Lots of the women become prostitutes. Sometimes the biggest men can get work on the docks on a day to day basis, but they're paid much less than any Mordanian dock worker. They live in the worst slums you can imagine, or under bridges, in doorways or culverts.

Borsen was City Thrun. His father was a piece of work, a thief, and they were always on the run. I'm sure there were plenty of times they slept on the streets. Borsen's mother, who sounds a decent sort, died when he was six under bad circumstances. He hasn't told me about that, but I overheard it one night, back when he was having nightmares and Menders would take him to his office and keep him there until he calmed down. Borsen would talk to him, and I was passing in the hall, going to the kitchen.

I can't pass on what I heard, because Borsen didn't tell me directly, and I don't think he wants anyone to know. I can tell you this much — Borsen lost everything he ever loved when his mother died. He blames himself for not being able to help her, even though he was just a little fellow.

So when you threatened him, even though it was a bowl of horse apples, he thought he was losing the people he's come to love and he went all to pieces. If you want some scolding, basically I feel like you hit someone a lot smaller than you who hasn't had the blessings in life you have. It was a cowardly act — there now, I hope you're cringing in shame. Just a little, anyway. But the important thing is that you made it up and I doubt you'll do it again.

I know how you feel. Remember when I was nine and got that gun as a present and went out, all wild to shoot it, and shot that poor mother thrush? Not even a damn game bird we could eat but a songbird, and worse, with babies on the nest. To this day I feel horrible about that, even though I tried to feed the babies. They all died, of course, and I never felt so ashamed in my life. People do these things, Willow, but it's pointless to go over and over them. Just learn from them and go on. That's what Borsen means when he says "we go on from here". It's good advice.

And just to let you know I see both sides, yes, everyone has been very much in love with Borsen and it showed. I can see how you got mad about it. Personally, I feel he doesn't need that much adoration either. It's not good for him because it will keep him childish. Just like you and I are always having problems with people forgetting that we're both big for our ages and expecting too much from us, people baby Borsen because he looks like such a little boy when he's actually your age and might even be older. So I think the whole rumpus will straighten things out a little. It will, as my Moral Philosophy lecturer says, 'Give people some perspective.'

No permanent harm done, Willow, if you don't allow it to be.

Now I have to get back to the damn books. And hasn't my letter writing improved! My journal got the highest mark this term!

Love,

Papa Bumpy,
Dispenser of Fatherly Wisdom to The Masses

CHAPTER 44
NOT PERFECT ANYMORE

Katrin held Snowflake's bridle and watched Borsen circle the pasture on her mare, Taffy. She had been trying to teach him to ride for weeks, after working to convince him to try to ride for a year. She was finally making headway.

Borsen was afraid of horses. Before he had glasses, he'd seen horses as large blurs. One had snapped at him when he was quite small, terrifying him as large square teeth had suddenly loomed out of the blur of his uncorrected vision.

Worse, he'd seen Demon throw Menders a couple of months ago. Demon had gone from fairly docile, which meant he only tried to bite Menders' foot every fifteen minutes or so, to demented bucking, corkscrewing and spinning in the blink of an eye. Menders felt it coming and rolled as he fell, then somersaulted to his feet with an assassin's lithe grace. But Borsen believed Menders was the greatest horseman alive, so if Menders could be thrown, what hope for the rest of us?

Katrin started Borsen out on Snowflake. After a couple of weeks of the boy nervously hauling at the reins, the normally placid pony became quite restive. Snowflake's occasional kick or headshake of protest only frightened Borsen more.

She finally struck on the idea of having him ride her mare instead. Taffy was trained to voice commands. Maybe once Borsen felt more confident, he wouldn't confuse the horse by hauling back on the reins in terror while urging it forward with his heels.

Borsen refused at first when she tried to get him to ride Taffy.

"What, ride on that sidesaddle?"

"Menders rides sidesaddle on the Mordanian saddles, like the Thrun do," Katrin observed slyly.

Using Borsen's idol as an example worked. "Can I have a Thrun saddle, like Menders does?"

"Learn to ride first," Katrin said. "Saddles can come later." She had no doubt Menders would buy a dozen of them for Borsen, if asked.

He nodded and clambered onto Taffy's back.

It works, she thought jubilantly, watching him make another circuit. Now he's thinking that hanging onto that saddle will save him, he's forgotten to curl his backside under and hold on like a monkey with his legs. She called Taffy down to a walk again, and then whistled for another canter. Borsen was smiling and automatically rocking to the mare's smooth gait, for the first time looking as if he might actually be enjoying the ride.

"Whoa, Taffy!" she called.

She kilted up her skirt, swinging aboard Snowflake. She rode over to Taffy.

"Now, swing your leg over her neck," she told Borsen, while she leaned over to undo the reins. "I know there isn't a stirrup there, but you're still going to hang on to the saddle with one hand. Hold the reins in your other hand and keep it right down by the pommel, in case you need to catch hold with it too. All right, Taffy, walk on."

She watched as Borsen smiled broadly as Taffy performed another gentle canter. He wasn't really guiding the horse, but he wasn't leaning back on the reins either. He actually had a talent for riding, once he forgot to be scared to death.

"I think we've sorted this out, Snowy," she said softly to the pony, whose ears swiveled back lazily. "I'll have to ride you for a while but that'll help you forget Borsen yanking your mouth. Then he can ride you again."

Just then two of the latest litter of boarhound puppies came tearing around the stable, yipping excitedly as they played. They barreled across the pasture and dove directly under Snowflake's belly. The pony, rudely startled from his pleasant near-drowse with his beloved mistress on his back, bucked viciously.

Katrin wasn't even aware of falling until she heard the terrible snapping noise and her right arm exploded in pain. She screamed before she could help herself, then slapped her own hand over her mouth, not wanting to frighten Snowflake to the point where he might panic and trample her.

She heard hooves thundering across the pasture and then the unmistakable sound of a horse jumping, and knew that Taffy had bolted. Oh gods, Borsen will fall too, she thought.

"Now then, Cuz, can you roll over?" Kaymar was there. He'd been right at the stable, watching them, though he'd been out of sight.

She nodded and did so, hearing his harsh intake of breath. She tried to look at her arm but he stopped her.

"Are the bones through the skin?" she asked fearfully. That meant infection – and worse.

"No, thank the gods, but it's a bad break, sweetheart." He stroked her hair.

"Where's Taffy... and Borsen?" she asked. Kaymar's face blanched. He stood abruptly, looking toward the house.

"He's still on her!" he cried. "They're going up the drive!"

"They jumped the fence?" Katrin gasped, trying to sit up. "Borsen stayed on?"

Kaymar was back by her on the ground.

"Do not sit up," he said fiercely. "Hear me? Just lie there and don't move."

***

Menders heard Borsen screaming for him and ran to the door to see the boy clinging to Katrin's mare, tearing across the lawn as if he was in the backstretch of a horse race. The little face was white with fear as he pulled Taffy up at the foot of the steps.

"Uncle, Katrin's fallen, she's hurt!" he cried.

"Move back!" Menders ordered jumping up as Borsen did so, shouting for the horse to go. They galloped back to the pasture. Taffy slid to a halt at the pasture gate, and Menders was off and over the fence by the time Borsen could get down and squeeze between the fence bars.

Kaymar was cradling Katrin's head in his lap.

"She came off of Snowflake," he said softly. "Her arm is broken, but no bones through the skin. It's a terrible break. I haven't let her see it."

Menders stifled a groan when he saw the arm. Katrin now had a joint where a joint shouldn't be, her forearm bent almost double in the middle. He forced a smile onto his face, and knelt by her.

"Well, you now will be able to scratch your right elbow with your right hand," he said, looking for other injuries.

"Isn't it disgusting?" she said, trying to sound cheerful. Her voice shook with pain.

Franz came running heavily across the pasture, bag in hand. He examined Katrin's arm.

"Oh my dear," he sighed. "This is a beauty, my girl, a real cracker. I've set worse, however, so let's get you feeling better and in the house." He opened his bag and extracted a small bottle of ramplane, holding it to Katrin's lips. She swallowed, and then closed her eyes, waiting for the medicine to work.

Franz took Menders aside quickly.

"The moment that ramplane starts working, we have to get that arm set or I might never get those bone ends back together. She'd end up crippled."

Menders nodded silently.

***

"She'll sleep the rest of the afternoon from that dose,"

Franz said, clearing up the medical paraphernalia he'd strewn about while setting and splinting Katrin's arm. "She's going to have a great deal of pain for a while. This is a very serious break. With her past history of fevers, I want her to stay in bed for a week. The more she rests now, the faster it will heal."

"We'll see to it that she stays put," Eiren responded. "I'm going to get some more pillows for her. She's going to want to sit up once she's awake." She left, her footsteps echoing down the hall.

"Now, just between you and me, how bad will it be?" Menders asked, sitting on the side of the bed carefully, stroking Katrin's forehead. She smiled, not waking.

He was shaken to his foundations. Setting the arm had been the stuff of nightmares. Even with the ramplane numbing the worst of the pain, poor Katrin had screamed as Franz worked over her. Menders had held her in his arms and talked to her – and knew for the first time the helplessness of a parent who is unable to assuage his child's suffering.

"It should knit well, she's young. It might end up somewhat weakened and perhaps a little shorter than the other arm. It's going to ache like blazes in the meantime." Franz said bluntly. "I have everything back where it belongs, but there's a great deal of damage, not only to the bones, but to the soft tissues of the arm. I can give her ramplane to help her over the worst of it but she's going to be an unhappy girl for a while."

Menders nodded. From the look of the arm, it was what he expected. He could only hope that Katrin would regain full use of it.

"Once it begins to knit, we'll start her with exercises to keep the arm strong and flexible. Don't look so destroyed, my friend," Franz said.

"You know how it is," Menders replied quietly, not taking his eyes from Katrin's face. "You worry, you plan, you try to keep them safe. Locks on the cupboards, guns stored away, poisons out of reach. Then they get bigger and want to do more, see more. You think you have it all sorted, and then…"

"I understand," Franz answered. "She'll be all right, Menders, I promise." He patted Katrin's hand and stood. "I'll be in my office, I need to make up some more ramplane syrup for her. Organize a rotating watch on her. Keep taking her temperature too, watch for fever."

Menders took Katrin's uninjured hand and stroked it. It was now a young lady's hand, despite the hard work she did around the house every day, making soap, tending chickens and milking goats. It was smooth and white, the skin soft because of the scented lotions she made and rubbed into her skin to counteract soapy water, lye and other harsh substances. At the moment though, he saw a smaller hand, grubby from catching tadpoles, tucked into his, and then even smaller, gripping the tip of his finger.

"I know you'll be fine," he whispered, lifting her uninjured hand and kissing it, "but it still breaks my heart to know you're hurt."

Deep in sleep she knew he was there and moved toward him slightly, her face turning upward.

"Everything is all right - sleep well, Little Princess," he whispered, rising and carefully adjusting the covers around her.

***

Katrin woke with a terrible taste in her mouth. Her right arm throbbed. At first she was confused. Then she remembered the fall, her broken arm.

She moaned. The bedside lamp was burning low. She looked at her bedside table and saw that water and a few bottles were there, but she couldn't bear the idea of trying to reach them, even with her good arm.

The door between her room and Menders' opened and he

was there, wearing his dressing gown. It must be very late.

He bent over her with a smile. She could smell the scent he used and memories of being carried everywhere by him as a little girl flooded back to her.

"Hello Little Princess," he said. He felt her forehead. "Thirsty?"

"Yes," she whispered, surprised to find her throat very dry and her voice hoarse.

"Ramplane does that to your throat," Menders said, pouring a glass of water and helping her with it. "This will help."

It did, but her arm was agonizing when she happened to move it. Katrin shuddered and couldn't repress a whimper.

"Let me see," Menders said gently, going around the bed and repositioning the arm for her. He then proceeded to pack it with ice from the basement ice store room, wrapping it in an old rubber apron that Kaymar used in his shed.

"The ice will numb the pain," Menders explained. "You've had a good long sleep and missed the experiments with keeping ice on it without drenching the bed and drowning you."

Katrin couldn't help smiling, in spite of the discomfort. "Kaymar can't make his rockets, for a while."

"Oh, I suspect he'll find another rubber apron." She could imagine the heated exchanges between Menders and Franz as they tried to fashion the ice sling, as such projects always brought out the worst in both of them.

"Are you hungry, sweetheart?"

"No," Katrin answered, glad to find that her throat was less raspy after the water. "I feel sort of sick."

"Not surprising. Now, Franz wanted to see you when you woke, so I'm going to get him."

A moment later they were back. Franz was in his dressing gown too but smelled of cigars, so he'd been awake.

He looked her over and took her temperature.

"Slight fever, but that's normal after a break," he said with a smile. "It's hurting, isn't it?"

"Yes. A lot. Thumping, like a hot, soft hammer."

"Well, I think we'll give you another dose of ramplane so you can sleep through the night. No point in lying awake in agony. It's going to hurt very badly for a while, Katrin. I think you'll be happiest sleeping a lot the next few days."

She didn't really care. She just wanted the pain to stop. It felt like someone was grinding her arm between two stones, and it wore her down to the point where she wanted to howl. Franz gave her more ramplane, made sure the ice was tight on her arm and said he would see her in the morning.

Menders sat on the edge of the bed beside her and held her good hand as the ramplane took effect and she went back to blessed, pain free sleep.

***

Menders let himself into Katrin's room to find her dozy and groggy again. It had been five days since she'd broken her arm. Franz wanted her to stay in bed longer, as she'd been running a continual low fever. He had given her a bottle of ramplane syrup to take when the pain got bad.

Menders knew she'd had a great deal of pain, but the worst had to be over by now. Katrin was too restless and spirited to enjoy being in bed for periods of more than a day. He had a feeling that the ramplane was being misused so she would sleep and not care that she was stuck in bed and bored stiff.

"Hello there, Little Princess," he said cheerfully, perching on the side of the bed. "How is it this morning?"

"It hurts."

"Yes, it's going to. Katrin, I want you to stop taking the ramplane, please."

Even under the influence of the drug, she was startled.

"Why, if it helps?"

"Because you're overusing it and misusing it," he

answered honestly. "You're trying to stay asleep because you don't like being confined to bed, my dear."

"Menders, my arm truly does hurt," Katrin said, struggling with heavy eyelids. He thought she sounded a little annoyed at the accusation.

"Yes, I know it does. It might hurt at times for the rest of your life. You can't just lie around in a ramplane haze forever, waiting for your arm to stop hurting. So I'm taking it back to Franz today."

"But what will I do when it starts up again? It's terrible, it feels like my arm is being mashed up in a machine!" Because of the ramplane, Katrin was near tears.

"Off to sleep with you now," Menders responded. "You're not fit to talk. We'll talk later, when you're awake." He sat with her until she slept, then rose and went to Franz's office, ramplane bottle in hand.

The doctor raised his eyebrows when Menders placed the bottle on his desk.

"We're having a problem," Menders said bluntly. "She's taking too much."

"I told her how much to take," Franz said with some concern. He lifted the bottle, looked at it, shook it a little.

"She's probably lost track. She's miserable and just wants to sleep and get past it," Menders said. "But I must keep her mother's habits in mind."

"I have something else to give her, but it's vile. You'll remember it, I'm sure."

"I do. I'd rather she have that, without the sedative effect."

"Do you want me to go speak to her?"

"No, she's asleep again."

"What? It's nine in the morning! Well, that's way too much ramplane," Franz said heatedly. "Gods, I never thought of it."

"Time to look for some distractions. You want her in bed for another few days?"

"I think I'm going to change that. Let's start having her get up and keep her occupied."

"Good. I'm hoping a letter from Hemmett might arrive. I wrote to him right after she got hurt to let him know some moral support would be a good idea. I'm expecting Kaymar back tomorrow, and if I know our Hemmett, there will be a communication forthcoming."

"I look forward to it," Franz laughed. Hemmett's missives were always funny and were very popular around The Shadows. They invariably detailed some mayhem at the Military Academy, usually involving Hemmett and his friend, Villison.

Later Menders sat on Katrin's bed as she woke up. He could see that the pain was bad because her face was lined with it, making her look older. She moaned.

"Hello again," he said, taking her good hand. "I've talked to Franz and he's going to let you get out of bed."

"That's a relief," she sighed.

"He's also going to give you something that will help with pain, but won't make you sleep. It tastes horrible but it does work."

She nodded and sat up. Menders helped her, not wanting her to jar the arm. Franz had taken his advice about using a Thrun-style splint on it, and had soaked a piece of leather and then wrapped it around the injured arm, where it dried to rock hardness. It supported the injured limb beautifully but made it impossible for Katrin to use it.

"I'm sorry about the ramplane, Menders," she said, surprising him. "I knew I was taking too much, but I felt compelled to do it. I just wanted to stay asleep."

He looked at her.

"This is something for us both to remember then," he said. "You will have to be careful with such things."

"Yes, I thought of my mother." Katrin sighed. "I'll just have to try to stand the pain, but it is really terrible, Menders."

"I know a Thrun trick that might help you. Tharan-Tul taught it to me when I was much younger than you. The Thrun call it a healing trance."

Katrin looked intrigued, though her forehead was still tight with pain.

"Would it really help when it gets bad?" she asked.

"Yes, it would. The trance doesn't do any actual healing, of course. It just distracts the mind so the body can heal. It makes you not mind the pain. It's easy to forget to use it when you're actually in pain. I went through that entire episode with my eyes when you were a baby and never thought about it once," Menders said.

"Really?"

"I was so afraid of going blind and of what would happen to you if I did that it never crossed my mind. Silly of me, because it would have helped me through what was not a pleasant experience. Now, here's this vile concoction of Franz's. It works very well for pain, but leaves your mind sharp. However, it is going to take every bit of your determination to get it down your throat." Menders held out the dose, but had her wait until he had a glass of water poured.

"Hold your breath and try to pour it straight down, avoiding your tongue at all costs," he directed with a grin.

She knocked back the dose and was absolutely silent for a second. Then she shrieked in horror and motioned desperately for the water. Menders laughingly handed it to her. She drained the glass.

"That is an instrument of torture," she gasped. "Nothing should taste that bad."

"And now, as it works very quickly, let's get you out of bed," Menders suggested, picking up her dressing gown. "Franz wants you to continue to take it easy but I think a change of scene and airing this room would be a good idea."

"Gods, it's thumping," she muttered as she slid her feet into her slippers. Menders helped her with the sling Franz had left for her, then picked up a walking cane he had put on the floor by the bed.

"There's nothing wrong with my legs, Menders," Katrin said, taking the cane with a laugh.

"You haven't been up on them for a week. You might be a bit wobbly and you don't want to fall and jar that arm."

"You think of everything," Katrin said with admiration as he ushered her into the lounge.

"If only that were true," Menders muttered to himself. "Now, I shall tell Borsen to come and regale you with news of his great riding prowess," he continued as he settled her upright on the sofa. "He's been coming right along, now that he's over his fear, and put Snowflake over a tiny jump the other day. He's been very worried about you."

***

Menders had learned to leave his body from Tharan-Tul when he was only a boy, when he still lived at Stettan. Whenever the abuse from tutors and nurses became more than he could endure, he would escape from his home to the Thrun, sometimes staying with them for days. There was always a beating when he finally went back home, but during his time with the Thrun he would be revitalized and strengthened to the point where he could endure the consequences of running away.

He'd fled to them when a tutor broke every bone in his right hand by thrashing it with a stick after catching him sketching rather than studying. The hand was monstrously swollen, the pain agonizing. Tharak found him sobbing in the shelter of a huge stone hand that stood alone on the plain. He took his friend to Tharan-Tul.

The young shaman fascinated Aylam Josirus. He walked with a marked limp due to a withered and twisted leg. He had blue eyes, something uncommon though not entirely unheard of among the Thrun. More than once when Aylam fled to the Thrun after abuse or rape, Tharan-Tul caught him by the chin and simply stared into his eyes. It always calmed Aylam and gave him a sense of peace, though the power of the lame shaman was frightening to a boy less than eleven years of age.

Tharan-Tul looked at Aylam's broken hand, then concocted a vilely bitter drink from dried plants hanging in his tent. He had Aylam drink it down, insisting that he take all of it though he gagged at the foul taste.

Soon Aylam felt elated and the pain in his hand receded. The shaman set the small bones, then carefully bound the hand in clean cloth. He wrapped it around with leather held with thongs and dipped it in water. Then Tharan-Tul had Aylam lie down, covering him with a fur.

Aylam had slept almost immediately, to waken later with his hand throbbing while arrows of agony shot up his arm to his shoulder. The leather had dried to rock hardness; he couldn't move his hand.

His sobs woke the shaman, who sat beside him.

"I can give you no more of the drink, you are too small to stand much," Tharan-Tul said. "But I can teach you a way to leave your body so that you do not feel pain. While you do it, you will be able to direct your thoughts to make your hand heal."

Tharan-Tul instructed him to breathe deeply until he felt great peace – and then talked to him until Aylam felt as if he had risen from his body and was somewhere at the top of the tent. He couldn't feel the pain from his hand, and eventually, with Tharan-Tul's guidance, he could feel the broken bones knitting together. He wasn't able to sustain the separation from his body long, but each time he opened his eyes and felt the terrible pain, Tharan-Tul was there, helping him leave his body again. By the end of three days he could enter the trance without help for as long as he liked.

He asked Tharan-Tul if there was danger of leaving his body forever, and the shaman laughed.

"No, the world will call you back until the appointed time comes for you to leave it and go to The Light At The Top Of The World," he said. "So long as you have work to be done in the world, you will always go back to your body. This is only a way to heal your body, not a way to leave it."

After that, Aylam often left his body at will. It had kept him sane when he was assaulted by his perverted tutor – where before he had gritted his teeth and screamed into the pillow the man shoved his face into, now he simply rose to the ceiling and felt nothing until the invasion of his body was over. Years later, when he became Menders, he'd used the shaman's technique to conquer bodily pain from training or injuries. He'd even refined the discipline to the point where he could separate his mind from painful activity. Yes, he felt the pain, but he didn't mind it.

Now he was teaching Katrin the same control of her mind and finding her a capable pupil.

"It starts with concentration," he told her. "You close your eyes and begin to concentrate only on your heartbeat and breathing. At first you'll hear things that go on around you, but that's all right, you just come back to listening only to your heartbeat and breathing."

She was doing as he said, her eyes closed.

"You slow your breathing gradually. Don't force it, take your time." He watched, fascinated, as she did as he said – rapidly. It was faster than he'd ever seen anyone learn the technique.

"At the end of each breath, before you breathe in again, there will be a moment where you feel like you're suspended, or floating," he went on. "Start concentrating on that moment. You'll begin to feel as if you're floating free from your body and soon all you will hear is your heartbeat and your breathing."

Her breathing had already slowed to a deep, steady respiration. Menders waited. She wouldn't be able to stay in the healing trance for long at first but she was going to master it quickly.

After a few minutes her breathing went back to normal and she opened her eyes.

"You won't be able to speak right away, so don't worry," he said. She nodded, and looked very pleased with herself.

"You can use that if you're in pain or sick," Menders told her. "Once you learn to do it, you can stay in the trance for a long time and concentrate on healing yourself."

"Is it all right to do it by myself?" she asked.

He nodded. "Yes, you can't come to any harm."

***

Katrin found the healing trance easy. It took her to a quiet and peaceful place where time didn't seem to pass. Sometimes she was aware of passing shapes, as if people were walking by in a mist, but she felt no curiosity about them and there was no indication that they noticed her. She would drift, thinking of her arm healing, dreaming of it being strong and whole again.

It was better than ramplane, which took away the pain and made her sleep, but left her with black and red dreams and the memory of voices that kept chiding her and telling her what she should do.

***

Dear Willow,

How is the fallen soldieress? Sounds ghastly. Such calamity and confusion. I am thinking of injuring myself in some similar spectacular way, so that we can discuss our scars like old soldiers.

I have been given fourteen days barracks detention. What is worse, I am being punished for being honest. I expect you to weep on Menders' neck over my sad tale.

A week ago, we were herded off to some frilly society do, as is often the case. Some Brigadier General was having a social brawl at his house and needed cadets to dance with his ugly daughters and their even uglier friends.

So there we are, with the dancing just beginning. I'm looking around for some girl who's halfway nice to lead out. So what happens but Ufronia Vildsteen comes flumping over to me and curtsies. Normally I manage to avoid the ones who do this, because I don't like it. I prefer doing the asking. Normally I let Villison take the forward ones, as he has no taste, but Miss Vildsteen's got me dead in her sights and Villison ducked when he saw her coming, the swine.

So, I lead her out. Willow, she's dressed like an unmade bed, with some ridiculous outfit that looks like a combination of summer bed curtains and sheets all coming adrift, with her great bosom taking the place of the pillows. She's built like two over-ripe summermelons in a satin bag and a small bag at that. Her neckline is so low and her corset is laced so tight that there is almost nothing left to the imagination, it's all popped to the top like doughy buns rising. Not attractive at all. Jiggle, jiggle, like a bowl of jelly on the tailboard of a drover's cart. Where is a fellow to look? And if you do look, you aren't a gentleman, blah blah blah blah blah blah blah.

So I'm hoping that it'll be a valtz or javot, one dance looking away over her shoulder and then pass her on to the next unfortunate. But no, the citified orchestra starts trying to play a holta. It's pathetic, toot-toot, no life in it or anything. I'm wondering how I'm going to get through this, with more of Ufronia showing than should be and all that bouncing around the holta calls for. I gird my loins.

We get started, I'm keeping my steps very tame, looking anywhere but at her, so I won't start staring or laughing. Or get my eye knocked out. Now, you're a buxom girl, so is Eiren, but when you do the holta, the real holta, you don't end up falling out of your bodice because you dress properly. Well, to my horror, Ufronia is popping out of her dress more and more with each step and she's smiling and fluttering her eyes at me. Every time I swing her or we come to the jumping part, she's just about to be naked to the waist. And in these stupid city holtas you don't change partners so I can't pass her along and flee.

The dance starts getting faster, so all these city folks start hooting. They don't give a good healthy yell like we do in the holta, they let out these little constipated yips and hoo-hoos that are the funniest thing you ever heard. I've been watching the floor so I don't see Ufronia's blubberous mounds, but when she lets out this wailing little howl, I look.

Willow, her right guhzonker is just about to flap loose from its mooring and she's hooting like a flatulent steam whistle. Worst of all, she's waving her arms around over her head. I'm dancing along, biting my tongue, watching her right business thrashing out of the top of her dress like a fish flopping around in a net. Then the music stepped up a notch and Ufronia really started to prance.

Both her mighty udders are bouncing and flapping up and down, in and out of her corset like a couple of hopfootle balls. I'm getting a view of them that only a nursing baby should have and I'm absolutely about to bust a blood vessel trying not to howl. She capers on, with her appendages flying up under her chin and Willow, I have wonderful control but nobody, not even Menders, could have stayed quiet.

I started laughing, haw haw haw haw, and just then the music stopped, and my voice was the only sound in the whole damned room. I couldn't stop, I just went on and on. Ufronia's bust had settled back into its casing, so nobody could really tell why I was doubled over and roaring. She gets mad and asks me what the hells I'm laughing at.

I told her I had the name of a good dressmaker in Erdstrom who could make a dress and corset so a girl didn't rise up out of them like the moons of Eirdon. She went mad and started calling me names. I just kept laughing and told her it wasn't like I'd just reached in and given them a jiggle without so much as a by your leave. She'd asked me to dance and then had them bouncing into the daylight and practically hitting me in the face.

Well, she goes and tells her mamma. It turns out her father is some bloody General and next thing I know, the Commandant has me up on the carpet in his office. So I explain the entire thing to him. He says he understands that there was provocation, but that I still had to stand fourteen days barracks detention for conduct unbecoming an officer and a gentleman. That I was expected to be gentlemanly under all circumstances.

So I left and what do I hear but him laughing his head off in his office! So I said out loud that he ought to confine himself to quarters for fourteen days, and he hears and asks me if I want to be confined for the whole month.

It's turned out pretty well though. Being confined to quarters has gotten me out of having to do maneuvers in this awful heat we've been having, so I've been working on some new sea chanties to play on my cromar.

So if the Commandant is reading this, nah nah nah nah! And I still say if he'd been dancing with She of the Massive Unrestrained Chest Balloons, he'd have laughed too.

That is my tale of woe, my dear. Not quite a badly broken arm, but my heart is sore. Do write to me to ease my pain.

Love,

Bumpy

Beneath Hemmett's scrawl was a postscript in an entirely different hand:

Dear Princess Katrin,

Your friend Hemmett has told me of your injury. I wished to convey my sympathies to you, and my wishes for a speedy recovery. He is weathering his confinement well, and it will probably not be necessary for you to weep on anyone's neck.

Faithfully yours,

Commandant Komroff

To Cadet Greinholz

Sirrah,

    I, Her Royal Highness, Katrin Morghenna, Princess of the Royal House of Mordania, wish to inform you that I am in receipt of your vulgar communication, and am appalled at your lack of gallantry in describing the elastic properties of the goddesslike bosom of your fair dancing partner. Your crude words and offensive turns of phrase have caused me to fall upon my sofa in a faint more than once. If your missive had reached me when I was on royal progress, doubtless I would have been borne home senseless in a cab.

    "Why, low person, would you include such vile and crude phrases as 'guhzonker', 'blubberous mounds', and 'massive udders' in a missive to a fragile and delicate lady of the blood royal? Know you not that such offensive images are as thorns in my pure and unsullied mind? I am highly offended, sir, and hesitate even to give you that honorific, as it is so painfully obvious that you are not worthy of the courtesy.

    "In future, low fellow, your communications with me must be of a more respectful nature, concomitant with my exalted rank and superior qualities. I would suggest that you have them accompanied by a minstrel or small musical ensemble, so that I may hear sweet melodies while reading your humble and properly delicate communications. Mark my words, or risk my wrath, oh spawn of the common soil."

    "Petra, that looks like I wrote it myself with my bad hand," Katrin grinned. She was still unable to write, as her arm was encased in the rigid leather splint. Petra had volunteered to act as her secretary.

    "What am I supposed to do with you saying ridiculous things like that and having to write 'blubberous mounds'? Blubberous isn't even a word. I'm not even sure how many 'b's it has in it!" Petra sputtered, wiping at her eyes.

    "Three, I think," Katrin laughed. "Hemmett just makes words up when he can't think of one. Like 'guhzonker'. Get off me, Dara." Katrin's boarhound was trying to insinuate herself onto the sofa where Katrin and Petra were seated, hoping she would get a chance to chew Katrin's splint. "You can't chew it. No! Bad girl!"

Dara gazed at them with grieving eyes and Katrin relented, holding out her leather encased arm. Dara began to nibble the end of the splint.

"Ugh," Petra said, picking up Hemmett's letter and perusing it. "I don't know how you can let her do that."

"I'm hoping that she'll eventually eat all of it and I'll be free," Katrin answered.

"It must not be hurting much anymore then."

"It still hurts like fury sometimes but I've learned not to mind that it hurts," Katrin explained, making Petra give her a puzzled look.

When Katrin could no longer force herself to swallow the bitter pain remedy but felt as if the bones in her injured arm were being ground in a gristmill, Menders had taught her how to deal with the pain without going into the healing trance.

"It's a matter of learning not to mind the pain," he said, "but without the trance."

Katrin had looked at him in confusion. "How can anyone do that?"

"It's a similar discipline, but you don't leave your body. You isolate your pain and don't allow yourself to mind it."

"Sort of like ignoring a headache?"

"Very much so. You've seen me use my hands to put nails into walls and trees, haven't you?"

"Yes." It was something Menders just did, she'd never really thought of it much. He held the nail in his fist, his arm moved so fast you could hardly see it and the nail was driven into the wood.

"Don't you think it hurts?" He'd looked at her intensely.

"I just thought your hands were strong enough…" She

realized that no matter how hard and strong his hands were, it had to hurt. "It does hurt, doesn't it?"

"It does indeed. But it's an exercise in mental discipline. I can separate myself from the pain enough that I can drive a nail into a tree trunk with only my hand. Good practice should I ever have to endure pain in a situation where there's no way to avoid it."

"Like the dancers!" Katrin had said suddenly. "They're in pain, but they still dance!"

"Exactly. You put the pain in a particular place in your mind, wall it off, and ignore it. You go on with what you're doing. The pain is there, you feel it, but you don't fear it and you don't mind it. Harder to do than the healing trance, but in the long run much more practical."

"How do I do it then?"

"I can't tell you, because what works for me won't work for you. You'll have to find how your own mind can deal with it. Find your own place in your mind. With practice you'll find that you'll be able to do it very easily."

Katrin found her own place and was able to manage, even when her arm ached incessantly.

Katrin read over the letter alongside Petra and they were giggling helplessly when they realized Franz was standing behind them with Menders.

"Oh! I'm sorry!" Katrin laughed, turning to see that Franz was holding an enormous pair of shears. "Decided to become a barber, Doctor Franz?"

"And what are you pretty maidens up to with all this snickering and hooting?" Franz grinned, brandishing the shears. "Noses will be snipped if you don't tell."

Petra, who wasn't quite accustomed to the varying forms of madness that ran rampant at The Shadows looked dubious, but Katrin burst out laughing.

"Defacement of the royal person will net you a hefty fine,

sirrah," she told him.

"You don't frighten me, because I know for a fact that you didn't have a stitch on when you were born," Franz replied. "Speaking of which, it's time to divest you of a part of your raiment."

"Oh good!" Katrin realized that he'd come to cut the leather splint off her arm. "Hurry!"

"I would, if there wasn't a bear on the sofa with you," Franz said, putting down his bag and nudging Dara, who snuggled down tighter, as if this would make her invisible.

"Dara, get down," Menders said in his "dogs will now obey" tone.

Dara slunk to the floor and stretched out full length, trying to be heartbroken.

Franz settled in place.

"Now, this isn't going to smell very good," he warned, having Katrin position her arm against his thigh, while working his evil looking shears under the first fastening. "It will have absorbed a lot of sweat. And have you been chewing on it?"

"Dara does."

"Ah. And what was all that tittering going on when we came in?"

"A letter to Hemmett." Katrin watched intently as Franz cut the first three lacings. Then the smell hit her.

Petra thrust the completed letter at Menders and fled, gagging.

"Oh gods!" Katrin gasped, trying to hold her breath. "I'm not dirty!"

"It isn't that, little one, it's just all the old dead skin and such – aghk!" Menders, who had kindly tried to be unaffected by the stench, fled across the room and opened the window as far as it would go, leaning out. Franz, going red in the face from holding his breath, cut faster.

"Doctor dear, you're hurting me," Katrin said, trying not

to breathe.

"I'm sorry, it's the stink or the pain."

"Go, go, *hurry*!" Katrin cried as the smell got worse. She turned away, pressing her face into the cushions, trying to breathe through her ears.

"Just a few more – ugh!" Franz said, having made the mistake of talking so much that he needed to inhale. He sliced through the last ties and gently forced the hard leather cuff open until it cracked. At the window, Menders retched and tried to cover it with a cough. Katrin wiggled her arm desperately and was free.

Dara plunged in, snatched the malodorous splint from Franz's hand, and charged out of the suite with it. Franz cut Katrin's bandages as fast as he could. Menders grabbed them as he held them out and tossed them out the window.

Just then, Eiren breezed into the suite, home from teaching.

"Hello darlings! Oh my gods, what are you doing, what is that smell!" She fled into her room, and could be seen holding a fragrant sachet to her nose while she tried to open a window with one hand. Menders dashed in to help her, explaining that it was the splint that smelled and not some very overripe dead rat.

Franz bumbled up, heaved open all the other windows and stood at one, drawing in huge breaths. Katrin couldn't help giggling. Poor man, he'd had the worst of it.

Suddenly Borsen and Tomar could be heard yelling from their workroom.

"What the... get that daft dog out of here, oh my Gods, what is that thing?" Tomar's voice had the edge of horror on it that could only be produced by a tailor who was having his precious, pristine bolts of cloth near to being touched by a reeking leather splint.

"Dara, give it to me... oh no, get out of here, get out!" There was a scrabbling of claws and then a slamming door, followed by some expert swearing from Borsen and the sound of windows being thrown open.

Dara's progress through the house could be heard, as she ran back down the stairs to the ground floor, causing a diatribe from Cook.

"What the hells do you have, you silly dog? Oh! Get out! Get out! Ordstrom, that dog has something dead, help! Get away from the food!"

Dara then romped with her prize into the Men's Wing, as a cacophony of slammed doors, opened windows and much masculine shouting erupted.

"She's got something dead!"

"Get it!"

"You get it!"

"I'm not touching that!"

"Oh hells, she's gone into the Family Wing. She's in Kaymar and Ifor's suite! Get out! Dara!"

"Get a broom, poke her, she'll come out."

"She bit the bloody broomstick in half! What is that thing?"

There was a doorslam.

"They're going to love that dog being in there with whatever that is."

Kaymar could be heard next.

"What have you bastards done now and why is it our suite?" he yelled.

"It wasn't us, it's that bloody dog of Katrin's with a dead grundar!"

Kaymar must have decided to evict Dara and her grisly prize, because a door could be heard opening as Kaymar yelled;

"Dara! Come out of here! Oh my..."

"Grundar shit, he's fainted!"

"Get out of the way!"

"Kaymar Shvalz bloody fainted? The toughest bastard in

the world fainted!"

"Get him out in the air! Where's the dog? Oh gods, it's under their bed!"

Katrin ran over to the window closest to the Men's Wing, laughing, and yelled, "Get my splint back from her! I want to wrap it up and send it to Hemmett!"

There was ringing silence from the Men's Wing, and then a tentative voice, Haakel's, drifted up.

"That's your splint? Darlin', do you still have an arm left, or did it rot off?"

***

"I'm afraid in light of the splint incident, your protestations to Hemmett about your frail delicacy pale a bit," Menders said to Katrin.

"I only wish I could show him my hideous arm as evidence of me pining away," Katrin replied, looking ruefully at her shriveled limb as Eiren gently bathed it.

"It'll look normal again soon," Franz told her. "It's being closed up for weeks in that splint that did it. Imagine a foot that you kept a shoe on for six weeks."

"Ugh!" Katrin said succinctly. "I'd rather not, thank you."

"Well, it's the same thing. Once the air is on your skin for a while and you can exercise it again, it'll look normal."

Katrin flexed her fingers a little and then rotated her wrist. Her arm worked, although it looked like it should be on a corpse. She'd overheard scraps of conversation and knew that the break had been worse than had been let on to her. Franz and Menders had been very fearful that her arm would be crippled.

Menders handed her a small ball that compressed when she squeezed it.

"What is this?" Katrin asked in amazement as she relaxed her grip and the ball returned to its normal shape.

"A new type of material, from Surytam, a sort of tree resin. You can clench a fist around that," Menders explained. "It will strengthen your grip again. Start slowly though, no point in hurting yourself."

"No, slow and steady, Katrin," Franz added, gathering his things. "I'm going to go have a look at Kaymar. It isn't like him to faint."

"He can't bear bad smells," Katrin said. "They give him a kind of fit."

She could have bitten her tongue off, because the festive atmosphere of the room cooled as Menders stared at her.

"How long have you known about this?" he asked, his voice very level.

Katrin tried to whip up a feasible lie, but knew it was hopeless.

"For years. We came across a felschat in the woods when I was seven. It spat toward us and Kaymar fainted," she said meekly.

"Why didn't you tell me about it?" Menders asked. Eiren put her hand on his shoulder but he shook his head, not taking his eyes from Katrin.

Desperately wishing she was several minutes back in time and had the opportunity to keep her mouth shut, she looked at the floor.

"I'll see what Kaymar has to say," Menders said angrily, starting to rise.

"He asked me not to!" Katrin blurted. "He knew you wouldn't let him guard me any longer if you knew – and it isn't smells like a rubbish heap that make him faint, but truly terrible smells, like that splint, or a felschat! I didn't want him not to be my guard and I could tell he didn't want you to take him off duty."

Menders stood, but Doctor Franz blocked his way.

"Not until I have a look at Kaymar," Franz said sternly.

He turned and left the suite abruptly, taking his bag with him.

Eiren busied herself clearing away the washbasin and soap while Menders looked steadily at Katrin.

"He's never fainted from that day to this," Katrin said suddenly. She felt stronger as she heard her own voice, and drew herself fully upright. "Perhaps it was wrong not to tell you, but it simply – I forgot about it almost immediately. Kaymar said the chances were so small that something like that would happen again that it didn't matter…"

"Katrin, you concealed the truth from me – that you were left unguarded while Kaymar was unconscious, and that you knew about his condition," Menders sighed. "I understand why you did it and that you likely forgot it in all this time, but things simply cannot be done this way, not in this situation, not ever."

"Sort it with Kaymar," Eiren said abruptly. Katrin started. She'd never heard Eiren speak so firmly to Menders. "She was seven. She forgot – children forget at that age. If there's anyone to have this out with, it's Kaymar. I have my doubts about the necessity of that."

Katrin was shocked as Menders bowed coolly and then left the room. She looked tentatively at Eiren, who smiled, though her eyes were angry.

"It's fine darling – a tempest over nothing. No harm has been done and Kaymar will talk him round. Why don't you go and do something with Borsen, or see if Cook could use any help. And don't worry. Once in a great while I give Menders a piece of my mind. Everything will be fine."

Katrin nodded and was glad to leave.

She looked over the stair railing and saw Menders walk out the front door. She went down to the entryway without a sound and saw that Kaymar was seated on the front steps, smoking a small cigar. Menders went to him and sat beside him. He didn't say a word.

Katrin leaned on the doorjamb, watching them.

"I imagine Katrin told you about my fits," Kaymar said gruffly.

"Not meaning to, really. She was excited over the entire affair of the dog running around with the splint and it came out as part of the conversation," Menders responded, taking the cigar as Kaymar proffered it to him. He took a puff and handed it back before leaning back on one arm, blowing out a slow stream of smoke.

"Cousin – there has been almost no chance that this would happen, and I've taken steps to be sure that it wouldn't happen. I couldn't predict that felschat years ago," Kaymar said.

"It's the unpredictable that concerns me," Menders replied.

"I had to make the best decision at the time. You know I'm the best guard she's had and will have. Considering the chances that I would run up against an assassin carrying a bag of rotten bones were practically none – I made the best call I could. You wouldn't have let me continue, so I decided not to tell you. I'm sorry I had to pull her into it, but there was nothing else to be done."

Menders said nothing. Katrin knew he was going to wait Kaymar out. Kaymar would talk, since he hated long silences.

"Oh for the gods' sake, Aylam, you know I'm mad as a pitchfork and you've had me guarding her for years!" Kaymar snapped impatiently. Katrin felt a ripple of shock over his use of Menders' first name. She'd never heard it spoken before.

"She's seen me talking to myself, she's seen me cutting myself. It hasn't happened here, but there have been times in the past where I was so mad that I was not aware of my surroundings. You took that risk to let me guard her – so I took the risk I did. It's far more likely I'll go off my head and start jabbering to a tree than that I'll run into something that stinks like that fucking splint did today!" Kaymar's voice rose and quavered. Menders reached up and put an arm around his shoulders.

"We're going to let it drop," Menders said quietly. "It's all gone under the bridge long ago and you're right – we aren't exactly surrounded by vile odors here. Eiren put me in my place a few moments ago. I don't like what was done but here we are."

"You wouldn't have listened to reason when Katrin was seven," Kaymar mumbled.

"No, I wouldn't have. Come on now, no point in getting yourself into a bad spell," Menders said soothingly. "I'll have a word with Katrin – I was rather hard on her when she first let it out. We'll go on from here. I need some things taken over to Erdahn. Do you want the job? That would give you a week away and some rest. It's just an errand, nothing more."

Menders leaned back on his arm again, stretching his legs in front of him. Kaymar maintained his hunched position for a moment and then sat up straight.

"I'd be glad to be away, until the laugh over my fainting fit dies down," he answered. "I see the humor, but for me it wasn't funny. I have a crashing headache." A petulant note had come into his voice and Katrin remembered Menders saying once that Kaymar had been horribly spoiled as a child.

"Go see a show. Go to Malvar's," Menders said gently.

Kaymar nodded. He puffed on his cigar and then turned toward Menders.

"You could go yourself, you know," he said. "You can go back and forth to Erdahn in one day in the boat. Take Eiren for an evening. How long since you had dinner at Malvar's?"

Menders shook his head. "I can't even say. I'm well enough here, for now. You go, stay a week, more if you want to. By then some new gossip will have erupted and everyone will forget today."

"Thank you, Cuz. And not just for letting me get away."

"I know." Menders patted Kaymar's back and rose in one smooth motion. "Let me get upstairs and see if Eiren has stopped looking stern."

"Send Katrin out to see me, would you?" Kaymar asked, sounding calm again.

Katrin shrank into the shadows beside the big clock as Menders walked through the doors. To her chagrin, he turned right to her.

"You heard him," he said, shaking his head a little bit. Then he kissed her forehead. "It's all right, Little Princess. Go show him your arm and talk to him for a while. You're getting to an age where you can be of great help to your cousin."

With that he was on his way up the stairs. Katrin went tentatively out onto the steps. Kaymar patted a space beside him and she sat down.

"I'm sorry," she began, but he shook his head.

"It would have come out today anyway," he said, looking over at her. "We got a good run without it being an issue. Don't blame yourself, because I don't blame you." He tossed his half-finished cigar out into the stones of the drive, where it emitted a thin stream of fragrant blue smoke. Katrin saw a small, round burn on the inside of his left wrist. Before she thought, she cradled his wrist in her hands.

"Why?" she asked, looking at the burn in dismay. He must have just done it!

"Sweetheart," Kaymar began, pulling away, starting to roll his sleeve down. Katrin shook her head, got up and went to the kitchen, gathering several towels and wetting them thoroughly. She returned and took Kaymar's wrist on her knee, holding the wet cloth over the burned spot, cooling it.

"Why?" she asked again, looking into his eyes.

Kaymar's forehead puckered in frustration. He shook his head abruptly.

"How can I explain madness to you?" he asked. "I – I hear voices in my head, Katrin. Not all the time, but at times of stress I do. They tell me things. They jabber away until my thoughts are so scattered and broken that there's no rest for me. I can't sleep. I start talking back to them. They torment me until I have no peace. I have compulsions to do things that I shouldn't, to be violent.

"I found long ago that hurting myself stops it all for a while. It's as if you're surrounded by noise that you can't ignore, that's shattering your eardrums – and it suddenly stops. It's peaceful. I don't know why it is, but cutting myself or burning myself actually helps me. Oh child, this is nothing for you to know about!" Kaymar looked away so abruptly that Katrin expected to hear the bones in his neck crackle.

"I'm fifteen, I'm not a child," Katrin replied, changing the cold compress on Kaymar's wrist. "I saw you cut yourself years ago – you just told Menders so."

"Eavesdropper," Kaymar chided.

"You both knew I was there," Katrin countered.

"Yes. As you were saying?"

"I'm old enough to understand. I'm old enough to help you if you need help. I go with Doctor Franz to see some of his patients who aren't well in their minds, but it's because they're old. I've wondered how you control your madness. I've seen the scars all over you – years ago, remember?"

"I remember."

"Were those to – control it?"

Kaymar sighed. "Yes. And to punish myself for things I felt very guilty about. That I won't tell you about, my dear. Not only are you too young to know about it, but it's my business alone and something I don't wish to relive. It may seem horrible to you, but it's a comfort to me to know that I have the power to control my madness. It's better than being lost to it and wandering around with the voices and compulsions clouding my mind. Any pain is better than that, Katrin."

Katrin nodded, shifting the compress as it warmed from Kaymar's body heat. Now she could see other old, round burns, scarred badly, over the crosshatched marks that must be from years of him cutting himself.

Suddenly she understood Kaymar's struggle. She had always simply accepted him as being different, but had never comprehended the toll such a difference took.

"Ah well, we got past Menders, didn't we?" Kaymar asked, his voice flippant and a lot more familiar than the strained tones he'd been speaking in. Katrin looked at him, startled.

"Oh yes, I get back to myself very quickly," he said, gently setting aside the wet cloth, blowing on his wrist to dry it and then rolling his sleeve down and buttoning the cuff. "I'll be good for a while now – and I'm off for a little holiday as well. I'll be back in a week or so, more than ready to work again. Don't you fret about any of this, now. Get on with life."

He rose and extended his hand for her to take. When she was on her feet, he inspected her withered right arm.

"It'll sort out in no time," he smiled. "Until then, take a tip from me – long sleeves."

***

"I have a letter for you," Kaymar said, peering around the door of Katrin's soapmaking shed with a particularly wicked expression on his face, obviously just back from Erdahn. He handed her an envelope, then produced a cromar and began to play a plaintive tune.

Katrin remembered her directive to Hemmett demanding that a minstrel play while she read any further letters from him. She laughed, wiped her forehead, and broke the seal on the letter.

Oh Most Fair Offended Princess,

Words cannot describe my agony upon learning that my endeavor to cheer you with the description of my chagrin at being partnered for a watered down holta with Ufronia The Dancing Cow has offended you and caused you to fall into fits of insensibility.

I have been lectured regarding the discomforts of the unconscious state by your noble cousin, Baronet Shvalz, who described to me his extreme discomfiture and subsequent fainting spell, upon being confronted with the odor wafting from an item previously worn upon your person. I am downcast, stricken and woebegone to think that I might have caused you one moment of any sentiment other than the most radiant joy.

Therefore, I debase myself before your delicate feet, a willing sacrifice to be put to whatever use you care to name. Punish me to the utmost of your abilities, my noble Princess, and I shall smile with happiness, knowing that my wretched faults are being expunged.

I grovel before you, a wretch worthy only of being pelted with dung. Have mercy upon me, fair Princess. Mercy!

Your vile worm,

Bumpy

Katrin staggered about, gasping with laughter over some of the choicer phrases and the sly dig at her feet, which were far from delicate. She was suddenly confronted by Hemmett leaning over the edge of the soapmaking shed roof, upside down. He grinned, saying, "oodle, oodle, oodle!" in a squeaky voice.

Kaymar finished his serenade, grinned and walked away, cromar over his shoulder.

"What are you doing here?" Katrin asked in astonishment. Hemmett cackled with satisfaction over the sensation he'd made, and somersaulted off the roof.

"You are observing, Madame, the cadet who had the highest exam score for the end of the year. My reward was release from school a week early, no doubt to avoid my assassination by jealous classmates. How about that, oh offended Princess, for the boy who reads slowly and painfully?"

"It's wonderful!" She threw her arms around his neck and

hugged hard.

"I'll say. I worked like fury, but I did it. Even the Commandant was amazed. And I say it's a great thing, because I get another week of summer up here in the cool while the rest of the fellows are slaving away in the heat. What soap are you making?"

"Something new, mint and lemon."

"Smells good enough to eat. So how are things? Let me see your poor arm."

Katrin held out the offending limb. It was still a pale shadow of itself, though it looked much better than the wizened mess of two weeks before.

"Poor thing," Hemmett said quietly.

"Oh, it's over. It's a half inch shorter than my other arm now and my elbow stays slightly bent but at least everything works," Katrin said staunchly. In reality, she was still shaken about the arm. The idea that some part of her wasn't what it used to be had a permanence that left her rattled and uneasy.

"Rotten when you bust something and it'll never be the same, isn't it?" Hemmett said. Katrin started. It was as if he'd read her mind.

"How did you know?" she asked.

"I never told anyone because I didn't want to worry Mama and Papa, but the very first month I was at military school, I busted a toe. Not just a little bit either, really busted it, the bone sticking out, blood all over the place. It was so bad they thought I wasn't ever going to be able to march and that would be the end of military school. It didn't heal worth a damn, so I had them take it off altogether."

Katrin muffled a scream of horror with her hands, staring at him. "No!"

"Sure did. It hurt less than having the damn thing there, all black and horrible and aching at night until I thought I would go mad. The doctor said it was a matter of time before it started to die and I said 'why wait?' Get it all over with, clean and done. So they gave me so much ramplane I would have cut my own leg off with a spoon on a dare and they nipped the thing right off. That toe was so bad it hardly bled, and it didn't hurt a whole lot after. Healed right up, and now it's like it never happened, except I can't count to twenty anymore."

Katrin laughed, though shivers of horror were running down her spine.

"Hells, Willow, it's better to have it all over with than go limping along with something gone bad and rotting," Hemmett grinned. "One short sharp pain, a good yell, and it's finished."

"Didn't Menders know?"

"I'm pretty sure that Sir told him," Hemmett said. "I asked him not to, but then I'm not of age. He has to tell Menders some things, doesn't have a choice. But he'd have let Menders know that I didn't want it getting back to Papa and Mama. They're getting old, they don't need extra worry, and it would have upset them even though it really wasn't that important."

"Having a toe cut off sounds important to me!"

"No, slowly dying from infection from not having the guts to have a rotten toe cut off is important," Hemmett answered. "And besides, it leaves a perfect gap that I can use to grip the end of a Hetzophian tangmare, which I sometimes play at night to annoy the lads."

Katrin had once heard someone play the very long, thin reed flute from the far away desert lands of Hetzophia. It had sounded like someone trying to strangle a goose. How typical of Hemmett to turn something like an amputated toe into a joke.

"You seem to have adjusted to it," Katrin smiled.

"The only thing that bothered me was that I wasn't perfect any more. Not that I'm saying I'm perfect, but my body wasn't ever going to be the same. Like your little arm here." He lifted it again and looked at it, shaking his head.

"Little it's not," Katrin laughed.

"To me, everyone is little, except for Tharak Karak," Hemmett said, releasing her arm and offering her his own to take. "Speaking of little, where's Borsen? I've missed him."

"He's grown a lot, but he's still small," Katrin laughed. "He's up in the workroom, toiling over a jacket for Menders. It's his own design and he's made the pattern for it himself."

"He's a smart fellow. Come on, let's get inside, you're the first person I came to see. I don't want Mama and Papa hurt and thinking I don't love them." Hemmett squired her away to the house, eager to begin his summer break.

***

Katrin had never been alone. Of course she'd been alone in rooms in the house, where it was safe, but even outside there was always someone within calling distance. The further she went from the house, the closer that person stayed to her. This summer, which had been warmer than usual, she had taken to waking up during the very short night and had gone into the garden alone several times – or so she had thought.

One night, after walking around the garden and spending some time sitting beneath the Assassin's Tree, she'd been startled to find Menders waiting quietly on the terrace in his dressing gown when she went back to the house.

"Good evening, Little Princess," he said with a smile.

"Did I wake you?" she asked.

"No, I was awake. I came out to be sure you were all right."

Katrin looked at him in amazement. "I was careful to be quiet. How did you know I was out here?"

Menders sat back in his wicker chair, smiled and folded his arms across his chest. "Oh, this old house and me... you know, we've been here for quite a while now. It's in my bones. I just sense when things are different - like the big clock in the entryway. I can tell you it's running about four minutes slow, just from the sound of it. I'll need to reset it."

Katrin strained her ears to hear the deep steady rhythm of the clock through the open windows. It was such a common background sound that she was usually unaware of it.

"I just wanted to walk around," she explained.

"And to be alone. I truly understand," Menders replied, his eyes kind as he drew her down to sit beside him. "But Katrin…"

"I know. It's not safe," she sighed.

"I'm sorry, but no, it isn't."

"But then if it's not safe here, then where is it safe? And when will it ever be?" Katrin blurted, the words tumbling from her, more confused than angry. "We have fences, trip alarms, foot patrols, mounted patrols, night watches, tower guards, body guards, dozens of heavily armed men! We're miles and miles out in the middle of nowhere!"

"I know. I know," Menders soothed. "I tell myself that it's all too much and I'm being over protective, while at the same time I agonize that it's not enough. But if there was even one small slip, if anything happened to you, Katrin, I don't know that I could bear it. So please, humor an old man."

Katrin looked at him and smiled. He was not old and she could never think of him as such. She also knew, beneath her frustration, that he was right.

"I won't do it again," she sighed. "I just liked being out here, in the quiet, smelling all the trees blooming."

"I'll tell you what," Menders said after a moment. "I happen to like midnight prowls too and I'm usually up late. I know it wouldn't be the same as being completely alone, but if you let me know when you want to dander around the garden in the middle of the night, I'll just sit here and you can wander."

"If you were up, I'd want you to come with me," Katrin smiled and Menders laughed a little.

"Well, you were my shadow when you were a little thing, so now I'll be yours," he teased. "Now, are you ready to go in or do I have time to smoke a cigar?"

"I'm not sleepy, but a cigar, Menders?"

"I have one a couple of times a year, and the occasional puff on one of the Men's cigars. It won't kill me to indulge myself," he answered. "Vices in extreme moderation, my dear, will do very little harm." He took the cigar from the pocket of his dressing gown and lit it.

"What is that like?" Katrin asked, watching as he puffed the cigar.

"You won't like it, but here," he said, handing it to her. "Don't draw it down into your lungs, just in your mouth so you taste the smoke."

She put it to her lips and knew instantly that he was right, even without drawing on it – she didn't like it. She handed it back to him, shaking her head. He laughed a little and put it in his mouth again. She sat with him until he finished it, happy to be with him and to be out on a beautiful night. It wasn't being alone, but it was the next best thing.

CHAPTER 45
ḶEPTHAM

"Now here's some news," Ifor said as he decoded a message from Bartan. "It seems that Princess Aidelia has been a bit more stable, lately."

"And the Queen?" Menders asked, leaning against the doorjamb of Ifor's office.

"Still drunk as a sailor on shore leave most of the time. Barty says at this point she's not a player at Court. Keeps to herself. Aidelia has a satellite Court around her, a strange assortment of oddbodys, but no-one who seems to be a real threat. As far as the Court is concerned, Katrin has disappeared. Many of them don't seem to know of her existence."

"That's the way I want it," Menders said with satisfaction. "The less people know of her, the better. Tell Bartan I still want a written report on the crowd around Aidelia. They may be harmless but a mob like that... anyone could slip in there."

"Right you are," Ifor replied, writing rapidly. "I don't think you'll ever make Katrin disappear entirely, but with things as quiet down there as they have been of late, we might manage some peace and quiet for ourselves."

Ifor handed the incoming message to his assistant, Olan, who filed it immediately, before it became lost in the welter of paper that was Ifor's desk.

"I'll get this reply off to Bartan tonight," Ifor continued, scribbling away.

"Excellent. Can I interest either of you in a journey to the Eastern Ocean?" Menders asked. He'd been thinking that Katrin needed to get out more. With the pleasant weather and the quiet political scene, he'd decided a small vacation might be in order.

Olan shook his head. "I'll stay here if I may, help Papa with some of the summer work," he said.

"Fair enough. Ifor?"

"I'm game. I'm sure Kip will be too."

"Get the Men together and we'll draw up our travel plans," Menders replied, trying not to smirk over Ifor's casual use of his nickname for Kaymar. Menders was leaving nothing to chance. Groups of the Men would travel with and ahead of Katrin's party, for her safety.

"I'll set a meeting for tonight, while everyone is on site." Ifor started making a list.

"I'll leave you to it," Menders said. He went up the stairs two at a time to tell Eiren.

From Menders' Journal:

It's trite to marvel about how quickly time passes, but I do marvel when I think of the children and how they have grown and matured.

Hemmett is the most seasoned and worldly of the three, thanks to his years away at the Military Academy. Despite his buffoonery and jovial nature, he is actually quite serious and levelheaded. He already shows the qualities that will make him a fine and decent man and a first class officer.

In the future, should Hemmett no longer wish to serve as the Commander of Katrin's Guard, his path through the higher ranks of the military establishment is assured. His success is certain, no matter what path he chooses. He makes me proud, always.

I can confide here that Borsen is the dearest to my heart. He is my son, my Little Man, the child I was supposed to have who has found me despite myself. He has blossomed and grown, not only in physical stature, but in confidence and self assurance. What he lacks in physical size he makes up in spirit and determination.

He approaches new ideas with enthusiasm and careful forethought. I see in him a reflection of myself, as if somehow I can erase some of the stains of my own past and give the world a child raised with the love, guidance and care that was denied me.

Borsen continues to speak of going into business, not in a small enterprise, but with grand plans. I feel he will have the competence and confidence to accomplish all he desires.

And then Katrin, the golden-haired Princess, the first child I chose to love as my own and who will always be a part of me. Her future concerns me most. She is bright and outgoing and she is no longer the baby and child who was easily distracted with childish things. She is a young lady about to reach full maturity. What direction her life will take is a quandary that looms large these days – for both of us.

A cloistered upbringing at the Shadows seemed the best way to keep Katrin safe from enemies of the royal line and the terrible political machinations that are commonplace in Mordania. This has served us well up to the present, but I know she is becoming restless with her confinement, as is appropriate at her age. The planned holiday to Leptham will help ease such restiveness, at least for a while.

Unlike her foster brothers, Katrin sees no clear purpose or direction for herself and although she has taken on the duties of The Shadows' housekeeper with admirable skill, has learned a great deal about the management of the estate and also shows her own enterprise in such projects as soap, candle and perfume making, I fear these interests will not entirely occupy her active mind for much longer.

She has shown no interest in becoming Queen and I have every intention of encouraging this attitude. Considering the disastrous effect being Queen has had on her mother and Katrin's own personality, I believe it would be the worst thing that could happen to her. As restricted as her freedom is now, becoming Queen would make her a virtual prisoner, if the traditional ways were followed. She would suffer terribly in such a situation. It must be avoided at all costs.

There is time to formulate whatever plans we may require in the future, but for now, in the quiet dark hours of the morning I think of Katrin, my most loved and precious daughter. Whatever am I to do with you?

***

Strolling along the beach, hands in pockets, feeling the sea spray and the crunch of fine sand beneath his shoes, Menders reflected that he couldn't remember a time when he'd felt this relaxed.

Leptham was a town on the Eastern Ocean. It was small, unspoiled and slow paced, unlike the more fashionable resort towns, or the larger industrial towns further south where ocean freighters and liners left for Hetzophia and Surytam.

The three youngsters loved the place. There was much for them to do. Hemmett lived in his swimming costume when he wasn't rostered for guard duty. Borsen followed his lead and was growing strong and hearty from hours of swimming and playing in the water. Katrin was more careful of her complexion, as she burned easily. She still spent plenty of time in the warm water of the ocean, when she wasn't gathering piles of shells or refereeing whatever contest Hemmett dreamed up, be it a swimming race or water fight. She loved to throw sticks into the water for Dara and the other boarhounds to fetch and wondered why other hotel guests gave the enormous wet dogs a wide berth.

Looking up the beach, Menders saw Borsen seated by Kaymar on the sand, with Ifor fishing not far away.

A few months before, Kaymar had spoken to Menders about Borsen, concerned that the boy could become a target for pederasts, given his loving nature and craving for affection.

"He's going to be beautiful soon, Menders, and then he'll be in real danger if he isn't given some direction and information," Kaymar explained intensely.

Menders had cocked an eyebrow. Borsen was winsome and a far cry from the skeletal child he'd been, but he'd yet to grow into his teeth, his ears stuck out, and he looked years younger than his age. "Beautiful?" he said doubtfully.

"Let's agree that I notice things that wouldn't occur to you," Kaymar responded sarcastically. "He's going to need to know the facts of life from the point of view of a nancyboy - that includes protecting himself from pederasts. You aren't going to be able to provide that. You don't want him coming to harm. Neither do I. Let me have a talk with him."

Menders had agreed readily, relieved. He'd considered the subject at times and had been at a loss as to how to open such a conversation with his nephew. His own miserable experience made such things distasteful to him, no matter how he tried to overcome it. He didn't want Borsen to sense his distaste. The boy was sensitive to the point of being psychic and would be heartbroken if he suspected his uncle's discomfort.

Borsen was listening intently and nodding appreciatively while the two of them worked on a sand castle. As Menders watched, Kaymar laughed suddenly and ruffled the boy's hair. All was going well.

Katrin and Hemmett were on the hotel lawn, playing a game of wicketball with two small children who were in residence with their widowed mother. Such games involving Hemmett were always anarchic, with various declarations of "new" rules and wild interpretations of established ones. With these two children he was careful and gentle, frequently declaring that people who didn't reach his waist got extra turns. Katrin laughed at his antics and helped the little ones with their mallets.

Katrin had attracted considerable male attention during their stay, particularly during the dinner dances at the hotel. Where many young girls her age would have flirted and been incredibly flattered, she remained cool and reserved. She danced only with the men in their party. When one young man continued to ask her to dance after she had declined politely, she had whispered to Menders that she needed him to snarl at her would-be suitor.

"You may dance with him if you wish," he'd told her.

"I don't wish. I don't feel comfortable. I'd rather dance with people I know," she answered.

"Then I shall remind the young gentleman that it is considered impolite to continue pressing his suit once a lady has courteously refused." Menders spoke quietly to the young man and sent him on his way.

After all, she's only just fifteen, although she looks older, he thought. Plenty of time for her to be interested in young men later. At least she knew what she wanted and didn't feel pressured to endure unwanted attention. When Hemmett was her escort there was no difficulty with would-be suitors. Surprisingly, Borsen had proven to be an even more effective deterrent, because when he was escorting Katrin, he suddenly exuded a sinister quality that otherwise did not exist in his makeup. He was not about to brook any nonsense from unwanted, over-attentive young men.

Eiren walked out onto the long verandah that ran the length of the hotel and Menders waved from the beach to attract her attention. She saw him, laughed, opened her sunshade and came to meet him.

"I woke up and you were gone," she chuckled as he kissed her and then laced his arm around her waist.

"I was restless and didn't want to wake you, but I did leave you a present," Menders smiled. She nodded and touched the new brooch on her dress, fashioned in the shape of a little bird.

"And so you've been beachcombing?" she asked as they turned back to the sea and stood there together.

"A bit. Watching the young people."

"Menders' brood," Eiren said teasingly.

"Yours too. I'm not too humble to say that they're a credit to us."

"Hemmett in particular. Gods, when I remember how he was when you came here, how wild and unkempt. Imagine what he could have grown into!"

"He was a terror only because he needed more discipline than he was being given. As soon as he was given some guidelines, he was fine. A handful, but fine."

"He's a handsome young man," Eiren said. "He's excited

more than a little attention from the young ladies and his response to them makes me wonder if he's losing his attraction to Katrin."

"That's an odd thing, because I happen to know that he had a couple of love affairs in Erdahn during the school year - nothing very serious, but definitely of a mature bent," Menders said. "The devotion to Katrin is continual, but it's friendly in nature. He only falls in love with her when he's around her, which makes me fairly confident that he's mistaking friendship and brotherly devotion for romance."

"Well, he has one more year left at the Academy. Maybe he'll find a young lady to bring home to The Shadows," Eiren said.

"I doubt it. Hemmett strikes me as the sort of man who marries late, like his father did. There's still a wildness and rawness in him. If the situation with Katrin becomes a problem, I will speak to him, because there is no romantic interest on her part and never will be. For now, I'm not going to fret."

"Good," Eiren said with feeling.

"As usual, we are of the same mind", Menders smiled, stealing a kiss. "No more chatter about children and raising children for now, love, except this. What do you think of making an extended journey abroad with this lot in a couple of years? Do you think that you'd like to see Surelia and Samorsa and... my goodness, Madame, you seem to be accosting me! Such impropriety, Madame! Shall I take such attentions to mean you agree with this proposition?"

***

"That's terrible!" Katrin said from the sofa, where she'd been playing a game of DeGratz with Borsen. "The children are so thin. Mistress Firenz tries hard, but little Masha told me that they have fish head soup a lot of the time. To think that their father died in the service and all Mistress Firenz gets is enough money to live in one room and eat fish heads."

"It's even worse for widows of enlisted men," Borsen told her heatedly. "There's no pension for them at all, Cuz. I met a lot of them when I was moving around with my family."

Menders waited, curious to see where this conversation led. The little family befriended by Katrin, Borsen and Hemmett had turned out to be in desperate straits. The mother, Mistress Firenz, had collapsed from poor nutrition and exhaustion two months previous. She and her children were at the hotel through the kindness of her sister, who had been appalled when she learned of the little family's situation. Katrin had overheard a conversation between the sister and Eiren and had immediately told Hemmett and Borsen about the plight of their new friends.

"What?" Katrin's voice rose in outrage.

"That's right," Borsen said. "Poor women whose husbands were enlisted soldiers don't get a thing if their man gets killed in a war. The women end up marrying the first man they can, or trying to make a living as charwomen or doing plain sewing or being prostitutes."

"Why does this happen, Menders?" Katrin asked, turning her horrified gaze in his direction.

"It's one of many injustices in Mordania," he answered quietly. "It's a terrible shame for this nation."

"If I were Queen, I wouldn't allow it!" Katrin cried furiously. Then she added, "Is that something a Queen can change?"

"Yes," Menders answered soberly.

"That would be a good thing," Borsen said. "Far too many people struggle in this country, considering all the money spent on having wars."

Though the topic was serious and in some ways painful, because Menders knew Katrin didn't want to become Queen and wasn't particularly happy about how being a Princess limited her opportunities, he had to smile. Borsen had a businesslike, practical bent that would serve him well when he had his own establishment. The boy seethed at wastefulness and injustice.

"Maybe you will be Queen someday and then you can change things," Borsen said in the silence.

Katrin shuddered involuntarily.

"I hope that never happens, but if I was Queen, I would see to it that soldiers' widows didn't live on fish heads," she finally said. "I'd see that nobody in this country had to live on fish heads. Why, Kaymar said he'd rather die than eat a fish head!"

"Why wouldn't you want to be Queen?" Borsen asked. "If I were King, I'd have some good times, I can tell you, and make up for years of being poor!"

"I just don't want to be Queen, that's all," Katrin said, her face clouding. Borsen looked over at Menders and Eiren in confusion. Eiren silently put a finger to her lips.

"Well, maybe if Kaymar ever got hungry enough he would eat a fish head," Borsen said, making such an ungraceful change of topic that Katrin laughed aloud.

"Being Queen isn't what you think it is," she said to Borsen, "and the Queen isn't what you'd ever think a Queen should be. Queens are people, like everyone else. There are good ones and bad ones. My mother is not a good Queen at all."

"You can get your head lopped off for that, Katrin," Borsen said, his eyes huge. "And besides, you don't have to be your mother. You could be yourself."

"Then we won't talk about it, so we don't get our heads lopped." Katrin turned back to the DeGratz game. Borsen, looking like a man who had narrowly avoided disaster, concentrated on his rapidly diminishing army of red game pieces with all the intensity of a great military commander.

Menders and Eiren managed a quiet and controlled exit of the suite and then staggered around the hallway, laughing silently at Borsen's warning.

"As if a spy was under the sofa," Menders gasped, then perfectly imitated Borsen's shocked tone "You can get your head lopped off for that, Katrin! Poor Little Man! I'll have to have a word with him about the real situation in the Royal Family, so that he doesn't torment Katrin about the wonders of becoming Queen."

"Careful that you don't say anything that could lead to head lopping. I'm very fond of your head," Eiren giggled.

***

Katrin went looking for Menders. It was early morning. Eiren was sound asleep but Menders wasn't in their suite. It was too early for breakfast, so he was prowling. Since he really couldn't prowl around a hotel, it was likely he was on the beach.

Everyone else seemed to be sleeping in after a party given for a newlywed couple who had included every guest at the hotel. There had been a big cake and dancing, with lots of wine for everyone. She'd tried a glass herself but didn't think much of it. Hemmett took more than one glass and got very happy indeed, but then he was allowed wine at the Military Academy and was more used to it. Menders had seen the face she made when she tried hers and made a point of whispering her that there was no law that said she had to drink it. So she'd left it, drank water along with Borsen and had a fine time.

Katrin dressed, taking care with her appearance and picking up her new sunshade, which matched her pink outfit. She went on the verandah, looking up and down the beach for Menders.

He was there, some distance from the hotel, standing looking out at the ocean with his hat in hand. He loved the ocean as much as she did and had been so relaxed and happy during this trip that he seemed much younger, as she remembered him from when she was very small – a laughing young man who would toss her in the air and who carried her everywhere on his hip. She knew that he liked walking out alone like this when he woke up very early, but he also never minded her finding him and going along. Katrin made her way down the steps and across the sand until he turned toward her and smiled.

"I'm glad to see you, Little Princess," he said, putting an arm around her shoulders. "You're up early this morning."

"I wanted to talk to you," Katrin said, falling into step with him as they walked away from the hotel.

"I'm listening," he said invitingly.

"I was thinking about what Borsen said – that if I ever became Queen, I could change things. Is that true?"

Menders looked at her.

"You know that Mordania is an absolute monarchy, so if you became Queen, you would, in theory, wield absolute power."

"In theory? I don't understand."

"It isn't a matter of simply saying 'do my will', because there is no way one person can run a modern country. There is a Council, as you know, various ministers, the military and other government bodies. But in theory, yes, a Queen could demand that these people do as she says and change things."

"Do you think there would be enough money to be sure that anyone who served as a soldier, or their widow, would have a pension?"

Menders raised his eyebrows.

"It's very likely that there is. The country is not run efficiently, Katrin. The Council tends to be corrupt and the Queen doesn't take an active role in running the country. A great deal of money is needed to wage war and we've been at war in one way or another for almost two hundred years. It's become a sort of national pastime with us. As you'll remember from your lessons, Mordania had to fight off the oppressive rule of the old Surelian Empire. We had to fight, first for our independence and then to protect our resources and territories. But now it seems we no longer know how to stop fighting. If the wars could be ended, there would be a great deal of excess money. It could then be used to improve things in Mordania."

Katrin thought about that. She knew how a budget worked because she ran the housekeeping at The Shadows. Some sort of balance was necessary for everything to run properly. You couldn't spend all the money on food or cloth or tools. It had to be spread around. It made sense that spending all of a country's resources on war would lead to other shortages.

"What is the situation now with the Queen – and Aidelia?" Katrin asked. "I know you keep track of it."

Menders drew her over to an enormous log that had washed up on the beach and was bleached white by the sun and water. He sat on it and patted the space beside him. She perched there and leaned against him while he put an arm around her waist.

"Your mother still drinks continuously," he said quietly. "She doesn't take an interest in national affairs, so the Council does as it pleases. Unfortunately, that means they feather their nests. Most of them are in some way connected to companies that make weapons and other things used by the military during wars."

"So it's to their advantage to have war!" Katrin cried.

"Yes. That's the ugly truth behind much of the war that Mordania engages in. Someone gets rich from it."

Katrin fumed but said nothing. Menders wouldn't have told her this if he didn't feel that she was old enough to understand it. She waited for him to finish answering her question.

"As for Aidelia, she has appeared to be more stable as she's grown older, though she's far from normal," Menders continued. "She's now eighteen and has a Court following of her own. It's obvious that she very much wants to become Queen, but she's no more fit for the role than the present Queen is."

"Gods, Menders, what will happen when she does become Queen?"

"Best not to think about it, my dear." Menders hugged

her close. "The women in your family are long lived. Despite your mother's drinking, she is a healthy woman. She should live a very long time, as her mother did. Even though she is ineffectual, an ineffectual Queen is far better than a mad one. Unless something very unusual occurs, your mother will be Queen for many years."

Katrin sat there silently, remembering that terrifying vision of her sister Adelia drooling and clawing at her in the dark corridor at the Palace. Even thinking of that creature being Queen and having the power to run the entire country was terrifying.

But if I were Queen, she thought, I would have the power to change things. I could stop the endless wars and improve the way the country runs. I would have to be unselfish and think about the country before myself, but I could do it. If only I wouldn't have to live in that terrible Palace and wear that horrible dress – and those teeth.

"Why does the Queen wear those false teeth? They are false, aren't they?" Katrin asked.

"They're false, yes – it's a rather ridiculous tradition that goes back to a time when the Queen was the strongest woman in a tribe. To appear fierce, they filed their teeth into points."

"Gods!"

"Yes, it's a wretched notion, isn't it?" Menders said. "The dress has a dual purpose. It shows the wealth of Mordania with all the gems and precious metals used in it, but it functions as armor should the Queen be attacked."

"It seems stupid to me. Couldn't someone be Queen without all that nonsense?"

Menders sighed.

"Traditions die hard, Little Princess," he said. "People cling to them. Mordania has always had a Queen with a fearsome appearance, and the appearance is the same from Queen to Queen. They also all use the same name, Morghenna. The rumor is that the Queen of Mordania is somehow of great age, perhaps even immortal. This was originally intended to frighten other nations so they wouldn't dare attack. It might be possible to change those traditions, but it would have to be done carefully so that people would accept the change."

Katrin was very quiet. She'd always understood that should things happen in a certain way, she would become Queen, but she'd never really thought it could happen. The Queen and the Court all seemed so far away.

"Katrin, it would be best if you didn't spend a great deal of your time worrying about this. I know it's something that you will need to think about, but as I told you, your mother is likely to live a very long time. There is no point in agonizing over it."

"If I did become Queen – do I have to do it?" Katrin asked.

"No. A Queen can abdicate and hand the crown on to the next person in line to the Throne," Menders answered.

Katrin sighed in relief and said, "Good."

Menders got up and stood before her.

"My Little Princess, if it ever came to it, that is what I would want you to do," he said, very seriously. "Like any parent, I want you to be happy, to marry for love, to lead a life that you can control and do with what you wish. Since you now know you don't have to accept being Queen, put the idea away from you and don't darken your days fretting about what may never be."

He put out a hand to help her up, and they walked back toward the hotel. Menders made a point of not talking about the Royal Family. Instead, they talked about Madame Firenz and how she and her children were going to be moved to her sister's home on an estate in Southern Mordania. But in the privacy of Katrin's mind, a thought kept surfacing – if you were the Queen, you would have the power to change Mordania. You could make it better.

***

Katrin and Kaymar strolled along one of the side streets of Leptham, whiling away a sleepy afternoon. When Katrin had proposed a shopping trip after breakfast, she'd seen Eiren preparing to rise from the chair where she'd been peacefully looking over several books of poetry she and Menders had bought, ever so slightly reluctant.

"No, don't get up," Katrin had said immediately, leaning over to put her hands playfully on Eiren's shoulders. "I don't have to go right now." She could see that Eiren was relieved, but sighed inwardly herself. She really wanted to go out and she couldn't go alone. Hemmett was off duty and had gone off with Borsen somewhere. Menders had fallen asleep and she couldn't bear to wake him. It wasn't often that he would rest during the day.

Kaymar looked up from the sofa where he'd been buried in a book for the last hour.

"I'm restless myself, Cuz," he said. "Why not let me take you out? Since the Irrepressibles won't be along, we can take a look at the perfume shop that Hemmett keeps refusing to go into."

Katrin smiled and looked over at Eiren, who nodded permission. Second to Menders, Kaymar was the most secure bodyguard she could have. When they went out together, they usually posed as brother and sister because of their similar coloring. Katrin was aware that that many people found Kaymar's mien sinister and frightening. She didn't mind, because it kept men at a distance. She'd become very aware that men looked at her during this holiday.

She went to her bedroom to freshen up, putting on her new hat. Kaymar liked her to look her best when she was out with him and she certainly appreciated the chance to step out in her finery.

When she returned to the lounge, Kaymar was already there, having changed into a white suit and straw hat.

"We'll probably stop for some lunch as well, so don't worry if it gets into the afternoon," he was saying to Eiren.

They had a wonderfully fragrant hour at the perfume shop he'd mentioned. The lady who owned it was most interested when Katrin told her that she made soap and scented oils at home and waxed verbose about different combinations of scents. She mixed up a fragrance just for Katrin that smelled like new mown hay and summer flowers, then concocted a wildly exotic scent for Kaymar, using Samorsan spices and wood fragrances.

"Now, my stomach is pounding out hunger signals like Menders' does, so shall we find somewhere to belly up to the trough?" Kaymar asked, pocketing their wrapped purchases as they left the shop.

"What an elegant invitation!" Katrin laughed, taking his arm.

He squired her to a Samorsan restaurant, where an exotic dark man bowed and showed them to a table. He said something to Kaymar in an undertone that made him laugh as he removed his hat and handed it over to be put away.

"What did he say?" Katrin asked.

"He just complimented me on my lovely bride," Kaymar grinned wickedly, winking as he picked up a menu. Katrin laughed into her gloved hand.

After some discussion and Kaymar warning her about the more incendiary dishes, they ordered.

They chatted idly for a while, watching the street scene outside through the window. Their food arrived and Katrin found that Kaymar hadn't been exaggerating. Some of the dishes were explosively hot, but it faded quickly.

"I've been considering asking Menders if there is any way that I could go somewhere by myself," Katrin said. "Just to a shop or on the beach."

Kaymar looked at her for a moment and then reached out for her hand.

"As Menders' friend, I'm going to ask that you don't do that," he said frankly. "You don't realize it but that would hurt him a great deal, because he simply will not be able to make it possible for you."

He saw the disappointment in her face.

"Katrin," he continued, "I'm Menders' second in command. That means I'm privy to everything Menders thinks or plans. He has tried desperately to find a way that you could do something on your own and it simply cannot be done where your safety would be always assured. He wants you to have as normal a life as possible and a fifteen year old girl should be able to do things on her own, but…"

"I know, I know. I'm the Princess," Katrin interrupted wearily.

"I'm sorry. This is one reason why, when you were little, I didn't play with you much so that you could have the feeling that you were doing things on your own and not constantly being shadowed. Haakel used to play with you a great deal. It helped him cope with losing his wife and children, but I never wanted to intrude on you."

"You… you can't imagine what it's like not to be able to say, 'I'm going to walk down half a block to the bookseller' and not have people forced to interrupt what they're doing to go along with you, even if they don't want to. Like Eiren today," Katrin sighed. "I knew she didn't want to go out, but she was going to anyway. I hate the idea that people are always pressured into servitude because of what I am."

"Although I've been with you many years now, I truly cannot imagine what it feels like," Kaymar replied. "And I saw how you reacted when you saw that Eiren didn't feel up to going out and I was proud of that. I know that you got the short end of the stick being the Princess. But remember, those closest to you are most interested in your safety out of love, not just a sense of duty."

"I know that and didn't mean to sound ungrateful, but... I'd give a lot not to be the Princess, even for just a little while," Katrin sighed, taking comfort in a dish concocted from chicken and onions that was dizzying to the taste buds.

"I'd give a lot to be six feet tall," Kaymar answered.

"Really?" Katrin was surprised.

"Of course. It's simply inconvenient being a small man. All your clothes have to be custom made, shoes too. Things are too high for you to reach." He shrugged. "I think everyone has something they would like to change about themselves. In your case, it's your station. I'd like to be taller. I'm sure Menders would give a lot to have normal eyes. Borsen would like to have a chance to grow more than five feet tall. But life goes on and is quite pleasant indeed."

He looked wicked, eating a dish that was so hot that Katrin had tasted it once and set it aside after a coughing fit brought tears to her eyes and made the waiter come running with a glass of water.

"I won't say anything to Menders then," Katrin said. "If it isn't possible, it isn't possible."

Kaymar looked pensive for a moment, then looked directly into her eyes.

"Katrin, you're old enough to know this now and Menders has given me permission to tell you. There have been plots against your life in the past," he said softly. "Now, don't get too concerned about it, because there is no particular threat at the moment. However, when you were small, things had to be extremely secure because there was always something afoot. Menders and I have seen to it that those threats have been eliminated, but we still have to be vigilant."

Katrin nodded and began to speak, but Kaymar held up a finger and continued speaking.

"We know about plots beforehand because Menders' Men is part of an enormous information network. What we can't predict is the lone madman. When you were just a little girl, a man jumped out of the bushes at The Shadows and attacked me with a knife. I ended up killing him."

Katrin stared at him. She'd never known about this!

"We never did find out what his story was," Kaymar continued. "It was as if he came out of nowhere and had no connections to anything. We don't know if he was after you, or me, or was simply mad."

"Why would he have been after you?" Katrin asked, crunching on a cracker provided with the chicken dish.

"He was wearing an Ephraemite pendant," Kaymar answered. "The Ephraemites don't like such as I, Katrin. Menders didn't think it possible, but I have always wondered if that man might have known about me."

"How terrible! Wait – is he Mr. Enigma?" She felt as if the air had gone cold for a moment, remembering that oddly marked gravestone in the estate graveyard, next to someone named Madame Holz. She'd always wondered…

"He is indeed," Kaymar answered. "That kind of thing is what we can't predict or prevent, other than to keep you guarded. I know that you would rather never be Queen, and in some ways that is the way we all feel. But my dear, you could be Mordania's best hope. Sane, kind, intelligent – such a Queen hasn't existed in living memory. Precious as you are to all of us, you are even more precious to this country. You must do what you can to preserve your life – and that means accepting restrictions."

"I've thought of that. Being Queen and changing things," Katrin said softly.

"Don't think on it much. Just be a young woman and finish growing up - and know that Menders does all he can to make your life as happy as possible."

Katrin nodded. "I'm surprised he let you tell me this," she replied, sitting back, her hunger finally appeased.

"I asked him if I could," Kaymar smiled. "Sometimes

people who aren't as close as parents are the best ones to talk about serious subjects. Menders has had to be so involved in your life that he can't be detached enough to talk to you about things that upset him deeply. Same situation with Borsen. My conversation with him would have been very difficult for Menders. For me it was easy."

Katrin nodded. Borsen had told her about Kaymar warning him there were men who would try to seduce him at a young age because he was so pretty and looked younger than he was. That was enough to disturb anyone and since Menders loved Borsen so much, it would have been a very difficult conversation to have.

Kaymar suggested they go back to the hotel along the beach road, where there were some games and a carousel. To her delight and immense amusement, he declared himself absolutely in the mood for a carousel ride. The two of them scrambled aboard the brightly painted horses, laughing themselves silly as they bobbed round and round, Katrin remembering how he'd stood next to her on the carousel at the fair so long ago.

Then he won several prizes for her, stuffed toys and cheap trinkets, and she barely restrained him from winning a bird in a cage, saying it would be nearly impossible to take it home on the train. They finished off the afternoon with enormous ice cream cones, walking along the boardwalk to the hotel, waving to Hemmett and Borsen, who were on the verandah trying to look dashing. Franz and Ifor were coming along from the opposite direction, carrying a large string of fish.

"Ah, we'll be cooking out on the beach tonight then," Kaymar said. He turned toward her and smiled.

"I wanted to thank you, my dear, for a lovely afternoon," he said. "With your permission, I would like to escort you from time to time in addition to Hemmett and Borsen, and yes, Menders has given me leave to ask you. It isn't the same as going places all by yourself, but it would be a bit of variety." He winked at her.

Katrin was delighted. "You may certainly escort me and let people think I'm your bride," she replied, giving him a graceful curtsey.

Franz and Ifor had reached them.

"Evening, Katrin," Ifor grinned. "Have a nice afternoon being squired by the dandy? Ready to scale some fish, Kip?"

"Not on your life, get away from me with those slimy things," Kaymar snapped, keeping a distance between the fish and his perfect suit. He despised fish in all forms, particularly if they were still wet and flapping.

"I'll help you, just let me get changed," Katrin said, laughing at Kaymar's expression. Now he either had to help with the fish or appear a complete ninny.

"Anyone who does not assist shall not eat," Franz proclaimed. He held up a rock grouper as long as his arm. Kaymar made a rude gesture and offered Katrin his arm to escort her to the hotel. She left him at the verandah. Hemmett and Borsen had been joined by Menders, who dispatched the boys to help with the fish scaling and gutting.

"And how was your afternoon?" Menders asked as Katrin kissed his cheek and leaned on the railing beside him.

"Wonderful. I've given Kaymar permission to be my escort. I am quite a woman of the world," she said airily. Menders laughed.

"It'll be good for you to have a change and good for Kaymar too," he said. "I always knew he would be a good friend for you once you grew into him. As you get older you'll want to go out more. This way, should you want to go to the village or just for a drive, you can go with him. I'm arranging for a little gig for you so you can drive out whenever you like."

Katrin threw her arms around his neck and hugged for all she was worth.

"Thank you," she whispered.

"It's high time you were able to get about almost on your own," he whispered back. "I wish it could be more, Little Princess, but it's something."

He made it sound as if it were nothing much, but to Katrin the thought of extra freedom was everything!

CHAPTER 46
FUTURE PLANS AND
UNEXPECTED SEPARATIONS

Shots rang across the quiet heathland around The Giants. Menders had brought the children here for special picnics over the years but at the moment the area was being used for the firearms training of the Princess.

More shots rang out.

"Katrin, you do see the target I'm talking about, don't you?" Menders jibed good-naturedly. Dara, Katrin's boarhound, whined and stretched wearily, tired of the noise.

"I think one of those shots came close enough to scare it a little," Borsen teased from his vantage point behind them, seated in the palm of a giant upturned stone hand, his sketchbook on his knees.

"I'm still learning, if you don't mind!" Katrin retorted, carefully reloading the gun with bullets Menders handed her. The wooden target stood thirty feet away, absolutely free of bullet holes.

Menders had watched her reaction closely when he presented her with the pistol several days ago. He thought she might be afraid or repulsed. To his relief she had been curious.

"I gave the other to Eiren many years ago," he'd explained. The two pistols were a set, each beautifully finished with carved ivory grips set with small jewels. "I thought it was time you had the other one for yourself, now that you and Kaymar will be roaming farther afield."

"Isn't Kaymar armed when he goes with me?" she'd asked.

"He is, but it can't hurt for you to have your own firearm."

"It's beautiful," Katrin had said, admiring the weapon.

"Almost not like a gun at all, more like jewelry."

"It is pretty and it's light enough to put in a purse or apron pocket. But you must never forget that it is deadly."

Katrin had closed the cylinder and replaced the gun in its velvet lined box. "I still take my knife with me when I go out."

"Knives are for close range fighting. This gives you a long range deterrent."

With a simple nod of her head, Katrin had accepted the gift and the ensuing responsibility. Getting her to accept the gun was easy, Menders mused now. Teaching her to shoot with accuracy was turning out to be another matter.

"Katrin, you can't just will the bullets onto the target. You have to aim at it."

"I thought I was."

Borsen chuckled. Not to be outdone, he'd sent away for his own pistol from the Mordanian Armaments Company. Kaymar joked that Borsen had chosen some little sparkly thing that looked like it should light cigarettes, not fire bullets.

"I fired that pistol Hemmett carries once," Katrin said, raising her gun to the target once more.

"That great big Breugan he lugs around? Too much gun for you," Menders replied.

"It was too loud, that much I remember." Katrin fired, missing the target again.

"Don't aim with your hand, Katrin, aim with your arm." Menders said. "The gun and your hand should be pointed like an extension of your arm. And don't squint. Both eyes open, look down the length of the barrel."

"Oh? All right then."

Katrin fired and a sliver of wood flew from the edge of the target.

"Better!" Menders said. "But you're fighting the weapon. Let it kick a little. Then draw down and re-aim at the target."

Katrin fired five more times. Holes appeared in the target.

"Getting there," Menders remarked with relief, glad to see some progress. He turned and watched Borsen pause in his drawing to study the details of the huge stone hand he was seated on.

Menders picked up his own sketchpad, making a rapid drawing of Borsen while the young man's attention was diverted. He had sketched Katrin cradled in the same stone hand when she was three as well as a long and lanky Hemmett at the age of nine. Now he felt as if he'd completed a set, with the third child of his "brood" caught on paper while cupped in the same colossal palm.

Katrin blazed away as Menders sketched, until Borsen called out, "Are you quite finished making us all deaf yet? I could use some lunch."

"I think that's enough for now," Katrin replied, unloading the gun and taking up an oilcloth to clean it.

"You're doing well," Menders said, appraising the target. Like most things, once she put her mind to it, Katrin learned quickly.

"Shooting at targets is one thing, Menders," she answered. "But I don't know that I could shoot someone, to kill them I mean."

"Chances are you won't have to," Menders assured her as he closed his sketchbook. "But I like to think that should you be threatened, you will have the means to defend yourself. Not just against people. There are wild animals around, don't forget."

"Animals are one thing, but to shoot another person…" Katrin put the gun carefully away in its case. Her voice was tense.

"Princess, I understand your reservations. Taking another human being's life is any civilized society's greatest taboo. It's not unknown for trained soldiers to flinch on the field and find they can't fire on another person." Menders took her hand, seeing her very real distress.

"I wonder how Hemmett copes with it? He mentioned it one time, in a letter, called it a moral dilemma." Katrin looked thoughtful.

"Write to him about it. You're both old enough to discuss such concepts. I think you should."

Borsen climbed down from his stone throne.

"Let me see what you have there young man," Menders said, reaching for Borsen's sketch pad. He turned the cover back and admired the drawing, glowing with pride. It was Katrin, caught perfectly in her long lightweight skirt, matching waistcoat and frilled blouse, striking an heroic pose as she aimed at the target. From the end of her pistol there protruded a small flag, with the word 'BANG!' on it. He showed it to her, saying,

"A perfect likeness. I'd like to have this for my office wall, if I may?"

"No uncle," Borsen responded, sitting down to unwrap sandwiches. "This is for Katrin's personal collection. I'll do another for your wall." He took back the pad, signed the sketch, then presented it to Katrin with great ceremony. "Here you are, your Royal Highness."

"Why thank you, sir!" Katrin took the sketch and admired it. Back at the Shadows, she put it away with her personal belongings.

***

After lunch, Menders relaxed and listened as Katrin chattered on about a party she had gone to days before and how Kaymar had partnered her for almost every dance except for courtesy dances with the host and his sons. She was still reluctant to dance with men she didn't know. That suited Menders. He would much rather she was reticent with the opposite sex than too forward.

Borsen set aside his sketchpad and leaned against Menders' side.

"I have a question for you two," Menders said very

casually. "I've already written to Hemmett about it. The letter should reach him today. Once Hemmett is finished with his school year, I've been considering taking the three of you abroad for an extended time - probably about two years."

Katrin sat upright and stared at him, her mouth open in an 'O'. Borsen looked up under Menders' dark glasses, trying to see his eyes. Menders laughed aloud.

"You think you have to ask?" Katrin gasped.

"Well, I don't know, perhaps now that you're a social butterfly here..." Menders teased. She put her hand over his mouth. He took it away gently and hugged her when she put her arms around his neck.

"You could attend a university in Surelia and perhaps Artreya, though that would depend on what is going on between Mordania and Artreya at the time," Menders explained. "We would look in on a few other places too. It would give you a chance to do some art study if you wished, or to attend lectures in philosophy or any other subject that takes your fancy. Borsen could take art study on as well, or spend some time learning about tailoring styles in those countries. Hemmett will get experience being your guard and he's welcome to attend any classes he'd like. And of course school isn't all you'll do. There are so many things to see that we'll be hard pressed to take it all in."

"Yes! Yes, yes, yes!" Katrin crowed with delight, almost giddy with excitement. "I want to see the all places I've read about, not just hear about them from other people!" She jumped up and spun around. "I want to go right now!" Dara leapt up to join the fun, shedding hair and barking.

"I think she favors the idea. What about you, manling?" Menders asked Borsen. The boy nodded mutely, wringing his hands a bit, as was his wont when overwrought. Menders knew that at this moment he couldn't remember a word of Mordanian, always a struggle for him when he was emotional.

"It takes time to put something like this together, and of

course we have to wait until Hemmett graduates," Menders explained, putting an arm around Borsen. "But you can be in on the planning. It's a definite thing, barring disaster – so please avoid disasters, my children."

"Who comes with us?" Katrin asked, dropping to her knees and fending off a barrage of licking from Dara. Menders flung a stick and the huge dog dashed away after it.

"Kaymar and Ifor, of course - Kaymar as your official escort, Ifor as security," Menders explained. "We'll have some of the other Men as well as Doctor Franz. It will be incognito, like our trip to Leptham was."

"Borsen, are you all right?" Katrin asked, looking at him worriedly.

"I'm completely overwhelmed, that's all," he managed haltingly. "I've traveled a lot, but not exactly to the sort of places you're talking about. And this time I'll be able to see things!"

"Now then," Menders said, taking out his watch, "if my watch is correct, we have just enough time to get out to the road and catch a ride with a certain schoolmistress." He rose and helped Katrin to her feet, while Borsen scrambled the food basket and blanket together. At Menders' whistle Dara came romping across the field with a very chewed stick the size of a small log in her mouth.

***

Dearest Bumpy

By now you know that Menders is going to take us abroad for two years! I simply cannot wait! Surelia, Samorsa, even Artreya! I want to see the famous golden dome of the Palace there, and walk along the harbor Promenade under the lanterns at night. They say the streets are paved with gold there – I'm sure that's not right but still, it's fun to think about! I have already begun to plan and dream, and plan some more! I was so excited the first night after I heard, I stayed up all night. The next day I embarrassed myself by falling asleep into the gravy at dinner.

On a more serious note, I now have a pistol to take with me whenever I'm not in the house. Menders taught me to shoot. He says I'm competent with it and not a danger to myself. That's almost a compliment. But it made me think of what you called the 'moral dilemma' of being a soldier and having to deal with the taking of life as a duty. If attacked, I do believe I would defend myself, but Bumpy... I just don't know that I could kill someone by shooting them at a distance.

How do you feel about it? Do you think you could kill someone like that? I know that with all the security that surrounds me it is very unlikely I'd ever have the need but I look at my pistol in its case, or in my hand, and I wonder.

But enough talk of such things, I have to plan for our great trip! I must pack! Yes I know still more than a year away yet, but a girl likes to be prepared!

Love,

Katrin, Overly Excited Royal
Princess Person

Heigh Ho, Royal Princess Person!

Yes I've heard about the planned trip, and think it's a great idea! I can't wait to get started. What say we spend some time looking up things to do and places to see? It'll help make the year pass quickly anyway. And not just museums and art galleries, please. I hear there's a very extravagant Changing of the Guard at the Palace in Surelia, as well as their famous armaments museum. Now that is something I would like to see, instead of a bunch of old paintings (unless they have naked ladies in them.) I think our trip shall be the grandest ever.

On a more serious note, yes I know the gun you speak of. Menders showed it to me one day, saying that it would be suitable for your use. Much more practical than the big pistol I carry, which Menders laughingly refers to as 'Hand Artillery'. But once you own a gun, there's the question of using it.

Should the need arise I believe I would do as a soldier must and that I would fulfill my duties and obligations like a soldier should. I like to think my training would count for something towards my behavior under fire.

I know that if your life was threatened I would do anything to protect you, killing without hesitation if need be. The same goes for any of the others who are close to me. I don't know that I could ever do what Menders and his lot did. Compared to the thugs they call assassins nowadays, he was a craftsman, a true artisan, and always had the ability to separate himself from his emotions – so I'm told. I think I'm more the reactive type and not cut out for such things. I don't know that I could 'remove' someone in that way, even someone I knew to be an enemy. I need a more obvious and immediate threat, I think. But enough of serious subjects.

Here it's all tiresome, marching and drilling and lectures and teaching lower classmen and more marching. We've had only one bright spot, quite a festival here at the term opening exercises. Villison decided it would be droll to bring a snake into temple and turn it loose during the ceremonies. There was a great riot, including Ufronia Vildsteen flapping about like a milchcow gone mad. I thought her guhzonkers were going to fly loose again and got a fit of the giggles. I ducked down quietly to snicker to my heart's content.

Sir strode up to where the poor little snake had wiggled, trying to get away from everyone rampaging about as if their karzis were on fire, picked it up by the tail and handed it to me to take outside, knowing I'm a hearty old country fellow and not about to scream and faint at the sight of a six inch long garter snake. Then he grabbed Villison by the neck and marched him out, while the priest, who is a million years old, deaf and blind, kept droning some awful prayer to Grahl. The little cadets from my tactics class giggled themselves sick. Am I ever glad that Menders never bothered with religious doings for either of us! What a bore.

Villison has been sent down for several weeks. How he's ever going to graduate, I don't know unless Sir pushes him through just to be rid of him. His mamma is in despair, because he's now at home and causing no end of *mischief. We're going to have to have him in your Guard because nobody else will ever employ him and the Army would just march him out and shoot him dead after a week.*

I'm ready to come home to The Shadows and get on with life. When this year is over, I'll be Captain Hemmett and ready to defend you against all contenders.

Meanwhile we can plan what to do abroad. Some of the fellows have already been to the places we're going to go, and I'll get them to recommend some things. Villison has been to Artreya and says the Three Elks Tavern is definitely one to take in.

Write back soon, I'm tired of school!

Love,

Soon To Be Captain Bumpy

***

"So what do you think?" Eiren asked, looking intently at Menders.

"I think it's a good idea and the opportunity has presented itself," he answered. "I will miss you terribly, my love, but it's not forever. There are vacations, and since you can go by boat, you won't be hours on the train or unable to get back here in the winter. If this is what you wish, let's arrange things so that you can do it."

Eiren sighed, not looking happy. He knew why. She was torn.

Eiren desperately wanted her school to become accredited, which meant one of the faculty had to complete an additional year of advanced schooling. Eiren had been on the waiting list for the course, but had expected another couple of years to pass before her turn came around. She had just received a letter announcing that a last minute vacancy at the Royal

Teacher's College in Erdahn.

Eiren had worked diligently to make her school successful and this was the logical next step. Many enquiries from potential students came to nothing because the school was not accredited. With accreditation, graduates of her school would be able to enter any university without having to go through a grueling examination process. Eiren's ambition to accept more charity pupils depended on the school attracting students who could pay tuition.

"Concentrate on the time you'll be here, not the time you'll be away," Menders urged. "It will be a wrench for Katrin, Borsen and me, but we'll write often and love you from afar. If you put it off until after we return from traveling, it will be two more years before you could even begin."

"That's true…"

"The sooner you go, the sooner you'll be back," Menders continued, repressing a terrible temptation to persuade her not to go. He didn't want to be without her, not for so much as a day.

Eiren breathed a sigh of relief and sat back against the headboard of her bed.

"I'll send my letter of acceptance."

"Good," Menders replied, making himself sound hearty.

"I know you don't want me to go."

"I want you to go, but I also want you here," he smiled, lying beside her. "But it isn't forever, Little Bird - and you can keep an eye on Hemmett."

Eiren laughed. No-one needed to keep an eye on Hemmett. He was starting his final year at military school, was very much at home in Erdahn and quite a man of the world.

"Well then, he can keep an eye on you," Menders grinned, putting his arms around her.

***

Menders took Eiren to the dock on the day she left for Erdahn. Katrin stayed behind at The Shadows. Genuinely upset, she couldn't face a formal good-bye. It would be the first time Eiren and Katrin were separated since Eiren had come to live at the Shadows.

"Now then, Little Bird," Menders whispered, putting his arms around Eiren, "this isn't goodbye, you know. Don't find yourself a handsome suitor over there."

"Never!" she whispered in his ear. "You're worth waiting for."

"Seems I've heard that before," Menders joked bravely. "So it must be true."

His embrace lifted her from the ground. Then he escorted her up the gangplank, kissed her a last time on deck and hurried back ashore before he became emotional and upset her further. He waited until the boat was out of sight.

Feeling at a loss, he drove slowly back to The Shadows.

Lately, dissatisfaction with a recent colonial war with Artreya had led to several factions once again working to remove the Queen and her Heiresses. Menders' network had uncovered a serious plot against Katrin's life. Most of the schemers had been found and eliminated, but the plot was the most advanced and sophisticated Menders' Men had exposed to date. It had involved a counterfeit summons to Court which Menders only just recognized as bogus. The intention had been to lure him to Erdahn with Katrin, so she could be murdered there.

The plot originated with the faction that had formed around Aidelia, so eliminating all the conspirators was impossible, as that would involve eliminating Aidelia herself – something Menders didn't dare risk. Removing Aidelia would make Katrin the Crown Princess, while costing Menders his life.

That meant he had to live with the knowledge that Aidelia wanted Katrin dead and was working toward that goal. As the Crown Princess, she could recruit sycophants to her cause.

Taking Katrin to Erdahn at present was unthinkable and he would not leave her at The Shadows, no matter how well guarded, to go himself. At times like this, he silently raged at his inability to handle the situation in a way that would settle things, once and for all.

Leaving the horse and phaeton at the stables, he strolled around The Shadows' grounds. Katrin was working in the soapmaking shed, carefully ladling creamy liquid soap into large wooden molds.

Chores and physical activity had made Katrin strong and graceful, something Menders was happy for, as tall women could often be ungainly and awkward. He had trained her to control her body since she was a tiny girl by teaching her dancing and deportment from toddlerhood. Her posture was magnificent.

She looked up at him and smiled. Her face had matured considerably in the last year. She greatly resembled her handsome father, though the cast of her mother and grandmother, both of whom had been beautiful women before becoming coarsened by excesses, was also on her features. Her expression was usually contented but lately there was an increasing tendency to pensiveness and sometimes sadness. The realities of her life weighed on her, despite her work on the estate and at the school.

"Are you done for the day?" Menders asked.

"I think so. I decided to stop moping and make myself busy," she answered. Her smile was tremulous.

"I know," Menders replied.

"What I hate is that it's my fault that you can't just go with her!" Katrin burst out. "You're stuck here because of me." She turned away and glared out over the gardens.

"Princess," Menders responded, touching her shoulder, "that is my choice. I'm not bound here because you're here. Most guardians of royal children don't even live at the residences. They have their own homes on the estates or elsewhere, and hire nurses, tutors and governesses to raise the child. I chose to live with you as your father and I continue to do so. Please don't take this on yourself."

"I didn't know that," Katrin said, turning back to him. Her face was pink with distress.

"It is the truth. Yes, it will be very hard with Eiren being away…" He stopped, as his voice was shaking. He swallowed and then went on. "But that isn't forever, and it won't be long before she and Hemmett are home for Winterfest. I wish we all could have gone to Erdahn, but it simply isn't safe for you," he said.

He stopped abruptly, wishing he'd bitten off his tongue.

Katrin looked at him.

"You mean it isn't safe because people want to kill me," she said bluntly.

"Yes."

"Is it my family?" she asked.

"I believe your sister may be involved. There is always some kind of plotting going on in Court circles, always some intrigue or another. We've kept you safe so far."

Katrin nodded, but tension showed in the line of her jaw. She sat down on a wooden bench.

"Why? What have I done? I swear… I will never understand such people!" Her voice was thick with anger. "Why should people want to kill me, people I've done nothing to?"

"It's hard to make sense of such stupidity," Menders responded after a moment. "And I know it's small compensation to realize it's not so much you personally, as the political threat you represent, because – "

"I know, I know…" She covered her face with her hands and struggled to control her breathing.

He had no words of comfort for her and that galled him. He could only wait patiently while Katrin worked through her anger. After a while she shook herself and stood, managing a small smile.

"I'm sulking when we should be trying to make the best

of things without Eiren here. For you, I mean."

"For all of us," Menders corrected her.

"I'm glad you're here," Katrin said suddenly.

"And I'm glad you're here. Now, let's go decide how we're going to withstand this particular drought." He walked her toward the house.

CHAPTER 47

SNAKES IN THE CELLAR

My darling,

    I'm settled in and because I can't sleep, am writing to you.

    The trip over was fine. Hemmett met me at the docks and escorted me to my lodgings. He seemed to think that he was showing me around the big city. He must forget that I lived here for three years! He promised to call for me on our mutual rest day so that he can take me around. It should be infinitely amusing and perhaps edifying.

    I hope you are well and not missing me too much.

    Why even write such a silly thing? I miss you, Katrin and Borsen terribly and I haven't even been gone for an entire day! I know you feel the same way.

    I happened upon some of my old classmates from my years here at college. They are also studying for additional accreditation. We talked about our lives and at first I was very excited to tell them about everything. Then I remembered what I have heard you say many times: 'Our business here is our business only.' Despite my pride in you and Katrin and all we've achieved, I chose to downplay it and even gave out deliberate misinformation. No mention of Princesses, or where the Shadows really is. I think my urge for subterfuge is due to the mood here in Erdhan.

    The city seems different, not like the place I knew. The most noticeable change is the increase in industry. There are many new factories and the older ones have been converted to steam generated power. The air is heavy with sooty smoke from many boilers and furnaces.

    All this business has brought a great number of people to the city. Some neighborhoods are jammed with jobseekers and those employed at menial labor, particularly City Thrun. The affluence of the new mechanized age has not filtered down to the lower classes. Many areas are overcrowded, the people dirty and poor. The mood of the city itself has changed too. It is somber and possibly malevolent.

I have heard open talk of dissatisfaction with the Royal Family, particularly regarding Princess Aidelia but also the Queen. There have always been dark mutterings, of course, but hearing people speaking so openly and with such hostility is disturbing. I shall busy myself with my studies and avoid all political discussion. I hope to finish as soon as possible so I can be home to you and all I love.

I will write to Katrin tomorrow. I just wanted to talk to you a little bit.

I love you so much.

Your Eiren

Dearest Little Bird,

I was so glad to have your letter, even though you were unhappy when you wrote it. What's this nonsense about hoping that I am not missing you? I miss you terribly, you miss me, and that's how it should be. We've been so close for eleven years now.

You have learned the art of secrecy well and I am proud that you chose to be cautious regarding what you disclose to others. I would dearly love for you to be able to proclaim your many achievements here, but you are right to be wary, considering the mood you sensed in Erdahn. Other reports I've received bear out the same thing.

The growing anti-royal sentiment is worrisome, and something that can no longer be hidden from Katrin. I've had to make her aware of the ongoing danger of attempted assassination. It's an end to innocence that is difficult to see and it has taken some of her bloom away.

My contacts in Erdahn tell me that someone is 'stirring the soup' there, causing the mood you find so widespread. We must be diligent but cautious in our investigations, so this mystery person won't vanish before being identified. It is damnably frustrating to do this at a remove, through other people. You may be one of my best sources of information there, my love, my other eyes and ears as it were. I know I can trust you to be cautious.

We are trying to settle into a new routine without you, but it isn't easy. I've moved back into my bedroom, as I cannot get used to being alone in your bed. Borsen and Katrin miss you so much!

I will busy myself with the autumn estate work and with some new things for Katrin to read and do. She is very restless at present and needs occupation. Any suggestions from you will be very welcome, because for the first time I feel somewhat at a loss to help her.

I have put your pillow on my bed. Your perfume still clings to it. I miss you so much, my love.

Your lover, your brother, your friend, your husband,

Menders

***

Dear Sir,

Be aware that the matter you had seen to earlier in the year seems to have recurred. At present, we are working to contain and eliminate it, but I thought it best that you be informed, in case you wished to give further directives.

Your other two matters are prospering. I enquired after them personally just this afternoon and was most pleased with their progress.

Your servant,

Ramschav

"Damn!" Menders roared. Kaymar's note indicated that the most recent plot against Katrin, originating in Aidelia's shadow Court, had resurfaced. Months of work by the combined forces of Bartan's assassins and Menders' Men had been completely negated.

A moment later, Franz looked round the door.

"Trouble, my young friend?" he grinned. The grin faded

as he saw Menders' face. He came in, easing the door shut.

"Snakes in the bloody cellar!" Menders snapped, flinging himself back in his chair.

"Eh?"

"That damned plot has come up again," Menders explained as Franz settled into the chair opposite his. "It's like snakes in the cellar. You think you get them all, but oh no, some have laid eggs and new ones hatch. We keep finding people supporting this plot and removing them, but it simply will not fade away."

"Then there must be someone you're not getting – someone behind it all. You said to me you thought Aidelia was too simple-minded to come up with a plot on her own, but that she could be manipulated. I gather that idea still holds with you?" Franz ventured.

"Yes. Kaymar has made detailed reports on the subject. He sees Aidelia when he goes to Court. She doesn't have the brains for this, so someone is putting her up to it. We can't get close enough to find out who it is without drawing attention to ourselves."

Franz was silent for a moment.

"You said you were 'removing' people. I usually don't pry into the details of your operations, Menders, but... does that mean what I think?" he ventured.

"Not necessarily," Menders replied calmly. "When a plot is uncovered, we carefully collect information, not just about those involved, but those they know as well. We look for weaknesses of character or situations we can exploit. Each person identified as a conspirator is assigned a rating as to their degree of involvement in a plot.

"The more timid ones and those on the fringe of things are often dissuaded by threats, intimidation, blackmail. A bloody handprint on a door does wonders for some. For those more deeply involved there are various options. Some find themselves framed for crimes and are dealt with by the courts – this is one reason why we look to exploit character weaknesses. For those who are the greatest threats, yes... they may be removed by physical means. Some have unfortunate accidents. A person might be removed by obvious assassination only if there is no other way. It draws unwanted attention."

"I had no idea it was so involved," Franz said. After another pause, he continued tentatively.

"You said someone might be exploiting Adelia. Suppose, just theoretically, you were to remove Adelia?"

'That may shut down that avenue of opportunity for our mystery conspirator, but I doubt we could get away with it, not without retribution. Remember, removing Aidelia would put Katrin in the position of being Crown Princess."

"Yes, yes... I know your reservations about that. But at times when I look at the ancestral lunacy that plagues the Royal Family, I sometimes think Katrin might be Mordania's brightest hope."

Menders sat back and stretched.

"Doctor, despite our disagreements over the years, I do value your opinion," he replied. "Tell me honestly, what do you think of the Princess?"

"Well, she's considerate, caring. She's a credit to your training and to how you've raised her."

"Go on."

"What else? Perhaps a little prone to procrastination, inclined to self-indulgence, but very intelligent with a keen inquiring mind."

"Would you say she's gentle-natured?"

"Oh yes, for the most part. She showed a jealous side back when she scared Borsen to death, but overall, she's a gentle girl."

Menders sat forward, fixing Franz with a firm gaze.

"Now, if I removed Adelia – and I have thought of doing

so more than once – Katrin would become Crown Princess, placing her at even higher risk from enemies of the Royal Family. That would force me to take the next step, removing not only the Queen, because she's a weak link, but all her allies and enemies as well. I would have to remove anyone who might oppose Katrin in any way and place her on the Ruby Throne myself."

"But she's not sixteen. She couldn't reign in her own right," Franz protested.

"Correct. So I would have to act on her behalf as Regent. If I did that with a free hand until she reached sixteen, I believe I could remove anyone who might oppose her rule. I would hand her a country that was governable and worth governing. But Doctor, that two year period would be a reign of bloodshed the likes of which this country has never seen - not even during the Surelian Occupation."

Menders stood slowly, tugged his waistcoat to straighten it, then went on. "I'm just the man to do it, too. I could gladly eliminate a thousand of Katrin's enemies."

Menders unlocked the large, black cabinet in the corner of his office, swinging the doors wide.

Doctor Franz saw that it was filled with hundreds of dossiers, neatly stacked and sorted.

"There you are, Doctor. Names, dates, places. Information on everyone who has had ambitions toward the Crown or aspirations to manipulate the Crown in the last fifteen years – and anyone connected with them, all cataloged and cross-referenced.

"Right now, if I released the information in these files, I could have several hundred people found guilty of treason and sent to the gallows, the block or the roasting spit."

Franz looked away. Menders closed and locked the cabinet, then sat at his desk again.

"A drink, Doctor? You look a little pale."

"I had no idea," Franz mumbled.

"Most people don't. Secrecy is very important."

Franz took the brandy and knocked it back, his hand shaking.

"If I tampered with the royal succession it would mean Katrin would have to know everything, as I'd be acting in her interest and in her name," Menders continued. "So Doctor, your honest opinion... do you think our Princess has the ruthlessness or the desire to rule to tolerate such a thing?"

"No," Franz answered firmly, looking up. "No, I don't see that as being in her character."

Menders sat back slowly, looking suddenly weary. "My thoughts exactly. Now you see part of my dilemma."

Franz nodded. "Is Katrin safe here, do you think?"

"Safer than anywhere else," Menders answered. "As long as I'm here, I don't think anyone will move against her. It's frustrating for me to do everything at a remove, but I don't dare leave her."

"What's the next step?" Franz asked. He set the empty brandy glass on Menders' desk.

"As always. We watch, listen and wait. Kaymar and Ifor are in Erdhan and a couple of the others as well."

"Is there danger to Hemmett and Eiren?" Franz asked, his face going rigid.

"I don't believe so. Their association with Katrin isn't that well known. As slick as this new party behind this plot is, I doubt he has the means to find that out. However I will take extra precautions."

Menders rose quickly and went Ifor's office where Haakel was working behind the desk.

"I want you to go to Erdahn now," Menders said without preamble. "Our plotters are back in action. Meet with Ifor, tell him I want you to cover Hemmett until further notice. Ifor is to watch over Eiren exclusively."

Haakel rose immediately, nodding.

"I'll have letters for you to carry within half an hour," Menders continued, before turning back to his own office.

My Darling Eiren,

I've just heard from Kaymar that there is someone actively plotting against Katrin's life. am sending Haakel to keep an eye on Hemmett. Ifor will stay with you.

I own a house in Erdahn, as you know. Please relocate there and set up house, looking as if you are living with Ifor. It will give the neighbors something to talk about, if you get my meaning. Since I know you can take care of yourself admirably, I am not overly fearful, but please, do not leave Ifor's sight. When Ifor needs a rest day, Kaymar will stay with you.

Fear not my dear, these are just precautionary measures. For your safety, however, please burn this note.

I will write you a long love letter this evening. For now I must write to Hemmett and get these letters and our friends in position out quickly.

Love, love, love,

M

Menders sealed the letter and sat back, suddenly feeling weary. He would have to tell Hemmett of this soon. The boy was no fool and would sense Haakel's presence sooner or later. For now he would delay. It was bad enough that the hint of such doings upset the smooth running of everything else!

This damnably frustrating business! Whoever had infiltrated the Court seemed to possess the wits and guile required to manipulate the Royal House while remaining hidden from sight. That was a serious new threat. Most conspirators got caught because they were bold and brazen, or self-righteous – and some were just plain stupid. Not this one. He was pulling strings from the shadows offstage.

***

Darling Menders,

I am settled with my new lover in our new abode and find that life has become quite interesting. Ifor is convinced that his duties include bringing me breakfast in bed every morning, which is spoiling me utterly. He also helps me study and is most solicitous of my welfare. When he's having a rest day, Kaymar is here, and has been insisting we put on a charade of me having two lovers rather than one, which is a bit more drama than I care for.

The neighbors seem to be divided between outrage and amusement. At first I wondered why you should want this subterfuge. Then I realized you wanted me watched by many eyes – and I certainly am! The neighbors are very keen to see the latest comings and goings at 21 Hodenstrassen, so I am under continual surveillance. No doubt you will be hearing about your scandalous tenant from other sources.

Kaymar suspects that the person of interest might be drawn by evidence of naughty doings, so he has been sleeping over with Ifor several times a week to make it look as if I am an insatiable lady who entertains two men at a time. I have taken to wearing my most daring outfits, to disguise the fact that I'm just a simple maid from the country.

Kaymar and Ifor tell me they are aware of a certain character they have seen loitering in the vicinity. We are acting all unknowing, but they are watching closely, as am I. Nothing much to tell you yet, only that he dresses terribly. It sets Kaymar's teeth on edge.

I am sending this letter with Kaymar, who will tell you more about this individual. I have seen Hemmett this week, and he continues as cheerful and funny as ever, very glad that you have finally 'brought him in on this'. He promises not to o anything bold or rash. He has also seen the same person hanging about, so I believe that we're on the right track.

I miss you so much, and all joking aside, you're a much better kisser than either Ifor or Kaymar.

Your Eiren

Menders looked up at Kaymar, still weather stained from

the boat trip and lounging comfortably in Menders' favorite armchair. Menders shook his head.

"Entering into the spirit of the thing, are we?"

"Use the right bait to catch the fishie," Kaymar answered flippantly. "I think I have an idea who the fishie is too. He's been a hanger-on of Aidelia's for a while. He's not always at Court and he's not Mordanian. Looks Artreyan to me, though the rumor is that he claims to be Surelian. Goes by the name of Therbalt. I haven't been able to get near him. Whenever I approach he manages to vanish, as if on very important business – and of course, I can't be overly persistent."

Menders scowled. He'd never heard the name. He flashed a look of betrayal at his cabinet – thousands of names, but where was the one he wanted?

"You've seen him around the house then?" Menders asked.

"I can't say for sure. If he's our loiterer, he's in disguise. We've only caught glimpses. Hemmett describes someone similar hanging about, but again, only glimpses. He's wily."

Menders leaned back in his chair and put his feet on his desk. "The name sounds contrived."

Kaymar took a piece of paper and pencil and began writing. Menders knew he was experimenting with the name, to see if it might be an anagram.

"What does Bartan say?" Menders asked, wondering if the Court Assassin had garnered more information. He was at Court far more often than Kaymar was.

"Bartan tries to stay away from those freaks clustered around Aidelia," Kaymar answered. "Big man, dark, about twenty-two years of age. Dresses like a fop, plush jackets, jewelry, oiled hair worn in curls. Speaks with a fake Surelian accent. Disappears for days at a time but always turns up again. At times I suspect he's there without us knowing it. Bright, though he doesn't act it."

Menders shook his head. "Doesn't sound familiar and if Bartan doesn't know who he is, no-one in Mordania is likely to."

Kaymar finished writing and pushed the paper across the desk to Menders, who picked it up and perused it.

Berthalt

Barthlet

Bartleth

Altbreth

"Those seem the most likely, without becoming very contrived. That's assuming he's using all the letters in Therbalt and isn't making a combination of two names like I do," Kaymar said. "Any jogging of memory?"

Menders shook his head. "Where's that crossword game Ifor gave Katrin last Winterfest?" He went to his suite with Kaymar trailing, and rummaged around until he found the game box. He turned all the flat marble letter tiles face up, selected the ones he wanted and tried to make names. Nothing clicked. Kaymar sat opposite and idly pushed a few tiles around, spelling out obscenities.

"Stop that," Mender said, glaring at him. "What if Katrin came in?"

"She'd probably tell me I'd misspelled this one here," Kaymar replied with a grin. "She's not a little girl now, Menders," he added.

"I'm well aware of that," Menders replied levelly. "Not only am I trying to keep her safe, educated, and actively involved in life, but she is also rapidly developing into a young woman and I would like to keep the atmosphere... Hells, I'm not discussing it. Stop what you're doing. Now."

Kaymar shrugged and rearranged the tiles. Doctor Franz appeared in the doorway.

"Games, at this hour, gentlemen?"

"Franz, you've been to Artreya haven't you?" Menders asked.

"Yes, for my medical studies. Some years ago, before we started endlessly knocking heads with them."

"Ah, the good old days," Kaymar mused sarcastically. His intense dislike for Artreya and all things Artreyan was legendary.

"Does this look like an Artreyan name?" Menders asked, waving his hand across the tiles he'd arranged. He changed some of the letters around. "Or perhaps this? Or even this?"

Franz frowned. "They all could be, or just the same, they might not be. What's Artreyan, really? It's a young country compared to Mordania or Surelia. Most Artreyan names are derived from Surelian names, or Fambrian or Samorsan. A lot of Fambrians moved there after the revolution failed."

"Explains where they get some of their half-baked ideas from," Kaymar muttered. He was stacking tiles into little towers.

"So Cochini became Cochine, Devereau became Deverett, Brumnelli became Brumnel... that sort of thing," Franz continued, ignoring Kaymar.

Menders frowned and added a few variants to Kaymar's list of names.

"I'll give them to Menck," Menders said, setting the list aside. "He can start cross checking them. How is Eiren holding up, in reality?" He gave the idly fidgeting Kaymar a hard stare.

"It's hard on her," Kaymar said, looking up from his towers. "She doesn't want to act as if we're her lovers, so we try very hard to give her privacy when we're not actually in public. She tries to laugh it all off, but she's very much your wife, Menders."

"I didn't think it would come to her easily," Menders sighed.

"No, she's a decent lady," Kaymar said sincerely. "I hope we get to the bottom of this soon so that she can get back to some sort of normal life. To be honest, she should stay at your house to finish out her school year and have one of us with her."

Kaymar rose and went to the window. "Menders, I don't think we're going to catch this character. He's terribly slippery, and he just disappears anytime Bartan or any of us get close," he continued bluntly.

"All right," Menders sighed. "Go let Cook feed you."

He sighed with frustration as Kaymar and Franz made their way to the kitchen.

CHAPTER 48
A GREAT PERFUMED FOP

Dear Simple Maid from The Country,

It is a great relief to find that I am a better kisser than either Ifor or Kaymar. My dress sense is better than theirs as well. I'm sure you've noticed over the years.

Please be very cautious regarding this person, my love. Take no risks. I would rather not catch him at all than take any chance of harm coming to you.

We are continuing as usual here, looking forward to you and Hemmett being home for Winterfest. Katrin is presently plowing through several volumes of philosophy that I recommended. I assumed she would take them one at a time. She's reading them all at once. Somehow her brain manages to sort everything out, so I say nothing. She is continuing with the music and art classes for the little ones at the school, and enjoys that.

Borsen is, as always, overworking. I heard a sound I couldn't place when I was up late the other night and finally traced it to the workshop, where Borsen was sitting at his machine, practically asleep, sewing another suit. I ended up carrying him downstairs in my arms like a child to deter him from continuing his somnambulant tailoring. He was asleep the moment I put him on his bed, and slumbered through disrobing and tucking in. His ambition and passion for his work worry me more than a little bit. He's still only a boy but pushes himself to the point where he would have no leisure if I didn't see to it.

So far I have said little to Katrin and Borsen about the present situation, as I don't want to cause needless concern. I only wish I didn't feel that this is the sort of disaster that will prevent us being able to take them abroad as planned. Enough of that for now. No point in borrowing trouble.

Kaymar has assured me that you are very much my wife and I am proud to claim you. I miss you so very much, my brave Little Bird.

All my love,

M

My darling,

Our mystery man approached me, turned up while I was between classes at school. Ifor was right there, but behind a pillar, because we had seen Mister Mystery lurking. Ifor pretended to go for some food, backtracked and was within arm's reach. I was much relieved to have my pistol in my pocket.

He's despicable, a great perfumed fop with the greasiest hair you can imagine. Tries to speak Mordanian as a Surelian would, but does so very badly. Introduced himself as Lord Therbalt of Surelia, so I tried some Surelian on him. He can barely speak it and has a hideous accent, so he's certainly not from Surelia.

He didn't say a great deal, but did a lot of leering and insinuating. Asked me if I was looking for a lover, for the gods' sakes! Truly stylish. He did not specifically mention you or Katrin, just made allusions to the fact that he's an important man at Court, etc. Ifor transcribed the conversation from his vantage point behind the pillar1 and is sending it along with this letter.

The school is having a short recess of four days in two weeks. I would dearly love to come home. I know it will be a matter of turning around and coming right back, but I'm desperate to see you. I don't mind telling you that this has all been frightening. I just want to let you hold me and tell me that it will all work out.

There, that's my lack of courage for the day. I must stop now, Kaymar is waiting to carry our letters to you. I love you.

Your Eiren

Menders rose and took his copy of *Kumpfler's Nobility* from the bookshelf. A few moments' searching let him know that there was no such person as Lord Therbalt of Surelia, or of any other nation for that matter. He hadn't expected there to be.

Kaymar stalked in and put Ifor's transcript of the conversation between Eiren and Lord Therbalt on Menders' desk. It contained nothing more than Eiren's brief letter indicated, so he scanned it again to see if anything had been said that was veiled or had a double meaning. Except for a couple of clankingly blatant sexual innuendoes, he could find nothing.

"Either the man is an idiot or he has something in place we don't know about," Menders said. "Showing himself like this is either a bold move or a stupid one... and so far he has done nothing stupid."

"He's contacted Hemmett as well," Kaymar answered. "He went by the Academy when Hemmett was in the yard, went to the fence and called him over with some tale of knowing Hemmett's father, wanted to pay his respects and the like. Hemmett made short work of him, showed him that cannon he carries around. Haakel made his presence very known. Therbalt fled precipitately."

Menders scowled angrily.

"Don't tear your hair out, Cuz. Bartan's on him at Court. He's been strutting and preening there quite a bit, and has drawn some attention he might not care to have. It could be that he's one of those types who can't maintain a façade indefinitely and ends up giving himself away," Kaymar drawled, stretching full length on the sofa.

"If I could just get over there!" Menders growled in frustration. He hated being stuck at such a remove, having to guess at what was going on, coping with long delays in receiving information.

"Menders," Kaymar said quietly, "stop thinking with your heart."

That startled Menders and he realized that Kaymar was right. He was becoming emotional because he loved Eiren and Hemmett, not because they were in immediate danger.

"I think he's trying to draw you over there," Kaymar continued. "Somehow, he's made the association between you and Eiren. He might have people in place to go after Katrin if you're away. They know if you're here along with all the rest of the Men that they will never get near her."

"I believe you might be right," Menders replied, "And if

he wants me there so that he can strike here, he would need to have assets in place in the area. Take notes."

Kaymar sat up and produced a notebook.

"Effective immediately, we double all standing and mounted patrols. I also want the mounted patrols going further afield. I want every farm on the estate checked at regular intervals. I want every outbuilding, corn crib, hayloft and henhouse searched. All the coal cellars and root cellars too. All unused buildings will be sealed under lock and key and the keys returned here."

Kaymar nodded, scribbling away.

"Mounted guards at the halt and patrolling the roads. No one gets on or off a train or comes by road that we don't know about. I want men in the village at all times, rotated there, watching for strangers. Seen any Revenants lately?"

Kaymar looked up, surprised, and shook his head. "Not in years."

The mysterious traveling people who called themselves Revenants had always given Menders pause, yet he could not say why. Their caravans turned up all over Mordania, often unexpectedly and then vanished just as unexpectedly. They traveled in other nations as well, but claimed to owe allegiance to none. There were rumors that they stole children to add to their numbers. It had been years since he'd seen them near The Shadows, and had put the word out through various channels that they had best stay away. Still, he wanted to leave no possibility unconsidered.

Menders went on. "Then, we sweep the woods. Every knothole, felschat den and manquar nest. If there's anyone within fifty miles of here who shouldn't be, we'll soon know about it.

"You know, I've been working on some new black powder rockets over the summer," Kaymar said suggestively.

"Yes, your eyebrows have grown in nicely, I see." Menders couldn't help a grim smile. Kaymar's pyrotechnical experiments often took their toll on the younger man's lashes, brows and mane of golden hair.

"Innovation is not without its mishaps," Kaymar said primly. Then he smiled broadly. "I've come up with an idea - trip wires attached to a flint wheel that would light a rocket, if tripped. The rocket would be in a metal tube, nailed to a tree. We have a lot of unused pathways in the woods. If we set trip wires, too high for most animals to set off but high enough for a man, it would alert us to anyone sneaking around out there."

Menders nodded. "That's brilliant. Do whatever it takes." He felt his mood lighten with the formation of a definite plan.

"Let's have a drink," he said. "I desperately need one."

Kaymar poured out two measures of brandy and settled on the sofa again.

"I'd be interested to see what change our heightened vigilance produces in our greasy mystery man," Kaymar said. "If he reacts, it will mean he has an agent somewhere here on the estate."

Menders went cold at the thought. An agent in the area, yes – but on the estate? He trusted those who worked for him. Considering this present threat, however, perhaps it was possible to trust too much.

"I want another background check on anyone new to the estate in the past six months," he responded quietly.

"Done," Kaymar nodded.

"What do you think of Eiren coming home for her recess in two weeks?" Menders asked.

"Since we're certain he knows of your association with her, it won't be as if we're leading him here by bringing her home. She misses you desperately and it has been horribly difficult for her to pretend to be involved with Ifor and me. It cuts across her grain. We can get her out unseen at night. With Hemmett staying on in Erdahn, it will ease our logistical situation."

"Then bring her home," Menders ordered without hesitation.

***

Menders laughed joyfully as Eiren ran down the gangplank of the boat, a little bag dangling from her hand. She flung herself at him and he spun her around.

"There's my love," he whispered, grinning over her shoulder at Ifor and Kaymar, who were following at a distance. "I'm so glad to see you!"

She clung to him for a few moments longer, kissing him with a vengeance.

"Am I still the best kisser?" he laughed when she finally let him go.

"By far. Let's not talk about it now," she said. Her color was not as glowing as usual. She looked thinner and there were definite lines of tension around her eyes.

At The Shadows, Menders escorted her up to their suite.

"You don't have to finish the year," he whispered to her as he cradled her head on his shoulder. "You can go back when things are settled. Sooner or later Bartan or Kaymar will get this Therbalt and then you'll be safe enough."

"I'm not letting him drive me away," she replied fiercely. "I set out to do something, and I'll do it. Kaymar and Ifor don't think I'm in danger, they think this character is just out to get information from me."

"It seems so."

She held him close, and he knew she didn't want to talk about it any longer – and to be honest, neither did he.

***

On Eiren's last night at the Shadows, Menders, Kaymar

and Ifor sat down with her to formulate a plan for her continuing stay in Erdahn. Menders would feel less like a grundar with a sore leg if there was some organization about the entire matter, though the sticking point was that they still had no idea who Therbalt was or what he wanted.

"I'm willing to continue to act as decoy," Eiren said. "I have a feeling he thinks that I will give him information, if I let him get close. There's some reason why he's approached Hemmett and me. It must be that he wants to get information about Katrin's whereabouts or habits."

"Katrin's location is not entirely secret at court. It's quite certain he knows she's here," Menders said.

"If he's what Bartan thinks he is, the leader of this faction around Aidelia, there is no reason why he would want to kill Eiren," Kaymar added. "More likely he wants to cultivate her, perhaps recruit her, because she would have information no-one else would have. But we have to remember, he could also use threatening or kidnapping her in an attempt to flush you out, Menders. If his goal is to eliminate Katrin, he will have to eliminate you first."

"The two of you will continue to stay with Eiren night and day," Menders ordered. "Eiren, one or the other will sleep in your room. Do not stir a step without one of them with you. If Therbalt approaches you, they must be near enough to help you. No heroics, my love."

Ifor spoke. "We need a plan for Hemmett as well. He likes to go around Erdahn on his rest days. I would prefer it if you sent him specific orders not to go out into Erdahn until further notice. It could be this scum's intention to flush you out by holding him hostage as well."

"Consider it done," Menders replied. "Hemmett is very keen to do his part, whatever it may be."

"If you gentlemen don't mind, I want to go and finish my packing," Eiren said, rising. Menders waited until she was out of earshot.

"If this Therbalt gets within striking distance, kill him," he said abruptly. "Do it as quietly as you can. I know he's slippery and I don't want attention drawn to us by a public display, but I want him eliminated."

"He's cagey," Kaymar replied. "Only approaches us in public, is always where he can be seen. We can't just kill a member of the Court outright – that would be the end of us all. We'll see what can be done."

Menders nodded. "I know this. Please watch over her. I know I don't need to tell you this, either of you, but it eases my mind to know that I said it, since I can't be there to protect her myself and have to depend on you to do so. So bear with me, if you would."

***

Menders reined Demon in and squinted, trying to identify the person approaching on horseback on the road from Erdstrom. He took out the small pair of binoculars he always carried in his hip pocket and peered through them.

The approaching horseman wore a yellow armband, which meant he had been cleared by one of Menders' patrols on the road. Yellow was the color for today. Recognizing the figure, Menders spoke to Demon and cantered ahead to intercept Thoren Bartan, the Court Assassin.

"Hello, Menders!" Bartan grinned, his hired horse prancing in dismay at the approach of Demon, who rolled his eyes and champed his teeth in a display of complete idiocy until Menders spoke to him.

"I'm glad to see you," Menders grinned back, relieved that his friend was cheerful.

"Not something I hear often in my line of work," Bartan joked, and pointed at Demon. "Call that thing a riding mount?

Looks like a bastard sheep."

Demon bared his teeth at him, wiggling his upper lip in the way of farlins.

"He's known as a bag full of piss and fire, but he's won every race in the area," Menders answered. "What brings you?"

"Are we alone?" Bartan asked.

Menders looked around and smiled at the open empty fields that flanked the road. "Apparently," he replied.

"Regarding our friend Therbalt," Bartan said, reining his horse to ride beside Menders. Demon tried lashing out and received a swat that convinced him that harassing the horse was not a good idea. "He heads the faction around Aidelia that wants Katrin eliminated."

Menders said nothing, clenching his teeth.

"Every time Aidelia acts up, the Queen reminds her that there is another Heiress to the Throne," Bartan went on, shifting in his saddle a little. "Aidelia controls herself better these days. She's not so likely to drool and speaks more reasonably, though she's clearly mad as a spoon. She drinks to excess, enjoys some very depraved pastimes that I would prefer not to go into. She desperately wants to be Queen. When she gets into a temper or does something destructive, the Queen mentions Katrin and the fact that she's not entirely dependent on Aidelia to be her Heiress. So Aidelia begins ranting and raving to that crowd of freaks she has around her about how she wants little sister removed. Since this Therbalt has turned up, there is direction to what she says, not just a lot of mad hot air as it was before."

"I'm glad to know this for certain. It's what I feared."

"From observation, it seems that this Therbalt is skilled at manipulating people," Bartan continued. "He's good at it. He's very much in Aidelia's good graces. In fact, he's one of the men she gives her favors to."

Menders said nothing, feeling sickened. Just the memory of Aidelia's stench – what sort of man could be intimate with someone that vile?

"He's very interested in seeing to it that Aidelia gets to be Queen," Bartan continued.

"Then his interest in Eiren and Hemmett is what we thought, an attempt to get information," Menders replied.

"It would seem so. Is that The Shadows? Gods, Menders!" They had ridden within sight of the big house while they were talking.

"It's quite a sight," Menders smiled. "Of course, it took quite a bit of work to get it to look like this. When we arrived here fifteen years ago it was completely neglected and full of dust and spiders. How long can you stay with us?"

"Only overnight, my friend. I'm on a mission. I've finally moved my wife away from Court and I'm going to contrive to spend a few days with her before going on. She's near Rondstein, at her parents' estate. She couldn't bear Court any longer, not that I can blame her."

***

Later, after settling in, Bartan handed Menders some letters.

"I called on Eiren and Hemmett this morning, in case they had any news for you, and I have a note for you from Kaymar as well," he explained. "They aren't urgent, no sign of our man this week. He hasn't been around Court either."

My darling,

It already seems like a year since I left you, though it hasn't been a week. I'm writing in haste, as Bartan has appeared all unexpectedly and says he will be seeing you tomorrow

All has been quiet, with no sign of our oily friend. It has been a relief to me, though I can tell that Ifor and Kaymar are on edge.

I have banned Ifor from sleeping in my room. He snores like a boar.

Kaymar sleeps silently, so he snuggles up each night in the trundle bed with several evil looking knives and two revolvers. He prowls quite a bit, not being a deep sleeper, but as you know, I can sleep through anything - except for Ifor snoring, which would drown out the mightiest symphony. Thank the Gods that you do not snore like that. Not having seen our obnoxious problem man, I have slept well enough, which is welcome.

There is little more to say except that I miss you and I love you and I can't keep Bartan waiting any longer. Write to me soon.

Your loving Eiren

Dear Menders,

I'm going to be quite the man around here, being called on by the Court Assassin! As it is, the fellows are very impressed by my having a bodyguard, even if he does try to be invisible most of the time.

I haven't seen Therbalt again, even at a distance and both Haakel and I have been vigilant. But I have the feeling we haven't seen the back of him, not by a long shot.

Otherwise, things have been dull except for one of the fellows' pillow exploding the other night. Feathers everywhere and a great rumpus.

Bartan has to go. I will write more this week. Love to Katrin and Borsen. Can't wait to come home for Winterfest.

Your friend,

Hemmett

N.B. The pillow didn't explode while the fellow's head was on it, but before he went to bed. I didn't do it, but I know who did. – HG

Menders,

Therbalt seems to have gone to ground – no sign of him at all. Eiren seems more relaxed, though she cast Ifor out of her room the first night he got on his back and started to snore resoundingly. Said he was vibrating the floor, which is entirely possible.

Enquiries as to Therbalt's whereabouts have come to nothing. I doubt anyone at Court knows where he is. Watch your back, just in case he's come your way, but my gut feeling is that he has some pies to put his fingers into elsewhere.

I will inform you immediately should he return. Take care.

Kaymar

CHAPTER 49
THERBALT

Eiren strolled down The Promenade, Erdahn's largest boulevard. Ifor and Kaymar were nearby, skillfully out of sight.

Therbalt was back. Kaymar had seen him outside the Palace that morning. It was three weeks since Eiren's return to Erdahn and she had begun to hope the repulsive man had gone away forever.

Her heart sank when Kaymar told her Therbalt had returned and she'd made up her mind to find out what he wanted. The endless suspense of waiting him out was grating on her nerves.

She felt sure, as she appeared to be living with both Kaymar and Ifor, that Therbalt believed she had broken off with Menders and would be a potential source of information about The Shadows. Or, as Kaymar put it, being a 'wicked little girl' when away from Menders was the type of thing that would draw Therbalt like a fly to honey.

She was frightened but she was also determined to stop the cat and mouse game that was disrupting her plans, threatening Katrin and driving Menders insane with frustration.

Eiren pretended to look in a shop window while watching the reflection of Therbalt approaching from across the street.

The ridiculous fop, she thought scornfully. He was wearing a scarlet plush jacket with gold braid that made him look like a burlesque show's notion of a Palace guard. His hair was even more absurd than when she'd seen him before, drooping in long looped curls that practically dripped with fragrant oil. He wore a hat the size of a platter, tipped over his eye in an attempt at rakishness.

He strolled up beside her and looked in the same shop window. Suddenly he froze with great affectation, looked at her and smiled, showing a mouthful of gold teeth.

"Why it's my charming acquaintance from the teacher's school!" he exclaimed, just as a gust of his perfume assaulted Eiren's nostrils. She couldn't help comparing him to Menders, who was always elegant and masculine, even if he was wearing an old pair of trousers and outworn shirt to pitch hay. Menders certainly never wore scent that smelled like a tart's handkerchief. There was a simpering effeminacy about this man that repulsed her.

She half-turned and bowed, lowering her eyelids coquettishly.

"I see you are without your – friends – this morning," he went on, looking her up and down. His fingernails were dirty and his hands were grubby under a plethora of rings. Many were obviously cheap fakes and most of his fingers were laden with more than one; small rings jammed onto the second knuckle of fingers far too plump for them to be worn properly. Gods, she thought, though Menders likes rings and sometimes wears quite a few, at least his fit – and they're real!

"How kind of you to notice," she murmured, curtseying slightly.

"A lady such as yourself should not be walking alone," he said with feigned concern. "Please, permit me to accompany you and see you to your destination safely."

She took the arm he proffered. She would burn her gloves the first chance she got. She didn't dare look round to see if Kaymar and Ifor were nearby. She knew they would be.

"Do I divine that you are recently from the country?" he asked, his voice unctuous. "You have that bloom that only graces country girls."

"How very perceptive of you," Eiren cooed, while thinking, of course, you idiot, anyone can tell a woman whose been raised in the country because we don't corset until we're grown and have normal waists, not like the pinched-in city women corseted from infancy. The extremes of city fashions appalled her with their lack of practicality.

"I'm very perceptive about women, my dear lady," he oozed. "You have that certain allure of the fresh, country bud... waiting to be plucked, as it were? Though you certainly have picked up a bit of city gloss here in Erdahn. Have you been here long?"

Gloss, Eiren thought sarcastically. Why, the city is the dirtiest I've seen it. Streets unswept, buildings grimy and shabby, air heavy with smoke and soot... what's glossy about that? Women go about dressed somberly like widows or garnished like tarts, their clothes overly tight, long trains always dragging and catching. For Eiren, Erdhan had lost a lot of its allure.

"I've lived here before, but have recently returned from the country after a period of some years," Eiren replied, watching him under the brim of her hat, pretending to be coy. She'd found the right words; his jaw tightened. She arranged her features to look pensive and forlorn and let her lower lip tremble slightly.

"I sense - was there some disappointment in love that caused you to return to Erdahn?" he queried. She could feel the muscles in his arm tightening under her hand.

"Why, how did you know?" she asked, making her voice sound like a little girl's, all wonder and surprise. They began to walk slowly towards the Teacher's College, Eiren stifling an urge to break into a run.

"As I said, I'm very perceptive about ladies. There is a certain piquant sadness in your eyes that touches me."

Oh, I wish Menders was here to pull your eyebrows out, Eiren thought.

"How sweet of you to care," Eiren said, lowering her eyes again, peeping up at him under her lashes.

"I do believe, however, that you have two admirers," he continued archly. Eiren simpered and made herself blush.

"Why my dear!" he cried expansively. "It is nothing to be

ashamed of! It's the man in the country who broke with you who should be ashamed. No wonder a woman of your beauty and quality has already found suitors? Or dare I be bold and say – lovers. The men of Erdahn know what to appreciate in a lady, including the quality of being daring."

"I thank you, sir," Eiren murmured. "It has been very difficult, and all very new to me, and coming so soon after…"

"Ah, my dear, it saddens me to see that you still feel the pain of the demise of your recent love affair. Should you ever wish to confide, remember Lord Therbalt as a friend who will always understand. Now then, I see we're at your destination, so I will leave you, with hope that we will meet again very soon."

He took her hand and kissed it, leaving a faint pink smear on the back of her glove. She curtseyed again, slightly, giving him a half-lovestruck look that elicited a smug smile. He doffed his platterlike hat, bowed with a flourish and then strolled away.

Eiren walked around a corner. When she was certain Therbalt could not see her, she slumped against the wall.

Kaymar materialized from the shadows. Ifor emerged from a side passageway.

"Are you all right?" he asked.

Eiren nodded, unable to speak for a moment as a wave of revulsion and anger swept through her.

"That was absolutely brilliant!" Kaymar crowed in a whisper. "Your 'I'm a poor rejected little country miss' act was priceless."

"Menders would have her head, and ours, on a platter for that," Ifor said.

"Ours, yes, but not Eiren's." Kaymar retorted.

"We have to do something," Eiren said heatedly, turning to Ifor. "This situation could drag on forever otherwise. Menders cannot risk leaving Katrin to come and see to things himself and I cannot live in fear and trembling of this man for the rest of a year." She stripped off her gloves in disgust, glaring at the pink smear. "The greasy wretch wears lip rouge," she snapped, flinging them down in the gutter.

"He's a piece of work," Kaymar agreed, patting her shoulder. "Don't let it rattle you, my dear. He wants information about Menders and The Shadows. There were plenty of hints dropped but you used just the right amount of dumb country girl to avoid them. So our suspicions are right and we can lead him on into a situation where he can be dealt with. I want an end to this too. I'm tired of being stuck here, sleeping in a trundle bed like your baby brother."

"Menders still won't like it," Ifor said. "And I don't think we should proceed without telling him."

"Please," Eiren protested, "don't tell him just yet. I know that isn't what he would want but he's being so cautious that this is going nowhere. It takes so long to get a message to him that the entire situation can change here before he has a chance to get instructions back. What I hope to do is make this wretched man so confident that I can lure him somewhere into a situation where... you two can finish him off."

Eiren felt herself go pale. Though she despised Therbalt for his intent to kill both Menders and Katrin, she felt sickened by the thought of arranging his death.

Kaymar placed a hand on her arm.

"Eiren, we all feel it. It's perfectly natural to quail when you're thinking about killing someone in cold blood, no matter how deserving they may be. When an assassin no longer feels that, it's time to stop being an assassin, because you're either going to become so blasé about killing that you become careless or you're going to begin enjoying it. I'm all for not letting Menders know what we're doing. Ifor, are you with us?"

"As if I could choose another course with you two decided?" Ifor said laconically. "If Menders goes spare, we'll just release Eiren on him. She'll let her lovely lower lip tremble and he'll go all shivery inside."

Eiren burst out laughing, even as she tried to scold him, thankful for the release of tension. He just stood there looking wicked.

"Would you like to go back to the house, Eiren?" Kaymar asked after he'd playfully punched Ifor a time or two. "I know you're very shaken."

"No. I came to Erdahn to go to school and to school I shall go," she declared. "I'm all right now. Shall we go to class, gentlemen?"

They melted away into the shadows, but she knew they would be with her, all through the day.

***

Eiren hated hiding anything from Menders. They were very close and were more than simply lovers to each other. They were friends, they acted as parents for Katrin, Hemmett and Borsen, they shared their lives almost entirely with one another. Menders didn't speak about his past but reveled in the happiness of hers. She respected his reticence about certain topics and rejoiced when he confided in her. She knew he loved her in all ways, as she loved him. Lying to him by omission now was weighing heavily on her.

She had encountered Therbalt "accidentally" a number of times recently and knew he was shadowing her because he turned up in so many places; as she was leaving class, as she walked to the library, while she was shopping. He would always offer an arm and his condescending and transparent "confide in me, my dear little countrywoman" routine. If he likened her to a bud in need of plucking just one more time she thought she might just scream.

He sickened her. She could tell that he truly did not like women, despite his guise of sexual attraction to her. He probably didn't truly like men either. Even Kaymar, who was difficult to rattle, admitted to being unnerved by the man. There was a strange other-worldliness to him that was difficult to read. Such a person could be capable of anything. As Kaymar said, if you cannot find what someone truly loves, then you should fear him, for he is likely to hate everything and everyone – and that hatred makes him infinitely dangerous.

She had fed Therbalt a morsel of information at a time, luring him to come looking for her again and again. She let him think he was winkling facts about Menders and The Shadows from her, though the information she had given so far was incorrect and entirely useless.

"Tell me, my dear," he said during one encounter, "I have heard of a man who is the guardian of the younger Princess. It is said he was involved with a young, attractive schoolteacher on an estate near Erdstrom. I was not sure, but could this possibly have been the man who was foolish enough to lose you?"

She blushed and nodded.

"I hear that he is a most formidable person," Therbalt prompted. "I do hope that he wasn't unkind."

"He was in withdrawing his affection from me," she quavered, utilizing Kaymar's trick of stretching the back of her throat in order to make tears come to her eyes.

"Ah now, my dear, it is never worth weeping over such as he," Therbalt said expansively. "I myself have had many affairs and frequently have endured a broken heart, but time always heals it. Now, when I think back on those times, I say 'what care I?' You have not hesitated to find gentlemen willing to console you. This is most healthy and shows an admirable resilience on your part."

Dear Gods, the idea that I would sleep with two men at one time is admirable in your eyes, Eiren thought.

"They were most persuasive," Eiren responded, eyes downcast. "And I found that I like it." She bridled and tossed her head up, meeting his gaze boldly, as if daring him to be put off by her libertine ways.

"Good for you! I think that it is much better for you than being mewed up in the country, trying to please a man who is so hard and ungiving."

"He could be very difficult," she sighed. "Most distant."

"Ah. That would be very trying to such a warm heart as yours. And the house, being kept in a place that is so very remote. Tell me, were you alone or does he employ many servants?"

"Oh there are a great many, all trained to arms," Eiren answered. "He traveled quite often, taking the Princess with him, leaving me behind." She was determined that he not have a clear or true picture of life at The Shadows. "They go incognito, of course."

"How interesting! I had heard that they are always in residence there, that he won't stir from the place."

"Oh no! That's what he would like everyone to think, but they are often gone, particularly in the winter months. He has permission from the Queen to raise Her Highness in any way that he sees fit."

"And the Princess... as I understand it, she's quite a precocious child?"

"No. I had the teaching of her for a while and she was unable to keep up with lessons," Eiren answered. "I had to give up on her, which angered him greatly, because he dotes on her and believes she is very gifted. But as a trained teacher, I assure you it is otherwise. Spoiled, overindulged, with a willful streak that's not been corrected. In general, not very bright or imaginative."

"Just like her sister. How very interesting," he muttered, and Eiren knew he'd risen to the bait. Good, she thought viciously, let him believe Katrin is not the threat to Aidelia that he thinks she is. Time to add the final tug on the line to hook this fish.

"In truth, I don't like the child. Not at all," Eiren

confided.

Therbalt smiled widely, reminding Eiren of a snake with gold teeth. "Well, well now - isn't that interesting?"

***

Bit by bit, with input from Kaymar and Ifor, Eiren wove an absurd picture of The Shadows for Therbalt, loaded with incorrect locations, foggy details and outright nonsense. She claimed that Menders employed an armed guard of sixty men secretly granted him by the Queen, that Katrin could barely read and couldn't write, that the road from Erdstrom was heavily guarded by more men of the Queen's army and that The Shadows was a veritable fortress with guns bristling on the roof and guards posted all around. She could see that he was confused and irritated, probably with whoever had given him intelligence about The Shadows. He never acted at all terse or angry toward her.

He was trying to romance her, though he had no inherent intuition of what a woman would find appealing. She led him along with tremulous sighs and longing looks, ignoring the temptation to scrub her eyes with soap after seeing him. She began to snuggle into his arm and smile up at him with a cow-eyed, lovesick gaze when she walked with him, while she told him lie after lie about The Shadows, Menders and Katrin. His expression told her he was delighted, as if it was all too good to be true.

Eiren could tell Therbalt was disappointed when she repeatedly described Katrin as simpleminded and could have cheered when he asked her if, in her opinion, the girl could ever be considered a suitable Queen.

"Only if Mordania wants a dullard for a Queen," she said in her most scathing tone, "I would be terribly surprised if the Queen's Council would consider her fit to be an Heiress. They would likely wish to pass her over for a cousin or such, if it ever came to it – but there's an older Princess in line to inherit."

"Oh yes, most unlikely that your former pupil would ever be called upon to take the Throne," he replied, and rapidly changed the subject.

Not wanting him to become bored, she deliberately appeared to withhold information about Menders. When asked if Menders had really been Lord Stettan, a great assassin with more than two hundred kills, Eiren suddenly went white and silent.

"Oh, my dear, I have upset you," Therbalt blubbered, feigning dismay. "Please forgive me! It is simply that I have become very enamored of you and wish to know everything about you. We shall speak no more of this man who has used and misused you so cruelly and has failed to appreciate the value of a lady so experienced and daring." He bent forward. Before she realized what he was about, he'd planted a sickening, slobbery kiss on her cheek.

Eiren had learned that anger was her best defense against the moments when Therbalt frightened or rattled her. She drew on it now.

I was a virgin when I first slept with Menders, she thought fiercely. I never wanted another man from the moment I first saw him, with his pure face and beautiful body and complex mind, and I never, ever will. If I could kill you now and not endanger us all, I would!

To Therbalt's eyes, she blushed and shivered. He couldn't know that the blush was a blood rush of rage and the shiver was her desperate attempt to keep from tearing her pistol from its concealed sheath and putting a bullet through his eye.

He reached around and tucked her hand more securely into the crook of his arm. She was infinitely grateful when he left her at school and she could rush to the ladies' room to scrub her face clean.

Kaymar and Ifor sat with her that night and went over and over the conversation, trying to divine Therbalt's intentions.

"Sooner or later, he must decide that someone is either lying, or misinformed," Kaymar finally concluded. "Either you, or whoever supplies his information about the Shadows."

"Wasn't there a woman, some time back?" Ifor recollected. "Ermia?"

"Ermina Trottenheim," Eiren said. "She left under a cloud long ago. I don't think she would…"

"Talk about the old days to someone she didn't know well? Or with someone overhearing?" Ifor said.

"I suppose it's possible. She didn't have much sense, though she tried to be manipulative – and she was most vindictive."

Kaymar made a note of the name. "I think we'll see what we can find out about her." He wrote several lines.

"Is this Lord Stettan someone Therbalt would be frightened of?" Eiren asked pointedly. She was answered by both men going silent.

"Yes, Therbalt would be very reluctant to approach Lord Stettan," Kaymar finally said.

"Would being told that Menders is Lord Stettan dissuade him from his plot?" Eiren pressed. "Or would it endanger Menders?"

The men exchanged a look and she knew then that Menders was Lord Stettan.

"It would definitely put Therbalt off," Kaymar responded. "Only a madman would knowingly go up against Stettan."

Eiren looked at him for a long time, but he only returned her gaze, his blue eyes radiating innocence.

"Then Menders is now Lord Stettan," she declared. "I'm very tired, gentlemen, so I am going to bed." She smiled, bid them good-night and went to her bedroom. She slipped off her shoes and silently backtracked to the hallway outside the kitchen, where they were still seated at the table.

"I can't believe she didn't know," Ifor said in a very soft

undertone.

"Menders plays his cards close to his waistcoat," Kaymar replied, his voice even softer. "He hasn't wanted her touched by all of that. She knew, of course, that he was an assassin, but I'm sure he's never told her that he's Stettan."

"Was Stettan," Ifor said. "He's not Stettan now. He's – well he's become Menders. And after all this time the name Stettan has lost significance outside of certain circles. The name wouldn't have meant anything to her, had she known before now – it would just be a name."

"Well she knows now and I'm not happy about that. It's something I wouldn't want anyone I loved to know. Damn that Therbalt bastard! Why can't we get him where we can eliminate him? He always approaches her when there are people around!" Kaymar smacked a hand down on the tabletop in temper.

"Like all slugs, he's slippery," Ifor answered. "Are you off to bed?"

"Not for a while. I'll give Eiren some time alone before I turn in. She needs some privacy. The strain is telling on her. If we can't resolve this thing soon, I'm going to tell Menders that he has to insist that she give up on school this year and go home."

Eiren crept to her room, undressed swiftly and got into bed. She lay there, looking at the shadows on the ceiling.

Yes, she had always known that Menders had been an assassin before coming to The Shadows. It was common knowledge in the neighborhood. She had never judged him by that, only by how he behaved. Her father had counseled her that a man was known by his deeds, not by his title or his occupation. A dung carter might be a good, decent fellow, her father said, while some great Lords were despicable and cruel.

Menders had made no secret of having been an assassin. He'd trained her to use a knife and gun as well as most of Menders' Men, hadn't he? But he'd been so young, barely twenty, when he'd left the profession – Lord Stettan with more than two hundred kills? How young had he been when he began?

It didn't change her feelings for him, but now, after this disturbing day, she wanted to curl up with him on their sofa before a warm fire and let him explain things in that deep gentle tone he used only to her.

Soon Kaymar came in, already dressed for bed, and went through his ritual of checking the window, then tucking his various knives and guns into the trundle bed. Kaymar slept with a private arsenal. He looked like a little boy in his nightshirt, clambering into the low bed beside her in the dim light - yet she knew that he was a most deadly human being. For all his kindness and sense of the ridiculous, he could be utterly ruthless if he chose.

"Kaymar, tell me about Menders being Stettan," she said quietly.

He sat up and looked around to see her peering over the edge of the big bed.

"My dear, I'm not at liberty to do so," he said. "It's been his express wish that you not know about that part of his life. I'm terribly sorry that Therbalt brought it up."

"I know now. Please enlighten me."

Kaymar sighed.

"Lord Stettan was the greatest assassin who ever lived," he said after a long pause, during which she knew he was hoping she would rescind her request. "He had the highest marks ever recorded at the Military Academy and Special Services training, and has yet to be surpassed. Only one other assassin has come close to Stettan's record. He began his professional career at fifteen and had over two hundred kills by the time he was twenty, when he disappeared."

"To The Shadows," Eiren murmured softly.

"Yes," Kaymar answered. "To the Shadows, to become the Menders you and I know... but as far as Mordania is concerned, Lord Stettan disappeared into thin air.

"If Stettan hadn't taken those lives then, Mordania would no longer exist," Kaymar continued after a moment. "He was famous for quick, clean actions. In fact, his targets never so much as saw him or knew that they were going to die. There was a political situation during those five years that was very dangerous indeed, and Stettan, by carrying out his missions successfully, had a great deal to do with securing Mordania's safe future."

"I've heard some of the Men speaking of '*The Surelian Solution*'. They were referring to Menders, weren't they?"

"Yes. That was a famous action and it became his nickname. But it's not what you think."

"Kaymar, I know that assassins aren't blood lusting lunatics," Eiren said heatedly.

"Don't let this knowledge come between you and Menders," he replied.

"Why would it?"

"You're a dear woman." Kaymar smiled, settling back on his pillow and closing his eyes.

The room had been silent quite a while when Eiren said,

"The assassin who came closest to Stettan's number of kills was you, wasn't it?"

There was no answer for so long that she almost thought Kaymar was asleep – except she could feel that he was awake, lying there in the dark, considering her question.

"Yes," he said finally, near a whisper. "Please don't ask me about that again, my dear. Good night."

Eiren lay awake for a long time. There were shadows on the ceiling, and Eiren imagined her husband, her lover, her friend, Menders moving through the shadows like smoke through the darkness, keeping them all safe.

CHAPTER 50
CHANGE ABOUT

Eiren finished buttoning the back of her amber dress and then asked Kaymar to turn around. He did, the amber skirts swirling around his feet.

"It's your color," she said quietly.

"Not a bad fit either," he responded, adjusting the set of the dress on his body. They'd had to resort to considerable padding to give him a bust, but it was working.

Kaymar had explained that when he was younger, he'd specialized in being a lady's maid who either collected information or, at the appropriate moment, turned into a deadly assassin.

"I'm a little long in the tooth for skirt roles now, but I'll do to target Therbalt at night," he grinned, brushing his long blond hair back and expertly tucking it under a red wig the same color as Eiren's plentiful locks.

Suddenly the absurdity of the situation struck Eiren and she started to laugh. Here she was, helping this lethal man dress up in her best clothes, watching as he fussily pressed hairpins into his storebought coiled tresses. She ended up having to sit down and realized that the laughter wasn't entirely born of humor.

"And now, would you care to take your dear sister shopping so that we may purchase two identical outfits?" Kaymar asked archly. It was an important part of the final plan that they dress identically at the crucial time.

Strolling down the Promenade, arms linked in sisterly affection, Eiren was amazed that people saw what they were meant to see — two women, sisters or close friends, out shopping for dresses. No one suspected Kaymar wasn't a woman. He even walked and moved like a woman.

They passed the gleaming, marble-columned façade of the

Rondheim Bank building. "It's a shame we have to trudge to all these different places to find two identical outfits," Eiren said. "You'd think there'd be one big store, where you could get everything."

"Perhaps someday there will be," Kaymar replied with a shrug.

***

Eiren's meetings with Therbalt had escalated. He now sought her out two or three times a day, always pressing her to admit that Menders was indeed Lord Stettan. He seemed stressed and nervous. She wondered if the information was vital to what he wanted to carry out.

She'd beaten around the bush, acting frightened and anxious. After he'd cuddled her and stroked a finger over her lips as if he was completely besotted with her, she stammered that indeed, Lord Stettan was Master of The Shadows.

She enjoyed the satisfaction of seeing Therbalt's face turn grey with fear. He covered clumsily, launching into a gushing soliloquy about how he was overjoyed that she had managed to escape the clutches of one as evil and dangerous as Stettan. He blubbered tiresomely that her secret was forever safe with him, that his high regard and tender feelings for her made him even more thankful.

She'd been able to smell the fear on him.

"You must not fear repercussions from him, my dear," Therbalt lectured her. "I wish to place you under my protection. You have done me a great service by giving me this information. You see, I needed to know the actual identity of the man living at The Shadows – desperately needed to know. I am in the service of the Queen, and it has become painfully obvious that there is a plot afoot from Stettan and his people to remove not only the Queen, but the rightful Heiress, Princess Aidelia, as well. Then this simple child, Princess Katrin, would be set up as Queen with Stettan acting as regent. Think of Mordania ruled by such a ruthless man with the blood of so many on his hands, my dear!"

If I saw such a dreadful job of acting on stage, I'd boo you off of it, Eiren thought, making sure that her expression was one of shock and horror.

"No, it would be a terrible thing!" she gasped. "It must not happen. I know more about Stettan than anyone. It must not happen!"

"My dear, am I assured of your loyalty to Her Majesty?" Therbalt asked, leaning very close to Eiren. She closed her nose to his rancid perfume.

"I am Mordanian and my loyalty to the Queen is unswerving," she replied with stunning conviction. In the sanctuary of her own mind she added 'because the alternative, her insane daughter Aidelia, is a horrifying idea.'

"Bless you my dear!" Therbalt whispered unctuously, spraying saliva in her face. He bent and put his arms around her, crushing her close. Eiren could see over his shoulder, where Kaymar, dressed as a loitering lout, was watching. She rolled her eyes in disgust. He doubled over in a silent laugh, then was upright again, his hands in his jacket pockets. Only a practiced eye could see that he held a gun trained on Therbalt's back.

"If only I had some idea how I could get to Lord Stettan," Therbalt blubbered on, standing back upright. "Have you any way to let me know the floorplan of The Shadows, even if you draw it out yourself? It would be invaluable to me – and to Mordania."

Eiren looked up at him, her eyes very wide and trusting.

"I do have a plan, drawn by Stettan himself. Out of sentiment I took one of his notebooks when he sent me away from The Shadows. There is a plan of all floors of the building in it. There have been a few changes since, but nothing significant."

He affected a look of solemn reverence and bent to kiss her hand.

"My dearest Little Bird," he whispered. "If you would trust me with this notebook ..."

Eiren nearly reeled in shock and waited until Therbalt stood upright so she could see his eyes.

No, there was no guile there. He wasn't good at disguising his thoughts for all he was expert at hiding his movements. Her letters from Menders, where he called her 'Little Bird', had all been hand delivered by Kaymar and could not have been intercepted. Years ago Menders had overheard her father calling her by her old childhood nickname, Birdie, and had devised his own loving name from that. He'd never called her that anywhere but in her bedroom and never before anyone else, not even Katrin. It was coincidence, certainly.

"I... I don't know. That would be betraying a great trust," Eiren answered.

"Ah, how noble of you," Therbalt soothed, "Even when you have been so terribly wronged."

"Yes, I have, but trust is important to me." She was careful not to appear too eager or compliant.

"Ah yes, rightly so, my dear."

"I must have time to think on it," Eiren continued, feigning distress at the thought. "I will give you an answer tonight."

He seemed annoyed at first, then smiled and produced a card from his pocket.

"You may reach me here, at this address," he said smoothly. "Until tonight - but I wish you to remember, dear sweet bud, that I, and all Mordania, are counting on you."

Eiren took the card with a silent nod.

"Once we have the matter of the notebook out of the way, we might then... discover each other," he whispered hoarsely. Then he was gone, leaving her quaking with revulsion.

Kaymar hurried over. She showed him the card.

"Tonight. He wants me to come to him tonight. With a

notebook."

Kaymar looked at the card, scowled darkly, then grinned. "All right then, we have him now! Tonight it is. I'll take you to class as usual, but we'll need to be home right after. We need to fit the parts together and go over them. As soon as class is over, come right out to me."

Eiren nodded solemnly. He walked her to her class and she sat down at her desk, feeling lightheaded. There was no turning back now.

***

Early evening found them sitting around the small parlor table. Ifor poured glasses of brandy and handed them around.

"Is this what they call 'liquid courage'?" Eiren joked. She assumed it was for her benefit, to calm her nerves. The day had passed with agonizing slowness, while her insides were coiled tight as a watch spring.

"A little distilled fortitude never hurt," Ifor explained. He lifted his glass. "To success."

They touched glasses over the table, then drank. Eiren shivered. It was strong, but very good. Despite his outward appearance of roughness, Ifor kept a very fine cellar in town, stocked with exclusive and expensive beverages.

"The fish is on the hook. All we have to do is land him," Ifor went on. "Eiren, later tonight you go to the address he gave you. You'll hand a note to the doorman to bring Therbalt out. Be sure he sees you up close and in detail."

"Should I go inside?" Eiren asked.

"No!" Kaymar exclaimed vehemently, his tenor voice harsh and strident. Eiren started and Kaymar obviously steadied himself. "This address… well, he's gotten a bit complacent the last few days and I managed to tail him there. It's a men's club for people with rather peculiar tastes," he continued. He flicked the edge of the card, lip curling in revulsion. "Best you don't go inside. Stay near the light of the door, let him come to you."

"Tell him you will bring him the book, but at a secret location. Somewhere private, that it's too unsafe to hand it over there where you could be seen," Ifor instructed her.

"Then you tell him you'll meet him here, at this address, in half an hour," Kaymar continued. He unrolled a plan of a city townhouse with a walled garden. "Should he ask, tell him it belongs to a friend who is away."

Peering at the plan, Eiren asked, "Whose house is it?"

"No-one we know or who knows us," Ifor explained. "No connection to anyone here. Belongs to a gentleman, lives alone, suddenly received a message of some importance that called him away unexpectedly. By the time he finds it's a ruse and gets back, we'll be long gone."

Eiren looked at them in amazement. "How did you do all this so fast?"

Kaymar chuckled. "We've had this place in mind for ages. We have keys, got the fellow out of there this morning with a beautifully forged note. The location is ideal. It has good access, is in a quiet and fairly well-to-do area, which puts people at ease. They think the rich part of town is safer, for some absurd reason."

She was still blinking in surprise, never having imagined that plotting a professional murder was so involved.

"The man there drinks a bit, so he sleeps heavily," Ifor added. "One night I went in, borrowed a few letters from his mother to copy the handwriting. He leaves his house key in his waistcoat pocket. I took an impression of it with a ball of hard wax, then filed a key blank to match. Been in several times at night, looking things over, getting familiar, making sure the key works. He has poor taste in art but has some nice Dysonian reproductions. Some good first editions too, but they were all over the place. I sorted them for him."

Kaymar laughed out loud. "How typical! How do you tell when Ifor Trantz has broken into your house? Your bookshelf is rearranged and your artwork has been appraised!"

Ifor smiled. Eiren felt better now, knowing the other two were so thorough and professional. Turning her attention to the plan, she asked;

"Once I arrange the meeting with Therbalt, what do I do?"

"You head toward the house we've staked out, but when we give you the signal that you're not being followed, you change direction and run home here as fast as you can. Then wait for us."

"Is that all?" She was both relieved and dismayed to have such a small role and to have to go against Menders' request that she stay within sight of Kaymar or Ifor at all times.

"That's more than enough," Kaymar answered. "He will come to the garden here, where he sees me dressed exactly as you were. Ifor will be with me, in hiding, and together - the end of Therbalt."

Ifor nodded.

"He's ours and the deed is done. We go out through the house, to our carriage at the front. A gentleman and lady are seen leaving a nice townhouse, with a large trunk. There's nothing suspicious about that, is there?" Kaymar continued.

"We pick you up here, head for the boat, then back to the Shadows," Ifor added.

Eiren nodded slowly. "And Therbalt?" she asked, almost fearing the answer.

"We feed the fish on the way home," Ifor said.

Eiren thought it through. They'd covered everything. It all seemed so simple, really.

"Shouldn't I be there with you? To help?"

"No!" the two men exclaimed in unison.

"Too dangerous," Kaymar pronounced. "If anything happened to either me or Ifor, Menders would grieve…"

"But if anything happened to you, even a scratch, he'd never forgive himself, or us." Ifor finished for him. He sat back and lit one of his brandy-cured cigars.

"Eiren, despite your brave heart, you're a schoolteacher and should stay that way. This sort of bloody business is what Ifor and I do," Kaymar said gently.

"I see," Eiren whispered. She listened to the parlor clock ticking away as tendrils of smoke from Ifor's cigar writhed toward the ceiling.

"What should I do if you don't come for me?" She looked up to hold their gazes with her own. "If something happens?"

Ifor reached across the table and gently covered her hands with his. "If we don't come by midnight, then you get a cab to the boat dock. Haakel will be there with the boat ready to go. He can take you back to the Shadows."

"We'll leave a dossier with you that explains everything," Kaymar said, his voice soft and colorless. "For Menders."

Eiren nodded, and swallowed hard. Ifor looked deep into her eyes. "You must promise us you will do this."

"Yes, you must," Kaymar said, placing his hands atop theirs in the centre of the table.

"I promise," Eiren whispered.

"Well then, that's settled" Kaymar said, suddenly bright and cheerful again. "So come now, sister dear, let us go and begin our preparations."

They released one another's hands and rose.

***

Eiren walked along the quiet dark street, willing her legs not to tremble and her stomach not to turn over. She'd given Therbalt the address where she would hand over the notebook, her nervous anxiety making her performance all the more convincing. He would be here in half an hour.

Ifor coalesced from a shadow and came to her. "It's all clear," he whispered. "No one followed you. Run along home, and wait for us."

"Where's Kaymar?" she whispered back.

"In place. I must get in my own position. I'm sorry we can't escort you home. Menders insisted we never leave you, but…" His big shoulders rose and fell in a shrug. "We can't be everywhere."

"I'll be fine," Eiren insisted. "But please, hurry back."

"See you soon," Ifor replied as he melted into darkness again. His dusky clothing made him almost invisible.

Despite gnawing anxiety, Eiren felt a strange elation, an almost perverse thrill, and knew that she could make a career of this sort of work if she had to. The only thing that concerned her about killing someone like Therbalt was that the concept didn't bother her as much as she felt it should.

She hurried on. She wasn't worried about going home alone; she was armed to the teeth. Ifor had cleaned and loaded her pistol, showing her how to wear a sash around her waist with the pistol tucked into it, in easy reach. Her wickedly sharp knife, the one Menders had made for her, was sheathed securely to her thigh, the handle accessible through a slit in her skirt. The knife gave her strength – she felt Menders was with her when she wore it.

"Gods forbid some drunken sailor comes tottering out of an alley and decides to give the pretty girlie a kiss," Kaymar had joked. She'd laughed in spite of her fear.

Eiren paused some blocks from the rendezvous address but many more from home. It didn't feel right to be going to safety without Kaymar and Ifor. A nagging presentiment she couldn't name and didn't want to analyze immobilized her.

She felt she wanted to – needed to be there, with the two men who had protected her more out of love than duty. She couldn't sit at home and wait for them, not knowing what was happening to them.

Eiren turned around and started back.

***

Eiren had studied the map in detail until she knew the layout of the "borrowed" property by heart. Therbalt would enter by the large gate behind the house to find Kaymar, dressed as Eiren, by the large sundial in the centre of the garden. Ifor would be in hiding a few feet away, behind the curved archways that supported the balcony overlooking the yard. There was a smaller entrance from a narrow side passage, hidden by a rose trellis. Eiren used this to slip silently into the courtyard, which was dimly lit from a single lamp post outside the wall.

The house was dark. Keeping to the shadows with her shawl drawn around her, she eased along the wall to the first of the archways.

How strange to see myself replicated in detail like this, she thought, watching Kaymar strolling among the flowerbeds, holding a notebook. To Eiren's surprise, what appeared to be a shadow beside her shifted. Ifor's voice, so low that she barely recognized it, said, "What the hells are you doing here?"

Eiren gave herself credit for not starting, shrieking or even gasping in surprise.

"I... thought I might help?" she ventured.

The shadow that was Ifor stood unmoving, but she imagined him looking at her with serious eyes. She knew he would not be angry, just saddened that she had not kept to the plan.

"Menders will have our guts."

"I know. I'm sorry. I just had to."

"Then don't get in the way." His tone was resolved. There would be no argument, not now. There was no time.

Nodding, Eiren shifted her position slightly, her foot

striking something. Looking down, she could just make out two large wooden pails, filled with water.

"What's the water for?" Eiren whispered.

"For the blood," came Ifor's level reply. "Hush now."

Therbalt walked through the gates, bowed to Kaymar and then moved close. Eiren could only see their silhouettes against the light from the lamppost in the street.

There were murmurs. For a moment Eiren felt as if time stood still. Then the peaceful garden erupted.

Eiren saw Kaymar's knife as a shard of silver light, slashing in an arc. He took Therbalt to the ground with one blow. Ifor erupted from the shadows and fell on Therbalt as well, metal flashing in his hand. It was over so quickly, almost too easily. Eiren stepped forward, instinct moving her hand to the hilt of her own knife.

Ifor rose and fetched a darkened lantern. He flicked it open, illuminating Therbalt's face.

"Fuck me! That isn't him!" Kaymar gasped, crouching by the body. Eiren rushed forward.

It was the same clothing, the long loops of oiled hair, the huge hat, the rings and reeking perfume, but it wasn't Therbalt. The man was older, heavier, with a lined face.

Time froze as the three of them stared at one another.

From a darkened corner, shadows coalesced into new form, moving fast.

A man rushed at them, jabbing a knife into Ifor as Kaymar struggled to rise, tripping over the long skirt he wore. Ifor grunted and fell as the assailant turned, then paused, confronted by the image of two Eirens, not knowing where to strike.

In the light of the lantern, Eiren recognized Therbalt instantly. Her knife scythed in a lethal arc. Only Therbalt's reflexes saved him from being decapitated as Eiren's blade sliced and left him with a gaping slash that ran from his left ear into the corner of his mouth.

He fell back, horror and shock in his eyes, emitting a high wailing shriek. Clutching his face, he turned and fled through the courtyard gate toward the street. Kaymar leapt into pursuit, tearing at the encumbering skirt to free his legs.

"See to Bear!" he yelled, then was gone.

Eiren fell to her knees beside Ifor and opened the lantern all the way.

"Oh my Gods, no!" Eiren gasped at the sight of his blood sodden shirt.

"It's all right," Ifor soothed her. "Bad but not fatal. You wounded him?"

She nodded, amazed at Ifor's calmness.

"Kip will finish it. I owe you my life," he said softly as she helped him sit up. The wound was in his shoulder, too high for his lungs, not enough blood for a major blood vessel to be involved – but enough to endanger his life if the bleeding wasn't stopped soon.

Sudden yells, panicked screams and shots were audible in the distance.

Eiren was helping Ifor to the house just as Kaymar ran back into the garden, his dress ripped and bespattered with blood. He looked like he'd fallen into a threshing machine, sporting multiple slashes and what were going to be impressive bruises.

"Bastard had a whole contingent of thugs waiting. They closed in on me," he groused, shucking off the dress and standing there in his contrived-bust undergarments, inspecting Ifor's wound.

"A lot of them won't be going home tonight, that's for sure. Bastards." He turned to Eiren sternly. "And as for you, my dear, just what got into your pretty head to come back here? Kaymar's eyes were very sinister as he stared at Eiren. Then they lit up with their usual mischievous brightness. He added, "But I am so glad you did. I think you saved us both."

Eiren blushed as Ifor staggered to his feet, wincing against the pain. "Later, Kip. We need to be going."

It took all three of them to bundle the body of the unknown slain man into a travelling trunk, haul it outside and hoist it up into the carriage. Before long, all was as before. They drove away into the night, comforted by the knowledge that though they had missed Therbalt, he would be frightened away for a while.

And marked for life, thanks to Eiren.

***

"You did what?" Menders roared.

"We did what needed to be done," Kaymar answered heatedly. He was weathering the storm of Menders' wrath alone. Ifor was upstairs, being tended by Doctor Franz. "We did what you would have done yourself."

"You stupid bastards!" Menders yelled, glaring across his desk at Kaymar. "I send you over there to protect her, and you do your damndest to get her killed? You bastards!"

"Oh shut up," Kaymar snapped. He eased down into the chair opposite Menders' desk, suddenly weary. The trip back had been rough, the boat moving at full throttle, tossed by running seas. His own wounds and trying to tend to Ifor's on the heaving boat had taxed his strength completely.

Menders leaned forward on his arms, glaring savagely across his desk at Kaymar.

"The fact of it is, if Eiren hadn't done what she did, you'd be digging graves for Ifor and me right now. We were royally had by that bastard Therbalt and if she hadn't… she saved us. She damned near got him, too!"

"That's beside the point!" Menders shouted.

"No, the point is you're pissed off because we did what you would like to have done instead of being stuck here guarding

Katrin and feeling powerless!" Kaymar's voice rose to a fevered pitch.

"Eiren could have been hurt!"

"Well she damn well wasn't!" Kaymar yelled, his temper fraying. "Ifor was. Eiren is not your little schoolteacher any more, Menders. She acted as you trained her, with courage and decisiveness. She's a damned fine woman, brave as they come and you should be bloody well proud of her, not standing there berating me for trying to do your work for you!"

Menders opened his mouth. Then closed it.

"I... I am proud of her," he admitted. "Of course I am."

"Good!" Kaymar hissed, pushing himself up from the seat with shaking arms. "See that you tell her so. Now, if you don't mind, Ifor's hurt and I must see to him, and as for me, well in case you were yelling so hard you didn't notice, I don't feel so good either. Excuse me."

He left Menders standing there, dumbfounded.

***

Eiren began unpacking her bag, hanging the clothing in her wardrobe. There wasn't much. Most of her things had been left behind, as she intended to return to Erdhan. Her bloody clothes had been sent to the laundry and she'd changed into a nightgown.

Word of their exploits was spread through The Shadows. Ifor's injury raised a stir, as did the story that Eiren had 'bloodied her blade', the assassins' term for being tested in combat. That gave her a sense of pride, as she knew she could now walk into the Men's Wing at any time and be accepted as one of them.

Menders came in quietly, closed the door and stood leaning against it, his hands behind him. Eiren smiled at him and went on unpacking.

He watched her silently for a time.

"Franz says Ifor will make a full recovery," he finally said.

"'Bad but not fatal' were the first words Ifor said to me at the time. So I knew he'd be all right."

"Yes, quite." Menders' reaction seemed controlled and Eiren wondered if that had been the wrong thing to say. Would it be a painful reminder of the fact that she had been there while he had not?

Eiren finally sat on the end of the bed, folding her hands in her lap, sighing.

"I expect we need to have this out?" she said. He nodded very slightly. "I expect there will be a fair amount of shouting and so on."

"No," Menders replied, quite calmly. He sat on the end of the bed, close beside her. "No... I think I've done enough shouting for one night."

"Good." Eiren reached across and put her hand on his. "I know what I did made you angry. I didn't do what you asked of me, and for that I'm sorry. But the truth is, I saw a chance to help, not just Kaymar and Ifor but you, Katrin, everyone. I do beg your forgiveness but in all honesty, should a situation like that arise again, I will not sit on my hands and do nothing!"

Menders turned to her, took her hands in his and held them firmly. "I'm very, *very* proud of you, my dear. Very proud," he said. Eiren was taken aback. It wasn't what she expected to hear at this point.

"Why, thank you," she responded meekly.

"Let me help you clear this bed," he whispered gently. "You're done in and need to sleep."

Eiren had thought she would never sleep again after slashing Therbalt's face, but found she could barely keep her eyes open long enough to slip under the covers.

***

Eiren woke and knew from the light that it was many hours later, close to sunrise. The room was now cozily warm. She turned and saw that Menders was sitting in the big armchair by the stove, watching her. He had the window shaded against the dawn light and wore his clear glasses. His white eyes seemed to glow a bit in the dimness.

He held out his arms to her with a smile. She went to him, folding herself into his lap with her head on his shoulder, his arms around her. He tucked her long nightgown gently over her feet.

"There's my Little Bird."

Remembering Therbalt calling her that, Eiren shivered involuntarily.

"What?" Menders asked.

"Therbalt called me that once. It terrified me until I realized that he couldn't know it's your name for me," she replied.

"Ah. No, he couldn't have known. There's a way you move your head at times while looking up at a fellow that is very reminiscent of a dear little bird. If you like, I won't call you that anymore."

"Don't you dare stop! I'm not silly," she smiled. He chuckled a little and cuddled her even closer.

"I've debriefed your fellow warriors and examined the body," he said. "Our mystery is solved. That was Lord Vannik. I've had a message from Bartan with some very interesting information he's just discovered. It turns out that Vannik's been behind this plot to remove Katrin. This Therbalt character is his protégé.

"Vannik's motives weren't purely political. He was sadistic and spiteful, and this Therbalt was a faithful pupil of his. Vannik had an incredible network, has manipulated things around the world for years, and no doubt Therbalt will inherit this operation. You placed yourself in terrible danger, my love. Those men had every intention of killing you once you turned over what they wanted."

"Menders, if I hadn't done what I did, we'd still be playing cat and mouse with Therbalt," Eiren said heatedly. "I only wish I'd cut his head off instead of slicing his greasy face."

"I know. I know, don't upset yourself. I'm proud of you. You have been incredibly brave and selfless."

"They want to kill my Katrin – and they want to kill you too. What else could I have done?"

Menders settled her head against his shoulder. After a short silence, he said "There is something more for us to talk about. Kaymar told me that you know who I am."

"Yes. I know that you were Lord Stettan and that you were a very successful assassin before you came here." Eiren could feel tension in him, and stroked his hair.

"I'm still Lord Stettan. I don't use the title, of course. I'm not proud of my family and don't relish the connection. I've used the name Menders since military school. I couldn't be a spy, because my eyes and the glasses make it impossible for me to disguise myself effectively, so I was strictly an assassin. I was a good assassin, Eiren. I was the best and no-one has exceeded me yet, though Kaymar came close during his service."

"You would have been the best. You never settle for less," she answered.

"Does it make a difference in the way you feel about me?" he asked, sounding a little uncertain.

"No." She sat up on his lap so she could look at his face.

"I saw you kill Madame Holz," she went on quietly. "That didn't change the way I felt about you. Why would knowing that you're Lord Stettan change anything?"

Menders looked like a stunned fish.

"You saw…"

"Yes. I was awake that night, because Katrin kept crying and I was angry with you for letting that woman be around her and for leaving Katrin to cry in that cold nursery. I got out of bed to go to Katrin, but I stopped when I saw you go into the nursery. You took care of Katrin, then you left and went downstairs. That confused me, because surely you knew that terrible woman was there. So I stayed in the hallway, watching. Then you returned and went in and drank with her. I thought you'd gone mad. Then I saw you kissing her...

"I watched as you took her down the stairs. I saw you kill her. I was glad! Oh, I was so glad! That was an evil woman and she would have done terrible things to Katrin. I loved you even more after you did it." Eiren's voice trembled with emotion.

Menders' expression was a mixture of perplexity and wonder. Then he laughed softly.

"My love, you are more terrifying than I, as Lord Stettan, ever was," he said. "When Kaymar told me how you led Therbalt on and kept him coming back for more by playing the libertine lass from the country, my hair stood on end. You had best retire from your career as spy and assassin now, or you might end up knocking Lord Stettan off his pedestal as the greatest."

"Don't be absurd," she murmured, letting him hold her again, resting her head against his shoulder comfortably. "If I have to do the same again to protect the ones I love, I will. I hope I never have to, but I will if need be."

"That's what the profession is about," Menders said quietly. "To protect what you love, you take measures most people couldn't. In my case, it was love of Mordania. I don't like the Queen and I don't like many things about the way the country is, but I love it and worked like a demon to preserve it in hope that someday it will be what it could be."

Eiren said nothing, putting her arms around his neck. He held her for a while, stroking her hair and occasionally kissing her. It felt wonderful to be home.

"One thing I do regret very much," Menders finally said as he ran a hand over her hair, "Is that because we are not married, you couldn't become Lady Stettan. If anyone deserves the title, it is you. I hope you can forgive me that."

"That's silly. I don't want a title, I want you," Eiren said, content, listening to the beating of his heart.

"My darling, that you always have," Menders whispered.

CHAPTER 51
TO BECOME A TAILOR

Borsen strolled along the long pier at Erdstrom on a very misty winter day. Few people were stalwart enough to brave the foggy chill but he found it intriguing and rather romantic. Normal seaside sounds took on mystery as they drifted, apparently sourceless, through the swirling grey clouds.

He was tired. He had just completed four days of examinations required to attain the rank of tailor in the Tailor's Guild of Mordania, and he knew without a doubt that his performance had been more than adequate. That didn't mean that the board would grant him the rank, of course. He'd realized that was going to be a problem the moment he'd gone into the room where the five board members sat and they had seen that he was Thrun.

No matter, he thought. If they knock my application back out of prejudice, I'll be back next year. Sooner or later, they will have to pass me through.

There was general approbation at The Shadows when Borsen announced that he'd applied to take the exams. That was followed by stunned silence when he stated his intention of taking the train to Erdstrom alone, even though that meant a week would pass before he could return.

He hadn't the heart to tell anyone the real reason he'd chosen to do so – that he wanted to spend some time completely on his own. It would have hurt far too many people.

Borsen had never been on his own in his life. His childhood had been spent trailing in the wake of his itinerant father, his woman and their growing brood of children. Then he had gone to live at The Shadows, where there were over fifty people within shouting distance at any given moment.

Borsen loved The Shadows. It was safe there. He was free

to be young and foolish if he wished. He liked the work he did and being with his beloved uncle was wonderful. But he had an overwhelming desire to be his own man, to accomplish things independently and to know that what he gained had been through his own efforts.

The loving atmosphere of The Shadows could be smothering. It would be easy, if he allowed it, to simply stay there forever, the adored pet of everyone, a fixture of Katrin's household. He would have a job for life, gracious and comfortable surroundings and more companionship and family love than he'd ever thought he would.

During this week alone in Erdstrom he'd had time to think. He'd hired a horse and explored parts of Erdstrom he'd never seen on family visits to the town, looking at elegant houses and their grounds. He also spent hours on foot, going into one shop after another, glad for the leisure and privacy to be able to look as long as he wished, without having to consider others' tastes and desires. He'd found ideas beginning to take definite form in his mind – what he wanted in the future, what he wanted to work toward.

He wanted something that, as far as he knew, did not exist. It would be a store, not a shop, where a person could go not only for a suit, but for shoes, hats, gloves, scarves, jewelry. And why not more, furniture, household goods, carriages? Not a general store – those were ghastly jumbled places – but high quality, luxury goods in beautiful and elegant surroundings. Kaymar, who traveled a great deal, said that he'd never seen such a place anywhere but would patronize such a store in a moment.

Borsen wanted money and fame and wasn't ashamed of it. He'd been startled when his uncle had given him an income. He had tried to resist at first, wanting to have earned every pennig of his own money, but Menders persuaded him to accept.

"This money, by rights, should have been given as support for your mother during her minority," his uncle explained gently. "My father had an obligation to support those children he fathered out of wedlock, but he never did so. In many ways, this will be righting a wrong. It will give you a start in life that your mother would have given you, had she been able to do so."

Borsen gave in. Menders taught him how to invest the money and his little fortune had grown impressively. He could buy anything he wanted. Beyond an exquisite wardrobe made entirely by himself and some indulgences for his room, he spent little, planning for the future.

Borsen also knew that he wanted luxury. He knew what it was to sleep outside on a snowy night, or to live in a tenement room infested with rats. He never wanted to face such conditions again. He was willing to do any amount of work to make a life of luxury for himself. Only Menders knew most of the story of Borsen's childhood, gently extracted from him during those nights when Borsen would wake screaming from nightmares. His early years had been a long, dark horror of cold, fear, insecurity, hunger, loneliness and abuse.

Borsen looked out over the grey ocean, seeing the house he would have someday. It would be near the sea, where he could hear the seagulls' cries and buoy bells coming through the mist like the voices of ghosts. Grand, but not so grand that it wouldn't be comfortable.

He'd taken an excellent hotel room, ignoring the stare of the desk clerk when a small, young Thrun man dressed in an exquisite suit had demanded and paid for the best.

Borsen was accustomed to being stared at, not only because he was obviously Thrun and because of his small stature, but also because in the last year he had become beautiful. Not handsome – beautiful. His face would have been considered beautiful on a woman, except for his perfectly kept Thrun-style jawline beard and moustache. He stood out in any crowd and made a point of doing so by his style of dressing and proudly upright bearing.

He'd gone into the Tailors Guild examination dressed in his absolute best, a handmade suit of an unusual golden grey silk, with a matching top hat. His heavy gold watch chain, a birthday gift from Menders, was much in evidence. A new pair of heavy gold hoops adorned his ears. He'd put a shine on his grey shoes that would make Hemmett's Commandant weep with joy, and carried his walking stick, which concealed a sword blade, in hand.

He could tell he'd impressed the examination board, though a couple of them made a point of curling their lips and making sure he knew they considered him an inferior being because he was Thrun.

Borsen proceeded as if nothing insulting had occurred. He presented his letters of recommendation and greatly enjoyed seeing eyebrows hitting hairlines as the board members, including the sneering ones, saw that he had the highest opinion of Lord Stettan, Lady Spartz, Baronet Kaymar Shvalz, First Lieutenant Hemmett Greinholz, Court Assassin Bartan, Lord and Lady Velten and Princess Katrin Morghenna of Mordania.

"Your current place of employment?" one sneerer asked, as if it wasn't clearly written on the paper before him. Perhaps he can't read, Borsen thought charitably.

"I am in the service of Her Highness, Princess Katrin Morghenna of Mordania," Borsen answered calmly.

Then the questions came thick and fast. The board members pretended they couldn't understand his accented speech and constantly asked him to repeat himself.

"Yes, I have been apprenticed since I was thirteen. I was not put to sweeping or running errands, but began immediately on seaming by hand. I am proficient with sewing machines, yes. My master, Tomar Fersen, has written at great length of the thoroughness of my training and my skills."

They perused Tomar's letter. A great deal of whispered conversation and argument went on. Borsen waited, showing no sign of concern or agitation.

"You are sixteen years of age?"

"Yes."

"Why have you not waited until you are of age to undertake the examinations?"

"There is no law or Guild rule that prevents someone of my age from becoming a tailor if he can demonstrate the required skills and knowledge," Borsen responded.

There was another whispered huddle, though Borsen noticed that one of the men, the only one who had remained silent, did not take part but was looking at him. Borsen nodded politely. He was rewarded with an answering nod and slight smile.

"How would one of your – derivation – attain the skills of tailoring?" one of the sneerers asked.

"I was mentored by people who do not allow themselves to be blinded by ignorant prejudice," Borsen responded politely. Out of the corner of his eye, he could see the silent man laughing to himself. "I have been given the training any other tailor's apprentice is given, and I have made the most of my opportunities."

There were red faces and more hissing conversation.

"We suggest that you are too young to attempt the examination," one man said.

"I will repeat myself - there is no law or Guild rule that prevents a sixteen year old from attempting the examinations or becoming a tailor." He had decided that he was sixteen this year, after Kaymar quizzed him closely about things he remembered and said that he thought Borsen was probably older than Katrin. Ifor had supplied Borsen with a skillfully forged birth certificate to that effect, quietly explaining that he needed such documentation as he became an adult, that it wouldn't do to be undocumented. Ifor had also reminded him that he was a member of the Royal Family, and would be considered of age at sixteen. That had sounded fine to Borsen.

The hissing began again, louder this time. Borsen heard

several choice phrases, including "dirty Thrun", "bloody little clever dick" and "let him show himself as a complete fake", but showed no sign. The Guild rules were dragged out and perused. Eventually they ran out of steam and just sat there, looking at him like so many turtles on a log.

"May I request that you gentlemen allow me to undertake the examination and let my answers and work prove my expertise?" Borsen suggested, lowering his voice ever so slightly so it had a seductive husk to it, a trick he'd learned from Kaymar. He could see the silent man laughing into his shirtfront again. "You may ask me anything pertaining to tailoring or request me to demonstrate any skills you wish. It is my desire to prove myself to you as a tailor worthy of Guild rank."

The silent man made an applauding motion and spoke, his voice a pleasant baritone.

"You can't prevent him trying, so stop bullying the young man."

They'd sputtered and hissed some more, but eventually gave in. They fired questions at Borsen for hours. He answered them all. They had bolts of fabrics hauled in, made him identify them, fired more questions about the handling of each fabric at him. He identified everything, knew exactly what should be done with each sample. The second day they gave him the written examination and he knew he had not missed a question. The third day they went over his presentation garments with magnifying glasses. They made him sew every hand stitch there was while they watched, dragged in a sewing machine that he had to clean and oil before it was workable and ran him through the repertoire of machine sewing.

On the fourth day, they had him cut and fit a casual jacket for the fattest member of the board. The man had an enormous belly and sway back. The jacket was to be roughed out, not finished. Borsen contemplated doing things by the book, but knew if he did, it would not fit the man's contorted figure properly.

He went with his instincts. He cut the garment as he would if he were in the relaxed and friendly workshop at The Shadows, not in this room that simmered with resentment. He cut the back of the jacket on the bias to flow gracefully over the man's sway back and massive buttocks. He weighted the hem with several washers he'd brought along in his pockets, so the jacket tail would hang straight. He sewed like a fiend, making the examiners stare as he drove the needle along the seams. He rejected the lining material they'd given him, saying briskly that it was cheap trash, and stunned them by selecting a heavy silk instead. He sat on the worktable all day, refusing to stop to eat or drink. He was determined to do more than they requested. The jacket would be finished, not merely roughed in.

Twice the silent man carried in food and water and set it beside him. Borsen, his gorge high from suppressed anger and tension, could barely choke it down. He made sure to thank the man, the only person who had treated him decently since this ordeal began.

It was a little before five o'clock when the jacket was done. Borsen gave it a final press and handed it over. The fat man slid it on.

"Would you make trousers for this?" he asked after a moment of staring at himself in the mirror.

Borsen laughed out loud, picking up his perfect hat and setting it on his silky, waist length hair.

"I will with pleasure," he replied as the fat man extended a hand for him to shake. "If it isn't convenient for you to travel to my workshop, I would gladly come to Erdstrom to make the trousers." The rest of the board were circling Mister Fat, ogling the jacket, picking at the lapels and cuffs. They should ogle. It was perfect. They asked about the bias cut back and he explained. Then they stood and stared at him.

"Let the young man go, he's exhausted," the silent man

said firmly. At that there was a general rumpus as they laughed at themselves and told him to run along, that he would receive official notification of his examination results by post in two weeks' time. They clustered around Mister Fat again, looking like hens that had just been given their grain. Borsen managed not to slam the door on his way out, went back to his hotel and drowned his rage and indignation in a long hot bath, followed by an enormous meal and a glass of wine.

His temper had cooled in the three days since as he'd gone on his solo excursions around Erdstrom. Now he felt philosophical. He knew that the board had demanded far more than they would of any other prospective tailor. It was likely he could protest the extreme requests they'd made. Tomar had told him that a written examination, some oral quizzing and perusal of the sample garments was all he had to expect. Tomar didn't understand how things were for Thrun. Borsen had been ready for the worst and was glad of it. He'd managed not to let them see how many times he'd been close to a display of temper – or of bursting into tears.

Now he took off his glasses, which were so bedewed by the thickening ocean mist that he could hardly see. He drew a piece of flannel from his pocket, an off-cut from a little nightdress he'd made for one of the estate children. He was using it to clean and dry the fogged lenses when he realized someone was approaching. He turned toward what was a dim shape to his uncorrected sight, gave his glasses a final polish and settled them on his nose.

It was the silent man.

"Good evening, Mister Menders," he said in the quiet tone which must be characteristic, bowing politely.

"Your servant, sir," Borsen replied, returning the bow.

"I must apologize for not introducing myself earlier. I'm Seran Ferensen. I saw you here and wanted to compliment you on your excellent performance this week - and to make a suggestion."

Oh, here it comes, Borsen thought, his confidence ebbing sickeningly. Try again next year, young man. Those bastards! I knew they'd never pass me even though I'm the best damned tailor they've ever seen!

"I cannot tell you the outcome of your examination," Ferensen continued. "That has to wait until you receive the official notification. However, I should like to suggest that in two years' time, when you are of age, you return and undertake the examination for Master Tailor. You would be assured of a pass, because that is the examination you were given."

Borsen, ready to use every bit of self control he had to avoid howling in despair, suddenly realized what he'd heard. The man was telling him indirectly that he'd passed, that he was a Guild tailor!

"Thank you, sir!" he beamed.

"You're more than welcome. You gave an impressive account of yourself and your talents," Ferensen responded. Then he looked closely at Borsen.

"I was wondering if you would care to join me..." he began. Then he cut himself off and stepped back, shaking his head slightly. "No, never mind. I wish you great good fortune in your future endeavors, Mister Menders." With that he tipped his hat, turned and walked rapidly away.

Borsen restrained himself from dancing wildly along the pier but did spin his walking stick repeatedly out of giddy glee. It wasn't until he was in the bathtub in his suite that he realized the import of Seran Ferensen's cut off question.

He was asking me to dinner, Borsen thought, sitting bolt upright in the tub. Gods! And he must have wanted more than that because he cut himself off so abruptly. Well of course, I'm sixteen and he knows it, but for a moment he reacted to me for myself.

He sat back for a while, contemplating the abortive

invitation and what it meant. He'd been perceived as an attractive man by someone he could easily have been interested in.

He let his mind drift on the idea of sleeping with Ferensen. Though Borsen had no experience, he had plenty of imagination and a great deal of information imparted to him by Kaymar. The thought was nice – very. But he wanted more. Kaymar had warned him against becoming involved very young or being promiscuous. Borsen already knew he wanted what Kaymar had – a good, steady, loving man who wanted to be with him for the rest of his life. Looks didn't matter, elegance didn't matter. What mattered was love and devotion, like what Ifor gave Kaymar and received in return.

So no, Mister Ferensen, I would not have gotten into bed with you, Borsen thought as he dried himself. I will wait until I have what I want, in all things, and that includes in a man.

Then, remembering that he was now a Guild tailor and the youngest person ever to have become one, and because he was sixteen and had forced himself to be much older for a week, he climbed up on the big hotel bed and spent several jubilant moments jumping up and down like a lunatic.

CHAPTER 52
A PAIR OF AMATEURS

Eiren returned to Erdhan and Menders tried to put his reservations aside. He was troubled. Despite his intense diligence, Vannik's plot had surfaced like a crocodile, carefully constructed, artfully executed. It had nearly cost the lives of two of his best and had placed his beloved Eiren in danger.

There had been no sign of Therbalt since the night of Vannik's death and the threads leading to Vannik's organization seemed to have been severed, leaving little trace of the plot that had been averted. There were no connections, no links to individuals or other factions. It was all too neat and clean for Menders' liking. He knew that somewhere a connection to unseen enemies went undiscovered.

Menders sorted recent events again, turning everything over in his mind while staring absently through his office window. In the distance, Marjana Spaltz's blue bonnet showed her progress across the fields. He wondered idly why she was up and around again so soon after her recent illness.

***

Sometimes Katrin seemed to hear voices in her head. As a child she had wanted to believe she was hearing the voice of her mother, trying to contact her. Why she thought this she couldn't say. If her mother, the Queen, wanted to contact her, all she had to do was write a letter.

After Kaymar had described his madness to her, Katrin had confided in him about the voices. She'd been shocked to see his eyes widen in fear – then he'd shaken his head vigorously.

"I've been watching you for hours almost every day since you were four," he said. "You are definitely not mad. You've never said anything about hearing voices before."

"I just accepted it when I was little." Katrin struggled to explain. "I – I thought it might be my mother trying to help me. I believed some very strange things when I was small."

"As do we all," Kaymar said with a touch of bitterness. He was not having a good day. Katrin had decided to ask him about the voices to bring him out of himself. He'd been muttering and fingering the knife at his side, as he tended to do before he cut himself. "What does this voice sound like?"

"Sometimes just whispers. Quite low pitched, like an older woman. Sometimes it sounds harsh."

Kaymar shook his head.

"If you'll remember, your mother's voice is remarkably like yours, medium pitched, very musical and gentle. Unless, of course, you're declaiming, which you both have a habit of doing," he said. Katrin shoved him, hard, and he shoved back, playfully.

"Don't get rough with me, Your Royal Highness, you could end up with more than you bargained for," he snickered.

Katrin was glad to hear him joke, but he was also being forthcoming and she wanted to get as much information from him as she could while his mood lasted.

"Sometimes it even sounds like more than one voice – like many women all whispering at once." She sighed in frustration. Now that she was talking about the voices, it all sounded either very stupid or rather mad.

"When do you hear these voices?" Kaymar asked.

"When I'm angry or very nervous," Katrin answered. "Sometimes when I'm in a situation that could turn dangerous. The time Trouble started kicking up his stall when I was saddling him, I heard them say he was going to kick a moment before he started. I got out of the way in time but if I hadn't heard them, I wouldn't have."

Kaymar studied her long and hard.

"Could be your own intuition," he said. "When you hear

the voices, do they tell you to do things to yourself, to harm yourself? Or do they deride you, ridicule you? Tell you to harm others?"

Katrin shook her head.

"I don't think you need to worry about them," Kaymar continued, looking relieved. "I don't like to use the words 'overactive imagination' because I've had them flung at me when what I deal with is anything but. I'm not that well educated, Katrin, so I don't know just how to put it into words. I would say it's your own mind, the part of it that you're not conscious of, perceiving things and warning you about them if there is danger."

Katrin had to be content with that. She didn't feel comfortable with the idea of telling Menders or Eiren about the voices. They would be alarmed and she felt that the voices meant no harm. She tried to analyze the phenomenon in an adult way. She came to the conclusion that what she heard resembled intense thought more than actual voices perceived by the ear.

The voices often let her know when someone was walking up behind her. She would turn around at their prompting, never surprised to find it was exactly who she thought it would be.

So as Katrin stood in her soapmaking shed, watching freshly poured soap cool in the mold as she prepared to dump out the remnants of the lye she had used, she knew with certainty that someone had come up behind her – and that the person was not someone she knew. Instead of the warm familiarity of a friend approaching, there was a feeling like the touch of a cold, wet hand on the back of her neck beneath her pinned up hair. The voices whispered in layers of alarm.

Katrin turned around slowly, the bucket of lye clutched in both hands. She was surprised to see Marjana Spaltz's familiar blue bonnet. Then she saw that the hollow-eyed woman wearing the bonnet wasn't Marjana Spaltz.

"Miss, is this where I can buy soap?" the woman asked. The gun in her hand pointed down towards the floor, wavering back and forth like a charmed snake. Katrin's eyes fixed on the weapon. Her own gun was in the pocket of her dress, her knife strapped to her hip. Both would take too long to reach. The only weapon immediately available was the bucket of lye in her hands.

"It is," Katrin said quietly. "Is there something I can do to help you?"

The woman looked directly at her and Katrin could see that her eyes were mad in the depths of the bonnet, desperate and frightened.

I could distract her enough to throw the lye in her face, Katrin thought, her mind suddenly frantic. She seems dazed or demented. But could I really throw lye into a woman's face, into her eyes? She shuddered inwardly.

"Yes, you can help me," the woman said, her face twisting into a dreamy and terribly mad smile. "You can die. That's what will help me." Her voice was small, almost whispery, as if she was one of those people who had never spoken up in their lives.

Katrin's grasp tightened on the bucket handle as the muzzle of the gun came up.

***

Eiren loved hats. She paused to glance in a shop window where a light green straw trimmed with a cream ribbon and a small cluster of silk snowflowers was on display. It would be marvelous against Katrin's golden hair, the perfect springtime hat.

"Excuse me, madame. Can you direct me to the train station?"

Eiren felt her muscles coiling with tension. You'd have to be blind to not see the train station from here – it was one of the largest and grandest buildings in Erdhan.

Turning, Eiren saw a tall woman with curling blonde hair standing only a couple of feet from her. She hadn't even seen a reflection in the window. The woman had been careful to stand where her image wouldn't be cast.

Then Eiren saw the knife. The woman held it at waist level. It was shaking. Caught off guard, there was no time to reach her own weapon. Menders' training took over.

She flung herself down, scything her legs around into the woman's knees, catching her off guard and knocking her to the ground.

Kaymar was there in an instant, kicking the woman's weapon away into the gutter as his own knife flashed out. He held it firmly against the stranger's throat.

***

"Please, madame, you're overwrought," Katrin said quietly. "Why would you want to kill me? Put the gun away and I'll do what I can to help you."

"He has my boy. My little boy, only two years old. He says if I kill you, he'll give him back to me." The woman's eyes jigged back and forth. Katrin tried to see a rhythm in the motion, an unguarded moment where she could jump out of the way or hurl the bucket of lye.

"If someone has taken your little boy, I can help you," Katrin said, trying to sound soothing. "I'm a Princess of Mordania. I have some powerful people here with me. Won't you put the gun down?"

"He said if I don't kill you, he'll rip my boy open," the woman went on, her voice bizarrely level and soft. The gun no longer wavered.

If being brave meant keeping calm while trying not to pass out or vomit, then Katrin was certainly feeling brave. From the dark recesses of her mind the spidery voices hissed.

"Kill her! Throw the lye, burn her eyes out!" the voices commanded.

"He must be a very terrible man," Katrin answered, her

own voice barely under control. "Tell me about him."

A movement behind the woman caught Katrin's eye but she didn't dare look in that direction. Another second revealed Borsen, advancing toward them from the goats' shed, a heavy axe handle in his hand.

"He's a demon, cruel as can be," the woman whispered. "He'd kill my little one even though he's the father. He loves nothing and nobody except himself."

"That is very wrong," Katrin soothed, seeing Borsen stealing ever closer. "The people here can help you, madame, but if you kill me, believe me, they will kill you and there will be no-one to care for your little boy. Put the gun away. Tell me where this man is and I will help you."

"In Surelia. You have no power there," the woman said mournfully. "You're just a ghost now, a shadow of things best left unbred. Better off dead, really."

Katrin thought the woman's rambling sounded rehearsed, like words she had learned to recite.

"I know people who can go anywhere. Please, my dear, put the gun away," Katrin answered, trying to sound comforting. The woman's mad eyes met hers and blinked.

Borsen, now within range, raised himself up and swung the axe handle. It struck the woman a heavy blow across her gun arm, knocking the muzzle down. Simultaneously, Katrin flung the bucket of lye, drenching the woman's dress and her own.

The woman screamed and brought her arms up to her face before doubling over. Borsen grabbed the hand holding the gun. It went off again, the bullet smacking the side of the house as Borsen wrested it away from her.

Ifor leapt in from the opposite side of the shed and knocked the woman to the ground.

"Get your skirt off, Katrin, you'll be burnt to the bone!" he shouted. Borsen pulled out one of his knives, and began slashing through the fabric of Katrin's dress, pulling the rapidly disintegrating cloth away from her.

***

Kaymar moved quickly, dragging the woman into a nearby alley before anyone passing by knew there had been an altercation.

"Who sent you?" he growled. Eiren stood by, holding her pistol ready.

The woman shook her head violently. Kaymar pressed his knife hard against her throat.

"It was Therbalt, wasn't it?" he hissed. "Tell me, if your life is worth anything to you."

"I'm dead now," the woman gasped.

"Under my hand you'll wish you were," Kaymar said. "You'd find you're actually very much alive. Talk!"

"He has my son. My little boy, four years old. He'll kill him if I don't kill her." The woman looked at Eiren.

"Who? Who told you to do this?"

The woman shook her head.

"Don't you understand?" she said quietly. "He's going to kill my son. He will do it without a thought, like swatting a fly, even though my boy is his son too. It doesn't matter anymore."

The woman stiffened and looked over Kaymar's shoulder, her eyes wide with fear. Instinctively, Kaymar and Eiren turned. A crunching sound reached them, accompanied by a sickening, sticky sweet stench as a soft rustling accompanied the woman falling to the ground. By the time Kaymar crouched beside her, she was dead.

Eiren closed her eyes in horror. A moment later, Kaymar was leading her from the alley, making her walk quickly toward their safe house.

"What the hells is going on? She had morric acid hidden in a tooth," he fumed. "It kills instantly. Assassins use it, but this woman is no assassin."

Eiren had no answers. She was trying not to be sick.

***

"I'm afraid she's dead," Doctor Franz said with a weary sigh, as he drew the bedcovers up over the burned face of the woman who had held Katrin at gunpoint. Menders had known it the second he'd walked back into the room. The open mouth, the hollowed tooth, the breath scented with morric acid, like crushed nightingale flowers - the deadliest poison in the world. Assassins' special issue – but this hapless woman had been no assassin.

Menders stood with his hands on his hips, looking down at the covered body. He'd have to bury her out near the woods, in the quiet corner next to Madame Holz and Mister Enigma.

The interrogation had gone nowhere. Franz had treated the woman's facial burns, bandaged her eyes and attended to her other injuries. Ifor had knocked her down hard and she was a sapling of a woman, scrawny and underfed.

"If you tell me who sent you, I will help you get your child back," Menders had told her quietly, finding it hard to believe he could feel compassion for anyone who had meant to kill Katrin – but this creature was purely pitiful. She was about as menacing as a kitten once she was divested of her cheap gun and a knife that wouldn't cut an onion. She shivered constantly, despite the blanket and towels she'd been wrapped in after the lye-soaked dress was taken from her. Her body would heal in time but her mind was another matter. At times she was completely incoherent, at others she wept uncontrollably. Her eyes, until bandaged, were unfocused and roving. She would whisper about her baby and rock back and forth.

Nothing could get her to give the name of the man who had sent her and who was threatening to kill her child. Menders had used every tone from threatening to tender. Doctor Franz had tried gentle persuasion. Even Katrin had spoken with her, but the woman was somewhere far away. Franz had finally given her a small dose of ramplane, as it was known to loosen inhibitions and tongues, but to no avail.

"There is no power on the planet like a woman's protective instinct toward her child," Franz had sighed to Menders. "I think nothing short of torture, possibly not even that, would make her talk. Her mind is destroyed."

Then the wretched creature, left alone for a moment, had poisoned herself with the morric acid hidden in her tooth.

What did it all mean? Menders thought angrily. This attempt on Katrin's life by someone not qualified to cut bread was pathetically absurd, but the fact that it had come so close to succeeding was maddening. Therbalt had to be behind it – but so far he was invisible. For him to strike so close to home with a completely incompetent amateur assassin was either a blunder or a ruse intended to deceive.

Whichever was Therbalt's motive, for now Menders was going to draw back his forces and close ranks at The Shadows. Ifor had taken the boat to fetch Eiren and Kaymar back from Erdhan.

***

"Could they have been some of Gladdas Dalmanthea's?" Haakel asked. Menders shook his head and Kaymar snorted in disgust.

"Glad Dalmanthea's girls are slick, they aren't shuddering emotional wrecks," Ifor retorted.

"The one who attacked me seemed quite sane," Eiren said, "but so rattled that she didn't seem to know what to do."

"Glad's girls are professionals. That woman wasn't," Kaymar scoffed.

"Gladdas and I have a pact not to go after each other,

we've had it for years," Menders added. "She used to be given contracts to kill me at least once a month. It got tedious, because she could never catch me and she was suffering financially because she couldn't collect the fees. Likewise, my attempts to bag her were like trying to nail custard to a wall. We finally made a truce. She's never accepted another contract on me."

"Who the hells is Gladdas Dalmanthea?" Eiren asked briskly.

Menders looked at her in apology.

"I'm sorry my dear, I forget you don't know all that we do," he replied. "Gladdas Dalmanthea is a spy-assassin. She's Artreyan by birth, or at least so we think. She's as slippery as a bucket of greased worms about details like that, has a million stories about her origins. She's not active herself these days, but runs a network of female assassins and spies – her own, she's a free agent for hire. Glad's ruthless, but she has her own set of rules and never breaks them. If she promised not to come after me, she will not come after me, full stop. No threat or amount of money would coerce her."

Eiren nodded, looking relieved.

"The story that both of these mystery women told is what puzzles me," Haakel mused. "Both claiming that some man had their child, that he was the father of the child. That's utterly bizarre."

"The ages of the children were different," Menders said. "It could be that it's the same father. I suspect Therbalt."

"It's the sort of sadistic thing that would amuse him," Eiren said wearily. "I'm sure of it."

"I thought this Therbalt was nancy?" Franz interjected. "Children with two women?"

"He is," Kaymar responded firmly. "But that doesn't mean he can't sleep with women. The rumor was that he slept with Aidelia. Nancies sleep with women all the time, for various reasons. Plenty of nancies in the nobility have wives and children."

"And there's another assassin out there. A real one. Therbalt expects us to fixate on solving the mystery of these two women, letting an assassin through while we're distracted." Menders got up and prowled around the room.

He was furious about the entire situation. Katrin had been in grave danger. Only Borsen's quick thinking and Katrin's calmness and distracting chatter had saved her. Ifor had gotten there quickly, but anyone startling that woman could have made her pull the trigger at point blank range. Ifor had been helpless to do anything from his position.

Menders knew he'd let things get too slack. Katrin had been without a guard close by and an amateur had managed to walk right up behind her with a gun.

"Hemmett, can you stay for a while?" he asked, turning back to the table. "I know your graduation is pressing, but I'd like you here."

"I spoke with Sir already. I brought assignments with me so I can keep up with my class," Hemmett answered firmly. "Late winter break is coming as well. If I can be of use, I'm here."

"It will risk your becoming top graduate," Eiren said quietly.

"I'm willing to sacrifice that if I'm needed here," Hemmett replied.

Menders swallowed. He knew how hard Hemmett had worked to keep top grades all these years.

"I need you to be with Katrin and Borsen for a while," he explained, settling on the edge of the table and looking at Hemmett. "If you could act as companion and guard for them it would be a great relief to me. They are going to be restricted to a painful degree, because until we know more, it's unsafe for them to leave the house. Being close to them in age will make you the best guard they could have."

"They're my sister and brother," Hemmett said with

finality. Menders knew his mind was set.

"Thank you, my son," he responded softly. Hemmett smiled.

"So you're going to lock us down?" Kaymar said sourly.

'Yes," Menders said with finality.

"I disagree," Kaymar said.

"I know, but it's not your decision," Menders replied.

Kaymar sat back and sighed. Both of them were too weary to argue. "I just don't know, Menders." He stretched and leaned back, then added, "All of us being cooped up here, bottled up like bugs in a jar... I just can't help get the feeling that this is exactly what Therbalt wants us to do."

"Perhaps," Menders said, thinking on it. "But it's hard for us to take the initiative when we don't know where to go with it. We can control access here. Triple the guard, regular patrols, no one in or out of the area for fifty miles."

CHAPTER 53
LOCKDOWN

Borsen padded down the hallway of the Family Wing in his nightshirt. He couldn't sleep and he was sure that Katrin was awake as well.

His uncle had outlined what they would have to do until further notice. It was severe. They couldn't leave the house. The winter shutters on all the windows were to be kept shut and bolted. Menders' Men were posted all over the house, anywhere anyone could get in and Hemmett was posted on guard in Katrin's bedroom. The strongroom door stood open. Borsen couldn't remember it being left open before.

Menders had also limited their movement within the house. Katrin could not leave the sight of an armed guard at any time. That meant someone had to be with her every second. The house was vast, and parts of it were not in use, so it made sense.

Kaymar was seated on a chair at the entrance to Katrin's suite.

"Can't sleep, little Cuz?" he smiled grimly.

"I want to see Katrin," Borsen answered.

"I heard her talking to Hemmett just now, so she's awake too," Kaymar said, nodding for him to go on in.

Katrin's lamp was burning and he could hear her speaking quietly to Hemmett. A glance into Eiren's room let him know she was sleeping. There was no sign of his uncle anywhere. He peeped around Katrin's doorway.

"There's Inchworm," Hemmett said with a grin. He was sitting in Katrin's easy chair, while she sat up in the bed. "Come join the sleepless party."

Borsen hoisted himself on the bed and leaned against a bedpost.

"I couldn't settle and Olan finally yelled through the wall

for me to quit moving around or he'd pound me," he said. "So I thought to come here."

"No-one will yell at you here." Katrin smiled. "You should come live on this end of the wing."

"I like my bachelor apartment," Borsen smiled back. Hemmett snorted with laughter, but winked at him. Borsen loved Menders, Eiren and Katrin, but preferred the quarters he'd had since coming to The Shadows.

They sat and talked quietly for a while. Borsen could tell that Katrin was frightened but putting on a good face. Hemmett was very calm and Borsen felt better just being near him.

"I keep thinking about those two little boys," Katrin finally said. "That woman… she wasn't lying and Eiren says the one who attacked her wasn't lying either. Everyone's busy protecting me, but what about those children?"

"Willow, there's no way to know where they are," Hemmett answered. "Menders will have his network on it. They're already making enquiries about those boys. He's going to do what he can to get this Therbalt and finish him. It's pointless to fret over things you're helpless to change."

Borsen watched as shadows of worry and doubt crossed Katrin's face.

He'd always understood the potential danger to her, from the time he'd come to The Shadows and become a sort of junior Menders' Man. Over time, his uncle had taught him knife fighting, marksmanship and many skills that spies and assassins used until Doctor Franz called a halt to advanced training with tumbling moves, fearful that Borsen's fragile bones wouldn't hold up to the pounding. He knew it was not only so he could protect himself, but for Katrin's protection as well.

Sometimes, he thought, too much has been kept from Katrin. Now that she's really in danger, it's a shock to her.

Soon Katrin fell asleep. Hemmett rose silently. He hefted Borsen down from the bed.

"She needs to rest," Hemmett whispered. "If you don't want to go back downstairs, you can bunk with me on my comfortable mattress."

Borsen was glad of the offer. He cuddled against Hemmett's broad back on the makeshift bed and finally managed to sleep.

***

Dear Sir Slippery Eel,

Some news for you at last, but not good. As suspected, the man you know as Lord Therbalt sent those two women after the Princess and your wife. He is in control of a very large organization, a combination of his own people and Vannik's. It seems it was his intention to throw Vannik to you all along, then to take control of Vannik's network. This is a man devoid of scruples or conscience, old friend, and though he presented himself to your people as a foolish fop, he is frighteningly intelligent. Crafty with it - and devious.

He is contracting not only on the Princess, but on you, your wife and the little fellow it's said you've adopted.

Be very careful, Menders. This man makes Vannik look like a philanthropist. My girls are trying to find out more and to see if the children you mentioned are with him. I had a girl working on a lead in Erdhan, but I have lost contact with her and fear the worst.

More as I find it.

Gladdy D.

Menders closed his eyes and crumpled the note in his hand. It was as he had feared – open contracts on all of The Shadows' inner family. Open contracts were the assassin's equivalent of war. Payment went to whoever fulfilled a contract, no questions asked or answered. Such an arrangement would bring out a lot of second rate operatives, little more than thugs. Menders had no fear of them. Between Gladdas' input and Menders' own connections, second raters would most likely be stopped in Erdhan.

But the contracts would also draw the attention of top notch assassins. Menders felt secure at the Shadows and didn't fear even the best assassin getting close while it was in lockdown, but as Kaymar said, the lockdown isolated them from events in the real world. Therbalt would surely slip away from them while they were stagnated and then would be poised, ready to strike at them later.

Menders stalked around his office in a raging fury, the desire to lash out at something – at anything – overwhelming. Somehow he had to take back the initiative, but at the same time he didn't dare risk weakening his defenses at The Shadows.

Snarling at the situation, he threw the ball of paper into the fireplace and watched it burn to ash.

***

A man slipped into the shelter of an enormous pine tree. He relaxed for a moment in the tentlike cavern created by sagging ice-coated branches, glad to be free of the endlessly falling snow.

He could see the huge house, The Shadows, clearly now. It hulked darkly against the sky, not a light to be seen. So the rumors were true. Stettan had the entire place locked down.

He smiled, fingering the tools in his pocket. They might be snugged up in there but a fire would bring them right out into the open. Then he could pick them all off and make Lord Stettan very sorry for all the miles he'd walked through the snow just to be able to creep up on the place between Stettan's damned endless watch patrols.

He packed several shells with gunpowder and fuel, then

carefully cut and seated fuses in the resulting firebombs. Water trickled down his neck where the snow on his collar was melting. He twitched irritably, hating the tickling, wet sensation. Why would anyone live up here in all this miserable snow and cold? He hunched over his work, not wanting any moisture to dampen the powder.

Finished, he stowed the bombs in his coat pockets, checked for his waterproof packet of matches and then pulled his collar up closer, sneering at the thought of going out into the falling snow. But then, the contract money he was about to earn would buy him a lot of time in a warm place.

He squeezed through a gap in the tree's branches, getting his bearings. Best to watch here where he couldn't be seen, get the timing on the patrols pacing the perimeter of the house and the roof. As soon as he saw the pattern, he could choose the best time to make the old estate house a place to flee from. Then his work would be like shooting chickens in a pen.

His hat was knocked forward over his eyes, then tumbled to the ground. A vicelike hand gripped his hair and a blade was at his throat.

"Didn't know I was there?" a snide voice with an uppercrust Southern Mordanian accent hissed in his ear. "Didn't Bartie teach you to stay upwind when you're on a mission? I could smell your stinking hair oil thirty feet away. Therbalt's starting to pay a pretty penny for assassins, isn't he?"

A lamp flared and was thrust in his face, nearly blinding him. He struggled, but the knife bit into his throat.

"It's Benton," came the same voice – the mad little nancy, Kaymar Shvalz. "I could tell the minute I picked up his stench."

As his vision adapted to the bright light, Benton saw a pair of furious white eyes glaring at him. The man who held the lantern was Stettan.

Benton began working his tongue frantically, trying to loosen the vial of morric acid lodged in a back tooth. He'd rather die than contend with that pair of men.

Shvalz smashed the butt of his knife against the hinge of Benton's jaw. His mouth gaped helplessly, the nerves controlling his jaw paralyzed.

Men were converging from everywhere as Stettan went through the assassin's pockets. Schvalz handed Benton over to a giant who must be Ifor Trantz and snatched the bombs away from Stettan, flinging them into a snowbank.

"Those would have blown the house into a firestorm," he snapped viciously. "Full of phosphorus."

"Get him inside without anyone seeing," Stettan commanded. "He's got a tooth full of morric acid – get it, and search him for anything else. Don't let Hemmett know he's here. Then leave him in the strongroom with Ifor. We'll be along."

Ifor Trantz took a vicious handful of Benton's hair and marched him toward the house.

***

The months ground on.

It was a slow winter. Therbalt wastefully sent men into the wolf's maw of Menders' Men. Kaymar extracted confessions from the surviving assassins, beginning with the turncoat, Benton, who had been one of Bartan's Assassins.

The work had taken a toll on Kaymar, leaving him brittle and muttering to himself. He was desperate to lash out and focused his frustration on Menders, provoking confrontations that often erupted into vicious brawling and long periods where they would not speak to each other. Menders finally refused to let Kaymar take part in interrogations, which made the situation between them even more tense.

Between Bartan and Gladdas Dalmanthea's operatives, Menders had learned that Therbalt was somewhere in Surelia, where he was deeply protected. Menders sent Kaymar after him with no luck. Bartan had dispatched men as well. Kaymar and Ifor had barely escaped that venture with their lives. Bartan's men had not been so fortunate.

The continual threats at home prevented Menders from making an all-out assault on Therbalt. He couldn't divide his forces and take the risk of leaving The Shadows vulnerable. Menders knew this was part of Therbalt's plan. It was exactly what he would have done in Therbalt's place. He fumed over it while making his midnight round of the house.

He spoke briefly to Ifor, on duty at the entrance to the Family Wing, then checked on Katrin, who was asleep.

"Everything is all right – goodnight, Little Princess," Menders whispered, kissing her cheek. She smiled briefly, but didn't stir. Hemmett was stretched out on the mattress that had been moved to the foot of her bed after Benton had been captured on the estate grounds. Such measures afforded little privacy for the Princess. She bore it stoically, though the situation had begun to wear on her temper. Hemmett woke when Menders came in, but just smiled and winked before closing his eyes again.

On the landing, Menders opened the inside shutters of the upper floor windows. Scraps of cloud raced before a baleful moon. Random snowflakes, lit like fireflies in the moonlight, flitted past the windows.

They were safe tonight, he felt certain. But other assassins would come. How many – and how soon, he did not know.

***

Eiren perused a letter that Menders brought her and then smiled at him.

"Miss Falcone has accepted my offer of a position at the school," she said, relief ringing in her voice. "We've gotten around the conundrum of having the school certified since she has the necessary degree!"

"I'm delighted," Menders replied, "though I'm sorry that you weren't able to get the degree yourself." Eiren had been forced to give up completing her year of extra schooling. There was no way she could make up the lost time and they were still confined to the house, though it was now well into springtime. The winter had been long and arduous for all concerned.

"No matter. The entire exercise was to have the school certified. Now it will be. And to be honest, I found it was a colossal waste, that course. It just went over the material I'd already learned when I was first at teacher's college." Eiren's face was so bright and happy that Menders knew she wasn't trying to make him feel better. She'd gotten her school certified and that was all that mattered.

"Then I think an all-out dinner tonight is in order, with toasts drunk to the school and Miss Falcone," he smiled. "It'll also be a nice sendoff for Hemmett, since he's going back to the Academy tomorrow." With winter recess over, it was time for the young man to take his place at the head of his graduating class. There had been fewer attempts by potential assassins of late, and none in the last few weeks. Menders hoped word that The Shadows was too tough a nut to crack had gotten back to Therbalt.

"I'll speak to Cook and lend a hand," Eiren said, rising and planting a kiss on his forehead. She left him alone in the suite.

Menders was glad for the letter. It had lifted Eiren's spirits no end. If only a similar letter would come for everyone in the household.

Things were depressing and difficult for all, particularly for Katrin and Borsen, who had been locked up for ten weeks. They did not complain, but they were both pale and quiet. Menders had heard them talking between themselves when they didn't know he was near. They didn't blame him, but they both longed to get out of the house. They also didn't want Hemmett to leave but assured each other that he deserved his chance to be top graduate. He'd completed his autumn term assignments by correspondence and still had excellent marks, but he couldn't afford to stay away from school any longer.

Both of them had become very dependent on Hemmett, who worked hard to stay cheerful and to shore their spirits up. Many nights Menders heard Borsen come up the stairs and steal into Katrin's room where he would curl up next to Hemmett on his mattress. The boy had been badly shaken by the attempt on Katrin's life and the capture of the additional assassins had rattled him more. Though Borsen was fearless in situations where his own safety was threatened, he was very protective of his family, particularly Katrin.

Katrin gravitated to her foster brothers for companionship and occupation. She was often to be found in the tailor shop with Borsen or bending over his sketches and plans for his prospective future business. She continued in her role of housekeeper and tried very hard to keep a lid on her temper.

When Menders saw Katrin and Borsen looking pale and sickly from lack of sun and exercise, he had to console himself with the knowledge that they were still alive.

CHAPTER 54
DELARCO

"DeLarco," Kaymar said flatly. He flung himself onto the sofa in Menders' office, looking grim, and tossed a letter on the desk. Menders picked it up and read quickly.

"Wonderful." Menders' heart sank. He went to his cabinet and withdrew the DeLarco file. This was what he feared most – a Surelian trained assassin, young, sharp and at the top of his game. Menders read through the file, sickened by the details.

"Pleasantly deranged, savage bastard, isn't he?" Kaymar remarked sardonically. Menders nodded, rose and closed the door to his office.

"Do we know who he's targeting?" he asked in a low voice

Kaymar hesitated before answering.

"Gladdy says Therbalt's taken out contracts on you, Katrin, Eiren and Borsen. I hate to tell you this… he specifies that he wants Borsen alive."

Menders went visibly pale. "Never," he said through clenched teeth.

"Don't go getting all fired up now, Papa Hen," Kaymar replied. "That's exactly what could lead to making a foolish mistake."

Menders composed himself. "Agreed. Tread carefully."

"Very. Now, here's how I see it," Kaymar continued, pausing to light one of the thin dark cigars he favored. "You're all steamed and wanting to hit back at him. That's probably what that little tidbit of information about Borsen was designed to have you do, fly around being emotional. Also, you're squirming with frustration at being sealed off from the world up here, while DeLarco's free to operate with impunity."

Menders shifted uncomfortably in his chair. Sometimes his cousin could see right into him and he always found it unnerving.

Kaymar waved a hand at the wall, indicating the countryside beyond. "He's out there. We can't let a man of DeLarco's caliber get close to us here – so we won't."

"Just what, exactly, are you suggesting?"

"We go get him first. It's time to go on the offensive."

"No."

"It's the only way."

"I can't risk losing the manpower, not if we are to maintain full protection here," Menders retorted, thumping a fist on the desk for emphasis.

"What we can't risk is letting someone like DeLarco get close to us here!" Kaymar snapped back. "If he gets as close as a hilltop with a view of this place, I'd not put it past him to build a big enough rocket, fire it and take out the whole damned house!"

Menders' expression shifted from anger to concern. His elegant eyebrows knit in a frown. "Could he do that?"

"You've seen what my rockets are capable of," Kaymar responded. "Other than detonating prematurely, blowing the roof off my shed and having me roll around in the horse trough to put out the flames, I mean."

Suppressing a smile, Menders was relieved that his cousin's absurd sense of humor could lighten the grimmest situations.

"What I mean is that he's mad enough to try something like that, Cousin," Kaymar continued, all smiles gone. "Those grenades Benton had with him would have burned The Shadows to the ground. Consider a rocket that could set fire to the place. We can't let DeLarco get close."

"I'll concede that but I still don't like reducing our manpower here enough to send a force after him."

"You don't need a force." Kaymar blew out a stream of smoke and grinned. "Two. Just two. Ifor and myself. We'll get him."

"I can't risk you two for such a mission. You were damn near killed when I sent you after Therbalt."

"That was different. Therbalt's snugged up in Surelia like a nest-spider with hundreds of men protecting him. DeLarco's here and without backup as far as Gladdy can tell. Also, you're not asking me, Cuz, I'm offering. And if you say no, I'll go and do it anyway as a free agent. Don't forget that I don't actually work for you."

Sitting back, Menders scrutinized his cousin, who was looking supremely contented through rising coils of grey smoke.

"How would you do it?" Menders finally asked.

"The answer is right there, on your desk – Gladdas Dalmanthea, our ace in the hole. We can't use our own people for fear he'll see us coming, so we go through her network. Since no-one knows you two are in collusion, we use that to our advantage."

"And then?"

"Getting in closer will be difficult. After all, he'll be expecting some move against him. So, I'll use his own indulgences as leverage."

"Meaning what?"

"I'll get to him through his own proclivities," Kaymar said, smiling. "After all Cuz, you know how winning and charming I can be." With exaggerated care he leaned forward and stubbed out his cigar in an ashtray. "Any further details, you would be better off not knowing. They might keep you awake nights."

***

Kaymar paced the rose garden path, hands in pockets, his face very blank while his mind was in frenetic motion. He was waiting for Ifor, who was about to come off duty guarding Katrin.

DeLarco was in the process of imploding, destroying

himself through continual indulgence of his sadistic urges, but it might be many years before he managed to finish himself off. Until that time, he was deadly. DeLarco was known to work for pleasure and the menu offered him by Therbalt's contract would be too tempting to pass up.

Making matters worse, the contract to bring Borsen to Therbalt alive was working on Menders. Though his cousin had agreed to stay calm and do nothing rash, Kaymar could see he was tempted to go after DeLarco himself. That was something that simply must not happen.

Ifor came into the rose garden, pausing to light a cigar. "How'd Menders take to the idea?"

"He doesn't like it. The longer we let him think about it, he'll like it even less. It'll have to be soon and if I have to I'll do it anyway, without his blessing. You know I have to, don't you, Bear?"

Ifor cupped his hands around a lit match, nodding. "I understand, Kip."

"There's only one way to catch this bastard," Kaymar continued. "I'll have to bait the trap with what he likes best. It could mean that I'd have to get into a compromising situation with him and I don't know just how far I would have to go before I could eliminate him. He's younger and larger. I could never beat him in a fight, so I'll have to get close enough to kill. There's only one way to manage that with someone like him. I wanted you to know how I was going to do it and to hear what you think."

Ifor took a puff of his cigar and looked away over the just-budding rose bushes.

"I've never been unfaithful," Kaymar said suddenly, his voice very soft.

Ifor looked at him. "I know that, Kip," he answered, just as softly. "I have what matters. I have your heart. What you need to do with your body – that washes away, Kip. It doesn't come between us. This is business."

"If Menders won't send me officially, will you still come?" Kaymar asked.

"Since when have I not? We're together in this, just like everything else," Ifor smiled. He looked back at the house.

"Time for all this to stop," he added. "This is no life, not for anyone. Hiding in shadows, scared of the light, like spiders."

"Then we'll need to go soon."

***

My dearest Mahmay,

I must tell you of a mission that I plan to undertake. Though I hate to trouble you, it is necessary that you know that this is a very serious business. I might not survive. I know that you would prefer to be prepared.

I have knowledge that makes me the best man for this mission. There is a very powerful person who is seeking to have Katrin, Menders, Eiren and Borsen killed. He has also taken out contracts on Ifor and me. We have not told Menders this – he is already half mad with anxiety over the threat to the children and has the entire household closed up with the winter shutters bolted. It has been that way since autumn.

This is a situation that cannot go on, my dearest mother. The safety of those I love is at stake, as is my own. I have an opportunity to put a stop to this threat. I know you would not have me flinch from duty.

So if this is to be goodbye, I want you to know that you have always been a delight and inspiration to me. You have helped me so much, Mahmay. I am proud of my Princess mother.

I hope to make you proud of me.

I have a clear heart, for I protect the future of Mordania.

Your loving son,
Kip
Baronet Kaymar Shvalz,
Prince of Mordania and Fambre

"It takes a freak to catch a freak!" Kaymar finally snapped.

"You're not a freak, damn it!" Menders retorted.

"Only because I choose not to be!" Kaymar flashed back. He stopped and forced himself to become calm, though his head was ringing with voices. He'd gone to tell Menders that he was going after DeLarco, only to have Menders balk at the plan.

"Menders, don't you remember when I first came here, still half-mad? Most of it was from having been sent out to kill so many times. You know that even the most well-trained and dedicated assassin feels guilt. He would be a monster if he didn't. The guilt was so terrible for me that I sought out punishment, but I began to like it instead – oh hells, why am I telling you this? You already know, you would never have let me come here and guard Katrin if you hadn't known everything about me!"

Menders turned away and looked out the window, saying nothing.

"I have moved in the circles this man does," Kaymar went on, refusing to flinch, though he feared losing some of the regard Menders held for him. "I know how to get close enough to kill him."

Menders didn't speak. Kaymar knew he was being manipulated to continue talking and suddenly felt content to do so.

"Menders, no-one else can manage this. I'm the only weapon you've got and we're running out of time. Either we end it now or the threat could go on for years. How long can we keep growing children locked up in a dark house?"

Menders turned toward him.

"Yes, I did know about that part of your life," he answered gently. "I believed you had put that behind you, as many of us left lives behind when we came here. As long as it didn't interfere with your dealings with Katrin and the other children, it was none of anyone's business. I'm more concerned for you than anything. Your happiness has been hard-won and I don't want it compromised, even if I have to go after DeLarco myself."

Kaymar felt of rush of affection and gratitude for his cousin, mixed with and horror that he'd spoken openly about eliminating DeLarco. Kaymar knew Menders wasn't equal to the task. He was too old. He'd been out of the game too long.

"Ifor understands that it's strictly business," Kaymar responded, hoping to derail Menders' last sentence. "He's willing to be my second on this mission.

"As for my being a freak – yes, I am, but it is only a part of me, a part I have voluntarily and gladly put away out of reach, because it brought me very little joy once the initial thrill was gone. It is no longer part of my life and has never been part of my life with Ifor. I understand people like DeLarco. I know what to do and what to say to get him in a compromising situation to finish him off. None of Menders' Men knows how to do that. Where will you find someone who does, Aylam?"

Menders started. Good, Kaymar thought. I'm not going to let you start closing off your ears as you are wont to do when hearing things you don't like. You forget that we're family, the same blood. Not only do I know more about you than you think I do, but in many ways we are very much alike. You just reacted to things that happened to you when you were small in a different way than I did. We both ran afoul of the same tutor, cousin of mine. In some ways, I might just know you better than you know yourself.

"Gladdy might have a girl or two who could do it, but DeLarco's nancy, he'd never rise to them as bait. To my knowledge there isn't an assassin out there the equal of me who is nancy and can do what I plan to," Kaymar continued.

He could see Menders was torn. Go in for the kill, Kaymar, he thought. The conflicting voices that had been chorusing in his mind faded away – only Kaymar was left.

"It's up to me now. That's what having a second is for.

Let me do this, Aylam," Kaymar said softly. "I serve Katrin and I serve you out of loyalty and love. It's why I've always refused to accept payment for what I do here. In this way I can serve you both as no-one else can. You gave me a home and your trust at a time when I was mad and desperate. This is a way to repay that.

"I can keep the ones you love safe. Borsen – I'd keep him safe. Please, let me do this, Cousin."

Menders studied him for a minute.

"Borsen?" he said quietly.

Kaymar answered, just as quietly. "He is like a beloved child to me, just as he is to you. He's what I was once, before certain things and people came into my life. I want Borsen to stay as he is - pure and natural and happy. The thought of something like Therbalt getting hold of him is more than enough to make me succeed."

Menders let out a long breath and stood. Kaymar rose with him.

"On one condition," Menders said. "You come back alive. No suicide missions, Kaymar. Even if you have to let him go, we'll get him another time. I need my second – my dear cousin – alive."

Kaymar nodded. "Agreed."

"When will you go?"

"Now. You have our current wills and letters for our families if things go wrong."

Suddenly Menders cupped Kaymar's face in his hands. He looked over his dark glasses into Kaymar's eyes.

"My troubled boy," he said roughly, fighting emotion.

Kaymar felt a glow of happiness. Menders referred to Hemmett as "my first boy" and to Borsen as "my late arriving boy" and considered both of them his sons. It was the first spoken acknowledgment that Menders considered Kaymar to be one of his boys as well, that the relationship between them was more than between cousins.

"Thank you," he said softly. "I have missed my Papa terribly since he died when I was fourteen. You have been a wonderful father to me."

Menders nodded mutely, dropping his hands from Kaymar's face.

Outside, Ifor was seated on their carriage, the tip of his lit cigar barely showing his overcoated form. Early spring nights were cold in northern Mordania.

"It seems you were going tonight, with or without my blessing."

"Yes, but it's nicer to have your understanding," Kaymar replied, wrapping his throat with a scarf, shrugging on a jacket. He worked his gloves onto his hands, then paused, looking at Menders, the smile fading from his face. "I have written to my mother, but I didn't tell anyone else that we are going. Should something happen… I trust you'll explain for me? Why I didn't say goodbye."

Menders, his lips pressed into a bloodless line, nodded solemnly. "I'll see to it." His voice was thick and hoarse. He took his cousin's hand and grasped it firmly. "Just save me the trouble by coming back."

"Agreed." Kaymar was suddenly his usual debonair and flippant self.

With a flourish he donned his hat, winked at Menders, then stepped out into the night, closing the door behind him with a solid thud.

***

"Have you seen Kaymar?" Katrin asked, leaning in the doorway of the tailor shop.

"Not today," Borsen replied, not looking up from the sewing machine. Clothing to be mended was piled high around him.

"Do you know what's going on?" Katrin asked, closing the door behind her.

He didn't answer. Katrin saw that he was gazing at his work even more intently than usual. She went to him.

"Tell me," she said quietly. "I know something is happening. I'm not a child. Someone here has got to treat me as if I can stand some bad news."

Borsen stitched determinedly on. His work was a comfort to him and had become a barrier between him and all things in the world that were hurtful or frightening. After a moment, Katrin reached out and put her hand over one of his.

Borsen stopped pedaling the machine. He swallowed hard and she saw that he was blinking rapidly, determined not to cry.

"He and Ifor have gone after an assassin that Therbalt has sent after all of us," he said, his voice harsh with strain. "Someone terrible. A freak, not like the assassins here. Someone who likes to torture people."

Katrin shuddered and closed her hand around Borsen's. He squeezed back hard, keeping his eyes on the work before him. She hated hearing such things, but knew she had to.

"Kaymar is very good at what he does," she said, trying to sound confident.

"So is the man he's after," Borsen answered between clenched teeth. "He's almost as good as Uncle was. Kaymar's going to have to get very close, because the only way to catch him is to… play his freak games with him."

"I hate this!" Katrin burst out fiercely, her eyes burning with fury. "I hate this!" Then she saw that Borsen was shivering with emotion and hugged his head against her. He put his arms around her waist and started to cry. Her rage fell away and the need to comfort him took over.

"It's going to be all right," she whispered. "Kaymar's smart. He'll come back." She tried to sound confident and calm, but failed. Two small, hot tears ran down her face. Several sobs hitched in her throat.

"Here you are – oh dear." Menders' voice startled them. In a moment his arms were around them both.

"My poor children," he said gently. He held them as they shuddered with stifled sobs and squeezed their eyes closed. He almost told them to go ahead and let it out, but they both wanted so badly to be grown up these days that he let them deal with the emotional storm in their own way.

When they regained their composure, he sat Katrin in Tomar's chair and looked at them.

"It seems you both know what Kaymar is planning to do," he sighed.

"I heard him and Ifor talking about it when I went to show them something," Borsen said forthrightly. "I wasn't eavesdropping. It was an accident. I didn't intend to tell anyone else, but... well..."

"We have all been under far too much pressure," Menders replied, patting Borsen's shoulder. "We wanted to spare you both the news, but that was probably not the thing to do. As you become adults, you will find that there are hard times like this when the ones we love are threatened. And there are hard decisions too, based on duty, loyalty, and sacrifice. Kaymar is our best and when he succeeds, our present troubles will be at an end. He has also promised me that he will not sacrifice himself. This is not a suicide mission."

"But he's going to have to..." Borsen blurted. Then his eyes slewed around to Katrin and he looked like he wished he'd bitten his tongue off.

One look at Katrin told Menders that she knew what that meant as well. It was inevitable that the children's voracious reading would expose them to the wider world and darker facets of human nature. He did not discourage this and had left the more 'adult' section of the locked bookcase open for some time. It was important that both Katrin and Borsen not grow up entirely naive.

"Sometimes subterfuge is part of Kaymar's work. Hopefully he will be able to eliminate this assassin before he has to get into a compromising situation. Ifor is with him and will help him. They are at their best when together," Menders answered.

"But what if this freak hurts him?" Borsen asked, his words coming out with effort. "Or kills him?" Katrin could see his hands were shaking. He started wringing them, which meant he was very upset. He adored Kaymar, almost as much as he loved Menders.

"I've known Kaymar since he was not much older than you," Menders explained reassuringly. "Motivation is important for an assassin. Kaymar is doing this out of love, for both of you, for all of us. That is what will give him the edge in the situation. Those of us who take on positions of service to Mordania know that we might risk the ultimate sacrifice. We do it so that we can make the world a better place. That is what being in service is about."

Menders rose and held out his hands to them.

"Now, my dears, I think it's time we went outside," he said. "You've been caged up in here for far too long. I know for certain that any threat to us is far from here today. The patrol has just passed. I think a jaunt around the garden would be perfectly safe."

Outside, Katrin found the world had changed. She had peeped through her shutters a time or two and seen glimpses of springtime, but the windows had been sealed when the world was still white. Now it was full of color! She immediately buried her nose in a cluster of roses. Borsen made a beeline to the herb beds and broke off several sprigs, rubbing them between his fingers and inhaling ecstatically.

Eiren saw them and came across the garden.

"Isn't the sun wonderful!" she said, kissing them both.

"Some more of this will bring the roses back to your cheeks."

Katrin turned her face up to the sun and smiled. Making the world a better place, she thought. To enjoy days like this.

***

Kaymar drew his razor across the skin of his cheek carefully, leaving a long slash. Blood beaded like rubies along the silver edge of the sharp metal. For some time now he'd carefully cut and marked himself, to have frequent fresh wounds like a practicing masochist would.

"Not on the face, Kip," Ifor sighed, coming in with dinner for them both, seeing the bleeding slash on Kaymar's cheek.

"It'll heal clean," Kaymar replied, rinsing the wound. "You worry too much."

"My job," Ifor grunted heavily, putting the food on the table of their very seedy tavern room.

"I'll tell people it's a dueling scar," Kaymar grinned. He dropped his pants, picked up a riding crop and viciously whacked himself on the rear several times, leaving a trail of welts on top of injuries from days ago. Ifor looked on silently, regretting Kaymar's ability – and sometime need – to harm himself. He didn't understand it, but he accepted it. He looked away briefly as Kaymar began to use sandpaper on his wrists, to make marks like manacles left.

"Leave off, come eat," Ifor ordered, keeping his back turned. He hated this process, necessary though it was.

"DeLarco is still at The Rooster," he remarked as they started their meal. "I saw him as I went by."

"Well he would be, wouldn't he?" Kaymar replied. The Rooster was a grotty tavern that catered to those with DeLarco's proclivities. There were several such establishments nearby. Kaymar wondered, when this was all over, if a series of selective fires might not do the city of Erdhan a measure of good. "It's his home away from home."

Kaymar knew DeLarco had noticed him during the times he had loitered around The Rooster's barroom, though the assassin had not made any advances yet. DeLarco had also not gone into hiding, so it was fairly certain he had no idea who Kaymar was. Kaymar had tinted his fair hair dark brown as a precaution.

"I think I have enough wounds," he said, shifting on his very sore bottom. Ifor handed over a pillow from the bed. He shuffled it under his backside with relief.

"What do you think about tomorrow night?" Kaymar flinched as Ifor froze for a moment and then put his fork down carefully.

"His place or here?" Ifor asked.

"His. Anyone that full of himself has things written down," Kaymar answered. "He'd have his writings with him. Once we finish him, we might be able to gather up information that would be valuable."

"Good." Ifor returned his attention to his dinner. The room was silent for several minutes.

"Thank you," Kaymar said softly.

Ifor nodded. Then he looked up at Kaymar with tenderness in his face.

"If you're going to do a nude scene, make sure your disguise is complete," Ifor smiled. "The moment you take your clothes off, you'll give yourself away."

Kaymar stared at him for a moment and then laughed aloud for the first time in many days. He started to rise, to get his hair dye and make sure that all hair on his body matched the dyed brown on his head.

Ifor stopped him, putting a hand on his damaged wrist.

"Have your dinner first. There's time yet," he said softly.

***

"I don't care for preliminaries," DeLarco said, rattling through a drawer and extracting various implements that Kaymar was all too familiar with. "Strip off. Fast."

The man likes to get down to business, Kaymar thought as he unbuttoned his shirt. For all DeLarco's haste, he was showing all the apparent impassivity of a surgeon or dentist about to go to work. Despite his revulsion toward the Surelian assassin, Kaymar also felt a peculiar fascination. Elegant face, refined posture, but the façade of outward elegance slipped all too easily, revealing stony menace and deliberate cruelty.

Kaymar slowed his undressing, making sure that Ifor had time to get into position. He had no desire to be completely on his own with this man.

DeLarco was frightening – even to Kaymar, who frightened most people. The Surelian assassin had ice water in his veins; there was little, if any, humanity in him. He'd already hurt Kaymar several times between the tavern and this room. There was no finesse in his sadism, none of the sophisticated role play that Kaymar had known in the past. He simply swung fists, pinched, twisted and gouged, bent fingers backward, smashed his prey into brick walls. There was nothing remotely sexual about his assaults. He existed to inflict pain.

DeLarco swung a fist but Kaymar managed to cringe away, letting the blow glance off his right ear. DeLarco was left-handed, something to remember.

"I said fast." DeLarco's inflection was even and cool. Kaymar made a show of unbuttoning his trousers and toeing off his shoes. He'd counted out the seconds. Ifor should be outside the alleyway window by now. Stupid of DeLarco to take a ground floor room.

DeLarco's breath quickened as Kaymar's scars were revealed.

"You've been around the track a few times," the assassin

said smugly, walking around Kaymar, flicking open a razor. "Some of those scars on your back must be ten years old or more."

"Yes," Kaymar whined, his tenor voice narrowed in the cringing tones of the perennial masochist.

"Did I say you could speak?" There was a sudden burning near Kaymar's left kidney. DeLarco had lightly drawn the edge of the razor in a long line across his back.

Kaymar shook his head, drawing on experience to make himself shiver ecstatically. He wanted nothing more than to simply kill the bastard, but by the time he drew his weapon, the long, steel dirk-bladed pin that skewered his hair into a knot at the nape of his neck, DeLarco would have his guts on the floor. There was a sheathed knife concealed up his karzi, but that would take even more time to attain. For now he had to go along with the miserable freak – until DeLarco turned his back.

Kaymar looked at the items DeLarco had tossed on the bed, hoping to draw the assassin's attention there. It worked, but not for long enough. DeLarco still wasn't completely at ease or certain that Kaymar was not a threat. He wasn't about to turn away.

"You don't seem particularly excited," DeLarco said, looking at Kaymar while his hand lovingly stroked the implements on the bed.

Gods, he wants me to be aroused, Kaymar moaned inwardly. I don't think I could be if they danced Ifor and several lovely Samorsan men around in front of me naked.

"I'm slow to warm," he sniveled.

The blow almost knocked Kaymar down. He stepped back to avoid a fall, turning away from the bed and in profile to the window. He made himself pant excitedly.

"You'll learn to speak when I tell you to," DeLarco said coldly, grabbing a pair of manacles from the bed. Kaymar got ready to move quickly. If his wrists were manacled he would never be able to reach his weapons. He'd have to buy himself time.

DeLarco darted in front of him, the manacles open. Kaymar moved across the room, raising a hand toward his bound hair, suddenly desperate to have a weapon in hand. As he did so, his damaged heart lurched painfully in his chest, making him freeze in his tracks.

DeLarco flung the manacles with lightning speed, striking Kaymar in the breastbone, knocking him breathless. He tumbled to the floor, curling himself away from what he knew would be a vicious attack from the Surelian assassin. His heart was whooshing desperately, every beat agonizing.

DeLarco launched himself across the room in the manacles' wake, ripping Kaymar up from the floor like a child's toy, swinging him into the wall with such force that Kaymar heard the plaster crack. He was thankful it wasn't his ribs. He slumped toward the floor again, but the assassin dug a thumb into the base of his throat, hard.

"Do you think I don't know who you are, Baronet Shvalz?" DeLarco hissed as he ground his thumb viciously against Kaymar's windpipe. "Did you honestly think a little hair dye and some self-inflicted bruises could hide you from me?"

Grahl's fucking teeth! Kaymar thought desperately. How long has he known? Since when? And how?

Kaymar thrashed violently until he was free, snatching the pin from his hair. DeLarco leapt at him silently, taking cuts on his hands as he tried to wrest the hardened steel dirk blade from Kaymar's grasp.

Kaymar continually retreated, desperately fighting to keep hold of the weapon. He wasn't as fast as DeLarco, who managed to trip him on one of their skittering transits of the room. Kaymar fell hard, feeling his breath explode out of his lungs for the second time in minutes, his heart knocking madly in his ears. DeLarco tore the pin from his hand and drove it into Kaymar's left thigh.

"Pretty playtoy for a pretty boy?" DeLarco snarled, his voice shaking with rage. "I know you have something better than this. You're not quite the fool you seem. I know where it is too. Yes, I know you, Mister Shvalz, all too well. Of course they'd send you after me. Who else? Did you think I didn't know? Did you forget that when you travel in my dirty little circles, for whatever reason, that you leave tracks?"

I will not have this bastard sticking his hand up my karzi, Kaymar thought furiously, forcing his protesting body to obey his will. He flipped over on his back, ignoring the agony as he tore the pin from his thigh, deafening himself to the damaged laboring of his heart. He clutched the blade, ready to stick it into whatever part of DeLarco presented itself first.

DeLarco grabbed his ankle, deftly keeping out of range of the dirk pin. He began dragging Kaymar across the splintery floor toward the nightmarish contraptions on the bed.

"Think you're mean? Your fame is certainly undeserved, Mister Shvalz," DeLarco grunted, hauling him along easily despite several well-placed kicks from Kaymar. The assassin grabbed a chain and swung it in a vicious arc, knocking the dirk pin from Kaymar's hand. It tinkled gaily across the room, rattling to silence in a corner.

DeLarco loomed over Kaymar, his dark features quirked into a glaring smile.

For the first time in his professional life, Kaymar felt terror. If Ifor didn't do something in the next few moments, DeLarco was going to kill him.

With this knowledge came a sense of calm. He found his mind working on two levels - one part bargaining desperately for his life, looking for any edge or escape, the other passively observing, thinking, 'this bastard's eyes have an evil gleam. They actually gleam, like something from a book! How odd.'

"I am so going to enjoy this," DeLarco smirked, lashing

the chain at Kaymar's face.

Somehow Kaymar caught the chain as it arced toward him. His hand snatched the metal and held it. He hauled himself from the floor with it, using the leverage to vault across the room, blood coursing down his leg. Barely able to breathe, he could think only of escape.

He got to the door to find that it was locked.

He'd known that. He'd heard DeLarco lock it after they came in. He should have run to the window. Ifor was there and could have hauled him through it. Worse, the dirk pin had rolled to the opposite corner. Short of somehow removing a knife from his backside, then getting it unsheathed, he was weaponless, naked and outweighed by his opponent in every way.

He was older now and time had slowed him. His heart condition betrayed him, his mind let him forget details and make deadly strategic mistakes. He'd lost his edge as an assassin and that was going to cost him his life.

"Running away? Legendary Shvalz? A coward, like all Mordanians," DeLarco snarled, snatching up a long steel bar with a hook on one end. "I'm surprised you don't have your big stupid friend with you, but that would require some forethought. You're boring me, so why don't we just finish this?"

Ifor, Kaymar thought abjectly, I didn't expect to die today, not like this. I can't keep running back and forth forever while this maniac chases me with his toys. My heart is going to give out. This bastard is a killing machine and he'll carve me up like cheese and never blink an eye. I'll never see you again, Bear.

DeLarco strode across the room, raising the steel rod so swiftly that it made a whistling sound. Kaymar readied himself, tensing every muscle to receive the blow. He had no strength to run or even to cringe.

DeLarco jerked upright, looking perplexed. His arm fell to his side, the bar dropping to the floor with a thud. The Surelian convulsed, then collapsed.

Protruding from his temple was a four inch piece of dully gleaming metal – the shaft of a small crossbow bolt.

Kaymar looked down at DeLarco. The assassin's eyes, mildly astonished, met his before the life in them went out – but not before Kaymar kicked him in the face. To his immense pleasure, one of DeLarco's teeth skittered away across the floor.

Ifor reached through a glassless pane, pushed back the window curtain and flicked the latch open.

"Kip, are you all right?"

"No," Kaymar replied, looking at his injuries and his blood on the floor. "But I'll live."

"I didn't think I was going to get a chance at him," Ifor said, climbing over the windowsill. "Thought I was going to have to jump through the glass and interfere. Good thing you led him over to the door, Kip."

"It was no genius on my part," Kaymar answered, pressing his hands against the puncture wound in his thigh, bending over and breathing deeply until the bleeding slowed. He could feel his heart slowing, the chest pain receding. "I panicked, forgot the door was locked. That was awfully close, Bear. I was in far over my head." He stood upright, then went to DeLarco's trunk at the foot of the bed.

"Sorry it took so long, but you two were running around like spiders on a hot griddle. I couldn't get a clear shot for fear of hitting you." Ifor put his hands on Kaymar's shoulders. Kaymar felt life pouring into him and stood motionless for a moment, rejoicing – then got back to business.

They hauled DeLarco's trunk into the middle of the room. The key was in DeLarco's pocket.

"We've got them," Kaymar breathed, unearthing several notebooks, an address book and many documents. Ifor rifled Delarco's pockets further, producing another notebook. It was all there – enough information about Therbalt's organization to make that greasy gentleman more than uncomfortable.

Kaymar searched the rest of the room while Ifor methodically stuffed DeLarco into the trunk after lining it with a tarpaulin he'd brought along. Any parts of the body that didn't fit, Ifor simply trod upon until they did.

"You aren't treading grapes, Bear," Kaymar chided as Ifor stomped vigorously on DeLarco's knees, preparatory to folding his legs into the trunk on top of the rest of him. Nauseating crunching sounds filled the room.

"For such a tough man, he uses a very small trunk," Ifor answered. Kaymar searched under the mattress, finding more documents and money. Ifor finished arranging DeLarco in his cramped berth and shut the lid, locking it securely with the key, which he proceeded to toss out the window. They could hear it jingle on the paving stones outside.

"I have just the address to ship him to," Kaymar said, brandishing a letter. "If you're ready, let's go."

"I know it's a nice night, Kip, but you might want to get dressed before going out on the street, if we don't want to draw attention," Ifor smiled. Kaymar had been searching the room in his birthday suit, dribbling blood from his wounded thigh and back.

Kaymar groaned in disgust, scrabbling for his garments. While he dressed, Ifor eased the windowpane he'd removed back into place, found Kaymar's dirk pin and handed it to him, then put something in Kaymar's hand.

"Here, you'll want this."

Kaymar looked at the tiny object in his palm. It was Delarco's tooth.

"Souvenir," Ifor said. Kaymar laughed softly, flung the tooth into a corner, then hugged the big man before helping him heft the trunk out of the door and into the night.

***

During the two weeks Ifor and Kaymar had been gone, gloom had settled over The Shadows like a cloak woven of bad tempers and frayed nerves. No word had come from Erdhan and though no-one spoke of it, everyone feared the worst.

Borsen had fretted himself into nightmares, causing Franz and Menders deep concern. Despite the manliness he projected since gaining his Tailor's Certificate, Borsen was still emotionally fragile and easily tipped toward ill health.

Menders and Eiren sat around a low table in the library with Doctor Franz and Katrin. Borsen was curled in an easy chair by the fire, dozing. The teapot on the side table had grown cold, once-warm pastries were left uneaten. The four sat around a table, playing cards with weary indifference.

"Whose bid is it?" Eiren asked unenthusiastically. She wished some word would come about Kaymar and Ifor, if only to ease the minds of the young people.

"Um, mine I think," Franz said. He studied his cards with minute care, then announced, "Four gold crowns."

"You have no such hand, sir," Menders said sourly. "You're a liar."

Looking at Eiren, Franz said, "How does he always know when I'm bluffing?"

Eiren shrugged, forcing a small smile.

"You're supposed to say, 'I call to see you', Menders," Katrin said.

"Is there a funeral? Something I don't know about?" Kaymar's voice, at its most flippant, came from the doorway.

There was a general explosion of people rising from chairs. Katrin and Borsen flung themselves at their astonished cousin, who found himself being embraced from both sides. Franz turned the lamps up high, took one look at Kaymar and left the room.

"Why the hells didn't you send word you were coming!" Menders snapped, his relief coming out as a bolt of fleeting anger.

"And lovely to see you too, Cousin," Kaymar taunted.

"We move with stealth and secrecy," Ifor pronounced from behind Kaymar, before going away up the corridor.

"Did he do that to you?" Katrin gasped, looking at the long, healing slash on Kaymar's cheek. "And your hair is brown!"

"Easy there, Cuz," Kaymar laughed. "Both were done by me, part of the disguise and the brown will wash out of my hair. Here, let go for a moment, both of you. Now, ladies first." He held out his arms to Katrin and hugged her. Then he did the same for Borsen.

"I'm all right. Everything's all right now. Unhand me, young sir." He laughed and ruffled Borsen's hair. He looked over at Menders, seeming shaken by the reaction of the youngsters.

"They knew all along," Menders explained. "I'm afraid you're going to have to put up with a festival of love for a while, Cousin. They've been terribly worried over you."

Kaymar frowned and Menders knew he wished Katrin and Borsen hadn't known. Then he laughed ruefully and gave up, allowing the "festival of love" to go on unabated as the young people clung to him.

"Oh, did you get him?" Katrin finally asked, looking up at Kaymar. Then her expression shifted to shame. "How terrible! Asking if you'd killed someone."

"I understand and it's all right. Yes, we solved that little problem." Kaymar grinned. "I don't know about you, but I'm starving. We came straight over on the boat after squaring some things away and sending off a parcel. Is there anything to eat? And here's the patient and lovely Eiren." He released Borsen and kissed Eiren's cheek. She fingered his fading black eye silently, but he shook his head, flicking his eyes toward Katrin and Borsen.

"Come on, you two," Eiren said to the children. "Let's put a platter of food together. I could eat a grundar all of a sudden."

"Me too." Borsen went with her through the doorway,

looking back at Kaymar happily.

"Ifor has taken the documents and notebooks to your office and locked them in the safe," Kaymar said to Menders, who came over and put an arm around his shoulders, now that everyone else had had a turn. "The bastard must have been collecting notes to write his memoirs. He wrote everything down. I have locations, names, plans, maps, all leading back to our friend Therbalt."

Menders felt as if his heart had stopped for a moment. Then a grin spread across his face.

"I've sent word to Surelia for Melnor to hold off with the explosives until you've had a chance to see what we have," Kaymar continued.

Franz came back in with his medical bag. "What needs seeing to?" he inquired with firm authority.

Kaymar shrugged and took off his shirt.

He was covered with bruises that had blossomed darkly during the return to The Shadows. Franz flinched and muttered something about poultices, taking a bottle from his bag while looking worriedly at the swollen wrist that had received the brunt of DeLarco's swung chain.

"Your heart sounds terrible," Franz scolded after plying his stethoscope. "Once we get you patched up, you are to go to bed and stay there for at least a week."

"After today, Doctor, I have no desire to do anything else," Kaymar answered, letting his voice sound less than jaunty for a moment. Doctor Franz sighed and patted his shoulder.

"What did you do with the body?" Menders asked, needing to know if a cover story had to be concocted.

"Ifor tucked him away in his own trunk and we sent it off to Lord Therbalt at the address conveniently supplied," Kaymar said with satisfaction. "Cartage to be paid by recipient."

Franz jerked bolt upright from where he had begun cleaning the slash on Kaymar's back, gaping, while Menders collapsed on the edge of the desk, so he wouldn't fall on the floor, and laughed wholeheartedly.

Kaymar Shvalz grinned with satisfaction and the ineffable air of a man who had somehow been reborn.

CHAPTER 55
TO PROTECT THE PRINCESS

"Cousin, she wants to go to Hemmett's graduation," Kaymar said insistently, leaning against Menders' closed office door.

"I know," Menders replied from behind his desk, shuffling papers and not looking up.

"Katrin wants to go, and what is more, she should go," Kaymar persisted.

"I know," Menders repeated with stern emphasis. "I'm against it."

"So am I, but I think she should go anyway."

Menders' head came up quickly. "Have you taken leave of your senses? With all that we've been through? With all that you've been through? With Therbalt still out there, somewhere? We haven't finished him off yet, you know."

Kaymar took two long strides across the room then eased himself down in the chair facing the desk. His body still ached everywhere from the abuse he'd taken from DeLarco.

"Listen, cousin of mine, I know all that as well as you. But look at us, two of the most.... no, the two most resourceful men I know. Are you telling me we can't think of a way? Obviously, she cannot go as the Princess but I think we could work up something if we opened our minds."

Raising his eyebrows, Menders nodded. "Go on."

"There's enough information in those documents I brought back to implicate more than two dozen active or would-be conspirators in Erdahn, correct?"

"At least."

"And, what can we do about it? How can we best use that information?"

"We can't," Menders said sourly. "I've passed on a

condensed synopsis to the Court Assassin's office, but as Bartan replied, they don't have the manpower or resources to act on it effectively."

"Correct," Kaymar smiled. "And if we were to act on our own, outside of the official sanction of the Court, a lot of people would be very unhappy."

"Exactly."

Kaymar was still smiling, the impish grin that told Menders his mercurial cousin had cooked up a plan during his week of enforced bed rest. "However, your Charter of Guardianship empowers you to take whatever actions are necessary to ensure the Princess' survival and safety, am I correct? So, if we were to take Katrin to Erdhan – heavily disguised of course – it would be your responsibility to ensure any known threats were removed first. No royal sanction needed, because in essence, you already have it."

Menders felt a smile tugging at the corners of his mouth. Kaymar excelled in turning viewpoints around. "You're right," he said. "I couldn't take the Princess to such a dangerous place without acting first to secure her safety. That's standard operating protocol. So I would be duty bound to eliminate her enemies."

"In fact, they'd have your head on a pike if you didn't." Kaymar smirked with self-satisfaction.

Menders suddenly felt better than he had in days.

Katrin had asked to go to the graduation and he knew it meant a lot to her to attend, just as it did to Hemmett to have her there. When he'd explained that he could not risk letting her go, she had countered him with a frustrated denunciation. She pointed out that nothing they did mattered anyway because for all their security precautions, some woman had managed to walk right up behind her and nearly shoot her at point blank range. That particular barb of truth, filtered through the critical point of view of a young girl, had struck Menders to the heart.

"We'll need to draw up assignments, travel orders and so

on," Menders said.

"Done." Kaymar took a folded sheaf of paper from his jacket pocket and handed it across the desk. "Just needing your review and approval. If we time this right, it coincides nicely with Melnor's planned incendiary attack in Surelia. If things go our way, we'll get Therbalt in the mix as well. Melnor might still winkle him out."

Melnor was one of Kaymar's protégés, trained in the art of explosive warfare. He was the first of a group that was becoming known as 'Kaymar's Men' or sometimes, just the 'K Men'.

Menders looked skeptical. "You think so?"

"I do."

Menders began signing the papers, making the orders official. It was as if he'd drawn up the documents himself; he could find no fault in the planning.

"What will you tell Katrin about this?" Kaymar asked after a short silence.

Menders' pen paused above a signature line that would seal the fate of yet another enemy of the Princess.

"I'm still debating that. Recently, she has shown more interest in knowing what's happening. But when I think of what we need to do now, I hesitate at giving her that information. I don't believe she has the stomach for it."

"It's not her stomach that worries me," Kaymar answered flatly. "It's her head. I don't think she's capable of dealing with such things and maybe that's best for her. But if she was ever made Queen…"

"We'll deal with the present actualities," Menders interrupted, signing more papers. "No point in fabricating trouble about a situation that may never arise."

"Agreed."

Menders scanned the documents assigning targets to various of Menders' Men, frowning. He looked up at Kaymar.

"Nothing for yourself?" he asked.

Kaymar's smile faded. "As a matter of fact, that's something I meant to talk to you about."

Menders sat back, listening.

"I've lost it, Cuz. Lost my edge. I found that out the hard way when I was up against DeLarco. He was younger, faster and meaner. I panicked. Panicked like a first timer, lost my nerve, felt overwhelming fear during a mission for the first time. I forgot he'd locked the door and ran to it trying to get away, trapping myself. I was in way over my head and should never have attempted it in the first place."

Menders rose slowly, came around his desk and then perched on the edge closest to Kaymar. He adjusted the set of his glasses carefully.

"There comes a time when all active assassins feel as you do. I'm aware that you know that I have lost my edge and could never function as an assassin again. You've been too gracious to say so, but I know you thought it," he said slowly.

Kaymar opened his mouth to speak but Menders raised a hand, continuing. "I hadn't the heart to show you this before now. It arrived the night before you and Ifor came home."

Menders drew a folded slip of yellow paper from his vest pocket and handed it to Kaymar.

Menders,

Kaymar's identity is known to DeLarco. He is in great danger. My girls are unable to locate either Kaymar or Ifor.

Gladdas D

"I decided to go myself, to try to intercept DeLarco, though it was probably already too late," Menders continued. "Eiren told me, mincing no words, that I wasn't up to it. I realized, reluctantly, that she was right. It was a very humbling moment for me. When I saw how DeLarco tore you up, I realized that he would have wiped the floor with me and sent my skin home in the form of a rug.

"I sent several men to Erdahn immediately after getting Gladdy's message – you were nowhere to be found. It takes so long – everything was probably all over and done with by the time I got that note."

Kaymar nodded and folded the paper slowly, then handed it back. Menders' torment at the time must have been considerable. There were traces of it etched into the fine lines around his eyes.

"They say the best thing after a fall is to get back on the horse," Menders said after a moment.

"Tell that to a jockey with two broken legs," Kaymar quipped darkly.

"You haven't lost your edge, you were just out of practice. I might be best suited behind a desk these days, but you… you're my best. I need you."

Kaymar thought it over.

"Perhaps… one more then. I'd like to finish what we've begun." Kaymar rose gracefully and sauntered out of the office without another word, the shift in his mercurial moods obvious.

Menders took the message from Gladdas Dalmanthea and placed it carefully in an open drawer.

Despite his outward flippant calm, Kaymar's chagrin over causing Menders anguish had been palpable during their conversation, as was his concern over his reduced prowess. The young assassin was not that young anymore, and no operative could go on forever. In time, Kaymar would need other pursuits to ease and divert his often overwrought mind. He had always prided himself on being the best, though by nature he was not cut out to be an assassin. For him to lose his pride in his abilities would bring on self-doubt, which would lead to self-loathing –

which could lead to his incipient madness driving him to torment and mutilate himself. Menders would watch him closely over the next few weeks.

"My troubled boy," Menders said softly, closing the desk drawer as gently as he would touch a baby.

***

In a rented room in Erdahn, Kaymar stood before twenty of Menders' Men, ten of Gladdas Dalmanthea's "girls" and as many of Bartan's Assassins, ready to pass on Menders' orders. They were simple. Every person incriminated by the documents found in DeLarco's lodgings was to be eliminated – no exceptions. No mercy would be shown.

"We have to finish this tonight," Kaymar said. "Menders is bringing Princess Katrin to Erdahn tomorrow, so it must be over by then. She will come in a closed carriage with Menders and Eiren, guarded by Haakel and two others. She'll be dressed as a widow. I want you three at the Academy at nine to be there when she arrives. I have more men posted in the hall itself."

There was a general murmuring of agreement at the news. Kaymar waited until the room quieted, then continued.

"You have your assignments. If you should find your targets are not where they are supposed to be, report back to Ifor immediately for another assignment. Do not let grass grow under your feet, ladies and gentlemen. We begin at six. Let's make a clean sweep."

With uncanny speed, the group dispersed. Not a trace was left behind – no telltale scrap of paper, no chalk dust or pencil shavings, no ash or cigar stubs. Within moments the room was empty, as if no-one had ever been there at all.

***

In Surrela, the exquisite Surelian capital, a trunk was delivered to Therbalt's second in command. The man complained about paying the cartage but capitulated when he saw the nametag identifying the luggage as belonging to DeLarco. He grudgingly offered up the money. Therbalt himself came in response to the news that the item had arrived and ordered it pried open when it was obvious the key was missing.

Within seconds, people were fleeing the scene ahead of a sickening miasma of rot and the sight of DeLarco's carefully folded body decaying in its final resting place, wrapped in rubberized canvas.

Moments later, timed explosive charges detonated and a series of explosions shattered the morning calm of three cities, completely destroying four townhouses, a tavern and a country estate in the process. Days of sifting through the rubble would finally reveal that a total of forty-three of Lord Therbalt's operatives had been killed outright.

Therbalt fled the moment he saw DeLarco's body, leaving his mistress behind to be destroyed as his townhouse went up in a roaring flash. Many days later, the woman's body would be recovered and identified as Ermina Trottenheim.

The blast knocked Therbalt unconscious. He fell to the pavement, where he was partially buried by rubble. He was passed over as dead by rescuers and slowly came to consciousness on his own, hours after the explosion. It was nightfall by the time he was able to sit up and move without vomiting. Burned, bleeding and nearly deafened by the blast, he finally crept through the darkened backstreets to one of his safe houses.

Later that night, Therbalt boarded a ship to Surytam dressed as a merchant seaman, nearly penniless, well aware that he must abandon his plans to take the Throne of Mordania. It was time to disappear.

***

The Mordanian Military Academy's Graduation Day was a busy time in Erdahn. Many people traveled large distances to attend the ceremony. Menders' Men, Bartan's Assassins and Glad's Girls slipped into the crowds seamlessly.

At six o'clock in the evening, a nude Kaymar Shvalz walked into a steam bath frequented by a certain minister of the Queen's Council. The man had corresponded at some length with Lord Therbalt about a "change" of Queens, actively encouraging the plot to take Katrin's life. Kaymar sauntered casually toward an empty bench near the minister, pausing behind him just long enough to thrust a push dirk into the base of the man's brain, killing him instantly. Kaymar then left the bath at a relaxed stroll, deciding not to lounge in the steamy heat after all. He hated the smell of such places.

At six-thirty, a lanky youthful gentleman gained entrance to Erdahn's most exclusive gentleman's club. He ordered a drink at the bar and stood chatting companionably with the barkeep. Soon he was joined by a well-known attorney, who had financed hiring DeLarco for Lord Therbalt. The attorney ordered his nightly brandy with soda. He exchanged a few pleasant words with the lanky youth and allowed himself to be distracted by a brief altercation between two club members, just long enough for a dose of flavorless morric acid to be deposited in his drink. The young gentleman drank up and said a pleasant goodnight to the barkeep, who was cleaning glasses before the evening rush, his back to the bar. The attorney was dead after his next sip of brandy, witnessed by the two Menders' Men who had provided the distracting altercation. Within ten minutes, all three had reported to Ifor Trantz and were dispatched to their next task.

An employee of the Rondheim Bank, who had dabbled in laundering money for Lord Therbalt, locked up the large bronze doors of his workplace and then bought a box of matches from a ragged young matchseller. She bantered kittenishly with him for a moment before moving down the street, calling out that she had matches to sell. He drew a cigar from his silver case, bit off the end and struck a match. As he raised it to the cigar, it exploded violently, neatly removing his head. The matchseller dodged into an alleyway and started to zigzag through back streets toward her next target.

By seven o'clock, a Lord Surentz, lounging in his bath, was suddenly rendered unconscious with skillfully applied pressure to the side of his neck. His head was lowered beneath the soapy water. His doctor later came to the conclusion that he had fallen asleep in the bath and inadvertently drowned. Surentz had been a solid supporter of Lord Therbalt's plans for eliminating the Queen.

Assassins fanned out across the city through the night, a lethal tide inundating the rich and influential citizens who had aided in the plot to kill Princess Katrin and her family. Plotters were stabbed, throttled, pushed down cellar steps, poisoned, made to look as if they had committed suicide, run down by carriages or thrust from windows. A total of twenty-seven traitors to the Throne were eliminated during that short summer night.

Sunrise was well underway when the last of the assassins reported to Ifor Trantz. He leaned over Kaymar, who was catnapping on a window seat. Despite his self-doubt, Kaymar had been out almost all night, taking on the most difficult targets himself.

Ifor smiled at the spectacle of Kaymar working open his pretty blue eyes.

"All of them," he said quietly. "We got all of them."

"Good," Kaymar said with satisfaction, stretching luxuriously. "Now, we have a graduation to attend."

Ifor handed him an envelope. "Menders just brought this along for you," he said.

Kaymar recognized his mother's handwriting and tore the envelope open. He had sent word to her as soon as the DeLarco operation was complete but had not remained at The Shadows long enough to receive her answer.

Dearest One,

Thank you for letting me know you have completed your dangerous mission. It is always best that I am aware of such things. I am glad that you so entrust me that you admit me into your confidence. How very proud I am of my brave and giving son.

It has long been known to me that your work can place you into danger and it is always with great relief that I find you have not been called to sacrifice yourself. We are lifting a glass to you as I write this. Your brother is greatly relieved also and sends his best wishes.

If indeed you are going on the world tour with our Katrin, please convince Cousin Menders to stop at Moresby on the way to Surelia. It is high time he saw that part of the Stettan estate that was lost to his father. We have been guests at his Shadows enough times, more than time to turn the tables!

Again, my dear, you make Mahmay so very proud. You delight me as you have from the day you were born, our red little Kipper. What a magnificent man you have grown to be.

Your loving mother,

Princess Dorlane Cheval-Shvalz

Kaymar smiled with pride and joy, carefully folded the letter and slid it into his waistcoat pocket.

CHAPTER 56
TO BECOME A SOLDIER

Katrin took advantage of the mirror in Commandant Komroff's office to make sure her fake mourning was as it should be. She hoped she would never have to wear garments like this all the time. As if a woman in mourning wouldn't be miserable enough, the dress was far from roomy, the straight fronted corset was a trial to the patience and the bonnet and veil were an endless fussy horror. The entire outfit was constantly in need of adjustment and repositioning. Why a bereaved lady would have to wear something that forced her to endlessly pull, tug, flatten and adjust, Katrin couldn't say. Perhaps it was meant to distract the mind from grief.

For the first time, Katrin wore all her hair up, which had taken an age and a hundred hair pins to achieve. Eiren had to send Kaymar running out for more pins, an errand that took him forever to complete, leaving Katrin waiting with her hair half up for over an hour.

For security, Hemmett hadn't been told she was coming. He'd taken the news that she couldn't attend his graduation stoically, although he'd been terribly disappointed.

After years of reading the ongoing correspondence between Katrin and Hemmett, Commandant Komroff had been delighted to meet the Princess. He declared her far too pretty to be a widow and proposed to her on the spot, an enormous twinkle in his eyes, laughing outright when she graciously declined. He told her that now she had the first of her proposals out of the way and could notch her belt. He was a funny, small, dapper man, not tall as she'd imagined, though his carriage and demeanor made him seem so. He had merry blue eyes and the wrinkles around them let her know that his face was more accustomed to smiles than frowns.

She'd been left alone in Komroff's office while Hemmett

was summoned to see the Commandant. The ceremony was only an hour away, so Hemmett would be peeved, probably worried about a last minute change of plans.

She heard brisk, determined footsteps and flipped the waist length, black bordered veil over her face, adjusting it so it fell around her in a sort of black pyramid. She turned her back, as if she was looking out the window.

There was a brisk rap at the door. It opened.

"You sent for me, Sir?" Hemmett's voice said, followed by, "Oh, I'm sorry, Madame."

Katrin turned toward him and flipped the veil back from her face. Then she gasped.

He was a grown man. Not only that, but a grown man wearing the full regalia of Army dress uniform, complete with gold braid and buttons, sword and pistol. When she'd last seen Hemmett, he'd still had the ghost of boyishness on his face, a certain youthful softness. In the last two months, that had vanished. It was a terrible shock, almost like being confronted with a stranger. For one moment she wondered what it would be like to kiss him.

"Willow?" He sounded completely baffled. He was familiar to her again. To her surprise, he closed his eyes and shivered for a second, going pale.

"What is it, Bumpy?" she asked, horrified that what was supposed to be a wonderful surprise was falling flat.

"Oh – just seeing you in that mourning – a goose walking over my grave. For a moment I thought – something had gone terribly wrong," he replied, opening his eyes again and grinning at her. "You're the last minute change in plans, I suspect?"

He caught her up, hugging her so hard he knocked her bonnet and veil off, so they hung by the ribbon that went under her chin.

"Aren't you the funniest little widder woman?" he teased. "Thank you for burying your grief long enough to come and see your humble subject graduate, Your Royalness." He put her down.

"Show respect, low fellow," Katrin laughed, trying to get her bonnet back in place. "I've already received a marriage proposal."

Hemmett scowled. "From whom?" he asked.

"Your Commandant, right after I got here. I turned him down," Katrin smiled. He blinked and then laughed.

"You could do worse, but imagine having to live here at this monkey house and fending off his bonded," he said. "Here, the bow on that thing is tangled. Gods, what an ugly hat."

"It's supposed to dissuade potential suitors," Katrin answered as he got the knot untangled.

"It would do that. It even dims you down. Got it. Here, put this fishnet back over your head. What do you have to do, nail it in place? Thank the gods I don't have to change my speech, it's carefully memorized. There's no way I could forget anything of it now. I'm so glad you came, Willow!"

***

The great hall of the Royal Mordanian Military Academy was an impressive sight, with flags hung from the high ceiling and red, white and black bunting looped along the walls and around the stage. Katrin and her group kept their distance from the main crowd until they were ushered to center row seats on the aisle. As Princess she would have been in a box seat up front, but from here she could see more of the crowd and watch their reactions, so perhaps this was better.

Katrin saw Kaymar and Ifor come in a side door, where they had a hurried conference with Menders. He nodded and shook their hands, then returned to his place between Katrin and Eiren while Kaymar and Ifor went to their seats in the row directly behind her. Bartan, the Court Assassin, came in through the same entrance, caught Menders' eye and nodded before taking a seat several rows away.

Katrin felt Menders relax. He reached over and lifted the widow's veil off her face, turning it back over the bonnet. Things must have gone well. He would never have uncovered her face otherwise.

The ceremony was long. Though there was much military pomp and great seriousness at this somber and important occasion, there was also a thread of light-heartedness due to the human touch afforded by the Commandant. He ran a tight ship, but he tempered discipline with humanity. When a cadet had trouble with a speech or recitation, the Commandant knew when to step in and save face.

"He's seems very thoughtful and kind," Katrin whispered to Menders.

"He is indeed. They are all his boys and their welfare is a personal issue to him," Menders answered. "No toughening here. Discipline, yes, but cruelty? No."

Finally, the Commandant rose and introduced Hemmett, who had been sitting at the head of the graduating class, looking incredibly dashing.

"It gives me enormous pleasure to introduce this year's top graduate, Captain Hemmett Greinholz," Komroff said solemnly. "To achieve that honor, Captain Greinholz has overcome an uncommon obstacle which makes it particularly difficult for him to read and write. Only through strong self-discipline and originality of thought has he been able to overcome this handicap to excel academically as well as in military disciplines. He has persevered in the face of debilitating odds to have the second highest scores, ever, in the history of this academy."

Katrin looked over at Menders, who remained impassive. She had heard enough to know who Hemmett had come second to. Katrin beamed with pride at the thought. Not only the cadet with the highest grades in his class, but second only to Menders!

"Not only that, but Captain Greinholz has proven himself a talented leader and a compassionate friend. Many of the young men here owe him a debt of gratitude for support and comradeship he has extended over his five year career at the Academy. At all times it has been an inspiration and pleasure to have him here with us.

"And now that I've completely embarrassed him, I give you this year's top graduate, Captain Greinholz."

Hemmett stood and stepped forward, saluted, and then removed his hat, stowing it under one arm, while the Commandant shook his hand warmly. Komroff took his seat and Hemmett turned toward the crowd, placing his hat on the podium, out of his way. The audience waited with hushed anticipation. Respected and admired by most, it was also well known that Hemmett possessed a powerful sense of humor. Would his speech be laced with jokes?

"I asked the Commandant how long I should speak. He said until booing started or everyone fell asleep, whichever came first. I promised to spare the audience too much agony, so I will try to be brief."

Hemmett grinned then and the audience, which had been stunned at his informal presentation, laughed. No-one could stay grim when Hemmett grinned; his smiles were infectious. The he grew solemn.

"Today Mordania is beset by enemies, both from without and from within. These are dark times. They test of our resolve and moral courage. They require calm resolution and clearheaded thinking from those called upon to serve our country in times of peril. We of the military are the first to serve and the first to sacrifice ourselves to a greater calling, for a greater good. This we do willingly, both as soldiers and as proud Mordanians. My graduating classmates and I only hope that such service, love and sacrifice will not be squandered needlessly, for the desire for material gain and the proud vanity of a few."

A murmur rippled through the crowd. Hemmett went on.

"Even now, the sons of Mordania are engaged in wars overseas, against enemies both real… and imagined."

The voices of the crowd were louder now and uneasy, for to question the deployment of Mordania's military forces was considered all but treason.

"The young men who are out there, fighting for us, look forward eagerly to a letter from home – just as I have done during the past five years away from those I love. Equally precious have been the letters that I've sent back in return, as they represent the bonds of love that remind a soldier of why he is putting his life on the line. Many letters I have written to a lifelong friend have made me reflect on why we in the military do our honorable and difficult job. So rather than drone on at you, I wanted to share one of these letters instead. It goes farther to sum up my convictions as a soldier of Mordania than any fine speech I could make.

"Dear Willow,

I've decided that I'm not good at writing speeches. I manage to make myself sound very pompous, with many a grand flourish and you know that is not like me. So I'm going to write a letter to you instead and let it be my graduating speech, because that way, it will be from my heart.

You once asked me what it really means to be a soldier. I think I can answer you now.

On the eve of becoming a fully commissioned officer, I've been giving a lot of thought to what makes a soldier. It is not the uniforms and protocols, maneuvers and parades. That is window dressing.

A soldier is defined by what he does. Once you strip away everything else, a soldier is a man whose life's work is protecting that which he holds dear – his country, his way of life and his loved ones. Nothing but a heartfelt commitment to protect the things he loves could make a man march unflinchingly into danger. This is a sacred trust, because those of us who have chosen a military life know that we are the first and last line of defense for Mordania.

After all, what is Mordania? It's not a shape on a map - it's the people who live there. When we soldiers risk injury or death, it isn't to protect a shape on a map. We risk our lives to protect the ones we love at home – our fathers, mothers, sisters, brothers, wives, children and lovers. No-one can love a shape on a map and brave death for it, but we willingly do so for those we hold dear. Mordania is full of people some soldier loves. Mordania is full of people some soldier is willing to sacrifice his life for.

And so I pledge in what I hope will be the last letter I have to write to you, that as a soldier I will always protect you and those I love – because in protecting those I love, I am protecting that which is Mordania. No sacrifice I am called upon to make will be too great, because it will be for the highest cause – keeping all I hold dear safe from harm.

Just as a soldier's true purpose is the simple one of protecting what he loves, a soldier's greatest desire is simple as well – to go home. And so Willow, I am, for the first time, going to achieve the soldier's dearest wish. I am going home, to begin the job I've worked hard to learn – protecting that which I love best. I'm returning home and to all that the word 'home' means, from the simplest dwelling to all of Mordania. There can be no higher duty and no reward more glorious than this.

Love,

Bumpy, Captain Hemmett Greinholz"

Katrin motioned to Menders, needing an extra handkerchief, but he indicated that he'd already given his to Eiren, who was dabbing at her eyes beside him. Kaymar reached offered one. Katrin took it.

Hemmett grinned directly at her from the podium as applause from the hushed audience started to swell. An old man in military uniform shouted, 'Send that boy out recruiting!' and had to be quelled by his embarrassed family.

Hemmett donned his hat and bellowed an order. The cadets rose, were given a last few words of congratulation by the Commandant, then marched from the hall in a perfect parade. Hemmett managed the barest wink as he went past where Katrin and the rest of them were sitting.

"That boy," Eiren gasped, putting away Menders' handkerchief.

"That's a man," Menders said, his eyes suspiciously damp behind his glasses. "A damned fine man."

***

Menders decided to stay for the reception and Katrin was thrilled. He seemed confident that the threat to her was entirely removed. He also admitted that little harm could come to Katrin or anyone else here on the Academy grounds, surrounded by the finest young officers of the graduating class, Menders' Men and every assassin of the Royal Court. With typical forethought, Eiren had packed one of Katrin's new gowns so that, free of her dreary widow's disguise, she could now be presented as Hemmett's country friend.

Katrin orbited the pre-dinner activities, watching Hemmett from a distance as he was congratulated by classmates, senior officers and family members of other cadets. Katrin noted that many young women flocked to him. He did look stunning in the white jacketed version of his full dress uniform. Across the room, Menders and Eiren were engaged in animated conversation with Commandant Komroff. Borsen was talking to two young officers by the buffet table, probably asking who made their clothes.

Katrin hung back, feeling ill at ease. She knew no-one but Hemmett and the family, and it didn't seem right for her to command all his attention now.

By threading through the crowd, she overheard snippets

of conversation. Hemmett's speech was the main topic of discussion. Some applauded his gumption to say what they thought needed to be said. Others were outspoken at his brazen questioning of military policy.

"Just who does he think he is, this puppy, to question the validity of the threats against us?" she overheard one crusty, old, much-decorated general proclaim.

"Oh, just the second highest graduate in the history of the Academy," a junior officer replied airily, looking away. He caught Katrin's eye and smiled. "One with more brains than the Chief General Staff added together," he added much more softly.

"Eh, what was that, Lugrentz?"

"Oh nothing, General... nothing." He smiled at Katrin again. She liked his smile.

Another senior officer expressed concern that the years' top graduate was being 'wasted' on a backwater assignment of low importance.

"He's been posted to go look after some damned Princess!" exclaimed a heavily bearded senior officer to a fleet Admiral in an impossibly white uniform.

"What, the mad one?"

"Eh? No! Some other blasted Princess! Princess Carlin, or some such."

"I didn't know we had another Princess," wheezed the Admiral, stroking his heavily lined face thoughtfully.

"Absolute waste of a top graduate, if you ask me."

Katrin slunk away. She felt bad about that. Menders had tried to ease her chagrin by reminding her that being Captain of her Guard was what Hemmett had always wanted and that she should be glad he wasn't being posted to active service. Top graduates came back from combat just as dead as other graduates.

"You seem a little lost, my dear." The voice came from behind Katrin. She turned quickly, not in fear but because the voice seemed familiar. The speaker, however, was not.

'Dowager' was how Katrin's mind catalogued the woman who had spoken to her, as if the word had been coined specifically for that person. The lady was elderly, heavyset, with a pale, lined face under a densely veiled hat, her iron grey hair drawn back tightly into a bun. She leaned on a silver walking cane, topped with a large sunstone. Her dress was old style, stiff fronted dark blue velvet with small blue beads modestly decorating the neckline. Why the veil? Katrin wondered. No-one wore veils in the evening these days. It simply wasn't done.

"Oh, forgive me," Katrin answered, curtseying gracefully. "I was just trying to keep out of everyone's way. You see, I really don't know anyone here."

The old woman scanned the crowd and smiled a little. "Nor do I." She extended a hand adorned with a ruby ring as big as Katrin's eye. "I am the Baroness Verclayden." Katrin took the Baroness' hand in hers, smiling.

"I am Emila de Cosini," she said quickly, drawing up her cover identity from memory. She'd practiced it for the expected trip abroad to the point where it was almost second nature. "A friend of Bu – Captain Greinholz, from the country."

"Are you now?" The voice was neither sarcastic nor curious. "From this country?"

"Y – er, no. Surelia, although I live here a lot of the time. With my father." Katrin pointed, then immediately tried to snap her hand back.

It was a stupid mistake. Menders was known here at the Academy. What if this lady knew him, knew he was not Signore de Cosini? The Baroness regarded Menders and almost smiled.

"Ah yes. I see the resemblance. Striking, though he is very dark while you are fair."

"My mother was Mordanian," Katrin explained quickly. She might be able to salvage her story. "That's his second wife, my stepmother."

"A Mordanian mother," the old woman said. "Of course.

That would explain your hair."

"Yes. She was very fair, like me, but her hair was a beautiful shade of red."

The woman shifted her weight and sighed.

"Would you like to take a seat for a while?" Katrin asked, concerned. There were alcoves furnished with comfortable settees behind the pillars flanking one wall of the room. Katrin led the old lady to one and helped her settle.

"You are a considerate young lady," the Baroness said with genuine appreciation. "So unlike... some others."

"I hope always to do the right thing," Katrin said.

"As I did, once," the Baroness said in a softer tone. Her veiled eyes looked out across the room, as if she saw something other than the scene before them.

"Now, tell me of yourself, my child. Where you live. And what it is you like to do." The lady shook herself, patted the settee cushion beside her and looked directly at Katrin.

Much to her surprise, Katrin sat down beside her and told her. She falsified certain details about the Shadows, but for some reason Katrin felt a compulsion to tell this woman all about herself. She spoke of her interest in music but lack of discipline to go further with it, her love of art but lack of perseverance at perfecting her technique and of her interest in teaching but shortness of patience with it.

"I really don't know what to do. I feel I don't fit in anywhere," Katrin sighed, amazed that she was expressing such a private trouble to this stranger. "Hemmett was always going to be a soldier, an officer. From an early age he knew exactly what he wanted to do. And Borsen has all sorts of dreams and plans and he'll make them happen if I know him."

"Borsen? That would be the elegant little gentleman with the long, dark hair?"

"That's Borsen. He's going to be great at whatever he chooses to do."

The Baroness smiled gently. "Greatness is not given to everyone at once. Many earn it. Others only find it when their time comes."

"Do you think so?" Katrin asked.

"I believe that is so, yes," said the Baroness. "Some of us miss our opportunity. Then all we can do is try to pass something on to someone else – a hope of greatness for the future."

Katrin didn't understand what the Baroness meant but sensed the sadness beneath her words.

"Would you be so kind and bring me something to drink?" the Baroness asked. Katrin smiled and rose, going toward a waiter with a trayful of glasses.

When she returned with a glass of champagne, the Baroness was gone. Puzzled, she looked around the alcove, although it was only large enough to hold the settee. There were no hiding places. She even began to look behind the settee and stopped herself. Hemmett's voice made her turn around sharply.

"There you are, Willow! You promised to let me escort you in to dinner and at the dance afterwards, to save me from the attentions of one Ufronia Vildsteen."

"Did you see an old lady here?"

"Here where? There are a lot of old ladies about."

"*Here*, here! Sitting right here. I was talking to her just a moment ago and now she's gone."

Hemmett took the Baroness' champagne glass from her hand and placed it on the arm of the settee. "How many of these have you had, Willow?"

"Very funny. It was for her, the lady. Baroness Verclayden."

"Never heard of her," Hemmett shrugged, as a distant chime sounded. "That's the call to dinner." He extended his arm for her to take. Katrin walked along with him, looking back over her shoulder and around the room, expecting some sign of the Baroness. There was none, as if she had never been there at all.

CHAPTER 57
ANOTHER NAME

From Doctor Franz's Journal:

> *Delightful interval attending Hemmett's graduation. It has been interesting seeing Menders during these two days. There has been a "housecleaning" performed by Kaymar and others, which I don't care to consider too carefully. The result has been a Princess able to attend Hemmett's event, a most happy young lady indeed. Menders, though very watchful, has also been happy, thriving on the change and the relief of knowing that considerable threats have been removed.*
>
> *Having Menders settled with the three children doing well is a great relief to me, particularly after the dreadful winter just past. It is to be hoped that we will have some peaceful days to come, particularly when the long tour that has been in the planning begins and Katrin can slip into anonymity.*

***

"I want to go abroad as soon as possible," Menders declared, leaning back in his comfortable seat on the steam launch. Doctor Franz looked up, smiled and pocketed the notebook he'd been scribbling in. The entire party was on board, returning to The Shadows after Hemmett's graduation.

"The Queen has granted permission to take Katrin, so it's best to move now, before she changes her mind or any other threats arise," Menders continued.

"Much harder to find a moving target," Kaymar added, preparing to make a sandwich for Borsen, who could be heard "shouting at the fish", Hemmett's euphemism for the boy's inevitable attack of seasickness anytime he got on a boat. Within fifteen minutes of his sick spell, Borsen would be ravenous again. Eiren removed the mustard pot from Kaymar's hands and took over the sandwich making, sparing Borsen's tormented stomach one of Kaymar's fiery, mustard-laden creations. "I was seriously beginning to fear you'd cancel the trip all together," Kaymar went on.

"I considered calling it off, naturally, with Therbalt still out there." Menders replied.

"Yes, I know," Kaymar replied with obvious chagrin. "Bear and I bollixed it sending DeLarco back home, gave Therbalt enough time to get away. Grandstanding like fools. We're truly sorry about that, Cousin. It was a stupid thing to do."

Menders shrugged slightly. It was true, but he knew the elation that followed a successful mission, where it was easy to do such things impulsively. In the same situation as Kaymar and Ifor, he would likely have done the same thing. Such moments of natural humanity worked against assassins – as he well knew.

He'd let Ermina Trottenheim go when his instinct had been to eliminate her, once he became aware of the potential of her manipulation and dishonesty. His lack of conviction in that case had and would continue to cost them all dearly.

It could be argued that he could never have predicted Ermina running across someone like Therbalt and endangering Katrin – but he had known she was potentially dangerous and let her go with nothing more than an empty threat because he'd been involved with her. He'd failed to eliminate a potential danger to Katrin and it had come back at him a thousandfold. He would be the last person to blame Kaymar and Ifor for a moment of human frailty.

"Katrin's so looking forward to the trip," Eiren said, replacing the lid on the mustard. "It would break her heart not to go. Remember how she spoke nothing but Surelian for a whole week, to practice?"

"And drove everyone mad with it," Kaymar snorted.

Menders rose and went to the galley counter, enticed by the smell of food.

"Yes, I know the trip is very important to her, after all her years of missed opportunities and restriction, but I was going to call it off anyway. Then I realized… if we are not there at The Shadows, but make it appear as though we are, then anyone looking for us will be looking in the wrong place. Gladdas has agreed to arrange a few imposters, so that an observer will still see a golden haired girl going around the place, as well as doubles for me, for Eiren, Franz, Kaymar and Ifor."

"Brilliant," Kaymar said with admiration. "Getting us out and on the move means we'll have the advantage."

"Exactly. No one will know where we've gone or are going next. We'll be able to change plans on a whim. We can see anyone trying to get close to us and scout out places ahead of time. May I have one of those?" Menders pointed at the sandwich.

"Of course," Eiren smiled, patting his cheek.

Menders kissed her hand. "What's more, the Charter of my mission to protect Katrin gives me great freedom and flexibility, something you reminded me of yourself, Kaymar."

Kaymar blinked and stiffened as if he'd been hit with a sandbag. He looked sharply at Menders.

"Cuz – has it occurred to you that your mission with Katrin is over and has been over for months?" he asked abruptly.

Menders stared at him as if he'd gone mad. Then his face went blank.

In Mordania, members of the Royal Family legally came of age at sixteen. Katrin had turned sixteen that winter, just after the The Shadows was locked down. In that somber time she had not felt like celebrating and the significance of her birthday had gone unnoticed.

Menders was stunned. His orders were no longer in effect. He was no longer Katrin's legal guardian – yet there had been no word from The Palace when he applied for permission to take her abroad.

He stared at Eiren, who was open-mouthed, a piece of

ham in her hand suspended over the half-finished sandwich. She stared back and then shook her head.

"She's not mature enough to be on her own," she gasped.

"Agreed," Kaymar added. "It's not as if she's going to turf you out, Menders."

Menders blinked slowly. "I had... never planned for this. Can you imagine? Me not having planned this far ahead? I'm appalled at myself."

Sixteen years, gone. Could it really have been that long since that baby had been put into his arms? It was. He was a free man, unshackled by any Royal Command. His tenure was over, his mission complete. Had he realized it while still in Erdhan, he could have gone to the Queen and requested another assignment. But no, the very thought was untenable.

Katrin was certainly not ready to be on her own and showed no desire to be. Her education was not complete. She needed protection and she certainly didn't need to come under the influence of her mother and sister at Court. Another motivation for the journey abroad was to get her away from Mordania for a while, to give her more experience, to let her grow up away from the continual worry that she would one day be summoned to Court.

Then there was The Shadows. His life had gone into making it what it was. Legally, of course, the house was Katrin's. He only had the running of it, but he loved it as he had never loved any other place. In that moment, he realized what The Shadows meant to him.

"I had no idea, until this very moment, just what being at The Shadows had come to mean to me, how important it has become to me. And to think, I once felt myself trapped there, put out to pasture," he murmured.

"You have done great things," Eiren said. "Made a home there for all of us, nurtured a community. It's something to be proud of."

"I had help," Menders replied softly, looking at her. "I cannot imagine what I would have done if I hadn't found you there."

Eiren blushed and smiled.

He shook his head to clear it and looked at Eiren again. "My dear, do you wish me to leave Katrin's service?" he asked firmly.

Her response was immediate and definite.

"No. She needs you – and you need her." She smiled, and he knew she spoke the truth.

"I'll go speak to her then," he replied, smiling back.

***

Katrin turned to look back at Erdahn in the distance. She hadn't seen much of it and that mostly from the carriage on her way to the dock that morning. They had passed the Palace and she'd been appalled by its condition. Once a gracious building, it was now disheveled and unkempt, just like the Queen inside it.

The town had a down-at-the-heels look too, nothing like the crispness of Erdstrom, which was becoming known as the "Second Capital". It was saddening, because Erdahn's boulevards could have been majestic and the parks should have been at their best in the late springtime.

"H'lo Cuz," came Borsen's voice beside her. She looked round to see him leaning on the railing, looking weary. He'd been copiously ill at the stern, so Katrin had stationed herself at the prow to give him some privacy.

"Feeling better?" she asked.

"Oh yes. I'll be a regular seadog for the rest of the trip," Borsen said. "It just takes me a while to adjust."

"Whatever will you do going to Surelia on a boat?"

"Same as now. Puke for fifteen minutes and then have a wonderful time," Borsen answered. "It never lasts longer. What are you doing out here?"

"I've never really had a look at Erdahn, so I was just watching it," she answered. "I'm ashamed that it's in such a state."

"It is bad," Borsen agreed. "With everyone leaving the Court a few years back, the town went right down. I can remember when you used to be able to get a tram anywhere. Now there are hardly any trams at all."

Katrin sighed. There was nothing she could do about it but it bothered her because it was her mother's lack of initiative that had allowed the fine old city to become so run down.

"Heigh-ho, here's the rest of the crew," Hemmett said, coming up to them, putting an arm around Katrin's waist and the other around Borsen's shoulders. "And how are my little brother and sister, bobbing around on the big salt briny? Finished shouting at the fish, Borsen?"

"At last. Have anything to eat?" Borsen answered.

"Sorry, no, but I saw Eiren taking over sandwich making from Kaymar, so I suspect you will be brought something that is not one of his mustard specials. Kaymar's never happy unless his tongue's aflame. Did you know this young fellow was gazing wistfully at a certain gentleman of my acquaintance last night?" Hemmett said baitingly in Katrin's direction.

"I was looking at his suit," Borsen replied calmly.

"All those soulful glances just at his tailoring?" Hemmett grinned.

"All right, but looking's free," Borsen snickered. "I didn't even speak to the fellow. I'm still young and innocent. You're the jaded man of the world, you old fart."

"Listen to Little Man abuse me," Hemmett said with false injury in his voice.

"You're a dreadful tease, Hemmett," Katrin laughed.

"Me? Never, fair Highness," Hemmett gasped, bowing comically, inadvertently grazing his head on the rail in the process. He swore and crossed his eyes for a moment and then leaned on the railing between them.

"Hemmett, where were the Special Services graduates yesterday?" Katrin asked. "I looked around, but I had no idea."

"They don't have graduations," Hemmett answered. "They're actually taking on missions when they're as young as fifteen, some of them. It's said that their graduation is when they complete their first mission, if they're spies, or their first kill if they're assassins. There were a few of them at the reception last night but since they're not supposed to become known, I'm not going to tell anyone who they were."

Katrin shuddered.

"It's a hard old world, Willow," Hemmett said. "If it wasn't for those fellows and those who came before them, it would have been a very different story for Mordania. I've found out a lot about Menders and about the history that we never see in the textbooks."

Borsen eyes grew huge.

"Tell," he demanded.

"Well, let's just say that he singlehandedly saw to it that Surelia didn't take over Mordania," Hemmett said. Katrin and Borsen stared at him.

"I'm not well educated, but Surelia hasn't tried to invade Mordania since Morghenna the Wise raised the army that expelled them from the country two hundred years ago," Borsen refuted him. Katrin nodded.

"That's what I mean, the history that isn't in the books," Hemmett explained. "You see, there's this whole other history that's all secret missions and clandestine operations. Katrin's grandmother, Morghenna the Terrible, was on the Throne forever. She lived to be about a hundred years old and she was an active Queen in her time, not like the Queen now. But when she got old, she let go of actually governing and then she had a stroke and was pretty much a breathing corpse for ten years. The Council were a bunch of old fools, just like they are now. Before anyone knew it, powerful people were dropping off like flies. Surelian assassins were wiping out the Royal Family and trying to get at Katrin's mother, who was the Heiress then."

Katrin stared at him, amazed.

"Yes, Blue Eyes, that's right. They killed off a lot of the people close to the Throne and they got some of the high-up military as well. They wanted to create a situation where there was considerable confusion as to just who was in charge, coerce as much of our military leadership as they could onto their side and then invade with their rather pathetic little army. At the time it could have worked. This was a couple of years before Katrin was born.

"Mordanian spies got the information back as to who was behind the entire plot. It turned out it was most of the high-ups in Surelia, many of them involved with an organization called 'The Old Family'. It was almost impossible to get at because they had good security and were spread all over the country. So they sent in Menders. By then he was already considered the greatest assassin who ever lived, even though he was only eighteen. He was a specialist at infiltration and had a record number of kills. A sudden rash of assassinations would have tipped the Surelians off that we were onto them, so things had to be done carefully. So in the end it all came down to Menders – just Menders."

Katrin and Borsen exchanged glances.

"No-one knows just how he did it, but somehow all of 'The Old Family' ended up at the same place at the same time, an estate in the Surelian countryside for a social gathering. It was a great big do, hundreds of people there – and by the end of it all the people who had been plotting were dead. It seems some were poisoned, some were caught in out of the way places and stabbed to death, but most died when the main building blew up in a huge fireball.

"That was the end of the 'Surelian Problem', as it was called. That's why Menders' nickname in the service is 'The

Surelian Solution'."

Hemmett shook his head, impressed with his own story.

"Gods!" Katrin breathed. It was awful, but also exciting. Borsen's almond eyes were almost round behind his glasses.

"Sir - Commandant Komroff to you - told me lots of stories like that. I think he really wanted me to understand Menders, what he did and why. Sir said Menders did many skirt roles, dressed as a shy little governess type complete with meek bonnet, moving almost unnoticed down a street. Then suddenly someone would slump down to the ground. The crowd would gather while little governess would toddle on all unawares. No one suspects that what appeared to be a little woman venturing along is really an assassin with a big knife.

"Sir also said that Menders would have made a wonderful spy if it hadn't been for his eyes making him so easy to spot," Hemmett went on, while Borsen hung on every word and Katrin held her breath. She was finally coming to understand some of the things that she'd always wondered about.

"He could get in anywhere. Up inside pipes and airshafts. He could climb straight up a wall, like a fly. When he went to the military academy he was a tiny little boy, only eleven, and puny. When we first went to The Shadows he really looked like a boy, like Borsen here, not fully grown. I can just remember it. He grew a bit after he was twenty, bulked up too. When he was an assassin, he was really small. He worked like the hells to build himself up when he went to the Academy. He went on his first mission when he was only fifteen. Sir says that he could see in the dark, like a langhur, because of his eyes..."

"He walks silently as a langhur too," Menders said behind them.

All three of them started and spun around. Menders was smiling. Hemmett let out a sigh of relief.

"I know you've kept it very quiet, Menders, but I'm proud of you," he said.

"So am I!" Katrin declared. "Singlehandedly saving Mordania? You should have a medal!"

"I am too!" Borsen added.

"Medals are for soldiers. Assassins don't get medals. And I didn't come up with The Surelian Solution singlehanded, for all they hung the nickname on me," Menders replied, standing there with his hands in his pockets as if the motion of the boat on the waves didn't affect him in the least. He could have been standing in the Great Hall at The Shadows.

"Many men who went in before me did the espionage work to identify the targets," Menders explained. "Some of them lost their lives getting the information back to Mordania – Ifor's partner, Falk, was one of them. That's how Ifor caught the bullet that's in his back to this day. Yes, I carried out the assassinations, but without the support of many, I wouldn't have succeeded."

"It was still a great thing," Hemmett protested.

"Perhaps. Mordania is still here and maybe someday it will be all it could be," Menders responded, joining them at the rail. "Doing what I did wasn't glorious. It was often frightening and upsetting. Being an assassin was a job I had once. It isn't the only thing I've done, by far. I've been Katrin's guardian and Head of Household at The Shadows for many more years than I was ever an assassin. I consider that much more important work."

"I don't see how," Borsen burst out. "Compared to saving a whole country?"

"It's much more important, because I've been fostering and nurturing life," Menders explained, putting an arm around Borsen's shoulders. "Helping stop the Surelian takeover was important, yes, but so is sustaining and guiding young lives. More important by far, in many ways." He hugged Katrin close with his free arm, kissed her cheek and then reached over and ruffled Hemmett's hair.

"Now, I came out here for an entirely different reason, not to relive past glories," he said, looking at Katrin. "It's something very serious, my dear."

"Come on, Inchworm," Hemmett said, starting to walk away. Menders reached out and stopped him.

"Stay. It's a family matter and concerns you all," he said. The boys settled back beside Katrin at the railing.

"Little Princess, something has completely slipped my mind for some months," Menders said, taking her hand. She looked puzzled and worried. "You turned sixteen this winter. Because you're a member of the Royal Family, that means that you're legally of age. It also means that I am no longer your guardian and that I am no longer bound by the order given by your mother the night you were born."

Katrin swayed slightly, Hemmett's mouth dropped open and Borsen looked as if the world was ending.

"You mean... you won't be Papa anymore?" Borsen said, his voice catching. He sounded like a very little boy.

Menders released Katrin's hand, removed his glasses and stepped back, slowly dropping to one knee before her, lowering his head to the opposite knee with his arms outstretched at his sides. Though her mind was reeling, Katrin was aware of the incredible control and grace of his movement. I must learn how to move like that, she thought. But what is he doing?

"I wish to request that you permit me to continue in your service, Your Royal Highness," Menders said, raising his eyes to meet hers. "I also request that you consider your answer well, for what is quickly done is not always quickly undone."

Katrin had her mouth open, ready to say 'of course'. Then she hesitated.

If she released him, he could go with Eiren and have a private life. She knew that their lives had been restricted by Menders' duty to her. If Menders was free, he could marry Eiren. They could go live somewhere else. There was time for them to have children of their own. It would be a wonderful thing for them.

But she couldn't imagine Menders without The Shadows – or the Shadows without Menders. He loved it, more than she loved it herself. He had created it; it was his more than it was anyone else's. If she refused his request, that meant she would be sending him away from The Shadows. She knew that would hurt him terribly.

She needed him as well. Katrin felt no more ready to be an adult than she was ready to fly to one of Eirdon's moons. He was her father, she loved him and sixteen was not old enough to be on her own, despite what the law said.

Katrin looked at Hemmett and then Borsen. Hemmett was carefully keeping his face expressionless. Borsen looked stricken and shrugged with a great deal of desperation. They could not help her with this decision.

She looked back at Menders and then felt her answer within herself, just as she'd known which strand of gems to pick up when Tharan Tul presented her with so many when she was only four years old. She saw through the grey of indecision to the glowing gold underneath.

"Yes, please continue in my service, as my Head of Household," she said, surprised to hear tears behind her voice. "It would please me so much for you to stay because you want to this time and not because you are ordered to – Papa."

Menders nodded, but remained on one knee despite the rolling of the boat.

"Was that enough? Was it formal enough to make it official?" Katrin asked.

"Normally there might be some inclusions such as terms of service and length of tenure, that sort of thing."

"Oh? All right then. I wish you to remain in my service, until… until the day one of us decides otherwise. Will that do?"

Menders smiled, remaining on one knee.

Katrin remembered. She put out her hand to him so he could rise. With perfect protocol, he took it, kissed it, and rose.

Then he smiled and took her in his arms.

"You are still my little one," he whispered. She rested her head on his shoulder. For a moment, there was no-one else in the world.

Menders released her and she wiped at her eyes, laughing a little.

"Very unexpected," she said.

"Yes, it was. Our esteemed cousin reminded me of your majority only a few moments ago. In case you were wondering, Eiren wants me to stay in your service as well." Menders blinked again and passed a finger under his glasses to wipe his eyes.

"I'm glad," Katrin sighed with relief. She did not want Eiren just dragged along willy-nilly.

Hemmett and Borsen both cleared their throats at once and they all laughed aloud. Menders stepped forward and leaned on the rail, standing between Katrin and Borsen. He put an arm around Katrin's waist and the other around Borsen's shoulders. Hemmett wrapped his arm around Katrin's shoulders and Menders raised his hand to grasp it, linking them all together.

"Well, my children, here we are at the point where you're beginning your lives as adults," Menders said. "The years have gone so quickly. Borsen, you are a tailor, a craftsman and an artist. Hemmett is a soldier, a distinguished officer and a gentleman. Katrin is a lovely and accomplished grown lady. I am so very proud of you all."

Katrin flushed with pride and saw Borsen and Hemmett doing the same.

The day was rapidly turning toward evening, the sky overhead darkening from deep blue to indigo. The three brightest stars showed as small points of light overhead, always the first objects visible in the evening sky. As the light faded, the other stars of The Weaver began to twinkle around them.

"Make the best of your time," Menders said softly, so softly that they could barely hear him over the noise of the engine and the splashing of waves against the bow. "It shall not come again. Once it passes, it is gone forever and never comes back – so make the best of it, brood of mine."

"Yes, Father," the trio whispered softly.

He had many names. And now, another – Father.

Aylam Josirus, Lord Stettan, The Surelian Solution, who used his dead mother's tribal name – Menders – as his only identity, held his children safe around him, looked toward home – and smiled.

UNTIL THE CIRCLE TURNS AGAIN

18663590R00426

Printed in Great Britain
by Amazon